J C SNOW

# THE Crane Moon Cycle

A DUOLOGY

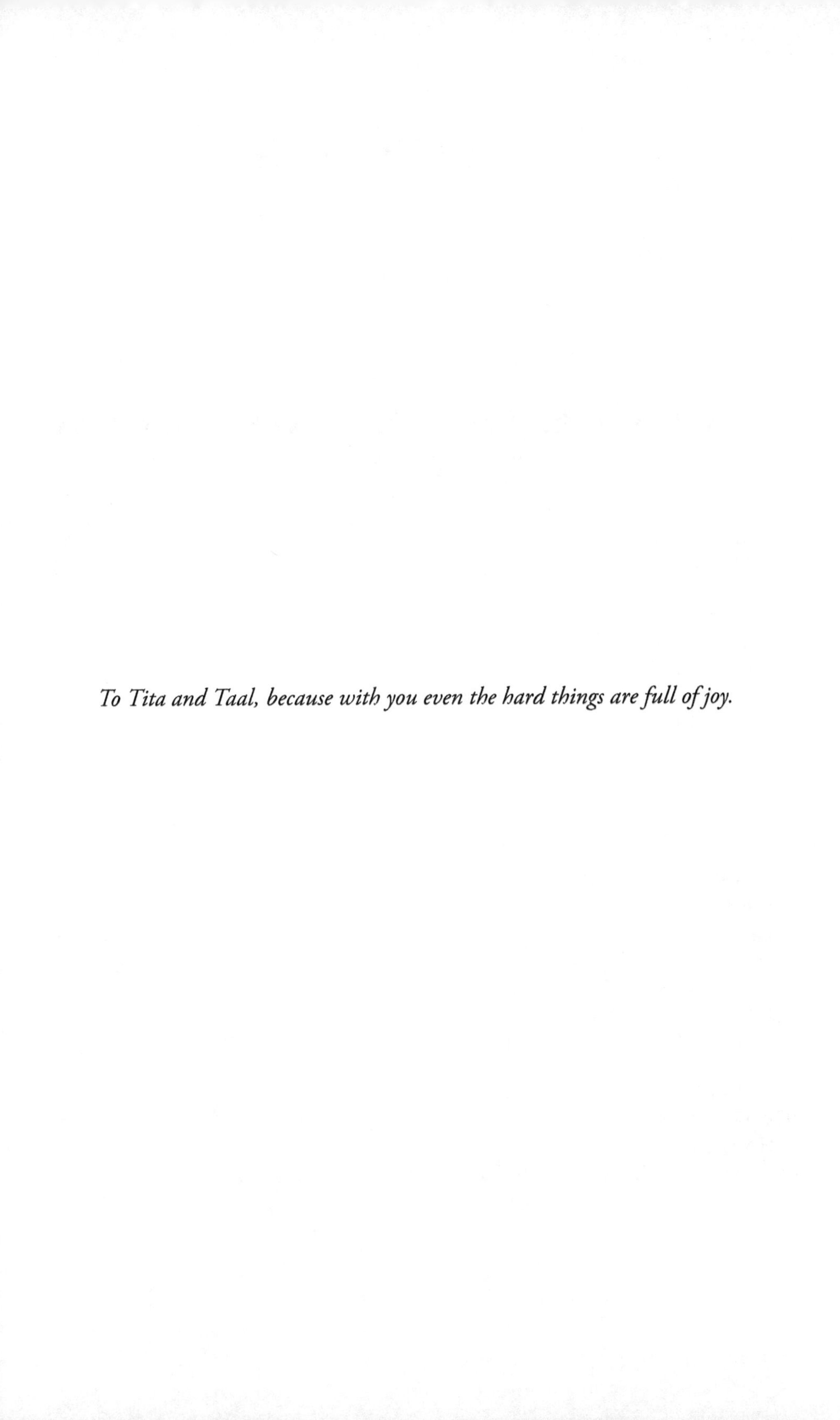

*To Tita and Taal, because with you even the hard things are full of joy.*

# CONTENTS

## BOOK ONE: THE PHOENIX AND THE SWORD

# CONTENTS

# THE Phoenix
## AND THE
# Sword

J C SNOW

# CHAPTER 1
## MEETING

BECAUSE THE BAR was small, smoky, crowded, and hot, with far too many people talking too loudly, and because she was tired from the day's training, Aili sat in a dark corner next to the counter and quietly watched other people have a good time. This was not a new experience for her. The bartender had long gotten used to ignoring her; she never spent much money, and he was much more interested in the men.

A woman with dark hair cut just to her chin, slicked back for the evening to look shorter, leaned in next to her. "You're not doing me proud here, Aili," Nora said, breathing deeply. She nodded toward a woman in a gauzy blue skirt entwined with a taller woman wearing pants. "How far did you even get? Did you kiss?"

"I did talk to her," Aili said defensively. She hated to disappoint Nora after she'd gone through such efforts to set Aili up with someone. "We didn't...Well, we weren't really interested in each other."

"You mean you stared at her and let her talk, right?" Nora rolled her eyes. "Did you even offer her a cigarette?"

"You know I don't smoke."

"Not the point, Aili. She does. It's your job to show your interest, right?" Nora patted her head. Aili was much taller, so Nora always took advantage while she was sitting down. "I'm tempted to give up, but never let it be said that I let my

1

best friend go out to a war zone without ever having any action in her life. Just get a kiss in before we leave, at least. Maybe there will even be someone who will write you letters when we're somewhere rescuing naval aviators in the Western Sea. Time's running out before we go. Is there anyone you do like? How about that one?" She tipped her chin toward a woman sitting in a corner booth, talking animatedly with two others, all giggling and hiding their mouths. "I know for a fact she came alone tonight. This is her first time; her friends brought her."

"And how do you know that?"

"Because I know her friends." Nora smiled at the girl, who smiled back. Nora smoothed her hair back, and the girl smiled more widely. "If you're not interested, mind if I give it a shot?"

Aili nodded. "We have to get back to base, though, ok? No more than another half hour here. You're going to need to fix your hair before we go back." *And put the regulation skirt on, and change out of what would almost certainly be a lipstick-stained shirt*, she thought but didn't say as Nora swaggered toward the corner booth. Aili sipped a little more beer.

The bar was mostly full of sailors ready to head out on the next carriers for the island war in the Great Western Sea taking their last opportunities to mingle with men they could secretly enjoy before months trapped on a ship. The women were much fewer, mostly locals. She and Nora had agreed not to tell anyone new they met that they were in training, but truthfully, since they both lived in Easterly anyway, Nora had already met just about every girl in the bar and Aili, who had been tagging along behind her for three years, wasn't very hopeful that there would be any surprises showing up in the next few weeks. Although, it would have been nice to have kissed someone, to have that memory before shipping out.

There was one interesting person, small and delicately-made, with dark eyes and shoulder-length, straight black hair. Not Anglish like almost everyone else in the room — most likely Daxian, or perhaps Kunorese. She thought Daxian was more likely. The bar wasn't far from Little Daxian, and surely any Kunorese people would not be out in public now for their own safety after the attack on the Western Islands. Some of the sailors had nonetheless decided that this person was a Kuno in their bar, and a group of the drunker ones was starting to make unfriendly noises while looking in his direction.

The young man himself, however, seemed unaware of all this. He looked through the bar carefully — eagerly examining faces, pushing through the crowd so he wouldn't miss any of the furthest corners — as though there was someone he expected to meet, and he was late for their appointment. He came close enough to the bar to sweep his eyes over hers along with all the others sitting there.

Even though Aili had never been interested in men, she felt that there was something very intriguing about this man's expressions and the intensity of his gaze. He looked delighted at seeing someone, and then suddenly startled and confused. The man pushed his way out toward the door, unfortunately bumping right into some of the more drunk sailors, who, of course, followed him.

Aili sighed and got up. On her way out, she tapped Nora on the shoulder. "Come on," she said, "let's head back."

"In a minute," Nora said, "in a minute."

Aili went outside to wait for her. A few men and women were scattered outside, talking and smoking, but not many, not loud. No one wanted to draw attention to this place.

Since no one was speaking loudly, no matter how drunk they were, it was easy to hear the sound of several threatening voices and one lighter one from around the corner, as Aili had half-expected, and she walked quickly toward the alley between the bar and the tottering wooden boarding house next door. There were four of the sailors with the Kunorese guy in the middle; they hadn't progressed from threats to fists yet, but it was only a matter of time. Aili was tall enough and experienced enough and just drunk enough that she thought she could handle at least two of the men, but four was a little too much, so she'd talk first.

She walked down the alley and sidled between them; "Hey fellas, you know this isn't—"

To her shock, one of the sailors suddenly slashed down with a knife, and even more shockingly, the Kunorese guy pushed her aside to take it in his forearm.

Except it wasn't a guy. It was very clearly a girl, and her arm was sliced down to the bone.

Aili yelled and pushed the bleeding girl behind her while kicking at the least protected parts of the sailor, who groaned and fell backward. "Get the hell away!" she shouted, but the other three started pressing in closer.

The voices around her sounded eerie in the darkness when she couldn't see their faces; the men circled around, their blood up. She had done enough fighting to know when things were getting dangerous, and this felt very much like one of those times. Aili tried to keep the girl behind her for her own safety, backing them both into the wooden wall of the alley. Very unhelpfully, the girl seemed to want to keep touching her, which was distracting, and kept trying to duck in front as though she thought that she could defend Aili even though she was much smaller.

Suddenly there was the familiar, oh-so-welcome sound of a gun cocking from the bright entrance of the alleyway. Nora said, "Aili, we're late. Boys, I know what ship you're from and who your officer is, get the hell out of here before someone makes a report."

The sailors shuffled out of the alley, their shore leave uniforms wrinkled and sweaty, giving Nora looks of deepest contempt. She smiled happily at them, the barrel of the gun never wavering.

"I love you, Nora," said Aili weakly, leaning back against the wall to get her breath.

The girl stood beside her, silently. Aili couldn't see her face, only the silhouette of her body against the light of the street. Definitely a girl.

"Where did you get the gun?"

Nora shrugged and carefully holstered it. Although she had drunk much more than Aili, she was far less affected. It was something Aili had always envied about her; she could keep a clear head through anything.

"It's mine. Obviously I don't bring the Navy one out with me. I stopped at our place in Easterly earlier to pick up some things. I usually have it with me when we're out late for just such occasions as this. How did you end up in an alley with four drunk sailors?" She craned her neck to see better. "Is there someone there with you?"

Aili pushed herself upright away from the wall, and, remembering Nora's advice to always be chivalrous, tried to determine how to hold the girl's arm and walk her out to the street. Which arm had been injured? When Aili put her hand on the girl's arm, though, she shivered and made a little gasping noise, so Aili immediately let go. "Sorry," she said awkwardly.

When they reached the street, Aili saw that the girl's face was shining — as though the most exciting thing in the world had just happened to her instead of nearly being killed by drunk Federation sailors.

"Hello there," said Nora, looking uncomfortable.

Aili realized belatedly that Nora, who was definitely the more patriotic of the two of them, probably thought the girl was Kunorese, and certainly, she would have been shocked to find Aili with pretty much anyone, given her total failure in that line to date. And it was as though the girl didn't see Nora at all. Even though it was really Nora who had rescued her, and all Aili had done was get her slashed by a knife, she stared only at Aili's face, with a huge, delighted smile.

The girl suddenly stepped closer, far closer than felt comfortable for Aili, and looked up into her eyes. She was very small, her head coming up barely to Aili's collarbones, and when she tilted her face upwards, her eyes dark but brilliant and her hair falling back from her forehead in a shining black wave, Aili felt as though she might faint, that there was something making her dizzy. She couldn't look away from her eyes.

The girl said something in another language. Aili looked helplessly at Nora, who clearly was not feeling helpful anymore and was staring pointedly at her watch.

"I don't speak Kunorese," Aili said.

The girl looked surprised for one flash of an eyebrow, but then smiled, and said, "It was Daxian, but of course we should speak Anglish, sorry. I forgot."

Aili tried to think about why the girl would think they would know Daxian either, and gave it up as a problem that would require her to not have drunk several beers recently. At least the Daxian Republic was an ally, so Nora shouldn't be upset.

"You got hurt," said Aili, trying to be professional. This was going to be her job, after all — fixing up people who got slashed and shot on battlefields. She reached out for the girl's bloodstained sleeve, carefully pushing it back from the wound to see how bad it was. Aili always kept a few necessities on hand just in case; she had the small kit with her in her jacket pocket.

But there was no wound.

The girl smiled, and took her arm back, smoothing down the bloody sleeve. "Healing and not dying, that's pretty much all I've got," she said, as though it were an accepted thing between them, something she had said many times before. Her voice was low and clear and vibrant. She was still too close, and suddenly she laughed out loud and said, "You're so tall! And your hair!"

Reaching up, she actually touched Aili's hair, golden-brown and bound up in a braid and pins. She left her hand on the nape of Aili's neck for just one moment too long. "I like it," she said, nodding decisively.

If Nora's eyes could have fallen out of her face, they would have. Aili could feel her own skin starting to heat up, but the girl seemed completely unbothered. She stroked Aili's ear gently with two fingers, smiling.

"I don't…know you?" Aili finally managed to stammer, though she didn't have enough self-control to grab the girl's wrist, or to do any of the things that Nora would have recommended had this been another girl who was not so strange and forward.

"What's your name?" the girl asked.

"Aili Fallon," she said. "And yours?" Chivalrous, chivalrous; Nora should approve.

"Tairei," she said, laughing, "you should call me Tairei. Aili," she added.

"That's a nice name."

Nora cleared her throat. "Aili, we have to get back. Really."

Tairei looked distinctly unpleased by this news, but nodded politely. "I'll see you again," she said, and smiled one last time at Aili before walking off down the street, her white blouse catching the streetlights.

Nora looked disapprovingly after her. "Femmes shouldn't wear men's pants," was all she said. "At least she's not Kunorese. Come on, we need to get back on base. We're going to miss the ferry now if we don't run."

The Sand Island naval base was a collection of recently-built wooden dormitories and giant airplane hangars, with a seaplane lagoon and a set of docks for the carriers and transports that came and went for the war against Kunoru and the Twin Empires in the Western Sea. Aili always woke up early because the window in her room faced southeast, and the morning sun hit her face as soon as it peeked over the horizon. Even without that, though, she would probably wake up early after spending the first sixteen years of her life on the farm, rising before dawn to do chores and help her mother.

Most of the people living on or visiting the base were men, and presumably men eager to have access to women, so the flight nurses in training slept in a dormitory somewhat apart from the others under the supervision of their chaperone who checked them in every night. She had marked both Aili and Nora down for demerits for their lateness and sloppy dress when they'd returned the night before. Nora grumbled; they had gotten in before the curfew after all, and had changed back into regulation dresses instead of the pants, button-downs, and vests they had worn at the bar. As they worked through that morning's physical exercises and then sat in class, listening to the teaching nurse's lecture on the importance of proper sanitation in field wound dressing, Aili found herself drifting off to the events of the night before. Nothing like that had ever happened to her — no woman had come close to her like that. Her pulse raced whenever she thought of it.

She liked to think of it.

Nora hissed, "Aili, pay attention!"

The training nurse said, "Trainee Fallon, please tell me the steps you would take to field dress a bayonet stab before moving the patient."

Aili took a deep breath and recited: triage, cleaning, sulfa, packing the wound. The trainer nodded, and Aili breathed out slowly, and immediately started thinking about that girl's face again. Tairei.

At the lunch break in the canteen, Aili brought her tray to sit with Nora, who looked quite proper and feminine in a tailored blouse and skirt, her hair curled nicely around her face, just as regulations would have it.

Nora looked over at Aili and rolled her eyes. "Hello, lovebird," she said dryly. "I'm guessing that wound care wasn't really on your mind this morning."

Aili smiled and shrugged. "How do you think I could find that girl again?" she heard herself say.

"You want to?" Nora asked, surprised. "After all this time that I've tried to get you together with someone, suddenly it's this weird Kunorese person you meet in an alley with a bunch of sailors?"

Aili shrugged, blushing. "She's Daxian," she said weakly.

"Not the point," Nora said, looking at her closely. "Are you actually blushing?"

"I want to see her again," Aili said, stubbornly.

Nora shook her head and began to eat. "I don't know why. She was really odd, the way she smiled at you that whole time. But if you did, you should hurry, because we're shipping out in a month. Assuming that someone has actually done her homework and will pass the final exam."

Aili's fork stopped partway to her mouth. "A month? It's posted?"

"There's still the exam, but yeah, all of us have been assigned in our cohort. They announced it today while you were in dreamland. We'll ship out in four weeks. So, if you meet your little friend again, remember not to tell her. Loose lips sink ships and all that."

A woman put her tray down on the other side of the table, facing them and smiling in a friendly way. To her surprise, Aili saw that this woman was also Daxian, though she didn't have much in common with Tairei otherwise; her hair was styled in curls instead of straight and loose, she was almost as tall as Aili, and she was wearing what looked like a pilot's uniform.

Aili inwardly burned with envy. She had wanted to enlist for pilot training, but they required a high school education. For various reasons that she didn't care to explain to the enlistment officer, she didn't have one. They had only accepted her for the nurse's training because she had been able to demonstrate practical skills. Again for various reasons, she had had a good amount of experience in setting broken bones and cleaning up flesh wounds.

Nora said, "Aili, this is Edna Lee, she's one of the Lady Aviators. I don't think you were here last time she was on base."

Edna smiled and reached over to shake hands. "Pleasure, Aili," she said. Aili noted her wedding ring and decided that she would not be able to tell her about Tairei, but Nora beat her to it.

"Edna, we met a Daxian girl at the bar in Easterly last night," Nora said bluntly, and Aili mentally put her face in her hands.

"Don't worry, Aili," Nora added. "Edna and I went to school together. She's from Easterly, she knows everybody and everything, no secrets, hey? So, we met this really strange Daxian girl, Edna — looked about our age, but I'd never seen her at the bar before. I was wondering, do you know her?"

Aili physically put her face in her hands.

Edna laughed. "It's all right, Aili, Nora's right, I'm safe to talk to about this. Anyway, I've got to fly back tomorrow. I'm ferrying bombers…logistics are a nightmare." She sipped her tea and nodded toward Nora. "But Nora, some discretion, please. You're on base, you could get in trouble if you're not careful."

Nora said, "Sorry, Edna, it's just so good to see you. I forgot it's not like we're back at school again. Are you and David moving back here?"

"Mmm," she said, "my parents are here, and now I'm flying in here a lot. We decided we might as well head back here. He's in Easterly next week looking for a place for us, and an office for him." She turned back to Aili. "So, I don't know everyone, but I do know most of the Daxian girls near our age from Little Daxian, anyway. What was her name?"

"Tairei?" Aili said, uncertainly.

Edna choked on her tea. "She said that's her name?" She shook her head. "You were right, Nora, this sounds weird."

Nora nodded. "I told you. This girl was strange. I'm worried about my farmgirl here, she's so innocent."

Aili looked back and forth between them, confused. "What's wrong with Tairei?"

"She knows you don't speak Daxian, right? The thing is, tairei isn't a name at all, it's…well, it's hard to explain in Anglish. We don't have Anglish words for these kinds of things, but it's more of a title of respect, it shows your relationship."

"Which is…?"

"Younger sister."

It was now Aili's turn to choke on her tea. Nora snickered.

"Don't worry," Edna said quickly, "it's not like a biological sister. More like you're in training together, it's a special relationship that's like a family, right?"

Nora and Aili looked at her blankly.

Edna rolled her eyes. "Nora, come on, I've explained this kind of thing to you before. The ones who are training you are an older generation, and there's special words for them too, but the ones who are training with you are in your generation, and you'd use tairei for anyone who's training with you in your generation but also who came in after you did. It's really weird to introduce yourself to someone that way when you've never met. She didn't explain why you were sisters, right? It's like she's claiming a relationship that doesn't exist."

"Would you come tonight and see if we can find her again?" Nora asked. "Because it's just…" Nora nodded toward Aili, who was staring at her plate in a stupor.

"Why not?" Edna smiled. "It's been a while since I've been able to visit Little Daxian."

Nora said, "We can get some food too? Take us to a good restaurant. I haven't been to a Daxian restaurant since you moved away. Have you ever had Daxian food, Aili?"

Aili started from her daze at being addressed directly. "Oh, no, yes, no, that would be good," she blurted out, and looked back down at her plate.

Less than ten minutes after Edna, Aili, and Nora settled into a round table at a tiny, packed restaurant in Little Daxian, full of smoke and loud voices, Aili looked up to meet Tairei's fierce, dark eyes. Tairei's eyes flicked over Nora, frowned briefly at Edna, and returned to meet Aili's. They hadn't even gotten a chance to discuss how they would find Tairei if she didn't appear at the bar again — in fact, they hadn't even ordered food — but here she stood, now wearing neatly-tailored pants and a blouse that Nora would consider femme-appropriate attire, Aili thought. Aili's throat closed up when she looked at her.

Tairei put a hand on her shoulder, and said, "Aili, it's good to see you, may I join you? Who are your friends?" as though they were the closest of companions already, instead of strangers.

Aili jumped up and pulled out a chair for her, again belatedly remembering Nora's frequent instructions for proper attentive date behavior. The effect was somewhat spoiled by her bumping into the man seated behind her — the place was just so small, and she was just so big and awkward — who broke out into a torrent of Daxian that sounded vaguely abusive. Both Tairei and Edna started talking back to him in the same moment and looked at each other, startled.

Tairei recovered first, smiled, and said something to Edna in Daxian, who responded and apparently started asking rapid-fire questions. Tairei smiled and answered all of them, but Aili noticed a little bead of sweat starting to run down from under her hair. This was, in itself, so fascinating that Aili just stared at Tairei's face and listened, entranced, to the language she didn't understand, completely ignoring Nora's expressions. At last, Tairei nodded her head politely toward Edna, who looked somewhat dissatisfied, and turned to Aili.

"Aili," Tairei said, "I think there's something here you'll really like. I'll order for you," and proceeded to yell something in Daxian at the waiter.

Edna looked surprised again, and Nora looked scandalized. In fact, every man and woman in the place stopped to look at her for a moment.

Tairei blushed a little bit. "Sorry," she said, "I forget sometimes that I'm not supposed to raise my voice in this…restaurant."

When their food came, it was placed in large dishes in the center of the table, with small bowls of rice for each of them, and Edna and Tairei took turns pointing Aili and Nora toward the things to put in their bowls. Tairei was especially insistent that Aili try something she called tofu. Aili gamely put it in her mouth and chewed and swallowed, but the texture was so very odd that she politely refused any more.

Tairei seemed, for a moment, quite startled by this. She looked seriously at Aili's face. "Really? You don't like it?"

"It's fine," Aili said diplomatically, drinking as much tea as she quickly could. "I like some of these other things better, though."

"Like this, right?" said Nora, waving a piece of roast duck on a fork. "This is delicious. And these are the noodles, right, from before, Edna? I remember these! I wish you were still around. This food is so great."

Edna said, "You can come here without me, silly goose. Just remember, that's chow mein. Just say that and you can get it on your own."

Aili watched Tairei out of the corner of her eye, a little worried. Quietly, she ate the tofu, and had some vegetables and rice as well, but avoided the duck; her smile had dimmed, and she looked preoccupied. When they had finished as much of the food as they could put away, she asked tentatively, "Tairei, do you want to go for a walk with me?"

Tairei's smile came back with the force of the sun rising, and Aili stared at her, then wondered if her mouth had fallen open.

"Yes," Tairei said. "Yes, let's walk. I'll– I'll– Yes, let's go." She grabbed Aili's hand, and Aili felt herself tugged to her feet — the girl was much stronger than she looked — as she waved helplessly at Nora and Edna.

It was fully dark now, Tairei's hand warmly entangled with hers.

"Do you know your way around here?" Tairei asked. "I haven't been here long. I just came from the Daxian Republic recently."

"I've lived in Easterly for a few years, but I don't spend much time in Little Daxian. When did you arrive?"

"Just last week."

Aili wondered how she had come; surely civilian ships weren't coming from the Daxian Republic now through the war blockade, but Tairei continued, "Is this your hometown?"

Aili shook her head. "I'm from a very small town. Nobody's ever heard of it, just farms."

"What's it called?"

"Fallon," she said. "Truthfully, it's not a very nice place; I was glad to leave."

"It's your surname, though, isn't it?" Tairei asked doubtfully. "Is it your clan home?"

"I guess so…My great-grandfather was one of the town's founders." Aili found herself not wanting to say any more about Fallon or her family, neither of which were pleasant topics for a romantic walk. "But what about you? Edna told me Tairei– It's not your name, right? Would you tell me your name?" She immediately thought that this was unforgivably awkward and wanted to slap her own face.

Tairei was quiet for a minute. "Why are you talking to Edna about me?"

"I don't really know Edna," Aili said quickly. "She's Nora's friend."

After a pause, Tairei said, "My name is Liu Chenguang."

Aili thought she sounded rather sad, and said, "I can call you Tairei if you want, though. It's already how I think of you."

Tairei smiled, but withdrew her hand; Aili's hand groped in the air for a moment before she found her pocket and tried to pretend that this was in no way complicated to manage. They were quiet for a while, walking from light to light pooling on the dark streets. There was a rich scent in the air, and then something medicinal and bitter.

Tairei raised her head and pointed with her chin. "That's the apothecary. I'm going to start working there tomorrow. I've been trained as a physician, but I can't really practice here. They'll just have me put the prescriptions together."

Aili said, "Is it like a pharmacy? I'm training to be a nurse now," and then remembered she wasn't supposed to tell anyone this. Well, Nora and her strictures were somewhere in a Daxian restaurant several blocks away, and Tairei was here now, pointing to a row of Daxian characters running up and down on a signboard.

"Come on," said Tairei, "it's still open. I can take you in and show you."

Aili looked around with interest at the wall full of tiny drawers, the counter showing roots and pills and oils, the scales and charts. "I wish I could read Daxian," she said, "I can't understand anything."

"I can tell you about things," Tairei said, and drew her finger along a chart showing a human body covered with mysterious figures. "These are the meridians that carry energy, and these are the acupuncture points, each point in combination with others addresses various disorders and imbalances in the body's energy…" After a while, she ran out of words, and smiled. "It's a very complicated system; it takes a long time to learn."

"It's fascinating," said Aili, mostly finding Tairei fascinating. She had soon gotten lost in the complicated lecture about elements and something called yin and yang, and wondered what kind of prodigy Tairei must be; she looked barely twenty. "It's very different from what I've been learning. It's mostly field dressings — not for chronic illness, just for wounds."

Tairei turned. "For wounds? What wounds? Field dressings?"

"Well, in the war."

"The war," Tairei said blankly. "Oh, yes."

"Didn't you just come from the Daxian Republic? Edna was saying that the Kunorese are occupying–"

"Yes, of course," Tairei said quickly. "I noticed that, of course. It's impossible not to notice."

It would definitely be difficult not to notice your country being invaded and occupied — and from what Edna had described, occupied with extreme brutality — yet Tairei sounded as though she had forgotten all about it, as though it wasn't anything particularly notable. Was she so traumatized that she was unable to think? Or perhaps she wasn't really Daxian at all? But she clearly spoke Daxian…Edna had spoken to her…and she suddenly remembered how the wound in Tairei's arm had simply disappeared. Why had she not even thought of that until now, as though a knife slash in an arm healing itself in a moment was a normal thing that didn't even deserve notice? Confused, Aili stared silently into Tairei's eyes.

"There's enough pain everywhere," Tairei said eventually. "After a while, it all blends together."

"I don't understand." Aili cleared her throat. "Was it because of the war, that you had to leave Daxian?"

"No, not because of that. I just had to come here."

"Why?"

"For you," Tairei said, simply, as though this was the most obvious thing in the world, something that both of them already knew. "For you, to find you, of course for you."

"What?" Aili said. She took a step backward. Tairei's eyes became anxious. "What, why for me?"

Tairei opened her mouth, and then closed it again. Finally, she said, "Don't you know why?" Her voice shook slightly. "You don't…know me?"

Aili stared, but nothing more was forthcoming. Tairei's eyes were very beautiful — that was all she could think of — but something wasn't right.

Tairei said, "You don't remember?"

Aili shook her head, which was starting to ache. It must be the alcohol at that restaurant; she knew she didn't have a good tolerance. She raised her hand to her forehead, and felt Tairei's hand cover it. Tairei was standing very close, too close, Aili could feel the nearness of her body, the pressure of her fingertips. Aili focused her eyes on a wall painting, partly illuminated by the streetlamps. In the dim light, the mural seemed alive to her.

"Are you all right?" Tairei asked. "Aili?"

"The painting," Aili said. "That painting – what is that picture?" Her head ached fiercely.

Tairei turned to look at the wall mural, painted in vivid colors. "It's just for a restaurant," she said, her voice thin. "It's a picture of a phoenix and a dragon."

She reached out for Aili's hand and Aili stepped back again, trying to get her balance, trying to stop her head from spinning. Tairei's fingers, warm and firm, were suddenly against the inside of Aili's wrist, pressing gently. "Aili, something's wrong?"

"I should get back to them," Aili said. "Too much to drink. It's late."

"I'll walk you back," Tairei said quickly. "You might get lost otherwise–"

"No, that's all right, I have a good sense of direction." This was not a lie; Aili had a very good head for knowing where she was and how she had gotten there, and the streets that had taken her and Tairei almost an hour of wandering and chatting through took less than ten minutes to bring her back to the restaurant. She almost ran back, away from this sense of unreality and dizziness and Tairei's hand over hers.

Reality was there, waiting for her, Edna and Nora outside the restaurant where she'd left them — Nora smoking a cigarette with her dark hair already losing its fashionable curl, and Edna looking worried. The pain in her head faded as though it had never been.

"I'm glad you're back," Edna said when she saw Aili. "There's something very strange about that girl. She's not telling the truth about who she is or where she came from. I think you should avoid her."

Aili said, "Yes, I agree."

"You do?" asked Nora.

Edna's mouth hung open, ready to argue more.

"I do," said Aili. "Let's go home."

Nora put her arm around Aili's shoulder. "Don't worry, little sister, big sister will help you find a better one before we ship out."

Edna and Aili said together, "Don't say that. It's weird," and started laughing.

As they got on the boat to cross the estuary to Sand Island, Aili looked back from the railings. Sure enough, a slight, dark-haired figure stood by the pier, watching the lighted ferry push through the dark waters. It only occurred to her, then, that she had left Tairei standing there in the street without even saying goodbye, and for some reason thinking this made her heart hurt. She put her head down against the wooden railing, took a deep breath, and looked up again. The figure had disappeared.

# CHAPTER 2
## TRAINING

THERE WERE LESS than four weeks left until embarkation, less than four weeks until the final tests. The days didn't leave much energy to visit bars at night anymore, and even Nora's amorous energy flopped asleep on the bed at lights out. The flight nurses would be evacuating maimed and bleeding soldiers from active battlefields on remote islands for long flights across the Great Western Sea to safe bases, and in addition to the medical training they needed to train in swimming, running, strength, orienteering, and using their issued guns.

Nora struggled swimming in the cold water of the bay, and Aili swam with her whenever they had a free moment, encouraging her to get her strength up and letting Nora use her as a test weight to prepare for the final watermanship test. They would need to be able to swim a mile — which truthfully seemed fairly inadequate if they crashed mid-Western, but Aili didn't mention it — and tow an unconscious person a quarter mile in ten minutes. Aili made Nora swim for at least an hour at a time, but still secretly worried that Nora wouldn't pass.

Aili had grown up swimming in the cold Helena River and in the rough, dangerous surf of the ocean at the river's mouth on the northern coast, so she anticipated no problems in that area. Truthfully, the medical training was also fairly routine — only systematizing what she had learned about treating wounds as a child through trial and error and providing her with better tools than she had had back home. Thus, she had ample mental space during class time and practical demonstrations to think about Tairei: when she went to sleep; when she woke up; when she was bored; sometimes when she should definitely not have been bored. It was infuriating, the way Tairei's eyes and smile were always waiting for her in her mind, and the way in which sometimes she would remember the figure waiting on the shore, quietly watching.

Nora's years-long crusade to set her up with interested girls had always begun well — with a good number of women quite interested in Aili's tall, blonde figure and something they interpreted as an air of quiet mystery — and had always flopped due to Aili's whatever it was: shyness or reserve or dislike of being touched. She had never felt drawn to anyone before. And now, there was this person, this strange and completely unsuitable person, occupying her mind only weeks before they left. Aili's fascination was only matched by Nora's growing concern about it.

"Aili," Nora said one day in the dormitory after Aili had missed three questions in a row in the classroom, "what's going on with you?"

Aili shook her head. "I don't know," she said.

"Still thinking about that person? Tairei?"

She nodded.

"Is it because she keeps showing up outside the gates and staring through the bars to see you?"

Aili blushed. "You noticed?"

"Of course I noticed, I've also noticed that you have to walk past the gates on errands you make up three times a day. I'm amazed they haven't just kicked you out of the program."

"I only saw her once or twice," she protested.

"You want to see her again, though." Nora sighed. "You know who else has noticed? The sentries. The chaperone. Half of our training cohort. Aili, we are on a military base in training, she looks Kunorese–"

"She's Daxian–"

"We all signed those papers about our romantic preferences. You know you'd get kicked out if anyone suspected." Nora put her arm around Aili's shoulders where they sat on Aili's bunk. Quietly, she continued, "Aili, I know it must be exciting to finally have these feelings, after all this time–"

Aili flinched a little bit, under Nora's arm, but knew more was coming.

As expected, Nora continued, doggedly, "This person isn't trustworthy. She gave you a false name. She pursued you and said that you should know her, and there's no possible way you know her. Edna says she is definitely not telling the truth about herself and where she came from. She said she changed dialects in the middle of their conversation, whatever that means, and now she's basically stalking you. You finally have a career — something to do that you can be proud of doing, right? You've come so far and you're ready to live a good life now. And that all goes down the drain if you trust the wrong person about this kind of thing. There will be other people, better people for you."

Aili didn't respond, looking down at her hands. *Nora is my best friend, my only friend,* she thought. *Nora knows me better than anyone else in the world.*

But she's wrong about this.

"You're ignoring me," Nora said, brown eyes narrowed. "I know you, Aili Fallon. You're so stubborn even though you never argue. You just do what you're going to do."

Aili smiled, knowing Nora wouldn't let it go until she did.

"That's better," Nora said. "In just a few days, it'll be the final exam, and then we'll leave. Are you going to visit your mother before we go?"

Aili sat up and said, "You really are getting all the hard conversations done at once, aren't you?"

"Might as well. It's not as though I get a lot of time with you where we can really talk. There's always other people around. If you don't want to contact your mother that's fine, you can stay here with me. But this might be the last chance. You might regret it if you don't."

"I've been thinking about it, I really have. I think...I think I should...but I'm..."

Squeezing her shoulders, Nora said, "We've talked about it. You don't have to go if your father's there, right? You can ask that friend of yours to just bring your mother to the restaurant to see you. He'll never know."

"He'll know," Aili said, absolutely certain.

"Well, he probably won't know before you're on a troop carrier in the Western Sea," Nora replied practically. After a pause, she added, "I know you've always missed your mother. You may not have another chance."

Aili nodded, and then said, "I should say goodbye to Tairei, too. The same reason. I might not have another chance."

Nora slapped her own forehead in exasperation. "Just let it go, Aili. I won't say any more. It's too late anyway. We'll be leaving soon, and you need to focus." She got up. "It's time for dinner. Are you coming?"

There was no possible way they would meet each other again; civilians weren't allowed onto the base, so Tairei couldn't come looking for her, and she... she couldn't go looking for Tairei.

Unless she did.

Aili stood up and said, "I'm signing off base for dinner tonight."

She didn't see Tairei in the restaurant, and it was too early for the bar, so she wandered toward the apothecary, as Tairei called it. The astringent, medicinal smell was stronger now, and through the windows she saw Tairei standing behind the counter, pulling roots and leaves and mushrooms and what looked like tree bark out of different little drawers and weighing them. Aili watched as she smiled at a customer and spoke something Aili couldn't hear, using a knife to cut the mixture up into thin pieces and wrapping it with white paper before handing it over.

Aili stood, unmoving. A rush of warmth and joy seemed to come from somewhere else but was most definitely inside her body, a tingling yearning to go closer that almost made her hair rise on her scalp. Tairei's hair was still loose and shining, swinging back and forth to cover her face, and once she put her hand up to brush it back behind her ear, Aili found her eyes following her hand… She took a few deep breaths before going inside.

When their eyes met, Tairei's brightened and glowed. "Aili," she said, "it's so good to see you."

Aili swallowed. "Do you want to get dinner with me?"

About twenty minutes later — after Aili had enjoyed watching Tairei get more roots and bark for prescriptions and listened to her explaining things in low-voiced Daxian to the customers, who looked oddly at the big, blonde person awkwardly wedged into a corner of the counter — the two of them walked down the darkening street toward an even smaller, but less crowded restaurant.

"I thought you might like this one," Tairei said. "It's more of a northern style. I thought that maybe that last restaurant's food was too unfamiliar to you."

"It was my first one. I've never had Daxian food before."

"Ah, yes," Tairei said, "I keep forgetting."

After dinner and drinks, Tairei laid some money down and asked, "Aili, would you like to walk with me?"

Aili stood up, hot all over as she imagined what it was she might like to do with Tairei, and stumbled after Tairei out into the dark street. She really had no ability to handle whatever liquor they served in those little bowls.

There was a curfew in place, so there were few people out now, most headed home for safety. The windows of the buildings were dark or covered, and the streetlights almost all shaded to avoid giving a target to a possible air raid. The

Kunorese hadn't raided the mainland yet, but everyone knew there were submarines off the coast. There might be carriers, too, and then the entire San Toma Bay would be a military target with all the bases and munitions factories here.

The darkness and hushed voices on the street felt strange — such a crowded place where it seemed that everyone was hiding. Aili shook her head, trying to clear it. Tairei took her hand and led her forward; she seemed to have extremely good night vision.

"We missed the sunset," Tairei said, unnecessarily. "But we can still go look at the stars? Down by the estuary, there's a good place. I found it the other day."

Aili's sense of direction told her that Tairei was leading her toward a part of town that most people would consider unsafe. She was personally quite familiar with it.

"How do you know your way around in the dark so well?" Aili asked. "I thought you'd only been here a few weeks."

Tairei said, "Careful, the sidewalk's broken there. I go out at night. To help people that I find in alleys, things like that. I don't sleep much."

"What do you mean, helping people?"

Tairei said, "I'm a healer. People need healing all the time, not only when they come looking."

Aili put her arm tentatively around Tairei's shoulders, and in the dimness could see the flash of Tairei's smile and her eyes shining up at her.

"You come here, alone, at night?" Aili asked. "Are you safe?"

"People do try things, sometimes," Tairei said offhandedly, "but I'm very fast. It's not a problem."

Aili frowned from the depths of her alcohol-fueled boldness. "Tairei," she said sternly, "you need to be safe. Who takes care of you if something happens? Isn't there anyone to protect you when you go out? I can. Do you want me to go with you?"

Then she realized that this wasn't much of a solution, as she'd soon be on a ship to an undisclosed island base, and added, "A gun, maybe? Do you know how to use one? I can ask Nora–"

"Why on earth would I want a gun?" Tairei asked. "I'm out there to heal people. Why would I want to put more holes in them? And in any case, I can't use a gun. The killing intent in those things is so high it would probably explode in my hand even if I just pointed it at a brick wall."

"Killing intent?"

"Never mind…well…you know…some things, they are weapons, but they can be other things too, right? They're not just for killing people. Like a scalpel, for instance. So a gun– Watch out!" Tairei pulled her to one side to avoid the carcass of some kind of rodent in the middle of the sidewalk. "A gun, it doesn't have any other purpose than killing. So, that means it has a high killing intent. It's infected by its purpose, and I can't use it. I've never even tried to touch one."

"I don't understand."

Tairei laughed. "You're drunk. It doesn't matter, it's not important. It's you I'm more worried about."

"About what?"

"The war you're training for. You said you'll be in combat areas. You were telling me." Tairei became serious. "When you're out there trying to help patients, what would you do if someone came at you with a weapon? Would you run?"

"Of course not, I'd try to protect the patient."

"With what? Polite arguments? Your body? What good does that do, in your situation?"

"What do you mean, in my situation?" Aili tried to clear her mind; Tairei sounded so worried. "Tairei, do you think that everything here is safe? It's not. There's nowhere totally safe..." Aili didn't know exactly how to say this. A war zone would be different than the streets of Easterly — of course it would, but home had never been a safe place either.

"Aili, truly, do you care so much about this war that you'll go lose your life for it?"

They had come to the edge of the seawalk now, but Tairei was looking at her, not at the stars.

"I don't want you to go. I want you to stay here, safe with me. Does it make a difference if I say it out loud?" Her eyes were dark and serious, pleading.

Aili said, "You're nervous." She could feel it in the sudden tension in Tairei's body. "Do you...I'm sorry," she said, and let go of her as she stepped back.

"No," Tairei said immediately, "it's not that." She looked around her. "There's something there. Someone watching us."

The stars over the bay were bright and clear in the absence of the city lights, but there was no moon, and around them everything was dark. Despite that, Aili could see Tairei's eyes shining, moving from one corner to another. Aili didn't sense any person nearby, though she was normally very sensitive to this kind of thing. Perhaps the liquor had made her fuzzy. Everything was silent — only occasional rustles of rats running through the dry leaves.

The rustling became louder, heavier, sounding almost like the beating of wings.

Softly, Tairei said, "Aili, get behind me."

Aili was slightly insulted. She was, after all, significantly taller and stronger, even if Tairei was one of those women who didn't like to be protected, which wouldn't at all be surprising. She put her hands on Tairei's shoulders again, and despite her protests, gently pushed her against the railing of the seawall so nothing could surprise her from behind. Then she stood in front of her, waiting.

Tairei was so sure that something was wrong, and for whatever unknown reason, she trusted Tairei. She did wish she at least had a knife. She was always better equipped than this before she started military training, but ironically, now she couldn't carry unauthorized weapons. "Do you have anything to protect yourself?" she asked.

Tairei shook her head. "You know I can't. I can't use weapons."

Something hissed from behind Tairei, where there shouldn't have been anything at all — in midair, above the water of the bay. Aili felt a shock through her body and moved before she was aware, pushing Tairei out of the way and jumping for the thing reaching for Tairei's back, bearing it down into the water underneath her before she even saw fully what it was. Luckily, it was high tide, so she didn't fall fifteen feet straight down onto sharp rocks. She heard Tairei scream as she fought the thing down into the cold, dirty, oily estuary water.

It was not a normal person; she was certain of that. It seemed to be half smoke and half slime, but somewhere in all the slipperiness and sludge, there were sharp teeth and bright yellow eyes, and something that wrapped around her forearm like a rope with glass shards, tearing at her skin as it pulled her beneath the surface. When the silt cleared slightly, she saw that it was a long tongue. Though a small voice in her mind protested that this thing couldn't be real, any shock was completely overwhelmed by her determination to kill it. She felt preternaturally calm, focused on the task at hand: to rip apart this thing that dared attack Tairei.

They had struggled down about five feet below the surface, black and dark, tangled in additional slime and sludge from the bottom, stirred up so there was barely a difference between the water and the earth as they fought. The only light came from the thing's yellow eyes glaring at her in the silty gloom. The shape of its body was hidden in the dark murk, but it was powerful and large — larger than she was. It seemed to have no problems breathing underwater, and to know that she herself couldn't. Its eyes gleefully blinked at her, and its tongue tightened around her arm, pulling her closer to what she now saw was a great mouth of irregular, needle-sharp teeth. Wherever the tongue touched her, it ripped and burned her skin.

She was a good swimmer, and she was strong, but that wasn't enough when she was held still and forced face-first into the mud. Aili groped helplessly in the sludge where the thing was slowly burying her alive, drowning and suffocating her with the filth of the estuary's bottom. Her free hand touched rocks, and bits of rubber, and trash, and then something sharp and hard. At last. A piece of metal. A weapon.

Aili brought it up slowly, knowing that the water's pressure would keep her from making any sudden moves, and stopped resisting the tongue dragging her into the needle-rimmed mouth. Just as she felt the first teeth pierce the skin of her entrapped arm, the thing's eyes glowing with delight, she carefully brought up the shard of steel from a long-destroyed ship and slammed it into the yellow disk.

The thing convulsed and released her, shuddering back into the black waters surrounding them. Aili shot to the surface, gasping for air.

"Tairei!" she rasped out when she had enough breath to do it.

"Aili!" Tairei's voice came, but nothing else; Aili couldn't see her.

The thing had dragged her several yards away from the shore. She swam over to the seawall and scrambled enough to grab the lowest bar of the railing, then pulled herself up, arms shaking. The arm that had been wrapped in the thing's tongue was a mass of blood and blisters, with yellow matter already pouring from pustules. It made her sick to look at, so she stopped looking. Of course, it hurt too, but that she could ignore.

She had left her precious metal shard in the thing's eye beneath the water, so when she staggered upright and squinted to see Tairei surrounded by four or five shifting, uncertain shadows, she had very few options. She simply ran straight in and used her momentum to bowl away two of them, catching the third around its middle, falling on top of it, and reaching out to grab its head with both hands and smash it against the pavement.

Tairei screamed again, and Aili felt Tairei's weight land on her back.

"What?" She startled, and then felt a sharp thump through Tairei's body that meant something had hit Tairei, hard.

"God*damn* it!" Aili yelled. "Tairei!"

The thing underneath her was not a person. Its face was covered in what seemed to be black feathers and its eyes were misshapen, one far larger than the other. The other half of its face was a short, sharp beak full of short, sharp teeth. Her effort to grab it by the cheekbones and smash it into unconsciousness was destined to fail.

Aili rolled to one side, doing her best to catch Tairei and protect her beneath her own body, but Tairei struggled frantically.

Tairei screamed, "No, no!" and pushed her back off violently, stumbling up. "Aili, just run!"

There were still four of the creatures surrounding them — all some uneasy blend of human shape and animal characteristics — giggling and hissing and clacking. Aili tried her best to get Tairei to back up against a wall so at least they would only have enemies in one direction, but it was too late. The most they could do was stand back to back.

Aili tried and tried to think, but nothing came to her. They had no weapons and there was no one nearby to call for help. The police would be unlikely to interfere in a fight in this part of town. Her arm hurt now, badly, her whole body shook, and she was having difficulty focusing her eyes. Pain shot up into her chest and throat from the damaged wrist and forearm, and her heart hurt with every uneven beat.

"Aili," Tairei cried urgently, but Aili couldn't really hear well now.

She fell to her knees, then to her hands, then down to the ground. Something laughed. She felt Tairei touching her, smoothing something warm and soothing over her arm, touching her lips for some reason. She tried to focus her eyes again. Was Tairei giving her medicine? Was Tairei crying?

Someone walked confidently out of the darkness. A man, by the shape, though it was too dim to see his face. He said something in a ringing, edged voice, in a language she didn't understand. The beings surrounding them growled and snapped, but one by one they disappeared — not walking away, but simply winking out.

Looking up at the stars, Aili could hear the soft susurrus of the water striking against the slimy stone of the wall. For some reason she hadn't been able to hear it, all this time. It was refreshing to hear. The pain in her arm was fading.

"Chenguang?" she called out.

Tairei's hand tightened on hers, but she didn't respond.

"Liu Chenguang," said the man, "you're taking risks out here, night after night."

"Get away," Tairei's voice came, hard and cold. "How dare you come near me."

"You're not even going to say thank you?" the man asked in mock-hurt tones. "I made the vermin leave. What was your plan to deal with them?" Coming closer, he said, "And what is–"

"*GO AWAY!*"

Aili felt Tairei jump to her feet.

"You don't come near! Get away from her!" Tairei's voice sounded raw, high-pitched, almost hysterical.

The man stopped as though surprised. Aili, moving her eyes though she couldn't move her head yet, watched him hold his hands up, protesting. "I'm leaving, I'm leaving," he said, placatingly. "We'll talk another time. When you're not so…overemotional."

Tairei responded with something that sounded very much like a curse word, even though the language was a mystery.

The man disappeared, as the others had.

She heard the beating of wings.

Aili tried to sit up, and she did feel much better, but sitting up was all she could do. She looked at her arm. She must have imagined those terrible, pus-filled wounds; there wasn't a mark on her.

"Tairei, where did they hurt you?"

Tairei was kneeling next to her, rocking slightly back and forth, head down almost to her knees, her arms wrapped around herself, not looking up.

"Tairei," Aili said, concerned. She reached out, pulling her into an awkward embrace, "Show me where you're hurt–"

"I'm not hurt," Tairei said through her muffled sniffling. "I'm not hurt. It's you that got hurt." She started sobbing — big, ugly, gasping cries, as though she could barely breathe.

Alarmed, Aili pulled her closer and tried to get her to calm down, calling her name over and over, but she couldn't stop. Moment after moment, it increased until Tairei was nearly screaming wordlessly, her body shuddering with each sob.

"Tairei!" Aili finally yelled, not wanting to hit her though they'd been trained that this kind of thing was best dealt with through a sharp slap. She shook Tairei gently, by the shoulders, trying to break the rhythm of sobbing cries and bring her back to reality. Tairei's shining eyes were red-rimmed and unfocused in the starlight, looking past her into the dark, as though she was seeing things that weren't really there.

"Tairei!"

Tairei put her arms around Aili in return and laid her head against Aili's shoulder, gasping, her muscles rigid with the effort of trying to control herself.

"No, not like that. It's all right, it's all right." Aili stroked her back gently, like she was a little cat.

Eventually, Tairei looked up at her; she was so very close, her eyelashes glittering with tears and her lips slightly parted as she breathed heavily.

Aili took a deep breath and closed her own eyes; she had never felt anything like this before, never touched or held anyone this way. Especially not someone that was looking at her with eyes like Tairei's. Aili swallowed and tried to think of petting the cat again.

"Aili," said Tairei at last, her voice soft and a little hoarse. "Aili, please don't go. Don't go, don't go." Her arms tightened around Aili's neck and shoulders. "I will do anything, anything, anything. Don't go to this war. Stay with me. Please stay with me, be safe with me. I can't even keep you safe here. You can't– you can't go."

Tairei's hands softly traced along Aili's neck, making her shiver, and then she said, "Your hairpins are all crooked. They're sticking you."

She pulled them out, one by one, while Aili sat there as though she were frozen. Aili stared past her as she concentrated on unbraiding Aili's hair, running her fingers through it, and Aili started shivering, and then Tairei's fingers stroked the edge of her ear, and she closed her eyes, and then. Then. Tairei's breath, Tairei's lips against her ear, so gently.

Aili gasped and blindly turned her head, finding Tairei's mouth, kissing her uncertainly, shyly, until she felt Tairei press forward against her. Aili held Tairei's face between her hands, then kissed down along her throat to feel the heartbeat beneath her lips, breath quick and uneven.

Body softening against her, Tairei called, yearning, eager, "Deming, Deming, please…"

Whatever had been happening inside her crashed and stuttered into coldness.

Aili broke off the kiss and opened her eyes. Tairei's eyes met hers, panicked.

For a moment the two of them sat there, frozen, staring at one another, sitting on the cold, bloodstained pavement in the dark, with no sound but the soft, slapping waves. Aili shivered all over with the shock of what had happened — what had stopped happening.

"Who is Deming?" Aili asked, at last. A sharp stab of pain lanced through her temple, and she held her hand to her forehead.

"Deming isn't anything. It's just a Daxian word for– for kissing," Tairei said quickly.

"Tairei," Aili sighed, "that's not even a good lie."

Tairei looked down at the ground between them. They were still entangled with each other.

"Deming is a name," Aili said. She didn't know how she knew this with the utmost certainty, but she did. "Deming is a person's name. I'm not that person."

Tairei shook her head, shivering.

Aili stood, shaking a little bit.

"Aili," Tairei said, pleading. She stood up too. "Aili, I…"

Aili wanted to say *We're done now, there's no possible explanation for you calling me some stranger's name while you kiss me*, but she looked at Tairei, so small and miserable after they had just been touching one another so tenderly, and she couldn't do it. She couldn't even keep her own dignity and walk away as Nora would certainly have advised. Instead, seeing the tears trickling down Tairei's cheeks where she stood with her head bowed, she carefully put her arms around her again and kissed her on the top of her head.

To her own surprise, Aili flushed again at the sensation of Tairei's hair beneath her lips. Aili took a deep breath, another one, the scent of bitter medicine and incense overwhelming her, and then carefully set space between them.

"Tairei, you're so upset. This isn't– this isn't– Look where we are," she said, trying to be a decent person.

Tairei's eyes settled back into consciousness from whatever frenzied world she had gone to and she took a deep breath. "Aili, I'm sorry. You don't– you don't– you don't want to…"

Of course she wanted to, but they were lying in the cold muck in the worst part of Easterly and they had just been attacked by god knows what, and Tairei seemed to be near some kind of nervous breakdown, and…She almost couldn't bring her mind to remember it, Tairei's voice calling someone else's name. Aili compromised by holding her protectively.

"What happened here, tonight?" Aili asked. "What were those things?"

The attackers, the dousing in the filthy estuary, the thing under the water, the man that had come. It all seemed unclear in her mind now. She had been drunk, after all; no doubt it was all just a fight. Nothing new. She had fought so many times just like this, at night, on the street. It wasn't anything unusual — and no harm done, she didn't even have any wounds — but something was not right. Not right at all. Her mind was as entangled and confused as her body, and that piercing pain kept coming and going behind her eyes.

Tairei swallowed. "I can explain," she said, at last. "But it's…very complicated. Can you let me think about how to explain it, please? Just…give me a little time."

Her hair still had that scent to it. Aili didn't dare come closer; something about that scent stirred her in every possible way.

"I need to get back to the base," she said, resolving to avoid everything in favor of simple reality. "I can't see you for a few days. We're in our final testing."

"I'm sorry," Tairei said, her voice still raspy. "You'll be tired tomorrow after…all this."

"I'm fine," Aili said, and physically she did feel fine aside from that headache and, sometimes, a shooting, stabbing pain in her chest. "If I pass, they'll give us two days of leave before we go. I'll see you then."

Tairei nodded, and though she didn't seem to want to let go, eventually she did and walked with her to the ferry. "I'll be waiting," she said. "I'll meet you in Little Daxian."

# CHAPTER 3
## DEPARTURE

ON THE DAY of the final watermanship test, rain poured down. Aili felt that this was really quite helpful, as they were already soaked and freezing cold before they jumped in. The water of the bay felt warm by comparison to the cold wind, though in reality, their body heat was being leached away rapidly. The wind whipped up huge waves as well. The final mile-long swim to shore left every one of the cohort — except those who had to be rescued themselves — literally dragging themselves on hands and knees onto the ramp and then lying there like dead things. Eighteen hours from crash simulation to final crawl to the deck, but it was done.

Aili and Nora both made it in. They lay there on the dock together staring at the dark afternoon sky, letting the rain crash down on them, and trying to breathe again until they were met by towels and the final evaluations from the trainers.

"I passed," said Nora, finally. "I did it."

"You did," said Aili. "Congratulations. Me too, by the way."

Giggling weakly, they collapsed onto their bunks. "What are you going to do during last leave?" asked Nora. "I'm going to spend it in Easterly."

Aili shrugged. "I'm going to Easterly tonight, want to come?"

"Absolutely not. I'm sleeping. I'll go nice and early tomorrow. Why are you going out again?"

"I just like Daxian food now."

Nora groaned. "No, not her. Haven't you learned your lesson?" she asked, and almost immediately passed out, still shivering slightly.

Aili piled another blanket on her, put on a sweater, and went to sign out. They had two and a half full days of leave. At noon on the third day, they would be given their uniforms with appropriate ranks and would embark on the ship.

It wasn't quite dinnertime, so Aili loitered around the places she had seen Tairei before: the restaurant, the bar, the apothecary, the ferry stop. It was just as well that she hadn't told Nora what had happened that strange night with Tairei, she thought. Nora would have tied her to the bunk before letting her go again. It was an uncomfortable feeling. She had never lied to Nora before, never even come close to lying. The only time she had ever concealed the whole truth from Nora…well, it had only been about bad things, shameful things. Did that mean that looking for Tairei — dreaming about Tairei — was a bad and shameful thing?

She stood still in the rain and stared at the painting on the wall again. The phoenix was a red bird with golden eyes, surrounded by elaborate flames. As the rain ran down it, the flames looked as though they were flickering in the last dim light.

With all the effort she'd put forth today already, and with the cold rain still coming down, her low body temperature kept cramping up her leg muscles. Just as the shops were beginning to close up for the evening, she had to sit down to catch her breath and massage her legs. She found a little bench up against a wall, probably used for someone to display their wares during the day, and leaned back against the bricks with her eyes closed, rubbing her calves rhythmically.

"Are your legs sore?"

"Tairei!"

Tairei was kneeling next to her, looking up, concerned. She reached out to continue to massage Aili's knee; Aili jerked in surprise and nearly kicked her in the face. Luckily, Tairei had excellent balance. She laughed and sat on the bench next to her, protecting them both with the umbrella she was carrying.

"I'm so glad to see you," Aili said, weakly.

Tairei looked like herself again — smiling, her eyes shining as usual, as though that night had never happened. Aili wasn't quite sure what to make of it. For days now, she had been remembering Tairei's tear-filled eyes and her sobbing gasps for air even more vividly than the impossible things that had attacked them or the strange man who had driven them away, both of which comparatively seemed unimportant.

Tairei seemed to know what she was thinking. "I'm all right," she said. "It was just…a lot to happen in one evening."

Aili nodded. Somehow, she didn't want to talk about it either. Let Tairei explain in her own time and way. This was the last day they would spend together for years at best — perhaps forever, if her luck was bad — she didn't want to ruin it with demands.

"What about your legs?" Tairei asked. "Do you want me to heal–"

"Ah no," she said quickly, "no need. I'm not injured, just tired. We had our final test today, to see how long and far we could swim. I'm just exhausted and my muscles are complaining."

Tairei smiled and pulled her upright toward a restaurant. "Aren't you hungry?"

After they had begun eating the rice and braised fish, Aili took a deep breath and said, "Tairei."

"Mmm?"

"Tairei, you know I'm leaving soon. The day after tomorrow."

Tairei's chopsticks stopped in midair, then continued toward the fish. "So soon," she said. Her eyes and face became very quiet, the shine in them at its lowest ebb.

"Can you choose not to go? Please?" she asked, at last.

Aili shook her head. "I'm committed. It would be desertion. And I wouldn't want to back out…this is…this is…"

She tried to find some words for it — to explain the ways in which she felt so unable to protect and help the people she loved in the past, how she wanted so much to be able to do it in the future. "I've never really accomplished anything good before," she said at last. "I'm able to do something meaningful, something important now, something that can…help people who are hurt. I don't mind taking risks to do that."

Tairei nodded quietly.

"Could you choose…not to go out at night while I'm gone?" Aili asked, even knowing what the answer would be.

Tairei just smiled quietly at her.

"Never mind," Tairei said. "Never mind it. Let's trust that we will see each other again when you come back. Let's…let's send you off with happy thoughts and memories. So you'll want to come back."

*I do*, Aili thought, looking at her. *I want to come back to this person.* She turned that over in her mind a few times. There had never been a person that she had wanted to return to.

"How long till you need to go?"

"The day after tomorrow."

"Then that's two days we'll have together, no matter what," Tairei said firmly. "And two nights."

Aili stared at her, chopsticks midair, mouth suddenly dry.

Tairei looked as though she was caught between laughter and tears, then put her own chopsticks to Aili's lips with the piece of fish she had just dipped in sauce. "Eat," she said gently. "There's something special I want to do with you. Before you go."

Aili choked on the fish and grabbed for the liquor again.

"Aili," Tairei sighed as she handed it over, "please get your mind out of the gutter, it's not that."

Aili spat liquor all over the table.

"Although," Tairei continued, now openly laughing at her and reaching over to wipe Aili's lips with a napkin, "I'm also open to that option?"

Her head down on the table, Aili prayed that Nora would never learn about this conversation. When she felt like she could look Tairei in the face again, she raised her head and coughed. "It's— it's just that I need to make a trip to see my mother. My mother lives in my hometown. It's not close," she said. "That's why I can't spend this time all with you…"

Then, she thought that sounded very presumptuous, and felt the blush that always showed in her skin. She reached over and gulped more of the liquor, which did not help.

"I mean," she said, after the burning went away, "I mean. If it were up to me…I would like…you're the only person I would want to— to spend the time with…?"

Tairei's face fell, then she said, determined, "I'll come with you. I can see your hometown and meet your family."

"No," Aili said loudly. "Absolutely not." She sat up straight, her whole body tense with the idea of Tairei in her family's house.

Tairei stared. "You— you don't want me to come?"

"It's not that," she said, tumbling down from her sudden clarity back into liquor-fueled confusion. "My home isn't a good place. That's why I've never been back. I won't go all the way home myself, even. I'll ask a friend to bring my mother out. She needs to know—" she stopped short, not wanting to say, *She needs to know I might die,* because she was fairly sure that Tairei would get upset and she didn't want to ruin their last evening together.

Tairei said, "I could come with you anyway. There's this thing I want to do with you, but I can't do it yet. The time's not right."

"Ah," said Aili as though she understood this completely, and ate more fish.

Tairei said, "Please, Aili. I have to come with you." Her eyes were fixed on Aili's, dark and sad. She added, "I'll follow you if you don't let me come with you."

Aili wavered. She truly didn't want to leave Tairei. Not so quickly, not without…it would be safe enough, surely. "You could come and just see the town. Not my hometown — another one, where my friend lives," she said. "And maybe I'll take you to see the ocean. Not Fallon. But the bus leaves tonight. Do you mind sleeping on the bus?" She found herself looking forward to that bus ride, to Tairei falling asleep on her shoulder.

Tairei beamed, relieved. "That's fine, as long as we're together." She added, "Do you think that we can find a quiet place, away from people, just us? Outdoors somewhere. After you see your mother."

"Oh, that would be no problem at all," Aili said, relieved. "The one thing I can tell you about my hometown is it's…very quiet."

The main street boasted twenty or so buildings, and other roads ran back with houses on them, but not many. Tairei looked around at the tininess of the place, amid the vast golden hills spotted with single oak trees and standing rocks.

"You can practically see the whole town from here. Is there anything you want to explore in particular?" Aili asked, smiling.

"Is this your home?"

"Just the closest town," she said. "It's a few miles walk from here to where I grew up, or maybe I can borrow a car. I thought I could settle you in here while I visit my…my mother."

She found that she didn't want to say home in the same sentence as Fallon or her family. This place wasn't home; in any real meaning of the word, it had never been home. She was already regretting trying to do this — spoiling her last moments with Tairei with this — but they were already here, and her mother… She should at least check on her, at least let her know that she was alive before she got on a ship with the possibility of dying in a distant country. They had never been able to say goodbye properly. No matter what, in the end, if she died her mother would get the telegram. She deserved to know that this was happening.

Tairei was watching her, concerned, but all she said was, "I'd like lunch. Is there a restaurant?"

"In the hotel. It's kind of strange there's a hotel, I guess, but in the old days people used to visit more…Anyway, most of their business is really the bar and selling food to folks. Not Daxian food though," she added quickly. "There's no Daxian people here."

"At all?"

"None. There are some Kunorese families with farms around, further north…"

They entered the darkness of the bar in the little hotel. The whole building had only two rooms on the first floor, and maybe four on the second. As their eyes adjusted, Aili saw the person she had been hoping to see: Old Mrs. Mitchell — looking feisty as ever with her graying blonde hair up in a bun — leaning against the bar to talk to Mr. Bullock, nursing a drink, and eating what looked like potatoes and ham.

Mrs. Mitchell looked over, and her voice stopped. Mr. Bullock looked up too.

"Aili Fallon," said Mrs. Mitchell. "Aili Fallon, I never! You've gone and grown up! It's been how long? Six years? And never a postcard or a note!" She hurried out from behind the bar to give Aili a hug.

Mr. Bullock kept staring from behind his moustache.

"Where are you coming from, are you staying? Have you seen your mama yet?"

"No," Aili said when she got her breath back, "not staying, and haven't seen Mama yet. Haven't been home. We just wanted to get some lunch. What've you got today?"

"Ham and potatoes, chicken pot pie, and some chicken soup, too, if you want that… Whatever you want, you let me know!"

When they had settled at a table with ham and potatoes — Tairei carefully poking it with a fork to separate all the meat from the vegetables — Mrs. Mitchell sat down with them. "Who's your friend, Aili?" she asked, peering to try to see Tairei's face better.

Aili didn't introduce Tairei, just letting Mrs. Mitchell run on as she knew she would.

Lowering her voice, she continued, "Aili, you know your mama's not in a good way. Your dad is still your dad. You should go see her as soon as you're done eating, all right? Your dad's not at home. I know for a fact that he went out of town yesterday with his drinking buddies. They'll be out for the weekend, no doubt, that's their usual way. You can take my car if you want to. Just don't go back to wherever without seeing her."

Aili swallowed. Well, this couldn't be any better; it was the best she could hope for, really. Her mother wouldn't need to risk leaving the house in Mrs. Mitchell's car and having that reported to her father later. Aili would be in control. She'd have a car. She'd be able to leave quickly.

"Ok," she said. "I'll go see her."

It would be quick.

"She'll be glad to know you're well and healthy, Aili. Will your friend go with you?"

"Is it ok if she stays here and waits for me?" she asked.

"Sure, sure, I'll give her a lemonade," Mrs. Mitchell said, and went back up to the bar.

"I want to go with you," Tairei said immediately.

"No."

"This is part of our time together," Tairei said stubbornly. "Don't leave me in a strange place with strangers and lemonade. I don't know how soon you'll come back."

Aili stared at her. She hadn't realized Tairei could be so argumentative. "It's better, Tairei, really…The place I grew up, it isn't a good place."

"I'm coming, Aili," Tairei said, as though it wasn't up for conversation. "I need to be with you."

"Why?"

Tairei looked back down at the potatoes, and said, at last, "Time is short."

"But…"

It was true, time was short; they only had a few hours left together. Her father wouldn't be there. It should be safe, and they would be quick. There was also a part of her that wanted her mother to meet Tairei — to have her mother know that she wasn't alone and friendless after everything.

"All right," she said, and Tairei raised her head and smiled.

The car bounced down the back road between the town and Fallon, crossing the little river and tracing along it into the valley that lay behind the looming rocks on the other side. The hills rolled golden around them, surrounding them and the green flat near the creek. Cows grazed around it, the standing rocks breaking through the soil in a pattern that no one could ever quite grasp. The fog came down, silencing everything, bringing an eerie stillness. The river seemed to come from nowhere and go nowhere, yet there was a path of water through the hills somewhere that they couldn't easily see. It was as though the hills were hiding all the ways one could go in order to leave that valley.

Tairei looked through the windows in silence, and at last said, "This is a strange place. Beautiful but strange."

When they pulled up to the white house on the steep hillside over the water, Tairei looked up. "There are a lot of crows," she said. "Are there always?"

"Yes," said Aili, getting out of the car and taking a deep breath. The sight of that house had been like a punch to her gut. It looked no more welcoming than it ever had, and more dilapidated than she remembered. The lace curtains stirred at the windows behind the porch.

"There've always been lots of crows here. They probably like being near the house because of that windbreak there. There aren't a lot of tall trees around except those. Someone planted them when the house was built."

Tairei looked some more, then turned to gaze back over the valley. There was a little frown between her eyes again. "There's something strange here. This should be excellent qi orientation, but it feels..." She shook her head.

Aili stared at the silent house. She could hear cattle lowing, far away. The crows calling. The wind whispering in the tall trees. Nothing else but the silence she remembered from her childhood, as though it were waiting for something.

This was Fallon: a group of six or so houses strung along the road, the hill at their back, the water in front, the rocks sharing a message no one could read.

"There used to be a flower garden," Aili said suddenly. "Maybe it got too much trouble to water, after I left." She looked at Tairei. "I should have told you...my mother doesn't talk much. I don't know how she is now. I haven't seen her since I left — I was sixteen then..."

Tairei took her hand. "It's all right. I'm with you."

Aili nodded and walked hand in hand with Tairei up the stairs to the porch. The front door was slightly open, no need to knock.

"Mama?" she called, tentatively. "Mama, it's me. I'm here to visit...I'm coming in, ok? I have a friend with me."

The scent of old wood, wax, mildew, meals eaten long ago, dust...Aili walked quickly through the sitting room. There was a radio now — she didn't remember that being there when she left — mumbling something to itself.

*It's good Mama has a radio so she's not so lonely*, Aili thought.

Down the corridor, past the stairs; it was too narrow now for Tairei to walk next to her. Through the door to the kitchen at the back of the house.

The kitchen had always been the best place — the place that felt more alive than the rest of the house — and it was where Aili's mother spent most of her time. There was something simmering on the stove, something with the scents of Aili's childhood. A tall, broad-shouldered woman, silver-gilt hair braided and pinned around her head, stood in front of it, apron tied neatly, carefully stirring. She turned around, and her blue eyes filled with tears.

"Aili," she said, and crossed the room in three wide steps, grabbed her, and held her in a hug. "Aili." There seemed to be no other words her mother could get out for a while, until finally, "I am glad."

Aili held her mother, a few tears on her cheek.

Aili's mother struggled again to find words. "Good to see you," she said at last. "Good that you left, good that you come back."

"Are you well? Are you ok?"

Her mother wiped her eyes. "I am ok," she said. "Just glad to see you, and know you are safe."

Aili pulled Tairei toward her. "Mama, this is my friend, Liu Chenguang."

"You have a friend," her mother said. "I'm glad. Welcome to our house, Miss Liu."

Tairei tilted her head to one side, as though considering something, then spoke in another language. To Aili's shock, her mother's face lit up and she began to talk rapidly, grabbing for Tairei's hand as she continued to hold Aili's and nodding energetically, pulling them both toward the table.

"You speak Sammish?" Aili said, dazed. "I barely even speak Sammish. There's no one else here who does…She's never had anyone to talk to, since my dad used to yell at her whenever she didn't speak Anglish."

"She wants you to know…" Tairei concentrated, then began translating almost simultaneously as Aili's mother continued. "I told her that you will be leaving soon, but didn't tell her why. She said she is so happy you are safe, and all this time she has been praying for your safety, and she doesn't blame you for leaving. She's glad you left, glad you got away, you should leave before he comes back—"

Aili was too stunned to explain to Tairei that she could understand Sammish, just not speak it well. "Please, tell her to come with us."

"Who is this that she's glad you got away from, Aili? She says that she can't leave, she doesn't have anywhere to go."

Aili found herself clenching her nails into her hands again. It was true. Her mother had nowhere to go; there was nowhere Aili could bring her, she had no way to support herself without Aili's father, and Aili was about to leave for the war. Who could possibly take care of her? Her Anglish was limited, she'd been isolated here all these years with a husband whose language was limited to slaps and curses, and she was — like Aili had been until she was sixteen years old —

too afraid of the consequences to run.

Tairei said something back to Aili's mother, but her mother shook her head, more firmly.

"She refuses, Aili. She says she doesn't want to be a burden to you, and she wants you to take some cookies she has made. You should take them all, and you should go. She says you have been the best daughter she could ever wish for, all her life. She wants you to know how much she is happy for you to live well."

Aili's mother's hands — long-fingered, large-knuckled hands identical to Aili's — were rapidly wrapping some cookies and treats into wax paper bundles.

Aili found her eyes so full of tears she could barely see.

"She says she wishes she knew you were coming so she could have made more, and there's also a shawl and a prayerbook she wants you to have. She'll go upstairs to get it," Tairei said as Aili's mother shoved the package into her hands and rushed off.

Tairei sat down in a chair, breathless, looking at her. Aili stood still in the middle of the kitchen, holding the cookies, her eyes squeezed tight to keep the tears in. At last, she took a deep breath and opened her eyes. She could hear her mother rummaging around upstairs, probably in that old cedar chest she had; that's where all her most special things were.

"Thank you," she said to Tairei. "I'm sad that I can't even talk to her. Not like that, so it's easy for her. I can understand, but we were never allowed to speak it. How do you know Sammish?"

Tairei looked at her, silently, her eyes very quiet and dark with the shine off of them. "Your name is Sammish, so I knew that someone in your family must be. It's not a common name. Usually, someone would have to talk to me so I know what language they speak. I just guessed this time."

When Aili didn't respond, Tairei asked, "This seems like a big house, do you have brothers or sisters?"

Aili shook her head, and finally said, "I had two younger brothers, but they died a long time ago."

"I'm sorry," said Tairei. She was very pale, as though all the blood had drained from her face. "I'm...I'm sorry, Aili."

"It's not your fault," she said, wondering why Tairei seemed so upset. She rubbed her eyes. Her mother looked just the same as she had when she had run away. It was so good to know that she was still safe and that she didn't blame Aili for leaving.

"When my mother comes back down, can you help me explain about... about the military stuff?" She had never written to her mother, in all these years.

A letter would have been too risky for both of them. "She won't understand it as well in Anglish. If you help, she can ask questions."

As they heard Aili's mother's footsteps coming down the stairs, the sound of a car engine came into the yard.

"Damn," said Aili under her breath.

Her mother's footsteps quickened desperately. She ran at full speed into the kitchen, shoving some fabric into Aili's arms, hugging her fiercely and quickly and kissing her hair, then said, "Go, go, go now, quick."

There was no point in running out the back door. He would already have seen the car.

Aili squared her shoulders and walked down the corridor. "Tairei," she said, a little too late, "you should go out the back, ok?

Tairei ignored her, following close behind.

The man who opened the front door was slightly drunk, but still very handsome — black hair with not a streak of gray, bright blue eyes, and a chiseled face that looked attractively flushed, rather than florid.

"Aili," he said, leaning against the doorjamb to get his balance. "Look who's back, huh? I knew you couldn't make it out there…Need to come back…I knew you would. I knew it." He fingered something in his pocket. "Get upstairs."

"Shut up and get out of the way," Aili said, her heart beating painfully with terror. "I'm not here for you and I'm not staying."

She was proud that her voice didn't shake. When she left, she had been so frightened of him that she ran away in the night, while he was passed out cold.

Tairei silently moved to stand in front of her, quicker than Aili could push her back.

Her father's eyes lit up. "You bring this for me? I got room." He reached out and grabbed for Tairei's arm.

Tairei twisted her hand and blocked him, grabbing his wrist, but that seemed to be all she could do. Once she let go, he would grab her again.

"Don't you touch her!" Aili got between them and pushed him away forcefully, furious.

He really was drunk, or maybe she was stronger than she'd been as a teenager.

At her touch, he lost his balance and flew back to slam against the wall, as though she had thrown him. A mirror fell off the wall and crashed next to him, covering him in shards of glass. He looked at her, open-mouthed and dazed, with blood on his forehead, but that wouldn't last long.

Aili grabbed Tairei's hand and pulled her out, practically pushing her in the car, then jumping in herself and cranking the engine.

One of the things she remembered about her childhood was that no one ever heard anything. Even though the silence over the valley was so complete that you could hear your neighbor cough at night, no one ever came to investigate the screaming and yelling at their house. No one ever saw anything either. No one ever came to check. No one helped them.

Once Tairei grabbed the wheel to keep them out of the ditch, Aili realized that she was driving blindly by instinct toward one of her safe places from her childhood. She stopped and put her face in her hands, trying to get her breath.

"This wasn't a good idea," Aili said, sitting up. "I'm sorry, Tairei. I shouldn't have brought you. My mother…I wish…"

Her hair had come unpinned and was falling around her face. Tairei reached up and put some strands back behind her ears, carefully, as though touching something very fragile.

"There's so much pain in your home," Tairei said. "I'm sorry for all that pain, for you."

"It's not my home," Aili said. "Nora is my home, if I have any home at all."

Tairei was silent, still stroking the hair behind her ears. "I wish," she said, carefully, "I wish. I wish I could save you from that."

Aili shook her head and picked up Tairei's hand to hold when she stopped touching her hair, hating herself for her uselessness and fear. "This is a bad place. I shouldn't have brought you here."

Even now she was too afraid to go back to that house, to see that man's eager eyes and share breath in a room where he also breathed.

"I'm glad you brought me. I'm glad you weren't alone." Tairei said, a little fierce. After a while, she looked out the window. "It's getting toward dinnertime now…Tomorrow you need to be back, don't you?"

Aili nodded. "We'll have to leave this evening, Mrs. Mitchell will drive us to the station, she said."

"There's still something I need to do," Tairei said, almost shyly. "Can you bring me to a place away from roads, and houses, and people? A place with a tree would be best."

"Of course," Aili said, shaking herself back into mental order. "There's a lot of places like that here. We can just leave the car here, just walk…A little less than a mile, there's a good place like that."

"Good," said Tairei, sounding determined. "That's good. Let's go now, Aili, please?"

Aili laughed a bit, getting out of the car and opening Tairei's door for her.

"Are you in a hurry?"

"A little," Tairei said, looking toward the angle of the sun moving toward the horizon. "A little bit of a hurry."

There was only one enormous tree, nestled between the steep hills. The coast oak was always green, even in the hottest summer, even surrounded by the grass turned to dry gold on all sides.

"I used to come here when I was young," Aili said, ducking under the spreading branches and touching the oak's thick, rough trunk. The branches spread out low and long from the trunk, wider than high — an easy tree for a child to climb, hiding from adults and the world outside. Aili found the rough bark comforting against her forehead, and looked up at the sky through the branches of the tree. The sunlight was thick and golden-red. "Well, we're here."

There was a nook between two high roots where Aili had liked to hide when she was young, which could fit her and Tairei if they were close to one another. "It's not that tall," Aili said. "Further north, there's enormous trees. You wouldn't believe them."

"Will you take me someday?" Tairei asked. "When you come back."

Aili nodded. "Yes." When she came back. They could start over then. "I would like to do that with you. When I come back."

Then, she thought of that name. *Deming.* A spasm of pain wrung inside her.

Tairei must have seen it in her face. She said, seriously, "Aili, I want to explain to you– I promised to explain. It's just…it's very hard. I don't know where to start. So I wanted to start with this." She lay her hands on either side of Aili's face and kissed her, not passionately, but yearning, hopeful.

Aili closed her eyes and felt Tairei's lips on hers again — like that time on the dark, wet street that night in Easterly — and pulled her closer, wanting to hold her. For some reason, she felt not joy and excitement, but a deep sadness welling up from somewhere she couldn't name. "Tairei," she said, at last, "Tairei, I'm not…that person. Is this even for me? Is it me that you want to be kissing?"

Tairei's face was so close that her lashes brushed against Aili's cheek. "It's for you, Aili," she said, "I promise, it's you that I want, I know who you are." She drew back a little bit. "Do you want me?"

"Yes," Aili said. This was too deep in her heart to deny or equivocate or protect her own dignity.

Tairei took a deep breath, and exhaled, slowly. "There's something…because

I want you to be safe–"

A voice came from outside the sheltering tree branches. "Aili, get your ass out here now."

Aili froze. He must have seen the car, parked where she had left it by the roadside.

Tairei stood up.

"Get out here!"

A gunshot rattled through the leaves over their heads.

"Did he just shoot at you?!" Tairei clenched her fists.

Aili stood, trembling in automatic obedience, but Tairei grabbed her arm as she passed.

"Don't bother," she said, her eyes glowing. Her hand felt hot on Aili's arm, as though she were suddenly running a high fever.

"Tairei?" she asked, turning toward her, frowning. "Are you all right?"

A second gunshot rang out. This one clipped Aili on the shoulder — just a graze, enough to make her cry out and bleed a little bit.

Aili's father laughed and his footsteps came closer, crunching on the grass.

Tairei held onto Aili's wrist with a grip like hot iron, and the blood running down from Aili's shoulder combined with that heat was making her dizzy.

"Dad?" Aili called, confused. Her will was in fragments, wounded by so much in so little time. If she was obedient, he wouldn't hurt anyone. If she was a good girl…

"Dad, just wait, I'll come out, just give me a minute."

Tairei bit her own lip until it bled, and leaned over to kiss the wound in Aili's shoulder.

Aili shook her head violently at the touch of her lips. "Tairei, what–"

"You!" shouted Tairei suddenly, turning her head to look out through the branches. "You nearly killed your own daughter!"

"She's mine to do whatever with," said the man. "You shut up, girlie, I have plenty here for you too."

Tairei laughed.

The laugh had such a strange edge to it — not of hysteria but of something else.

Tairei shouted, "You have thirty seconds to live."

"What!?" Aili tried to pull her hand out of Tairei's grip, harder, but she couldn't get away. She needed to do what her father said, then Tairei wouldn't be hurt–

The sharp-edged, strange laughter stopped almost as quickly as it had started.

Tairei turned back to Aili and met her eyes. "I'll explain later. Aili, we've run out of time, please trust me."

Then, suddenly, Tairei raised her other arm to her mouth and ripped her own wrist open with her teeth.

Aili screamed, "*Tairei!*"

The blood poured out, spurted out, leapt out, decorating the leaves and the grass and Aili's body. The tear in Tairei's arm didn't close.

Tairei didn't look at her or let go of her hand, though Aili desperately fought to put pressure on the dreadful, ragged wound. Her face was not like Tairei's face anymore; the gentleness and playfulness that Aili had always seen there was gone, and in its place was something hard and furious and empty.

She could hear her father running beneath the tree branches, stomping over the golden grass that was dappled with blood. But something was happening to the blood — where it had fallen on the grass, it began to smolder. Where it was pouring from Tairei's arm, it fell like a waterfall of sparks, surrounding them in a whirlwind of tiny fires.

Tairei turned back to Aili, raised Aili's arm to her bloody lips, and bit down, not gently, but strong enough to tear Aili's skin and rip the veins beneath. Aili screamed again and struggled, but even with one hand, the smaller woman was stronger.

"Aili," Tairei said, her eyes narrowed and fierce, "I will keep you safe, you understand? That's all I want. For you to live a good life. You'll be safe. I'm sorry. I'm sorry for everything."

Tairei held Aili's bleeding wrist against hers. The sparks quickened, increased, mixing with Aili's blood and making it burn in her body. All she could see was the river of fire surrounding them.

"*Tairei!*" Aili screamed again. "Chenguang, what are you doing? Stop it, stop it right now! Get away from me! Let go! I–"

And then, Liu Chenguang, still holding Aili's hand, erupted into a pillar of fire.

# CHAPTER 4
## HEALING

THE LEAVES OF the tree were green and rustled in the wind.

Everything else was black.

Aili was lying on the charred ground, staring up through the leaves of the tree. It seemed untouched by anything, as though it hadn't noticed the explosion, or whatever it had been.

Tairei—

She sat up, the blackened grass crackling beneath her, and leaned with her hand on the tree trunk for balance until she was on her feet. Was it still the same day? Had a night passed? Was it still morning, would they get back in time? Mrs. Mitchell would drive them back to the station. She couldn't miss the embarkation.

"Tairei!" she shouted. Aili coughed a little, but not as though she'd just been through a conflagration, breathing the smoke of the valley's incineration around her. "Tairei!"

There was no answer.

She grabbed at her wrist. There was no pain. There was no mark at all. Her shoulder, where the bullet had grazed it, was unscarred, unhurt.

Had she lost her mind completely? What had happened?

She turned around and around in the bowl of the little valley. The black burning covered everything to the rim of the hilltops and then stopped, evenly, as though it were an ebony bowl with golden decorations. As though the fire had expanded out and then simply disappeared, down to its last sparks and embers.

The charred grass wasn't hot; the ground felt cool, even damp. Had it rained? Had the fog come through?

She walked out across the crackling blackened grass. The crows were gone. All life was gone. There was no answer to her calls.

Perhaps Tairei had woken up first. Perhaps she had left.

But Aili knew this couldn't be. She knew Tairei would not have left her here. Tairei would not leave her alone.

The blood, and the fire.

Aili laughed a little bit because she had to do something or she would scream, or cry. Then, she decided that she should, indeed, scream and cry.

"TAIREI!" she screamed until her throat was raw. "CHENGUANG!"

Eventually, there was nothing else to do but trudge out of the ebony bowl, across its golden rim, and back out into the world. The tree rustled, green, behind her as she climbed. Just before the rim of the bowl, in the golden grass that hadn't burned, she found a fallen figure, but it wasn't Tairei.

It was her father.

She squatted down next to him and observed, clinically.

He had not died painlessly. There must have been a wave of heated air and smoke that had overcome him as he ran; he had clawed at his throat as tears ran down his sooty face. He had not been burned, except perhaps inside, where the lung tissues had been unable to take in air. He had suffocated, he had known he was dying. He must have been frightened. It must have hurt.

She found that this didn't bother her at all.

Aili tried to think of something that would make her feel sorry, or at least that would make her feel some pity for this person who had died in pain, but there was nothing. Her heart was cold.

"You were right about me, Dad," she said finally. "I'm very glad you're dead, and I hope you rot in hell."

She still didn't feel anything.

As she drove Mrs. Mitchell's car back to town, she realized for the first time that her clothes were half burned off her, hanging in torn rags. There were no burns at all on her skin beneath. She managed to sneak into the hotel and change quickly in the bathroom; she held the burned remnants in her hands for a few moments, then looked more closely. What was left of her right sleeve was bloody. Tairei had cut her after all. That part hadn't been a dream. Not cut her — bit her until she bled. But the cut was gone now.

Tairei was gone.

She just had to move one step at a time. One step. Nothing here was solvable. Tairei was gone, and her father was dead on the hillside. She couldn't leave these burned clothes here. People might connect her with what had happened, even though she had no idea what had happened. She stuffed them into her duffel bag and took them with her, along with the bag Tairei had brought.

"Where's your friend, Aili?" Mrs. Mitchell asked, firing up the car for the trip to the station.

"She ran into someone she knew when we were out. She's going to go visit them for a few days. We'll meet back in Easterly sometime," Aili said.

It seemed as though she was watching all of this from somewhere else, through a glass that made everything seem distant and quiet. She vaguely remembered this feeling from her childhood, when things were bad at home. She was in her body, but not; her body was doing things that it needed to do, and her mind was doing whatever needed to be done to protect her, including, apparently, lying as though it felt nothing at all about the person who had been so special to her just a few hours ago.

She suddenly, vividly remembered kissing Tairei that strange night in Easterly — Tairei's mouth and skin and hands, and the pulse in her throat under her lips, and Tairei's voice calling her someone else's name. Deming. That felt real, as though there was a hot spike in her heart; she actually groaned a little bit and hunched over. But then, it was gone. The glass was back over everything, keeping it far away from her.

She threw the burned clothes away in Easterly before she went back to the base. Nora wasn't there yet, though other women were. Talking, chatting excitedly, putting on the new uniforms that had been laid out for them, and packing the few personal belongings they would be allowed to bring.

This was all happening through the glass.

Aili smiled in greeting, but that was already as much as she could do. She put on the uniform and unpacked her duffel and trunk, which held almost nothing anyway, then picked up Tairei's bag because she couldn't bear to throw it away with the burned clothes. Tairei's bag held a change of clothes — a shirt and pants that smelled like her, that scent of bitter medicine and incense. Aili looked at them for a long time before carefully folding them and putting them into the bag she would bring onto the ship, along with her own clothes. There was a book, too, in Daxian characters, and a pendant made of jade on a string of braided red silk. The pendant was a little smaller than the palm of her hand — a flat circle containing a bird with outstretched wings. She put the pendant on and hid it under her uniform. The book went in the bag, too.

Then, there was nothing left to do but lie on the bed and wait, so she did that, staring unblinkingly at the ceiling.

"Aili," said Nora's voice. She sounded concerned. Nora sat next to her on the bed. "Aili, what's wrong?"

Aili looked at her very slowly. She couldn't seem to make words come out of her mouth. Nora wasn't Mrs. Mitchell. Lies didn't want to be told to Nora. At last, she said, "Tairei left."

"Is that all?" Nora put her hand on Aili's forehead. Her dark eyes were worried. "Aili, did something happen? You look…" Like you did when I found you, Aili knew she was going to say, but didn't.

"Ok. I'm ok." With an effort, she sat up. "I visited home. With Tairei."

Nora gently slapped her arm. "Aili, what the hell were you thinking? Was it bad?"

"It was bad." She thought for a moment. "I don't know what I was thinking. I shouldn't have brought her there."

She remembered kissing Tairei, and the fire, and pulled the glass back over everything. "My mother gave me a shawl, though. It's in my bag."

"Aili."

"Also cookies. My mother made cookies. You can have some."

"Aili, stop it."

She laid down again and stared at the ceiling some more.

Nora kept her hand on Aili's arm, refusing to let her go. "Aili, snap out of it. You can't be like this when it's time to board. They'll take you out and put you into a mental ward for observation. I'm not joking."

"I know."

"Is this just because Tairei left? Was it because of your dad? Did he try something?"

"Yes," she said. "I can't talk about it. Just let me be for a little while. I'll be ok, I promise. When they call us."

The ship loomed, enormous, over the tiny figures queuing to board in regimental order. There were twelve flight nurses going, all from their cohort, and they were placed in their tiny, shared quarters before the men boarded. Aili managed to look alive as they were given their rank pins and ushered into the bunks to await departure, pretending to be excited and nervous like the others. She couldn't play it too convincingly, but she had always been quiet so no one really noticed much difference. Their quarters had nothing like a window — this was a ship of war, not a cruise — but they could hear the roar of the engines starting and feel the lurch as they left the dock at last.

Their officer came to tell them they could take a turn on the deck as they passed the Sunset Gate, flags flying proudly. Ship discipline would provide times for deck, times for training and shifts in the sick bay, times in the mess hall, and times for other duties as assigned. But for now, they were able to stand together and watch the bridge pass over their heads, unbelievably high, and squint their eyes toward the sunset pouring its red-gold light onto them.

Aili took a deep breath.

Nora squeezed her arm. "It's really happening, Aili. We're really going. We did it."

"Yes," Aili said, and she smiled a real smile. She would not think of Tairei anymore. That was all there was to it. It was all behind her, as her home had been left behind when she ran away those years ago. There was a way of shutting a door in her heart so that she could live again. Nora had helped her do it before, but she knew the way of it now. This was a familiar territory. She took a deep breath again, pretending that the sunlight was liquid and she could drink it, bathe in it, be healed by it.

"You'll be ok," said Nora. "Just think about the future."

"Are you scared at all?"

Nora snorted. "Hell no I'm not scared, why would I be scared? This is a real adventure, Aili. This is the best thing we've done in our lives so far."

Nora was shorter than Aili by almost a head, but sturdy and strong; the cold wind blew her thick dark hair all over, tangling the curls. The official nurse's uniform when not wearing the flight suits was wide-legged pants and a matching jacket, with a cap that was unlikely to stay on in this wind. It suited Nora's style well. She stood with her legs spread and arms akimbo, looking into the Western Sea as though daring some yahoo on the streets of Easterly to come say that to her face. That was just Nora, as always.

Their main duties were taking shifts in the sick bay to deal with the array of accidents and illnesses that happened on board over the weeks it took to reach their destination: cuts and burns, broken limbs, waves of cold and flu and anything else contagious. Often, they just sat there and played cards; the other nurses — aside from Nora — flirted with the doctors who were also doing busywork and counting supplies. The orderlies were darker-skinned men from the rural provinces, mostly soft-spoken and trying not to draw attention to themselves. Aili recognized this strategy since it was more or less how she had survived her childhood. They had names on their tags like everyone else, but no one in sickbay called them by name; the doctors called all the orderlies *boy*, talked down to them, and told them to run errands that shouldn't have been asked, which they did unquestioningly. Aili recognized this, too. It made her feel a sense of kinship, though like the other nurses, she didn't talk to them.

One of the orderlies was extremely good-looking — tall with very deep brown skin, high cheekbones, and expressive, intelligent eyes — and once, one of the nurses decided that, despite everything, he was a worthy recipient of some flirting glances and conversation. The doctor on duty immediately sent the orderly to go swab out the latrine. Aili's eyes met his as he left, and he raised his eyebrow at her in an expression she couldn't interpret. She shook her head, not wanting the doctor to pay any more attention to the man, but after that, she saw him regularly, and it seemed as though he was watching her as well.

Nora also noticed it. "Why's that orderly always looking at you?" she asked quietly after one shift. "It's making me uncomfortable. Should we report it or something?"

"No," she said at once, "he's not doing anything. He's probably watching everyone. It's his job to keep an eye on things, isn't it? He's not bothering me at all."

"Has he gotten friendly with you?"

"Are you joking, Nora? Of course not, he's never even spoken to me."

"It's just weird…"

"You're reading too much into it."

Nora sighed. "You know what's weird, really? Being in a place full of desperate men when I'm only interested in Nurse Sarah."

"Nurse Sarah is only interested in Dr. Jones."

"Yeah, I know." Nora sighed again. "I knew it would be hard, but not this hard! There's even guys hitting on me, so you know the bar is low. And they're definitely looking at you, tall, blonde, and intimidating as you are. So just be careful, ok? Things happen on ships."

Aili nodded. "I'm always careful."

One night shift, very late, there was an accident in the boiler room. Three men were brought to the sick bay badly scalded, all in shock, one already near death. Aili started soaking bandages while Nora went with the doctor to prepare the surgery for grafts. There was only that strange orderly on duty, the one who always watched her. Since he was alone, Aili helped him carefully lift the burned men one by one into warm saline baths to give them some relief.

The one that was worst off had taken the steam blast directly in the face; he had breathed it in, burning his throat, and the airways were swelling.

"He'll suffocate soon," Aili said. "We should trache him. I'll confirm with the doctor. I'll be right back."

The orderly nodded, silently holding the man up to keep as much of his body from touching any other surface as possible.

When she came back, however, the man was breathing easily, and the burns were beginning to look better.

"The saline bath is very helpful," said the orderly blandly.

Aili didn't know when she had gotten so suspicious of everything in the world, but there it was. She looked at the orderly, meeting his eyes.

He raised his eyebrows at her again. This time he spoke directly to her: "That's a nice necklace you have there, Lieutenant Fallon."

Aili realized that Tairei's jade pendant had somehow fallen out of her uniform blouse, probably when she twisted to help pick up the men without hurting them. "It belongs to a friend," she said.

"Oh," he said. "Yes, I thought so. Where's your friend now?"

"She– she disappeared. In a fire."

"Ah," the man said, as though this was completely unremarkable. "Well, I suppose it was the time."

Aili's heart nearly stopped in shock. "What?"

The man ignored her question. "Come over here," he said, leading her to the second burned person; he had passed out from shock as well. "Let me show you a little trick I learned to help with burns. Not everyone can do it. Your friend with the pendant could do it."

"What? What are you talking about?"

He bit his finger until blood came out, dripping softly down toward the palm of his hand as he moved toward the injured man on the bed. The orderly smiled reassuringly and said, "It's all right. It doesn't hurt me, or him."

Tairei. Tairei ripping open her arm, the blood everywhere on the golden grass.

"Don't," whispered Aili frantically. "Don't do it. I don't need to see– You can't, the fire–"

"Why should I not do it?" He gently spread blood on the burned skin. "There's no fire involved."

Blood speckled the burned lips of the man as the orderly put his fingers inside his mouth, deft and quick.

Aili took a step backward, then another one and another. "What are you doing? Who are you?"

"How long have you spoken Niforu?" asked the orderly casually.

"I don't speak Niforu. I don't even know what that is. I only speak Anglish." Aili was still whispering. She couldn't take her eyes off his bloody finger, which immediately healed itself. The cut was gone as though it had never been. The blistered skin was already healing on the burned man.

Like Tairei. Like Tairei's knife cut that disappeared. Like the wounds on her own arm that night in Easterly, gone without a mark, Tairei smoothing something warm on her skin, putting something between her lips…

"It's an East Shanyu language," the orderly said. "You've been speaking it with me for the past few minutes now, very fluently. No accent at all." Suddenly, he grabbed her hand. "Your turn."

"No–" she said, "I'm not–" Her heart's door was shut, and her mind's door was closing rapidly now too. The glass over reality was getting thicker, more opaque. "You can't make me."

He laughed gently. "You're quite right, I can't make you. Don't you want to try?"

"No," she whispered. "I don't want to try." To her shock, she realized that they were now speaking Daxian.

"Stop hyperventilating, you're going to faint," said Nora's voice. "I know the burns are awful to look at, but it seems like they're going to be ok. The doctor's prepped for grafts now, but look at them now, the saline baths must have done the trick, right?"

Nora walked over to the worst patient, the first, and added, "Even this one, breathing easily now." She ignored the orderly as though he didn't exist, and he stood back as though he were actually invisible, looking calmly over her head. "Only this one, he might still need grafts."

While the other two patients were now sleeping comfortably in their baths, their skin turning a gentle pink, this man was writhing even while unconscious. Every time he moved, the burned and blistered skin tore. The water was full of red streams from the cracks in his legs and feet.

The orderly looked down from the contemplation of space and met her gaze, his eyes compassionate and encouraging. The man in the bath made a little wheezing moaning noise.

Nora winced. "Let me set up a morphine drip," she said, and turned to the back counter.

Faster than she thought she could move, Aili suddenly found herself next to the man in the bath; she had a scalpel in her hand and slashed it quickly across her palm. With one shaking finger, she traced her own blood over the man's face, dripped it onto his lips.

His breathing eased immediately, but Nora was already there, inserting the drip into his hand, and already, the skin on the arm was healed enough for her to easily find a vein.

"See," she said, "he's feeling better. They'll all be fine, Aili, don't worry so much."

"Yes, you're right," she said. She washed her hands in the sink, the blood draining down off of her hands. Her unblemished, unmarked hands.

The doctor came back and expressed pleasure at the improvement; obviously, the nurses must have miscalculated the degree of burning, these men would all be fine. "Write it up, nurse," he said to the air, and went back to his office.

For the remainder of that shift, the orderly ignored Aili completely and she did her best to ignore him. She and Nora went back to their quarters soon after, and Nora immediately fell asleep. The other nurses were either sleeping or headed to sickbay for their own shifts. Aili couldn't do anything except stare into space and scream in her mind for Tairei.

Experimentally, she reached out with her hand and found the sharp edge of a screw that had come loose from the bulkhead. It had torn her sheets a few days ago; she'd reported it so it could be repaired, but it was still there. She drew her hand back and drove it down, hard, at an angle. She could feel the slash through her skin — a tiny cut, but deep enough that she could feel the blood dripping. Aili wiped her hand against the sheet, and in the dim safety light that stayed on all night, she could see the stain.

But when she lifted her hand in front of her eyes and touched the spot with her fingers, there was nothing. The cut was gone.

She slammed her head against the pillow a couple of times and then stopped. There was no point, people might hear.

She needed fresh air; she needed to be alone, to think; she needed to talk to that goddamn orderly. He had done that on purpose — had made sure she saw. He had recognized Tairei's pendant. He knew something. He knew. He might know where Tairei had gone, what had happened…how could she find him?

She staggered up and hit her head on the top bunk, seeing stars, but the pain was gone even before she could yell in surprise. "Well, that's a plus, I guess," she said out loud.

"What?" Nora asked, sleepily.

"Nothing." She left the bunkroom, taking the steep, laddered stairs up toward the deck. She might not find the orderly, but she could at least get to the point where she could breathe fresh air and see the stars.

No one was supposed to wander the ship at night, but there were lots of excuses that people used to be able to get out of the crowded, smelly bunk areas, and she wasn't alone standing in an out-of-the-way spot and breathing deeply. In the darkness, the great Bridge of Souls blazed across the whole sky, and the beginnings of black turning to deep blue in the east teased that dawn would make it all invisible soon. But the stars would still be there. Even if they couldn't be seen, the stars were there. Their paths continued.

Aili looked down at her hand again in wonder. "Tairei," she whispered softly. "Liu Chenguang."

She had failed in her life in so many ways — failed to protect the people she loved — but Liu Chenguang had not. Tairei had protected her at a cost Aili couldn't comprehend, but she would pay it. She would find Tairei again and protect her in turn. The door in her heart had broken, and with her mind quiet and her heart full, she looked at the stars.

# CHAPTER 5
## DESTROYING

AILI'S EFFORTS TO find the orderly again petered out. There were over two thousand men on the ship and the flight combat nurses were supposed to avoid all of them. She didn't want to ask directly about him because it would lead to trouble of one sort or another — certainly for him, if not for her. She was able to discover that the orderlies really were just recruited from the mess hall staff, which was where almost all the provincial enlisted men had been assigned. The orderly must have been sent back to the mess hall because he wasn't showing up in sick bay anymore; she never saw him in the kitchen, either, but the ship had more than one galley and perhaps he had been assigned to a different one.

A few days later, Nora saw her holding a book in Daxian characters on the bunk while the other women were on duty and sat down next to her. "Can you read that?" she asked, surprised.

"No, guess not. Guess that's something you have to learn," Aili replied.

"Well, of course it is," Nora replied. "No one just magically learns Daxian."

Aili laughed.

"What is it, did Tairei give it to you? Or Edna?"

"It was Tairei's," Aili said. "I don't know what it is. Tairei left some things behind...anyway, I took them to keep them safe. There's this, too." She pulled the pendant over her head and held it in her hand. It felt warm from her body, smooth to her touch.

Nora examined it. "It's pretty," she said, finally. "Do you want to talk about what happened with Tairei, Aili?"

Aili considered for a moment, then put the pendant back over her head. "I don't really understand what happened at the end, to be honest. But we kissed and she called me someone else's name."

"Oh my god." Nora shook her head. "That woman…I knew it. So, that was the end of it?"

"I don't know if it's the end of it. We separated and then I had to leave, so I don't know…I'd like to find her again."

Nora looked at her, surprised. "You– Well, fine then. Can you write to her?"

"No, I don't know how to get in touch. I don't know where she went. When we get back home, I'll look for her in Little Daxian. That's all I know how to do." She wondered if Tairei would try to find her again, too, wherever she was.

"Hmph." Nora shook her head. "Well, Aili, all I can say is you're a forgiving person. Or else that woman must be a really good kisser."

Aili snorted. "As though I have any basis for comparison."

"My point exactly." Nora looked at her carefully. "You look…better."

"You mean not catatonic?" Aili smiled.

"Yes, exactly. I was really worried about you when you came back, and when we boarded. So, I'm guessing, she's a good kisser? I have to watch out for you; you're my little sister." Nora reached out and ruffled her hair, making the braids get messy. "My little girl, all grown up."

"Shut up," said Aili, pushing her off the bed.

Two of their other bunkmates came in and began taking their bags out of the storage lockers.

"You girls ready to go?" asked one. "We're going to be making port late today, the word just came down to get ready. They want us to go straight to the airstrip in flight gear — they're going to take us right off the ship. I don't know where we're going from there, but there's an airstrip ready somewhere and I guess some evacuations to get to."

Nora looked over. "Aili? Why are you staring at your hand?"

Aili smiled. "Ready, Nora."

The first evacuation was smooth, just like they had practiced back in Sand Island. They didn't have to go onto the battlefield, and they weren't under fire. Field medics had already brought the wounded to the airstrip, triaged for evacuation; all they had to do was keep them alive through the multi-hour flight back to the base and settle them into the infirmaries.

After that, they were always on alert. It didn't always go so well. On one island, they landed under fire, while the marines were still coming up onto the beach and being shot in the surf. It was complete madness, finding men floating in the water who were still alive and dragging them up onto the beach beneath covering fire. Aili found that this was an ideal situation for blood healing, however; no one could see what she was doing through the seafoam and bullets, not even the men she was healing, and the blood washed away immediately after doing its work. She wasn't stealthy enough to manage it in the close quarters of the plane, where the men, orderlies, and other nurses were always close by.

By the time they boarded — bringing only the men she hadn't been able to heal, since the others were miraculously able to walk and grab their weapons as soon as they hit the sand — she was dizzy and lightheaded and had to lie down in a bunk herself.

"What happened to your hand?" Nora asked, sitting next to her. "Lucky we have a spare bunk for you. What happened? Did you slash it on coral or something? Remember they told us you could get coral poisoning?" She picked up Aili's hand and looked at it. "Those are deep. You might need stitches."

"Really?" she asked, dizzy. She held her own hand in front of her face and tried to focus on it. Sure enough, there were slashes in it, like a raw chicken that someone was planning to stuff garlic into. The saltwater had cleaned it out and it wasn't bleeding much, but she realized that it throbbed painfully.

"How weird." It was unusual now, to feel pain that didn't go away. Why wasn't it healing? She frowned at it. "I feel kind of...drunk, maybe?"

Nora shook her head. "Stay here till I can get back to you. I need to check IVs. No getting up till I say, got it?"

"Got it!" she giggled. "What the hell is happening..."

The man in the bunk across from her looked over. "Same question, little lady, same question!" He wiggled his bandaged foot at her. "I saw you drag my buddy out. Looks like he was ok?"

"I dragged a lot of people out," she said honestly, focusing on making her words make sense in Anglish. "And everyone I dragged out was ok, so yes."

"Wish you dragged me." He winked at her. "Looks like maybe you'll have a few days recuperation. Want to get a drink with me when we're off duty?"

Aili looked at him, trying to imagine it. Instead, she imagined Tairei's facial expression if she knew Aili was getting asked out by random marines and naval aviators several times a day, not counting the ones who just copped a feel when she walked by.

"No," she said at last. Belatedly, she added, "Thank you." Then she looked at her hand again. Maybe it was starting to close up a little bit? But why was it still there at all?

Nora decided to go ahead and put stitches in Aili's palm on the flight back, and then she did indeed have a few days of recuperation before she was sent out on an evacuation again. She spent them relaxing near the mess hall, trying to politely fend off men and lurking around in the hopes of seeing the mysterious orderly, but he never appeared. The wound in her hand healed very quickly — much more quickly than normal — but not immediately.

Was whatever Tairei had given her limited? Was it wearing off, somehow?

But the next evacuation, the healing still worked. She saved it this time for the most heavily wounded, just in case she really was running out, and felt fine for the whole flight.

A few weeks later, the nurses were told in the preflight briefing that they would be landing in a secured airstrip, but this time they would be going with the combat units into an active battlefield, so they had the choice to carry weapons or not. Nora would, she knew. They would be responsible for bringing the wounded back through the jungle along with the extra orderlies assigned to their units to help with transport.

Aili looked up and saw the orderly sitting there, looking very serious, along with several other men she remembered from the sick bay on the ship. His deep brown eyes met hers, but he made no movement to indicate that he knew her. The evacuation planes were lined inside with bunks three high; once in the air, it was expected that the nurses would be moving around, not sitting down, so there wasn't much in terms of comfort from the bumps and noise of the plane's roaring engines. She would have had to get pretty close to the orderly to talk to him, and she couldn't figure out how to do it unobtrusively. He didn't approach her, instead staring calmly down at the floor of the plane, his arms folded over his chest.

An hour into the flight, there was a huge crash, and the plane banked suddenly sideways. One of the pilots yelled and the plane dove hard. Aili screamed in shock despite herself, grabbing onto one of the bunks for balance. One of the nurses who had been walking down the aisle was thrown headfirst, her forehead striking the metal skin of the plane with a sickening cracking noise. She lay crumpled against the wall, her head bleeding, but before anyone could get to her the plane keeled heavily to the side.

"Mayday, mayday, mayday!" she could hear the pilot yelling.

Aili pulled herself toward the cockpit and looked out through the windshield at a sky full of explosions like flowers. A small plane dived toward them, its guns blazing. She ducked as the gunfire came through the windshield. One of the pilots sank down, covered in blood, held by the harness to his seat.

The other pulled back on the controller, yelling, "Prepare to evacuate! Water landing! Water landing!"

Aili let go of the handle and let herself half fall, half tumble back toward where the parachutes, life jackets, and life rafts were held ready. "Water landing!" she yelled at the people waiting there.

The orderly was holding the arm of the woman with the bleeding head wound, but she was standing on her own now.

The pilot seemed confident they would land, not need to parachute, but just in case, they all watched silently through the small window of heavy glass, trying to gauge how high they were. Not high, and dropping quickly — they were already close enough to see not only waves, but the individual ripples of bullets and debris falling into the water like evil rain from an unimaginable sky. A part of a human torso fell silently to one side as they glided in toward the water.

"Brace!" yelled someone; they all grabbed whatever stanchion or handle was nearest. The entire plane screamed and shuddered and banked and crashed and jolted violently, and at last, they were still, except for a gentle tilt and a sloshing noise.

Aili took a deep breath; her arm had been a little strained as they were thrown around inside the plane, but no real injuries.

"Out," yelled the pilot, running down the aisle toward them. "Open up, get out the rafts."

There were plenty of rafts — enough to evacuate a fully loaded plane with sixty patients — and they launched them all to provide more options in case some were sunk. There were people in the water from other planes and ships, many already dead but some waving hands to be fished out. Aili and Nora were in the same raft, but in the evacuation, she had lost sight of the orderly and couldn't locate him as the rafts diverged and spread out in the water.

The broken plane behind them slowly sank.

Once they set up the distress beacon and began rowing, there wasn't much else to do. Nora and Aili both took turns despite the protests of the men on board, but it was exhausting work in the hot sun. The rafts were all equipped with water and emergency rations, which by common consent they tried not to use; there was no knowing if the land they found would have fresh water or food available. There was also no knowing if the land would be held by Federatives or by the Kunorese.

"What happened?" Nora asked eventually. "We couldn't have been anywhere near the battlefield yet. It was only an hour plus in the air."

The surviving pilot wasn't in the raft with them, but there were a few marines who had come aboard from the ocean. "Convoy of ships was attacked," said one of the men. "You all were just collateral damage. Wrong place, wrong time."

A small, red bird suddenly landed on the hull of the raft. It tilted its head to one side, observing them with golden eyes, then flew away again.

"We must be close," said the rowing man. "That's a land bird for sure. Follow it. That's the best way to find an island."

The little red bird fluttered ahead of them, vivid against the turquoise ocean, never quite out of sight until a green triangle heaved over the horizon.

"Land," said Nora, unnecessarily. She looked rather seasick and had sat out the last bout of rowing.

Aili's hands were blistered, but since they healed almost as soon as she stopped rowing, she kept offering to take a turn, feeling a little guilty that it wasn't as painful for her as for the others. She looked back over her shoulder at the red bird, who seemed to be as excited by the sight of land as they were. It suddenly shot ahead and disappeared into the green wall that bordered the shining white beach.

"What do you think?" whispered one marine to another. "Don't see any flags or any sign…"

"You wouldn't," said the other, grimly. "Anyone got weapons, get 'em ready to fire. Girlies, get ready to duck."

Nora shot him an evil look and took out her gun. Aili just kept rowing. The two marines knelt at the front of the raft, guns pointed toward the beach, carefully sweeping this way and that.

"What happened to all the other rafts?" someone asked. "Are we the only ones that made it?"

"There's one over there," said someone else. "On the beach by that crooked tree. But…"

"Damn," muttered one of the marines. He aimed at something in the trees and pulled the trigger. At almost the same moment, he fell into the water with a splash. The water, which was so clear that you could see the white sand at the bottom, immediately turned red. The man sank and didn't come up again.

Nora moved up to the front to take his place, crouching behind the low edge to try to get some cover.

"Sitting ducks," muttered the surviving marine.

"Should we swim?" Aili asked uncertainly. She didn't see how they could beach without all being shot in the water at the convenience of whoever was hiding in the trees.

"They didn't shoot till we did. They may want prisoners." The marine shuddered. "Let's take some down with us."

It wasn't at all clear who he was talking to, but he slipped into the water and huddled behind the boat, using it as cover and as a balance for his weapon. Whoever was in the raft now immediately became part of the cover, so one by one, everyone else got into the water as well.

Aili stayed where she was, rowing.

"Get in the water!" hissed Nora.

"If no one's rowing we're just going to float back out to sea," she hissed back. "We're not close enough to shore yet. I'll get out when the waves will carry us." She wasn't sure whether the protection Tairei had given her would really heal her from something as serious as a bullet and kept flinching in the middle of her back as she rowed, but nothing happened. When she could feel the tug of the waves bringing them in, she slipped quietly into the water as well. They turned the boat sideways to provide more room for them to hide behind it and let the current bring them into the surf. It wasn't a violent beach like the ones she knew from home, where the waves crashed and threw the cold foam dozens of feet in the air, with sharp rocks underneath. There was nowhere to hide on a beach of small, gentle waves coming into soft white sand.

At last, they couldn't hide anymore; the gradual slope had brought them to the shallows, and they had to stand. A voice came over the sand toward them, shouting for them to surrender and drop their weapons. No one but Aili understood what the voice said.

The marine went first, running ahead onto the beach to meet the ragged, dark-haired figures that converged out of the trees, shooting carefully. One of the figures fell onto the white sand and didn't move again. The marine also fell, bleeding heavily and moaning. Someone from the land side came and looked down at him, nudged him with his foot, and then took out a long, sharp knife and cut his throat.

Aili looked at the blood pouring onto the sand and listened to the voices of the Kunorese, who were trying to decide whether to shoot the remaining people or take them prisoner.

"Don't shoot," she said to the others in the raft, then yelled out, "Don't shoot us! We're medical personnel." She was only half-aware that she was speaking Kunorese.

Nora stared at her as though she were a stranger.

Aili saw it out of the corner of her eye, and her heart sank, but she continued, in Anglish, "Everyone, if you have a weapon, throw it on the ground."

Nora very slowly threw down her gun, as did two others; either no one else had a gun, or no one else was going to disarm.

The man standing across from them shouted in Kunorese, "If you are really medical personnel we will accept your unconditional surrender! Do you surrender?"

Aili looked around helplessly. "They are asking for unconditional surrender. Do we agree?" She was shocked to realize that she and Nora were actually the highest-ranking people left. The marines were dead, and the remaining men were lower-ranked pharmacists, medical assistants, or orderlies.

No one spoke.

"Nora?"

"I agree," said Nora. She didn't say anything else, like *since when do you speak Kunorese?* or *who are you?*

There was no other noise for a moment except the waves whispering into the sand. The two bodies lay on the beach in spreading red pools.

Aili suddenly remembered and called out, "Before we surrender, we need to know what happened to the other people on that raft." She pointed to the one that had been beached before they came, empty and crooked on the sand.

The man replied, "You do not need to know that, and you do not have a choice. You can surrender or be killed. If you surrender, kneel."

Nora squeezed her hand, standing next to her. Without looking at her, she whispered, "If you get back and I don't, promise me you will visit my mama and tell her what happened, ok? Nothing really bad — just that I was brave, or whatever. And that I love her."

Aili squeezed her hand in return as they knelt together, along with the other men from the raft. The Kunorese soldiers came closer, and suddenly, from somewhere behind her, Aili heard a gun cocking.

"No," she whispered, but it was too late.

Not everyone had disarmed after all.

One shot was enough to bring a barrage of return bullets from the Kunorese. The sound was simultaneously overwhelming and tiny, guns roaring, bullets whining past, and men screaming and dying everywhere, all falling into the greater silence of the endless waves.

Nora and Aili tried to stay together and take cover, but there was no cover. No safe place. Bullets flew in every direction, and in any direction they ran, they were likely to be shot before they were recognized.

"White flag," hissed Nora, but there was nothing white nearby.

Aili grabbed the first aid kit and hoisted it over her head as some kind of *don't kill us* symbol. The men who had been in the raft with them fell to the sand, one by one, and both Aili and Nora ran back toward them instinctively after all their training. Simultaneously, they crashed to their knees in the sand next to the closest groaning body. All of this felt familiar, now. Both she and Nora moved with confidence, as though it didn't make a difference whether they would be shot or not, their hands moving in sync to check pulses and look for wounds.

"Dead," said Aili, moving on to the next one. "This one's alive. Nora, do you have anything for a tourniquet?"

"Grab the dead one's belt," Nora said, and then someone yelled in Kunorese behind them.

"Here it is," said Aili, passing it over.

"Tie that tighter. I'll hold him down. You're doing ok, buddy!" Nora said encouragingly to the man gasping on the ground; his leg had been shot through the bone, just above the knee. "You're gonna be just fine."

"Do you have a scalpel? Anything sharp?" Aili asked, wanting to do something more effective, in fact literally itching to do so; in a minute she would just start biting her finger, the way she had seen the orderly do.

"Surgical kit, in the raft," Nora said. "I've got this guy. Go grab it. We'll need it."

She was back at the raft, her hand on the surgical kit, when she heard the order to execute the prisoners.

Everything seemed to happen quite slowly, then — so she could remember it well later, perhaps. She turned around and ran through the heavy sand, holding the scalpel in her hand so she could stab someone with it, or cut their throat, as she heard the first bullets.

The men on the ground were shot in the head one by one. The fourth bullet was for Nora, who was standing up now, her hands in the air to show that she was unarmed. It went through her forehead cleanly, and she fell over very, very slowly.

The soldier doing the shooting kept on working, methodically. One by one.

Aili felt something come out of her throat that was like a scream, but soundless, because after she heard those bullets, nothing made any sounds anymore. She slashed her hand while she ran toward Nora, who could not possibly be dead.

She would heal her.

The Kunorese soldier was suddenly in her way, a gun pointed at her face. There was a loud noise and a terrible, sharp pain. For a moment, her eyes were filled with blood, and she felt herself falling, but as soon as she was on the sand, the pain was gone.

She wiped the blood out of her eyes and started crawling toward Nora. The soldier had already turned away and was looking back toward the trees, shouting in Kunorese.

But Nora — Nora was still alive. She would save Nora.

But Nora was dead.

Nora lay quietly looking up at the bright sun with blind eyes and an obscene hole in her forehead.

Shaking, Aili sprinkled some blood on the wound, on Nora's eyes and lips, but nothing happened. She looked around, dazed.

Nora was dead on the ground, but wasn't that also Nora, standing at the edge of the trees, waving at her? She was mouthing something, perhaps she was saying *goodbye*, but Aili couldn't hear it because the silence all around her was so deafening.

Nora turned around to leave.

Aili stood up, stumbled over a body on the ground. Wasn't that Nora's body?

But Nora was there, through the trees. Aili could see her leaving — she had to follow her, she couldn't let Nora go.

She felt sharp pains in her shoulder, in her leg, through her hand, but nothing that would stop her. Everything healed.

The Kunorese soldier was in her way again, eyes wild, yelling that there was a ghost, a demon. He raised his gun again; he would stop her from following Nora.

She screamed and raised her left hand — the hand covered in her own blood — and brought it down hard in the air.

A whip of fire burst out and ensnared the Kunorese soldier, who started begging for mercy, for his mother, for the pain to stop, but the fire didn't stop there. As though it had a life of its own, it scattered and sought out all the living beings it could find, Federative and Kunorese alike, and wherever it fell, they burned. Their voices clamored, a cacophony in her mind, their skin breaking, and then falling silent, one by one. She watched all of them turn and leave the beach; behind them were bundles of burned flesh.

She knelt by one of them, her hands shaking, and slashed her hand again and again, deeper and deeper, blood spurting all over the body on the sand. Her hand continued to heal, but the blackened corpse in front of her would not move.

A red bird fluttered to the ground in front of her.

She heard the orderly's voice: "Stop. They're dead. There's nothing you can do for them now. You'll only weaken yourself if you keep trying."

Aili screamed, not knowing whether it was with her body or her mind. The red bird hopped closer. The orderly's voice was very slow, very calm. The golden eyes looked into hers steadily.

"You need to get away from here. Follow me."

Like a sleepwalker, she followed the red bird as it flew inland toward the mountain at the island's core. The undergrowth was thick, and there were still bullets flying. The red bird flew ahead of her but had to keep returning as she was hit and stumbled, or had to push through vines and undergrowth. When the slope became steeper, she simply knelt down and stopped moving.

The red bird landed in front of her, shimmered, and became the orderly. Aili watched this happen dully and without interest. The orderly looked at her, frowning, and reached out to touch her wrist with two fingers. She flinched back.

"Ok, let's rest. You need to recover. You've used a lot of power." He sat down with his legs crossed, feet on his thighs. "Can you cultivate?"

"What do you mean?" she asked.

The orderly said, "Cultivate. It means to gather spiritual power. You'll recover more quickly if you know how."

"I don't understand."

"Ok, ok then," he said. "Just be quiet for now and rest."

She hadn't been resting for more than fifteen minutes when she said, "I have a lot of questions."

"I'm sure you do." He unfolded his legs and sighed. "I also have a lot of questions, so I may not have answers for you, but go ahead."

"Where's Tairei?"

He choked. "Tairei?"

"She…she…" Aili swallowed. "Liu Chenguang?"

"I can't believe…" The orderly shook his head, smiling a little bit. "That person. Tairei. All right, if she's Tairei you should call me Tainu."

"Elder martial brother," Aili said automatically, and then stopped. They had been speaking Daxian; she hadn't even noticed.

Tainu cleared his throat. "Tairei is most likely in the spirit realm. That's where we go when we are reborn."

"Start that over and explain to me what it means."

"Got it." Tainu smiled gently, encouraging. "You know, in ten thousand years, I've never actually needed to explain this to anyone?"

Aili stared at him.

"Tairei and I, we are spiritual creatures," he said. "Our natural home is in the spirit realm, and when we go through rebirth we return there, but it's a very dangerous place, since we can't defend ourselves–"

"What do you mean, rebirth? You can't defend yourself? What about the fire?"

He shook his head. "That fire…we can't control it. It only comes at our time of rebirth, and all we can do is try to contain it — time it so it comes when we're in a good place, away from mortal beings that can be hurt. Normally, we enter rebirth fire every thousand years or so."

Aili looked at him, stunned. She decided to let go of the thousand years and focus on what she had done. "But I…I used that fire to…"

"I know," he replied. "I saw it. But that's nothing that we can do. What you did, using the fire to attack…we can't do that."

He watched her and waited for her response, but there was none. "You're not quite like us, but I don't know what all the differences are yet. You seem to have the gift of languages, like us, and you can heal yourself and others, like us. You can use weapons, unlike us, you can produce the rebirth fire as a weapon. That's completely strange. We can't use weapons at all. I couldn't even slap someone if I tried– Well, watch." He leaned over toward her, very quickly, and swung his fist toward her face.

It was as though a strong breeze had picked him up and spun him around, away from her. She felt the wind of his hand passing her cheek. He laughed; his laughter, like his voice, was warm and kind, and she felt herself soothed in spite of everything.

"So, our self-defense abilities are very limited. We can block, but we can't make any aggressive moves toward any living being. Basically, we can run, and when we transform, we can fly." Tainu transformed again into the red bird, then back. "Those are my two forms here in the mortal realm. The mortal body, we call it. In the spirit realm, my transformation is a bit different. That's my true body. So my next question for you is, can you transform?" He looked at her expectantly.

She stared back. "How?"

"You just…do it." He did it — man to bird and back again. "Just, you know, think about it, and it will happen?"

She stared at him some more. "That's it?"

"Just your intention should do it…?"

She gave it some intention. Nothing happened.

"Well, maybe there's something I'm missing, but let's assume that you can't transform for now. That may make it difficult for you to enter the gate I'm thinking of. We'll have to just see."

"What's the gate?"

"Phoenix gates are gates of pure fire. Fire without mortal intention. There's sky fire, lightning or wildfires started by lightning; earth fire, volcanoes; and spirit fire. That's our rebirth fire. Entering the pure fire allows us to enter the spirit realm."

Aili looked up the slope. She couldn't see the top of the mountain from where they were. "Are you saying you're taking me into a volcano?"

"That's all I can think of," he said, spreading his hands. "I'm a few centuries away from rebirth fire right now and this place seems too damp for wildfires, even if some lightning were to hit. But there's a volcano here. Very handy."

She nodded. She still felt dazed and sick, and when she remembered Nora's dead face, the fire burning and the screams in her mind, and the sharp pain of the gunshots that should have killed her, she had to flinch away inwardly and not think about it anymore. Nothing made sense, and so going into a volcano with an orderly who turned into a red bird seemed perfectly fine and sensible.

But Tairei…Tairei would make sense of everything, if she could find Tairei then all this would be fixed somehow. "And then we'll see Tairei?"

"Well, it depends on where the gate brings us in the spirit realm, but once we're there, I'll be able to take you to her. Of course, it will take longer if you can't transform. We'll have to walk." He added, "Keep in mind she may look different when we find her. After rebirth, we spend some time as children in the spirit realm, we need that time to culti– to gather power for our adulthood. It's a very dangerous time for us, so hopefully she's already gotten to a refuge. Normally, we'd also change our mortal body after rebirth, but knowing her," he rolled his eyes, "she'll have kept the one she met you in."

"Why?"

Tainu asked, surprised, "You don't know?"

"No," Aili said, suddenly angry. "I don't know. I don't understand what's happening." She felt her eyes tear up. "Why did Tairei– why– this is the part you have to explain most."

"This is the part I can't explain most," Tainu said. "I can't, Aili. Tairei needs to explain things to you."

His voice was so final that she reluctantly nodded.

"All right," he said. "Now, you. You obviously were not born a phoenix–"

"A phoenix?"

"That's what we're called," he said patiently. "What happened to make you… like this?"

She tried to explain and Tainu listened, quietly, his eyes growing larger and larger.

Finally, he held up his hand. "Go back," he said. "So she met you only a few weeks ago?"

"Yes."

"And you told her that you were about to leave and go into a war zone without weapons or combat training?"

"Yes, I told her that because that's what was happening," she said.

Tainu swore quietly and put his hand over his eyes.

"What is it?" she asked. "What's wrong?"

"All right," he said, breathing out. "I don't think that she was likely able to make good decisions. Let's put it that way." He shook his head and stood up. "You seem to have gotten some energy back. Let's keep going. Just…when you see her, be kind. That's the most important thing."

"Why would I not be kind?" she said, getting to her feet as well.

"I don't know." He turned to walk up the pathless mountainside. "I just know she can very easily be hurt by you. That's all. Everything she did, no matter whether it was good or bad, just remember that she's very…vulnerable. To you in particular."

Tainu muttered to himself every time they got stuck in vines or mudholes, which happened fairly frequently, and they were both scratched and bitten by insects and snakes, which was annoying but, for them, not dangerous. They didn't have to go all the way to the top of the crater. Tainu led her into a deep crack in the side of the mountain, which rapidly grew hotter and hotter. It opened up deep in the volcano's core. Up above, Aili could crane her neck and see a misshapen circle of blue sky, deepening now toward sunset. Below, very far below, she could see a trace of red light. Both of them could feel the heat and smell the sulfur and acid. Aili coughed once; Tainu just looked down.

"This is where it would be helpful for you to transform," he said, after a little bit of staring into the abyss and thinking. "Try again?"

She tried. Nothing.

"Ok, well, we'll have to work with what we have, then." He looked at her closely, as though weighing her. "Are you afraid of heights?"

She shrugged. "Doesn't seem like it."

"All right. This is as close as I've been able to find to get us to the actual pure fire. I can fly down. I'll do that and hover above the fire. You just jump, and when you get down there I'll fly in front to take you through the gate."

"Jump," Aili said flatly. She couldn't even see the bottom of the hole.

"It won't kill you," he said helpfully. "Even if you can't get through the gate and just hit the magma, I'll be there to heal you."

"How exactly are you going to drag me out of the magma? You're the size of a large sparrow."

Tainu didn't seem to be insulted. "Well, I'll figure something out. I can get bigger if I need to. Just don't bother, usually…The transformations do take quite a bit of spiritual power."

Aili looked at the bottomless hole. "'It won't kill you' isn't all that reassuring. And are you sure it won't?"

"Well, no," he said. "I don't know how much power you have, if you have the same kind of healing ability we do, or if you're still mortal really. I'm not even sure you can get through the gate. It's all trial and error. There's no manual, you know."

She hesitated at the edge. "No manual?"

"It's not like somebody gave us an instruction booklet. We just figure things out as we go."

"All right then." She took a few steps back, ran, and threw herself over the side.

Tainu yelled "Idiot! Wait, we have to time it!" He ran for the edge and jumped, transforming as he fell.

# CHAPTER 6
## SPIRIT REALM

THERE WAS A valley of gold, and in the valley was a tree. The gold was like ocean waves, and when the wind blew it made a sound like distant music.

The tree was enormous, towering up to the sky, with leaves of deep golden-red. At its foot was a small woman with lightly tanned skin, shoulder-length black hair and black eyes, and great feathered wings the color of the tree's leaves. She sat still at the foot of the tree in a lotus position, her eyes downcast and her body unmoving, but the wings seemed to be awkward for her, not obeying; fluttering around, stretching, as though they were uncomfortable.

A man flickered into being at the top of one of the golden hills, blue-eyed and brown-haired, and walked down steadily toward her, his handsome face decorated with a broad smile. When he passed through the golden grass, something seemed to be moving underneath it, as though the land was like water and he was not walking on it, but wading through it. At the foot of the tree, however, as the grass grew short, his feet were moving quite normally. He, too, dropped into a lotus position, but he held his face in his hands and grinned at the woman cheerfully.

Finally, she opened her eyes and looked at him.

"Hello!" he said, delighted.

She closed her eyes again.

"It's lovely to see you, Liu Chenguang," he said. "You remember me, don't you?"

She ignored him.

"How about this?" he said. His body seemed to waver and shift as though seen through a heat mirage, and instead of a tall blue-eyed man, there was a smaller man, pale features extraordinarily perfect, with sharp black eyes and long black hair partly bound up with a jade pin. This man wore long robes with wide sleeves made of deep green silk, layered with inner robes of contrasting colors, and closed with a wide, embroidered sash.

He fell back into the lotus position again. "That's much more comfortable, I have to say. I've been wearing an illusion enchantment for a while now. It gets old."

She still ignored him.

"Do you still hold it against me?"

She kept her eyes closed. "Zhu Guiren, whatever you did to me is long done. It's not as though I'm a mortal, you couldn't actually kill me."

"So, no hard feelings then?"

She got up, flicked her wings, and started walking away from him.

In amazement, he asked, "Are those things really just to look at?"

"Shut up."

"Was this really your plan? Reunite with that person, and then this? You're here in this bizarre form…doing what? Sulking? Meditating? Waiting to meet me?"

"Get away from me."

"Or you'll do what, exactly, phoenix? Bleed on me?" He snorted.

She stopped at the edge of the grass, where it started to grow long, and fluttered the wings again, but nothing happened. Then, the wings disappeared.

She turned around, came back to the foot of the tree, and started climbing.

Zhu Guiren put his chin back in his hand, his eyes following her. "You're kidding."

Liu Chenguang found a sturdy branch about twenty feet above the ground and resumed her lotus position. He leapt up after her, light as a feather, and sat opposite her.

Her eyes snapped open. "What do you want, demon?"

He held his hand up. "Just to talk," he said, seriously. "That's all. I'm curious. Or I'm bored. However you want to think about it, really. Done is done, right? That's what you phoenixes say."

"Done is done," she recited, "and pain is pain." She closed her eyes again, and the demon fell silent.

After a while, she said, "You're right, my plan was pathetic to start with and it didn't go very well. So if you need to know, demon, I am actually in quite a lot of pain right now and would like you to go away and leave me in it, because you are definitely not helping. Capture me if you want to capture me. Otherwise, leave me be."

Zhu Guiren looked at her body carefully. "I don't see any wounds."

She snorted. "It's not that kind of pain."

The demon put his head to one side. "I know, I'm just messing with you. Demons feel pain too, you know. But it's only physical, for us. Did you know that?"

"I can honestly say I have never given any thought to the feelings of demons."

Zhu Guiren laughed. "That's a little unfair, isn't it? You know that unlike you, I can actually die. Surely my pain should be of interest to you? At least as much as a mortal's?"

Below them, an invisible sun was setting. The sky changed from azure to emerald, then to a deep green, nearly black. The golden grass started waving on its own; the music it made now sounded rather sinister.

The demon stood up, lightly balancing on the tree branch. "What's your plan, phoenix? Shouldn't you have gone to a refuge by now?"

"I can't," she admitted reluctantly. "I can't transform, and I can't fly, and I can't sense where the refuges and gates are."

"Wow," he said flatly. "This plan of yours is of truly legendary proportions. Just because I'm bored, I'll keep you alive overnight."

He leapt down to the ground and took up a guarding position at the foot of the tree. As the night became complete, the woman in the tree could hear a hissing sound coming closer, weaving through the grass toward him.

He was unconcerned. "Liu Chenguang," he called, "while I'm taking care of this little vermin problem we have, why don't you make a better plan?"

But the woman in the tree did not answer. She leaned back against the bark, perfectly balanced, her eyes closed. In the light that flashed through the leaves from something that was like a star, but not quite, her face shone with tears.

As she fell, Aili felt a strange sense of exhilaration. It was only a few seconds, but there was nothing to worry about now; everything that could be done had been done. Her brothers were gone, Nora was gone, her father was gone. Falling was as though she was leaving it all behind. All her life, done and undone. It was behind her now.

The heat started to crisp her clothes and hair. Next to her a red bird dove with folded wings like a falcon, its head stretched toward the fire below them. The bird flicked its wings and suddenly was directly ahead of her, below her, falling at a constant speed that matched hers; she could have reached out and grabbed the scarlet tail feathers.

*"Don't,"* said Tainu's voice. He sounded strained, as though he couldn't manage anymore. The wings of the bird stretched very carefully against the blistering wind, very slightly outspread, bit by bit; they started to catch fire, first a flow of individual sparks, then a rush of golden-white flame that surrounded her with a comfortable warmth, as though she were enclosed in the tail of a comet.

The molten rock beneath them rushed closer and closer, the heat incredible, and then suddenly, everything around them was black.

Aili spilled out onto something hot and spiky in bright sunlight, a red bird zipping up into the air above her as she rolled and tried to catch her breath. Behind her, she saw a glowing ring in the air — an outline of white-hot fire that immediately faded away.

"Get up, get up, get up!" The bird swooped back down, trying to grab her by the hair, but she managed to stand on her own and wave her hand in the air.

"What's going on?"

"Run! Follow me!"

Running. That, she could do. She pounded behind the red bird at top speed, breathing evenly to keep herself focused. "Where– are– we– going?"

"There."

The only thing she could see that was "there" was a line of hills in the distance.

They were not close.

She kept her breath measured for running and turned around only once.

Behind them was a line of shadow like a wave on the ocean, and like foam on the ocean, there were bits that were flying and reaching out ahead. Some of these bits, in the split second she had to see, seemed to have faces, but the faces were all alike, and all monstrous. Whatever this thing was, it was one being, not many. The faces had eyes and noses, but no mouths; the mouth was the wave itself, growing higher and higher behind them.

*Never turn your back on the ocean,* she thought, panicked.

Aili dug her toes into the earth, which felt like deep sand dragging her down even though it looked like ordinary golden grass. The grass ahead of her got longer, and she realized it wasn't quite ordinary. It was as sharp as razors. As the grass blades slashed through her uniform pants and the skin of her legs, her blood spattered all over them. They made a gleeful, high-pitched laughing noise. Her skin healed immediately, but the slashing continued, and she started to feel a tingling in her muscles.

She couldn't tell if the wave was catching up. Instead of looking, she put her head down and ran for her life.

Before they reached the distant hills, they started to pass boulders — first, small ones, then larger and larger, some as large as houses. They reminded her of the standing stones near her home, set into the gentle hills without rhyme or reason, but these were a crystalline blue, not the rough, gray rock she was familiar with. The red bird swooped off to the left, and she followed it, but now they were running parallel to the wave and it immediately took advantage. The smallest bits of shadow were splashing near her feet when she saw the red bird perch on a single blue rock straight ahead.

"Get in, get in! Just keep running without stopping!"

The crystal face loomed up in front of her and she ran full-tilt into it, not even taking time to wonder what it would feel like to smash her skull on a rock. Suddenly she was surrounded by a dim, filtered light. The red bird landed beside her, transforming into Tainu's tall form. He still wore the uniform of an orderly, torn and dirty, gray and ragged against his warm, brown skin. He looked down at himself in distaste, picking at his collar with two fingers.

"Ugh," he said. He took a deep breath. "Well, we made it."

Aili bent over, gasping, to catch her breath before looking around. "Why— why were you worried?" she asked at last. "I thought we can't die?"

"I don't know about you, to be honest. You're a special case." Tainu stretched, and then went toward the back of the room where there was a standing wardrobe; he reached into it and started rummaging around. "Thank goodness, there's some stuff to change into here…"

He came out with a dark blue tunic and trousers and casually started unbuttoning his shirt.

"Do you want some privacy?" Aili asked. "To change?"

"Eh, it's ok, you're not my type," he said. "You should change too. Here." He tossed her another tunic and leggings. "It'll be loose on you and tight on me, but at least it doesn't stink."

Aili realized that her clothes were not only ripped, but also stiff with blood — her own and others' — and she couldn't get them off fast enough. She found that with the opportunity to get something clean on, she didn't particularly care about privacy either. With clean clothes, even in such a bizarre situation, came some ability to think.

"Who put this stuff here?" she asked. "Is it for…phoenixes? Do people stock this like a rest station?"

"I have no idea," Tainu said. "Probably not phoenixes. We don't do long-term planning, and we're not here that often. This is someone's house. We shouldn't stay that long."

"This is what now?" Aili looked around, instantly uncomfortable.

"Some spirit being's home. There are a lot of beings that belong here. Plenty of them never enter the mortal realm at all. It's not interesting or needful for them."

"Don't they…lock their doors?"

"Not well enough to keep me out, luckily," he said. "I know a few ways to break a ward. It's not my first time with this, believe me."

"Ok," she said, "fine. But before we leave, what was that thing?"

"There are a lot of dangers here. And to answer your previous question, I don't know what your situation is, and I guess we won't know unless sometime in the future, you can't be healed from an injury. But for phoenixes, in the mortal realm, we can't truly be killed. If we have an injury we can't heal from, we'll be reborn. That's how it is for us. In the spirit realm, though, death is death for us. This is our home, and our bodies here are versions of our true bodies, no matter what we might look like. There are beings here that hunt phoenixes. That's why–"

"Hunt you? Why?"

"For power." He shrugged. "It's not like they tell me their reasons. Anyway, that's why the period of childhood is very dangerous for us, because we have to spend it in the spirit realm. And *that*," he added, linking his hands and cracking his knuckles, "is why there are refuges with strong wards to protect phoenixes after rebirth. I'm hoping that Tairei is in one of them by now."

He closed his eyes and whispered something under his breath.

"What?"

"Quiet," he said, and whispered again. He turned his head from side to side, as though listening carefully, and then nodded. "She's here. In that direction, over those hills."

"Aren't we going to be chased again when we get out?" she asked.

"This is why we normally fly," he admitted. "I don't have a lot of solutions, aside from flying. On the other hand, though, I don't think you're as defenseless as I am. Let's experiment."

He rummaged through another wardrobe, then a chest in a back corner.

"Aha!" Tainu took out a long, thin piece of metal. It took Aili a moment to realize that it was a sword.

"There you go!"

"You are…you're serious? I can't use a sword."

"Sure you can. I believe in you!" He grinned widely.

Gamely, she hefted the sword, which was surprisingly heavy, and gave it an awkward swoosh through the air. It clanged sadly down on the stone floor.

Tainu laughed and patted her gently on the shoulder. "There you go. Remember, the end of this is that you get to see Tairei again, right? Just give it your best shot. Anything that comes near us, attack them."

She lifted the sword awkwardly in her right hand; her wrist ached briefly. "Can't I just hit them with fire again?"

"No idea. Feel free to give that a try too. I'll ride on your shoulder and fly away if anything comes."

Aili had to laugh. "Are you and Tairei really the same kind of thing?"

"We're siblings," he said, slightly insulted.

He took her hand, muttered something under his breath, and pulled her through the wall of the crystal boulder again. On the other side, he briefly turned and bowed toward the stone and murmured something again. He held his hands together with his fingers bent in odd positions, then clapped them together.

"What's that?" she asked. "I didn't understand it."

"Really?" he said. "That's interesting. It's our native language. We only use it for spells and blessings. Anyway, that was just my giving payment for what we took. I put a spell of safety on the house and its inhabitants. It will warn them of danger for the next quarter cycle."

Tainu turned back and held his hand over his eyes, squinting at the hills, golden against a brilliant green sky. "We're lucky, the sun just rose when we arrived. We have a whole day to make progress. I think we'll find her in less than a week. Doesn't feel like she's that far…although I've never walked before, so I guess I'm not a good judge of distance…" He shrugged. "Well, off we go." He transformed and flew up to her shoulder.

They trudged up the hills, the crystalline blue rocks poking up from the golden grass around them, and then, were surrounded by only rocks as though they had passed some kind of tree line. It wasn't cold — in fact, it was quite hot, the sun's reflection off the crystalline faces enough to burn — but Aili couldn't shake the idea that she *should* be cold, surrounded by these lumps of what looked like glaciers.

When she turned back near the top of the first peak, she could see the golden plain spreading out beneath them, shot through with rivers. At least, she assumed they were rivers, although they were colors she had never previously associated with water; one seemed to be just a ribbon of fog, and another one to be made of sparkling lights. She blinked and rubbed her eyes.

She turned back to the path to see Tainu looking closely at her, now in a human form. "I've never seen a mortal here before," he said abruptly. "I don't know how it will affect you. Are you all right?"

"No," she said. "But I don't think that's really about the spirit world."

Tainu walked next to her for a while. "We're unlikely to meet much here. The high peaks aren't home to any malicious beings. It's only if we were very unlucky and a demon flies right over us."

She nodded and kept walking.

"Your friend died," Tainu said. "Wasn't that your friend? The one on the beach that you were trying to heal the others with?"

"Yes," she said. "Nora."

"I'm sorry," he said, "about her death. You should know that there's probably nothing you could have done. Even if you were ready to heal immediately, with a wound of that kind, she was probably dead before…before you could have done anything. Even before I could have done anything, if that makes you feel any better."

"Why did you lead us there?" she asked.

"I didn't know that there were people on the island that would attack you," he replied sadly. "I should have thought of it, but I'm not omniscient. I just wanted to guide you to land, and there wasn't any other land."

She didn't answer for a while. Then, she said, "I was shot in the forehead too, but I'm still alive."

"Tairei somehow gave you that protection, I think," Tainu said, "for just such a reason. In case she wasn't there to heal you in time. It seems as though you have the same self-healing ability as a phoenix. So, at least in the mortal realm you probably can't die."

"Is that something that happens a lot? Are there other people like me?"

"No," he replied. "I don't know how Tairei did it. There's no one like you."

That phrase seemed to echo in her mind a bit; she shook her head to clear it.

"I wish I had something to carry this in," she said, irritated at the awkward weight of the sword. She had to carry it slightly away from her body so she didn't slice herself by accident, which was annoying and had already happened several times.

They had started to descend from the peak now, and it seemed as though the mountain range was really only one ridge deep. Below spread another golden plain, this one dotted with more forests. The leaves of the trees were dark purple and black, sometimes shimmering with iridescent blue.

"Why did Tairei come to me?" she asked at last.

Tainu answered with a question: "Were you happy to see her?"

She thought about it — the very first time, when she saw her in the bar, and then in the alley afterward. It had been so fast. Mostly, she remembered Tairei's eyes: such beautiful eyes, smiling at her, shining.

"Not happy, exactly," she said. "More that I couldn't turn away from her. I only felt…I needed to be near her."

"Well, you can assume it was similar for her," Tainu said, after a long pause. They had come down into a copse of trees, threaded by a brook that threw off bits of lightning. Some of the trees were scorched. "Can you run and jump that? There won't be a bridge."

She nodded, backed up, and started running, while Tainu transformed and flew to the other side. Just as she leapt, something landed on her from above, screeching.

Aili rolled to one side to avoid falling into the lightning stream. The thing was not feathered; it was more like a snake, about ten feet long, but with multiple tails and heads. It must have been waiting in the tree branches over them. One head buried its fangs in her shoulder, while several of the tails wrapped around her legs so that she was immobilized except for one arm.

Luckily, this was her sword arm.

Her body seemed to know what to do. Aili reversed the sword and stabbed down toward her own body, impaling the thing beneath her bitten shoulder where its belly lay against her back. It shrieked and sent another head to bite her sword hand, but she tore and ripped at its torso until it let go and fell to the ground. She jumped up and slashed out at a head.

"No!" shouted Tainu, who was sitting on a branch.

It was too late. The head was gone, and the thing grew two heads in its place.

"Are you kidding me?" she yelled.

"Throw it in the stream!" he shouted back.

"How am I supposed to pick it up?" The heads were all coming for her now, and the thing was obviously annoyed. Where she had torn at its belly, something thick and bright was coming out; wherever it dripped, there was a hissing noise and the ground turned black.

"Don't let the blood touch you!"

This also came a little late, but after all, she would heal. She spun in the air, came down, and slashed again, this time at the main trunk of the body. She had a sense that there was something else she should be doing — something more effective than a sword, but what else could there be? She certainly didn't have a gun.

"This sword is terrible! Tainu, I need a different sword–"

Immediately, Aili wondered where that had come from. She froze. "I don't know how to use a sword," she said, bewildered, looking at her hand holding the sword as though it knew what it was doing. "Why– what–"

The creature slithered forward to bite her again; Tainu came down to beat his wings in the thing's face, distracting it, but it seemed that was all he could do. He baited it to follow him, coming dangerously close to the fanged mouths and darting back, tempting it closer to the stream.

When she saw what he was doing, she understood. Aili waited for the right moment to rush forward, then gave it a powerful kick, leaping to twist in the air and strike with both feet.

Of course, it was far too big to be affected, far too heavy, but somehow it seemed as though her body had more power than it logically should. The thing *flew* from her strike and landed in the lightning, shrieking and burning.

Tainu fluttered to her shoulder. "Run," he said, and she did.

"How did I do that?" she asked, fitting the words into the rhythm of her running. "Fight like that?"

Tainu flew slightly ahead of her. He didn't answer until she slowed down, in an open area again. "This isn't really safer," he said. "We need to keep going. I need to get us both in a refuge or under a strong ward by nightfall."

Aili stood stock still. "Tell me. Tell me why I can use a sword. That's not from Tairei. She can't use weapons, she told me."

"I promise you, you'll understand everything soon, Aili," Tainu said urgently, "but the sun is setting. We don't have time. The night is more dangerous. We can find Tairei as long as we're able to stay safe. She's not far. She'll explain it to you. I can't. I really can't do it."

Aili stood there, watching the sun near the horizon, paralyzed. "For a minute," she said slowly, "while I was fighting, I felt like I was someone else. Not like someone was taking over my body, but like I didn't know who I was. That I'm a stranger. To myself."

He didn't answer.

She looked at him, and asked, "What is it? Why is this happening to me?"

"Don't think about it now," he said. "You need to survive now. To get to

Tairei. Just think about that."

He transformed back into a person, and cautiously put his hand on her shoulder. "Aili, I'm doing my very best to help you. I don't think it will help you to think about this much now. Can you help me help you? Can you just focus on getting through these next few days, and don't let those questions occupy your mind?"

She didn't answer. Of course she could. She was very good at drawing glass over the truth. She took a deep breath and said, "All right," and they continued walking toward the forest.

When the sun rose, Tairei was still alive. Day after day after day.

Each morning, Tairei woke up and started walking aimlessly through the world. She had found clothes right after coming through the phoenix gate at rebirth, a loose shirt that her wings ripped holes in the first time she tried to transform, and loose trousers that came halfway up her calves. Since she wasn't that tall for a mortal, clearly they had belonged to something rather small before she invaded their home and found them. She couldn't find a refuge, she couldn't fly, she couldn't rest or feel safe. She couldn't even cultivate, because she needed to sit still to cultivate, and every day, she had to keep walking.

Unfortunately, she didn't have the privilege of walking alone.

"What are you looking for?" the demon asked one day, following behind her as he always did.

Tairei shrugged. "A way back to the mortal world." *I need to find Aili*, she added inwardly, but didn't share this with the demon. She was much more worried about Aili than herself, even though she was so unexpectedly crippled after rebirth. What had happened to Aili? Had she been able to protect Aili, was she still alive? Had anything she had done borne fruit at all?

"I can help you with that," Zhu Guiren offered unexpectedly. "We have our own gates, and I can take you through."

"I don't want your help," she said, and walked faster. She said this even though she knew in her heart she would already be dead or captured without his protection. The dangers of the spirit realm for phoenixes were insurmountable without the protection of a refuge. Nonetheless, having him near her and hearing that smirk in his voice made her want to scream in disgust and fury. It was exhausting to hate someone so much.

When it came right down to it, she didn't understand his motivation to protect her. She didn't know what his plan was this time, and she absolutely didn't trust him anywhere near Aili. Taking him back to the mortal realm with her would be even more of a mistake than doing…what she'd already done.

The demon caught up to walk next to her. She walked further away.

"Listen," he said, "there's a demonic gate not far from here. It's not one I control personally, but I can get you through, no problem."

She shrugged. "Stop talking. I don't want to hear your voice or see your face, Zhu Guiren." She tried to transform again, and the wings came back. That was it. She stood still and beat them heavily; they made an impressive wind, and that was all. No flying.

"They do look pretty, though," Zhu Guiren said in a faux-complimentary voice.

"Shut up," she said automatically. She transformed back again. The wings were heavy despite their total uselessness. It was easier to walk without them.

"You know," he said, trailing behind her again, "someone with less self-confidence than myself might be put off by your unfriendliness."

"Zhu Guiren, what were your last words to me?" She whirled around, enraged.

He didn't have the grace to look ashamed. "I believe I said something along the lines of 'don't be so trusting next time.'"

She clenched her fists at her side and turned around again so she wouldn't have to look at his smirking face. "Please just kill me. It would be better than having you follow me and talk to me. I can't wait to find a refuge and get inside it and keep you out."

"Well, live in hope, then. If I don't kill you something certainly will unless you find one of your precious refuges."

"Being a demon must be really boring, you really have nothing better to do than this. How shocking that you have no friends."

"Who needs friends? I just need entertainment, and here you are providing."

She kept walking, determined not to answer him anymore. Every few hours, though, he managed to get a rise out of her.

*I hate the spirit world. I never really realized it before.*

She hadn't had an uncomplicated rebirth for the last three cycles. Before the current disaster, the last time was…Her mind quickly shied away from remembering. In any case, she had left as soon as she attained spiritual adulthood, which she'd done as quickly as possible by cultivating nonstop. She hadn't wanted to risk missing that person's return. The time before that, she'd been driven out by demons chasing her before she found a refuge. She'd still been in childhood when she fled into the mortal realm. And then…

There were too many memories. Yet, after eight thousand years, the memories that mattered were only Hong Deming.

That night, she managed to find another world-tree and climb high enough to avoid any grounded predators. Zhu Guiren spent his evenings guarding from climbers. So far they hadn't met anything winged. So far, she'd been lucky.

She settled into the lotus position and began to cultivate, but her mind was distracted: Aili's face the last moment she had seen it, as she dissolved into the fire of rebirth, her blood mingling with Aili's. Aili looked so terrified. Even Hong Deming had never known what she was, and Deming had known her for years. She had forced Aili into knowing so much, so fast, but she had seemed able to handle it. Aili never seemed surprised or shocked, even when they were attacked, even when she healed her. Surely that meant that, at some level, she remembered? Surely it wasn't all gone? Surely that person still…cared? Would still want to see her, whenever they were reunited again?

Zhu Guiren called up from the base of the tree, "Do you not ever need to eat? I'm hungry."

"I don't need to eat yet. I'm cultivating," she said. "There's some fruit up on the higher branches."

The demon leapt up. "For the record," he said, as he touched his feet to her branch and flew past her to a higher one, "I do not particularly care for fruit."

"Hurray." She had no idea what demons normally ate when they weren't pretending to be human. Phoenixes weren't food for demons; demons captured phoenixes for other reasons. She assumed, however, that typical demon fare was disgusting because demons were so generally awful.

"Tairei?" called a familiar voice.

Her head jerked up, and she leapt down from the tree in one bound. *"Aili?"* she half-whispered.

Aili was there, wearing something she must have found in the spirit realm. Her dark gold hair was down in one thick braid, lying over her shoulder, and she was carrying a sword, of all things. There was blood on her clothing. She looked…nervous?

"Aili," she whispered again, and threw herself forward, wrapping her arms around Aili's body and nestling her head against her shoulder. She felt Aili's arms come around her uncertainly, and gently pat her back, as though she wasn't quite sure she wanted to do this.

But it was enough. Aili was here, she was alive, she could feel her heart beating. Tairei closed her eyes and pressed harder.

"What happened to you?" came another familiar voice.

She looked up to see her sibling frowning at her and smiled, overjoyed.

"You can call me Tainu, by the way," he said.

She couldn't help snorting with laughter before she buried her head in Aili's shoulder again. She hugged her harder to be sure she was real. Her sibling had brought Aili through the gate somehow. He had known; he had helped as he always did. Aili wasn't responding to her touch, but that was all right. As long as she was here, as long as she was safe, it was all the best it could be.

"You can thank yourself for that," Tainu continued. "Tairei? Really?"

"It– it seemed…funny?" she said at last.

He shook his head. "Why aren't you in a refuge? How are you surviving–"

Zhu Guiren leapt down from his high branch, a red fruit in his hand and another in his mouth. He smiled. "That would be me."

He moved to Tainu's side, almost too fast to see, and held a knife against his cheek. The knife looked as though it were made of ice, and he carefully drew it down against Tainu's throat. "Shall we play, little phoenix?"

Tainu turned quickly, grabbed his wrist, and stabbed the knife at Zhu Guiren's throat in return. It shattered into a glittering, powdered dust before it grazed his skin.

"Well played!" said Zhu Guiren. "Phoenixes certainly are evolving these days."

Tainu looked him up and down, his expression furious. "Leave my sibling alone. How dare you even come near after what you did?"

The demon raised an eyebrow. "Have we met? I don't see why it's your business, phoenix."

"Do you have no shame at all?"

"Not really," he said, and bit his red fruit so the juice ran down his chin. "Why do you ask?"

"Get away from my sibling," said Tainu flatly.

Zhu Guiren smiled and began eating his second fruit. "Make me."

Tainu turned away from him and began walking. "Tairei? Let's go."

Aili had frozen, staring at Zhu Guiren, and begun to shake uncontrollably.

Tairei tried to hold her still and keep her from collapsing. "Get him away from her," she said through clenched teeth.

Zhu Guiren strolled over and placed himself directly in front of Aili's gaze, still eating his fruit. Tainu leapt in front of him to try to block Aili's view, but Zhu Guiren just kept circling, looking her up and down.

He bit the red fruit again. "What did you do to this one? Apparently, you're

the only one who really appreciates me, Hong Deming."
Aili's eyes rolled back in her head, and she fell to the ground.

# CHAPTER 7
## RED BIRD

AILI FELT TAIREI's arms around her back, Tairei's head pressed just beneath her shoulder so hard Aili had trouble getting her breath. Maybe there were other reasons she wasn't getting her breath. Tairei looked just the same — not different at all, only tired and sad — and it seemed as though all Tairei wanted was to hold her and say her name.

Aili didn't know what she wanted.

She cautiously put her hands around Tairei in return, awkwardly patting her back as though to comfort her. Tairei held tighter. Aili gathered herself to try to say something, anything, as she carefully lay her hands flat along Tairei's shoulder blades, touching her with her fingertips and then the palms of her hands, feeling her warmth and the contours of her body underneath a shirt that seemed very thin — and had shockingly huge holes in it, she realized just as her fingers reached inside and brushed against Tairei's smooth skin. Both of them jumped a little bit, and Aili snatched her hand back immediately and looked up.

There was someone else there now. Someone looking at them.

This person walked toward her, talking, but she couldn't hear the words. There was a rush in her ears like the ocean waves crashing on the rocky shore that drowned everything else out, a violent and unstoppable current. The person was a Daxian man in old-fashioned, storybook clothing — handsome, with perfect, jewel-like features and dark eyes, his black hair falling smoothly down toward the small of his back. He was smiling in a friendly way as he talked soundlessly, but her heart contracted around that hot, stabbing spike, and pain ripped through the space behind her eyes.

Tairei was trying to talk to her too; she could see Tairei's expression growing more and more frightened, her own body shaking uncontrollably even though Tairei's hands were now on her shoulders, trying to hold her still, hard enough to bruise. The ocean waves grew louder and louder. Tainu moved in front of her, but she could still see the man's face.

Through the sound of the waves beating on the continental shelf, endless and imperative, she heard two words.

*Hong Deming,* the man said.

Everything became silent.

"Hong Deming!"

He looked up from where he was counting his arrows. "I've got four left," he said obediently.

His older martial brother, Shen Lu, shook his head. "We've got to get more than this. Taiqian will scold us."

The two of them were out in the snow, supposedly practicing their archery skills, but they also needed to bring back some food to the camp. It wasn't enough that they were both able to hit a target while leaping from one treetop to another, or leaning off the back of the horses if they had been in the plains. They were in winter camp in the mountains, among warriors now, and far from their home where food was easy to come by. The emperor's army seemed in no way eager to provide provisions. Hunting was imperative.

"What are we doing here, anyway?" Hong Deming asked. "When do you think we'll go home?"

They walked on top of the snow, not breaking its crust, practicing their lightness skills as they went. Shen Lu was the eldest of the disciples, and at twenty-five was highly skilled. Hong Deming was not quite sixteen, and still learning, but quite good for his age. He walked without much care or attention — his lightness skills already well enough developed to leave no tracks ordinary people would be able to see — leaping up occasionally onto a higher tree branch for a better view. His bow was in his hand, arrow on the string.

"I don't know," said Shen Lu grouchily. "Taiqian was called to consult with the emperor about the war. When they've made whatever plans they need to make, we'll return. There are other sects here, and he'll meet with their sect leaders as well. So, lots of meetings. There's a rabbit, taine."

Hong Deming had already shot; the arrow landed in its eye, spreading a pool of blood across the white snow. He leapt down from his tree branch to add it to the game bag. "Do you think we'll see anything bigger? Deer or elk? Boar?"

"You wish," Shen Lu replied, still grouchy; he had only shot one rabbit so far, out of the five in the game bag. "There's too many men camped all around these mountains."

"Why aren't we having these meetings in Zhashan?"

"Why are you always asking questions about things that aren't your business?"

Hong Deming flushed and bowed an apology. "Sorry, tainu."

Shen Lu waved his hand. "Never mind. You're really too easy to bully, taine."

Hong Deming, meanwhile, walked toward another red spot in the snow. "Did we miss one of the kills?" he asked, confused. "Where did that blood come from?"

But when they reached it, it wasn't a blood mark at all; it was a small, red bird, shivering in the snow.

Hong Deming reached out carefully and cupped it in its hands, lifting it out of its snow nest. "Look. It must have fallen out of a tree. It doesn't have all its feathers. I don't think it can fly yet."

He looked around the bare trees and bushes. "Do you see any other birds? Or a nest?"

"No," Shen Lu said without much interest. "Are you going to skewer it? It's a little small to bring back for dinner."

Hong Deming laughed. "Of course not! Look at it. It wouldn't even make a mouthful. And anyway, it's so…cute."

"Cute," said Shen Lu flatly. "Well, it's fluffy."

Actually the little creature wasn't fluffy at all; the snow had dampened and bedraggled all its red feathers, and it was shivering constantly. It looked up at Hong Deming, its golden eyes almost slits. He looked back down at it, curling his hands around it more tightly to give it warmth. He bent down and blew on it a little bit too.

"Elder brother?" He looked up and saw that Shen Lu was already walking on, bow at the ready.

"We need two more rabbits if everyone's going to eat tonight," Shen Lu said. "Come on, leave it."

"But it'll die! Look how small it is. I don't see any nests at all. And it's injured, too, I think. Look at its little wing. Probably something caught it and brought it here. It doesn't have any way to get home."

"Leave it to whatever caught it, then. Maybe we should use it for bait?"

"What, for a fox? Elder brother, that's disgusting. Who eats foxes?"

"Well, it's just going to burden you if you're going to hold it in your hands all the way home. You need two hands to shoot. We're here to catch animals for our dinner. Not save them from being dinner."

"Well, this one won't be dinner," Hong Deming said. Carefully, he opened his outer robe slightly and made a little pocket just above his sash, loose enough to keep the little bird from being crushed when he moved, but enclosed enough to keep it warm and safe. "There."

He quickly twisted, and shot again immediately. "And now we only need one more rabbit."

Shen Lu had to laugh at him. "Hong Deming, does it make any sense that you just killed an animal while also saving one? How are you going to pick which one you save? Are you going to save all the animals now?"

"Just this one," he said. "This is the one that was in front of me for saving."

The next day, the little red bird was still there when Hong Deming woke up. He had scrounged a little clay pot — the kind to cook rice in — and put some soft bits of cloth and straw into it so it would be like a nest. The little creature looked much better, all fluffed out, brilliant red and bright-gold eyed, looking up at him from inside the pot.

He had to laugh. "Look at it, elder brother. Isn't it cute?"

Shen Lu rolled his eyes. "What are you going to feed it?"

"I don't know. What do little birds eat?" He scratched his head. "Rice?"

Shen Lu settled his sash and grabbed his sword. "Get yourself ready, taine. Taiqian is waiting. One of the emperor's counselors is coming for a visit. Wear the formal robes, and make your hair look decent."

Hong Deming nodded and dove into his baggage for the heavy formal robes of the Crane Moon sect, with several layers graduating from white at the inmost to deep blue in the outer robe. Their usual uniform was lightweight and strong, suited for exertion and lightness practice with only two layers and a simple sash, the sleeves caught tight for archery. The only mark they normally wore was the flying crane in a circle, embroidered over one breast. The formal one was of much heavier silk, with embroidery all down the front and around the hems of the long, open sleeves — suitable mostly for standing around in and sweating while honoring important occasions. After struggling to get it on, Hong Deming tried to stroke down his hair as well. The pincrown that held hair back from his face was probably crooked, but his tainu had already left, so there wasn't anyone to help him fix it and he was already late, so…hopefully it would look all right? He picked up his sword. It was an ordinary one — he hadn't yet achieved a spiritual sword.

"Be good, little bird," he said, carefully petting it on the head with one finger. "I'll be back soon, and I'll try to get you some rice."

He went as quickly as he could over to the tent where he could see his sect father seated behind a small banquet table, awaiting the visitors. Tainu was standing behind him at attention, and he quickly went to stand at Taiqian's other shoulder, ready to serve or run errands as necessary.

Taiqian nodded at him and remarked, "Shen Lu, help your taine. It looks as though he knocked his head crooked on the way here."

Shen Lu leaned over to fix the pincrown, and quietly smacked Hong Deming on the back of his head while he was at it. Hong Deming grinned at him.

Taiqian continued to speak, looking forward. "Today, we will receive the emperor's envoy. It appears that he is trusted for his counsel and cleverness. He does not come bearing a formal message, and so we do not need to receive him as the speaking voice of the Son of Heaven. His request to visit us was deliberately made in such a way as to make clear that this conversation is to feel us out rather than making clear demands of us. I want you two here to be silent and to observe."

"Yes, Taiqian," they said in unison.

Hong Deming looked at Shen Lu under his lashes, wondering, as he had often since they left the Crane Moon sect home, why it was that only he and Shen Lu had come on this journey — the oldest and the youngest disciples. He had never asked because, as Shen Lu told him often, he asked too many questions about things that were not for him to understand or decide.

The servants put out the articles for tea, and then were dismissed for privacy. They stood still for what seemed like quite a while, waiting for the envoy to appear. When he did, Hong Deming struggled to keep his mouth closed. This person was by far the most beautiful man he had ever seen. Hong Deming observed in awe and wondered what it felt like to be as beautiful as an ascended immortal.

The envoy's shining eyes took in each of them. "Sect leader, thank you for your kind welcome." He saluted formally. "I have heard much of the intelligence, strength, and wisdom of the Crane Moon sect."

"Zhu Guiren, you are too kind. These disciples are sloppy and poorly trained, the fault is mine." Taiqian acknowledged his salute and gestured to the table.

Hong Deming went over to pour his tea, but Zhu Guiren's eyes were only for Taiqian now.

Their conversation touched on the situation of the emperor, who had ascended the throne under mysterious circumstances that neither of them seemed to want to say outright. Hong Deming, paying attention as Taiqian had told them, noticed that Zhu Guiren seemed to be insinuating that something had happened that Taiqian must know about, but was refusing to say it out loud. Taiqian's face grew stern at various points of this jousting conversation, and Zhu Guiren would always skillfully back up until the peace was renewed. The envoy spoke of the need to defend the people from the warlords that surrounded the borders, and the requirement of personal trust between the emperor and those who would support the coming of peace and tranquility. The generals of the army, he hinted, were not to be trusted completely, and so the emperor looked to the cultivational sect leaders, who were pure of heart and didn't desire power in the secular world, to provide advice and guidance in these troubled times.

Taiqian stroked his beard thoughtfully. Hong Deming, observing carefully, knew that he was completely unconvinced. Anyone familiar with the affairs of the cultivation world knew that the sect leaders were just as self-interested as court officials and were constantly competing for dominance with one another, but it was at least true that none of them wanted to be emperor or start a new dynasty.

However, Taiqian said to Zhu Guiren, "My poor advice could be of no use to the Son of Heaven, even if he were to ask for it. Even the servant of the Son of Heaven surely is more familiar than I with the important affairs of the dynasty. The Crane Moon sect is a righteous sect, and our desire is only to pursue the Pathless Way and to serve the righteous Son of Heaven."

Zhu Guiren must have noticed Taiqian's deliberate refusal of alliance and implication that the Son of Heaven wasn't righteous, but nonetheless kept his face pleasant. "You are too modest, sect leader. I will share your modesty with the Son of Heaven." He sipped his tea and added, "You are far from your temple, here. We are grateful that you came at the summons. Will you be here much longer?"

Taiqian replied calmly, "We are not certain how long we will remain. The skills of the cultivation sects are not to fight alongside the warriors in pitched battles, as you know. We cannot advise on military strategy except from studies of the ancient battles, which surely we are not as expert in as the generals of the Son of Heaven. Our insignificant value must lie in our care for the common people, and in providing spiritual protection from evil beings."

"Ah, the common people!" Zhu Guiren smiled. "There is certainly a way in which you can be helpful to the emperor immediately. Might the Crane Moon sect consider visiting some villages down the mountain? Several have been attacked by bandits taking advantage of the unrest here. Because the generals must use their forces to patrol the border, bandits within the nation are able to move about unchecked."

Hong Deming's eyes lit up, but Taiqian's face was expressionless.

"I will take my disciples there to test their training," he said. "Unfortunately, our weak skills may be inadequate. May I have an opportunity to report back to the honored sir when we return?"

Zhu Guiren stood and bowed. "I will not keep you longer. Many thanks for your welcome." He saluted formally and withdrew.

When he was sure that the envoy had left, Taiqian stood. "Well, little ones, we have something to do now, at any rate. Shen Lu, it's still early in the day. Let's go now and see what there is to see."

As they went to change into their regular uniforms and gather their weapons, Shen Lu said, "Taine, what was wrong with you? You were gaping at the envoy like a half-wit the whole time. He couldn't help but notice it."

"Wasn't he handsome?" Hong Deming carefully turned away while unknotting his sash.

Shen Lu replied, "Hong Deming, get a grip on yourself. Is that all you notice in a person?"

Hong Deming blushed slightly.

"Well, you're at the age," Shen Lu laughed.

"What age?"

"The age at which you can't think about anything else," Shen Lu said dryly. "Lucky for you, the Crane Moon cultivation path doesn't require bodily purity. I think you would have a failing career in front of you. Don't worry," he added, "everyone goes through it — nothing to be embarrassed about."

Hong Deming tried to fix his hair again in order to hide his face behind his arms.

"Just tie it up, you're really too young for a pincrown anyway, that was just to go with the formal robes," Shen Lu said, already dressed and tapping his fingers against his sword.

"Oh, my bird!" Hong Deming said, running over to see as he tied up his hair. "Little bird, we have to go, but I brought some of a bun for you." He crumbled it up for the bird in its little clay pot. "We'll be back…when do you think, tainu?"

"Not that your pet bird needs to know," Shen Lu said, "but a few days, most likely. The first village down the mountain is just a couple of hours' walk at most. Taiqian had me look at maps when we arrived here. Just put the pot near the door so the creature can get out when it wants to. I'm sure it doesn't want to spend its life in a tent."

Hong Deming nodded and straightened up, quiver over one shoulder, bow over the other, and sword in hand. "I'm ready."

As they walked out, Taiqian caught their eyes and nodded, but all he said was, "Be prepared for an ambush. I am sure there was a reason we were sent in this direction."

Two hours of walking later, however, all they had found was a village that was unharmed and had no news to give.

The next day they came to a second village, full of corpses.

They had seen many such sights in their travels, but it hit Hong Deming hard regardless. This had happened very recently, and it didn't seem to be bandits; bandits would have taken the women and older children, but here they lay dead in the dirt or in their burned houses. This was simply war gone where war would always go. Hong Deming didn't have many memories of his childhood before Taiqian brought him to the sect, but the clearest was of a village like this one where he had sat down on a burned piece of wood next to a corpse and waited to die.

Taiqian put his hand on his shoulder, silently.

Suddenly, Shen Lu said, "Taiqian, there's—"

There was a boy, perhaps twelve years old, sitting up dazedly in one of the burned houses. He looked over at them, his eyes serious. "I couldn't help them," he said in a very grave voice.

Hong Deming ran over to him. "Are you all right?" he asked, kneeling down. "Are you hurt?"

The boy shook his head. "I'm fine," he said. "Nothing hurt me."

"Who did this?" asked Taiqian.

The boy replied, "I don't know who they were. Men with swords and fire."

It was about as much sense as they could expect from a little peasant boy wearing torn, dirty clothing. His hair was pulled back from his face with a ragged cloth and his face was filthy, as would be expected, but even though his shirt was ripped and bloodstained, he did seem uninjured and surprisingly calm.

Hong Deming looked inquiringly up at Taiqian.

"Little boy, are your parents here?" Taiqian asked carefully.

He shook his head, eyes downcast.

"Do you have family somewhere?"

He shook his head again.

Taiqian looked serious. "What is your name?"

He looked up, his eyes bright even through all the dirt and soot, and wiped his face with his fingers, making stripes on it and looking very fierce. "Liu Chenguang."

There was no one else alive in the village; they would have to find someone to leave him with. The boy walked silently behind Hong Deming as they retraced their steps.

Hong Deming listened as Taiqian and tainu discussed the situation in low voices. Apparently, it was unclear whether the emperor actually was the emperor or not; he had not waited for the nine bestowments to signal his plan for usurpation, and there had been no signs from heaven on the beginning of his reign. Instead, things like this kept happening — incursions, invasions, bandits, assassinations. The world was not at peace.

Shen Lu lowered his voice further. "Taiqian, do we need to take any kind of action?"

Taiqian was silent, and then said even more quietly, "Before the emperor ascended, he brought the child emperor of the old dynasty under his supposed protection and moved the capital. At that time, he asked for the help of the cultivation sects. No one was willing to step forward. Without the clear mandate of heaven, how can we know where justice lies? The last two emperors of the previous dynasty were weak, and the realm was disintegrating. That is the truth. There was no safety anywhere. If there had been, then people like Hong Deming would be growing up safe, in their own families. That is why if the new emperor had tried even a little bit to support a righteous order — even after killing the child emperor he was supposed to protect — many of the people would be satisfied. But his power is insecure, and thus, he continues to become more violent and less trusting even of his own people. And he is always under attack by those trying to establish rival dynasties. The best we can do is to try to keep our own people safe."

"Taiqian, is that enough?" Hong Deming asked. "Shouldn't we try to protect the common people?"

Shen Lu hissed, "Taine, it's not your place."

"It's a good question," replied Taiqian. "But we are not an army. How many disciples are there in the Crane Moon sect?"

"Twenty-three," answered Shen Lu immediately.

"We are not a large sect. Many are larger, with greater numbers — even some with a few hundred disciples and ranked teachers and grandmasters. And each disciple who cultivates enough spiritual power to attain some qinggong is able to fight with greater strength and skill than any ordinary man. For some disciples, they can best ten or twenty ordinary men. For the highest ranked, even more. A cultivator who has achieved a spiritual weapon might defeat a hundred or more ordinary men. But an army is thousands on thousands strong. The arrows are like a cloud in the sky. The swords are like the stars. The ants will move the mountain in the end." He shook his head. "To protect the common people... only the emperor can do that. Only the Mandate of Heaven can provide safety and stability for people like those today, who died under bandits' swords, or the swords of the barbarians, or the Prince of Fei from the north."

Hong Deming said, "That's why we came? To see if the emperor has the Mandate of Heaven?"

"Yes," said Taiqian. "If he does, despite all he has done, I will support him against those establishing rival dynasties. In the past, at least, he has shown himself to be a great general."

They walked silently for a while. Then, the boy in the back piped up; he must have excellent hearing, Hong Deming thought. "How do you know if he has the Mandate of Heaven?"

Shen Lu said, "Address Taiqian respectfully."

"Taiqian?" the boy asked, questioning.

"No, you're not a disciple. Don't call him father. You can call him sect leader."

"Sect leader," the boy repeated obediently, "what does the Mandate of Heaven look like?" He was small and had to clamber over a deadfall while he was speaking, but he sounded very serious. "How does it help the people?"

Hong Deming reached out to help the boy balance, but he jumped lightly down on his own.

Taiqian said, "The Mandate of Heaven can look like many things. One is clear and glorious victory in battle. The new emperor had many victories, but none associated with his taking the throne. Another is miracles and heavenly movements. That, we also have not seen. Another would be good weather, prosperity, peace and stability among the common people, which clearly is not the case. Without this clear mandate, the emperor is vulnerable to many enemies, and there is continuing disorder. If there is a mandate, then all flows as it should."

The boy nodded seriously, as if he understood what Taiqian meant. Hong Deming did; there was no mandate, no victory, no miracles, no sign from heaven. And, even in simple, human terms, the new emperor was uneasy in his power, undermining his own foundations with his persecution of his most powerful followers, whom he feared might become threats.

Taiqian said, "That's enough talk on that topic, children. We're nearly back to camp. This is not something to be discussed where others can hear."

"Yes, Taiqian," chorused Hong Deming and Shen Lu.

"Yes, sect leader" said the boy.

"Come with me," Hong Deming said to the boy when they arrived back at the camp late that evening. He went directly to their sleeping tent. "There's something to show you."

The little red bird was gone. Hong Deming was very disappointed. "It was so cute," he said, holding his hands curved to show how small it had been. "Bright red, with golden eyes. I hope it's all right. I hope an animal didn't come eat it…"

"I'm sorry it's gone," said the boy.

As he came in, Shen Lu said, "Taine, don't be so silly about that bird, probably it just got better and flew away. As it should be. Liu Chenguang, go over to the servants' tent. Taiqian wants you to be bathed and to put on clean clothes."

"Yes, master," said the boy obediently.

That evening, Taiqian spoke with Liu Chenguang during dinner. Since they were traveling, meals were informal, and Taiqian ate with them at a shared table in his own tent. Liu Chenguang's hair had been taken out of its rag wrap and washed, now falling in a long ponytail from the top of his head. Clean and in overly large servant clothing, he was a good-looking boy with an air of intelligence, rather than a peasant urchin. Hong Deming reflected on the difference that good presentation made in the world and sighed.

"How old are you, child?" Taiqian asked.

The boy was shoveling rice and vegetables in his mouth at a terrifying rate, but carefully avoided the rabbit meat that Hong Deming had provided. Hong Deming watched, impressed.

Liu Chenguang swallowed and said, "Sect leader, I don't really know. Maybe fourteen?" He looked very small for fourteen, but if he had been malnourished as a child, that would explain it.

"Where is your family from?"

Liu Chenguang had already put another mouthful in, and nearly choked trying to answer before Hong Deming passed him some tea. "Sect leader, please forgive me, but I don't really know. That's why I also don't know exactly how old I am. My earliest memories, I was already alone. And I wandered. Sometimes I was chased, or came to bad places, like today. So, I can't tell you where I'm from, or my family. My name…probably someone gave me when I was a baby, and I learned it, but am I really from the Liu clan? I don't even know that."

He spoke like a well-educated adult, not like a peasant child at all; it was remarkable when combined with his extremely bad table manners. Clearly, he was an intelligent child. Taiqian looked at him appraisingly. "If you have nowhere else to go, you would be welcome to join our sect as a servant. We have many people who are part of our community, aside from the disciples."

Liu Chenguang bowed his head. "Would I call you martial father, then? And Hong Deming and Shen Lu would be my elder martial brothers?"

Taiqian shook his head. "I couldn't consider you as a disciple," he said bluntly. "Cultivation needs to begin much earlier than fourteen in order to form a well of qi. At your age, it is unlikely you would be able to do it."

The boy looked at him, almost smiling. "Could I try?"

"No one can stop you from trying," said Taiqian, frowning a bit. "But becoming a disciple is another thing entirely."

Hong Deming and Shen Lu had been silent throughout all of this. Hong Deming was disappointed that the boy wouldn't be joining them as a disciple; he didn't have any younger martial brothers, as he was the youngest himself. It would have been good to have a taine — someone to play with. But, as Taiqian had said, fourteen was too old. Hong Deming himself had been taken in at four or five. He tried to imagine how it must have been for Liu Chenguang to live on his own all this time, without any family or sect or clan to care for him, and looked at him with sympathy.

"Have some more of the mushrooms, since you like them so much," he said, and put some more in Liu Chenguang's bowl.

Liu Chenguang looked up at him and smiled.

Hong Deming thought that he wasn't as beautiful as Zhu Guiren, of course, but he did have truly remarkable eyes — shining and full of clarity, lashes long and dark.

"Thank you, Hong Deming," he said.

# CHAPTER 8
## ARCINIANG

Tairei cried out, "She's not waking up, she's not waking up!"

Tainu laid his fingers on the inside of Aili's wrist. "Her qi is chaotic. Can you direct it, Tairei?"

Tairei put her trembling hands on Aili's shoulders, then slid her fingers down her arms to check the meridians. Aili was unresponsive — her heart beating, her lungs breathing, but nothing else. Tairei sent qi into the meridians, concentrating, but it was as though Aili had fallen into the ocean, deep and full of currents and waves, pushing her from place to place. How could you calm the ocean?

Tainu knelt next to her. "Just throw her a lifeline, keep a smooth flow…"

"I know what to do," she gritted. She knew, but she was so weak now, recently reborn, without an adult's cultivation.

"Let me," said Zhu Guiren, walking closer. "You know I'm good at this, Liu Chenguang–"

"Don't you dare touch her, you filth." She flung herself across Aili's body and spread the wings that had suddenly appeared, unbidden.

"What the hell are those?" yelled Tainu in shock. "You have– What?"

"I don't know either." Tairei arranged herself so her wings covered Aili almost head to foot — so Zhu Guiren couldn't see her — and put her fingers on the proper acupoints again. She breathed deeply. "It's better now, it's calmer."

"Let her sleep then," said Tainu, rising to his feet. "She's been through a lot

95

with no real rest. When you're sure she's stable, go cultivate. You, demon."

"I have a name," Zhu Guiren said.

"Whatever. Demon, I'm setting the wards now."

"You can set wards? Why hasn't she been setting wards?" Zhu Guiren asked peevishly. "Every night I just stay awake waving my sword around and killing things. She hasn't been very helpful at all."

"Again, whatever. Demon, I'm setting the wards. You'll want to back up."

Zhu Guiren tilted his head and grinned. "Make me."

Tainu took a step toward him, then another. He looked down calmly at the demon's face.

"You're in my personal space," said Zhu Guiren.

"How nice." Tainu took another step, so they were standing nearly chest to chest; Tainu was slightly taller. He stepped forward again, and the demon stepped back.

"Wait a minute," Zhu Guiren said. "What–"

"One more step please."

"No, I–"

Tainu reached out and tousled his hair. "You're really very cute."

Zhu Guiren rapidly took three steps backward, nearly stumbling in haste.

"Lovely." Tainu quickly shifted through a set of hand seals, then reached down and slapped the ground. A circle of light with the tree at its center spread out to surround Tairei, Aili, and Tainu in a glittering dome, then faded. The demon remained outside. He reached one finger out, then jerked it back as though it had been burned.

"You think that's strong enough to last the night? Even with everything you've done to it, that's still a mortal soul and it smells like fresh meat. Worse things than me will be coming."

"Well, if you can't handle them, I'll bring you in the ward, demon."

"That's not what I– ugh, forget it." Zhu Guiren turned his back on them and stomped a few steps further away. He stretched out both his hands, a sword of ice and smoke in each one. "Fine."

Tainu curled himself into a lotus position, his hands set in their seals, concentrating to maintain the ward.

Tairei's wings trembled as she held Aili's acupoints; the qi surged dangerously, then settled. Aili's body became still, her breathing deep, and Tairei relaxed slightly. "I think she's asleep," she said.

Tainu nodded from his warding posture. Quietly, he asked, "Why is that demon with you?"

"Do you think I can get him to leave? It's not as though I can fight him," she said bitterly. "He showed up immediately after my rebirth and he's just been following me."

"Just following you? Nothing else?"

Reluctantly, she admitted, "He's been protecting me at night. And sometimes during the daytime. Whenever anything attacks."

"Why?" Tainu frowned.

"I have no idea." She looked down at Aili and said, "I refuse to be grateful to him."

Tainu looked out through the wards toward where Zhu Guiren stood with his back to them, a sword ready in each hand. "Every night? Has he slept?"

"Who knows. Every night, I hope he'll be dead in the morning."

Tainu withdrew his gaze and nodded toward Tairei's wings. "Tell me about the…whatever those are."

Tairei settled into a lotus position and carefully placed Aili's head in her lap, ready to send her qi if necessary. "I was like this when I woke up. I didn't have a child body at all. Just this, the same as my previous one. And if I transform, this is all that happens — these wings. I can't fly with them, and I can't sense the refuges. I've just been walking around aimlessly, trying to run into something that would get me back to the mortal realm since I don't have enough cultivation to produce a phoenix gate yet."

"You can't transform at all?"

"This is me transformed into my true body," she said, flicking a wing. The wing disappeared. "Then this is me in the mortal body. No other difference."

Tainu shook his head. "Can you do anything to that body? Change the gender?"

"Nothing. The body is stable and immovable, unchangeable by my will. Transformed or not, this is it."

After a moment, Tainu snickered. "You're going to get tired of that equipment in a few centuries."

"Shut up," she said, but the corner of her mouth quirked up a little nonetheless. "Seriously, what's wrong with you? That's all you think about in this situation?"

"Well, we could use a little humor," he said. "How about Aili? Has her mortal body changed at all from going through the rebirth fire? She can't transform at all, as far as I've been able to see."

"I don't think so," she said uncertainly.

"You don't think so? Are you familiar with her body or not?"

Tairei said, "No."

Tainu looked at her with great, sad eyes.

Blushing, Tairei waved one hand in the air. "Tainu, I don't want to make light of it. She didn't remember me or her previous life, but I could tell that there was something underneath. And this life– there has been so much pain for her before I even found her. Whenever we got close to talking about…things…she'd start to say she was in pain. I was worried about a qi deviation if I pushed it too quickly. I didn't know what to do…what would help her remember…what would harm her, and I didn't have time." She looked down. "I'm not used to not having time."

Tainu nodded. "I don't want to make light of it either. When she told me the circumstances…I've been very worried about you, to be honest."

Tairei shook her head fiercely. "I don't want to cry right now. Let's not talk about it too much. I'm glad to see you. I've never been so glad to see you as I was tonight."

"All right then. You should cultivate. I think we should get back into the mortal realm as soon as we can manage it."

From outside, the demon called, "Does anyone want my opinion?"

"No. Go away," said Tairei.

She held Aili's head in her lap, unable to cultivate or focus on anything, her mind wandering over the past. Long ago, she had healed people as Hong Deming had healed a red bird — whatever was in front of her to save. It flew from her and was gone, and she was not changed, it did not remain in her heart. When she healed now, she saw all the loss and inevitable end, the burden of the years and the terrible swiftness of the days. They had thought there would be time, and then there was not.

She regretted it.

Aili coughed a little bit, and Tairei carefully lifted her to lie more upright, supported against her shoulder to breathe more easily. Her dark blonde braid was itchy against Tairei's skin, little curls escaping from their confinement like flames from coals, so she pushed it to the other side carefully, not wanting to accidentally pull her hair. Tairei kissed her forehead gently; Aili's sleeping hand squeezed hers very slightly, then relaxed again.

"Tairei," Tainu said quietly. "You need to cultivate. She'll be safe."

Tairei nodded and sat upright, carefully laying Aili back down, her wings still furled around them.

Tainu asked, "How long do you think you will need to cultivate to reach your adult level of power?"

"I don't know if I will. I don't know if my power will be what it was before this. I estimate two months, perhaps twice that. Everything feels different with my power now."

Tainu nodded, considering. "I can't hold a ward that long. We'll have to find a refuge."

"That's what I was going to say," called the demon from beyond the ward. "There are more attackers every night, and the mortal soul will draw different beings than just a phoenix. I can handle demons, but there are some things that will be more…challenging. Tonight will be bad. I know your pet can't fly, but walking is also an option."

"Shut. Up," gritted Tairei. "Can you not speak without being insulting?"

"No," he said bluntly. There was a sound of a hissing scream from beyond the wards.  "Please excuse me. Fun's beginning."

"The purpose of the ward is that you shouldn't have to do that," called Tainu.

"I'm not allowed in the ward, remember? Oh, no you don't."

Another hiss. Another scream.

"Also, that ward can't hold off everything that's on its way. It'll be overwhelmed if you just sit behind it all night. I'll at least take the edge off. Then maybe you'll be nice to me."

"I'm being nice to you now," said Tainu. "I'm talking to you like you are a sentient being with whom conversation can be had."

"Ha, good one!" A strange noise of wings and howling arose outside, battering the ward. Tainu stood and abruptly changed his hand seal formation.

"Ugh, disgusting. I hate those things."

Something was beating against the ward's boundary near the ground, making it waver and shiver back and forth.

Tainu eyed it closely. "There's a cthonic being trying to get in," he called.

"That's not good," called the demon, gasping slightly.

"Are you all right?" Tainu came closer to the edge.

"Just too many at once. I'll switch to arrows–" Suddenly, he screamed, visceral and short.

Tainu shouted, "Demon?!"

There was a sudden thud as Zhu Guiren's body was thrown against the ward by something both large and powerful. He slumped down to the ground, unmoving, leaving streaks of blood bright in midair, unable to fall to earth through the boundary that repelled demons.

"Tairei," Tainu ordered, "strengthen the ward. Just do whatever you can, I need to bring him in–"

"No," she said.

Tainu narrowed his eyes at her. "Tairei, either you can strengthen the ward so I can get him, or I'm going to drop the ward to get him and then we're all going to die."

"Fine," she said, furious. "Fine." Tairei put her back to the boundary and spread her wings, carefully mirroring the curve of the ward, her hands held in the strongest seal she could manage. Sweat broke out on her face. "Get him."

Tainu crawled out through the shimmering light and dragged the demon in under her wings. Zhu Guiren was covered with blood, his face and arms and legs a myriad of small, deep cuts, as though he had been put into a whirling tunnel of swords or teeth. He was also missing his left hand, cleanly removed just above the wrist. Blood poured from the wound to the rhythm of his heartbeat.

"Ah!" Zhu Guiren opened his eyes, unseeing. "It hurts."

"It's all right, I'm here," said Tainu.

"That's good." The demon tried to focus his eyes. He looked up and reached toward Tainu's face with his remaining hand as though to touch him.

Tainu flinched back.

"Of course," the demon said, a little bitterly. He sighed. "Come closer, I need to tell you something."

Tainu leaned over, carefully, although not to listen. "Hold your sword still," he said. "Hold it tight in your hand."

"Closer."

Tainu leaned closer.

Zhu Guiren whispered, "My true name is Arciniang."

"Arciniang," said Tainu, very softly, and nodded. "Arciniang, hold your sword tightly."

The demon clenched his remaining fist around the sword. Tainu reached over and slashed his own hand against it, deeply, and began to anoint the demon's wounds with his blood.

Looking at his face, Zhu Guiren asked, "Will you tell me your name?"

"Hell no," said Tainu, touching the demon's lips with his blood, his eyes darting from one wound to the next. "Why did you tell me yours?"

"I don't want to die with no one knowing my name."

"So much drama," Tainu said. "You're not going to die. You have two phoenixes next to you."

"I'm completely fine with him dying," said Tairei from where she was guarding the ward.

"Ok, you have one phoenix." Tainu continued to carefully paint his blood on the demon's body. "You are quite ripped up. What was it?"

"A soul-devourer. Here for the mortal soul." Beneath the bloody smears, the demon's face was blushing with embarrassment. "I didn't realize that phoenixes could heal this kind of thing. That you could heal a demon."

"Of course we *can*. The opportunity rarely arises, given what demons are normally trying to do when near a phoenix."

"Can you forget I told you my name?"

"Ha, never. It's buried in my heart for all time." Tainu held up the stump of Zhu Guiren's left wrist. "This, though, I can't fix. Since we are in the spirit realm, whatever part of your true body this is, it's gone forever."

"Damn." The demon lay still. "That's…unfortunate. Inconvenient."

"I'm sorry."

"No, it's all right. What you did really feels amazing. My body feels great otherwise."

"Well, I'm done doing it." Tainu sat back on his heels. "Normally, I'd advise you to get some rest after injuries like this, but I'm guessing that's not happening."

"Nope. Fully cured, satisfied customer." The demon stood and shook out his ripped, bloodstained sleeves. "I am now officially angry. Who the hell do they think they are?" He reached out his remaining hand with a sharp gesture and grasped a seven-foot halberd made of ice and smoke. "Excuse me."

He vaulted through the ward, one hand on the halberd, and swung it viciously against the darkness that had crowded up at the edge. Tainu watched him as he threw his head back and shouted something in a language the phoenix couldn't understand and then smashed the pole of the halberd against the ground. Ripples of blue-black light shivered up the ward, along the earth, into the sky; suddenly things that seemed like stars were falling all around him — stars with flames of black and red and purple, resolving into beings with wings and horns and tails. All of them knelt with their various ill-assorted bodies and bowed what passed for their heads toward Zhu Guiren before he shouted again. Then, they attacked the shadows.

Through the cacophony of screams and howls and hisses and the sounds of flesh being parted, Tairei looked at Tainu. "Did you know he could command other demons?" she asked.

"How would I know?" Tainu watched the demon as he settled back into supporting the ward. "Did you know?"

"No. Zhu Guiren has never told me the truth about anything in my life."

Thoughtfully, Tainu said, "He's certainly arrogant enough."

"I heard that," the demon yelled over his shoulder, swinging the halberd. "Can I get a little more respect from you two now?"

Tairei was silent, settling back down to cultivate next to Aili.

Tainu considered. "No," he called back. "I think we're good."

# CHAPTER 9
## WELL OF QI

THE NEXT DAY Taiqian, Shen Lu, and Hong Deming made another foray out to the lower villages, leaving Liu Chenguang behind with the servants. The first two villages they visited were grateful for the visitors but had escaped attack; the third had been attacked twice and had driven the attackers off. Taiqian decided that they would wait in this village to see if the bandits would try again.

Hong Deming was eager to head home and leave this cold, snowy, brutal place behind. He supposed this was what it was like to walk beyond the bounds, homeless and defending the common people with the sword. It was much less heroic than he had anticipated, and there was a lot of boredom waiting for something to happen. Every day, he faithfully practiced his cultivation — moving through the sword forms, settling into his cultivation pose — but other than that, there was nothing to do. There was no inn, so they stayed in an old woodshed, and the villagers didn't have much in the way of food, either. They brought out their best, and Taiqian reminded his disciples to show proper gratitude, but still it was going to be a hungry waiting.

A few days later, two of the sect servants came down, bringing some additional food supplies in case their wait lasted longer. Liu Chenguang came as well, to run errands and do small tasks for them as he learned how to be a proper sect servant. He was bright-eyed, and already looking healthier than he had when they found him. Hong Deming was delighted.

Once Liu Chenguang had finished cleaning up their morning meal each day, there wasn't much for him to do until lunch time, so he tagged after Hong Deming into the woods above the village, climbing trees with him and finding things buried underneath the snow. Hong Deming found that Liu Chenguang really knew quite a lot about how to find food in the forest. Usually he could bring back a basketful of leaves, or a cache of nuts, or edible bark, or mushrooms — enough to make the glowering senior servant nod and approve, and enough to make their dinners of stored grain and hunted meat much more interesting. In return, Hong Deming tried to show Liu Chenguang how to use the sword, since that was the Crane Moon sect's cultivation path.

Liu Chenguang was surprised to learn about this. He watched Hong Deming moving through a basic sword form, frowning a little. "Isn't the sword for killing?" he asked bluntly. "How do you use it to cultivate spiritual power?"

"Well, of course it's for killing, but you can use it for cultivation too," Hong Deming replied, sweating a bit as he moved into a more advanced form in an unacknowledged effort to show off. "And then when you fight you'll also be a better fighter. You move the qi inside your meridians using the sword as a focus point and tracing a pattern that connects with the spiritual qi of the universe."

He leapt up and twirled, sending out a brief, contained energetic pattern around him. "If I was doing that full strength," he boasted, "it would have taken down all of those trees."

"How interesting," Liu Chenguang said politely. "I thought cultivation was about sitting still and meditating to gather spiritual power."

"Well, there's that too," he admitted. "If we were at home in the sect, we'd spend all morning doing that. New disciples have to do a lot of it till we've formed our inner wells. That's what stores qi when you cultivate."

"When we reach the sect, can I try to do that too?"

"I don't know, Taiqian said you're too old. And there are some other things too, about how he chooses disciples. Not everyone can do it even if they're young. But since you have free time here, why don't you try it while you don't have any work to do? And I'll teach you the first sword form. Here, take it." He grabbed Liu Chenguang's hand and wrapped it around the sword hilt.

Liu Chenguang jerked back as though he had been burned.

"What's wrong?" Hong Deming asked, concerned. "Did I hurt your hand?"

"No, no, it just gave me a little shock…I've never held a sword before. It feels…" Liu Chenguang tilted his head to one side thoughtfully. "…strange. Has this sword ever killed anyone?"

What a bizarre question. Hong Deming frowned. "Well, probably. Not by me. It's a sword that has belonged to the sect for a long time. It was given to me when I reached a certain point in cultivation. It doesn't have a strong spirit, though. I'm not yet able to control a spiritual sword. So, even if it did kill someone, it shouldn't remember."

"You've never killed anyone?" Liu Chenguang asked. "I thought that was what you people did all the time."

"I'm young," he defended. "And what do you mean, 'you people'? You mean cultivator people?"

"People with swords. That's all I've ever seen people with swords do. That's what weapons are for, aren't they?"

Hong Deming held his sword close to his eyes. It was true; it was a beautiful thing designed to kill efficiently and well. Probably, it had killed people before, and one day soon, he would also kill people.

"But we don't kill people for no reason," he said out loud. "At least, our sect doesn't. We're a righteous sect."

"Hmm," said Liu Chenguang. "Well, dead is just as dead, whether you did it for a reason or not."

Hong Deming shook his head. "How do you think we'll protect the villagers here if they're attacked? I'll certainly be killing people. Or doing my best, anyway."

Liu Chenguang reached out cautiously and touched the sword hilt again. Hong Deming wrapped his fingers carefully around it, then curled his own hand around Liu Chenguang's fist; the boy's fingers were fine and long, and felt very warm inside his own. Hong Deming found himself blushing a little bit when Liu Chenguang looked inquiringly up over his shoulder to where Hong Deming stood slightly behind him, helping to hold the sword parallel with the ground.

"It's very heavy," Liu Chenguang said, with a little surprise. "I wouldn't have guessed how heavy it is."

Hong Deming unwrapped his fingers from Liu Chenguang's fist and the sword point dropped to the ground. "When you've cultivated more, it won't feel so heavy. Cultivation gives you additional strength through gathering the qi. And your muscles become stronger too, from drills and exercise. It takes time to develop, and also the flexibility for lightness skills, that's why we have to start young."

"And the…well of qi?"

"That's the core that holds your spiritual power," he explained, feeling quite accomplished. "You have to develop it when you're very young. Once you're older, it's impossible. I don't know why."

"How do you know?" Liu Chenguang experimentally tried to lift the sword and swung it in a heavy, clumsy arc.

Hong Deming easily caught the blade between his fingers to stop it, although with that little strength behind it, the edge would have barely scratched him. "How do you know what?"

"If you have a well of qi?"

"Taiqian tests you," he said.

Liu Chenguang nodded and tried to lift the sword again. "Probably I haven't got one," he admitted. He handed the sword back to Hong Deming. The hilt felt a little sweaty.

"Don't worry," Hong Deming said, "you can still stay with us at the sect, if that's what you're worried about."

Liu Chenguang smiled. "I'm not worried," he said. "Come with me, on the way here I saw—"

Something flashed past his face and he jumped back, startled.

Hong Deming stared shocked as a line of red spread across Liu Chenguang's cheekbone. Liu Chenguang touched the blood coming down and frowned, opening his mouth to speak again.

Hong Deming yelled "Down!" and pushed him to the ground, simultaneously grabbing for his bow and shooting several arrows in succession in the direction that had sent the arrow at Liu Chenguang. More arrows came their way. He dropped his bow and started blocking with the sword, cutting the arrows out of the air.

"Liu Chenguang," he said, not sparing time to look behind him. "Jump up, grab my shoulders. I'll carry you!"

"What?!"

"Just do it!"

He felt Liu Chenguang's weight against his back, negligible, and he put his mind toward lightness. "Arms around my neck, legs around my waist — I can't spare hands to hold you," he said quickly, sheathing the sword and grabbing the bow again, three arrows ready. He leapt up for a branch ten feet over his head, easily landed on it, and then pushed off toward the next tree, running through the branches as though on a road.

To his surprise, he heard Liu Chenguang's voice in his ear — laughing, of all things. "This is wonderful!" he said. "Like flying without wings!"

Hong Deming had to laugh back at him, even as he stopped, turned, and sent the three arrows toward the pursuers. He could see them now, coming out of the undergrowth to follow them. They seemed like ordinary people, not cultivators — no real threat to him. Three arrows found three throats, and down they went. If it hadn't been for needing to get Liu Chenguang out of the way and warn the village, he could have just stayed and probably taken care of them all, he thought.

Liu Chenguang's laughter stopped, suddenly. Hong Deming kept moving through the trees, far more quickly than their pursuers could, but he felt Liu Chenguang's body twisting back away from his shoulders as though he was looking behind them.

"They're dead," Liu Chenguang said coolly. "But we're going so fast anyway, did you really have to kill them?"

"It slowed them down. And they shot at us first, and they were still shooting at us. It's not just that we needed to get away," he tried to explain. "They're certainly on the way to attack the village..."

Why did he feel vaguely ashamed of killing those three bandits? It was a fine bit of archery, actually — three on one string — he would have thought the boy would be impressed. Liu Chenguang's hands carefully grasped his shoulders, his legs wrapped tight around his waist; he was really very light.

Liu Chenguang's voice came thoughtfully. "I see."

They were at the outskirts of the village now, and the tall trees drew back. Hong Deming jumped down lightly and continued running, still with Liu Chenguang on his back.

"Taiqian!" he yelled as they came into the village's single street. "Get down," he said to Liu Chenguang. He disentangled himself and went to stand near a courtyard wall. "Taiqian, tainu, they're coming!"

Taiqian and Shen Lu ran out to join him. None of them wore any kind of armor; if your quickness and sword couldn't protect you, then you might just as well give up cultivation and go home.

"They caught us in the woods. I shot three, but I think they'll still come," Hong Deming said quickly.

"They may come from more than one direction," said Taiqian. "We'll wait here."

They didn't have to wait long. There were about fifty of them — all men in military armor, but without military discipline or officers. Deserters from various armies, likely, or else they had attacked an isolated outpost somewhere and fitted themselves out. Hong Deming quickly used up all his arrows, then moved to the sword. He thought, as his sword cut through the first man's upraised arm — armor or no armor, a cultivational sword with qi behind it wasn't easily blocked — that he would be able to tell Liu Chenguang his sword had killed someone later, when it was over.

"Try to keep some alive, remember," called Taiqian, observing their work and occasionally blocking an over-ambitious bandit one-handed.

Shen Lu quickly reversed his sword and smashed someone in the face with the hilt. "Sorry, I think that killed him anyway."

Hong Deming laughed, but he saw that Liu Chenguang stood at the corner of the wall, watching with a rather sad expression on his face.

*Hmmph,* he thought to himself, *he should be worried about us, not crying about these stupid murderers.*

Nonetheless, he knelt low and grabbed the next comer's leg, twisted so his knee was out of joint, and then kicked him sharply in the head. "Got one," he said, and got his sword ready again.

He heard screaming from inside the village walls and saw Liu Chenguang suddenly turn around and run.

"Go," called Taiqian, and he nodded and went.

Liu Chenguang was ahead of him, ducking into a house with its door broken down. Inside, there were three or four bandits and a woman desperately trying to shield her children, a dead man on the floor in front of them. The attackers were particularly interested in the daughter — a girl of about twelve. Liu Chenguang, completely unarmed, was trying to block them with some ineffective grabs; his forearm and shoulder were already covered in blood.

"Get out of the way!" Hong Deming yelled. "You're going to get killed!"

The men turned to see someone who was ready, willing, and able to cut them into twitching pieces of meat and let go of the girl's arm. Hong Deming cut one of them nearly in half, then took the second one in the throat on the backslash. The third tried to push past him, but Hong Deming took him with a palm strike to the chest; the man coughed blood and fell over.

"That's two alive," he said to himself, then turned. "You idiot, Liu Chenguang! Just stay here. Stay out of the way!"

"All right," came a calm voice from the dim corner of the house.

"And get a bandage on your arm!" he yelled before running back outside.

He found Taiqian and Shen Lu well in control of the situation. Each of them had accounted for at least ten bodies and there were Hong Deming's two survivors, plus Taiqian had gotten one alive as well. The remainder had fled.

Shen Lu sent a last cast of arrows toward them; no good would come of keeping them alive, since they would have no other way of survival than continuing to attack villages and travelers. "Are there any more in the village, taine?"

"I didn't see any," Hong Deming said, flicking his sword sharply to clean the remaining blood drops. "I think I have another survivor, too. Liu Chenguang is with him."

"Why are you bringing a servant along with you all the time?" Shen Lu asked.

"It was just an accident. We were in the woods together–"

"Really?" Shen Lu raised his eyebrows. "What were you doing in the woods?"

"Just playing. He's interesting to talk to."

Shen Lu shook his head. "Well, let's get some information from these people."

He and Hong Deming dragged their captives back to lie against the courtyard wall, away from the corpses.

Taiqian stood there, waiting. "Go get your other one, taine."

When he returned to the house, the woman and her children were mourning over the dead man inside. Liu Chenguang had already dragged one corpse out into the street, which must have been something of a challenge — the man certainly outweighed him by half and again — and brought out not one, but two prisoners, tied with ropes he had found somewhere. Shockingly, the one Hong Deming had gotten across the throat had survived, looking dazed from blood loss. In the dim light, he must have miscalculated the distance, though Hong Deming could have sworn that he had felt the pressure of the skin giving way to the sword edge at the time. He shook his head.

"Liu Chenguang, let me see your arm," he called.

Liu Chenguang came over obediently. "I'm fine, nothing got me."

"But I saw your arm all bloody?"

"It just spurted out from when the husband was killed. I'm fine."

Hong Deming looked at it just to be sure, then at his face. The line from the arrow was healed already; it wouldn't scar. "You were very lucky. My elder sect brother reminded me I shouldn't be bringing you into dangerous places. I'm glad you're safe. You look very pale, though." He wished he could check Liu Chenguang's pulse the way sect father or a more advanced practitioner could, but he didn't know how to do that yet. "I think your qi isn't good now. Come with me, let sect father check you."

Liu Chenguang nodded wearily and reached out to lean on his arm. He was really weak after all; it seemed like he might fall down.

"Does the sight of blood upset you?" Hong Deming asked. He'd never met anyone like that, but he knew that some people fainted when they saw blood.

The boy smiled, looking at the ground. "No, I'm fine with blood. I just… don't feel well. I think maybe I'm not very strong yet…"

Hong Deming deposited his prisoners along with the others along the wall. Taiqian had begun interrogating the men. They had little to lose at this point, given that they had been caught in the act of slaughter and pillage of unarmed people, and were part of a group that was responsible for rape and murder as well, although all of them insisted that they themselves hadn't done such things. The men against the wall knew that their only choice now was between an easy death and a hard one, and were not particularly brave, so it wasn't difficult to get the location of the bandit camp and the history of where they'd gotten their armor.

When they were done, Taiqian stroked his chin. "Send Liu Chenguang back with a message while we continue to the next village," he said. "We're not executioners, and I wouldn't hand any honorable brother over to the magistrate, but there's no sense setting these ones free. Have Zhu Guiren send people to come pick them up."

Hong Deming said, "I don't think he can travel on his own, Taiqian, he seems unwell." He pulled on Liu Chenguang's arm to bring him closer. "Anyway, we can all travel faster than he could. It doesn't seem fair to send him with the message to Zhu Guiren."

Taiqian frowned. "Boy, are you sick?"

Liu Chenguang seemed unable to open his eyes, swaying on his feet. Hong Deming held tightly to his arm, and then put an arm around his shoulders to try to keep him upright, alarmed. "He's getting worse. Taiqian, can you check?"

Suddenly, Liu Chenguang coughed up blood.

Taiqian grabbed for his wrist with two fingers, pressing gently, then opened his eyes wide. "I don't understand this," he said. "Have him sit down." He placed his fingers on Liu Chenguang's heart meridian and began transferring spiritual energy.

Shen Lu and Hong Deming watched, confused.

Taiqian transferred qi until the color came back into Liu Chenguang's face and he began to breathe normally, then removed his fingers and spoke. "He has a fully-formed well of qi, but it's empty. He's used all his qi and nearly fell into a coma. I've never seen such a thing. Even if he can form the well, he shouldn't be able to access all his qi without training to overcome the body's safeguards. How could he, at his age…and empty? Hong Deming, did you notice anything unusual with him today?"

"I…I let him hold my sword…he said it was very heavy…"

"Did he use qi to try to guide the sword?" asked Taiqian, without a word of the blame Hong Deming felt he deserved.

Shen Lu glared from the side.

"Not that I noticed. He said he probably didn't have a spirit well because it was so heavy. And he seemed all right afterward…He just became like this after the fight…" He looked guiltily at Liu Chenguang's closed eyes.

"Did he fight? Was he wounded?"

"Just the scratch on his face from an arrow, but that was when we were in the woods. Was it– Is it poisoned?"

Taiqian shook his head again and stood up. "Carry him. Old Ling will bring the rest of our belongings back to our camp. I need to consult on this."

Hong Deming gently pulled Liu Chenguang's limp form onto his back, holding him carefully, and followed Shen Lu and Taiqian swiftly into the woods.

Two days later, Liu Chenguang still hadn't woken up. Hong Deming was terrified. This was his fault; letting an untrained person without cultivation hold the sword must have injured him in some way internally. He hovered around the servants' tent constantly, asking irritating questions of the senior servant, except when Taiqian, exasperated by his obsessive guilt, sent him out to find more meat. He came back with six rabbits, threw them at the senior servant to preserve, and sat down outside the tent again.

"You need to go cultivate," Shen Lu said. "Get off your rump and get to work."

Hong Deming obstinately folded himself into a lotus position, holding his sword parallel to the ground in both hands. "I'll do it here. It's not as though we have a temple or cultivation ground anyway."

Shen Lu rolled his eyes. "Taiqian's doing everything that can be done. You shouldn't have let him hold the sword. That's true, and you'll need to face the wall and reflect for a while when we get back home, but Taiqian is sure that's not what caused the problem. It's none of your business. And it's unseemly for you to pay so much attention to a servant." Shen Lu looked at him carefully. "Taine, is there…something you want to tell me? About you and Liu Chenguang?"

Hong Deming looked back at him, completely clueless. "About what?"

"Taiqian's consulting the other sect leaders this afternoon before we leave for home tomorrow," Shen Lu said as he walked away. "He'll find someone with some ideas for the boy. Don't worry."

When Taiqian returned, it was not with a fellow sect leader but with Zhu Guiren. Zhu Guiren, it transpired, had been paying a visit to the leader of the Peaceful River sect when Taiqian arrived, and after a bit of dancing around discussing political issues and attempting to get Zhu Guiren to leave the room in a very polite way, Taiqian had mentioned the strange case of Liu Chenguang. Zhu Guiren immediately explained that he was not only trained as a physician, but had a particular scholarly specialty in issues regarding qi deviation and rare cultivation problems. Taiqian had, somewhat unwillingly, brought him back to examine Liu Chenguang directly.

Hong Deming bowed to Zhu Guiren when he arrived, speechless again at how beautiful the man was, but Zhu Guiren swept past him without a second glance, ducking into the servants' tent with Taiqian. Without any sense of shame whatsoever, Hong Deming quickly went around to the back, where he knew Liu Chenguang's cot was against the canvas, so he could hear better.

For a while, there was nothing — just "hmmmm" and "interesting…" in Zhu Guiren's cool voice. At last, he explained, "Sect leader, this boy has a very unusual pattern to his well of qi and meridians. I have only read of this in old books. I haven't ever seen it before. He was born with his well already formed, but he has not yet cultivated enough to fill the well for his own safety. Because he didn't need to cultivate to create and fill the well, it is drawing directly from his own vital qi. The only way he will survive is to cultivate intensively for several years. If you continue to give him spiritual energy, enough to awaken, and then bring him back to your sect as a disciple for training, that would solve this problem."

There was silence.

"I am not sure that would be convenient," said Taiqian eventually.

Hong Deming covered his mouth in shock.

"It's not clear to me what caused his sudden crisis," continued Taiqian. "There's something odd about him, even before this happened. He is a present-able, intelligent boy, yet his origins are very mysterious, and his behavior and conversation are strange. I had intended to bring him back to Crane Moon as a servant since he had nowhere else to go, but I was already thinking that that might be the wrong decision. One of my disciples seemed almost bewitched by him."

"Really?" It sounded as though Zhu Guiren was laughing. "Both of your disciples are young enough that they must get bewitched fairly easily."

Taiqian didn't laugh in return. "I don't know if this person should be brought back to our sect even as a servant, and now you are telling me that I should take him as a disciple. Given the strangeness of his meridians, is there anything else I should know about his cultivation path?"

"Well, it's likely that he will heal very easily and quickly from wounds," Zhu

Guiren said. "This is an effect of being born with the well already formed, but again, it is drawing from his own life force to do so. In addition, it is possible that he may not be able to cultivate with the sword at all. In the scrolls I've examined describing this condition, it often seems that those who suffer from it… For most of them, they die young, but those who do cultivate seem unable to use weapons well. However, it is very likely that he would be able to cultivate the healing path."

"Crane Moon is a sword path, so we'd be useless to him in any case. Peaceful River is a music path, but I don't know any sect that focuses on healing."

"No," Zhu Guiren replied, in his cold, rather haughty voice, "it's not a path that sects have really developed. The ability to follow it fully is too rare. A true healing path is something he couldn't find within any sect today. However, if you could support him in developing his cultivational foundation, I would be willing to take him as my apprentice later on, when he's stabilized his qi."

Hong Deming's eyes grew wide.

Taiqian didn't respond.

Zhu Guiren continued, persuasively, "To have such a disciple attached to your sect would be a great advantage to you. You don't know yet what a true healing path can accomplish. He will be able to heal any wound, any illness — a true divine physician. There are other powers associated with this path that may develop further for him later in life, but there has been no such person in the cultivation world for centuries, according to the scrolls. Such a disciple, in these uncertain times, would be worth having."

Hong Deming wondered why Zhu Guiren was arguing so hard in favor of the boy staying with the Crane Moon, but desperately hoped he would succeed. It would be wonderful to have Liu Chenguang around all the time; much more fun than Shen Lu or the other older disciples. He only wondered why Taiqian was so reluctant. Did he not like Liu Chenguang? And if Taiqian thought he was bewitched, well, that was ridiculous. He'd just made a bad decision in offering Liu Chenguang the sword. It was completely his own idea and his own fault — he would have to make that clear.

At last, Taiqian said, still without a commitment, "Why can't you take him now?"

"I'm not a cultivator myself," Zhu Guiren said, "only a physician of mediocre ability. I could not guide him into developing the spiritual foundation as you could. I could not teach him to cultivate as he needs to. My service to him would be in learning the classical texts and prescriptions, learning to read pulses and diagnose — the things any adequate physician can do. I can also introduce him to my studies in the ancient manuals of qi deviation and cultivational health, though for me these are only theoretical as I am without any spiritual power. Nonetheless, to him, with the cultivation he will have as an adult, they'll be very useful."

Hong Deming pressed his ear even closer to the canvas wall; he thought he could hear Liu Chenguang's even breathing, very close to the cloth, closer than the voices. He closed his eyes and reached out gently to where his shoulder was pressed right up against the side of the tent. He touched it gently and thought, *don't worry, Taiqian is kind and wise. He'll give you another chance. I'm sorry I got you in trouble like this.*

Just as he let go, Taiqian said, "Very well. I will provide spiritual energy to wake him. We will return to our sect, and if he is willing to follow the path you have outlined, I will accept him as a disciple of the Crane Moon. I will need to continue to trouble you for guidance on his path."

Zhu Guiren said, "Of course, of course. If it is convenient, I will come to visit in a half year to check on him."

Hong Deming scrambled away as Zhu Guiren and Taiqian moved toward the entrance. He came around the front and was able to stand, looking innocent, next to the horse shelter by the time they exited.

Taiqian looked over at him without smiling. "Hong Deming, see Master Zhu to the gate," he said.

Hong Deming went up to Zhu Guiren and bowed. "Sir, I'll lead you out," he said, hoping his voice conveyed some gratitude for his care for Liu Chenguang.

Zhu Guiren's distant eyes brushed over him with a brief, inattentive nod, but his beautiful face, usually so cold, looked extremely pleased.

# CHAPTER 10
## CRANE MOON

Several hours later, Liu Chenguang sat up in the cot, drinking some broth and making a face. He smiled when he saw Hong Deming duck in through the tent entrance. "Can I call you tainu now?" he asked.

Hong Deming settled next to him. "Not yet. You haven't completed the ceremony. When we get back to the sect, you'll bow to Taiqian formally and then he will be your sect father and we'll be sect brothers, and you can call him Taiqian, and I can call you taine, too, but not till then. What's wrong with the broth?"

"Nothing, I guess. I don't usually eat meat." Liu Chenguang sipped some more. "It just feels strange for my body. But Taiqian– I mean, the sect leader insisted we're traveling tomorrow, and I have to have enough strength to ride a horse."

Hong Deming said, very formally, "I'm sorry that I had you hold the sword."

"Why? That's not what made me fall down," he said, smiling. "Sect leader said a physician came to see me. Apparently, it's something about my well, which it turns out I do have. I'll cultivate and get better. And then I'll learn to be a healer. Everything is perfect."

Hong Deming wrapped his arms around his bent knees, feeling very much the same. "The physician who came for you is Zhu Guiren. He's an envoy from the Son of Heaven. You'll study with him when you're ready. I wonder if he'll bring you to the court?"

"What's he like?"

"He's very cultured and refined and elegant, and he knows a lot about the empire. I didn't know he was a physician until he came to see you. And he's very handsome."

Liu Chenguang made a face. "Why does that matter?"

"It doesn't, I guess. But wait till you see him. I've never seen anyone even close to his looks — like one of those characters in tales of deities and spirits."

Liu Chenguang shook his head, smiling, and sipped the broth again. "What an imagination you have. Have you ever seen an immortal?"

"Have you?" Hong Deming was very curious.

Liu Chenguang laughed a little bit. "No deities. Only people."

The Crane Moon's sect home was located in a remote, mountainous area, south and west of the old capital. Built high up on ledges and backed by a cliff, it centered around the temple and cultivation ground, with buildings and grounds on several different levels overlooking a narrow river gorge. Crane Moon wasn't a particularly large or important sect; it was known in the cultivation world for its age — Hong Deming was a disciple of the twenty-eighth generation — and the power of its sword cultivation. Among newer, larger, or more powerful sects competing for prominence and power in the cultivation world, the Crane Moon was far from the center of things. Nonetheless, there was a certain romance to it. Whenever they visited other sects, Hong Deming always felt a sense of pride that he had been chosen to follow the Crane Moon path.

Hong Deming stretched with relief as they completed the climb up the warded stairs and returned at last into the main courtyard, leaving the horses at the stable below the mountaintop. They followed Taiqian in good order: Shen Lu, Hong Deming, Liu Chenguang, still in his servants' clothes, and finally, the servants themselves, who instantly dispersed to their own quarters. The other members of the sect — martial uncles and aunts of Taiqian's generation, and the martial brothers and sisters of Hong Deming's — all greeted Taiqian formally as sect leader and followed him into the great hall of ceremony to feast and to see Liu Chenguang's acceptance as a disciple.

Liu Chenguang bowed three times formally to the ground, quite gracefully — he had been practicing all along the way to demonstrate good manners — and Taiqian formally accepted him, receiving his service as symbolized by a cup of tea. Liu Chenguang was now bound to obey Taiqian in all things, as a father and teacher, for the rest of his life. He would belong to the Crane Moon sect forever and Taiqian, in return, would care for him as a child and teach him, while the whole sect would protect him. When Liu Chenguang rose from the final bow, his face was very solemn, and his eyes were dark. Hong Deming remembered his own acceptance ceremony; he felt that there had been more joyousness about the whole thing. This time, all the older disciples were looking at one another, though no one dared to speak, and Taiqian's acceptance of Liu Chenguang as his final disciple was spoken without warmth or a smile. Hong Deming tried to catch Liu Chenguang's eye and look encouraging without success.

At last, the banquet became more relaxed, and the disciples were able to move around and chat with one another.

Hong Deming turned to Liu Chenguang, who was seated at the lowest table near him, and smiled. "Taine," he said, teasing, trying to get him to smile back.

Quietly, Liu Chenguang said, "Tainu." He looked very small in Hong Deming's outgrown sect uniform; there hadn't been any new ones ready, since no one had expected Taiqian to take a disciple again. His eyes still looked very serious. For the first time ever, Hong Deming thought he looked a little frightened.

Hong Deming reached over to his bowl and put in a few more mushrooms. "Here, taine, you'll need to build up your strength. You can have all the mushrooms you want now. Isn't the sauce good? We couldn't have this on the road, but the food will be much better now that we're home."

Liu Chenguang looked down and poked at the mushrooms unenthusiastically, then brought some to his mouth.

"Tomorrow you'll start cultivating and training with us—"

"Taiqian told me this afternoon that I'll go into seclusion tomorrow," Liu Chenguang interrupted quietly. "What's that like?"

"Seclusion?" Hong Deming frowned. "That's normally for very advanced disciples. It's silent meditation, alone in one of the spiritual caverns…"

He himself had never cultivated in seclusion, and wouldn't until he was ready to cultivate a spiritual weapon; it was the last test before spiritual adulthood. He was inwardly shocked that Taiqian would send Liu Chenguang into the caverns so quickly. People sometimes went into qi deviation during seclusion, but for those with the strength to bear it, seclusion was the best way to focus and advance quickly in cultivation — more than cultivating as part of one's regular life and interactions with the world.

"I suppose he thinks that's the best way for you to catch up, it's for your own good. Did he say for how long?"

"Two months, to begin."

Hong Deming choked. "Two months? Starting tomorrow? You won't be training with us at all?" He had been looking forward to trying to teach Liu Chenguang the sword again.

Liu Chenguang nodded and ate some more mushrooms. "I'm used to being alone," he said, finally. "It's not that difficult for me to be in seclusion, probably, it's not different from what I'm used to." He looked up and smiled bravely. "I'll be fine. When I come out, can I look for you?"

"Of course. Who else would you look for? I'm your tainu. Come with me. I'll show you all around the place before you have to go to the caverns tomorrow." He pulled Liu Chenguang up by the wrist and smiled at him, trying to get Liu Chenguang's eyes to shine again. "Come on."

He brought Liu Chenguang to see the dormitories, where each of the disciples had their own small room; the kitchens; the cultivation ground where they practiced meditation every morning and the sword path in the afternoons; the library full of scrolls and books; the music rooms where they learned qin; the archery grounds and the meditation gardens; the armory full of ancient weapons, though of course, they couldn't go in; the hot springs inside the mountain at the lowest level; the staircases and bridges that connected the pieces of the sect together, usable for defense as well as beauty.

"Look," he said, "this is my favorite place. I come here to just…imagine the world, sometimes."

It was a wall at the second highest level of the sect, which was built back against the mountain beneath the houses of the sect leader and head disciples. The wall around that level made a second curve here and leapt back out to enclose a tiny garden, capturing a trickling waterfall from the highest level in a shallow pool. From the pool, the water ran out again through a little channel and cut through the wall at the cliff's edge; the stream continued as a fall into the air, turning into mist a thousand feet above the ground below.

The little garden had only one small tree and a few green plants. Aside from the basin and the channel for the water, there was no sign of deliberate human planning. The tree had grown wild, as had the grass. There were no benches, or anywhere to sit except the wall itself.

"Look," Hong Deming said, "this is the best time."

He brought Liu Chenguang to stand near the cliff wall, where the water came down from above, and turned him to look toward the sheer drop beyond the outer wall, where the mist of the fall that never reached the ground was blown upward by the wind from below. As the sun neared its setting, red beams came through the gorge and diffused in the mist — not like a rainbow, but with every droplet sparking like a jewel, moving and changing like stars in unpredictable patterns that seemed to always be on the verge of making sense.

Liu Chenguang sighed. "Thank you." He didn't smile, but his eyes shone again, as bright as the drops of mist. He looked out at it until the light faded, then turned to Hong Deming.

Now, the smile was there, and Hong Deming breathed, relieved in his heart.

"Tainu, you...I'll see you in two months." Liu Chenguang bowed and turned away.

There was plenty to keep Hong Deming busy after Liu Chenguang entered the caverns for seclusion. He was still effectively the youngest disciple, and at sixteen was nearing the completion of his foundation training. He had been neglecting his music and calligraphy in favor of archery, sword, and horsemanship while he had been gone — a journey of nearly six months total — but all of these were cultivational skills through which he could develop, express, and use qi, and his teachers insisted he work constantly to make up the lost time. He rarely had the opportunity to think that he finally had a taine, even if his taine was kept in seclusion all the time. It was only when he had a few moments of quiet, in the walled garden, or while playing qin, that Hong Deming would remember that his taine was here, but alone and silent in the dark.

Taiqian gave Liu Chenguang only short breaks before sending him back to the caverns, again and again, for longer and longer sessions. Whenever Liu Chenguang came out, though, it was true that he seemed stronger, and he was always cheerful and happy. In those months when he wasn't in secluded meditation, Liu Chenguang read the works that Zhu Guiren had assigned to him on his visits, studying in the sect library. After a couple more efforts to teach him basic sword forms that failed miserably — holding the sword seemed to make him extremely uncomfortable and set him back in cultivation, according to Shen Lu — Taiqian consulted with Zhu Guiren and decided to teach him only lightness skill and to play the qin for cultivation.

Every few months, Hong Deming would look up from whatever he was doing, whether sword or study or archery or music, and see Liu Chenguang standing nearby, his eyes shining, smiling and waiting for him to notice. When his taine was not in seclusion, he and Liu Chenguang spent all their spare moments together. He would visit Liu Chenguang in the library to hear him explain theories of medicine and quiz him on acupoints and meridian paths, or they would wander in the mountain woods above the temple, looking for herbs and flowers with particular medicinal virtues and talking. Liu Chenguang had very strange views of the world, and Hong Deming always enjoyed hearing him make his unpredictable statements. They would be walking by a stream, and Liu Chenguang would suddenly kneel down and point to a rock that he thought was particularly interesting or exclaim at the tiny fish swimming nearby. He had an immense capacity for stillness and could lie on his stomach examining a flower for an hour at a time, yet at the same time, was full of energy held in check, just ready to be unleashed to run or jump or climb trees.

Once, they found a rabbit in the woods, injured by a predator. Liu Chenguang practiced his healing skills on it, showing Hong Deming how the wound would be washed and poulticed with boiled, crushed herbs.

"Now, you bandage it," he said, his voice cracking a little; it was mostly settled now into a light tenor, but occasionally would return to his boy's register. His long, fine fingers dexterously wrapped the injured leg with a strip of cloth. "I'll do it loosely so he can get it off by himself later. Just to keep the poultice on for a while...I've been practicing this, but it's my first time trying with a living creature. It does feel different! Stay still, little thing. If it was a person, we'd have him stay quiet in bed for a few days, but since it's a rabbit, he'd probably be so terrified that it wouldn't be helpful for him. So I think it's best to put him back in a safe place, we'll cut some grass and put it in there with him, and in a few days he'll be well."

He looked up, smiling. "Do you think it's silly for me to save a rabbit? After all, you shoot and eat them all the time."

Crouched next to him, Hong Deming smiled back. "It's different when it's hurt in front of you. I'm not hunting now, anyway. We have plenty to eat. Look, it's so soft." He reached out and stroked the rabbit's ears, but the little thing shivered, its eyes glazed.

"It's too frightened," Liu Chenguang said. "Just let it be. Rabbits can't tell a friend from an enemy."

"Hah, if you're a rabbit the whole world is your enemy. Of course it's frightened."

"Where do you think its burrow is?"

Hong Deming looked around. "There's a hole at the bottom of that tree," he said, and looked in it. "I can see rabbit fur caught in the edge here. This is probably safe, unless it belongs to some other rabbit."

Carefully, he lifted the creature up and put it gently into the hole. "If this isn't your home, brother rabbit, forgive us. This is the best we can do."

Liu Chenguang knelt down and put handfuls of grass in. "Here you go! Be well, my first patient." He grinned up at Hong Deming. "It would be nice for you to remember this one next time you're out hunting and try not to shoot it."

"I'll do my best, but if it's not wearing that bandage, it will look like all other rabbits. At least I'm a better shot than whatever tried to get him. Little rabbit, if I come for you, it'll be quick and painless."

Liu Chenguang pushed him gently. "Stop that, you're scaring my patient." He stood up and brushed the grass off his robes. "Come on, let's go wash off. My hands are all covered in blood."

As they walked together toward the lake, Hong Deming asked, "You don't eat meat — is that because of your cultivation path?"

"Partly…It's not good for me to hurt any beings, or to benefit from hurting any beings," he said, tripping slightly over a root.

Hong Deming grabbed his elbow. "Are you all right? Why are you tripping? You didn't use any qi for that, did you? Master Zhu said you're not to use qi for healing until your cultivation is complete."

"No, no, I was just thinking about things, not looking where I was going." Liu Chenguang continued, "It's really good for me to be learning from him, from all these books, so I can do other things besides use qi…I can save it for really important things that way. For things that can't be healed by any other method."

"Will you really be able to heal anything like Master Zhu said?"

"Yes," he said, bluntly and confidently, no room for doubt. "There's nothing I can't heal. Even now, I could. It's just that I don't have enough qi stored to do it safely yet for serious things."

Hong Deming walked quietly next to him, hands behind his back, considering Liu Chenguang's profile. "Will you tell me something, honestly?"

Liu Chenguang looked at him, surprised. "Of course. I've never lied to you. I never will," he said seriously.

"Did you heal that man in the house? The one I got in the throat, that time we were fighting the bandits. The time you collapsed."

"Yes."

"Why would you do that? He had just tried to rape that girl. He had killed that man. He was a murderer many times over." Hong Deming frowned. "I'm not angry, but what was the point? What if he'd killed you? What if he'd killed me? And his life was going to end either way…"

"I don't know. It was just an instinct when I was younger. Just something I did whenever I saw people hurt. That village you found me in — do you remember?"

"Of course I remember."

"I'd been trying to heal people, but the bandits came back and they hurt me too, so I was unconscious for a while as I was healing. I'd probably just woken up when you came…and I still healed that person in the house, even though I knew exactly who and what he was. I don't know. I know it doesn't make sense. I understand now why it doesn't make sense to you. I can't really justify it. Of course I know he was a criminal and he would be executed if he wasn't killed by you directly…it's just…you know. Like the rabbit. The one in front of me."

Liu Chenguang walked a little further, frowning thoughtfully. "There's something I heard once: done is done, and pain is pain. What that man had done in the past…That couldn't be undone, whatever pain he'd caused. But if he's in pain in front of me, I can do something about that. Maybe I'm the only one who can. Who knows what he will do if he lives? Perhaps good things. I can only choose to heal, or not."

Hong Deming shook his head. "Think about the consequences, though. Should you really heal everyone you see? Some people will just cause more pain in the world. Some people probably shouldn't be saved."

"Some people probably shouldn't," Liu Chenguang agreed. "But I have to save them anyway."

They reached the stream and knelt down next to each other to wash their hands; Hong Deming looked over at him, thinking how easy it would have been for that bandit to kill him that day. What would it have been if he had come just a minute later, with the three men hacking at the unarmed boy trying to block them with his body? His heart hurt a little bit.

Liu Chenguang smiled at him. "You're so serious," he said, and splashed water at Hong Deming's face.

"You are going to pay for that." Hong Deming narrowed his eyes at him and reached out to pull him into the water by his sleeve.

Several years after Liu Chenguang's arrival, Hong Deming accompanied him quite high on the mountain, helping him look for a tiny flower that only grew between rocks up above the tree line. By the time they found the lichen and Liu Chenguang had carefully collected the little flowers into a small linen bag, night was already starting to fall.

"Come on." Hong Deming looked up at the sky. "We're going to have to be fast going back down. This is a good time to practice your lightness skills."

Liu Chenguang made a face. "I'm tired," he said. Then, smiling, "Do you think you can still carry me on your back?"

Hong Deming looked him up and down seriously. "Well, if I had to, probably. But I'm too lazy today, so move your own feet."

Liu Chenguang laughed and leapt forward, moving from rock to rock down the cliff quicker than a mountain sheep, touching each stone with just the tips of his feet before moving forward.

Hong Deming jumped after him, trying to get ahead. "Ha!" he yelled. "Shameless, you went first without waiting–"

Liu Chenguang turned in midair to say something back to him, but missed the next landing point and tumbled a little way down the cliff.

"Taine!" Hong Deming shouted. He put more qi into his movements, nearly flying down to meet him.

Liu Chenguang had righted himself after bouncing off a couple of rocks and continued to leap down to more level ground, but Hong Deming could see that his movements were uncoordinated. In a moment, he would lose lightness completely and fall to the ground, still from a great height. He managed to catch up, put an arm around Liu Chenguang's ribs, and complete the movements to the bottom of the cliff.

He lay Liu Chenguang down carefully and reached for his lower leg, which was at a strange angle below the knee.

But Liu Chenguang, very pale, pushed his hand away. "It's all right. Don't worry. It'll be fine by tomorrow."

"What are you talking about?" Hong Deming asked, a little angry. "The bone is broken. I can see from how it's lying. And there's blood, too…it must have punched through the skin. How will it be all right tomorrow if we don't clean and splint it?"

To his shock, he saw Liu Chenguang reach down, his hands around his own leg, and wrench it into position.

"Ah," he said briefly, turning even paler.

"Don't pass out," Hong Deming said, alarmed.

"No, no, it's good now." Liu Chenguang panted a little bit, and color came back into his face. "Remember, I have that healing path. This is part of it. My body heals itself quickly. When I have my full cultivation, this kind of thing would heal in just a few moments, but as things are now…probably I'll need to stay here overnight." He looked around at the darkening sky.

"You can't stay here by yourself, taine," Hong Deming said firmly.

Liu Chenguang looked at him strangely. "Are you worried about me? You don't need to be. You can go back down. It's all right."

"You're not thinking well. How can you defend yourself if anything comes? You can't use weapons and you can't move. Should I carry you?"

Liu Chenguang shook his head. "I'm sorry, tainu. The leg shouldn't be moved or jostled. I wouldn't be able to hold on to you."

Hong Deming stood. "I'll get firewood."

"Is my qinggong really that bad, tainu?"

"Sloppy," he called back over his shoulder. "Can you eat meat if I shoot something?"

"Better not right now. Don't worry about me," Liu Chenguang said.

When he returned, he had brought not only a rabbit for himself but some nuts, berries, and mushrooms for Liu Chenguang. He took out a piece of cloth and laid it all next to him; Liu Chenguang looked at him, eyes wide.

"Well, make sure none of it will kill you," Hong Deming said, "but that's all I could find." He had already cleaned the rabbit and put bits of it on skewers around the fire. "It's too bad you can't eat this. Isn't it good for wounds to eat meat?"

"Not for me, tainu. It's really very different for me, but thank you. There's plenty here that I can eat. You've gotten better at avoiding poisonous mushrooms." He picked up some nuts and ate them slowly. After a while, he said, "Tainu, you take really good care of me. I'm grateful."

"It's just what I should do," Hong Deming said. "But it would be better if you had good skills. Then I wouldn't need to worry about you so much."

"You worry about me?"

"A little…just knowing that you can't use a sword or anything."

"Most people can't."

"But I don't know most people, so I don't worry about them," Hong Deming said, smiling. He reached over to poke Liu Chenguang in the shoulder. "Only my taine."

After a while, Liu Chenguang asked, "When I'm in seclusion, what do you do?"

"Pretty much the same thing I do when you're out of it. Practice the sword. Practice calligraphy and qin and archery. Only, I don't spend as much time studying in the library."

Liu Chenguang hesitated a moment. "Do you spend time with other people the way you do with me when I'm not in seclusion?"

"Well, of course. All the other disciples. But when you're not in seclusion I want to spend time with you, since it's not often…" He trailed off, realizing that when Liu Chenguang was in seclusion, life really was pretty boring. "Anyway, there's no one else who likes to go in the woods or do different things like you do. Don't you want to get to know some of the other disciples better, too?" he asked. "We're all a family."

"I haven't even met any of the female disciples," Liu Chenguang said. "But all my tainu…none of them pay much attention to me, except for you."

"We're the youngest of this generation, that's all," Hong Deming said. "They'll choose some more young disciples soon. More of the seniors are ready to teach, I think."

He took a stick out of the fire and began to blow on its bits of rabbit meat. "Did you know that Shen Lu is going to get married soon? He met a disciple from the Peaceful River sect a year ago, and it's all set. She'll come here to live, since Shen Lu will be the next sect leader."

Liu Chenguang was quiet for a while. "Look at the stars," he said, looking up and carefully lying down to see better. "It's so clear tonight."

Hong Deming finished eating his rabbit and lay down next to him. "Yes, look there — a falling star…"

"Master Zhu assigned me some astronomy readings this time, but they didn't talk much about falling stars. At least, not that I've read yet."

As the fire died down, the cold began to increase; they were still very high up. Hong Deming began to draw on qi to keep himself warm and looked, concerned, over at Liu Chenguang. "Taine, are you cold?"

"A little bit," he said, teeth chattering.

Since they didn't have any blankets, he put more wood on the fire, but the cold became more intense. He moved over closer to Liu Chenguang and said, "I'll help you keep warm, taine, all right?"

"All right," he said.

When Hong Deming put his arms around him carefully, trying to avoid touching his hurt leg or jostling him, he could feel Liu Chenguang's entire body shaking uncontrollably. "Shhhh, be still. I still don't know how to share qi."

"Hah," said Liu Chenguang, "I do know how. I just am using all my qi to heal my leg."

"I know. Don't feel bad about it." He leaned back against a rock and drew Liu Chenguang further under his arm, draping his own robe around him. He'd have to use qi to stay warm himself and to generate warmth for Liu Chenguang as well. "Go to sleep, taine."

Liu Chenguang said, "Thank you for worrying about me."

"Mm," he said, feeling sleepy and comfortable. "So silly. Don't show off skills you don't have next time. I know you're good at other things."

Liu Chenguang's hair smelled pleasant — a blend of medicinal herbs and incense. He yawned; producing so much warmth was tiring. "We can…we can work on the qinggong another time…"

After a while, Liu Chenguang asked, "How old are you now, tainu?"

Hong Deming had set his concentration on using his qi to create enough warmth for both of them and had planned to fall asleep that way, but Liu Chenguang's questions kept distracting him. When he lost his focus, he realized that somehow their bodies had become closely intertwined, and he felt a little awkward. Liu Chenguang was still small, but the weight and shape of his body half-lying on his own was no longer that of a child. He coughed and tried to straighten up a little bit, refocusing on warmth. "I'm almost twenty, I'll have my adulthood ceremony soon."

"Oh. You told me before that when you've had your ceremony you'll go to the Peaceful River sect too, won't you?"

"That's what Taiqian wants for me. He wants me to spend a few years focused on qin cultivation under their sect leader. I'm already advanced enough here."

"And you'll have a spiritual sword?"

"Yes, certainly that will be soon. I'll have to go into seclusion for that myself."

Liu Chenguang looked up at him. "I'm eighteen. Zhu Guiren will come soon to make the decision, but Taiqian thinks I probably only need one more period of seclusion before my cultivation foundation is set. Then, I'll leave with him to study. I don't know when I'll be back."

"You'll come back someday," he said, confidently. "We both will. This is our home." He looked down at Liu Chenguang, at his eyes, shining in the starlight beneath his lashes.

Liu Chenguang's eyes were always bright and interested in the world, but now they looked rather soft and sad.

Impulsively, Hong Deming said, "Don't worry, taine. We'll always see each other again. Eventually, you'll be done with all this time of seclusion and your life will get easier. I know it's been hard for you." He carefully pressed on his shoulder, comforting. "With Zhu Guiren, you'll see so much of the world. Maybe even the emperor and the court. You'll learn so many things and meet many new people. You won't need to worry about whether you can do the same things we ordinary disciples can because you'll be able to do so much more. There are thousands of people that can use swords, but you will be a divine physician.

There's no one like you, taine."

Liu Chenguang smiled. "There's no one like you either, tainu."

He felt absurdly warmed and checked to see if he'd been overdoing it with the qi generation. He patted Liu Chenguang's shoulder again. "Shh. Time to sleep."

# CHAPTER 11
## SECLUSION

Liu Chenguang had been in his final time of seclusion for a month already when Taiqian directed Hong Deming to enter.

As a very young disciple, Hong Deming had entered the spiritual caverns soon after he first formed his well of qi for a brief ceremony, but never since then. Secluded cultivation was reserved for particularly important steps in a cultivator's life, and highly-advanced practitioners that had reached a plateau in their cultivation would sometimes enter seclusion for years at a time in order to reach a breakthrough. Aside from this, a young cultivator in the Crane Moon sect would normally enter only when they had reached the point of developing a spiritual weapon.

Hong Deming knew that it would be dark and quiet and that there was a risk, as for everyone, of qi deviation during the intensity of this cultivation period. Beyond that, he had no idea what to expect.

Taiqian led him through the winding corridors inside the mountain, concentrating on finding an area that would be most appropriate for Hong Deming's cultivation. He ended up choosing a cavern with a small, clear stream running over a bed of silvery pebbles. The sound was peaceful, enticing — Hong Deming liked it immediately. He saluted Taiqian silently; Taiqian departed in equal silence.

Until he had a spiritual sword, he would not speak, or eat, or drink, or leave the cavern.

The darkness was complete. The only sounds were the quiet trickle of water, his own breathing, his own heartbeat. In a lotus position, he slowed both and practiced quieting his mind. There were many scriptures appropriate to seclusion, but he found that none of them suited his inner direction. Instead, he opened his mind completely to silence — only the sound of the stream, only the pebbles being slowly worn away into their new forms.

At first, he saw lights and images in his mind, and he let them go and come as they would. None left a mark and eventually, they, too, disappeared. Repeated words, phrases, obsessive thoughts, came and fell down into silence. His emotions — sorrow, loss, fear, anxiety, joy, memories of the past, imaginations of the future — all observed and released. He felt his stomach contract, longing for food, sometimes even making noises demanding it; eventually, that also wore away, like all the senses of his body. Like the pebbles beneath the stream. Like the water in the veins of the earth, he directed the qi of his body through his meridians, gradually sensing its increase in strength and purity.

There was now no boundary between his body and the darkness, and no difference between darkness and light. The qi within his body was no different than the qi of the living world around him. Like the water of the stream, it came from one place and went to another, but was all of one being in the end.

His awareness touched on other living beings, and he felt something.

Out of the darkness, beyond time, he felt something new — something in his heart that had no name, a longing for which he could place no object. Unlike all that had come before, this longing disturbed his equanimity. It called his heart out from his body, and his body out from life into the dark to seek what he so desperately needed, what he could not put a name to. Would he even know it when he found it? He flailed in the darkness, seeking in all directions for the thing without which he could not live. His heart called out in desperation, crying for something undiscovered and unknown.

His breathing broke its rhythm.

With the shift came the need to control his breathing again, and with the need for control came the loss of connection to the qi rushing through him.

Hong Deming was consciously aware that he was spiraling into qi deviation; the qi in his meridians surged beyond his body's capacity to contain it. As though from a great distance, he knew that his body was in pain. There was a small, glowing figure doubled over, convulsing, blood coming from the seven orifices. This body did not have a connection with his ability to control it, no matter how much he desired to do so. The borders had been blurred and broken. He could no longer set the boundaries of the qi flooding in and overwhelming him.

Suddenly, there was a second body rushing in, a body with intention and awareness and control. This body knelt down and touched his face with fingers that shone blood red. He could feel it touching him — his eyes, his nostrils, his ears, his lips — anointing him.

With a rush, he was back inside his body, gasping for air. He could feel hands on him, hear breathing that was not his own, though he couldn't see anything at all. But in the complete darkness, touch and scent and hearing were increased beyond any normal sensitivity. From the breath, from the shape of the fingers lightly touching his lips, from the faint scent of herbs and incense, he said, without thinking, breaking the silence of seclusion for both of them, "Liu Chenguang." His voice was hoarse with disuse.

The fingers on his lips were removed, then placed firmly on his heart meridian, still in silence. He could feel Liu Chenguang's long hair brushing his wrist; he must be leaning over closely. Hong Deming shivered all over with the increased sensitivity to touch. He could feel, now, the warmth of qi entering from Liu Chenguang's fingers — a stream that went throughout his meridians, calming and healing everything that was there, all the chaos smoothed out.

"Don't. Not good for you," Hong Deming said, and tried to move his arm, but Liu Chenguang firmly grasped it, and he was too weak to move away.

When the fingers were removed, Hong Deming was able to bring himself back into a lotus position without pain. His mind felt clear and peaceful again. He regretted that he had broken Liu Chenguang's seclusion and had even required him to use qi for healing, but he had truly needed it. He didn't think that there was anything he could have done to save himself. Cultivators risked death in qi deviation from seclusion. He had known this going in. Only because Liu Chenguang had been there, had taken the risk of injuring his own cultivation to save him, was Hong Deming still alive. There was nothing he could do about this now except determine how to repay Liu Chenguang in the future.

As he felt Liu Chenguang move next to him, he reached out and took his wrist, smoothing out his closed fingers and palm. Carefully, he wrote the character for gratitude, en, in the palm of Liu Chenguang's hand. The hand remained in his own for another moment, warm and quiet, peaceful, then was softly withdrawn.

He heard the steps, felt the warmth of the living person withdraw from his cavern, still in silence, leaving him alone.

There was no way to know time's passing in the cavern, but there came a moment when he reached his hand into the darkness and felt it close around the hilt of a sword; he named it En. *Gratitude.*

He then stood up and walked out into the world again with the sword in his hand.

He had been in seclusion for six months.

Hong Deming formally presented the sword to Taiqian and told him its name and what had happened in seclusion without hiding either his qi deviation or the fact that he owed his life to Liu Chenguang.

Taiqian looked serious about this. "Liu Chenguang did not mention this when he left seclusion, and has already departed with Zhu Guiren for his further training," he said slowly. "I will write to Zhu Guiren and tell him. It may be important for him to know in case it has serious effects for him later."

Hong Deming felt as clear and calm as a still pond, but the realization that Liu Chenguang was no longer at Crane Moon was a stone that caused ripples in his mind.

Taiqian must have noticed this in his face. "Are you distressed that your taine has gone?"

"I wanted to thank him properly."

"You'll have a chance in the future. You owe him a debt, certainly. Zhu Guiren told the truth that day when he said that someone on the healing path would be an asset to our sect. Your life is already repayment for having offered him a home here." He added, "When Shen Lu becomes the sect leader, I will enter seclusion myself for a while, but he knows about Liu Chenguang's special status. I'll be sure that he knows as well that he has shown himself to be a devoted and loyal taine to you in this way."

In his post-seclusion clarity, Hong Deming realized what lay beneath these words: Taiqian had doubts about Liu Chenguang, and these doubts were shared by Shen Lu. Why would this be, when Liu Chenguang was so obviously a good person? But, he also felt clearly that this was not the time to ask, even if he had the status to question Taiqian about such a thing. He only said, "I'll always be grateful that he is my taine."

"You named your sword En for this reason. For your gratitude for him."

"Yes, that's why."

Taiqian nodded slowly. "In regard to your qi deviation, it seems that it was caused by an unrestrained longing. Did the desire have an object?"

"No. I couldn't tell what it was that I wanted or needed, yet it seemed that if I didn't have it…" He tried to put it into words. "It seemed that if I didn't have… whatever it was…that everything would fall apart, somehow. Nothing as simple as death, but that everything would…" He trailed off, helplessly. "The fear of not finding what I was seeking — it made me so terrified that I lost control of everything."

"Unrestrained desire without an object…this is what you will need to work on during your next phase of cultivation," Taiqian responded. "It may be that you need to discover what it is that you truly desire, or it may be that you need to let go of desire entirely. Both of these are possible cultivation paths, and desire can take many forms and have many objects, not all of which are acceptable or attainable. But, to desire so deeply and not know what it is that you desire…that path is clearly not one that you can continue to walk indefinitely. This is what your sword seclusion has shown you. For this self-knowledge, be grateful to your sword as well."

He bent his head. "Yes, Taiqian."

"In two weeks, it will be time for your crowning as an adult. Spend time between now and then on getting to know the ways of your new sword, and on qin. Nothing more than those two things. After your adulthood ceremony, you will travel to the Peaceful River sect for training with qin cultivation." He added, "Peaceful River sect is less strict than the Crane Moon in some ways. While you are there, make wise decisions, but don't judge harshly or be too quick to refuse their invitations. Crane Moon's path is strong, but narrow, like a sword blade. Sometimes, it's good for the spirit to experience the world differently before one comes back home."

Hong Deming looked at him, confused.

Taiqian shook his head, smiling a little. "You know that your sect mother came from the Peaceful River sect. So does Shen Lu's wife. It often happens that leaving Crane Moon to visit another sect or to wander beyond the bounds is a time to explore human relationships, and that is appropriate at your time of life. You are an adult. Your decisions are your own. Only marriage needs to be approved by the Crane Moon. That's all I want you to know, speaking as your Taiqian — that it's not forbidden, even if it's not the way we live here within our own sect home."

"I don't think…" he said, stumbling. "I just have never…I don't think I'm ready to consider marriage yet."

"No need until you are ready." Taiqian stood up, handing him back the sword. "Liu Chenguang will never achieve a spiritual sword. Though he is my youngest disciple in name, you are my youngest in the Crane Moon sword path. The name of your sword is appropriate. I, too, am grateful that you have completed your cultivation and can now go out into the world."

Hong Deming placed the sword by his side, knelt, and bowed his head to the ground, palms flat. The words he spoke were formal, but they were truly in his heart as well: "This humble person is grateful to Taiqian for his life and teaching. This insignificant person will strive not to dishonor the Crane Moon sect."

The crowning ceremony was accompanied by a feast of departure not only for Hong Deming leaving for Peaceful River, but for Taiqian entering secluded cultivation; Shen Lu, Hong Deming's tainu, would now be sect leader and Taiqian to a new generation of disciples. The feast was thus a double celebration.

No one seemed to remember that Liu Chenguang was really the youngest disciple, not Hong Deming. He felt this a little painfully — that no one but him seemed to remember Liu Chenguang at all, or care that he wasn't present. Nonetheless, Liu Chenguang would always be his taine. Nothing on earth could change that. There would be years and years ahead for them to be together at the sect. The others would realize what a wonderful person he was, and that even if his cultivation was different from everyone else's, he was valuable for that very reason.

Hong Deming left the next morning, riding toward Zhashan, first down the gorge path, then down progressively larger and busier roads and highways to the great capital — or, the capital that had once been, before the new Son of Heaven moved it to Gunan.

Zhashan was a city almost in ruins after its repeated sackings, lootings, rebellions, and forced removals. Hong Deming sat outside of the walls that remained, watching the few inhabitants trying to reconstruct their lives, the scavengers trying to find whatever they could to fill tonight's cookpot. This had been a city of almost a million people, he had read in the library of the Crane Moon. Monasteries and abbeys, palaces and ponds, marketplaces, brothels, foreigners and flowers and fruit trees — all were now gone.

Zhashan was where Taiqian had found him as an abandoned child. He thought he might be able to find the place, or the people that cared for him, but this was clearly impossible. Out of those million people, he would never know who had given birth to him or given him his name. He watched a small child eat spoiled vegetables from the ground and his heart ached, but when he offered dried fruit from his supplies the child ran in terror.

After wandering the rubble-strewn streets, he continued his journey toward Gunan. The highway was growing more crowded, and bandits preyed on wealthier travelers. Since he was a cultivator from a righteous sect, he was called upon to protect various groups, and didn't mind doing so in return for food and conversation. One such group was conveying a young woman and her dowry to her new husband in Gunan, and although they had initially had many guards, it was so obviously an excellent target that they had already been attacked multiple times since setting out. Hong Deming wasn't naturally given to solitude; after his seclusion, the lonely journey, and the depression of seeing the ruins of Zhashan, he was eager to spend time with human beings again, hearing them laugh and tell stories and share food together.

"Handsome one," called one of the lady's maids to him as he rode along their column, "come visit with us!" She stuck her head out of the carriage, smiling at him admiringly.

He smiled back and slowed his horse so he could ride alongside her.

"Handsome one, what's your name?"

"Hong Deming," he said. "And you?"

"Oh, they call me Peony," she said. She had pale skin and black hair caught back from her face with very tiny brass pins, and clearly wasn't a woman completely without worldly experience; she was well made-up, wearing a heavily embroidered dress and shawl. "I'm the maid of the Lady Su, who is the first concubine of the house. The girl being married is her daughter. Lady Su sent me along to ensure that all is well with the marriage and that the girl is happy. I suppose you can say I'm her maid now, though I'm older than she is."

Hong Deming found her very funny. It was just like the stories he'd heard from his elder martial brothers about the men and women of the world outside the sect; he hadn't believed that people would actually talk like this and be this obvious, but it appeared that this woman was bored enough to attempt to seduce an unknown cultivator hired to guard the convoy. He tried to decide whether he was interested, and discerned that he was not in the least. But at least it was not boring to hear her talk and attempt to invite him to come into the carriage without saying so, getting more and more brazen about her intentions as time went on.

Eventually, since he did actually have a job to do for these people, he excused himself and rode up and down the column slowly, keeping an eye on the woods to one side and the road to the other. He wondered if his presence alone would be enough to deter bandits, but he didn't look that impressive in simple traveling robes with an unremarkable sword, bow, and quiver. It was unlikely that the embroidered symbol of the Crane Moon on his robe meant much to anyone at this point.

When the bandits did attack, it was something of a surprise for them; about twenty came rushing out of the woods to one side as the convoy entered a narrow stretch of road, blocking off the road in front with another twenty and far outnumbering the guards of the convoy. Arrows were already coming out of the trees. He sent a few back in answer and blocked the rest with his sword, leaving only a few to strike the carriages or in the dirt.

The difficulty, as Hong Deming saw it, was protecting two sides at once; which should be first?

Woods, he decided. The arrows were annoying, and endangering his charges. He rode through the attackers, slashing from one side to the other, using as little qi as was necessary to control the sword. These appeared to be ordinary people; there was no need to use the full power he would bring to a battle with a true cultivation opponent. For something like this, he hardly needed to exert himself. Several bandits fell easily, blood spurting wherever the sword went, and those that survived retreated into the woods. By that point, he was at the front of the convoy and cut through those attempting to block the road with similar ease. He then shooed the carriages through at top speed and fell in behind them.

This all took only a few moments; he had not even needed to dismount. He flicked the blood from En's blade and settled in as rearguard just to see if any of the bandits had any further ideas. Then he thought of something himself.

"I'll be right back," he called, and cantered back, looking for a survivor. He knelt down next to a man cradling his arm in shock. En had carved a piece out of the bandit's upper arm, though truly it was only a flesh wound.

"You'll survive." He realized that the bandit, staring at him pale and terrified, was younger than he was — perhaps only a skinny seventeen. His weapon, he saw now, was only a rusted blade, such as a farmer might use to cut wood. Are all the others as prepared as you?" Hong Deming blurted out.

"We're starving," the boy said. "That's all. Why would we do this if we had any other choice?" He rocked in pain, closing his eyes.

For a moment, disconcertingly, Hong Deming thought of Liu Chenguang, who would have been able to heal him, for good or for ill.

"Just kill me. There's nothing I can do about any of it."

Trying to put authority into his voice, Hong Deming said, "Tell the others to stop attacking travelers. This is the only end they'll come to if they're not captured and executed for brigandage first."

"Execution, no execution…we're all dying anyway," the boy said, his eyes glinting up from beneath his lids. "So lucky for you — you have food, you're so smart, so powerful, you can kill us, whatever. Every day we live through an attack, we eat. Every day we eat, we live to attack again. There's nothing else to do. So just kill me or stop talking." He grunted, rose to his feet, and staggered away.

Hong Deming watched him go.

He thought of the beauty of the Crane Moon sect: the quiet library, the jeweled mist in the sunset, the cavern with the clear stream, Liu Chenguang's hand in his in the dark. Hong Deming looked at the sword in his hand, which was now clean of blood, a bond with the deepest realities of existence that allowed him to kill starving boys without even breaking a sweat.

Was there anything else he could have done?

Why had his elder martial brothers never talked about this, when they talked about the world?

He found that he really wanted to talk to Liu Chenguang.

Like Crane Moon, the Peaceful River sect was dedicated to the Pathless Way. It had long been located in an ancient abbey in Zhashan. Like all the other residents of Zhashan, the sect had been forced to move to Gunan a few years ago. Though Gunan, too, was ancient, as a result of the relocation of the imperial court, the whole city had a sense of raw, unsettled frenzy about it. Hong Deming asked through the streets until he found where the Peaceful River had set up its new sect location — an abbey built outside of the city walls on a hill set back from the river, planted with peonies. The track wound up steeply between the flowers, giving the sense of rising up above the world into the heavens. As he passed under the gate, he turned to look back at the sun across the river, the valley full of shadows as the sun neared setting.

"Why do I feel so melancholy?" he asked no one in particular.

"I have no idea," a voice answered. A young man stuck his face out from behind the gate pillar, where he had apparently been sleeping in the shade. "But it's nothing that some good liquor and conversation shouldn't cure, I'm betting." He smiled, hopped up to his feet, and bowed without the slightest bit of embarrassment at having been caught sleeping on guard.

"I'm Mo Xiang, fourth disciple of the seventh generation of the Peaceful River sect," he said. His hair was up in a pincrown, but his manner was so playful that it was hard to believe he was an adult. After the images of corpses and starving children and ruined cities that had kept intruding into his mind throughout the journey, day after day, Hong Deming found him almost dreamlike.

Mo Xiang reached down and picked up a qin. "Please forgive me for seeming overtired, but it's a hot day, and I can only play the qin for so long among the flowers and sunshine before feeling as though staying awake to guard against enemies is really pointless." He winked. "And after all, we are not expecting an enemy; I've been here the past several days to greet a friend. Who I think, judging by that embroidery on your robe, is you. Would the gentleman honor me with his name?"

Hong Deming had to laugh. "I'm Hong Deming. I've been sent–"

"From the Crane Moon, yes. Your sect leader sent a letter to expect you weeks ago. Were the roads bad? Oh, come up. You must be tired and hungry." He gestured toward the path, which continued to climb and twist between peonies and rocks. "There's a ward here. It's not all dependent on my meager skills to defend the sect. You'll have to follow me closely so I can bring you in. Just leave the horse…see, there's a place there to tether the reins? The servants will come bring it to the stables later."

He set the qin on a convenient boulder and began to play a haunting melody. Hong Deming felt a shifting of the energy of the air — something was being opened in front of them, although until it was open he hadn't realized it was closed.

"Maze ward," Mo Xiang casually called while playing. "Outsiders just get lost and then dumped outside the boundary. It's not harmful to anyone, but why make you go through that? All right, that's enough, come on."

Hong Deming followed him up the winding path, impressed with Mo Xiang's skill. Behind him, the river valley was filled with shadows, but the hilltop was bright and filled with the sound of music.

Mo Xiang brought him to a small cell with a window looking out toward the mountains of Crane Moon, which he could no longer see behind the great gates of the Sorrowful River. He bathed and changed into clean clothes, then sat near the window, his chin in his hand and the world laid out before him — cities and rivers and mountains, shadowed and bright, without any boundaries visible on it — and imagined that Liu Chenguang was there to look at it with him.

# CHAPTER 12
## DISTRACTION

DESPITE HIS BRAVADO, Zhu Guiren eventually had to return to Tainu's ward in exhaustion. No more soul-devourers had come, but the attacks from demons and yaoguai had been unrelenting, and he had, after all, just lost a hand, although he acted as though this was no more than a minor irritation. Despite hating him, Tairei said nothing when Tainu dragged him back inside and told him to go to sleep before further strengthening the ward.

Tairei settled herself again, closing her eyes, one hand on Aili's hair. She wasn't even trying to cultivate now — just wallowing in memories that hit her harder than they had in centuries with Aili in front of her, next to her, touched by her. When she leapt down from the world tree and saw Aili walking in from the darkness next to Tainu, sword in hand, the expression on Aili's face, the way she held her body, all of it had literally knocked the wind out of her. She had had to gasp for breath as she ran forward, almost hysterical, to touch her and make sure she was real.

Her mind had seen Hong Deming in that very posture, weary and confused and lost, covered in blood after that first battle outside Gunan. He had run toward Hong Deming then, tripping over the corpses. Hong Deming had flicked the blood from his sword, looked out over the corpses, and said none of the blood was his, but he had been hurt inside. All the certainty of his world had gone. Back then, she had seen it in his eyes; she could see it now in Aili's.

Hong Deming hadn't let him touch him then. He had been so cautious about touching one another at that time, she remembered. But Aili was here now. She could touch Aili. She was real, she was alive. She sighed, and stroked Aili's hair, gently. She wanted to say *I'm here. It's me; it's Liu Chenguang, your little martial sibling. I am real. You can count on me…*

But after all, in the end…

She wanted to kiss her, but Zhu Guiren was awake again. The demon was humming softly to himself, eyes closed, as though very pleased with the way all the world was going. Tairei looked at him with disgust.

"Why did you make up all that?" she asked suddenly. "All that stupidity about me being born with a cultivator's well of qi, the healing path— all of it?"

"Don't you admire my creativity?" Zhu Guiren opened his eyes. "Use your brain. Why do you think I did it? Obviously because it benefited me."

"In what way?"

"Why are you so stupid? Didn't I teach you to figure things out?" He yawned. "Think about it. What was the result of all that? What happened?"

"Taiqian accepted me as a disciple. I stayed with the sect…"

"Exactly. It was perfect. Even you didn't know I'd made it up. You thought I was a human doctor believing in myths. Mistaken, but you went along with it because it benefited you too. I knew you couldn't resist the chance of having a place to cultivate to adulthood that would be safe and warded from demonic attack. And then, when you had your full power, you'd trust me. I'd know where to find you. It saved me all the time and effort of capturing you."

He nodded. "It was a spur-of-the-moment thing…I hadn't planned to have a phoenix. I wasn't the one that had been chasing you in the spirit realm. I wasn't the one who had driven you into the mortal realm before you had completed your regeneration, but as soon as I saw you, as soon as I knew what you were, I knew how I could use it. No demon has ever had an adult phoenix to use before. And you did it willingly. Stayed near me, obeyed my orders…"

Tairei was quiet, trying to bite down on her rage. Tainu was watching them. Tainu would be upset; for some reason her sibling wanted her to be polite to this creature. *He protected us, he's lost his hand,* she chanted inwardly to calm herself. Then she said, "I didn't stay because I wanted to cultivate. I didn't stay for you. And I never fully trusted you."

"Who cares?" He shrugged his shoulders. "It still all worked out the way I planned. Why tell me now?"

"Because you should know you're not as smart as you think you are. You think you are controlling people, controlling events, but things are really happening for other reasons."

Zhu Guiren said, "Whatever. As long as I win, I win."

"You didn't win, you stupid, self-satisfied piece of garbage. You didn't win."

The demon looked at her, eyes wide. For the first time, his face showed something other than his usual expression of pleased arrogance.

Tainu's voice came calmly: "Demon, stop provoking her, or you can leave. Can't you even understand what you've done?"

Zhu Guiren's face fell for a moment, and then he said, "I made it as painless for her as I could."

Tairei said, "I wish so much that I was able to kill you for saying that."

Zhu Guiren turned toward her in what seemed to be genuine surprise. "I kept you unconscious for almost all of it–"

"Shut up," she hissed. "Shut up, shut up, shut up."

"Shut up," Tainu said firmly. "Get out."

The demon stood up and pushed through the ward.

"Do you think he'll come back?" Tairei asked after a while.

"Do you care?"

"I want him to leave. His face makes me want to vomit," Tairei said fiercely. "And don't you dare tell me done is done. There's no possible pain he could be feeling that I could care about."

"I'll be honest, Tairei, I think we are going to need his help."

"No."

"For Aili's sake."

Tairei fell silent.

Tainu continued, "Whether he helps us or not, we need to move today. He can't defend us for another nightfall regardless, it'll just get worse. We need to get to a refuge. My wards are under attack, and I can't hold much longer."

They both looked outside the wards, which under Tainu's increased strengthening now kept out even sounds, like a very thick pane of flexible glass. In the brightening sunlight, Zhu Guiren fought, one-handed, with a snake demon. It was as though someone had painted a moving picture for them. He finally managed to decapitate the thing and stood there, breathing heavily, head down. Then, something shaped like an enormous scorpion leapt on his back; he threw it to the ground and speared it with his sword, switched to the halberd, and swung it at waist level at a misshapen shadow they couldn't see clearly.

Tairei remarked, "I quite like watching him be attacked by other demons, actually. Let's stay here."

Tainu snorted. "Those are the little ones. At nightfall, the chthonic beings will come for Aili again, and he can't do much against those. There haven't been any really powerful demons yet, either, and even so, he's exhausted. Even for a demon losing a part of the true body must hit hard. He won't really recover until he gets some rest, and I can't hold this ward another night."

He stood up, walked through the ward, and dragged Zhu Guiren back inside. Tairei quickly shifted to take the burden of the ward from him, but she couldn't hold it long either, she had never been as strong as Tainu.

"Come in, come out, make up your mind," the demon said. His face was pale and sweaty, and he had a few wounds on his back from the scorpion thing.

"Turn around," Tainu said, biting his finger. He brushed some of his blood on the wounds. "Demon, we need to get to a refuge."

"How fast can you run?" Zhu Guiren asked. "Because the minute you step outside, there's a welcoming committee eager to take you for a ride elsewhere."

"I'll distract them. They'll follow me. Your job is to get these two to a refuge," Tainu said.

Tairei was as surprised as Zhu Guiren looked. "I don't want to go with him," she said immediately.

"I am the distraction," Tainu said patiently. "He's the protection. You can't fight, you can't fly, and you'll need to carry her. *Can* you carry her?" He looked Tairei up and down, clearly just realizing that she was far too small to carry Aili.

"I can carry her," said the demon.

"You will not," said Tairei, furious.

Tainu ignored her. "Can you carry her and fight?" he asked Zhu Guiren.

"Of course. I've got a useless arm anyway." He waved his handless arm in the air. "Perfect for carrying unconscious mortal-phoenix hybrids."

Tairei turned away; she couldn't stand the sight of him. After a moment, she said, "I also can't find the refuge."

"I know," Tainu said. He put his hands on Zhu Guiren's shoulders and turned him around to stare at him, considering, for several moments.

Zhu Guiren seemed uncomfortable, but he didn't look away.

Eventually, Tainu asked, "Can you protect them?"

"Of course," he said immediately. "These little things aren't a match for–"

"Will you protect them?"

"Yes," Zhu Guiren said seriously, still looking at Tainu as though fascinated by his eyes. "I promise I will."

Tainu nodded and placed two fingers on Zhu Guiren's forehead, just above and between his brows. "Can you see it? The path?"

"Yes. I see the way."

"Hold Tairei's hand when you get there, otherwise the wards won't let you in," Tainu said. "The wards of the refuge are much stronger than the one I made here. They're completely different. It will kill you if you try to force your way in. Don't mess with it."

Zhu Guiren nodded, still looking at Tainu.

Tainu turned away and said, "Tairei."

Tairei sat next to Aili and stared out through the ward, refusing to look at them.

"Tairei," Tainu said, "take him in the refuge with you. You promise?"

"I don't trust him."

"Then trust me. Take him in the refuge with you. He won't be able to fight the soul devourers that will come for Aili. He'll need protection too."

"Then he can just leave. He doesn't need to stay near us. I don't want—"

"Take him inside the refuge," Tainu said, his voice both gentle and implacable.

She closed her eyes. "Tainu, don't."

"Tairei," he said quietly. "Promise. We need his help to save Aili."

"All right," she replied at last, though the words choked her.

Tainu nodded. "All right then. I don't know if the wards of the refuge will keep out the soul-devourers that will come for Aili, but they're much stronger than these, and they'll repel anything demonic. That'll give us something of a rest, anyway. Tairei, you'll probably get there before I do. Start cultivating right away."

She nodded.

"I'll meet you there. As soon as I'm gone and they've followed me, start running. The ward will dissolve."

Without waiting any further, he walked out past the wards. Immediately he began running, followed by an assortment of demons and shadow figures that rose out of the grass.

Zhu Guiren immediately stepped forward, his sword in his hand.

"Wait," said Tairei.

Tainu began running faster, his long legs taking him into the razor grass.

"He's bleeding," said Zhu Guiren sharply.

But before he could follow, between one step and the next, Tainu's form shimmered into an enormous, winged being, its feathers the color of blood and sunlight. As it shook out its wings and took flight, golden light trailed it like a shadow. The demons touched by the light shrieked and withdrew for a moment.

The invisible ward dissolved; they could hear the beating of the wings like slow thunder, the wind from them rushing through the grass and trees and nearly knocking them over. The golden shadow spun above them as the phoenix called out, a music that shook the world to the horizon, stirring the bones and the blood of all living beings into awareness.

Like a comet in daylight, the phoenix's wings struck fire and it sped away.

All the demons followed it — running, hopping, flying, slithering. Around the tree where they waited was only clean silence.

Zhu Guiren kept watching until the last light had faded. "He's…he's very powerful," he said at last.

Tairei smiled, feeling affectionate. "Well, he's a little bit of a show-off, but I suppose that was necessary. It will certainly cover our tiny existence for a while."

"That would be why we never capture adults…" he said slowly.

"He's the oldest of us. Or at least the one of us who can remember the farthest back."

"How old is he?"

"You should ask him." Gently, she raised Aili's limp form into a sitting position. "Come take her," she said, reluctantly. She kissed her forehead quickly — hoping Zhu Guiren didn't notice, hoping it was all right.

"Keep her safe," she said, as he stooped and picked Aili up over his left shoulder.

"Let's go," he said, turning in the opposite direction from where Tainu had flown. "It's this way." Sword in his single hand, he led the way into the tall grass.

Tairei followed.

# CHAPTER 13
## PEACEFUL RIVER

Hong Deming was welcomed by the sect leader of Peaceful River and given a qin to work with. The disciples of Peaceful River were dedicated to their own cultivation path, but compared to the austere world of the Crane Moon, it seemed to be a path of joy and pleasure. The days were filled with music, and the nights, quite often, with wine and poetry as well. It was all a balm to his heart after the darkness of the past year.

The cultivation of the qin required a deep silence of mind and focus of the body, the movements subtle and small compared to the large, active movements and risky cultivation of the sword path. It was almost as though the younger disciples needed to balance this with active celebration and play.

Unlike at Crane Moon, the female disciples joined the males in their studies, and often for the nightly celebrations, with no elders forbidding it. Hong Deming found this bizarre at first, but got used to it quickly. The women were intelligent, skilled, and strong in their way. Some were even studying the sword or archery along with qin, though not at the cultivation level of Crane Moon, and he was happy to help them practice. This became more comfortable after a few of the women disciples had tried to interest him in more intimate activities and he refused clearly; apparently, they spread the word, and after that, the female disciples treated him just as the men did — with friendliness and humor — which set him at ease.

The only places the women disciples didn't accompany the men were to the pavilions and houses of pleasure in Gunan. Since the Peaceful River sect was close to a great city with all a city's attractions, and since their cultivation path didn't require bodily purity, a good number of the younger disciples regularly visited the pleasure quarters. They always went to the most respectable ones, known for their music as well as other entertainments — never to the cruder or more vulgar places. Hong Deming felt uncomfortable with this practice for reasons he couldn't fully understand himself, but he didn't want to offend his friends or stay at home alone, so often he would go as well, though he always stayed in the main room listening to the music and drinking.

"Why don't you ever go upstairs?" yawned a rumpled Mo Xiang one night, back down after a session. "They've got all kinds here. Whatever you like."

Hong Deming shrugged.

"Are you really that stoic? How can you be surrounded by such beauty and remain unmoved, week after week? I'll bet you a jar of wine that I can find the one you'll like most." Mo Xiang looked around; he waved over one of the musicians — a pretty girl with her hair pinned in complex coils and dressed in lightweight silks who had been playing a stringed instrument on a low dais at the center of the room. "This is Jade Blossom. She's talented in many areas!"

Jade Blossom raised her lashes briefly in a shy smile. "I've noticed the gentleman listening several times," she said in a cultured voice. "Might the gentleman be interested in music? Or perhaps in poetry?"

"Thank you, I'm honored to hear you play and sing." Hong Deming didn't smile back. "But I wouldn't want to deprive the room of the pleasure of hearing you to while away the hours."

Jade Blossom smiled again, offered a curtsy, and returned to the stage to begin another song.

"Hmmmm…" Mo Xiang looked around the room again. "No…no…probably not…I've got it!"

At Mo Xiang's drunken wave, a slim young man came over to them carrying a jar of wine. His hair fell smoothly down his back, accentuating his gentle features and shining eyes. He gracefully reached out and poured wine for both Mo Xiang and Hong Deming. As he offered the cup to Hong Deming, he smiled, and one of his fingers gently brushed Hong Deming's hand as though by accident.

"What is the gentleman's pleasure tonight?" he asked. His lips curved very slightly as he looked at Hong Deming, who blushed.

Mo Xiang, watching carefully, said, "Oh, my friend is looking for someone he can chat with while he waits for the others. Perhaps you could offer him a game of chess?"

"Do you enjoy chess?" the young man asked Hong Deming. "I can play many other games as well."

Hong Deming blushed even more.

The young man smiled. "My name is Wu Fan. May I have the honor of knowing the gentleman's name?"

"I'm Hong Deming," he replied, but it was difficult to get it out past the constriction in his throat. This person's physical closeness — his quiet, intimate voice, his dark eyes — combined with the entire air of the place and the sounds Hong Deming could sometimes hear from upstairs was making him feel heated and awkward. He gulped. "It's– it's all right. I'm happy just listening to the music while I wait."

Mo Xiang smirked and went over to a distant part of the room to drink with another beauty, leaving Hong Deming with Wu Fan alone in their corner. Wu Fan moved closer on the bench, close enough that Hong Deming could feel the warmth of Wu Fan's body through the thin robes he wore.

Wu Fan listened quietly to the music for a while along with him, then leaned over and whispered: "This song is very tragic, isn't it? Lovers seek but don't find. I prefer songs where the lovers find one another, don't you?"

The warm breath in his ear made Hong Deming shiver as his body reacted far ahead of his mind. He moved to the other side of the bench.

"Is there something wrong?" Wu Fan asked. His eyes looked directly into Hong Deming's — dark and inviting — reminding him of something he couldn't quite place.

Wu Fan reached over with one hand, and gently touched the sleeve of Hong Deming's outer robe, pulling it very slightly. "Would you like to…go somewhere else?"

Hong Deming took a deep breath, trying to gather himself together. "I– no." He breathed again. "I'll stay here. You must have other things you need to do and other guests to see to."

Wu Fan smiled and got up, perhaps even a little reluctantly. "I hope I'll see you again. Another night, perhaps we could spend more time together." He bowed, as self-contained as any lord, and moved off to speak to another man.

Mo Xiang came back over when he saw Wu Fan had left. He tapped Hong Deming with his fan. "What happened? It was going so well! You still owe me a jar of wine. I found the type you like, didn't I?"

Hong Deming pushed the wine jar over to him, acknowledging defeat.

Mo Xiang poured them both another bowl. "Now I'm interested in this. As a friend, I have to look out for you. I knew you were human like us, not a stone! Crane Moon must just make you anxious about these things. You really don't need to be. So you like beautiful young men — it's nothing to be ashamed of. If it were a problem, people like Wu Fan would be out of business. Why not do him and you a favor and take him upstairs? He doesn't go with just anyone, you know. He's the most exclusive person they have. He can pick and choose. Top-shelf." He tossed down his bowl and poured himself another. "Are you afraid of the price?"

Hong Deming felt his stomach turn. "There shouldn't be a price."

"There's always a price," snorted Mo Xiang.

"He's not…it's not real." He drank his own bowl as well and pushed it back over.

Mo Xiang laughed, not offended. "What's real in this world? Pleasure is real, so why not share it with one another?"

Hong Deming shook his head. He was a little drunk at this point and more than a little frustrated, both by his body's reaction and his inability to explain how he felt. "Anyway, it's not him that I like."

"Ah, there it is! That's why you're all high and mighty and idealistic. Well, it all makes sense now. Who does he remind you of? Someone here, or someone back at your sect? Have you confessed to this person yet?"

Hong Deming drank down the last bowl of liquor. "I need to go out. I'll get you another jar when I come back in." He walked very carefully out into the courtyard, breathing deeply to try to clear his head. The yard was dimly lit by a few lampions hung strategically in the trees to provide privacy for couples among the paths and shrubbery. He followed a path that led to a decorative pond to find the shining scales of dark fish breaking the surface. He breathed again and looked up at the sky. There was no moon, but the stars were bright.

He was still hot and flushed all over, as if the warmth of Wu Fan's breath and body were next to him. He wasn't a child, his body functioned as it should, yet he'd never had such a reaction to a person before — never experienced that rush of physical desire. He'd been coming to the brothel with the disciples for weeks. Why tonight? What was it that made him so eager for Wu Fan? Yet at the same time, it wasn't for Wu Fan, not really, because he didn't want to pursue it. It felt wrong, mistaken. Something made him send Wu Fan away when he thought he might respond to him.

And then, he remembered Wu Fan tugging gently on his robe and wondered how it might be if he just let that happen. Why would it be wrong? Why did it feel wrong?

"Tainu?!"

A slender young man with long, smooth hair, gentle features, and shining dark eyes stared at him in shock. He wore a scholar's robes and carried a gourd at his waist: the mark of a physician. "Tainu, why are you here?"

Hong Deming swallowed hard. "Taine, why are *you* here?"

It had been more than a year.

He looked at this person — his eyes and lips, the shape of his body; in that time, he had grown taller, but he was still delicate, still had that quiet, fearless air about him that Hong Deming remembered so clearly. Eyes that shone and laughed, his smile at all the wonders of the world. His scent and breath in the dark.

This person.

Hong Deming's fingers twitched. He brushed his hand over his eyes, trying to get his balance.

Liu Chenguang came over to him, standing close to see him in the dim starlight. "It really is you? I never thought that *you* would–" He cut off whatever he was going to say. "Teacher Zhu brought me to Gunan, but he's busy with the court now. I'm just practicing my skills." He indicated the gourd hanging below his sash, which drew Hong Deming's eyes down to an area that brought uncomfortable thoughts into his mind immediately.

He closed his eyes. Coughing a little, Hong Deming said, "Zhu Guiren allows you to come to brothels? What kind of training is he giving you?"

Liu Chenguang laughed. "No, he has no idea. He doesn't care about these people. Actually, he'd probably be angry if he knew, but he's at the court for days at a time. It's boring just to sit around and read books. But there's often illness and injury in places like this... Anyway, I didn't think you'd be...here."

Hong Deming realized what Liu Chenguang must be thinking but didn't really know how to correct it, and felt a little defiant as well. "Of course I come here, why would you think I wouldn't come to places like this? The people from the Peaceful River sect often come here so I–"

Liu Chenguang stepped a little bit closer. His scent of incense and herbs surrounded Hong Deming — the scent that had last come to him in the dark of the caverns, with the feeling of Liu Chenguang's hair brushing his wrist. Now, he was close enough that he needed to look up into Hong Deming's eyes. Liu Chenguang's eyes were brilliant and shining, catching all the light of the stars like the fish in the dark water. His black hair fell back from his forehead as he examined Hong Deming closely, a tiny frown between his brows. "Are you all right? You look a little unwell."

Liu Chenguang's focused gaze was making him dizzy. Hong Deming's hand was suddenly possessed. Without his conscious intention, he reached out with one finger and touched that little furrow between Liu Chenguang's eyebrows.

Liu Chenguang froze, his lips slightly parted as though he was planning to say something else, but had forgotten language.

"Stop frowning," Hong Deming whispered. His fingers traced the delicate shape of Liu Chenguang's eyebrow down the side of his face, stroking under his jaw, and then Hong Deming bent down and kissed his lips.

Liu Chenguang's shock kept him standing still; his parted lips opened more fully, and Hong Deming tasted him, his tongue exploring his mouth. The hand on his throat slipped back to the nape of his neck, beneath his hair, holding him in place. Hong Deming felt his own body push helplessly to press against Liu Chenguang's. His other hand stroked through Liu Chenguang's hair down to grasp the small of his back, all the while kissing him harder, his tongue becoming greedy for Liu Chenguang's mouth, making it hard for either of them to breathe.

Suddenly Liu Chenguang gasped for air, and stepped back, breathing heavily. "Hong Deming. Hong Deming, what—"

Hong Deming suddenly woke up from his daze and stuttered, "You— you are— Liu Chenguang, I—"

Liu Chenguang was still breathing hard and unevenly, staring at him with those eyes. "It's not— I—"

"I'm sorry. I— I drank too much." Hong Deming pulled himself back, taking another step away despite his entire and complete desire to push Liu Chenguang against a nearby wall to continue to kiss him and do…other things.

"I know, I could taste it," Liu Chenguang blurted out.

Even in the darkness, Hong Deming could see him blush. Hong Deming closed his eyes in shame, and then felt Liu Chenguang moving closer again. He swallowed. "I'm sorry, taine. That shouldn't have happened."

This was all his own fault — coming to a place like this thinking it wouldn't affect him, allowing his body to be stimulated knowing he wouldn't have any release, what had he been thinking? Now, he'd crossed this line with Liu Chenguang. Had imposed himself on the person he truly valued and cared for, as though Liu Chenguang was available for his taking. If he could have sunk into the earth, he would have.

"It's all right, tainu. It's— I was— I was just surprised. I didn't…" Liu Chenguang seemed to be struggling for words.

"It's nothing. Nothing. Just me being drunk. It didn't mean anything," he said quickly. He couldn't imagine that Liu Chenguang — who was so kind and gentle with everyone, who he'd known since he was a little child — could understand the kind of desire that was still surging inside him. Liu Chenguang was so innocent, and he himself had been innocent until just a moment ago. He now knew that he wanted Liu Chenguang so badly that his entire body ached and that it wasn't because Wu Fan had been touching him; Wu Fan had made him excited because he looked slightly like Liu Chenguang. Imagining Liu Chenguang stroking his hand, warm breath whispering in his ear, taking him upstairs…There was no way to hide this from himself anymore, but he could at least spare Liu Chenguang from knowing the ugly details. He coughed awkwardly and took several more steps back.

"But I–"

Another voice cut through the courtyard — an endlessly haughty, cold voice. "Student Liu, what are you doing here?"

Liu Chenguang quickly turned away. "Teacher Zhu, I'm here visiting a patient." His voice shook very slightly.

"Who gave you permission to leave our quarters?" Zhu Guiren came into the dim light of the yard.

Hong Deming looked at him, wondering how he had ever thought this person was the most beautiful in the world. His features were perfect, but his bearing was so distant and removed. In addition, he was now in charge of Liu Chenguang's days and nights, responsible for his safety and training, and somehow Hong Deming felt that he wasn't to be trusted with something so precious.

"I did not approve you coming here. This is not a place that anyone associated with me should be seen. Who is your patient?" He looked over, and his facial expression changed to surprise.

Hong Deming saluted. "Master Zhu, I am training with the Peaceful River sect. They often come here. I was only saying hello to my taine. I'm not the patient."

Zhu Guiren nodded, dismissing him. "My greetings to the sect leader of Peaceful River. I will come to visit before the court reconvenes. I hope that your training is going well. Student Liu, we will leave first."

Liu Chenguang said, quietly, "Tainu, I'll leave now."

"Taine, I'll see you another time," he replied helplessly. What else could he say in front of Zhu Guiren's cold, angry face? There was so much else he needed to say, but couldn't. He watched them walk out of the courtyard, Zhu Guiren still berating Liu Chenguang in a low voice.

His mind was a whirlpool of images and emotions, and his body was still uncomfortably aroused; he didn't dare to go back into the brothel. After he splashed some cold water from the pond on his face, drenching his hair, he walked back to the Peaceful River compound alone in the dark.

The next morning, for the first time since coming to Peaceful River, he woke up with a hangover.

Mo Xiang peeked into his room as soon as he started moaning. "How much did you drink? Not more than usual while you were with me! Did you drink more when you got home? Why did you leave without getting me?"

Hong Deming just groaned and put his face down in the pillow.

"Stay there. The sober tea is ready, like always." Mo Xiang dashed out to the kitchen and brought back a teapot and cups. "I, of course, never need this. But I guess you do. How much did you drink, really?"

Hong Deming finished a cup, then held it out for more. "I came back and drank two more jars."

"By yourself?"

"That I remember."

Mo Xiang shook his head. "All right, talk to your elder brother now. Was it Wu Fan? Did you regret walking away? Don't worry, he liked you. I can tell. If you go back, I'm sure he'd be willing to talk with you again. And more than talk with you."

"Not…not that."

"Then, it's the person you like?"

"I saw him last night. He was there." He rubbed his eyes with both hands and held the cup out again.

Mo Xiang winced. "He's a courtesan? He was with someone else?"

Hong Deming laughed out loud. "Oh no, much worse than that. He was just passing by, and I…" The smile fell off his face. "I was drunk, and acted like a drunk person, and made a fool out of myself. He probably hates me now."

Mo Xiang waited expectantly to hear something more dramatic. "That's it? You are so easily discouraged."

Hong Deming shook his head. He didn't want to tell anyone else, ever, that he had grabbed Liu Chenguang and physically forced him to kiss him. He couldn't imagine that Liu Chenguang would ever want to speak with him again. He also couldn't forget what it felt like to touch him…like that…

He put his head down into his hands. "Ugh. No more."

"Well, time for cultivation anyway. Get your qin. We'll be sparring today."

"Wonderful." He sighed and reached over for his qin. Going through high-level sword forms and knocking over a few trees felt more like what he wanted to do today, but no one at the Peaceful River sect was very comfortable with him doing such things.

After the morning's cultivation practice — where Hong Deming was soundly beaten in qin battle by several Peaceful River disciples in a row since he wasn't paying attention — he went into the largest courtyard to get some aggression out with the sword. As he moved through a basic sword formation, then a more advanced one, En began to shine energetically, the qi moving in proper patterns between his body and the sword. He started adding lightness skills: leaping several feet in the air and hanging like a hummingbird for a few minutes at a time, practicing the sword form while held by qi rather than earth.

"Tainu, you have your sword now?"

He crashed onto the pavement of the courtyard and rolled several times.

"Oh, I'm sorry!" Liu Chenguang rushed over to help him get up.

Hong Deming frantically waved him away and stumbled to his feet on his own, using En to hold himself upright and try to regain some dignity. "Taine," he said helplessly. He could feel his face flushing bright red.

Liu Chenguang stood there, smiling shyly. His hair was up in a pincrown now, so he had had his adulthood crowning ceremony, but the rest flowed down his back. He didn't wear a doctor's cap — only the gourd hanging from his sash so that observers could recognize him as a cultivator rather than a true scholarly doctor. He really had grown quite a bit.

The moment this thought crossed Hong Deming's mind, he remembered exactly how tall Liu Chenguang now was in relation to his own body and blushed even more, closing his eyes and desperately trying to think of something else. "I'm sorry," he said at last. "For last night. It was...wrong of me."

"Of course," Liu Chenguang said quickly; he blushed too. "There's nothing, really, I–"

"I didn't mean it," Hong Deming said just as quickly, talking over him. "You aren't– I wouldn't ever think of you in that way. It was just the liquor..."

"Oh." Liu Chenguang continued smiling, but the hand he had reached out was drawn back. "It's all right, then. Let's...let's go back to the way we were before?"

Hong Deming nodded, relieved, and took a deep breath. "I never thanked you properly for saving me when I was in seclusion. I don't know how to thank you. When I came out, you were gone already."

"Yes, I completed my seclusion and you were still in the caverns…then Teacher Zhu came and tested my qi levels. He said I had completed my foundation, so Taiqian sent me off with him to study medicine intensively. We've traveled all over. Teacher Zhu is always running errands for the emperor. We just came a few weeks ago for the court, and he's locked up with that most days now. He brought me today because he needed to visit the sect leader anyway."

"What for?"

"I don't know. To be honest, I don't really pay attention to all that. And most of it is secret — the things he discusses with the emperor and the court officials. That's why he doesn't take me to court with him. Otherwise, he takes me everywhere."

"Really?" Hong Deming felt very unhappy with this situation.

"Yes," Liu Chenguang continued uncaringly. "He says it will help me learn to understand people better, but it doesn't because I can't really follow all the politics and I wouldn't want to if I could. It's such an ugly side of humanity. Even when he tries to explain to me, my mind just stops paying attention, and then he tries more, so I end up having to go everywhere he goes and then listen to him talk all day and night."

Hong Deming was very, very not happy.

"But I wanted to come today, so I could see you. Can you show me the sword? It's your spiritual weapon?"

"Yes," he said, and brought it over close so Liu Chenguang could see it. "Its name is En," he said, a little embarrassed now. He had imagined this many ways, but none of them had included meeting Liu Chenguang after drunkenly kissing him in a brothel the night before. "Because of you."

"Because of me?" Liu Chenguang's eyes came up to his again.

Hong Deming swallowed. "I don't know how to say thank you enough, but I'm grateful for you, always, and it's because of you that I was able to complete my cultivation. So I named the sword En."

Liu Chenguang was silent, looking at the sword. En was a slender blade, shining white and gold. It seemed to be pleased to be near Liu Chenguang, surrounding itself with a dance of light. He looked up again, his long eyes opened wide, and met Hong Deming's eyes, for once seeming unable to say anything.

"Are you Liu Chenguang?" came Mo Xiang's voice.

Hong Deming looked up to see him glancing back and forth between the two of them, frowning.

"Yes, is my teacher looking for me?"

"Master Zhu requested that you join him in his meeting with our sect leader," Mo Xiang said. "I'll bring you there, please follow me in."

Liu Chenguang nodded, smiled one last time at Hong Deming, and followed him off. Just before they turned the corner Mo Xiang looked back at Hong Deming and winked.

Hong Deming grabbed En and started the basic formation. Again.

Later that night, Mo Xiang brought a jar of wine over to his room along with two bowls. "So, that's the person."

"How do you know?" Hong Deming sighed and drank.

"First of all, it's completely obvious in the way you look at him. You're not at all subtle, my friend. Also, he looks a little like Wu Fan, so he really is the kind of person you like. I don't know why I'm the one that keeps providing the wine here. You owe me."

"I know."

"I wanted to say…" Mo Xiang drank down his bowl and looked at him seriously. "I hope you don't take this the wrong way. I'm speaking as a friend. But you know that my older brother is often at court. He's actually mentioned your friend to me before. I just didn't know that's who you were thinking of — I've never met him before. But…"

Hong Deming looked up from the bowl of liquor. "What is it?"

"Well…the court gossip is that he's…well…he and Zhu Guiren…Everyone says so. They're never apart. Zhu Guiren won't let him out of his sight for more than a few minutes. They share a room together when Zhu Guiren's at court."

Hong Deming drank quickly, then poured himself another bowl and immediately drank that.

"And you know how Zhu Guiren's very beautiful. They say that he could easily have had the emperor's favor at one time but he left the court for several years, so that's why now everyone is talking about this person Zhu Guiren keeps at his side and, and…"

"It doesn't necessarily mean they are…" Hong Deming drank two more bowls of liquor while Mo Xiang fiddled with the jar.

"I know," Mo Xiang sighed. "But you have to admit…Zhu Guiren's very powerful and influential at court, and my brother says he can be very vicious when he's crossed. You shouldn't do something that would draw his attention to you."

"Who cares about that?!" He grabbed the jar from Mo Xiang and poured the remainder of the liquor down his throat directly, since bowls were too slow.

Mo Xiang watched, eyes wide.

"Zhu Guiren– he's nothing to me. The court doesn't mean anything to me. Why should I care? If I want to do something, I will. It's all just gossip. Court gossip. You've told me before, those people always– always say bad things about others. They're always looking for the worst interpretation of things."

"I know." Mo Xiang said. "But honestly, forgive me for saying it, and with your best interests in mind, I think you would be better off just visiting with Wu Fan."

"It doesn't matter, anyway," Hong Deming said, as firmly as he could. He was both burning with jealousy and starting to feel as though the room was twirling around him; his eyes had refused to focus since the fourth bowl. "He's my taine."

Mo Xiang stared at him. "What do you mean, it doesn't matter?"

"He'll always be my taine, forever," he explained thickly. "That's all that matters. I'll always protect him. I'll take care of him. He– Liu Chenguang…"

Mo Xiang reached over and tried to hold up his face as he pitched forward onto the table. Through his buzzing ears, he heard Mo Xiang say, "I'll forget all about this conversation, all right? All right?"

Then, everything went black.

# CHAPTER 14
## ATTACK

For several days, Hong Deming stayed at home with the Peaceful River sect. When Mo Xiang invited him to the brothel again, he didn't go. He focused on his qin cultivation, or sometimes sat quietly at the gate of peonies, looking toward Gunan. When the air was clear, he thought he could see the roofs of the Imperial Palace.

At last, he decided he had to do something. Who knew when Zhu Guiren would take him away again? He needed to know; he couldn't just spend the rest of his life not sleeping unless he was drunk.

He asked Mo Xiang where to find the best jadeworkers and went out to visit the market with some of the money he'd earned from guarding the convoys to Gunan. Then, he went toward the Palace and told the guards at the gate that he had a message for Liu Chenguang, Zhu Guiren's apprentice. Of course, he wasn't allowed into the imperial compound; he didn't expect to be let in the gates. He waited impatiently outside, but it was less than an hour later that he saw Liu Chenguang come through the gates, looking around for a messenger.

Hong Deming swallowed and stood up. "Taine."

Liu Chenguang's face lit up. "Tainu!" He nearly ran over, completely forgetting his own dignity, his heavy silk court robes swinging around him wildly.

Hong Deming had to smile; it was so like him.

"Tainu, you're here," he said breathlessly. "Are you here to see me, or do you really have a message?"

"To see you. I brought you something. A thank you gift." He handed over a package smaller than the palm of his hand, wrapped in silk.

Curious, Liu Chenguang carefully unwrapped it and held it up: a jade circle carved with a crane with outspread wings. "It's beautiful. It's the Crane Moon, isn't it?"

"I saw you aren't wearing any sect symbols...I thought this might be a good thing for you, to help you remember us when you're away for so long. And I wanted to give you something to say thank you..."

Liu Chenguang held it up to see more closely. "I could never forget. And you don't need to say thank you to me. Not for anything. Not ever."

His words sounded so serious, not what he had been expecting at all. "Taine," Hong Deming asked, "are you all right?"

Liu Chenguang smiled, more genuinely this time, and found a silk cord in the package to attach the ornament to his sash, hanging the jade circle as a decoration beside the gourd. "It's beautiful," he said again. "I'll wear it when we go...wherever we're going next. Teacher Zhu said we'll be leaving in a day or so. Somewhere up north this time, across the Sorrowful River."

"Isn't that dangerous? Why is Zhu Guiren taking you across the border? Can't you stay here?"

"Do you want me to stay here?"

"Do you want to stay with Zhu Guiren all the time? Is that why you're going?" he asked before he registered what Liu Chenguang had actually said.

Liu Chenguang looked down and shook his head. "Have you been listening to rumors about Teacher Zhu and me? I have to hear them all the time at court. He's my teacher," he said, suddenly very fierce. "Only my teacher. He's not anything else to me but my teacher. But if I'm going to stay a part of the Crane Moon sect—"

"Why would you not?"

"—then I have to obey Taiqian, and Taiqian has assigned me to the authority of Teacher Zhu until he says I can return to Crane Moon. So, I have to obey. The agreement was the condition on which Taiqian accepted me as a disciple. I have to honor it." He looked up, eyes flashing. "Do you really think I'm following him for any other reason? I'm not the one who thinks he's the most handsome man ever to walk the earth."

Out of everything he said, Hong Deming decided that this was the most important thing he had to clear up. "I don't think he's that handsome anymore."

They stood staring at each other for a minute, and then Liu Chenguang started snickering. Hong Deming started laughing too, and suddenly, everything was all right again. Liu Chenguang's laugh made everything good.

"Taine, why should you cross the river? Can't anyone persuade him?"

"Well, there will be many things to see and learn. I don't know why we have to go on this trip, but I don't usually know, to be honest. He doesn't tell me about what the emperor wants. But Teacher Zhu is an excellent mentor. I can't complain for that reason. Here at court, he gets me access to scrolls and cultivational manuals and ancient writings in the Imperial Library I've never even heard of. On our travels, he has me practice healing all kinds of things. Whatever we come across…he's still very careful though. He monitors my qi each time. And he has never…never done any of those things that people say about him. He has done his best by me as his student, and I owe him respect for that." He sighed. "However boring it sometimes gets. Tainu, I'd rather be with you."

Hong Deming felt his heart warm. "I'd rather have you with me too."

Liu Chenguang smiled at him, his eyes again shining as they should.

He must have been staring, because Liu Chenguang asked, "What are you looking at? Is my pincrown crooked?" He reached up to his pincrown, trying to adjust it.

"Nothing," he said. "It's fine. Wait, now you're making it crooked…" He reached over too, and their hands brushed each other. He jerked back quickly.

Liu Chenguang laughed.

Suddenly, he heard the guards at the gate come to attention; someone said, "Over there, sir."

Zhu Guiren came striding toward them, his face cold as always. "Student Liu," he said, his voice melodious though his eyes were hard. "This evening, we will discuss the cultivational manual I assigned you this morning. You may leave."

"Yes, Teacher Zhu," Liu Chenguang said, and left without another word.

Zhu Guiren turned to Hong Deming. For the first time, he met Hong Deming's eyes directly, and seemed to see him. "Hmph," he said, after a moment. "You are the youngest sword disciple of the Crane Moon. Liu Chenguang is your taine."

"Yes," he said, without any honorific or address, deciding to be as rude as he could get away with.

Zhu Guiren's cold expression softened. "Three times now in just two weeks, I've found Liu Chenguang with you when, for almost a year, he's been with me at all times, never showing a special interest in anyone. He feels closer to you than to others, I think."

Hong Deming looked at him steadily, refusing to let this man see that this news warmed him all through.

"You are also the one that he risked breaking his own seclusion for, undermining his own cultivation."

Hong Deming nodded. "I will always be grateful to him. And I want to protect him. Keep him safe in return."

"You're wondering, therefore, why I'm taking him with me on all my travels for the emperor's cause," he said shrewdly. "You're thinking it would be better for me to leave him here, or somewhere else that's safe."

"Yes," he said again.

"You must understand that Liu Chenguang's cultivation is not yet as stable as it must be to support his healing power. This is partly because of his use of his qi to heal you during your secluded meditation. I must watch him very carefully to ensure that he is able to use his own qi without falling into a coma again. If it does, could you heal him?"

"No," he said, shaken. Was Liu Chenguang so injured from helping him?

"I can," Zhu Guiren said. "I have the knowledge and the skills and the medicine that can heal him even from that state. I keep him with me constantly to observe him and to be ready for emergencies. In time — perhaps a year or so — I will be certain that he is safe. I know that you want him to be safe as well. So remember that his safety, for now, lies in staying close to me."

At close range, Zhu Guiren was as perfect as he had been at a distance, but nonetheless it was obvious to Hong Deming that his warmth and openness was feigned. He was not distracted by this, but the news that Liu Chenguang was not yet healed disturbed him deeply.

"I understand," Hong Deming said at last. "I want him to be safe."

Zhu Guiren nodded, satisfied.

He didn't see Liu Chenguang again before Mo Xiang's brother informed him that Zhu Guiren had departed on the Son of Heaven's business, taking his favorite along. Mo Xiang added that several mutually-antagonistic factions at court were delighted by this, and that a few others were now weakened. Court politics made Hong Deming's head spin, but Mo Xiang was able to simplify things enough that he could follow the basics. Since the emperor had slaughtered all the imperial eunuchs of the previous dynasty, a power vacuum had arisen in the palace and in the civil administration. Various relatives, concubines, generals, counselors, nobles, princes, and governors filled it, all vying for power and imperial attention. Zhu Guiren was part of a faction advocating to stabilize the new dynasty through military conquest. This was opposed by governors of strong cities who didn't wish to become stepping stones for the dynasty and preferred their independence, as well as the enemies of the dynasty itself, who were always a threat at the border and often sent assassins.

"It doesn't help," Mo Xiang whispered, "that the Son of Heaven himself isn't a good master to work for or obey. It sometimes seems that his most loyal supporters are the ones he turns on and destroys. And he insults people in other ways too, even by assaulting their wives and lovers…"

Hong Deming didn't dare to speak, and wished he wasn't hearing this. People were executed for far, far less than this kind of conversation. "Hush," he said, "enough. If you're not worried about yourself and me, at least worry about your brother."

Mo Xiang nodded and drew back. "You're right. You're right, enough of that." He shook it off. "Anyway, my brother said that this time, Zhu Guiren has been sent north of the Sorrowful River into enemy territory. No one really knows why, or what his purpose is there. He's useless as a spy. He's too memorable when you see him, and too well-known as a servant of the emperor, so it must be some kind of diplomatic mission. Did your friend…?"

"Liu Chenguang doesn't know anything. He's got no mind for politics. He's just training as a physician with Zhu Guiren."

"Ah, I see."

"And there's nothing between them," Hong Deming added firmly. "Tell your brother to stop spreading those rumors."

Mo Xiang looked at him almost pityingly. "Hong Deming, never go into the court. Promise me. You're far too simple for this. Don't you realize it makes no difference at all whether it's true or false? If the rumor is useful to someone, it will have a life either way."

Hong Deming found that remembering the warmth of Liu Chenguang's body and the taste of his lips was impossible when he focused on the complexities of qin cultivation, and as a result, Hong Deming's qin cultivation was improving by leaps and bounds. He could now play the qin defensively to establish wards against both human and spiritual encroachments, and offensively as well, though he was still far behind the Peaceful River disciples. Day by day, he continued with his practice.

Once, he even dared to accompany Mo Xiang back to the brothel to listen to music and to look at Wu Fan, since he couldn't see Liu Chenguang. Now that he knew what he really wanted — however impossible it might be — he found that Wu Fan no longer looked as much like Liu Chenguang as he had thought, and he could even sit with him calmly and discuss music and art when Wu Fan had no clients to engage. Wu Fan's occasional forays into flirtatious or suggestive behavior were simply ignored as though they hadn't happened; Wu Fan himself was too skilled, and indeed too popular, to press him beyond this, though sometimes he looked at Hong Deming oddly.

A few weeks later, Mo Xiang invited him out again. This time, he refused. Most of the younger male disciples went with Mo Xiang, leaving the women and the older men to sleep. Hong Deming took his qin up to one of the highest points of the sect compound — a moon-viewing platform facing away from the city and the highway in the valley below — and began to play there. Not to cultivate, but merely to enjoy the music. He knew he wasn't very good yet and would rarely play where the Peaceful River disciples could hear, but he found it very pleasant and peaceful to the spirit, rather like calligraphy.

After he had played himself out, he relaxed with his back against a pillar, looking at the stars and thinking of nothing in particular, which, as usual, led to thinking of Liu Chenguang, and then to Crane Moon and going home. He knew that true mastery of qin cultivation would require a lifetime, but he wasn't that talented, and it wasn't his sect's path. At some point, the Peaceful River sect master would send him home — back to Taiqian and Shen Lu and his other martial siblings. There might even be new little disciples, and he could help teach them. Eventually, Liu Chenguang would come home as well, Zhu Guiren had promised, and then…

When he woke up, the moon had set and he was sitting with cold, cramped muscles. He stood and stretched, recognizing it as the fourth watch. Dawn would come soon. Mo Xiang and the others should be coming back. Hong Deming turned back toward the path, yawning, then frowned. He heard a noise that didn't belong at Peaceful River. He put his head to one side and heard it again: metal clashing.

Before he was consciously aware, he had called En to his hand and was leaping down the hillside toward the peony gate. The sounds grew louder; it seemed as though there were many swords, but only a few voices, screams and shouts. Qin music clashed against sword, but only the strongest qin players could contend against a skilled sword cultivator for sheer aggressive power. They would need him. This was one of the reasons, he knew, that Peaceful River had made a practice of welcoming guest cultivators from Crane Moon.

As he leapt from wall to wall, as fast as he could, he caught up with the sect master and the senior disciples running down the paths.

"Why didn't the wards give warning?" he shouted; he knew that the peony gate should have alerted those on watch.

The sect leader said, "If they followed closely on our disciples, and they didn't notice…they may have brought them into the wards as guests, unknowing." He stopped and struck his qin, one hard note that echoed. Above them, the wards flared red in a perfect dome, then faded. "I've strengthened them. No more can come in," he said, and began running again.

Hong Deming didn't have his bow and arrows, so he couldn't send warning flights down onto the mob that was caught outside the peony gate now. It seemed as though they were ordinary bandits, but the sword clash he had heard was not that of ordinary metal swords. Some of the attackers, at least, were cultivators. En began to glow golden, sending off sparks in anticipation. Despite the terrible view of the attackers already within the gate — heavily outnumbering Mo Xiang and the remaining Peaceful River disciples, who were drawn into a circle formation in the center of the first courtyard — he felt a sense of excitement. He had never truly matched with another sword cultivator in a life-and-death battle. This was what he had trained for all his life.

Running and jumping to come in from above, he used his lightness skills to send sword energy down through the packed crowd of attackers, leaving a swath of blood and body parts through the ordinary bandits. The cultivators looked up, and several leapt up to deal with him as he landed on the opposite courtyard wall.

"Hong Deming!" Mo Xiang shouted in relief from within the defenders' circle. He struck his qin, sending out energy that blocked a sword stroke. "You're here! What took you so long?"

Hong Deming laughed and parried a stroke, then turned for another. "Mo Xiang, you shouldn't spend so long in brothels, it's almost morning," he called back, and slashed down again; he had attackers on both sides, and occasionally jumping in from above or leaping up from below to strike at his feet. There didn't seem to be a lot of chivalry involved, but En was delighted with the challenge.

Soon, the sect leader and senior disciples arrived, setting up a second circle that ground the attackers between the two groups of qin attacks with Hong Deming running about as well and striking whatever particularly powerful sword cultivator he could find. There wasn't much in his mind aside from the weight of En, managing his qi and lightness: flipping, jumping, parrying, sending out the sword light, blocking. He was using his skills to the utmost against worthy opponents at last, and it was all he had hoped it would be. Every so often, he would notice that the courtyard looked rather slippery in the dark, but aside from that, he couldn't see the damage he was doing very well. He only knew that no one had yet gotten a blade on him, and given that he'd fought off at least eight attackers, he was rather pleased with himself.

"Hong Deming!" the sect leader called. "The wards are weakening. Go deal with the gate!"

He rushed down to the gate, where he saw two Peaceful River disciples, male and female, lying dead across the threshold. Beyond, the attackers had reorganized themselves: more ordinary bandits, and more cultivators. This time, one of the cultivators also used qin, strumming a melody to undo the wards — a handsome, powerfully-built older man with a sword strapped over his back. His robes were white and green.

"Jade Bamboo," Hong Deming muttered to himself, remembering his lessons as a child. The Jade Bamboo was also a righteous sect; why were they attacking Peaceful River?

A loud voice shouted, "Send out the traitor Mo Xiang!"

The Jade Bamboo cultivator came at him immediately, sending out a powerful qin strike. Hong Deming didn't block in time, not completely; qin was hard to block, since it came in such large, dispersed attacks. The qin energy caught his throat, left shoulder, and hip, and he leaned over, coughing and gasping for breath — enough time for several swords to come at him. He ducked, spun, leapt, and came down hard, his injured hip aching, but a great surge of energy from En rushed out ahead of him. It took down three swordsmen, who fell to the ground coughing blood; for the fourth, he used the actual blade, nearly cutting him in half. The attacker had been so close that the hot spurting blood soaked through his robes. Disgusting, but he had to keep cutting a path down and down.

At last, he looked up and saw that he had reached the last of the attackers on the path. The survivors were fleeing — ordinary folk on foot, the cultivators with lightness; the leader of the Jade Bamboo was among them. Hong Deming followed them with his eyes to see where they would re-enter the highway below, then saw that the highway was choked with people.

People were fleeing Gunan.

Leaping to the top of the peony gate, he looked toward the city. Fires were set in the nearest quarter, and there were attackers, tiny at a distance, grappling with defenders and watchmen on the walls.

Mo Xiang suddenly was up on the gate with him, eyes shaded to pierce the dim, smoky distance. The sun was not yet risen, but it was no longer completely dark. "Are they attacking the city?" Mo Xiang asked, shocked. "But when we left—"

"What's happening?" Hong Deming asked. "Why did they chase you here?" Without waiting for an answer, he bowed to the Peaceful River leader who was looking sadly at the dead disciples as he picked his way down the path between them. His blood still up, he said, "Sect leader, I would like to go help defend the city."

"Go, then, if you want to," the sect leader said, his voice tired. "Come back when you desire as well. You are not my disciple, and I do not exert my authority over you in this. Mo Xiang, you must stay. Your business is with defending the sect."

"Yes, Taiqian," said Mo Xiang.

Hong Deming jumped down and began running, sword in hand, toward the highway.

The gates of Gunan hadn't been prepared for an attack, so the enemy was already inside, wreaking havoc among the houses nearest the wall. Hong Deming found a few gate guards backed into a corner; he killed the people surrounding them and took them on as his backup. Few of the people attacking had armor, and none of them had military discipline. It was only because of the cultivators inexplicably supporting them that they had been able to take down the city guard.

As they ran through the streets, Hong Deming striking freely, he asked the rescued guards, "What happened? Why are they here? Who are they?"

The bewildered guards shook their heads, eyes wide. Three cultivators blocked the street ahead of them.

Hong Deming said, "Leave now, look for ordinary enemies, bring word to the palace guard."

The soldiers ran.

Hong Deming straightened and grasped En, ready but starting to feel the effects of fighting nonstop. There were other cultivational sects in Gunan, other swordmasters, even the imperial guard; why did it seem he was the only one fighting?

To get a little breathing time, he shouted, "Why are you here? Why are you attacking Gunan?"

One of the cultivators came toward him, sword flashing, and then a second;

the third held back, looking for an opening.

Hong Deming decided to take a different tack. Cutting down the first two with slices to the throat and abdomen, he sent a sword pulse toward the third, who was caught by the sword energy and dropped to his knees, spitting blood. Hong Deming leapt over, grabbed him, and jumped to the nearest rooftop.

"Why are you here?" he demanded.

The man wore the Jade Bamboo robes. He glared at Hong Deming in impotent fury. "Traitor," he managed, continuing to cough blood, and then, "Those who threaten the dynasty must be punished."

"Who was threatening the dynasty at Peaceful River? In Gunan? Isn't this threatening the dynasty, to attack the capital city?"

The man spat at him.

Hong Deming shook his head, tied him up with his own sash, and left him there for later. There were still bandits rampaging through the streets, and the cultivators were ahead of them. He went back to the slash-and-kill practice that constituted fighting against people without cultivation, trying to grasp some sense of what the goal of these people was, aside from causing havoc. The only specific areas he could see them focusing on were the cultivational sects scattered across the mansions, abbeys, and monasteries of Gunan — not only Peaceful River, but also several smaller and lesser-known sect houses located in the city itself. He saw one, the Divine Lotus sect, on fire, corpses scattered around its broken gate. Another several streets over, the Clear Mirror, was under attack as he ran by, its disciples on the walls, shooting at the cultivators attempting to leap up with their lightness skills.

Well, that would explain why there were no cultivators fighting back in the streets. They were all busy trying to defend their own sects. He spun, leapt, slashed, stabbed, and used En to send wide pulses of aggressive energy through the crowd, over and over again. There were so many, where had they all come from?

And then, he saw Shen Lu. He shouted, "Tainu! Tainu!"

Shen Lu spun around, his Crane Moon robes spattered with blood; he sent a sword pulse at Hong Deming, who ducked.

"Tainu, it's me! What's happening? Why are you here?"

Shen Lu's eyes cleared of bloodlust and recognized him. He pulled Hong Deming over into a corner, away from the fighting, and yelled in his ear, "Taine! Why are you here? What happened at Peaceful River?"

"They've been attacked. We fought them off."

Shen Lu swore. "Taine, this is hard to explain right now. The Peaceful River shouldn't have been targeted–"

"What do you mean, shouldn't have been targeted?" As he said it, he felt a crawling sense of horror on his spine; he looked wide-eyed at his tainu — now his sect leader — whose eyes ranged coldly over the street fighting.

Shen Lu picked up his sword again, then seemed to think twice. "Taine, I can't explain now. Go back to Peaceful River and wait for me."

"No, all the people– Look, they're being attacked! We have to–"

"Fine, protect the people. But stay away from fights with cultivators. The Jade Bamboo and Stone Phoenix are our allies."

"But– I– how– They're attacking all the sects in Gunan!"

"Not all of them. Taine, I'm your sect leader now. Don't argue about things you don't know about. These are my orders," he said fiercely, "and if you don't obey them, I will cast you out. Do you understand? Go back to Peaceful River. You can fight looters on the way but no cultivators." He pushed out of their corner. "Go now."

Hong Deming looked at him, his sword half-raised, eyes blank.

Shen Lu shook his head. "Taine, trust me. This is to protect you," he said, calling his own sword and heading back into the street. "Go now."

On the way back to the gate, Hong Deming killed thirty-five looters — ordinary people who were unable to resist a cultivational sword.

Hong Deming stood in the cobbled area just outside the gate of Gunan. There were only corpses here now, scattered all along the city walls on each side of the gate. The sun had risen, throwing long shadows over the twisted bodies and pools of blood on the stones, soaking into the earth.

There was a person picking among the corpses, a gourd and a jade pendant hanging from his sash. One by one, at each body, he knelt down and felt their pulse, long hair falling forward over one shoulder. Sometimes, he would do something with his fingers, touching their mouths or the wounds on their bodies; Hong Deming couldn't see what it was in the sharp, shadowed light.

Hong Deming's lips moved without making any sound.

"Tainu! What happened? you're covered in blood–" The person ran toward him, tripped over a corpse, and stumbled forward. Everything about his body was filled with anxiety, his face pale.

Hong Deming looked down, slowly. He was indeed covered in blood. Soaked in it. The blue of his outer robe was a dappled purple. "None of it's mine," he said, looking at Liu Chenguang. He flicked En mechanically to get the blood off it and thought, how strange it is that it's so clean, and I'm so filthy.

Liu Chenguang reached out to touch his arm, distressed.

Hong Deming took a step back. "No," he said, not sure what he was refusing. "Tainu–"

"Get away from him!" A sword came for Liu Chenguang's head from behind. Automatically, Hong Deming leapt to block. "Mo– Mo Xiang? Why?"

Liu Chenguang looked on, eyes wide. For the first time, Hong Deming realized that his taine carried no weapons at all. Not even a knife.

Mo Xiang's breath came hard. "Zhu Guiren did this. He brought them from the south. He said– he said that the Peaceful River are undermining the emperor. Zhu Guiren did it. You must have known!" he screamed at Liu Chenguang

Liu Chenguang looked at him, bewildered but seemingly unafraid.  "No. No, that's not right. Teacher Zhu– Teacher Zhu wouldn't have…And we were just in the north, across the Sorrowful River–"

Hong Deming kept in front of him; Mo Xiang's swordsmanship was not up to his standards, but he also carried the qin, which would make it difficult to fully protect Liu Chenguang. Hong Deming's mind had woken up again with the sudden dive back into combat. He said, "Mo Xiang, you know Liu Chenguang is only studying with Zhu Guiren as a physician. You know that he doesn't take part in Zhu Guiren's work for the emperor. Whether Zhu Guiren did this or not, he wouldn't have known about it."

"How could he not know?" Mo Xiang asked hatefully. "He's his bed partner, isn't he?"

Liu Chenguang snapped, "Shut up." He pushed Hong Deming out of the way, or tried to; Hong Deming outweighed him significantly. "How dare you? That's a lie!"

"Taine, stay behind me," Hong Deming said sharply. "Mo Xiang, that's enough. Whether you believe Liu Chenguang or not, I will fight you if you attack him and you are not…" He took a deep breath. He had never actually done this before; never made the kind of boasts that set up the competitive hierarchy of the cultivational sects. "You are not qualified to match me," he said firmly.

Mo Xiang's face crumpled. "Damn you, Hong Deming." He sheathed his sword and turned away. Over his shoulder, he shouted, "Don't come back to Peaceful River!"

Hong Deming looked around again.

From behind him, Liu Chenguang reached out, carefully, for his blood-soaked sleeve. "Hong Deming," he said, "now be honest, are you hurt?"

"No, I'm fine. But I don't have anywhere to go now. Shen Lu is in the city. He told me to go back to Peaceful River…"

"Do you think that person was telling the truth, that you can't go back there?" Liu Chenguang spoke in a calm voice, guiding Hong Deming over to the side of the road as though he were blind. "Sit here, I'll clear a place." He indicated a spot under a tree with only a few corpses and began dragging them farther away.

Hong Deming leaned down to help him, then collapsed with his back against the tree, staring out over the carnage.

"You can wait here," said Liu Chenguang. He put his hand over Hong Deming's briefly, then added, "I was looking for survivors. I'm going to keep looking for people that I can save. Promise me you will stay here. Don't wander off. Promise?" He looked very worried.

Hong Deming let Liu Chenguang's hand remain for a moment, then withdrew; his hand was spattered with blood. "Sorry. I'll stay, you don't need to worry about me. Where's Zhu Guiren?"

"I don't know. We were coming back today and I saw…well, this. I couldn't keep going without trying to help, but Teacher Zhu needed to continue to the palace."

"There's attackers in the city."

"I'm sure he'll be safe," Liu Chenguang said indifferently, "Zhu Guiren is in dangerous places all the time. He has lots of ways…"

"He takes you into dangerous places?" Hong Deming frowned; this cut through his strange lethargy.

Liu Chenguang knelt next to him. "Tainu, you don't need to worry about me so much. I am also used to dangerous places. Just because I can't use a sword doesn't mean I can't keep myself safe."

Hong Deming watched him among the corpses, paying equal attention to each one whether cultivator or common person, attacker or defender of the city. After he passed, occasionally someone would sit up, or stand to walk away, but there were few. Most of the people remaining on the field had been too seriously injured to be evacuated and had bled to death before Liu Chenguang arrived. Every so often, he could see Liu Chenguang look back, hand shading his eyes, to be sure he was still sitting in the darkness between the trees, and then continue his slow, painstaking work.

When Liu Chenguang was far across the square, working down the wall on the other side of the city gate, Shen Lu found Hong Deming and sat next to him under the tree. He handed Hong Deming a flask of liquor, which he drank down without really tasting. After a while, Shen Lu said, "Taine, you stink. The first thing you need to do when we're done here is go into the city and take a bath. And burn those robes."

Hong Deming nodded. "Into the city…not back to Peaceful River?"

"No. I've managed to smooth it over so our sects will remain allies, but you can't go back there after challenging Mo Xiang. He's not willing to back down and you defeating or killing him would be disastrous right now." He handed Hong Deming a bag. "Here's your things. They won't let you keep the qin."

"That's fine. I have one at home." He watched Liu Chenguang, now a very small figure far in the distance, bending down over the bodies again and again. Shen Lu followed his gaze, then rubbed his face as though he was very tired.

"Taine, do you know why you're not the sect leader?"

"What?" Hong Deming turned to him and frowned. "Why would I be the sect leader? I'm the youngest disciple. You're the oldest. We all always knew you were going to be the sect leader."

"No," Shen Lu said, "actually, that trip when we found Liu Chenguang, Taiqian was observing you to see if you could become sect leader in the future. Didn't you ever wonder why he took the youngest disciple on a dangerous journey, not some of your seniors? Even then, he was considering you, and he kept observing over the years. And, although you are an idiot, it must be obvious to you that your cultivation is higher than mine." The last was said with some bitterness, but not too much. "I'm the eldest, of course, but the succession doesn't necessarily go that way. The strongest disciple would also be a candidate. But Taiqian decided that you were not suited."

Hong Deming waited.

"I see it too. I've seen it since you were a child. It's as though there's something missing in you. Something a person has from birth, but you don't have it…" He shook his head. "An insult means nothing to you. There's no anger in you, no desire for vengeance. Your cultivation is high and your skills are good, but you are reluctant to use them because you regret the consequences and you have no desire to use them to prove yourself or raise the sect. You have no sense of injury and necessary redress at all."

It was not true, that he had no anger. It was just that… "Taiqian saved me," he said, trying to explain. Did Shen Lu really think that in all those years of training, all the harsh discipline of the sect with no other children to share it with, he had never been angry? He had been an orphan in a city destroyed by war, and without Taiqian's whim to pick him up from the market of Zhashan, he would have been enslaved, or a beggar on the street, or dead before he was six years old. How could he dare to be angry? It was only gratitude, that was all; he must always be obedient, must show himself worthy of Crane Moon, must always be the best.

"When a person like Mo Xiang attacks you, attacks your taine, you are reluctant to fight him. You should be angry, taine. You are not angry. You've probably already let it go in your heart when you should be remembering it, thinking about how to deal with this enemy in the future. Thus, too, you are unable to make decisions that would injure others. Too unwilling to destroy an enemy, and too kind to make hard choices in hard times. You are missing that from your childhood, and you've never developed it. That was the first reason." Shen Lu looked back out at Liu Chenguang. "The second reason is that person you keep staring at."

"What? Why?" At last, he could ask this question of Shen Lu — the one he could never ask Taiqian: "I've always wondered, why didn't Taiqian like Liu Chenguang? Why doesn't anyone? He is such a good person, he's...why not?"

"Why is this not obvious to you?" Shen Lu threw his hands up in exasperation. "That is not an ordinary person, Hong Deming. But you don't seem to notice. What kind of danger is that in a sect leader, that you can't even recognize something that is abnormal when it is right in front of your face?"

"He saved my life," Hong Deming said stubbornly. "He's never done anything to hurt anyone, to hurt the sect. He's always obeyed. He's never said an unkind word about any of you. What's wrong? What more do you and Taiqian want from him?"

"Taine, *think*. Do you think that an orphaned peasant child with the language of a scholar and a unique cultivation path somehow comes across a cultivational sect leader in the wilderness by accident? And do you think he really cares about whether he's a sect disciple or not? He came to us for his own purposes, Hong Deming. Taiqian agreed to take him because Zhu Guiren said his healing abilities would be an asset eventually, but he never trusted him. And nothing I've seen since is convincing me otherwise. Look at him, Hong Deming. Can you see what he's doing? How is he healing those people? And why is he doing it? These people were just attacking one another. Surely some of them were in the wrong, but he's healing everyone that can live without a care for their responsibility for this disaster."

"That's— Of course he is! How could he know? And why should he have to make that kind of decision, tainu? That's not fair, he's not an executioner—"

"I know he saved your life, but taine, how could he possibly have done it? Not that I wish you had died in seclusion, but qi deviation isn't cured by wishing."

"Tainu—"

"Taine, he spent years of his childhood in seclusion and he's not insane. Do you think that's normal either?"

"Then why?" he demanded, frustrated. "Why did you put him through that? Just because Zhu Guiren said so?"

After a moment, Shen Lu said, "Zhu Guiren gave the order, but Taiqian wouldn't have done it if he thought that Liu Chenguang was in any way a normal human being. A normal human child, even a child born and raised in a cultivational sect, would not have survived it. Taine, you have to think. Whoever this person is, he has a purpose that we don't fully understand. He has never opened his heart to us or really trusted us."

"That's not true. Tainu, that's not true at all. You never tried to get to know him. He has trusted me, and I trust him."

Yet, he wondered, too; Liu Chenguang had never shown any interest in developing a relationship with anyone else in the sect. He had accepted everything without demur, but also without showing anything of his inward feelings to anyone but Hong Deming.

Liu Chenguang had reached the last corpse and turned back down the length of the city wall toward them. He would reach them in a few moments.

Shen Lu stood up. "Taine, there's no point in continuing this conversation. Taiqian and I have consulted about the future of the sect, and it is relevant for you in particular now. You must not return to Crane Moon yet. Taiqian and I agree on this. Since you also can't stay at Peaceful River, you should take the opportunity to wander beyond the bounds."

Hong Deming didn't ask why this was; Shen Lu's voice had the ring of authority, and he knew he wouldn't be told. "For how long?"

"At least a year. Two."

"Does the sect leader have any particular assignments for this humble disciple?" he asked formally.

"There are many reports of demons coming out of the mountains with the instability and turmoil of the lands. Report to the Stone Phoenix sect house outside Bian. You should know that we are now allied formally with Jade Bamboo and Stone Phoenix sects, although what a mess that is. It'll take quite a bit to cover that you killed several Jade Bamboo cultivators..." He sighed. "Our alliance has decided to support the emperor in establishing a stable dynasty. There are plans in motion to make this happen; we're not central to them, but we have a specific role. In any case, you are likely to be targeted by survivors, because they, unlike you, will want to take vengeance for their losses. Try to develop some anger. Try to learn to see enemies as what they are."

Hong Deming just stared at him. "It's true, tainu. I couldn't be a sect leader."

"Yes, Taiqian made a wise decision there," Shen Lu said, apparently not noticing the sarcasm, which was not generally Hong Deming's style. "I'll leave first. I don't really want to talk with that person." He walked off before Liu Chenguang came close enough to recognize him.

Hong Deming remained standing until Liu Chenguang came close enough to speak. "Taine," he said, seeing the signs of exhaustion in Liu Chenguang's face, "you're pale. Are you all right?"

"I'm fine," Liu Chenguang said. "It was just a lot of work at one time, that's all. There were some that could be saved. Now that's done, it's you I'm worried about."

"There's nothing to worry about. I'm not hurt," he said. Liu Chenguang's closeness warmed him, helped heal the sickness in his heart after talking with Shen Lu. "But I can't go back to Peaceful River, and I really need a bath."

# CHAPTER 15
## THE INN AT GUNAN

HONG DEMING AND Liu Chenguang wandered through the city, looking for an inn. Hong Deming was glad to note that the fighting had ended, and most of the surviving wounded had already been taken from the streets; those that remained were clearly very dead and were being gathered up as well. He hadn't wanted to watch Liu Chenguang check every corpse in Gunan, especially as a good number would have been his own responsibility.

The streets were still splashed with blood, and not all the fires were out yet. The looters had seemingly settled for several high-ranked brothels when the cultivation sects had proven too difficult. They would have valuable property — not the least of which was their inhabitants — and were only well guarded against over-enthusiastic patrons. Hong Deming saw that the Delicate Orchid pavilion was one of those burnt.

Liu Chenguang looked over at the yard. Through the broken gate, they could see the willow trees overhanging the pond, choked with ash. "Was there someone you cared about there?" he asked, a little catch in his voice.

"Just one person I knew," Hong Deming said, thinking of Wu Fan. "But you must have known others. You came there that night…" He looked away.

Liu Chenguang's gaze moved over the courtyard, raking over the building. "The fire was intense," he said at last. "Anyone still in there is unlikely to have survived, but I don't see many bodies. Hopefully, your friend escaped."

"He wasn't a friend, exactly, but I hope he escaped." He turned and kept walking.

Past the quarters nearest the gate, the damage became more focused. Only specific cultivational sects had been targeted.

"It's still so obvious," Hong Deming said.

"What do you mean?"

Belatedly, he thought maybe Shen Lu hadn't meant for Liu Chenguang to know this, but then, with a burst of anger, he decided that Liu Chenguang was a disciple and he damn well deserved to know. "Shen Lu told me that this was planned. It was to cover attacks on the cultivational sects that don't support the new dynasty. Our sect is allied with others in support of the Son of Heaven."

Liu Chenguang frowned. "Teacher Zhu may well be involved then, but why Peaceful River? They support the emperor, as far as I know…"

"Aren't you shocked?" he asked.

"Not shocked exactly. Traveling with Teacher Zhu has been an education in that way…The dynasty is unstable, people are not safe, and after years of this, there's a need to take action to make things better. That's what I've gleaned from what I've heard, anyway…There are so many refugees on the road, so many poor people…Did you know that in the Wan Zhao rebellion, when Zhashan was attacked, hundreds of thousands of people came and slaughtered and looted? Starving farmers turned into bandits…and we still had a dynasty, then. The Feng had a few decades left to go." Liu Chenguang lifted his robes to step over a corpse. "So much death, tainu. So much suffering. Teacher Zhu says that it's only with a stable dynasty that holds the mandate of heaven that we can avert it. That's what he says to everyone, at least in public where I can hear. So, I'm not shocked that action is being taken to strengthen the dynasty."

"But wasn't it…wrong? For the Crane Moon to ally against cultivators? To help attack a city? So many innocent people died." *So many were killed by me,* Hong Deming thought, *innocent or not.*

Liu Chenguang stopped after walking in silence, seemingly unable to answer. "Look, here's a good place."

They were well beyond the damaged quarter now. This inn was well appointed and peaceful, as though in a different world from the corpses at the gate.

"Tainu, wait here. Let me get the room and then bring you in. You'll frighten them. They won't rent to you." He smiled. "This is another education from Teacher Zhu: how to choose a good inn."

Hong Deming watched him go up the steps and decided that he hated Zhu Guiren with all his heart.

After a while, Liu Chenguang came back out, waiting until the front counter cashier was looking away to lead him upstairs. The room was pleasant, with a window of translucent paper panes filtering the afternoon sunlight, a large bed platform, and a table for tea.

"I've already sent for hot water," Liu Chenguang said. "You should bathe up here."

For a moment they stood staring at each other. The silence drew out.

Liu Chenguang cleared his throat. "I'll have them send up extra water, so you can…get really clean. Leave the dirty robes. Do you have clean ones?"

Hong Deming gratefully held up the bag Shen Lu had brought.

"I'll go, then." Liu Chenguang turned to the door.

"Will you come back?" Hong Deming asked quickly.

Liu Chenguang turned and smiled. "Of course," he said.

Hong Deming felt something warm him inside. Everything would be well, as long as Liu Chenguang would be there and would smile at him like that.

After he left, Hong Deming stripped off the bloody robes and threw them outside the door in disgust. He wiped himself off with a bathing cloth and settled into the bathing tub after getting off the worst of it. He poured water over himself till it turned cold, thinking about what to do next; he was so exhausted that nothing seemed to come to mind. When he thought of Shen Lu's calm explanation — of the Crane Moon collaborating with bandits to hide an attack on cultivators — he felt sick to his stomach. The corpses in the street and the burned houses lingered in his mind, too, as he washed the blood from his body. He did hope Wu Fan had gotten away, somewhere safe.

The image of a ruined Zhashan kept haunting him. His birth family had been killed in the Wan Zhao rebellion. At least, Taiqian had thought so…

And Liu Chenguang…how could it be that there was so much hatred for him in the sect, so much distrust? Did he sense it, did it hurt him to know? Or did he really not care at all? Out loud, as though Shen Lu could hear, he said, "Tainu, I'm not that stupid. I know he's not like other people, but why does it matter?" Why did it matter so much that Shen Lu would simply walk away without even greeting his own taine? Why did it matter so much that his own willingness to accept Liu Chenguang's oddities was proof that he was incapable of good judgment?

His body was beginning to ache all over and he felt the drain on his qi from the nonstop fighting. The water in the bath had turned pink, and he was glad that Liu Chenguang had arranged for the second tub so that he could fully rinse off before staggering toward the bed to collapse.

He was startled awake by Liu Chenguang's voice above him. "Tainu, the food's here. You should eat. It's gotten late, almost dark."

Hong Deming struggled to get out of the bed, but winced and fell back; his arm and side wouldn't bear weight, and his entire body felt bruised and battered.

"What's wrong?" Liu Chenguang came over and stopped still, staring down at him.

Hong Deming looked down at himself. He was wearing only an inner robe after the bath and it had opened slightly, exposing enormous, multi-layered bruises over his throat, collarbone, and shoulder. His entire left side was shades of dark red, blue, and purple.

Liu Chenguang knelt next to the bed, staring at the bruises, biting his lip till the blood showed. "You said you were fine," he accused. "Why didn't you tell me? It wouldn't have gotten this bad if I'd taken care of it right away. Can you even move at all?"

Truthfully, moving felt quite difficult. He tried to get up again, but the bruises had now set deeply and his muscles and tendons didn't seem to want to respond. "I'm fine," he said nonetheless. "Really. It's just from a qin attack. I–"

He broke off into inarticulate gasping because Liu Chenguang grasped him by his right shoulder so he couldn't move and leaned over to kiss the bruise on his throat. It almost felt as though Liu Chenguang was licking him, his mouth moving over his throat and below to his collarbone, kissing, pressing gently, the blood and saliva soothing his skin. Wherever Liu Chenguang's mouth went, intense pleasure followed through Hong Deming's body, heating him beyond his ability to bear.

"Ah, please," he begged. "Please, I can't–"

Liu Chenguang looked up, blood bright on his lips. He didn't look particularly aroused; he looked furious, his long eyes narrowed. "Where else? Where else are you hurt? And don't lie this time."

Hong Deming shook his head, still trying to get his breath. He was fairly confident that if Liu Chenguang did that to his hip, he couldn't be responsible for the consequences. "There's nothing. Nothing–"

"Get up then," Liu Chenguang said coldly.

He couldn't.

"Tainu!" Liu Chenguang yelled in exasperation. "Fine then."

He laid his hands on both sides of Hong Deming's face to hold him still again, bent down, and kissed his lips. Hong Deming tasted the salt of his blood as Liu Chenguang's tongue slipped effortlessly between his lips and teeth. He groaned, grasping Liu Chenguang's shoulders and then the nape of his neck, holding on tightly. Liu Chenguang's hair fell down around him, teasing at his bared throat and chest and engulfing him in his scent and warmth. Liu Chenguang's body responded to him, not struggling to get away but pressing closer. He heard him gasp as well, the two of them softly breathing and panting together. He moved his hand down Chenguang's back to his waist, bringing them closer; it seemed to him that they couldn't get close enough.

"Chenguang," he breathed, opening his eyes at last to look at him.

Liu Chenguang's eyes were partly closed, hazy and unfocused, his bitten lip swollen, but the bleeding had already stopped. "Deming," Liu Chenguang responded, and kissed him again, gently, eyes still half closed.

Hong Deming watched him, entranced by the sound of his name in his mouth and the shape of his lips, his dreaming eyes.

"Don't lie to me anymore. If you're hurt, tell me right away."

"I'll want to get hurt all the time now," he said.

Chenguang laughed and laid his head down on his breast, half-lying on him. He couldn't see himself under Liu Chenguang's hair, but the bruises felt much better.

"I hope you don't give this treatment to everyone, though."

"Just to you…"

There was a knock at the door. Both of them started and sat up — it was quite easy now, Hong Deming noticed; being kissed by Liu Chenguang was evidently a magical panacea — flushed and disarrayed, trying to quickly make themselves decent.

Liu Chenguang dashed across the room to Hong Deming's luggage and threw an outer robe at him, then went to the door. "Yes?" he asked, clearing his throat.

"Master, sorry for the disturbance, but there's someone here that–"

"Student Liu," interrupted a cold voice that Hong Deming now thoroughly detested.

"Teacher Zhu," Liu Chenguang sighed. He opened the door.

Zhu Guiren swept in, wearing court robes. His eyes landed first on Hong Deming, sitting demurely at the tea table. "You survived the unfortunate attack on Peaceful River, I see."

Hong Deming said, "Thanks to the efforts of the disciples of the sect, we did fend off the attackers successfully."

Zhu Guiren nodded, clearly dismissing him. "Student Liu, I've completed what's necessary here. We need to depart with the Crane Moon sect leader to-night. We will require their protection on the road back, after today's events. There will be attacks from the scattered disciples of the surviving targeted sects. My name has unfortunately been associated with this."

Liu Chenguang said, "Of course, I'm ready. Hong Deming was injured to-day–"

"Have you healed him?" he cut in, as though Hong Deming wasn't right there. "I told you, no more healing until the work is complete."

"I've been healing people all morning, actually," said Liu Chenguang coolly. "And I'm fine. Check if you don't think so."

Zhu Guiren declined to touch the arm he held out. "Student Liu," he said sternly, "I am still your teacher, and you must trust that I know more than you do about this. The issue is not only whether you can survive healing others, ran-domly and constantly as the opportunity presents itself, though I'm not sure you can, but how this will affect your powers in the next few months."

Hong Deming looked at Liu Chenguang, whose expression was rebellious, then back at Zhu Guiren.

Liu Chenguang shrugged. "Well, it doesn't matter. Either way, I'm fine. Hong Deming and I will be coming, of course. Just let us gather our things. I'm sure you need to change out of court dress before we leave, Teacher Zhu."

"Oh, is he coming too?" Zhu Guiren raised his eyebrows. "I was under the impression that his sect leader had given him other commands."

Liu Chenguang turned and looked at Hong Deming, speechless.

He nodded reluctantly. "I'm to seek yaoguai. I can't return to Crane Moon for a year, at least."

"A year," Liu Chenguang echoed. He looked back at Zhu Guiren. "How fortuitous."

"Within a year," Zhu Guiren said blandly, "if all goes as planned, the current unrest should be addressed adequately by the stabilizing of the dynasty. At that point, cultivators might be able to return to their sects with the re-establishment of law and order and the guarantee of safety for the common people."

Hong Deming looked back and forth between them. Certainly, he thought to his own satisfaction, no one would think these two were involved, seeing them talk together. It seemed to be pompous demands on one side and outspoken re-sentment on the other. Liu Chenguang showed Zhu Guiren none of the warmth he had when he smiled at Hong Deming, which was a lovely thing to think about, but there would be at least a year before they could be together again.

"I'm not going to Crane Moon," Liu Chenguang said. He sat down to emphasize his words. "I'll stay with Hong Deming. We'll wander together."

Zhu Guiren opened his mouth, then closed it again and looked at Hong Deming. Eventually, he said, "Student Liu, you have to complete your cultivational healing for yourself before you can go out into the world. I know how to get you through what will happen in the next year—"

"What will happen in the next year?" Hong Deming asked sharply.

"Nothing. Nothing will happen that I won't be perfectly fine doing," Liu Chenguang said, glaring at Zhu Guiren.

"One more year, Student Liu. One more year, and everything will be done. Then, you'll be able to go do…whatever it is you want to do. A year isn't so long, is it, when it's your life at stake?"

"My life is not at stake!" Liu Chenguang shouted in frustration. "I am perfectly fine! I know my powers better than you."

"Do you refuse, then, to do what I order you to do? Your sect leader placed you under my authority."

"Then let Hong Deming come back with me. Let him come back to Crane Moon with me," Liu Chenguang said stubbornly. He met Hong Deming's eyes, fierce and pleading.

"I can't, taine. I'm forbidden to come." He held Liu Chenguang's gaze, trying to communicate things he couldn't possibly say in front of Zhu Guiren.

Zhu Guiren added, "That wasn't my decision, Student Liu. You can't blame me for it, and I can't change it."

Liu Chenguang clenched his hands into fists and stared at the floor. "Will you release me, Zhu Guiren," he asked through his teeth, "and tell Taiqian that I am able to be on my own?"

"Not yet. One more year. And Liu Chenguang," Zhu Guiren added, using his full name, "you know that if I release you, you still owe obedience to your sect leader. I am only carrying out their authority through delegation now."

Liu Chenguang stared silently at the tea table.

Zhu Guiren raised his eyes to meet Hong Deming's. He said, "Student Liu, you need one more year of work with me, in an intensive environment, to stabilize your cultivation and avoid qi deviation in your healing path. You need to be in a safe and protected place where I can help you in case of emergency."

"There will be no emergencies," Liu Chenguang said.

Hong Deming spoke, trying to be polite, although he truly wanted to smash Zhu Guiren into little pieces: "Master Zhu, please leave first. I will bring my taine to the gate to meet you and the sect leader in one hour."

Zhu Guiren nodded and swept out.

Defeated, Liu Chenguang stared at him from the tea table. Hong Deming readied himself for one last attempt to say what he meant, to make things good between them after everything that had happened. The silence stretched as Liu Chenguang looked at him with sad eyes.

At last, Hong Deming said, "I wish more than anything that you could come with me, or I could come with you. But your being safe means more than that. That's the most important thing to me — for you to be safe."

Liu Chenguang finally smiled and shook his head. "Why do you think I don't want to let you go anywhere without me, after seeing what a mess you got yourself into today?" He stood and walked over to Hong Deming, reaching out to touch his hand cautiously. "Deming, before, were you drunk?"

Hong Deming smiled and took his other hand as well, lightly tracing the shape of Liu Chenguang's fingers, his delicacy and strength. "I wasn't drunk. Were you?"

"I wanted to kiss you for so long. That's all," Liu Chenguang said, and blushed a little bit. "I took advantage. You should know, I really don't normally heal people that way. By kissing them."

"But you use your blood to heal people?" Hong Deming gently stroked the dark hair back sticking to his skin, his forehead a little warm and sweaty. It made his heart beat harder. "Your hair is a mess, Chenguang."

"My blood has healing powers, yes," Liu Chenguang said, smiling up at him. "And if my hair is a mess, it's completely your fault."

"It's your cultivational path?"

Liu Chenguang hesitated slightly. "That's the best way to explain it. Does it frighten you, that I can do that?"

"No. Nothing about you could frighten me, Chenguang." Hong Deming gathered him into his arms, where he fit completely perfectly. Liu Chenguang tipped his face up and Hong Deming very softly kissed him on his eyebrows, his nose, and his lips.

"It truly doesn't bother you, that I'm not like other people?" Liu Chenguang asked through all the kissing.

"No," Hong Deming said. He thought to himself that it was a wonderful feeling, to kiss Liu Chenguang gently like this — as though they unshakably belonged to each other and could count on having all the time in the world for everything else.

Liu Chenguang seemed to have a contradictory thought; he nestled more closely, teasing his waist with his fingers, and said, "I wish that we could have a lot of time together right now, in this pleasant inn, with this very convenient bed."

Hong Deming flushed.

"However," Liu Chenguang sighed, "I suspect that Zhu Guiren is waiting downstairs because he doesn't trust you to bring me, really." He tangled his hands up in Hong Deming's hair, tugging him down to kiss him more thoroughly.

Breathing a little more quickly, Hong Deming closed his eyes, and let himself feel everything about him: his tongue, his lips, his hands, his body's weight against him, his skin warming where they touched. Liu Chenguang made a little whimpering noise that went through him with a shock of heat, and urgently he kissed back, his hands and mouth growing more demanding.

"Ah," Liu Chenguang said at last, breaking it off to get his breath. "Deming, promise me that you will come to Crane Moon as soon as you can."

"A year," he said, taking in Liu Chenguang's eyes, dark and wide, fixed on his own. "It's not so long."

"Too long." Liu Chenguang kissed him one last time.

Hong Deming brought Liu Chenguang to the gate as he had promised and gave him up to Zhu Guiren, Shen Lu, and the senior Crane Moon disciples who had accompanied him. None of them looked at Liu Chenguang with any warmth. He sat quietly on his horse, looking at the ground, dressed in his scholar's robes with his gourd and pendant. No one spoke to him or welcomed him. Zhu Guiren talked with Shen Lu near the front of the column, ignoring him.

Hong Deming walked over to them, feeling the anger that Shen Lu told him he was missing; the most precious thing in the world was being delivered into their hands and they treated him like this. "Excuse this disciple's presumption, sect leader, may he speak with the sect leader before leaving?"

Shen Lu looked surprised. "Yes, of course."

Zhu Guiren seemed to be unwilling to withdraw, ignoring the atmosphere. Hong Deming glared silently at him until at last he nodded shortly and moved away. Hong Deming then stared malevolently at his back.

"What is it?" Shen Lu asked impatiently. "We need to head out while we can take advantage of the moonlight. I want to get us well away from here."

Now that it had come to it, he didn't know how to say it except bluntly. "Tainu, please, take care of him. Don't treat him this way — like a thing that doesn't matter. He's your taine too."

"It's like that?" Shen Lu looked at him, then looked over at Liu Chenguang and shook his head. "Taine, you…Well, it's not unexpected. Taiqian was hoping that you might find someone else at Peaceful River, but it must be something fated for you."

"Can you let me come with you?" he asked, low and desperate. "Since you know how it is?"

Shen Lu shook his head. "It's better if you're away for now. For him too. He needs to focus on his cultivation, Zhu Guiren says. And what would you do anyway, if he's in seclusion, or cultivating intensively, or whatever it is that Zhu Guiren has planned for him? You would just distract him and make things more difficult." He reached out and patted his shoulder consolingly. "Since it's important to you, taine, I'll do my best to be kind. And you know he will be safe. Where could be safer than at Crane Moon? You should be grateful that Zhu Guiren is willing to bring him to us for this last year and stay with him. You know Master Zhu has much to do. He's giving up a year for it."

Hong Deming stepped back, watching Shen Lu mount his horse and ride forward, the column following. Liu Chenguang and Zhu Guiren were near the end, just before the senior disciples of the rearguard. Liu Chenguang raised his head as they passed and smiled at him — one last smile — and he smiled back.

*Only one year,* he thought. *Only one year. That's all.*

When he couldn't hear the hoofbeats on the road anymore, he mounted his own horse and rode in the other direction.

# CHAPTER 16
## REACHING THE REFUGE

TAIREI FOLLOWED ZHU GUIREN blindly through the razor grass to the shore of a river. Rivers in the spirit realm were unpredictable, and many were not normal water, but spiritual energy with different effects.

Zhu Guiren put Aili down for a moment and looked at it, frowning. "The path leads across here," he said, "but I don't see how to cross."

This place was unfamiliar to Tairei as well. Whenever a phoenix was reborn, they would be moved into the spirit realm by the phoenix gate, but the fire could bring them anywhere within it. This time — probably since she'd been in a new part of the mortal world at rebirth — she had awoken in a part of the spirit world that was completely strange to her. She knew no paths, recognized few plants, and there were no landmarks she could orient toward.

The phoenix refuges were scattered around the entire spirit world, hidden from view and findable only by the phoenixes themselves. There were not many phoenixes; less than one hundred and fifty, Tainu had told her once, spending most of their cycles hidden in the mortal realm and returning to the spirit realm only when forced to by the rebirth fire. Of course, there were many more refuges than phoenixes — established everywhere for a phoenix's safety since a phoenix might appear anywhere — but still, a few hundred or even a thousand refuges scattered throughout the spirit realm didn't necessarily mean a refuge was close.

In the life in which she had met Hong Deming, she had been reborn as usual but had not been able to reach a refuge before demons found her, forcing her back into the mortal realm before she had reached adulthood. Demons were already chasing them now, and if Tainu's distraction didn't work or if they didn't find a refuge before nightfall, they would be in a very precarious position.

Zhu Guiren said, "I don't want to go up- or downstream. This must be the quickest path to cross."

Tairei knelt at the shore, reaching out cautiously to touch the water with two fingers. She closed her eyes to concentrate. "It doesn't seem to be corrosive or spiritually damaging," she said at last. "If we could fly, this would be so much easier."

"Of the three of us, I'm the only one with that option and I'm not the one in danger," he said. "Well, I don't see anything we can use as a boat. Can you swim?"

"Not very well, but I think I can make it across this one. It's not very wide…" She shaded her hand and looked across; it was really only a little over a hundred feet, perhaps, and there didn't seem to be a strong current. And damned if she was going to let Zhu Guiren carry *her*. She'd rather drown. "But can you swim while you're carrying Aili?"

Zhu Guiren sent her a look that she remembered well from their travels around the Sorrowful River valley. "Of course," he said haughtily. He considered his robes, then shrugged and took off the outer two layers, leaving him in a thin underrobe with narrow sleeves. Tossing the outer robes over to her, he said, "Carry that for me."

Tairei rolled her eyes and made it into a neater package. Out of nowhere, she found herself saying, "Did you know Hong Deming really admired you once?"

"No," he said indifferently. "Let's go." He waded into the river water and began to swim an awkward sidestroke, holding Aili under his handless arm on his chest so that her face remained above the water.

Tairei wished she were taller so she could do this. She hated that Zhu Guiren was doing for Aili what she couldn't.

On the other side, having dog-paddled over after him — luckily nothing had attacked them in the water, because she really couldn't swim — Tairei silently handed him his robes. They were soaking wet, but he carefully wrung them out and put them back on.

"You look ridiculous," she said.

"As though there's anyone I need to impress here." He looked around, a sword in his hand once more. "If we do need to fight, I'm going to need to put her down quickly," he said. "Don't get upset if she gets a few bumps."

They walked again in single file, Zhu Guiren following a twisting, spiraling path through a flat, open meadow; it must be a requirement of the wards, to navigate through a maze. After a while, he asked, "You hate me because he died?"

Tairei looked at him, marveling at his denseness. "I hate you because you lied; because you destroyed our life together; because you ruined his life and his family; because you organized the destruction of thousands of other lives and their families and all they had; and yes, of course, because he died," she said. "The more I know about you, the more there is to hate."

Zhu Guiren hefted Aili a little higher on his shoulder, frowning as though this was a very complicated thing to understand. "Did you hate me when you first met me, or only after all that happened?"

"Why would I have hated you when I just met you?" She remembered that time, the first time they were formally introduced, right after coming to Crane Moon. Taiqian had brought him to stand in front of the gathered disciples and bow to Zhu Guiren as his future teacher. Hong Deming had been off in a corner, staring wide-eyed at Zhu Guiren rather than at him even though it was the first time they'd seen each other since his arrival at the sect. It was unlikely she would forget *that*. Zhu Guiren's perfect face and elegant demeanor drew everyone's eyes; he didn't speak kindly or warmly, his voice precise and cold. Though she hadn't known that he was a demon, she had known that what he was saying was completely false. She was not some kind of rogue cultivator with a unique cultivation path. She was not human at all. Yet, it fit so well — provided such an excellent explanation of who she was that mortals could understand.

It allowed her to stay near Hong Deming.

So she acted as though she believed it, and she obeyed.

But she didn't hate him, not until almost the very end.

"I didn't hate you," Zhu Guiren was saying. He had led them beneath some tall trees with dark purple leaves, so they were effectively walking in the dark. She could barely see him walking ahead of her, his facial expressions invisible. "I actually…liked having a student. It wasn't all lies. Aren't you glad that I taught you medicine? And astronomy?" He seemed uncertain. "I tried to teach you about politics, too, so you would understand how worthless mortals are. I could see you getting entangled…I taught you things I knew would help you in the future, when we were…done."

"I found the book of the Way of Heavenly Benevolence in the imperial library," she said. "Oddly, you never introduced me to that one."

"Ah," he said, floundering a bit. "Well. Master Shao was a little too idealistic. Not a good match for you. You were already too much…that."

"Why are you even here?" she asked, frustrated enough to finally ask it, as though she could hope for any honesty from him. "Why did you come to find me in Easterly?"

"I wasn't looking for you. It was just a coincidence. But I protected you, remember? I have no idea why you had to scream at me to get away."

"Do you think protecting me from a few random yaoguai makes up for what you did to us?" she asked, enraged. "Who the hell asked for your protection? Do you— you stupid—" She cut herself off. There was no point trying to talk to him. No point at all.

He didn't respond, perhaps wanting to save his breath as the hill steepened dramatically. Tairei jumped forward to help balance Aili as Zhu Guiren clambered over a rocky part.

After she had calmed herself enough to talk like a rational person, she added, "We're already inside the outer wards that would have alerted anyone in the refuge that someone is coming. I could feel when we crossed."

"I need a rest," Zhu Guiren said. He placed Aili down on the ground, then sat next to her, panting.

Tairei sat on the other side of Aili's limp form and held her hand. After a moment, she realized that Zhu Guiren was staring at that — her hand, holding Aili's.

"What?" she asked defensively. She thought of bringing her wings out again so he couldn't look at them, but she, too, was tired; they had been going for most of the day without a break.

"I didn't hate you," Zhu Guiren said again, as though it was a very important and necessary point. "Everything I did, I tried to make it easy for you…It was only a few years of your thousands of years of life. Only a little bit. I…aren't you fine now?"

She stared at him in contempt and considered spitting in his face, but turned back to Aili in the end, stroking her hand.

"I had to do it," he continued, "because I was doing something very important. Something I needed to complete…"

"Did you hate Hong Deming?" she asked coolly. "Or any of the other people whose lives you ruined?"

"No! That's what I'm saying. That's what you don't understand. I didn't hate any of them. I didn't do things just to hurt them. They were just…just…raw material." His voice petered out as he looked at the ground. "They were just there. Helpful or annoying or inconsequential. Hong Deming was annoying, but I didn't hate him."

"Do you see–" she said, very slowly, "–can you wrap your genius brain around the fact that whether you hated him or not made no difference whatsoever with what you did to him? To me? To everyone you touched, or spoke to — people you never even knew about who were caught up in all those machinations of yours? Have you given even a moment's thought to Hong Deming in the past thousand years?"

"No. Why would I?"

Tairei gritted her teeth. "Hatred or indifference is the same. You destroyed us and didn't even notice. You didn't even care." She bent down and kissed Aili's hair. "You're not worth my breath. You're certainly not worth my forgiveness, if that's what you're looking for."

They sat in silence until at last, Zhu Guiren said, "Let's keep going." He picked up Aili again, grunting, and started upward without looking at Tairei.

Halfway up the slope, a large, winged yao came down and swooped at Aili's head. Tairei screamed in shock. Zhu Guiren put Aili down rather carefully and yelled something vicious up at the sky that she couldn't quite catch.

The winged demon came down, transforming into a smiling, golden-haired woman who called out a sword. "Why are you hoarding these delicious little treats?"

"They're mine," Zhu Guiren said, sounding bored. "Off you go now."

The woman walked toward Tairei and Aili. "A phoenix and a…whatever that is. What is it, an experiment?"

"In a sense," said Zhu Guiren. He stepped in front of them.

"Our clans are allied," the woman said. "The phoenix is fair game if you can't protect it for yourself. If I kill you, your clan won't retaliate."

"That is not a problem you'll have to consider, since you'll be dead." Zhu Guiren leapt toward her. He aimed first at her right arm, but she was very fast, dodging around him to get to Tairei.

She smiled and grabbed Tairei's hair. "I've heard that you have a long and involved way of dealing with phoenixes. I'm more straightforward."

Then she yanked Tairei's head back and viciously stabbed her in the throat.

Tairei coughed and choked on the blood and pain. She fell to all fours on top of Aili, hoping to protect her. For a moment, she blacked out from blood loss, which was to be expected with this kind of wound; she knew the demon had attacked so that she wouldn't have the energy to transform and flee, though of course she wouldn't have been able to anyway.

When she was able to see again and the wound had closed, Zhu Guiren and the demon woman were spinning and leaping around each other almost too fast to see. Qi trailed in the air like fireworks as they threw spells and talismans at each other, as well as striking with the swords. At last, Zhu Guiren managed to strike the woman's upper arm, heavily. The woman screamed and brought her wings back out, transforming into a black eagle, dripping blood from the sky as she flew away.

Zhu Guiren limped back over to them, panting and coughing. Tairei got up, covered in blood. Aili was drenched in her blood as well; she must have bled out almost completely before she healed. He was also injured — a slash to his thigh and a talisman mark on his handless arm — but he didn't ask Tairei to heal him. Instead, he bent down, silently, to pick up Aili again.

As Zhu Guiren reached for Aili's waist, her eyes opened suddenly, a bright and terrifying blue in her blood-streaked face, and a golden sword appeared in her hand.

"Zhu Guiren," she whispered, her voice hoarse and strange.

"Aili?!" yelled Tairei. "Wait, Hong Deming!"

Aili's sword stabbed upward, piercing Zhu Guiren's chest, as he was bent over her. Zhu Guiren gave a gurgling scream and fell backward; the golden sword disappeared into thin air, his blood spurting from where it had been. Aili's eyes closed again.

"Aili?!" said Tairei, running to her. Then, reluctantly, "Zhu Guiren?"

He looked at her silently, then closed his eyes. Blood ran down from his lips.

"Damn you, Zhu Guiren," she said. She was tempted, just for the flash of a heartbeat, to watch him die. It would be so easy. But even as she thought it, she was already slashing at her hand with Zhu Guiren's sword. She anointed the wound on his chest, then reluctantly placed her blood between his lips.

It didn't take long before he opened his eyes. Tairei was already back beside Aili, holding her hand. He watched them quietly for a while before he stood up and walked over. "Let's go," he said, and bent down to pick up Aili again.

They walked up the steep, forested hill, to a lawn of short moss interspersed among the hateful razor grass that fronted a stone cliff in the hillside.

Zhu Guiren spoke at last. "This is it. This is where the path ends."

Tairei let go of the last shred of hope that she could get rid of him; she had promised her sibling. "Give me your hand," she said.

He reached out, still looking away from her; she pulled him forward until she felt a sense of resistance in the air, then paused until the refuge recognized her. Tainu had been confident it would, despite the weakening of her powers. Yes, the refuge acknowledged, yes, this is a phoenix, after all.

She opened her eyes to see the gate outlined in light on the stone in front of her and began walking forward, pulling Zhu Guiren after her. "Stay close to me," she said, feeling the wards begin to activate against him.

He gasped once, in pain. She could feel his pulse racing; this must be difficult for him.

"It will be all right," she heard herself say.

He didn't respond, his fingers spasming in her hand. Then, he only said, "Ah," and fell to his knees.

The thickness of the wall wasn't so great that they should still be inside it; clearly, the wards were not going to let a demon in. Tairei swore, realizing that she couldn't let go of his hand or he would be trapped between the ward shields forever.

"Don't let go of Aili." She bit her other hand, then drew several characters in her own blood on Zhu Guiren's forehead and started chanting softly. She wasn't as good with spells as her sibling was, but she had good instincts. He had always told her that.

Zhu Guiren's breathing smoothed out, and he staggered upright again. "Quickly," he said.

They came through into a small cavern — very small for three, and soon to be four, people — smoothed in a perfect sphere around a golden-blue fire that burned in the middle without any visible source of fuel. The walls were shining and smooth, and purely black. In them, the flames of the golden fire reflected and refracted endlessly, seeming to hint at symbols and figures deep in the stone that disappeared as soon as one tried to see them more closely.

"Here we are," Tairei sighed with relief.

Zhu Guiren half-fell down, lying Aili on the floor, then collapsed either into unconsciousness or a deep sleep. Tairei checked Aili, who seemed stable, and then Zhu Guiren; he would recover, she thought. She looked at him for a moment, remembering those days traveling with him, learning from him. They had never been friends, only teacher and student, but she had learned so much from him. He had been right, after all. She had trusted him.

It only made everything worse.

Time passed differently in the refuges than in other places, Tairei knew. There was no hint of day or night or seasons. In that sense, it was somewhat like the spiritual caverns at Crane Moon, though those were crude and brutal compared to the refuges — just enforced night and deprivation of the bodily senses.

The refuges didn't deprive, but enhanced and focused, intensifying the power of the spirit realm so that cultivation would move more quickly. As Aili and Zhu Guiren were unconscious, she settled herself into some good, hard cultivation.

"Who made this?" Zhu Guiren asked, waking up suddenly.

"I don't know, they've always been here."

"How long have we been here? Where's Tainu?"

"I don't know," she said, opening her eyes and frowning at him. He looked uneasy. "Are you worried about him?"

"Why would I be worried? I'm sure the giant bird is fine," he said pettishly.

"I'm sure he is too." She closed her eyes again. "He really will be fine, but when he arrives. he'll probably be tired. Just let him rest."

Zhu Guiren tapped his fingers on the crystalline floor in an unpredictable pattern, making an echoing noise. Tairei's eyes flew open again.

"Sorry," he said, not sounding sorry at all. "What is this made of? The substance is so hard…"

"Why are you so interested? Finding ways to undermine the refuge so you can catch phoenixes later? Don't bother — they're impregnable."

"Nothing's impregnable," he muttered. "It's not very comfortable for me. There's some pain, and pressure on my body just being here, even though you took me through the wards. I can tell it's anti-demonic, but what about the soul-devourers?"

"I don't know about that." Tainu suddenly appeared next to the wall. "We've never had a mortal soul in one of these before to attract them, so it's never been a problem." He slid down the wall and tipped his head back, eyes closed. Against the black wall, his dark brown skin made him seem like a silhouette surrounded by an aura of dancing golden lights in the stone.

Zhu Guiren stared at him. "You're tired."

"You noticed," Tainu replied, his eyes still closed. "Yes." He sighed deeply and turned his head to the side to look wearily at Tairei. "Did anything happen?"

Zhu Guiren looked at the ground and started tapping his fingers again.

Tairei said, "We were attacked by a demon. And Aili woke up for a split second and stabbed Zhu Guiren with En."

"What?!" Tainu shook himself to a more upright position. "She…"

Tairei nodded. "I couldn't have been mistaken — it was En."

"I also couldn't have been mistaken," said Zhu Guiren, "she stabbed me with it. Oh, and yes, there was a demon I fought off."

Tairei noticed that he seemed more like himself now and felt oddly relieved; it had been strange to have him quiet and withdrawn.

Tainu said, "We haven't gotten to talk about this yet, but Tairei, you should know that she can use weapons. And she can use the rebirth fire as a weapon."

Zhu Guiren and Tairei both stared at him.

"But no phoenix can use a weapon," Tairei replied. "Do you have any idea how hard I tried?"

Zhu Guiren said, "I hate to point out the obvious, but this person is not a phoenix. You can't assume that what she is or does will be the same as what you do. Just because you did whatever it was you did to her doesn't make her a phoenix. She's a mortal soul with heavy demonic affinity."

Now, Tairei and Tainu both stared at Zhu Guiren.

"Demonic affinity?" asked Tairei finally.

"All mortals have it," he said impatiently, "it's why they're so fun for us. Well, most mortals, anyway. Hers is heavier than most, so in addition to the normal mortal inclinations…" He stood and walked over to where she was lying, moved his hands in a sharp gesture, then reached out as though he was grabbing something in the air. "She's bound into three separate arrays. That's a record, as far as I know. No living being I've ever seen was bound into more than one, and to be honest, I already knew that she was bound into one. There are some ghosts, for lack of a better word, that are bound into two. She has three…incredibly bad luck for her."

"What's an array?" Tairei asked. "What does it do to her?"

Absently, Zhu Guiren said, "It's difficult to explain in a few words what it is. Demons at a certain level of power can set up an array to cultivate resentment more efficiently by capturing souls in suffering. Mostly souls of the dead, but living people can be bound into arrays as well."

He looked briefly at Tainu, then away. "The effect on a mortal living being is…not good. It's more likely than not that they experience a lot of suffering, or they cause a lot of suffering, or both. It depends on how strongly she's bound and how long it's had an effect on her…how strong the array is and how strong the demon who made it was. There are a lot of variables. With three, it would be hard to determine how they might interact with one another and which ones came from which life…" He trailed off, tapping his fingers against his handless arm.

"Can you just say what it does to her?" Tairei asked, holding tightly to Aili's hand; if Aili had been awake, she likely would have winced, but Aili slept through it all.

Zhu Guiren shrugged. "Brief life, unhappy death."

Tairei looked down at Aili's face, pale and silent.

Tainu spoke at last. "Tell me why you were confident she would have at least one."

Zhu Guiren looked at him. "Isn't it obvious? Hong Deming was bound at his death by me."

"No," Tairei said fiercely. "No, he wasn't. He was bound by me."

Zhu Guiren frowned at her, then bent down to look more closely at Aili. His hand moved in the air again, his fingers grasping and pulling at invisible threads in the air. His brows knit more seriously. "Liu Chenguang, what exactly did you *do?*"

Tairei shook her head. "Isn't it possible that some people have a phoenix affinity?" she asked.

Zhu Guiren snorted, still looking at Aili and running his fingers through the air. "Who would want a phoenix affinity? Just meat that doesn't die."

Tainu and Tairei both stared at him in silence.

"Oh, come on," he said, "don't be offended. I'm treating you like family here."

"You have a family?" asked Tainu.

"Of course not. But if I did, I would certainly talk to them like this." He tugged hard at something invisible in midair. "I'd also probably try to kill them, so, you know, you two really are like family to me..."

Tainu stood up and walked back out through the wall.

Zhu Guiren's hand froze in position. "Did I say something?" he asked.

"Are you asking me that as though it's a serious question?" Tairei glared at him and settled back into a cultivation pose.

"I was joking," he said.

"It was a terrible joke and you are giving us terrible news, so it wasn't funny. It's pathetic that I have to explain that to you, Zhu Guiren. How did you survive at court all those years?"

He shrugged. "I didn't show them my true personality. Everything about me at court was a lie."

"Lucky us." When Zhu Guiren continued silently staring at the wall where Tainu had disappeared, she said, "All right, if you really want to know, you shouldn't joke with Tainu about family. Family is very important to him."

Zhu Guiren sat up, clearly surprised. "How can that be? You don't have families. You don't have parents or children, you're not born..."

"He always wanted the phoenixes to be like a family," Tairei explained, "but most of us...we're not made that way. Most of us aren't very good at relationships."

"Unlike you," said Zhu Guiren.

"Unlike me," Tairei said. "Obviously I am amazing at relationships. Please get away from me now." She looked down at Aili and closed her eyes to cultivate.

Zhu Guiren tapped his fingers on the floor of the cavern a few more times, then went out, pushing against the wards, which clearly did not like him.

He found Tainu just outside, his back against the rock of the refuge. "You shouldn't be out here without me," he said, "it's not safe for you."

"Demon, I've been walking this realm since before you were spawned," he said, looking down the slope at the trees, "don't tell me where I can and can't go."

Zhu Guiren sat down next to him. After a while, he said, "I was born, not spawned. But we don't really have families. It's all very…violent. Highly organized and very violent. So it's not…I didn't…there wasn't…" He struggled to say something complicated, his voice starting a few times and then stopping. Tainu finally turned to look at him. He managed, "I don't know how to be with people without trying to hurt them."

"I don't know how to be with people without trying to heal them," said Tainu in return.

They sat quietly for a while.

Tainu said, "Ah, I see. Clever."

"What?" Zhu Guiren rubbed his forehead where Tainu was staring. "Oh, Tairei did that."

Tainu bit his finger and leaned over toward him, writing firmly across his forehead. Zhu Guiren felt something tingle beneath the warmth of Tainu's blood. "Mine will be more effective," he said. "You should be able to come in and out now with minimal pain."

Zhu Guiren nodded, surprised.

Tainu picked a small flower in the moss. "Not everything about the spirit realm is awful," he said. "But for us, we can't really be here unless we're inside the refuges, so we never get to see it."

Zhu Guiren took the flower from his hand, and looked at it carefully. "I don't remember flowers in the spirit realm," he said. "Growing up in the clan, flowers are…not a priority. I always preferred being in the mortal world."

"Why are you staying with us, then?" Tainu asked. "The mortal world beckons. You've already lost a hand for this. You're not a phoenix, you could go through a demonic gate any time you want. Tairei and I have to stay until she has enough cultivation to generate a phoenix gate, I can't since I haven't gone through rebirth recently. Why are you here? It must be obvious that you're not welcome."

"Your way of showing me I'm not welcome is to let me come into a phoenix refuge with you," Zhu Guiren said, nettled.

"So?" Tainu probed.

"Well, it's confusing, demons would have pulled out my heart and made me eat it, you're giving me mixed messages." Tainu laughed. Zhu Guiren frowned at him. "Why are you laughing? Aren't you worried that this is all a plan of mine to catch phoenixes?"

Tainu met his eyes thoughtfully, the smile leaving his face. "No," he said simply. "I'm not worried."

"Well, you're an idiot, then." Zhu Guiren looked back down at the flower in his hand.

"You could have captured Tairei at any time before I arrived. You could take both of us now, if I didn't fly fast enough, we can't fight you. Now you have Aili as a hostage. Whatever you wanted in that line you would already have done. That's what I don't understand."

Zhu Guiren was silent, staring at the flower.

"What was the best time of your life?" Tainu asked suddenly.

Zhu Guiren said, without thinking, "When Liu Chenguang and I traveled around and I would teach him things and we would talk."

Tainu said, "What was good about it?"

The silence stretched out.

"The best time in my life," Tainu went on, when he didn't answer, "was early in my third cycle. Around eight thousand years ago, in mortal time. Tairei was probably just coming into consciousness then, she's the youngest of us…anyway, we're usually solitary, and I hadn't ever been with other beings for any long amount of time, even though I was two thousand years old by then. But there was a village…they learned who I was and what I could do, but they weren't afraid of me, and they didn't try to take advantage of me. They just…welcomed me. For myself and no other reason. We laughed and we cried and told stories and ate together and worked together and argued together and went on adventures and then told one another about them…They were my family."

Zhu Guiren said, "It was like that, a little bit, with Liu Chenguang."

Tainu nodded.

"But Liu Chenguang didn't know who I was, so it wasn't the same," Zhu Guiren said pedantically.

"So you want to do that again? With Liu Chenguang knowing who you are, this time? To have a family?"

Zhu Guiren shrugged.

"Do you think she can forgive you?" Tainu said. "Do you think any of us can? Or should?"

Zhu Guiren was quiet, and then changed the subject. "Where was the village?"

"It doesn't exist anymore; even the place where it was is covered by desert. The language we spoke is gone. Even another phoenix couldn't speak it with me, I think." Tainu's voice sounded sad.

Zhu Guiren asked, "What happened to your…family?"

"I kept them safe from harm, of course. But eventually, one by one, after they'd lived for a century or thereabouts, they came to me and asked me to stop healing them. Mortals aren't made for immortality. They couldn't bear the weight of the years, the memories. So, one by one, I stopped. And one by one, they died and left me." He looked at the flower again, in Zhu Guiren's hand, and reached out to touch it. "But they weren't afraid to go, they were ready. So that was my gift to them, that they didn't fear death."

Zhu Guiren looked at Tainu's fingers, touching the flower.

"I sometimes wonder," Tainu said, "if mortals now are more afraid of death than they used to be. More cruel. My family wasn't cruel, because they weren't afraid."

"Maybe," Zhu Guiren said. He lay the flower down gently. "Resentment builds on resentment, suffering on suffering."

Tainu said, "So that's what the array is." He said it without blame, and so Zhu Guiren answered without guilt.

Zhu Guiren said, "Yes."

# CHAPTER 17
## YAOGUAI

Hong Deming spent several days riding down the road away from Gunan, away from Crane Moon, and away from Liu Chenguang. The things that had happened in Gunan, the drunken kiss in the brothel, the attack on Peaceful River, the time in the inn, the feeling of Liu Chenguang's body against his, that sense of deep peace and trust that they would be together…it all began to feel like a fever dream in the quiet emptiness of the days. It was only at night, when he lay wrapped in a blanket and looked at the stars, that everything was real again, because Chenguang would also see those stars, and would think of him.

During the days, though, he had a task to do: to fight the evil beings that Shen Lu had directed him to find. He'd certainly never seen any such thing, only human beings killing each other, but he was eager to avoid killing human beings again. Once cultivators specialized in exorcising and destroying evil beings, yao-mo and yaoguai, demons and monsters, on the path to ascension to the heavens, and his childhood had been full of the ancient stories, but it seemed that being a cultivator now was about the battles and plots and resentments of human beings. He hated it, hated killing other people.

Let there be some demons. That, he could feel good about unleashing En upon.

Not knowing quite how to go about it, he decided to leave the main highway for the smaller roads and villages, traipsing down the lesser-known paths, asking if anyone was suffering from demon oppression or evil spirits or ghosts or yaoguai. In these little villages, separated from the great cities, faced with a handsome young cultivator in silk robes with a spiritual sword, the people didn't even laugh at such questions, but answered seriously. It wasn't until the fifth village that several people mentioned a local lake that had just developed a strange aura, where two children had recently drowned. Their mother, sobbing, said, "Both of them could swim. Why would they drown? Why would they even go into the water? It's not hot out, they weren't fishing…"

When he reached the shores of the lake, it was almost twilight, a good time to see if anything would happen. He sat down cross-legged, En across his lap, waiting.

In the dark, the lake was a dismal place. There were no insect or animal noises, he noticed, and the water didn't reflect the stars coming out in the sky. When the water rippled and the thing came out, there were no noises of waves lapping against the rocks, as though whatever was in the lake was no longer water at all, but some viscous, thick substance.

The creature wasn't near him, but it knew he was there. "Cultivator," it said, "are you here to kill me? How delicious."

"Do I need to kill you?" he asked it. Truthfully he was quite sure he did; the yaoguai stank of corpses and oozed resentful energy. But it seemed polite to inquire, since it hadn't attacked him first. It didn't seem as though it would be very fast as it pulled itself creeping up the shore. He stood up, En in hand.

"I will tell your fortune," the thing whispered, and crawled up the bole of a tree. The tree withered and died. "It is easy, it is written all over you." The creature opened its eyes, something like a huge salamander. Its eyes glowed hypnotic in the dark.

Suddenly, far faster than he could have imagined, the yaoguai leapt at him, its legs growing longer and clawed, its glowing eyes hidden behind the opening maw. It swiped at him, and as fast as he was in spinning away, as good as his lightness skills were, as strong as En was, nonetheless it caught him on the arm with one claw, ripping his flesh open just below the shoulder.

He yelled out loud in shock rather than pain. In all of his years of training, in the various skirmishes and battles he'd experienced, no one had ever managed to get a blade on him.

Once he got over the surprise, he was thrilled.

He leapt to the top of the tree the yaoguai had been climbing on, holding En out to get a better look by its light. It was both scaled and slimy, something like a water creature, something like a worm, except for those ridiculously long claws, half as long as its own body. It looked up at him, grinning through its three rows of teeth. "Cultivator, cultivator," it sang, "come down and play, cultivator," and then it was in the air again, fast as lightning, whipping its claws and its tail – he realized too late the tail had a sting – and spinning toward him, zipping toward wherever he himself jumped. He slashed out En with a sword pulse, and the golden light struck the scales and bounced off. The yaoguai laughed.

"You are that one," it said, "I will have a double reward for this, I will eat your delicious bones and the master will give me a gift, he has said so, he has said!"

"What master?" he asked, and jumped beneath it, rolling on the ground, to try if the sword pulse would work better on its belly. It did not, but he got a faceful of slime for his troubles. He jumped up again, spitting and retching at the foul taste.

"Hah, you are a funny one! I have eaten six cultivators so far in my travels, they taste much better than ordinary people. No one tried rolling underneath me before." The creature didn't seem to be particularly intelligent. According to what he had read in the library and learned in his training, a yaoguai such as this one was not originally a spiritual being, but a creature of the mortal realm that had failed in its cultivation, half-finished, supporting itself with blood and resentment. Its power was limited. In terms of sheer strength, he really should be able to kill it, except he had never done this before, and wasn't quite sure how.

Without anything else coming to mind, he jumped on its back and stabbed En straight down into its spine. The yaoguai screamed and scrabbled back with its claws at an impossible angle, nearly impaling him before he spun off, leaving En embedded in its scales. He now had two deep slashes, one in his arm, one in his back. "Too slow," he berated himself.

The creature screamed again and spun in circles, then rolled on the ground, forcing En in deeper. But the sword alone wouldn't kill a yaoguai.

Hong Deming breathed deeply and placed his hands into the demon-destroying seal, closing his eyes, and envisioning En. Within the creature's body, the spiritual energy he sent into the sword spiraled out, golden patterns moving into its spiritual resentment and purifying it.

When he opened his eyes, the yaoguai's body was webbed with cracks of golden light, as though it was made of fire covered over in smoke. It shrieked, louder and shriller, then dissolved.

The lake reflected the stars again.

Hong Deming sat down next on the shore in the mud and laughed endlessly at he didn't know what, then winced. En returned to his hand, and as he caught it he saw the long, bleeding slash from the yaoguai. It was slightly tinged with a hazy, dark smoke, a demonic wound polluted with resentment. He would need to cultivate to purify it, and the one in his back as well.

*Liu Chenguang would be so angry at me,* he thought, and smiled as he placed himself into a lotus position. "Chenguang," he said out loud, just to hear his name.

It was lonely, wandering the back paths between the little villages and isolated farmsteads. It wasn't like on the highways where he would see other people every day, or even travel with them. When he found a village that needed a monster or demon dealt with, he would often stay there for a week or so, ostensibly to recover, but really, as he eventually realized, because he so desperately wanted to hear human voices again after the silence of the forest. Truly, he was not cut out to be a hermit.

He wrote letters to Chenguang sometimes and sent them to Crane Moon via the network of messengers and casual contacts that joined the sects whenever he came across an allied cultivator in his travels. He wrote about the yaoguai, about the occasional bandit attack on a village that he needed to break up, about any beautiful thing he saw in the woods. Hong Deming wasn't a great writer, so the letters weren't very poetic, and he couldn't figure out how to say things that were romantic very well, but it was some way to try to reach out back to where Liu Chenguang was, to keep their connection, even though Liu Chenguang was going through whatever Zhu Guiren had planned for him now. To make sure Liu Chenguang knew that he hadn't forgotten, that he was still thinking of him, all the time, every day.

After several months of this, he decided to leave the mountain villages and return to Bian to report to Stone Phoenix, as Shen Lu had directed. He had a sense that he had done what he could with these small yaoguai; he had destroyed or suppressed a good number, and surely there was an endless number more, but many of them had mentioned a master in their conversations with him. The yaoguai always wanted to talk while they were fighting, perhaps because they had often been trying to cultivate into human forms when things all began for them.

On the third day down from the mountains, he came across a bandit camp.

In all his journey, during which he'd clashed with bandit groups several times, he had yet to come across a place where they lived when they weren't attacking villages or travelers. Here it was, not very different from most other poor villages — a few huts, a few fields. The differences were in the people. A few dozen young men and older men and even a few women, sitting around gossiping or eating or practicing archery; dozens of women and younger children, dressed in rags, doing the work of the day, most showing signs of being beaten or worse.

Hong Deming decided to ride up in the middle just to see what would happen.

As expected, the bandit leader immediately ordered an attack, while the people in rags threw themselves on the ground and begged for mercy and freedom. Hong Deming was quite willing to get it for them, especially after he saw a young girl of no more than nine crying, her ragged skirt stained with old blood. He didn't need qi for this, only a sword, not even lightness skill.

He dismounted to give away any unnecessary advantage and called En. "Come on then," he yelled, "if you think you're capable!"

A good number of the bandits had very elevated ideas about their capability, which he quickly disabused them of. As much as he hated unnecessary killing, he no longer had a lot of regrets over killing bandits, whatever Chenguang might say. Any suffering they had undergone to get to this point was surely balanced by the suffering they had inflicted on others.

Once those people were unconscious or dead, the remainder ran away into the forest, and for the most part, the ragged captives did as well. He would have been glad to guard them back down to the highway, but after all, he wasn't equipped to do much more for them, not even feed them. It was just as well. He flicked the blood off En and mounted up again.

"It's you," said a voice behind him.

He turned around and saw a slender young man, dressed in rags perhaps slightly cleaner than the others, long hair knotted and braided behind his head. "Wu Fan?" he asked, stunned. "Is that you?"

"It's me," he said, with that smile he had used in the brothel, gentle and caressing. "It's been a long time. Can I come with you?"

Since there was only one horse, Wu Fan had to ride behind him down the mountain, which felt awkward to Hong Deming at least. But it would have been much worse to have him riding in the front, since that would have made it obvious that Hong Deming was not as oblivious to Wu Fan as he would have liked to be. Wu Fan didn't bring this up, simply holding on to him while they rode silently, sometimes leaning against his back. Hong Deming was very aware of the warmth of his body, and the feeling of his hands, and it was very lucky that they didn't run into any other bandits on the way down the mountain.

That night, Hong Deming shot a rabbit for them to eat, and Wu Fan helped him skin and roast it. "I learned to do this in the bandit camp," he said, "it's not something they teach you at the Delicate Orchid." He smiled. "Although I'm not alive because of my cooking."

"I'm glad that you survived," Hong Deming said, awkwardly, after they had eaten. "I saw the pavilion burnt, and I wondered if you were safe…"

"It hasn't been very pleasant," Wu Fan said calmly, "but truthfully, in some ways, not much different than the Delicate Orchid. Just rougher, and less food." He must have seen Hong Deming's expression, and he said quickly, "Not you, I remember you, you were very kind to me, back then." Wu Fan reached out and touched his hand, then brought it to his lips. "Thank you," he said, simply. He brushed the back of Hong Deming's hand softly with his breath, then let go.

Hong Deming took his hand back, silently.

Wu Fan looked down, and smiled. "Well, you're not totally uninterested, anyway."

"Thanks for noticing," he said, flushing. "You don't need to thank me in that way."

Wu Fan said, "It's not just to say thank you."

Hong Deming looked away.

"Ah," Wu Fan said. "I see. You're in love with someone." When Hong Deming stayed quiet, he continued, "Just so you know, I'm very good at my job."

Hong Deming shook his head. "I deeply regret that I must refuse your kind offer," he said, trying to give him some face.

"Why? Because you think I'd be upset you're imagining someone else the whole time? Believe me, you wouldn't have the energy."

Clearly, Wu Fan had no face to lose. Hong Deming said, trying to make light of it as Wu Fan did, "Really, I don't…want to." Since his body was openly denying this claim he got up and turned away.

"All right then." Wu Fan let it go as easily as he had raised the topic.

Hong Deming, still looking out into space and trying to distract himself from various images of Wu Fan doing various interesting things, asked, "Where do you want to go now? I'd like to get you there safely."

"You're very kind." Wu Fan settled himself gracefully into a seated position. Despite the dirt and grime on his face and his tangled hair, he still managed to appear beautiful. "Well, there's not much point in me going back to my home village, my parents sold me when I was six. Since at least I can read and write, the best plan I've been able to come up with is to develop a relationship with a merchant, and learn the business for myself." He said this calmly and as though it was quite easy to imagine. "Perhaps I should return to Gunan, it might be easier to get started with old clients…" He looked up at Hong Deming, smiling. "Don't look so shocked, it's not as though I have other skills. Can I farm? Can I fight? Can I be a government official? I only know one way to feed myself." He shrugged. "At least if I was a woman I could go have children for someone; but for someone like me…well, even if this hadn't happened it was time to think for the future, I'm getting too old. Most clients like us younger in the brothels."

Hong Deming couldn't think of any real response to this. "Tell me where you want to go, and I'll get you there."

"Where are you going?"

"I was going to visit a cultivational sect outside of Bian," he said. "But I don't really have any specific goals, I can take you back to Gunan if that's what you want."

"So you've just been wandering around the mountains, attacking bandits?" he asked, confused. "This isn't on any road to Bian."

"Not bandits, exactly…but sometimes."

"Yaoguai?"

"Yes, some." He no longer felt embarrassed about this, the people in the mountains didn't have problems believing him.

Wu Fan also nodded. "I never saw such things in the city," he said, simply. "But I think that's because in the city, the people are the demons…in the mountains, you can see what they look like when they don't need to look like people."

Hong Deming looked at him with more respect. "That makes a lot of sense," he said.

"I've seen demons in both places," he murmured, "but the ones that live among humans, the ones you can't tell apart from people, they are much worse than the ones with teeth and claws." He closed his eyes briefly, then opened them. "That's enough of that, then," he said briskly. "Do you have a spare blanket?"

He didn't, but he gave Wu Fan his to wrap up in, and stayed awake watching the stars.

It took four more days for them to reach the Stone Phoenix sect house, but Hong Deming bypassed it to bring Wu Fan directly into the city. He said that there was an old friend of his there, a courtesan from the Delicate Orchid who had come here to establish her own house. While, as Wu Fan insisted on saying, he was probably too old to get in the business directly, perhaps he could work for her in managing the house or training new talent. Hong Deming felt very strange about it all, yet Wu Fan wasn't wrong. He wasn't a eunuch, at some point he would outgrow the youthful beauty that attracted many men to brothels, and then what was he to do? A female courtesan or even an ordinary prostitute could hope to be redeemed by a doting client, or by producing a wanted child. A male courtesan, no matter how celebrated, would never have a client with that kind of devotion.

"You know your own business best," he said uncomfortably when they had found the pleasure quarters and Wu Fan's friend's pavilion, and there was nothing else to be said. "I'm sorry I can't offer you any more help."

"Hong Deming." Wu Fa stopped and turned to look full at him, his eyes serious.

"Yes?"

"You've been good to me, and I'm grateful. The only thing I could give you to thank you, you don't want, so instead…I wanted to tell you…" Wu Fan seemed to be turning over his words carefully. "This person, the person you really want, don't wait too long. I don't know why you can't be together already, but you need to settle this for yourself. My work means I've had to study a lot about these things, I've seen a lot…I know enough to tell you this, it's a burden on your heart. Even when you look at me, I see it in you."

"I don't–" He wanted to deny that he looked at Wu Fan, then realized it was pointless and looked at the ground instead.

Wu Fan ignored the interruption and continued. "If you're afraid this person doesn't want you back, you still need to know this, or you'll never be able to live without false hope. If you know they like you too, whatever obstacles there are, you need to overcome them. Go confess to them if you haven't, go be with them if you have, if you've had an argument make it up, apologize even if you're not in the wrong. Life is too short and unpredictable. You don't know when it might be too late."

Hong Deming was silent.

Wu Fan touched his hand. "This is the last time I'll offer."

"No," he said. "You're right. I should go find him."

Wu Fan nodded and turned away. "Thank you," he said, one last time, and walked up the stairs to the pavilion, gracefully, his head held high.

It hadn't been a year yet. Hong Deming rode to the Stone Phoenix sect thoughtfully, considering the gift Wu Fan had given him. Life is too short, after all. Why should they be forced to waste a year of loving one another, when years might be so few? He would go back. Even if they wouldn't let him enter Crane Moon, he would remain in one of the closest villages. Let Shen Lu say whatever he wanted about it, nothing said that wandering beyond the bounds started only one hundred miles out from the sect wards. He could wander in the gorge guarding against yaoguai there and waiting for Liu Chenguang to come out of seclusion if that was necessary.

Once he made that decision, he felt much more focused on getting the current task done: telling the Stone Phoenix disciples about the yaoguai he'd hunted in the mountains, and getting their insight as to the possible "master" of the evil spirits.

The sect leader of the Stone Phoenix recognized him as an allied cultivator, and welcomed him into the sect guest quarters. One of the senior disciples, who introduced himself as Ti Jinghua, sat down with him to offer tea, and to take a record of his yaoguai encounters in the mountains. It turned out that the Stone Phoenix specialized in yaoguai battles, and it was they who had noticed the increase in activity among all sorts of evil beings over the past several years.

Ti Jinghua wrote diligently as Hong Deming described the yaoguai he had fought, asking specific questions about each: how large? What shape? What color? Did any of these change during the battle? Where were they found? Did they flee or attack when challenged? What time of day? What damage had they done previously? What techniques were used? What had been useful, what had been ineffective? How long did the battle take? What was the result? Did the cultivator receive any injuries? And last, did the yaoguai speak, and if so, what did it say?

By the time they had completed going over the fifteen yaoguai he had fought and defeated in the past months, Hong Deming was ready to collapse in exhaustion, but Ti Jinghua was jubilant. "Excellent, excellent," he murmured, "there's a lot to learn here."

"Like what?" Hong Deming sipped his tea.

Although Ti Jinghua was a senior disciple, and had fought yaoguai himself, his air was far more that of a scholar than a fighter. Right now he was excited and eager to teach. He said, "There is a pattern. The yaoguai are moving into new areas, thus encountering new people who do not know how to be safe around them, thus leading to greater loss of life. Second, the yaoguai are becoming more aggressive. Not one of the yaoguai you fought tried to flee you, all of them attacked first and didn't try to escape even when you clearly had the upper hand."

"Is that unusual?"

"Very much so, yaoguai are cowardly more often than not. I suppose it's possible that there were yaoguai who tried to avoid you completely, which would make a different picture?"

"If so," he said, thinking back, "then in that region, those yaoguai were not attacking people at all. Every time I had a report of a yaoguai, I found it and it fought me. As you say. There were no reports where I didn't find the responsible yaoguai."

"Very diligent," he murmured. "So the pattern is definite. And thirdly, they all spoke."

"Also unusual?"

"Not necessarily, depending on the level of strength of the yaoguai. These were all of third rank strength according to the hierarchy we use in our Stone Phoenix records, but they were not weak. Such yaoguai do not always choose to speak, they can strategize whether it is worth their while. Yet every one of them spoke to you, and every one mentioned a master." He tapped his brush-end against his chin. "Thus we can assume that there is such a master, the master would be of first-rank, probably yaomo rather than yaoguai, an evil spiritual being rather than a being created through incomplete cultivation. Second-level yaoguai, and perhaps also other yao and yaomo depending on his strength, are his immediate subordinates. These mountain beings are simply along for the ride, hoping for rewards. The master wouldn't give these beings any instructions that he truly needed carried out, they're too unreliable and too remote."

Hong Deming looked at the table. "Several of them mentioned…"

"Yes, I remember," he said, "they said 'you are that one,' and that there would be an extra reward. Thus we can assume that this master desires your death, probably along with that of many others. Your death is almost certainly not his primary goal," he said analytically, "I don't mean to insult you, Hong Deming, but you can't possibly be that important to a first rank yaomo."

Hong Deming nodded. "I'm certainly not insulted," he said. "I'm going back after this to Crane Moon, what word should I bring?"

Ti Jinghua gave him some more tea and ordered the servant to bring more to eat, then left him while he consulted with the sect leader. When he returned, he looked solemn, and gave Hong Deming a written letter, sealed. "This is for your sect leader," he said, "for you, the gist of this is that there is a demon lord, a strong yaomo, moving among people. The yaomo is likely to have a human form and is unrecognizable as a yao. Given that the yaoguai recognize you and attack you, it is likely that the yaomo has had some encounter with you or with the Crane Moon sect or Peaceful River sect, as these are the only places where you have been in your life. It may not be about you personally," he said, consolingly. "If the yaomo has decided that the Crane Moon or Peaceful River sects are its enemies it may have ordered yaoguai to target anyone they find; it's just that you are the only one from your sect that has reported this to us."

Hong Deming took the letter, shocked. All of these things were happening under the surface, and who knew? When had he ever met a demon? He shook his head. Ti Jinghua said, "Don't be so surprised. If all sects paid more attention we would know more about these things, they are always there. Other sects do not always consider the yao world even though as cultivators defending against it should be our first priority." He bowed and added, "Your guest room is ready for tonight, and your horse will be ready for your departure tomorrow."

Hong Deming slept well, unworried about great yao or yaoguai attacks. He now had a perfect, watertight excuse to go back to Crane Moon and report to Shen Lu.

# CHAPTER 18
## RETURN TO CRANE MOON

HONG DEMING RODE up the gorge past the little village at the foot of the mountain, and left his horse there to be stabled, then began his climb up the first thousand steps. His heart was beating wildly, not because of the exertion, but imagining Chenguang's face after so many months, so much earlier than he would have thought. Perhaps a little bit of worry, about Shen Lu and Taiqian's reaction, but after all he had been sent back with a message by their ally, the sect leader of the Stone Phoenix. Even though he would have ignored their orders and come anyway they didn't need to know that, everyone's face could be saved this way. It was ideal.

At the first, lowest gate, he was challenged by two of his tainu on guard, who were visibly shocked to see him. "Hong Deming? Taine?" blurted out Shen Feng, Shen Lu's biological brother, in shock. "You're not supposed to—" He exchanged glances with Xia Zhiming behind him. "Go back down, taine," he said, "back to the village, you can't come up."

"I have a message for the sect leader," he said. "From Stone Phoenix, I'm charged to give it only to the sect leader from my own hand." This was a complete fabrication, of course, but he had already decided to insist on it.

"Wait here," said Shen Feng. "I'll go get tainu."

About half an hour later, during which Hong Deming politely remained silent while Xia Zhiming ignored him, Shen Lu hurried down behind Shen Feng, his face thunderous. "Taine," he said sternly, "you were warned, how dare you disobey my commands?"

Hong Deming formally saluted. "This disciple brings a message from the honored sect leader Qin Yuan," he said, offering it with both hands.

Shen Lu took it with little grace and opened the seal, reading through it. Afterward his face was calmer. "I see," he said. "You've done well on your journey, taine, the sect leader speaks highly of your skills and diligence." He tapped the scroll against his other hand for a moment, as though thinking what to do. At last, he said, as Hong Deming had hoped, "Come on up for one night so you can discuss this with Taiqian. He will want to hear details directly from you. Afterward, you must go back down, Taiqian and I may have new commands for you because of this development."

Hong Deming bowed again and followed up the next thousand steps. When they reached the gate to the second level, the largest one which held most of the buildings, Shen Lu looked at him directly. "Liu Chenguang is in seclusion," he said abruptly. "He will be in seclusion for at least three more months, according to Zhu Guiren."

"Thank you for telling me," he said, his heart sinking; but he had known it would probably be like this. Later, he would tell Shen Lu his plan of staying in the villages close by. Or perhaps not, perhaps he would just do it without telling him. He wondered if Liu Chenguang had received any of his letters. "When did he enter seclusion?"

"Almost as soon as we arrived," Shen Lu said, continuing through the gate. Hong Deming tried to hide his shock. "Don't worry, it's not like a normal seclusion, Zhu Guiren and Taiqian check on him regularly. It's part of his cultivation path."

"If they can see him—"

"No," Shen Lu said firmly. "No one else is allowed to enter, not even me. Only Taiqian and Master Zhu." He shrugged; his resentment at being left out was so evident that Hong Deming believed him. "Master Zhu says that Taiqian is assisting with his own spiritual power, since he himself doesn't have any, to direct something that has to be done at this juncture. Or something like that, it doesn't really make sense to me, to be honest, Zhu Guiren is full of words…"

Hong Deming went to his own little cell, where he found his old bed, books, and qin, just as he had left them. It seemed like a lifetime ago, that he had left seclusion with En, and then been sent out to Peaceful River.

Later on came word from Shen Lu that Taiqian was unavailable to meet that evening, but they would breakfast together in the morning to discuss the

Stone Phoenix's report and what was to be done about it. That was even better, he thought. After a good night's sleep he'd be much more prepared to talk with them and convince them to let him stay close by. He asked the messenger, a new little disciple only seven years old, his first martial nephew, to have the kitchen send up a tray for his meal.

Liu Chenguang's cell was just down the hall, though he had rarely used it compared to the amount of time he spent in seclusion. When it seemed that no one else was around, Hong Deming stole into it — no one locked doors in the sect dormitory — and sank down on the bed. It still had Liu Chenguang's scent of herbs and incense, even though he couldn't have slept in it for months now. The room was permeated with him. He curled up on it, breathing deeply, eyes closed, imagining that Chenguang was there, lying with him.

For some reason his eyes were wet, why? He would see him soon enough.

Chenguang's books were still on the rack. He had little appreciation for poetry, there were mostly medical treatises, star charts, and some history. The book of the Master of the Pathless Way was there, of course, and a heavily marked copy of the book of the Master of Heavenly Benevolence, which probably Chenguang shouldn't have had in a Pathless sect, where had he gotten it? Surely not from Zhu Guiren.

The letters he had sent were all there, in a neat pile. Someone had opened them, had read them. He touched them briefly, then left.

At dusk, he was in his favorite place, watching the sunset spark in the waterfall mist, when a woman came up to greet him. He looked up, surprised. The female disciples at Crane Moon had a separate place, except those who were married to senior disciples. They lived together with their spouses in individual homes on the third and highest level of the sect, but even they didn't come down into this area unless for a particular reason. The servants on this side of the sect home were all male as well. Yet this woman was dressed as a sect servant, her hair pulled up into a servant's simple coil.

She prostrated herself, shaking, as though something had terrified her.

"What is it?" he asked, frowning.

"You're Deming," she said. "You sent the letters."

He frowned even more; a servant shouldn't be using his personal name like this. "*Hong* Deming," he corrected.

The woman knelt up so he could see her face. She was very beautiful, with large dark eyes and delicate features, but her face was blotchy with tears. She whispered, "Please, master. Liu Chenguang?"

A chill ran down his back, all the hair on his arms rising. "What is it?" he asked, also whispering. There was something wrong, there was…

He had known it in his heart. There was something wrong.

The servant whispered, "Go to the spiritual caverns when the sun sets."

"Tell me first," he said.

"You, you will need to take him away," she said. "If you care about him, you can't leave him here. You must take him. Please."

The sun was already set; the fire in the waterfall had turned to grey mist.

"I will meet you down at the stables," she said, "I will have a good horse ready." She turned and fled along the wall, back toward the women's quarters.

Hong Deming ran for the entrance to the caverns.

No one went to the caverns to play or to explore; there was no ward, no guard. Normally.

Now there was a ward.

Hong Deming swore and ran back to his room for his qin, feeling as though time was running out on something, though he couldn't imagine what. Liu Chenguang had been in seclusion for months already, would be for months more, Taiqian was checking on him, what could have gone wrong? With the qin in his hand, running back to the entrance, dodging to avoid the notice of other disciples who were out on their evening walks after dinner, chatting animatedly about this and that, he wondered why he was so certain that he could trust that strange servant woman. It was only because he had already known, he had known there was something, some reason he needed to return. Those tears in Liu Chenguang's bed, where had they come from? He had known.

At the ward, he set himself with the qin across his lap and closed his eyes, sensing the patterns. This couldn't be rushed, however much he wanted to; a wrong note would strengthen the ward and alert whomever had set it. When he was confident that he understood how the ward had been set, he plucked out a short, echoing melody, and broke it.

There was a noise in the cavern of multiple breaths, and something else, a sound that picked at his memory but that he couldn't identify. He followed the breaths through the dark, and felt his way along a wall, realizing that the darkness was becoming only dimness, and then becoming bright. A room, only one room, one cavern, had been lit with spiritual lights, dancing about its ceiling to illuminate three people. One of them stood by the wall, hands behind his back, observing the second person, who was using a spiritual sword to carefully cut into the arms and legs and torso of a third person, a nearly naked person. The sound he had heard, the sound without a name, was the sound of the sword cutting deeply into the flesh. The cuts went on repeatedly, over and over again, as they healed and they were cut once more, an endlessly repeated execution.

The person being cut was a young man, obviously unconscious, his frame small and thin, wearing only the light, short trousers usually hidden beneath robes. His long black hair fell unnoticed from the low couch where he lay onto the floor, where it puddled like ink. Where the sword cut, blood oozed and poured and spurted, caught into channels cut into the stone couch like the channel of the waterfall by the cliff where he had just been sitting. All the captured blood poured in a slow, thin waterfall from one corner of the couch into an open bowl, making occasionally a low burbling sound. Hong Deming stared at the blood fall for a frozen moment, unable to look again at Liu Chenguang's naked body.

Hong Deming launched himself at Taiqian, not even taking his sword out, tackling him to the ground bodily and throwing Taiqian's sword into a corner. He realized, dimly, that he was screaming.

After Taiqian was on the ground he went for Zhu Guiren, standing by the wall. For this he used his sword. Just before En stabbed him in the heart, with a clang Taiqian blocked him.

He retreated and stood in front of Liu Chenguang, gasping for air in distress, his rhythm of breath completely broken. "I will kill you," he said. "I will kill you both."

Zhu Guiren sighed and pushed Taiqian's sword away where it blocked in front of his face. "Hong Deming. This is part of his cultivation–"

"THIS IS NOT CULTIVATION!" he roared. "What are you doing to him? How could you? Taiqian!"

Taiqian looked at him with no hint of warmth. "You were told not to be here," he said. "This is why, we knew you would act this way. We didn't want to worry you. However, all of our care was evidently for nothing." Suddenly he shouted, "Useless disciple, why are you not kneeling to ask for my forgiveness? How dare you lay your hands on your sect father?"

"No," he said, his voice shaking with rage. "I will not."

Zhu Guiren, his voice smooth, said, "Now, now, as your Taiqian said, we knew this would distress you to see, thus you should never have seen it. But now that you have, we can explain. You know, I believe, that Liu Chenguang's–"

"Do not say his name," he said, low and fierce. "You are not qualified."

Zhu Guiren coughed. "Very well. This person's cultivation includes a certain power in the blood. This power is actually too high for him to manage and will eventually destroy his meridians and kill him. This process of bleeding allows us to remove some of the overflowing qi. Believe me, he will heal from it. Look now, you see? The cuts are already closed."

He risked a brief glance. They were closed, that was true. But there were also scars, Many, many layers of scars.

"You are seeking death," he whispered.

"What?" Zhu Guiren asked, apparently taken completely by surprise.

"Hong Deming," said Taiqian. "Be silent."

He was silent, but didn't release En.

Zhu Guiren glanced at Taiqian, then continued. "In addition, as you know, we are working to support the new dynasty in order to bring stability back to the Divine Land. Liu Che– This person's blood may help in that it is an ingredient in the elixir of immortality, which we can then present to the Son of Heaven. Your sect leader understands. Liu Chenguang has agreed to all of this."

Hong Deming stared at Zhu Guiren, his cold and perfect face, and considered trusting him. Then he looked back at Liu Chenguang. He was so thin. Beneath his closed eyes were dark circles like black bruises. The scars covered him all over, everywhere but his face and neck; pink scars that were new, white scars that were older, red scars from tonight, still trickling and oozing blood.

"No," he said. "You tricked him, or you drugged him, or he didn't understand." He took a step backward, released En, then turned swiftly and picked Liu Chenguang up bodily. He was pathetically light, and didn't wake up. He smelled like blood and death. "I am taking him," he said. "If you try to stop me, I will kill you both right here."

Taiqian sent a sword pulse at him, and Hong Deming quickly shifted Liu Chenguang over one shoulder to have his sword hand free, blocking the strike. Forcing himself to bottle up his rage and keep his breathing smooth, he leapt out of the way, behind Taiqian, and sent a sword pulse at him in return. It missed, but shattered the stone couch. Liu Chenguang's blood poured from the bowl all over the floor in little rivers, and Zhu Guiren fell to the ground, trying to gather it up with a small crystal chalice.

He was closer to the entrance to the cavern, but he didn't dare turn his back on Taiqian, so Hong Deming gently lay Liu Chenguang down again on the rock, and then ran to meet him, slashing his sword down. Taiqian blocked and blocked again, then shouted in rage and slashed down toward Hong Deming's wrist, but Hong Deming spun, sent a sword pulse at Zhu Guiren to keep him away, and then landed behind Taiqian's back and reached out to quickly strike his acupoints, temporarily paralyzing his legs and arms.

Taiqian fell heavily to the stone, and Zhu Guiren crawled toward him, one leg dragging limp from Hong Deming's second sword pulse, making tracks through Liu Chenguang's blood. His eyes met Hong Deming's, glittering in such open malevolence that Hong Deming froze.

Taiqian shouted, his face twisted in fury, "I repudiate you. You are no longer a member of the sect. Every cultivator's hand is turned against you from this day, false son, traitorous disciple, thief of the sect's teachings."

Hong Deming's heart hurt for one moment, and then it was gone, a white scar. He said, "I don't care."

He ran out and leapt down the cliff, rock to rock, tree to tree, carrying Chenguang's body from which his soul seemed to have fled. If he hadn't felt the heartbeat through the visible ribs, he would have thought him dead.

At that thought, he almost lost his qinggong, but then recovered, and kept racing down.

The servant woman was there, outside the stables, a saddled horse with bags of provisions on a rein next to her. "Go, go," she whispered, looking all around. "When Liu Chenguang wakes up, tell him that there is a yaomo here. You must take him far away. Take him to the eastern sacred mountain."

Hong Deming nodded and mounted up, putting a robe the servant woman offered onto Chenguang's unresisting body. The servant woman brought out strong silk ribbons and tied Liu Chenguang's hands to the saddle, then wrapped his legs and tied them together beneath the horse's belly: uncomfortable had he been conscious, but a wise precaution since Hong Deming might need his arms free to fight. "Are you coming?" he asked.

"I would only slow you down, I will find my own way and meet you there," the servant woman said. "Go now."

"What is your name? How do you know—"

"There's no time. He'll know who I am when you give him the message. Go, go!" She whistled something at the horse, hard and shrill, and they were off.

In a nightmare, Hong Deming galloped down through the gorge, holding Liu Chenguang against him as much as he could to shield him from the roughness of the ride. Once out of the gorge into the wide flatlands around the Cui River, he veered off the road into the forest, riding along the riverbank in the hopes of finding a ferry to bring them across. His mind was a snowstorm of blank white and wind, thinking only of how cold Chenguang's body was, how he had lost so much blood, how he was dressed only in a single robe against the chill of the night, how they would soon be followed and when word got out every cultivator would be bound to attack them. How to reach Mount Shi without using the highways that went past Zhashan and Gunan where they would certainly be found. How there was a yaomo at Crane Moon.

He didn't dare try to swim the horse across the river, not with Chenguang like this, so he had to lose hours riding along the bank until he found a boat that some fisherman or ferryman had left unguarded. He would have to leave the horse, but there were always more horses in the world. Laying Chenguang gently on the bottom of the boat, he removed the saddle and tack from the horse and threw it in the river, and took the saddlebags of provisions on his shoulders, then slapped the horse's rump so it would run. It would, unfortunately, probably run back to the sect, but it seemed too cruel to kill it. Hopefully some peasant would find it first and take it home, muddying the trail.

On the other side of the river, he cut a hole in the bottom of the boat, then sank it.

Still dazed, he carried Chenguang into the forest of the mountains on the other side of the river, cradling him bridal style since he was still too deeply unconscious to hold on, the saddlebags over his shoulder. With his qinggong Hong Deming could move much more quickly than an ordinary person, and went quite far before the weight and his sick heart told on him. At last he had to admit defeat, at least until he could sleep and cultivate and rejuvenate his qi.

He didn't dare to make a fire, either, not when searchers would probably already be out. He dug into the packs for blankets and extra robes, and wrapped Liu Chenguang in them. Then, on second thought, he sat beneath a tree and held him, sitting up, with Chenguang's back to his chest, comforted in his arms. He placed the blankets over them both, so that as much of Chenguang's body as possible could be held and warmed. He looked down at Chenguang's pale face, drooping against him, and bent his own head down, as though he could be a shield for him against all the cold and the darkness.

A long time later, but still well before dawn, he felt Chenguang stirring against him, and his heart leapt. "Chenguang," he called gently, kissing his hair that was still clotted with blood. "Chenguang, wake up, Deming is here."

His eyes opened, bleary. "Tainu," he said, "what…" He tried to sit up, and couldn't. "What happened to me?" His eyes fixed on Hong Deming's, confused and uncertain.

"I took you from the sect," he said. "Taine, they were hurting you."

"What do you mean, you took me?" He tried to sit up again, and succeeded slightly, his eyes focusing a bit more. "Tainu, what happened, why are you here, where are we? Are we in the woods?"

"In the woods, somewhere, across the river." He hesitated. "Hiding."

"I was– I was in seclusion?" He raised a shaking hand to his own forehead. "That's the last thing I remember, going into the caverns, what happened? Why am I like this?"

Hong Deming paused for a while, trying to think how to say it. "Zhu Guiren was having Taiqian…cut you, all over your body, making you bleed," he said. "He said you agreed to it as part of your cultivation."

"I didn't agree to it," he said, frowning, "but it shouldn't matter…it shouldn't…"

Hong Deming swallowed, trying to get the picture out of his mind; he was afraid it would always be there. "They were…collecting your blood. Zhu Guiren said that they could make the elixir of immortality out of it."

"He said *what?*" Liu Chenguang's voice became sharper, more like himself. "I would never have agreed to *that*, that's just ridiculous, there's no such thing, and he knows it too, we've talked about it."

"He said you would help by bringing the mandate of heaven for the emperor."

"What?" He leaned his head against Hong Deming's chest, exhausted again. "Tainu, I don't understand, what is he talking about?" Tears suddenly leaked from beneath his closed eyes. "Tainu, why do I feel this way? My body hurts… all over…"

Hong Deming's heart ached. He tried to gather him up, as gently as possible, murmuring, "Taine…"

Liu Chenguang was crying without any sound, tears falling. "Everything is burning, my body is burning all over, tainu, I'm frightened." He ran his hand over his own forearm, feeling the raised scars, bewildered. "There are scars, how can there be scars, how can it be?"

"Shh, shhh…" Hong Deming rocked him back and forth, trying to comfort him. "It's only scars. Scars mean you're healing," he said meaninglessly, "you will feel better soon, you're away from there now." He wished he had killed them all. "You're getting warm because you are getting feverish, that's all, it's better than before, you were so cold…"

Liu Chenguang looked up at him, eyes fever-bright. "But tainu, I can't get fevers, I can't…"

Hong Deming held him, kissed his forehead, brought his hands into his chest to warm them. "I'm here, taine," he said, "sleep, tomorrow will be better."

At last Liu Chenguang settled again into normal, if somewhat fevered, sleep, his heart beating strongly, his body alive against him even if so fragile. Hong Deming kissed the top of his head, all that he could reach now that he was nestled down, curled up to rest on him. He leaned back against the tree for a few hours of sleep, until dawn.

The next morning, Liu Chenguang was noticeably better. If his cultivational powers of self-healing were still damaged, they were still certainly better than most people's; after a night sleeping in the woods, preceded by months of blood loss and torture, he awoke with the fever broken. Hong Deming still held him in his arms, unwilling to let him go, as he examined his own arms and his body silently in the dawn light.

Liu Chenguang looked up at him from his position leaning against his chest when his self-examination was complete. At last he said, his voice calm and clinical, "They must have given me something, some kind of drug or spirit-blocking spell. Even with what they were doing to me, even for as long as they did it, I shouldn't have scars like this."

Hong Deming simply nodded, not caring about the mystery of the scars. Having seen what they were doing to him, he wasn't surprised by them at all. How many nights over the past months must they have cut him, to have so many of such varying ages? He bit back his rage. "We need to keep going," he said, "but we also need to hide for a while till you can get your strength back."

"It won't take long," Liu Chenguang said, confidently, but he still couldn't quite walk on his own when they got up. Hong Deming made him ride on his back for most of the day, and he could feel that for much of it he was sleeping. That was fine, as long as he could still hold on. Sleep was the best thing for him, the thing he would most need to heal, and he was still so very light to carry. Hong Deming had seldom crossed the Cui before and he wasn't completely certain of his ground, but he thought that within the day he should reach a village partway up the mountain, one with an inn and an apothecary.

He woke up Liu Chenguang as they came to the outskirts, and he was already recovered enough to walk the rest of the way into town, so as not to make too much of a fuss. Liu Chenguang was wearing a very dark blue robe, almost black, that the servant woman had found somewhere, and with his incredibly pale skin and unbound, blood-tangled black hair he looked like a very beautiful ghost exploring the daylight world. The villagers stood up in the fields to watch them as they walked by. Liu Chenguang looked down at the ground, embarrassed.

"It's my turn this time," Hong Deming said, encouragingly. "I'm at least as good as Zhu Guiren at finding an inn."

Liu Chenguang smiled. "Tainu, if there's more than one inn in this place I would be very surprised."

"True," he admitted. "I will get us the best room in town."

It was not as fine as the inn they had visited in Gunan, of course, but there was one good room with a decent bed and table, it was clean, and they sent up hot water immediately. Liu Chenguang stripped without any consideration of shyness and got right in, eager to wash the dried blood off his skin and hair. Hong Deming watched with his eyes wide and then turned around.

"Come help me," Liu Chenguang called. "I hate this feeling, this blood on my skin, help me get it all off." He held up a bathing cloth, already washing with his other hand. "Can you ask them to send up some dried herbs for the bath, too? And more water?"

He yelled out the door at the innkeeper — they were the only guests — and returned to where Liu Chenguang was scrubbing at his skin with the cloth. "Not so hard, you'll open the wounds–" he said.

"No, that can't happen," Liu Chenguang replied, "they are closed now for good, I can feel a little bit of power coming back. Can you check?" He held out his arm, and Hong Deming checked the pulse. He wasn't an expert, but he could feel that the qi was settling back into normal patterns, and sighed with relief.

"Are you still in pain?" he asked, picking up the bathing cloth and carefully stroking Liu Chenguang's back with it, trying not to press too hard.

Liu Chenguang shivered, and laughed, turning his head back over his shoulder to smile at him. "Not like that, tainu, or we will be doing something else besides bathing soon."

Hong Deming turned bright red and dropped the cloth into the water, then had to feel around inside the tub for it, touching Liu Chenguang in all sorts of inappropriate places. Liu Chenguang finally reached down and found the cloth himself, handing it back to him. "Deming," he said, "it's all right, really. I'm not hurt any more. I don't know what they did to me, but I'll heal. Please don't be scared for me, all right? You don't need to worry that I'll break." He reached out and touched his arm briefly. "Just get the blood off of me. Can you pour water over my head? My hair feels disgusting." As he obediently rinsed out his long hair, Liu Chenguang added, "So that's what it feels like, to be sick…how awful. No wonder people are so desperate for healing."

"You've never been sick at all?"

"Never…just those times when I had the weakness of my qi and I was unconscious, but that was just like sleeping, I didn't feel anything. It's so awful to feel pain in your body when it doesn't go away."

The second batch of hot water came up, this one with herbs to give a nice scent. Liu Chenguang stood up to rinse and then went to the second tub, standing, pouring more water over his hair a few times. Hong Deming took his unspoken invitation to look openly at him and thought, despite the scars — all turning white now — how beautiful he was, every part of him. He felt his body becoming aroused and closed his eyes for a few moments to get things under control. He hadn't slept more than a few hours for two nights now, with all the exertion of taking Liu Chenguang from the sect and their flight here, and before he realized it, he had fallen asleep sitting up.

It felt like the deep night when he woke up, still sitting in the chair. At the table, he saw Liu Chenguang sitting fully dressed in that dark blue robe, now with his hair clean and the scent of herbs rather than blood. He must have gone out to the apothecary, he was preparing something at the table, chopping and grinding herbs and putting them into small paper wrappings. He looked up at him and smiled. "You're awake, tainu," he said. "The innkeeper's second daughter has a weakness of the liver, I'm making some medicine for them to give her."

Hong Deming stood up and stretched, yawning. "I needed to sleep, what about you, are you getting medicine for yourself?"

Liu Chenguang tapped a second batch of packets. "I pre-made these so we can take them on the road with us, they'll help strengthen my blood and purify it, I can't tell what drugs they gave me but these will help." He looked up expectantly. "Where are we going?"

"Mount Shi," he said, sitting down at next to him, and aimlessly picking up one of the packets. He was a little worried about how Liu Chenguang would take this, and a little curious as well. "Did you read any of my letters?"

"You wrote me letters?" Liu Chenguang's eyes warmed at him. "No, they put me into seclusion right away when I arrived. Did you bring them with you so I can read them?"

"No, there wasn't time." He thought more. "Liu Chenguang, do you know a woman who is a servant at Crane Moon?"

"No?" he replied curiously.

"I just came, it hasn't been a year but I didn't want to wait so long." Liu Chenguang's eyes warmed even more. "I had a message for Taiqian and Shen Lu, that was my good excuse to come back…I didn't know anything was wrong with you until a woman servant came to me. She knew me even though I've never seen her. She said 'You wrote the letters.' How would that servant woman know? How could a servant woman even read?"

Liu Chenguang's eyes sharpened, but he didn't respond.

Hong Deming continued, "She was the one who said I needed to get you out, she sent me into the caverns to find you, and she told me to give you a message. She said you would know who she was."

Reluctantly, Liu Chenguang said, "She's most likely my relative, my older sibling. She must have come looking for me when I was in seclusion, I didn't know she was there…"

Hong Deming, shocked, said, "You have relatives?"

Liu Chenguang shook his head. "I haven't seen my sibling since before I met you, that's not important. What was the message?"

Hong Deming didn't want to let this subject go, but there truly were more urgent matters. "She said you needed to go to Mount Shi, and to tell you that there is an evil yaomo at Crane Moon. A demon."

Liu Chenguang's face became, if possible, even paler. The packet he had been holding in his hand dropped to the table. "You have to get away," he said, his voice low and shaking. "Hong Deming. If there's a yaomo—"

"It's all right, Chenguang," he reached out and held his hands in both of his, folding them together. "It's all right. I've been fighting yaoguai all this time. I know how to do it — there's nothing to be afraid of…"

"You don't understand. A demon will never give up. It will come after me to the ends of the earth, as long as it has a trace to follow." Liu Chenguang put his head down on top of their folded hands. "I need to— I need to fully recover, then I can get away and hide, I'm not able now— Hong Deming, you can't stay near me—"

"No," he said sharply. "Taine, listen, I'm not leaving you. I'll get you to Mount Shi. Will that be safe for you?"

"Safer, not completely safe…but it's so far. Deming, please." His eyes were wide and terrified. "I can't bear it if you're hurt for me."

"Could you get there on your own, taine?" he asked. "Be honest."

Liu Chenguang was still for a few moments before answering, seeming to consider his own resources. "Being honest, not now. I need a few months to fully recover before I could…on my own."

"I am not leaving you anywhere for a few months," Hong Deming said. "I am not leaving you anywhere for even a day. A few hours is all you're going to have to yourself until we get to Mount Shi."

Liu Chenguang shook his head. "Tainu, I can't…I can't defend myself." It seemed as though it took a great deal of effort for him to admit this. "I can only run and hide. Do you know how it would be for me, if you were hurt or killed trying to protect me?"

"It's not a safe world," he replied. "I've been away for you for more than half a year. And I've been attacked by fifteen yaoguai–"

"Fifteen!"

"–and who knows how many bandits, I stopped counting. Before that when Peaceful River was attacked, cultivators as well attacked me. And I'm fine. And none of that was because of you. It will be all right, taine. Don't worry so much."

Liu Chenguang shook his head again. "Fifteen yaoguai? So many. What's happening?" He accepted without demur that the yaomo and yaoguai existed and were a real danger. There was no surprise in his voice.

Hong Deming looked at his face, pale in the candlelight, his dark eyes thoughtful and distant, and wondered, *Chenguang, who are you, what are you? Where did you come from, before we found you? Why does the yaomo want you, why will it keep pursuing you?*

In the end, though, he didn't ask because it didn't make a difference at all. This person was his person, always.

Instead, he said, "Liu Chenguang…I shouldn't call you taine anymore, and you shouldn't call me tainu. I left the sect. We're not martial siblings anymore."

"I'll call you tainu if I want to," he said stubbornly. "But Deming, what happened? The sect is your family. Family is important."

Hong Deming noticed that he didn't say *the sect is our family,* and felt sad for him. But that was all in the past now. "I attacked Taiqian because he was hurting you, and took you away. I disobeyed him and injured him. He repudiated me." He didn't go into the fact that as a traitor to the sect, all cultivators from the Crane Moon and their allies would challenge him on sight. If Liu Chenguang didn't already realize it, he wouldn't add to his worries. "We can't go back there, Chenguang."

Liu Chenguang knelt next to him. Hong Deming looked down at his eyes, dark and longing, and felt his heart move inside him, his hand reaching out to touch Chenguang's hair. From the bath he was wearing nothing to keep his hair back, and a long lock flowed uninterrupted down in front of his temple past his collarbone, blocking the edge of his eye a little bit. Carefully, with great care because he wanted so much to do more, Hong Deming picked it up, warm and smooth, and stroked it back behind his ear. He kept two fingers on his ear, trac-ing its curves, feeling the heat of Chenguang's skin, watching him shiver slightly and breathe in at his touch.

Liu Chenguang reached up and touched his cheek, then drew his fingers down to his lips. Hong Deming softly kissed Liu Chenguang's fingertips. Liu Chenguang leaned forward, his eyes half closed, to meet his lips with his own. "Deming," he said, breathing into him, "didn't you know? Since the beginning, since we met, since we were children, I've only stayed for you."

# CHAPTER 19
## FLIGHT

THE NEXT MORNING, Liu Chenguang couldn't get out of bed immediately, for which Hong Deming blamed himself and ran down to the innkeeper to demand an extravagant congee for breakfast and hot water for bathing. By the time the hot water arrived, Chenguang was laughing, sitting up and tossing pieces of leftover ginseng root peel at him from his medical packets. "I'll have to make you a tea to fix your anxiety and keep your vitality strong," he said, and threw another piece of ginseng. "Have them send up hot water in a teapot too."

Hong Deming blushed and said, "Are you all right? I didn't mean to hurt you."

"I told you, I'm fine, it only hurt for a bit," he said. "I'm well now. Very well." He smiled innocently, eyes sparkling. "Would you like to make sure?"

"*Chenguang*," he said, and silently recited some scripture. "Enough, eat breakfast, we need to plan."

Hong Deming used his chopsticks to draw a map of tea on the table. "Mount Shi is here," he said, "and the quickest road to it is the road east along the Sorrowful River, but that road is heavily-traveled and passes the great cities. The slower way, if we are trying to hide, would be to stay near the edges of the northern mountains and travel that way, but it would be much more difficult. I'm not even sure we could ride all the way."

Liu Chenguang looked carefully at the tea map. "I'm familiar with a lot of these paths," he said, "the high ones through the mountains. There are also paths we could take around the cities."

"Do you think Zhu Guiren is a yaomo?" Hong Deming asked suddenly.

Liu Chenguang nodded slowly. "It is possible it's Taiqian," he said, "but Zhu Guiren is more likely, of the people at Crane Moon. I've never seen any sign of demonic power from him, he says he doesn't have any spiritual power at all, but if he is a strong yaomo of course he could hide it if he chooses to. And he...he never wanted me to be away from him. A yaomo would be like that if he had... me." He looked up and said, "He was very angry whenever he found me with you, and I couldn't understand it. I think he thought you might take me away." He smiled. "Which of course you have."

Eventually they decided on the plan of staying as close to the mountainous areas as possible, traveling over ridges by foot using their qinggong, slower but harder to find, they hoped. Hong Deming wanted to avoid meeting cultivators above all.

Unfortunately, however, staying in the mountains seemed to attract yaoguai instead.

Ten days later Hong Deming wiped his forehead and looked down at the latest contender, a creature that seemed to have cultivated from a poisonous vine. Its thorny tendrils still whipped around even though En had cut it into dozens of pieces, some of them growing new limbs and trying to attack one final time. He took a deep breath and put his hands in the demon-quelling seal, and sent qi into En, stabbed into the creature's largest part, for the tenth time in ten days.

Liu Chenguang came up to him from where he had been waiting off to the side. "I'm so useless," he said, frustrated. He put his hands on Hong Deming's back to transfer qi to him, but Hong Deming shook him off.

"You don't have enough," he said, leaning on En.

"Neither do you," Liu Chenguang said, his eyes sweeping over the yaoguai pieces dissolving on the ground. "Every time you have less for the final strike. I can tell."

Hong Deming sighed and reached out for him. Liu Chenguang squeezed his hand. "I have some medicines I can give you," he said, "and acupuncture tonight to stimulate the meridians. I'm getting better, soon I'll be able to help you more. Do you have any injuries?"

"Just this, a thorn got me," he said, pulling his hair aside to show a festering scratch on the back of his shoulder, leaking red and yellow fluid, and showing red threads running out into his flesh from all directions.

"It must have been very poisonous," Liu Chenguang muttered, and bit his finger to spread blood on it. But nothing happened. Liu Chenguang swore vociferously. "Still nothing, when will it come back?" He leaned forward and sucked the poison out of the wound, spitting it out on the ground vehemently. Then he reached into his sleeves for a healing powder and sprinkled it on. "Deming," he said, seriously, "we may need to go down to the highway after all. You can't keep going on like this."

"Would it be safer for me to have to fight cultivators?" he said, a little angry. "No matter what I'll still be fighting."

"It would be safer," Liu Chenguang said firmly. "These yaoguai are harder to fight than humans, even strong humans, and they take too much of your spiritual energy to disperse them. If you have a serious injury, I can't heal you right now." He took his hand again. "Deming, we're trying to hide, but I think these yaoguai have been sent, they are looking for us, we've been attacked so frequently, and we're not deep in the mountains at all to be encountering them so often by accident. I think we need to accept that hiding is useless now, and try speed instead. We need to go down."

Hong Deming kicked at the remaining dried leaves of the yaoguai. "I don't want to fight people," he said at last. "People I may know."

"I know." Liu Chenguang looked up at the sky. Gently, he said, "Deming, you can leave me. Just find a cave, set a ward for me, I'll cultivate and heal on my own."

He shook his head stubbornly. "No. I won't leave you again."

"I wouldn't be that much safer at Mount Shi. It's only a sacred place with a strong ward, that's all."

"No. Mount Shi is so far away, surely the yaomo will give up chasing you by then."

"No. He won't."

Hong Deming turned to go. "All right then. We'll go down and get horses."

Liu Chenguang stood and watched him walk down the slope, then sighed and followed him into the trees.

Days later, they were on the highway between Zhashan and Gunan, going as fast as they could. Hong Deming hadn't brought much money, so they couldn't afford to change horses regularly or ride these into the ground, as he would have liked to; they needed to let them rest sometimes at a walk rather than galloping all day. While they'd been in the mountains they'd been able to sleep on the ground, and gather food for free with Liu Chenguang's foraging skills, but now they would have to stay in inns and buy food as well. So many opportunities to be caught, so many places where they were leaving a trail to be followed. Hong Deming's skin crawled every time they passed a traveler on the road, or rode past the turnoff to a sect house.

Mo Xiang caught them at evening, just before Sanmen, on an empty stretch of road.

"Hong Deming!"

Hong Deming closed his eyes briefly. They had been so lucky, and they had come so far, but their luck had run out.

Mo Xiang stood on the road in front of them, and raised his qin. "Traitor and betrayer. Please," he said with exaggerated courtesy, "show me your skills."

Liu Chenguang stepped back out of the way. "You're next," Mo Xiang added. "Prepare yourself."

Hong Deming couldn't very well say that Liu Chenguang couldn't fight, but this made it crucial that he defeat Mo Xiang quickly, before he was able to attack Chenguang. He drew En. "Come then," he said, "I look forward to learning from you."

Mo Xiang's qin strikes came fast, doubling one upon the other, filling the entire space of the roadway. Hong Deming was tired from traveling and the residual spiritual weariness of the fights in the mountains, but his qi was almost fully restored. Sword against qin, he needed to block the qin attacks that Mo Xiang sent from all directions, before he could find an opening to attack himself. He sent a pulse of sword energy toward the qin, but Mo Xiang had already jumped aside, using his own qinggong. Hong Deming had often lost qin battles at Peaceful River, and Mo Xiang was one of the best. A sword was more powerful on attack, but the qin was very difficult to completely defend against with only a sword.

Hong Deming took a qin strike to his back and then to his shoulder, unable to block everything when three qin strikes came from three different directions; Mo Xiang's qinggong was very impressive, allowing him to strike and leap to a new position and strike again almost faster than Hong Deming's eyes could follow. Hong Deming flipped into the air and tried to gain a high position, but a powerful qin blow took down the tree he had landed on, and he had to leap again.

He held his flying crane position in midair for a moment, sending three sword pulses out, one to where Mo Xiang was, two to where he thought he might be next, and came down to lightly touch the ground and leap away. Another qin strike took him in the knee, a bad strike for him, and he had to fall to the ground and roll away, but one of his own sword pulses had taken Mo Xiang in the chest, and he was coughing blood.

Hong Deming staggered upright. He couldn't put any weight on his knee yet, but he leapt from the working leg straight upward to avoid a qin strike. It passed beneath him, and he flipped backward to land, again, on his weak leg and fall, again, and have to roll. This time, Mo Xiang went for him with a sword, and caught him on the forearm; if he had had a better angle, Hong Deming would have lost his left hand. Hong Deming's blood spattered heavily on the ground.

Out of the corner of his eye, he saw Liu Chenguang move forward, distressed. "No!" he yelled, hit his own acupoints to stop the bleeding, and rolled back up, spinning with En to send a sword pulse and then a slash: the pulse at the qin, the slash at Mo Xiang's right arm. It took him deep in the elbow, and he staggered backward.

With that wound Mo Xiang could no longer use the qin beyond single notes, and would have to switch fully to sword. This meant that he had lost, because he was far below Hong Deming in sword skill, and must have known it. Nonetheless, he refused to yield, leaping up with his qinggong and coming down, shouting out his battle cry and slashing down with his most powerful strike. Because he couldn't move quickly on the bad leg, it caught Hong Deming glancingly in the shoulder — glancing, but enough to cut deeply into the muscle above his collarbone. It was the same shoulder that had already received a qin strike. That arm was now completely useless, and although Hong Deming could fight with either hand, now one was unusable, the other still bleeding from the slash to the wrist.

Hong Deming gritted his teeth, hit the acupoints on his shoulder and chest with the bleeding hand that still could move, and spun to release a final sword pulse at Mo Xiang, using much more qi than he ever had before in a single sword strike. It threw Mo Xiang into the air and back more than ten body lengths to crash heavily against the ground, bleeding from all his orifices and vomiting blood.

Hong Deming limped over to him to see that he was still alive. Liu Chenguang also came up, pale, and lifted a bleeding hand to Hong Deming's worst visible wound, the cut into his collar and shoulder muscles. He felt that something happened; the bleeding stopped and the pain lessened, but it didn't instantly heal. Liu Chenguang clenched his fists.

"Mo Xiang," Hong Deming said, struggling not to fall over, "I've beaten you."

Mo Xiang spat blood and mucus at him. It landed on his lower robe, making a glutinous red stain.

Hong Deming stared at him. He knew he should kill him, for their safety, for Liu Chenguang's safety.

"Will he live?" he asked Liu Chenguang.

Liu Chenguang knelt down and tried to check his pulse, but Mo Xiang spat at him as well and jerked his arm out of his hands. "He may," Liu Chenguang said finally. "If someone comes to help him." He looked up at Hong Deming. "I could help him."

Hong Deming looked at Mo Xiang again, remembering. Mo Xiang looked at him bleeding and nearly unconscious, his limbs all at strange angles, eyes full of hatred.

"It's because of you," Mo Xiang suddenly said, his voice thick with blood. "Because of you. My brother is dead. Zhu Guiren had him killed. You told that piece of stained filth next to you and he told his master."

Liu Chenguang said, "Hong Deming never mentioned your brother to me. I don't even know who you are."

Mo Xiang spat at him again.

Hong Deming said at last, "Do it."

Swiftly, Liu Chenguang struck Mo Xiang's acupoints to freeze his movements, checked his pulse, struck other acupoints to stop and start bleeding, and took some medicinal powder from his sleeves, carefully sprinkling it on the visible wounds. Then he bit his finger, and touched his lips.

"I don't have enough power now to heal immediately or fully," Liu Chenguang said quietly, "but he won't die of these wounds." He stood up.

"Let's go," said Hong Deming, walking back toward the road. "Take his horse with us, we need a spare."

Neither of them spoke much for a while. It was night now, but they rode hard, past several towns on the roundabout paths, at last finding an inn near midnight in a small village.

That night, Liu Chenguang tried again to heal Hong Deming's wounds. His blood closed them fully, but it was not a full healing, there was still pain and Hong Deming didn't have a full range of movement. "I don't think my blood is healing the internal wounds," Liu Chenguang, said, his voice low and frustrated, "from the qin. I'm not able to do what I want to do yet."

Hong Deming lay quietly on the bed, aching all over, his heart as well as his body. "Mo Xiang," he said after a while. "He was my friend at Peaceful River. He must have thought…thought I told you that his brother doesn't like the emperor…but…"

Liu Chenguang sat next to him, and interlaced their fingers, looking at their hands together. "I'm sorry," he said at last. "All this has happened to you because of me. You've lost so much."

"Don't cry."

"I won't cry, why should I cry." Liu Chenguang stared fixedly at the opposite wall for a moment. "Tomorrow turn around and go back, I can go from here on my own."

"Don't be ridiculous." He was too tired to soften it. "There's no point, Chenguang, I can't turn around now and say 'I'm sorry,' no one is going to accept that apology unless maybe I bring you back with me as proof of my repentance. This is not the kind of thing where Taiqian makes me face the wall and reflect on my shortcomings."

Liu Chenguang said, "Then take me back with you. When I'm recovered I can escape on my own, I promise you I can."

"How long do you need to recover."

"Six weeks, I think?"

Hong Deming closed his eyes, exhausted beyond belief. "This is a stupid conversation. I won't do that. Come here and lie next to me." He felt Chenguang's body next to him, warming him, Chenguang's scent surrounding him, his hair brushing his arm as he lay on his side next to him, carefully extending an arm across his chest to hold him without touching the huge bruises from the qin strikes. Hong Deming brought his own hand across, heavily because of the aching pains, to touch his head briefly. "Just sleep, taine," he said, too tired to think well. "It will be all right."

He drifted off, knowing that next to him, Chenguang was watching him through the darkness.

The next morning, his bruises were better. As he had half expected through his exhausted haze from their conversation last night, Chenguang had gone before he got up, leaving a note that he was going on his own and Hong Deming should go back. Hong Deming saddled both his horse and Mo Xiang's as the spare and caught up to him before the sun was halfway to noon. After they yelled at each other a few times, they kept going, east toward Mount Shi.

Mo Xiang had spread the word. Hong Deming fought four other cultivators, two from Jade Bamboo and two from Peaceful River, in the next three days. Liu Chenguang was able to heal them, so Hong Deming hadn't yet killed a cultivator in this endeavor, but he knew it was a matter of time.

They were racing toward the sunrise, the eastern sacred mountain, and Hong Deming began to feel that perhaps they would make it. Mount Shi was visible across the horizon now. They were almost into Hai'an, and they rode late every night and rose early every morning.

Hong Deming woke up, his head aching and all his muscles feeling strangely slack. His balance felt off, and when he reached out he couldn't summon En. "Chenguang?" he called out, dazed. "Taine? Is there something wrong with me?" He blindly held out his arm for Liu Chenguang to check his pulse.

No one touched his arm or replied.

Still not fully able to focus his eyes, he felt around the bed. Except where his body had lain, the mat and blankets were cold. No one was there.

He staggered up, holding on to the wall, and began to call out loudly. "Chenguang? Where are you?"

There was no answer.

He steadied himself, trying to calm his heart, which was galloping painfully in his chest. He wouldn't have tried to leave on his own again, they had already dealt with all that. Surely Chenguang had just gone down to the baths, that was all. He would be back in a moment. Hong Deming breathed deeply, trying to regulate his body again, and at last felt that he could both see and control his movements.

Liu Chenguang was not in the room. Nothing was disarranged, and his belongings were still there, except the clothes he had been wearing at dinner, and the jade pendant.

He sat at the table, trying to remember the night before. He didn't remember getting into bed at all, actually, or falling asleep; his last memory was of a maid bringing tea and a simple meal of rice and vegetables for them to share. Liu Chenguang had especially liked the braised tofu, he remembered. For a meal at a low-rank inn, it had been quite well flavored.

He put his head in his hands. Obviously, they had been drugged. For whatever reason, they had left him alive, but Liu Chenguang was gone.

He got up again, and reached out to summon En. This time, it came to his hand.

Hong Deming walked down into the kitchen. "Who cooked our dinner last night?" he asked quietly.

He had no patience for kindness now. He went through the kitchen staff like the wind through the grass, trying to leave as little permanent damage as he could but unwilling to be too gentle. At last he determined that the food they had eaten had been likely safe when it was cooked — others had eaten the same meal with no ill-effects — but that no one could recall the maid who had brought it up to them. The maid assigned to their room had not done it, but no one could remember who it was.

Hong Deming went outside, panting for air. His head still hurt, he still felt weak, and his terror was rising, making him unable to think, unable to wait, unable to make a plan. He would just have to look for their tracks, follow them, try his best, they could only go so far with lightness skills, they would have to get horses eventually, but where could they have gone, why had they taken him, what did they need? *Why?*

He returned to their room in a panic, to grab their belongings, to bring Chenguang's things too because surely he would want them when he found him. There was a woman already there, dressed only in an inner robe. She was holding Chenguang's extra robe in her hands, looking at it curiously.

"Get away," he said, then changed his mind.

The woman was extraordinarily beautiful, her features and skin perfect, her hair unbound down to her knees, her robe very thin, showing the shape of her body beneath. She smiled at him, and moved closer, reaching out a hand.

This gave him the opportunity to put his hand on her throat and push her roughly against the wall. "Where?" he hissed. "Where did they take him?"

She laughed, unafraid. When his hand loosened slightly, she suddenly reached out and sensuously drew her fingers across his collarbone. "How pretty," she said. "I don't know where they went. My master doesn't tell me such things. Which is just as well for him, as now I can't tell you no matter what you do with me." She smiled and added, "What would you like to do with me? I will be much better for you than that one."

She suddenly kissed him, full on the lips, her tongue slipping between his teeth and delicately touching inside. Furious, he pushed her away and spat, wiping his mouth fiercely. She laughed and licked her lips. "Delicious," she said. Her face changed, harsh and angry, though no less beautiful. She grabbed his face with both hands and hissed, "Brief life, unhappy death."

The woman turned in his hands to a tiny fox, its fur soft as silk. It squirmed out of his hands and leapt out of the window. Hong Deming stared for a moment, swore and rubbed his mouth again, then ran out to find the horses.

That night, he hadn't found any traces, but had had to kill two yaoguai, cultivated crow-beings who had near-human form, who had dived at him from the sky at the same time. Their cultivation was high and he took several wounds to his arms and one to his torso, The yaoguai had nearly disemboweled him. One of the horses was dead, and more crows came to feast on it, cawing at him mockingly. He sat next to the road and put his head in his hands for a moment, despairing, but then staggered up and mounted again, riding back west. Surely they would take Chenguang west, back toward Crane Moon? It was his only guess. The panic in his heart was rising. As when he had entered the caverns to find Chenguang that night at Crane Moon, he felt that he was running out of time.

The next day, he was challenged in the road by Shen Lu.

"No," he said. "Tainu, I won't fight you."

Shen Lu sighed. "Don't call me tainu. Hong Deming, I will attack you and you can defend yourself or not. You've left us no choice in this." He raised his sword and saluted.

"Tainu–"

"You are not qualified to call me tainu, Hong Deming," Shen Lu said, and made his first strike.

Hong Deming leapt the blade and its pulse and came down, leapt up again with En in his hand. "Tainu! Shen Lu, they were torturing him, I had to take him– please, do you know where he is, where they took him–"

"Shut up." Two more sword strikes. Shen Lu was aiming for the wound in his belly from yesterday, making him move quickly to reopen it. Hong Deming winced as he felt the edges tear and the blood begin to ooze out. Another strike. He used En to parry and leapt backward. The wound was affecting his qinggong, he couldn't be as fast or agile as usual. "What made that?" Shen Lu asked, conversationally. "It's pretty ugly."

"Yaoguai," he gasped, "two of them. Shen Lu, did you know, did you know what they were doing to him?"

"I didn't. And I don't want to know now." A slash came for his ankles, Hong Deming jumped up and flipped, nearly screaming as the wound in his belly tore completely, tore wider, the muscles separating in blood. He hit his acupoints and landed, and at last had to attack, sending out a sword pulse. Shen Lu parried and continued, "Whatever he was doing, Taiqian is Taiqian. Loyalty and obedience are what you need to concern yourself with. What he orders, you obey. It doesn't matter. You've never understood this."

"Where is he now, where did they take him?" he asked desperately.

Shen Lu moved forward in a flurry of rapid sword strikes, this time aiming at the unhealed wounds of Hong Deming's shoulder and arms. Hong Deming parried, dodged, and leapt, feeling blood dripping down onto the earth beneath him. "This is a question that doesn't concern you," said Shen Lu. "That's something else that you never understood." A cut came across his chest, burning through the skin to his ribs. Hong Deming grunted and hit the acupoints.

Realizing at last that Shen Lu would indeed kill him, he finally attacked with all the strength he had left, throwing qi into En's strikes and rushing forward. Shen Lu had said it himself, Hong Deming's cultivation was higher. With a supreme effort he put the pain out of his mind and slashed a pattern that would cage Shen Lu into one specific area, forcing him to move in a predictable defensive pattern and show a weakness, with the final cut through his thigh designed to disable him.

But because his qinggong was limited, because he was wounded, because he was not able to focus properly, he hit the femoral artery instead of the tendon and muscle, a killing strike.

Shen Lu struck his own acupoints, but the wound was too deep to stop the bleeding completely.

Hong Deming knelt next to him, frantic, pressing on the wound. "I'm sorry, I'm sorry, tainu," he said, "please don't die."

Shen Lu put his own hands over Hong Deming's. "Hong Deming," he said, "don't call me tainu." He moved his hands out of the way and pressed himself. "Go to the next town and send a doctor back."

They both knew a doctor wouldn't reach him in time. Hong Deming remained next to him, helpless. "If Chenguang were here he could help you," he said. "I didn't mean, I didn't want to fight you, tai– Shen Lu."

Shen Lu's pressure on the acupoints and the wound was failing. The blood didn't spurt anymore, but oozed out, pulsing softly with his heartbeat, creating a great pool where he lay and Hong Deming knelt, crying. "Hong Deming," he said after a while, "you've killed people before, I'm not your first, don't sit there like a child weeping over a broken toy." He thought a little while, his mind wandering. "My wife is back at Peaceful River, send her the letter in my saddlebags. I wrote it before I went out to find you, Mo Xiang brought word, you've been followed…I knew I probably couldn't win against you, taine. But I'm the sect leader, after all."

Hong Deming was silent.

"That person, I wish we never found him, I wish Taiqian never brought him back," Shen Lu said with sudden vehemence. "It's because of him, all of this, what happened to you, he ruined you, taine."

"It's not his fault," Hong Deming said. "I love him, tainu, what else could I have done?"

Shen Lu's face was nearly bloodless now, his eyes unfocused. "You're very stubborn, taine." An endless time went by. Hong Deming held his hand and waited. "They took him across, the Fei have been attacking cities north of the Sorrowful River," he said at last. "The imperial army has been fighting for two months now. Zhu Guiren says that person has an ability, he'll be able to break the Fei army with one blow. Mandate of Heaven."

"But he can't even fight," Hong Deming said. "You know it, tainu — he can't even hold a weapon–"

"I just tell you what I know. I don't need to know everything, I'm not like you. Leave it, taine," he said. "By the time you can get there he'll probably already be dead, or he will have done what Zhu Guiren says he can, and either way you'll be forgiven after that if you confess your guilt…Let it be, don't interfere anymore." Shen Lu tried to squeeze his hand, but he had no strength left. "Taine, I also did what I had to do. I don't have regrets."

He didn't speak again.

Hong Deming finally arranged Shen Lu's limbs and placed a ward shield around his body, to keep it from animals or corruption until it was found. He placed the letter to his wife on his chest, under his hands. He knew he would never be able to send it.

That day when Chenguang had tried to run away, along with the note he had left packets of medicine for Hong Deming, labeled with their use and how to take them. He rummaged through Chenguang's bag and found them, one labeled for wounds as a poultice. He looked at the wound in his belly for a while, holding Liu Chenguang's needle and thread and considering whether he could stitch it up himself. Thinking about this took him a very long time; it seemed as though it were a hard decision. He finally decided that he couldn't, and put the needle and thread down on the ground and forgot about them. Then he needed to think about whether he should stop somewhere for a doctor to do it. It also took him a long time to think about this. He sat on the ground by the horses, just out of view of Shen Lu's body by the roadside, staring at the medicine packet, and then at the wound, a long slash from the yaoguai's claw that at one end might have gone completely through the inner wall of his abdomen, he couldn't really tell, at least nothing was falling out. The bleeding was slow, but it wouldn't stop. He tried to hold the edges together and considered, then finally bandaged it tightly with the poultice herbs. He forgot to actually make the poultice, he just put the herbs in the bandages and tied them on. He thought that if he passed a town with a doctor, he would stop and ask for help then.

He pulled himself onto the horse, wincing, and started riding toward the Sorrowful River, looking for a way to cross into the territory of the Prince of Fei.

# CHAPTER 20
## THE SORROWFUL RIVER

HE WAS ABLE to find a doctor before he crossed the river. The physician looked very serious when he saw his wounds but sewed him up and gave him medicine anyway. "Your vitality is greatly weakened, and you need to reinvigorate your vital energy. Rest. Don't exert yourself," the doctor said, hopelessly, and took his silver. Hong Deming didn't feel much better, but at least the bandages were tightly done and clean now. Just past that town he found a ferry to take him across and began riding aimlessly, trying to find clues as to where the armies of the Fei and the Son of Heaven were circling about one another. He heard that there had been fighting throughout the circuit, but he always arrived late to the battles. This slowed him down, as he had to walk through the corpses left on the field, looking for Chenguang's body. The first time he had to do this he nearly lost his mind, but it soon became easier through practice.

The days grew shorter and colder, and the trees lost their leaves. Hong Deming sat dazed under one, after searching the most recent battlefield, too tired even to start a fire. He had no idea where to go next, he would follow the trail that seemed to belong to the dynasty's forces, but this was always a guess. He carefully unwound the bandages around his middle, rubbed the ointment from the doctor on the oozing red wound, and then put clean bandages on. There was a lot of weakness in that area of his body since the muscles had been cut, which would be a severe disability when next he had to fight. Nonetheless, he hoped it would be sooner rather than later. These days and weeks were growing together, and whenever he thought of Chenguang he saw that image of his naked body, cut and bleeding on the stone couch. There was no one to stop them from doing that now.

He got up to his feet, grabbed En, and began walking. It was good to give the horse a rest occasionally, it was in almost as bad a shape as he was after the endless weeks of travel and short rations. He saw a rabbit dash off through the underbrush, and remembered he would need to shoot something for the day's meal. Grabbing his bow and arrow off the saddle, he moved softly through the woods, arrow on string. At a movement, he shot and missed.

Hong Deming looked at the arrow quivering in the earth, astonished. He never missed.

Walking over, he pulled the arrow out of the ground and noticed something bright red next to it: a small red bird with golden eyes, looking up at him.

"Hello," he said, and bent down. "Are you hurt? Why aren't you flying?"

But it immediately spread its wings and took flight.

Shortly afterward, he successfully shot a rabbit, skinned and wrapped it, and went back to where he'd tethered the horse to make a fire and cook it, well away from the corpse-littered field. He ate about half of it, stowed the rest for later, and mounted up again, riding toward the way he guessed the dynastic forces had gone.

The red bird was suddenly fluttering in the air in front of him. It dashed at the horse's face, making it shy and turn back. The bird, as though surprised, flew slowly in the other direction.

Hong Deming started forward again. The red bird again blocked the horse, and flew in the other direction.

After this had happened a third time, and a fourth, Hong Deming gave up and followed the bird, down the track of the other departing army.

The bird perched on a tree ahead, its golden eyes watching him. He greeted it respectfully, wondering if it were a yao. Ti Jinghua, back at the Stone Phoenix, had said that there were yao that didn't harm humans, though he'd never met one. Remembering the tiny, silken-haired fox, he watched the bird uncertainly, but it didn't try to interfere. Some long-tailed crows flew down and chased it away.

The trail of the army was easy to follow, with occasional dead horses or men to one side or another. He could even follow it under the light of the moon. On the third day, he heard a clash of swords and screams ahead of him, behind some low hills, notable only because the landscape was generally so flat. For once, he hadn't come too late. He rode to the bottom of one of the hills, tethered the horse, and crawled up to the top to view what was happening, the wound in his belly screaming at the unaccustomed movement.

In the shallow valley below, an immense confusion of forces were fully intertwined in an orgy of mutual slaughter, killing each other in a little stream that ran red down the middle, in the marshes on either slide, throughout the small town already nearly burned to the ground, in the fields, in the stables, in the outlying farmsteads, among the copses of leafless trees that hid nothing of the events. He couldn't easily tell which side was which, or who was who. The banners were mixed together, the soldiers' uniforms were torn and bloodied, the officers were shouting and screaming as much as anyone. On a hill to one side he saw the general, as he supposed, of the dynasty, so far as the banners went; they were too far away to identify any individuals. There was a squadron of archers there as well, and some reserve forces. On a hill farther away were the generals of the Prince of Fei, waving signal flags for whomever might be able to watch and interpret them.

Everyone else was in the blood cauldron.

Near a copse of trees, tiny from the distance, there was a person without armor or weapons, his robe a dark blue, his hair flowing down his back, pressing against a tree trunk, ducking and running among the trees to avoid swords and spears. This person had a little qinggong, and sometimes leapt into the trees himself, but then had to come back down because of the arrows immediately flying toward him.

Hong Deming stood up, called En, and ran down the hillside.

These were ordinary people. There were no cultivators on either side, and En cut a bloody swathe through the first line. Anyone who stood between him and the person in the blue robe was cut down. He didn't wait to see if they were friend or foe, they were all foes, Chenguang was a rabbit and the whole world was his enemy. However, this meant that both sides began to target him equally, and there was no safe place for him. As the soldiers of both sides closed in around his back, and he was immersed in the blood cauldron, spears and arrows began to fly. He couldn't block all of them, all of the time. He felt an arrow take him in the back, not too deep, not a killing wound, not yet. He tore it out and kept running, slashing with En and sending sword energy forward, always going toward the trees.

Liu Chenguang was bleeding heavily from a wound in his arm. He hadn't noticed him yet.

"Chenguang!" he shouted with all his breath. "Chenguang, I'm here!"

He saw Chenguang look up, his face striped with blood from a wound on his forehead, and scream despairingly.

"Go back!" he shouted. "Deming, go, I'm fine!" Distracted, Chenguang took a sword slash into his leg and fell forward to one knee.

Hong Deming killed the attacker and picked Liu Chenguang up. "Chenguang," he said, and looked at his leg. It wasn't a fatal wound, but it wasn't healing, why not?

"Deming," Liu Chenguang said, his face deadly pale under the bloody stripes, his hands clutching desperately to Hong Deming's arms despite his words, "no, Deming, leave, please leave–"

An arrow came for them, and Hong Deming blocked it, but there were more, and he couldn't block them all. This one hit Hong Deming in the chest, on the right side.

Chenguang screamed and for the first time Hong Deming saw him try to use a sword. Liu Chenguang rushed forward, limping on his bleeding leg, and stood in front of him, trying to block arrows. When someone came to attack him and he slashed down, the sword disintegrated in his hands. Hong Deming leapt in front again and blocked the return sword, cutting the attacker in half. "Chenguang!" he shouted. "Get behind me and stay there!"

With shaking hands, Liu Chenguang picked up a bow and arrow from a corpse, drawing with an arrow set. When he released the arrow, the bow broke, and the arrow snapped in two. Liu Chenguang screamed again in rage and fury and turned to him, begging him, "Deming, Deming, please, please go–"

Hong Deming considered whether he had enough energy left to simply pick Chenguang up and carry him out with his qinggong, and then realized that he didn't, and he knew he didn't when he came in, and the sole purpose of being here was to die with him. Realizing this made his mind clear, and almost joyful, except that Chenguang would die too, and that he couldn't bear to see. "Stay behind me, taine," he said, his voice calm.

More arrows came. He remembered what Taiqian had said that day very long ago, about the arrows that were like clouds, the ants that could defeat a mountain. En swung again and again, blocking, sending out sword energy. Corpses piled up in front of him, blood like a thin waterfall, he remembered Chenguang's blood in the cavern, flowing from the stone couch. He retreated step by step, feeling Chenguang behind him, and then they stopped with a strong tree at their backs. Chenguang came out and stood next to him. The soldiers were still for a moment, afraid of the sword, but it would be no more than that last moment.

He felt Chenguang's eyes on him, pleading, but he didn't say anything, didn't try to take his hand, not wanting to distract him. "Chenguang," he said, one last time, "get behind—"

The cloud of arrows flew out, and he blocked some. But not all. He felt the hot pain of an arrow in his throat, several in his chest. These were killing strikes. With his last power of movement, he turned and gathered Chenguang under his arm, twisted, and fell forward on top of him to shield him.

He could see Chenguang's face beneath his, his eyes full of tears, his mouth moving, but he couldn't really hear sounds anymore. The last thing he wanted to see in this life was Chenguang's eyes, so he watched them until everything grew dark.

Liu Chenguang felt Hong Deming die, his body shuddering into stillness, his breathing rattling into nothing, the light leaving his eyes as they grew fixed and dull. Then he lay there beneath him, feeling the dead weight of Hong Deming's body grow cold because he couldn't bear to miss the one last moment when his body was warm and remembered being alive. Tears fell like blood, the blood that continued to run from the deep wounds in his arm and leg.

Once the cultivators were dead, the soldiers went to kill each other elsewhere on the battlefield, looking for other meaningless places to defend and die for. Liu Chenguang lay beneath Hong Deming until a red bird fluttered to the ground next to him. Liu Chenguang turned his head to look at the bird, in silence.

The bird transformed into a woman, the servant woman Hong Deming had met at the Crane Moon sect. She knelt next to the bodies. "I'm sorry," she said. "I thought he could rescue you."

"Then you could at least have come earlier and healed him, why weren't you here to save him?" Liu Chenguang said. Hot tears fell from his eyes again. The servant woman reached forward and began to pull out the arrows that had pierced Hong Deming's back, then gently pulled his body off of Liu Chenguang. There were arrows in his front, in the throat and chest, that had been broken in his fall onto Liu Chenguang. She pulled those out too.

Liu Chenguang slowly sat up. The servant woman said, "You're still bleeding, why are you not healing?"

He gave an angry cry that was half a scream. "If I could heal do you think I wouldn't heal him? They've been bleeding me for months. I've got nothing left."

The servant woman shook her head. "I've been chased by yaoguai for days, we need to go. Can you transform?"

"No I can't transform, why are you asking stupid questions, if I could transform would I be here with the person I love dead in front of me?" He reached out and pulled Deming's body against him, holding him, and rocking slowly back and forth. "He died for me, Tielende. He died for me. He died for nothing. For nothing."

"It's not nothing," the woman said. "He loved you, Eftahede."

Liu Chenguang rocked back and forth. He reached out and moved Hong Deming's robes aside to look at his wounds, touching them one by one. "He was hurt when he came already, this would have killed him eventually if I couldn't heal him," he said softly, tracing the wound in his belly. "His body must have been full of sick blood when he was fighting, he must have been in pain for so long." He traced the wound in Hong Deming's throat, and ended with his fingers on the arrow wound in his left breast. "This is the wound that killed him." He leaned down and kissed it. "Deming," he said. He bit his lip and kissed it again. "Deming…"

"Eftahede," said the servant woman, "he's dead. There's nothing you can do. He's gone now. He's not suffering anymore. There's no pain here for you to heal."

Liu Chenguang looked up. "Is there no pain here, Tielende?" He reached again to Hong Deming's fatal wound, reaching inside as though to touch his heart, and touched his own lips with Hong Deming's smeared blood, already clotting and drying.

The servant woman watched with a calm face and narrowed eyes. "What are you doing, Eftahede?"

Liu Chenguang reached out with shaking hands and picked up En. He cut a piece of fabric from his white inner robe, and then cut it again into two long narrow strips. "I don't know." Liu Chenguang took the strips of cloth and smeared them with Hong Deming's blood, then trailed them through the bleeding wound on his own leg, soaking them deep red.

"Eftahede," said the servant woman, very gently, almost pleading, "this man's soul is on the journey that all mortal souls take. Don't pull him off his path."

Liu Chenguang bit his lip, reached over and kissed Hong Deming again, anointing him with his blood, on his eyes, on the tip of his nose, his lips, the wounds in his throat and breast.

"Eftahede," the woman tried again, "he's dead, sibling. In a thousand years, will you even remember that such a person once existed?"

Liu Chenguang looked at her, and the woman lowered her head. "I will remember," he said, fiercely, very soft.

He tied one of the bloody ribbons around Hong Deming's wrist, and the other around his own. The servant woman watched, and was silent.

Liu Chenguang kissed Hong Deming one last time, then lay him down, as though he were sleeping, though he never let go of his hand. Not looking up, he said, "The yaomo will be coming soon, I think. You should go now."

"Can you not come with me?" she asked.

"No," he said. "Even if I had the strength, this is over for me, Tielende. I want it to end. I want to go with him."

Very, very gently, as though speaking to a child that can't comprehend death, the servant woman said, "Eftahede, you know you can never go with him."

"I know," he said. "But I will not walk away from where he died."

"I won't leave you alone," the servant woman said. "I will be here with you."

"It's not necessary." When the woman didn't move, Liu Chenguang said, "At least transform, go to the other end of the valley. Don't let him get two of us. It doesn't matter how close you are. I'll know you're here."

After a moment the woman nodded. Liu Chenguang said, with his eyes closed, "Take the jade decoration on my sash, keep it safe for me."

The servant woman untied the jade crane ornament. With it in her hand, she transformed into a red bird and flew away.

For an unmeasurable time, Liu Chenguang lay partly on Hong Deming's body, his head against his breast, his hair falling over his shoulders, as though they were falling asleep together, as though he could hear his heartbeat. A stray arrow came and struck Liu Chenguang in the back, but he didn't move. Blood seeped out slowly from the wound. The sounds of the battle around them didn't stop, sometimes closer, sometimes more distant, but no one paid attention to two corpses among thousands.

Suddenly there was a foot between them, kicking Liu Chenguang over onto his back. The arrow ground in the wound and pierced through his chest before breaking. He gasped a little bit; the arrow was in his lung. Dark blood was dripping from his lips.

"Still all in one piece, I see," said Zhu Guiren disapprovingly. "Ah well."

Liu Chenguang looked toward the sky, ignoring him.

Zhu Guiren squatted down next to him. Conversationally, he added, "I'd like you to know that this was not how I initially wanted to end things. You should have just died in the battle, cut to pieces here. But Taiqian's on the way to clean things up, and truthfully it's probably better that way for me. More convenient for the timing."

Silence.

"It's all right if you don't want to talk. I'm sure you don't have much energy left. It won't be long." He looked at Hong Deming's body. "I see your little friend didn't make it. I've been trying to kill him for quite a while now, but he wasn't supposed to be here today at all. My subordinate at that inn will have some explaining to do…the irony is that if he hadn't come today, I would have let him live. It's only you I need."

Liu Chenguang choked a little bit, blood dribbling out of the side of his mouth. After he spat, he said thickly, "Let me hold his hand."

Zhu Guiren raised his eyebrows. "That's a dead man, phoenix. Holding his hand won't change anything."

He turned his head to look into Zhu Guiren's eyes. After a moment, he said, "Please."

Zhu Guiren stared back, then laughed. "Fine." He picked up Hong Deming's cold hand and placed it in Liu Chenguang's. "Ugh, how disgusting."

Liu Chenguang just watched Hong Deming's face, quietly, as though hoping against hope that he would notice him holding his hand, trying to warm him, trying to store up a memory of this face against any future need. "Did you ever say anything to me that wasn't a lie?" Liu Chenguang asked.

"Many things. I told you many truths about human beings and how they are with one another," Zhu Guiren said. "You just didn't want to listen. Typical phoenix." He reached out with one finger and flicked him on the forehead. "Next time around, don't be so trusting."

Liu Chenguang heard footsteps, but didn't look away from Hong Deming. The footsteps came up behind his body, and stopped. Taiqian's face looked down coldly. He stepped over Hong Deming's body to speak to Zhu Guiren. "Zhu Guiren," he said, "what was the point of all this? You brought us here, weeks of my time, and promised that Liu Chenguang would be able to end this war decisively, with one blow. As far as I can tell, he's completely useless."

"Not quite, sect leader," Zhu Guiren replied. "There is one more step. It should have happened during the battle, but as it was interrupted, it needs to be completed now. As I have explained before, Liu Chenguang's ability to unlock his true powers, to be able to attack as strongly as he can heal, is being blocked by the weakness of his meridians compared to his inner power. The meridians have to be completely severed, then they can regrow appropriate to the power he holds."

Taiqian looked down at Liu Chenguang, lying there stained with blood, with a complicated expression. "Zhu Guiren, you've shown me that Liu Chenguang's blood can heal others, and that he can heal himself, but look at him now. It seems that the power is weakened, not strengthened."

"That's why this final step needs to be taken exactly now, before the body heals again," Zhu Guiren explained. "If you leave him in this state, without taking the final steps, his body will eventually heal itself completely, but it will still be unable to attain the full power he is capable of."

Liu Chenguang continued to watch Hong Deming's face, holding his hand, as though this conversation had nothing to do with him. On the hillside above the battle, the servant woman pressed her face further into the ground. Her body shook a little bit, but then she was still.

Zhu Guiren nodded to Taiqian. "Continue the cutting, as before," he said.

Taiqian took up his sword, a little reluctantly, but began slicing. After the first few cuts, Liu Chenguang started shivering and crying out softly, though he never looked away from Hong Deming's face. Everywhere the sword touched, Liu Chenguang's skin and flesh opened, and blood oozed out slowly, dripping into the earth. Some of it fell on Hong Deming, warm where he was cold.

As the blood fell, behind Taiqian, where he couldn't see, Zhu Guiren held his fingers in unrecognizable hand seals, shifting swiftly from one to another while softly murmuring under his breath. Liu Chenguang's voice fell silent.

"He's unconscious now," Taiqian said, at last. "I think he doesn't have much blood left."

"The last step is dismemberment and decapitation," Zhu Guiren said calmly. "In that order."

"What?!" Taiqian stepped back, his face disgusted. "I'm not an executioner, Zhu Guiren—"

"It's the only way," Zhu Guiren said, encouragingly. "And after all, he's unconscious now, isn't he? Don't wait too long. If he heals, you'll have to do it all over again."

Taiqian raised the sword, then stopped. "You do it."

"I can't," Zhu Guiren said, "it needs to be a high-level spiritual sword, you know I can't use one. My expertise comes from long study, but I don't have a spiritual weapon, I have no spiritual power of my own."

Taiqian raised the sword again, quickly, then, one-handed, slashed down. The sword was extremely sharp, and he put a great deal of qi behind it, to sever with one strike.

At the first cut, Liu Chenguang woke up briefly and screamed, his voice hoarse, his vocal cords raw with blood. But by the second cut, he was already unconscious again.

Three cuts. Four. Zhu Guiren held his hands still over the earth and chanted softly. Just before the sword swung down for the last time, at the moment Taiqian raised the sword above his head for the killing stroke, a black long-tailed crow appeared where Zhu Guiren had stood, and drove itself away to the west with a speed greater than any earthly bird.

Five cuts.

The fire poured outward, instantaneous, overwhelming, an explosion that caught up Taiqian, and the body of Hong Deming, all the corpses on the battlefield. It rolled over the valley, dynasty and rebel alike, alive and dead, incinerating them in an instant. It rolled up the hills and captured the generals, the reserves, the waiting messengers. The fire raged into the sky, no end visible to it, a pillar connecting heaven and earth.

The last bits of Hong Deming's observing soul dissolved in the flame, and the last thing his soul would remember was a small red bird turning into sparks, rushing upwards, dissolving along with him.

# INTERLUDE
## BETWEEN LIVES

"Doctor Liu! Doctor Liu!"

He looked up from his counter, where he was carefully compounding a prescription for a woman at risk of a miscarriage. "Yes, I'm here," he replied.

"Doctor Liu, there's news from below, grandfather wants you to come."

He completed the prescription and handed it to the child. "Bring this to Master Shen for his wife. Tell him that she is to boil it, cool it, and drink every hour today. She should remain in bed all week. That is very important. Be sure to tell him that."

"Yes, Doctor Liu. I'm going!" The young boy ran out, excited to have a mission to take him from the work in the fields.

He walked down through the stone-paved street of the village toward the headman's house. Headman Fang was standing outside, gray beard waving in the wind.

"Doctor Liu," he said, "you're here. Please come in."

They sat down together; the old man offered weak tea, the best he had. The village was isolated and poor, and in recent years trade had been bad. Nonetheless, after drinking, he said, "The heavens have blessed our village to have a divine doctor among us. But I know you will leave us soon."

Liu Chenguang drank his own tea. "What makes you say so?"

"When you came here, I was a young boy. Now my hair is gray, and you are still a young man. I remember that my father told me, when you first came, that you had been here before. His grandfather told him of the divine doctor Liu, who he remembered from his own childhood. Who cured all illnesses for us and disappeared without warning."

Liu Chenguang drank again. "Perhaps this is true, perhaps not. Who can say what happened in the lifetime of your esteemed ancestor?"

The headman continued, "You are right to say so, Doctor Liu. My ancestor's ancestor built the shrine to the divine doctor here many generations ago. My father said that it was because the divine doctor had been here then too, and all the village hoped he would return. And so you did. We are grateful. And I do not want to be greedy or disturb your peace. What you have given— You have saved our lives from all the accidents and suffering of human life, except old age and war."

"I have done my poor best."

"Doctor Liu may be concerned that perhaps the village would be unhappy that he does not age. That the foolish people would trouble him for elixirs of immortality and other things that are not appropriate for mortals. I promise you that it would not be so."

Liu Chenguang looked out from the porch where they drank at the little village: the fields around it, the laughing children chasing dragonflies. There was no sickness here, no untimely death. There was peace for the people here, at least.

He drank again.

The headman pressed on. "Doctor Liu may worry that the foolish people would tell others about him, boasting about our blessing. That he would be troubled by those coming from far away to demand what can't be given. I promise you. I promise you, this would not be so."

Liu Chenguang replied, gently, "Your grandson told me that there is news from below."

The headman sighed. "The northern barbarians are coming closer. There are many battles, many raiders. They are settled around Eifeng now, not so far. Soon, they will come here. The rumor is that they raze cities and towns to the earth to make pasture for their horses. They are unstoppable. What if they come here? Doctor Liu, divine doctor, can't you remain to protect us?"

"Headman Fang, I can't protect you. I am not a martial god. Not any kind of god. I am only a doctor. I can only heal." He said softly, then stood up and bowed formally. "Thank you for your kind words. You are correct that I must leave now."

Headman Fang tried to kneel down to prostrate himself, but Liu Chenguang reached down to lift him up.

"Don't. It's not necessary, not appropriate. I'm only a person."

"Will you come back?" he asked. "We will keep the temple for you, we will burn incense for you. We will keep your house clean–"

"It may be a long time, but I will come back. Remember not to tell anyone about me," he said, "or I won't be able to stay."

"Yes, yes," he said, delighted. "We will be discreet, divine doctor. Thank you, thank you!"

Liu Chenguang still remembered the lightness skills of the Crane Moon, and of course he could have transformed and flown, but it occurred to him to keep that aspect of things secret. He might need an escape route at some point. This journey would be better done on a horse. He obtained one from a farm near the highway and began riding, asking along the way where he could find the Mitang army. He no longer wore his hair like a cultivator — the cultivation sects had disappeared, so most people would not recognize it except as someone enacting an ancient tale — but for this journey, he decided it would be more effective. Better if word went before him. He put up his hair in the pincrown again, letting the rest flow down behind his back, and exchanged his scholar's tunic for the flowing, lightweight robes of a cultivator. Instead of a sword, which he still could not hold, he kept the gourd at his waist, along with a jade pendant figuring a crane with outspread wings. He could at least look like a proper cultivator.

First, he went to the siege of Eifeng.

He made himself highly visible, dramatically healing people near death on the battlefield — both Daxian defenders and Mitang attackers. Soon enough word reached the Mitang general, who ordered him captured. This was exactly what he had been hoping for, so he didn't try to escape.

All he would say to the general was, "I am a messenger from the spirits. I am sent to the Great Khan. Cease your warfare until I have spoken to him."

Nothing would make him say more than this.

As he had hoped, the general was superstitious enough to listen and send him to the Khan. Whether he stopped attacking Eifeng while Liu Chenguang was on the road, there was no way of knowing.

At last he stood before the Great Khan, an enormous man with a deceptively cheerful attitude. "Eh, little man, why are you here?" he asked.

Liu Chenguang bowed formally. "Great Khan, I am sent from the spirit world to offer my protection to you."

The Khan laughed out loud. "Ha, you will protect me? How?"

Liu Chenguang took a deep breath and readied himself. "Tell one of your men to cut my throat."

The Khan raised his eyebrow. "You, there. Do it."

One of the guards immediately leapt over, pulled Liu Chenguang's head back by his hair, and slashed his throat with a saber. The freezing, burning pain shot through him, and he fell to his knees, blood spurting to the floor. The room darkened before his eyes, and he felt his body slump to the ground.

Then, he woke up.

Several of the guards — big men, afraid of nothing — screamed out loud as he climbed to his feet. At least two shot at him: one arrow through the chest, one through the shoulder.

He fell to the ground again, swearing under his breath; he hadn't expected to be attacked twice, although he probably should have. Rising to his feet once more, he reached up a hand and broke off the head of the arrow piercing through his chest and jerked it out, wincing. The one that had hit his shoulder hadn't gone through completely, so that one he had to drag out, despite the barbs. "Ah," he gasped, but then it was over. And after all, it probably had a bigger effect that way, he thought.

He raised his head and bowed again to the Great Khan. The guards, pale beneath their tans, backed away, murmuring to one another.

The man in the chair leaned forward. "You can recover from any wound?"

"I can recover from any wound," Liu Chenguang said, resisting the urge to rub his throat. "However, I advise you not to behead me. I will survive that, but everyone within three miles will die immediately."

"Ha, that could be useful in its own way."

"You would not survive the attempt. The heavens forbid it."

"Good enough. You can give me this protection?"

"There are conditions," he said. "You must find a way to establish your dynasty without destroying the Daxian people and their cities. Consider, after all, the benefit to you. Farmers will provide food, tribute, taxes for you. Much better than a land where you can only ride horses and graze."

"You're not the first to say so." The Khan looked over toward another Mitang warrior — a huge man with a long beard. "Feru says the same. But the cities resist us. They must be destroyed."

"Find another way," Liu Chenguang said bluntly. "So long as you don't destroy the cities or villages, or loot the countryside, or rape the women, or massacre the people, I will protect your life. No illness or wound will hurt you."

Feru leaned over to the Khan and whispered.

"Can you give me the elixir of immortality?" he asked.

"Certainly," Liu Chenguang said. "However, for that there are additional conditions. The Elixir of Immortality is only effective if, for the next ten years before I give it to you, and then for all of eternity, you refrain from war, hunting, eating meat, and sexual relations of any kind." After a moment of reflection, he added, "Also, no alcohol. Not even fermented mare's milk."

The big man glared, then laughed out loud, slapping his thigh in amusement. "To hell with that!"

Liu Chenguang bowed, hiding his smile. "The Great Khan speaks wisely."

He was placed in a room without windows, the door locked, while the Khan considered. Liu Chenguang sat quietly in a corner, thinking. As usual at such times, he thought of Hong Deming — wishing he could talk with him again, tell him about what he was doing, about his efforts to try to stave off the suffering they had seen together. Hong Deming would have been upset that he'd been shot twice. He would have to explain why that was important. Hong Deming would try to protect him, but that wasn't always possible. He would need to understand that.

It had been such a long time.

He was used to such thoughts; in their own way, they were comforting.

As he had expected, sometime around the fourth watch the door opened and Feru entered, bending over so as not to strike his head on the lintel. Liu Chenguang remained seated.

"Your manners have declined since this afternoon," the big man noted, seating himself on the floor opposite.

"I am in a jail cell, talking to my jailor," he replied. "I choose to be courteous to the Great Khan. I don't need to be courteous to you."

Feru grinned. "We understand each other. The Great Khan is amenable to your terms. What is required?"

"I must remain close to him. I will diagnose him now and cure whatever ills he currently suffers. From this, I will know what is likely to come to him in the future as well. I guess already that he is declining from alcohol use."

"He has been told this by other physicians."

"I can keep this death from him."

Feru snorted. "For that alone, he would spare twenty cities, the old drunkard. However, he asks that you also extend this protection to his sons."

"I can't defend them when they are at war unless I am at their side." He didn't mind offering this; it would ensure that he could rein in the army from the field, rather than solely through the Great Khan's messengers. "I will not leave the central plain for any long period of time. The Great Khan, I understand, has sent his armies elsewhere as well."

Feru nodded. "The southern dynasty is resisting, although the final outcome is inevitable before the armies of the Great Khan. I will do my best to ensure that the damage is minimal. You and I are allies in this."

"It's good to have allies," he said. "I can't be everywhere, but if I receive news that this bargain has been broken — if there have been massacres or destruction by his order, or the orders of his sons, the Great Khan should know that his death approaches, and the death of his sons as well."

"You don't need to worry." Feru scratched his beard, then asked, "Why are you doing this? Are you not a patriot? Are you not angry that the Mitang people will rule the Daxian?"

"I am not a patriot," he said, "and I don't care who rules who, so long as the people are safe from harm."

"Are you truly sent from heaven? Are you a divine compassionate one?"

"What difference does it make?" he asked, smiling. "I have heard that you have compassion for the people as well. Does that make you a deity? You use the powers that you have to avert suffering, so far as you can. So do I. That's all you need to know." After a moment, he added, "Long ago, I was foolish. There are things I need to atone for."

Feru nodded as though he understood. "Very well. Come with me."

Forty years later, Liu Chenguang sat on a high cliff near a trickling waterfall. The fall came down from the cliff behind him, trickled across the ledge on which he sat, and then fell down below. As the sun descended, its rays filled the gorge and lit up the mist where the waterfall dissipated into the air. Golden-red sparks glimmered and disappeared, glimmered and disappeared.

Once, there had been a little wall at the edge of the cliff and a carved channel for the waterfall, but these things were largely worn away by time. From where he sat, he could see the remnants of stone walls above and below, some with the outline of houses and courtyards. They had long been destroyed by fire and sword. This must have happened before he returned from rebirth, even before the rise of the Ning dynasty, centuries before; it had been like this when he first came back. The fire, and whoever had attacked, had destroyed the library, the buildings, the armory. Only the spiritual caverns remained — in darkness, as they had always been, waiting for someone to enter. There was nothing left of the Crane Moon but the jade pendant he wore.

He watched the sparks glimmer and disappear as the sun set, and leaned back against the cliffside as the stars came out. Eventually, he felt the heat of his tears slowly trickling down his face; he didn't raise his hand to wipe them. Soon he was sobbing, gasping for breath. It had been so long.

This was the only place where he allowed himself to cry.

Liu Chenguang leapt down the cliff and walked the mountain paths to the village. The temple was still there; incense was still being burnt for the divine doctor.

An old man saw him walk down from the forests. "Doctor Liu," he called, "Doctor Liu, welcome back! Welcome back!"

He was gray-haired, but hale and healthy. Liu Chenguang was glad to see it. "Little Fang," he said, smiling, "I'm here."

# CHAPTER 21
## TAIREI AND AILI

AILI OPENED HER eyes and looked into Tairei's. "Chenguang," she heard her voice say, hoarse with disuse, as it had been after she came out of seclusion. After he had come out of seclusion. She felt a rush of warmth all through her body, as she always had whenever she saw Tairei. Now, she knew why. She stopped herself from reaching out to touch Tairei's face before the movement began.

Tairei's eyes shone. "Aili," she said.

Not Hong Deming, but Aili knew that was who she really meant.

She sat up and held her head. "That…My head hurts…"

Tairei reached out to touch her, concerned. "You've been asleep for a long time. Nightfalls and nightfalls."

"I remember everything," Aili said, her head still in her hands.

Tairei reached out again, more tentatively. "You…remember?" Her voice was hopeful.

It made Aili's heart hurt to hear how much hope she had.

"I remember," she said, and met her eyes.

She and Tairei looked at each other, neither certain how to begin.

Belatedly, Aili realized that the cavern they were in was not very large, and that Zhu Guiren and Tainu were sitting on the other side of a blue and golden fire, watching them. Zhu Guiren looked a little worried when their eyes met, which made her feel somewhat better. She had a vague memory of stabbing him with En — quite a pleasant thought, even if it had only been a dream.

"Come on," said Tainu, getting up.

Zhu Guiren settled down with his chin in his hand. "Oh no, this is going to be good. I've earned this. I'll have a scar forever."

"Now, voyeur." Tainu grabbed his ear and started pulling.

"Ow, ow, ow! I'm coming, stop it! What about the wards? You shouldn't go out like this?"

Aili could hear him complaining for quite a while — the only sound as she and Tairei looked at one another. She saw the hope slowly dim in Tairei's eyes as she looked into them, and looked, and didn't speak.

At last Tairei said, very softly, "I knew when you came back into the world. I could feel it. But you were far away. I spiraled out from where I was, systematically. It turned into a game of hot and cold. You know that game? Where if you get closer, the other person says 'getting warm'? But you were so distant that the sense was so very subtle. It took a long, long time. And then, I stood on the shore of the ocean and felt that you were on the other side. I had no way to cross the ocean, and I felt that time was running out. I knew that my time of rebirth was coming soon, and when that happened, I would need to be away from you in the spirit realm. I had already missed your childhood…you were already an adult. Because of the war, there were no ships. I couldn't…And when I found you, you didn't remember me. I was sure you would have remembered me, would have felt something…did you…not feel anything?"

Aili felt her throat constrict, but didn't respond.

Eventually, Tairei continued, "Almost as soon as I found you, you were going to leave. You were going to go back onto a battlefield, and I couldn't stop you. I was almost out of my mind with terror. I felt like this was some kind of cruel punishment. That you would die again, at the same age. That I wouldn't be able to stop it. So, I came up with this plan to protect you…To keep you alive."

"You could have explained it to me. You could have asked me." Aili realized that out of everything, that was what she was going to talk about; it wasn't what really mattered. It was helpful, though, to feel a little bit wronged, a little bit angry — helpful because her heart was lost and broken; helpful because she still loved this person, and this person did not love her.

Tairei was silent. "I'm sorry. I wasn't…I wasn't able to think that far ahead… about what it might mean to you. All I could think was that you wouldn't die."

"What did you do to me, exactly?" Aili asked eventually.

"I don't really know. Both times, I just…I did what seemed right to me at that moment. I didn't…I didn't know what would happen." she said. "When you died…"

"I saw it in my memories." She couldn't bear to hear Tairei describe it.

Tairei nodded, looking at the ground. "So you…your soul was still there? You saw everything?"

She remembered it: seeing Liu Chenguang lying under his dead body, despairing, being cut to pieces by Zhu Guiren. She clenched her fists so hard she felt the blood in her palm.

"How could you do this?" she asked, her voice rising. "How could you do this to me and not know what you were doing? What would happen to me? What am I now?"

She realized that she was actually, truly very angry after all.

"You– you lied to me! You didn't tell me what you were. I was glad to die, Liu Chenguang. Did you know it?" she asked. "I was glad to die because I thought we would go together. I thought…I came to die with you. Didn't you understand?"

"Don't *you* understand?" Tairei said, suddenly flinging back her head. Tears flew like jewels in the blue firelight with the violence of her movement. "Do you not understand that I can't die? That I can't– You were– You died for me for no reason at all. I had to watch it happen because I'm so useless. Did you think how I would feel, watching you, feeling you die?"

"Could I have had any idea you would have survived?" Aili asked, almost shouting. "That you were some kind of immortal thing? That I could have just left you there and gone on my way and met up at an inn later when you had gotten through it–"

"I tried to get away from you and keep you safe! I told you!" Tairei shouted back. "I told you to leave! You knew that I could heal myself–"

"You damn well weren't healing! You were bleeding all over! How could I have known that I was dying for nothing?"

Tairei's face turned pale beneath her tears, all the blood draining from it.

Aili felt her heart clench and turned around, unable to look at her pain. She struck the wall of the cavern with her hand and swore. Bits of fire escaped from between her fingers, running up and down the crystal walls with nothing to burn.

"All right," Aili said at last, in a low voice. "I would have stayed with you anyway. Even if I knew. I would have wanted to try to protect you from them. From the pain you were in. I would have died anyway. I knew at the time, Tairei. That's the truth. That I wouldn't survive. I knew it when I came to try to get you."

"You were in so much pain then," Tairei said. "I saw the wounds you had…"

Her voice trailed off. "I never knew what had happened to you, after they took me at the inn. I didn't even know how long it was. Zhu Guiren kept me drugged until they brought me onto the battlefield."

Aili shook her head. "Tairei, you don't want to know."

"I do."

"There were two yaoguai at once," she said, keeping it to the bare minimum. "One of them wounded me in the stomach. Then I killed my tainu. After that, I don't think I was thinking clearly."

Tairei didn't drop her gaze, but her face was even sadder than before. "Shen Lu…I'm so sorry. So sorry for everything."

"Why didn't you tell me?" Aili asked, looking past her at the black rock of the wall and the constantly-changing golden figures deep inside it.

Tairei took a deep breath. "Aili, for a thousand years, I have wished I did. Every day. But at the time…at the time, I didn't know how to say it. I was afraid that you wouldn't love me anymore if you knew. I'd never…I'd never been with people before I met you. Not really. I was like a mountain yao — living in the wilderness, only crossing paths with human beings once in a while. I didn't want you to see me the way they did. As something that needed to be avoided, or only sought out if they wanted something." She sighed. "I was afraid…"

"You were afraid of the wrong things," Aili said.

"Tell me the truth. Would you be dead now if I hadn't done this? Would you already have died?"

"Yes," Aili said. The bullets that struck Nora had struck her too. There was no doubt, she should have died for the second time without ever seeing Liu Chenguang again.

"Then I'm not sorry." Tairei came a step closer. "I am sorry if you hate me for it, but I'm not sorry that you are alive. I will never be sorry for that. If you're alive…If you're alive, then that's all that matters to me."

She was close enough that Aili could hear it when she took a deep breath, and then continued. "Would it have been better if had never come to look for you? You could have lived a good life without me. Maybe you could have…fallen in love with someone, grown old with them…"

"Stop," Aili said, desperate. There would never have been anyone else, but she couldn't say that; it wouldn't help anything.

"I can leave you alone if that's what you want," said Tairei.

Aili looked into her eyes — red-rimmed with tears, but so determined. Something like the feeling of glass over her heart, but more like ice, coldness. And yet, there was warmth too. Something almost painful that yearned to come out into the light. Something that tasted of longing and hope and fear. There was too much.

She was Hong Deming, and yet she was not. The man with a kind and gentle heart, the man whose soul was so open, the man who protected the people he loved — he had been betrayed and failed and died, suffered and failed again, and she was no longer that person. A thousand years later, her lives were only a long, shameful defeat; she was a useless coward, and the people she loved were destroyed around her.

Tairei was standing straight and rigid, her hands clenched at her sides.

Aili saw this and felt that soreness in her heart again, and at the same time that clarity and distance. "This feels familiar," she said, finally.

Tairei closed her eyes.

"Hong Deming is dead, Tairei," Aili said, very quietly. "The person you were in love with has been dead for a thousand years. I am not that person."

Tairei shivered and hung her head low.

"I remember…" Aili said. "I remember everything. I loved you. I really did love you. You were everything to me. You were the best part of my life from the day I met you. I didn't say it well then — how much I loved you. At least I can say it now."

In the firelight, she could see the glimmer of tears, falling from Tairei's chin like little sparks. She steeled herself to continue. "If I had known when I died, that you would…I didn't die so that you could feel guilty forever, or keep loving a dead person. I wanted you to live. I don't want you to torture yourself for this. It wasn't your fault. Let it go. Just…let it go. There's nothing else you need to do. Stop carrying the burden of my life and death with you. For a thousand years, Tairei…I wish…"

But she was no longer the person Tairei yearned for, and she couldn't ever be again.

Tairei nodded, jerkily, once.

Aili took a deep breath. "I am going to go out. I won't go far. I'll come back soon. You stay here."

Without waiting for an answer, she walked out past the wards that she recognized through the tingling in her skin. The sun was close to setting. About a hundred yards away, she saw Tainu sitting under a tree, still casually holding Zhu Guiren's ear.

"You two can go back now," she called, her voice steady.

The demon said, "Finally."

Tainu stood up, brushing off his legs. He looked at her, but didn't say anything before going back into the cave.

Just before he went inside the wards and became invisible to her eyes, Zhu Guiren looked back, his eyes bright and curious. "I always wondered why you did it. There was no way you could have won. You must have known you were going to die and he would die too, as far as you knew anyway. Why bother?"

Aili didn't respond; she stared up at the sky, moving toward twilight now. It was full of things that were not stars, glimmering and dashing around one another in complex patterns.

Zhu Guiren shrugged and disappeared behind the wards.

Almost immediately, he came out again. "He told me to leave," he said, sounding offended. "Liu Chenguang is crying. I don't understand. Didn't she get what she wanted?"

Aili looked at him in disgust. When he came to sit next to her, she moved away.

"Don't go too far," he said, "tonight's wave will be coming. Did you know we get attacked every night here? The spirit realm is full of entertainment. At least you'll be able to help with defense more than those useless things."

"Since I'm here now, can you stop torturing us all with your existence and just go?"

Zhu Guiren beamed. "You remember me!"

"Yes, this is why I'd like you to be dead."

"This is not an uncommon response to me," he remarked. "But I didn't reach my advanced age by being easy to kill. You used up three lives' worth of luck for that one shot. You won't get another one."

He twisted his hand and pulled a knife of ice and smoke out of nothingness. "On that topic…that is, my particular skills and what you can and can't do around me. You can lie to those phoenixes since they're stupid and innocent and unused to deception. You can possibly lie to yourself. You can't lie to me. I'm too good at it. So, stop pretending you're not Hong Deming and that you don't have…whatever feelings you have for little Chenguang."

"I am not Hong Deming. And how the hell do you know anything about my feelings?"

"I know nothing at all about your feelings. I just know lies when I hear them." He began tossing his knife and catching it in his single hand. "That little phoenix will believe you, and it will break her heart. She is the stupidest I've ever met, even among phoenixes. So trusting." He caught his knife and held it at Aili's throat; Aili already had a knife at his — a knife that glowed golden.

She whispered, "You are not qualified to speak about her."

Calmly, Zhu Guiren said, "Your speed is decent. I will admit I didn't see that coming. However, it proves my point."

Aili brought her knife closer to his throat. "Tainu is not here now, and I'm not going to heal you. Zhu Guiren, please remember that I would love to kill you."

"If you wanted it that much, I'd already be dead."

She pressed the golden knife more firmly, feeling the tautness of his skin beneath as he swallowed. "You might also remember that I don't care if I'm dead, and it's not at all clear that I can be killed. This is not an even fight for you."

A line of blood appeared under the knife. She tried to calm herself so she wouldn't cut his throat accidentally out of sheer trembling rage.

"Actually, you probably can be killed. At least here," Zhu Guiren said. "The spirit realm is the only place where a phoenix can truly die. Why do you think they're trying so hard to hide? Why do you think I'm trying to protect them? Unlike you, I don't do pointless acts of heroism. If those useless things couldn't be killed, I'd be on my merry way."

More blood trickled from under the knife. "You. Do. Not. Speak. About. Liu Chenguang."

Zhu Guiren pressed his own knife against Aili's throat in return. "Fine. I won't say anything about Liu Chenguang. I will only say things about you. These are things you need to hear, and neither of those phoenixes are able to tell you because they are–"

Aili's knife bit deeper.

"Fine. I will not mock phoenixes in your hearing."

She pulled the knife away.

"Talk. Politely."

"All right." He rubbed his throat and flicked his hand; his dagger disappeared. "I have every plan to tell Tainu about this outrage, by the way. Have you been trained in knife-fighting? In your current form, I mean."

"Training is not quite what I'd call it," she said, thinking about the bus station in Easterly.

"Do you know how to use a spiritual weapon?"

"No."

"But you just did both of those things. Because Hong Deming knew how to do one of them and you knew how to do the other, you combined them to pull a spiritual knife on me. You are not separate from Hong Deming. You are continuous: mind, soul, heart, body."

"How can our bodies be continuous?"

"I'm not going to explain the theory to you. Your little brain would explode. But the training you received as Hong Deming, the skills you developed, even the spiritual cultivation, is within the body you have now, along with everything you have learned in this life, in this body. It's not just cognitive. It's not just memories. You are the continuation of that person. Don't tell yourself otherwise. That's the lie."

She stood. "I am not Hong Deming."

Zhu Guiren looked up at her. "You are more than Hong Deming, yes. You have lived more than Hong Deming had when he was killed. But you are Hong Deming, and he is you. You are not separate beings. I don't really understand why you don't get this. You have the memories."

"No."

He rolled his eyes theatrically. "Phoenixes…all intuition and no skill. She literally has no idea what she did or why it worked. One day, I'll get the little phoenix to tell me exactly what steps she took and then I'll probably be able to analyze what happened and tell you more details. Meanwhile, don't waste my time. Your skills and abilities as Hong Deming are still with you. You've just never tried to use them properly in this body. You're a cultivator. You have the ability to create a spiritual weapon, just as I do." He held out his hand, and his sword of ice and smoke appeared in it. "It's a part of you, in a sense. It will take the form of whatever weapon you are most skilled with, or that you feel connected to in a given moment. You were a swordsman and an archer. I expect you could use either a sword or a bow."

Aili thought of En. It was true; En had been a part of her, the deepest part in some ways. She had never tried to summon anything but En, yet she had just pulled a knife on Zhu Guiren. "Why are you telling me this?"

"As I told you, first of all, to prove to you that you are lying. I don't enjoy lies done badly. They irritate me. Secondly, because we are going to be attacked tonight, and the attacks are getting worse each nightfall. I think that tomorrow, we'll also be attacked during the day, and probably more or less continuously from there on. We don't know for sure how much the refuge can take if we don't drive off some of the attacks. It will be useful to have you as backup, on the off chance that I need a break."

She looked at him. "You're lying to me now."

"Fine. Third reason. For the overly-trusting phoenix I'm not allowed to talk about."

Aili walked away. Chenguang's eyes in those last moments of Hong Deming's life wouldn't leave her; their eyes were the same — Liu Chenguang's beautiful shining eyes and Tairei's eyes just now, filled with tears, trying to be brave. How was it that she herself was so different from the person she had been? Body and soul, continuity be damned, she was not the same as Hong Deming.

"Leave me alone," she said, not sure who she was talking to.

"I'm serious," called Zhu Guiren. "Don't go too far. There are things here that are coming specifically for you—"

"Let them come." Now all the pain seemed to be pooling in her heart, like molten rock, hot and burning and full of sharp points ripping at her insides. She knelt and put her head on to the ground. "Let them come."

Sounding a little frantic, Zhu Guiren yelled, "That's not the best defensive position."

"Shut up," she whispered.

Something ripped across her back, like nothing she'd ever felt before; not like a single claw, or a sword, or an arrow, or even like a whip, though a whip was the closest memory she had to this if a whip could have teeth and intention. It tore across her back in several directions at once — ripping her skin like scissors through crumpled paper — and at the same time savaged her with a spiritual attack, a freezing coldness that hissed inward toward her heart.

She leapt up and threw a rock at it. The rock bounced off. Aili staggered and nearly lost her balance. Blood poured down her back and the coldness spread, slowing her down.

"Are you serious?" yelled Zhu Guiren. "Don't just throw rocks! Call the damn sword!" He was attacking the thing a few dozen feet away. It was huge, multi-tentacled, and covered in shifting, razor-sharp thorns — like a slug, but with legs that came and went irregularly along its length. Its eyeless head was crowned with a row of horns; its huge mouth was glowing a strange, bruised purple that made her feel sick to look at.

Zhu Guiren's sword bounced off of it just like the rock had. He tumbled out of the way of its lashing claws and shouted, "It's immune to demonic weapons. I'm just like a mosquito to it. You really need to use yours and see—"

The thing struck him in the abdomen with a razored tentacle; he spat blood and fell to the ground, unmoving, with a gaping wound in his belly. It turned its maw toward him, then back to Aili, as though Zhu Guiren was no longer of interest.

She tried to center herself and remember how this was done; she closed her eyes, reached out, and felt the hilt between her fingers.

"En," she said, and opened her eyes. Grateful. This was the right thing.

With En in hand, she ran forward, quick and even, remembering qinggong, the lightness skill. She leapt on the thing's back, still dripping her own blood everywhere she went, and sent out a sword pulse at the thing's skin. It felt like a bag full of water; she couldn't feel any structure or bones to it at all, and it made her feel a little ill to stand on it. The thing made a burbling noise and she nearly vomited. There was something so utterly *wrong* about it.

Her blood falling on it sent it into a frenzy. It reared up and turned its misshapen maw around toward her, twisting to follow her every move, the vast irregular mouth growing closer and closer to her. Aili sent a sword pulse into it, and it burbled again; along with the noise came a stench of battlefields and unburied corpses. This time, she actually did throw up. The thing was not bothered by her vomiting into its mouth.

She slashed hard, sending qi in a spiral of golden light from En into the thing's innards. A horrible, indescribable noise filled her ears. The thing flung itself from side to side in protest, but it was as though it couldn't stop itself from trying to swallow her, sword and all. Now that she was almost completely inside its mouth, its razor-like, shifting teeth tearing into her all over, she slashed again and again, cutting whatever passed for its lips and tongue into pieces. Her own blood covered it like a slick of oil, the stench overwhelming her. En's glowing, golden light shivered out from her hands, but it wasn't enough.

*Ah,* she thought, her skin shredded into a thousand strips, *I remember now. I don't only have a sword.*

She placed her hands together and sharply drew them apart, shouting something — she didn't know what — and then the fire was blazing in her hands.

Yes, that's right. En was gratitude. This was utter fury. *Shen Lu,* she thought, *if only you knew.*

Aili called En back, bowed her bleeding head, and placed the fire within the spiral of spiritual qi. The golden light of En now had a fiery edge of rage to it; it rampaged through the body of the creature, tearing it into pieces and incinerating it in a hill of flame. She yelled at the joy of that vicious anger, taking vengeance for every cut it had given her.

When it had burned itself into nothingness and the stink of it had dissipated, Aili dropped to the ground, covered in blood. The thing was gone, but the night was full of wailing. Collapsed next to her, Zhu Guiren was trying to cover the bloody rip in his abdomen.

*Ha, see how that feels, Zhu Guiren,* she thought. Nonetheless, she reached over with a shaking hand and smeared her blood onto him before passing out.

Aili woke, warm and safe, and realized that Tairei was sitting on the floor of the cavern, holding her in her arms against her chest. She looked up and saw Tairei's eyes looking down at her, her lips red with blood.

"Chenguang," she said, and struggled to sit up. Her head hurt. Everything was blurred together. Chenguang and Tairei, but they were the same person; they were not the same, because one person was her lover, and the other was not. Both of them loved the person she no longer was.

"My head," she said, and raised her hand to it.

"Does it still hurt?" Tairei asked, concerned. "You should be…you should be all right by now…"

"Did you try to heal me? Why are your lips bloody?" Aili dazedly put her finger to Tairei's lips. "You don't need to do that anymore, do you?"

Tairei blushed. "I just…I just kissed you…but you're covered with blood. It wouldn't have done any good for me to try to heal you now. Phoenixes can't heal one another."

From the other side of the fire, Zhu Guiren called, "As I keep saying, not a phoenix. Don't make assumptions."

Tairei and Aili realized at the same time that they had no privacy whatsoever and looked away from one another.

Tainu came over, sending a glare toward Zhu Guiren, who rolled his eyes.

"Tairei," he said, "cultivate. We can't leave here till you're done, and I think we're all eager to leave."

Tairei nodded and helped Aili sit up so she could settle herself into a lotus position.

"You too," Tainu said to Aili. "You used a lot of power doing whatever that was. Cultivate. You remember how now, right?"

She nodded and sat next to Tairei. Tairei looked at her beneath her lashes, then closed her eyes so they both could concentrate.

Tairei did her best to cultivate instead of letting her mind wander, but it wasn't working very well. She had been terrified watching Aili battle the soul-devourer through the golden fire which allowed them to see outside of the refuge. The beings had been exiled to the spirit realm thousands of years before and were desperate for mortal souls after so long; there would be more and more coming, drawn by Aili's soul, until she could complete her cultivation and they could leave.

When Zhu Guiren had brought Aili's body back through the wards, for a moment she forgot that Aili would be able to heal herself and fell to her knees, cradling Aili's bloody body against her. Remembering the feeling of Hong Deming's body after death — the stillness and the coldness — she bit into her own lips to do whatever she could.

As though realizing that she was on the edge of complete insanity, Tainu said sharply, "No, Tairei. Don't panic. Remember, she'll heal."

Nonetheless, she kissed Aili fiercely on her bloodstained lips, holding her tightly until her blue eyes opened in confusion. She had completely forgotten that Tainu and Zhu Guiren were watching.

Of course she knew that this body was not the body she had loved when Hong Deming was alive, but this was still her person. The body didn't matter. The kiss was as it should have been. How could Aili not understand this? The body was the way in which they loved one another, but the body wasn't the person that she loved; Hong Deming's body was dead, but the person she loved was not dead. Whether what she did back then had been wrong or right, and even if this person would never forgive her, she rejoiced that she had done it.

She regretted that she had called Deming's name when Aili kissed her back in Easterly, but Deming's name had been the one she knew; Deming's name had been her talisman all these centuries — far more than his body, which was gone forever. She knew that. Aili's name, beautiful as it was, it was new to her. She had to get used to it.

Tentatively, she said, "Aili."

"What?" Aili's voice came from beside her, sleepily.

Tairei looked over and saw that Aili had slumped to the side, lying on the cavern floor. So much for cultivating. But she needed sleep too.

She lay down next to her. They were not touching each other, but it was enough, for now.

Tainu sat in his lotus position, watching Tairei and Aili sleep, while Zhu Guiren watched Tainu's face — tired and thoughtful and a little sad.

Tainu noticed that Zhu Guiren was staring at him. He raised an eyebrow. "What?"

"Nothing." Zhu Guiren looked away.

"Is it possible to free Aili from the arrays she's bound to?" Tainu asked after a little while, tone considering.

"Maybe," Zhu Guiren said, tracing a pattern on the floor of the cavern with one finger. "I need to do some calculations."

"Calculate away."

Zhu Guiren continued to trace something no one else could see on the shining black stone; golden figures rose and fell inside it. He said, "I don't know if it's something…I think I will need…"

"Do you want me to help you?"

"Yes."

"All right, then."

Zhu Guiren looked up to meet his eyes again, but Tainu had already turned away. On the cavern floor, Tairei and Aili lay sleeping next to one another. One or the other of them had reached out, and their hands were intertwined.

# CHAPTER 22
## FIRST ARRAY

TAIREI WOKE UP first, since she hadn't been wounded. Zhu Guiren and Aili still slept deeply in the darkness of the cavern, but she saw Tainu was cultivating.

"Tainu," she whispered. The echoes ran around alarmingly.

"Are you all right?" he asked.

"No."

"Do you want to talk?" he asked, unfolding his long legs. "We should go outside, let them sleep."

"Is it safe?"

"We'll sit right against the rock. We can just fall backward if anything comes," he whispered.

Outside, the sun was shining.

"There are flowers," she said, "I never knew."

"What did you want to talk about?" His face was still very tired, and he rubbed his eyes.

"Last night, or whenever it was…after Aili had woken up, you started saying that I didn't understand. What don't I understand?"

"You don't understand because you are a phoenix," he said patiently. "For us, changing mortal bodies and being reborn is simple and easy. Our life and sense of who we are isn't disrupted. She is not a phoenix, as the demon keeps reminding us. I don't know how this feels to her, but it's obvious that it is not simple.

And what the demon said about those arrays…Her soul is bound, and that's…well…she's had a hard time."

Tairei was silent. She picked a flower and started tearing it into little pieces.

"What's done is done. You don't need to second-guess it, but she needs to find her own way through this. I don't want to see you hurt any more than you have been." He added, "I can see that she doesn't want to hurt you either, but I don't think she can give you what you're hoping for."

"I just want him back," she said. "To be together again. And now she remembers us, remembers who I am. Why is it not simple? Doesn't…does she not love me anymore? Does she blame me for dying?"

He shook his head. "Tairei, didn't you listen to what she said to you? What you told me? She has told you as bluntly as she can without being cruel. For her, I think that all she knows is that you want Hong Deming back. And you can't have Hong Deming. Not from her. Not from anyone."

"That's not what I meant," she said.

"What did you mean, then?"

Tairei tore up another flower.

He touched her hand gently. "You knew her for what, three weeks? You've been waiting a thousand years. Be patient — we're good at that. It will be what it will be, and you can't make it be something it cannot." Tainu tugged at her hair. "Get in there and cultivate, and we'll talk more. I'm going to enjoy the sunshine for a bit and think."

Time in the refuge passed without markers. Tairei settled into deep cultivation, deliberately shutting off her senses so she wouldn't be distracted by Aili's voice and not rousing unless someone shook her physically. Aili regularly went out to fight the soul-devourers, saying she had the hang of it now; she looked haggard, but Tainu let her go anyway, figuring she needed some way to get her anger out. It was obvious to him that she was very angry, even if she wasn't taking it out on Tairei.

Zhu Guiren sat opposite Tairei, back to the fire, using a stick he'd gotten from the forest and charred in the fire to scribble figures on a piece of his inner robe that he had torn off. Whenever the piece of cloth was full, he would sigh and tear off another one. At one point, he took out his sword and sliced his arm, seeming to consider the rate at which blood dripped out. He muttered to himself and wrote more figures.

"Do you want me to heal that?" Tainu asked.

"Oh, yes," he said, sticking out his arm without looking. "Thanks."

"What are you working on?" Tainu bit his lip and went over to smear the cut with his blood. "By the way, you almost hit a major artery. You need to be more careful if I'm not next to you. What if I was cultivating? You would have bled out, and I wouldn't have noticed."

"You're right. Stay there." He took his sword out and sliced again; this time he did hit an artery.

Tainu watched him, eyebrows raised, as he held the arm up and seemed to be counting until he passed out.

When he woke up, Tainu remarked, "It wasn't actually a suggestion."

"I needed to see the difference in the rate of flow," Zhu Guiren explained. "My blood is the key to undoing an array. I need to know how much I can get in a certain time frame."

Tainu laughed. "Demon, don't you know that if I'm with you it doesn't matter? I can heal you — your blood is more or less an endless supply."

"Really?" He tapped his thumb against his mouth, looking thoughtful.

"Are you chewing on your thumb?"

"Am I?" Zhu Guiren looked down at his thumb. "Yes, I am. Anyway, I'm working on the calculations I told you about. For the arrays. I'm still not sure... There are three. I think that one has a strong hold but is a weak array. That one, I'm confident I can break. The other two, I'm really not sure. They're...complicated."

"Do you need to actually break them? Can't you just cut the connection?"

"Arrays don't work that way. All in, all out. I theoretically figured out how to break arrays, but I don't know of any array that a demon has actually broken. This isn't done — usually, we just steal them from one another. They're valuable property. So...the owners of the arrays are going to show up and fight me as well."

Tainu frowned. "That's a problem, since you are both our fighter and our array-breaker."

"Will that one come with us? Aili?"

Tainu looked over at the empty place where she normally slept; she must have gone outside to kill things. "I don't know. She's not in good shape."

"As a fighter, she's not bad. Sloppy, but powerful. Better than skilled but weak," Zhu Guiren said judiciously.

"It's more her state of mind..." Tainu paused. "Actually, I wonder if it's the arrays that are affecting her? She seems to be so angry."

Zhu Guiren snorted. "Really, Tainu, do you think mortals don't get angry without demonic intervention? She's probably awash in resentment at this point. In fact, she's going to start attracting demons herself if she doesn't calm it down. Everything in range is going to see a tasty resentment snack. Aside from everything else, violent death is a source of resentment on its own, and when I was carrying her through the river, I happened to feel massive scars on her back, so she's had quite a bit of abuse in this life as well."

Tainu started. "What?"

Zhu Guiren said, "She's been heavily whipped at some point. Probably more than once, judging by the scars. Didn't you know?"

He shook his head, frowning.

"In any case, the arrays might be influencing her, yes. But they would only influence, not cause her anger. I actually think that whatever Liu Chenguang did to her is probably protective, keeping her from losing control or degenerating into deliberate cruelty, which is what the arrays would be attempting to do to her. But they could only work with what's already there."

"She would never be deliberately cruel," came Tairei's voice. "Never. Even in her first life, even at the moment of her death. So it's not because of anything I did. That's just who she is."

She unfolded from her cultivational pose and stretched. "Tainu, I'm done. Let's go."

They had to wait until Aili was done killing things. Tairei watched through the golden fire; it was a soul devourer again. It was true, Aili had gotten the hang of it. She let the thing get her in its awful maw, tearing her into bloody strips, then called En and the phoenix fire at the same time to rip it to shreds from the inside, yelling something incomprehensible the whole time. After, she fell over, a bloody mess, and looked up at the stars till she recovered, stood up, and went striding off toward the forest to look for something else to fight.

"As I said, powerful but sloppy," Zhu Guiren commented. "How can you give her all that power and not give her any guidance?"

"On what, using weapons?" asked Tainu. "We're uniquely unqualified."

This was not something anyone should do enough to get the hang of, Tairei thought. "Do you think," she asked uncertainly, "that's the only way to kill it? Or does she just…like doing it that way?"

Zhu Guiren seemed to consider this for a moment. "Nothing I've known of can kill a soul-devourer. That's why they were banished here, and not killed. It may well be that's the only way. She's using spiritual power, as an exorcist would, but also her own blood with its healing powers and the phoenix fire, both of which are probably particularly deadly to that kind of thing. It's a death-thing, and phoenixes are…life things, I guess."

"Very poetic," muttered Tainu.

"Also," Zhu Guiren continued, "speaking as someone who is very qualified with weapons, I would say that she likes doing it that way. She's certainly not showing any inclination to find a way that's less messy."

Tairei just shook her head, looking after Aili, where she had disappeared into the forest.

Around dawn, she came back up the hill, En in her hand, head down. She must have gone somewhere to bathe; her hair was damp in its single braid and the blood had been washed off of her skin, though her clothes were still essentially bloodstained rags.

"You're awake," she said to Tairei. "Are you all right?"

"I'm fine now," she said, feeling awkward. She looked up at this grim, blood-stained person with her unreadable, blue-grey eyes, remembering the wet cobblestones in Easterly. She still remembered how Aili's hair felt in her hands — marked and bent by the heavy braid, cold and wet from the water of the bay, but her ears were warm to touch. It felt farther away than her lifetime with Hong Deming.

After that, of course, Aili had kissed her — that wonderful, terrible time when she accidentally called her Deming. Was that why she was so distant now, did she think that…?

"Tairei," Tainu said, "pay attention."

Zhu Guiren cleared his throat meaningfully. "Aili is tied into three different demonic arrays," he said. "After examination, the first and weakest array is, in my opinion, near the place where she was born–"

Tainu leaned against the rock, arms folded over his chest, smiling at him.

"–in– in this life."

"What's an array? What are you talking about?" Aili asked. "Why has no one mentioned this to me before?"

"Ah, you've been busy," replied Zhu Guiren, waving his hand in the air, "killing things. And Tairei's been cultivating. We thought it would be easiest to just go over it all together so we wouldn't have to do it twice."

"We?" Aili frowned.

"Me and Tainu," he said.

Aili and Tairei both turned to look quizzically at Tainu.

"What?" Tainu asked.

"Anyway," Zhu Guiren continued, "the array is the weakest of the three and–"

"Go back to 'Aili is tied into arrays,'" Aili interrupted. "What does that mean?"

Zhu Guiren sighed dramatically. "All right, although truthfully this is more information than you need. The cultivation of demons depends on resentment–"

"What's resentment?"

"What it says — the energy mortals produce when their desires are unfulfilled. Do you want the entire list? It'll take a while." He stared at Aili.

She shook her head.

"Now," Zhu Guiren cleared his throat, "resentment occurs naturally in the mortal realm–"

Tainu snickered.

"WHAT?"

"You're funny," he said.

"This is not a funny conversation! This is very serious. Do you want this or not?"

"Want," they chorused.

"The arrays come from and shape the corruption of qi, causing the resentment of mortality to increase over time. They're built upon events of deep resentment. Unjust and violent death, usually, but sometimes other kinds of suffering. The array captures the resentment of that event, as well as the mortal souls that died, within it and essentially replays the event, thus inscribing it into those souls and providing a constant source of nourishment for demons. There are many levels of strength depending on its geographical extent, the number of souls caught into it, the strength of the demon that created it, whether a demon manipulated human beings so as to bring the array event about…" He looked at them. "Questions to this point?"

No one had questions, but Aili looked a little sick.

"Once an array has been established, living beings can be tied into it to further increase the resentment," Zhu Guiren continued. "Aili's been bound into three arrays. The first one, I believe, is connected to her birthplace in her current lifetime. Being born within the geographic node of an array, or to someone who is mortally connected to an array, is a strong binding for an individual. The nature of the array is that living beings bound in it are more likely to suffer unfairly, or to enact unjustified suffering upon others, or both. The type of suffering or violence depends on the strength of the array and how close one is to the center of it…" He trailed off.

Tainu and Tairei were both staring at Aili, whose skin had paled to complete bloodlessness. Tainu caught Zhu Guiren's eye and shook his head minutely as Tairei reached out, clearly concerned, and Aili moved away.

Zhu Guiren cleared his throat again. "It's because of this that we want to break the array. So things like that won't be…happening to Aili," he finished, awkwardly.

Still looking at Aili, Tairei said, "I agree, let's do that. What do we do now?"

"The real work will be done by me. Breaking the array requires a demon's blood and spells. Tainu will support me in case I need healing, and, if she's willing, Aili can step in to help with protection in case we're attacked during the spellcasting," Zhu Guiren said.

Aili didn't respond.

"Aili?" asked Tairei uncertainly.

As though she was just waking up, Aili said, "What?"

"Never mind." Zhu Guiren exchanged glances with Tainu. "You two can just watch. Like I said, the first one is the weakest array, even though it's a strong bond. We just have to get to the physical location of the array in the mortal world."

"Aili's birthplace?" Tairei asked. "It was near where I– where we– well, you know," she said, nodding at Tainu. "Where I last entered rebirth fire."

"That makes it easy," said Tainu, standing upright from his lazy lean against the wall of the refuge. "No point waiting. The demon is ready to get to work. Let's go."

Every phoenix could generate the rebirth fire once after entering the spirit realm for regeneration, which would return them to the location of their rebirth fire in the mortal world. In the lifetime where she had met Hong Deming, Tairei had been forced to do this before she had completed cultivation, weakening her for years afterward. Having completed cultivation now, though, it was as natural as breathing. Her wings appeared and spread wide as she moved her hands into the seal for opening the gate, and a circle of white-gold flame appeared in the air before her. "You all go first," she said.

Tainu took Zhu Guiren's hand, which evidently surprised him. "In case there's a problem taking a demon through a phoenix gate," he said, and pulled him through.

Aili looked at her silently.

"Go ahead," Tairei said. "I'm holding it open. I'll come as soon as you're through."

After Aili had disappeared, Tairei folded her wings and threw herself forward. She landed in a roll on the other side, crunching over old burned grass and new green seedlings. Aili was there, waiting for her, and reached out a hand to help her up. Tairei took her hand, looking at the coast oak, still green in the center of the little valley. Only a few black marks showed on its trunk. The late afternoon sun poured down from a cloudless sky.

"It's been months, at least," said Aili. "The grass is coming up again. It must be winter now, rainy season…" She looked around. Tairei remembered that she had burned Aili's father to death here, with the rebirth fire, and winced in case Aili was looking for the corpse. But Aili didn't say anything else.

A little bit away, Zhu Guiren and Tainu stood talking. Zhu Guiren said, "Aili, let me check something." He moved his hand carefully in front of her, focusing on an area in the center of her chest, and seemed to tug minutely on something in the air. "There it is. The central node of the array is not far. That way," he pointed, satisfied.

Aili nodded. "I was born in the house I grew up in, about a mile away in a straight line. Just follow me."

They followed her out of the valley toward the northeast in silence, single file, skirting one of the hills until they came to the little creek. Then she followed that into the valley.

She looked toward the white house on the hill. "Is it in the house?"

Zhu Guiren, seeming oblivious to the strain in her voice, tugged again on the invisible thread. "No. It's there, right by the stream. But the house would have been deeply affected, it's very close to the central node."

"Ah," said Aili. She looked around. "The cattle are gone. Let me…let me check on my mother before you…do it."

Without waiting for an answer, she started up the slope toward the white house. Tairei followed her closely.

The door was locked. Aili knocked hard; when no one answered, she broke a windowpane in the door and reached in through the glass, cutting herself a bit.

"Careful," Tairei said, but of course, the cut healed almost immediately.

Aili opened the door without looking at her and went inside. Everything in the house was dusty; it smelled of mildew.

"Mama?" Aili called.

They checked everywhere in the house, but there was no one there and no sign that anyone had been there for a long time. They ended up in the kitchen. There was mail on the table — some opened, some not. On top of the pile was a telegram. It notified the parents of Lieutenant Aili Fallon that she was missing in action and presumed dead.

"I was only gone for a few months…"

"Time in the spirit realm doesn't always coincide with time here," Tairei said. "But it hasn't been too long, I'm sure. Not…years."

Aili sat down on the table and put her head in her hands, breathing hard. "My head hurts," she said eventually.

Helplessly, Tairei put a hand on her shoulder. Aili didn't respond.

At last, Tairei said, "Let's do what we came to do. Then we can go look for your mother, all right?"

Aili got up without looking at her and went back outside.

Zhu Guiren stood at the edge of the stream where the cattle used to drink, sounding almost anxious. "Be ready. Timing will be important, and I need to do this on the first try or things will get much more difficult."

Aili and Tairei stood away from him, Tainu closer; all of them waited.

After several moments of standing still, looking down at the trampled earth with his arms folded across his chest, he said, "Damn, this is going to be complicated with only one hand. Tainu, come stand by me."

Zhu Guiren took a deep breath and held out his sword, then thrust it into the ground in front of him. He murmured something, and suddenly a cup made of ice appeared in his single hand. "Damn. Damn, none of you can hold this…"

He knelt, put it on the ground, then placed his handless forearm against the blade of the sword, slicing a deep gash that began spurting blood immediately. He held it over the cup of ice, filling it with bright red arterial blood. Filling the cup took much more than the size would suggest.

As soon as his blood reached the rim, he held his arm out to Tainu. "Fix," he demanded.

The blood in the cup began to smoke slightly.

As Tainu bit his finger, a cloud of crows descended from the trees and hills around them, beating their wings against Zhu Guiren's face and trying to overturn the cup.

"Trash," the demon muttered, and stood, grasping the sword.

"It's not done," warned Tainu.

"Oh, just keep going, I don't need two arms for this," Zhu Guiren replied. His eyes glittered. "Sorry for the inconvenience to you."

Tainu shrugged and continued to hold his arm, anointing the wound with his own blood to heal it while the crows swarmed them.

"Those crows, they're always here..." said Aili. She couldn't stop her voice from shaking.

"They're not crows. Come out, failure!" Zhu Guiren yelled from within the midst of the shrieking birds. The crows stopped beating against them and gathered a few feet away, their wings and feathers melting together into an indiscernible mass, then coalescing into a figure that looked almost human, but not quite. Its legs were shorter than its torso, its arms, still covered with dark feathers, bent like wings, and its mouth opened wider than any human mouth could.

It didn't seem to have eyes, but it turned its face toward Zhu Guiren. "Master, master, please don't," it begged. "It's all I have. I'll share it with you. I'll share it–"

"Don't call me master. Get back to your teacher and confess your shortcomings," Zhu Guiren said coldly, "or I'll destroy you permanently. Your shoddy work offends me. I don't want to share it. I want to clean up the mess."

The yaoguai screamed and threw itself on the ground. "Master, master, please!"

Zhu Guiren closed his eyes and began chanting.

The yaoguai suddenly launched itself at him, its claws elongating impossibly — longer than its entire body — while its head opened wider and wider.

Zhu Guiren continued chanting. Without opening his eyes, he pulled his standing sword from the earth and slashed down just as the claws tugged at his robe.

The creature screamed one last time and fled, trailing purple fire.

"Weak," Zhu Guiren snorted. He tossed down the sword to pick up the cup of blood, holding it at the level of his heart. The smoke immediately thickened and began to trickle out, circling around his body. It crawled across the ground as he chanted, a strange wheel with Zhu Guiren at the center. The tendrils of smoke began to curl and twist around each other, deliberately and without a discernible pattern, as though each had its own consciousness. There were beads of sweat standing out on Zhu Guiren's forehead as he swayed slightly; Tainu still held his arm and tightened his grip, keeping him upright.

"Stop! Stop! Don't come!" Aili raced past Zhu Guiren to a group of ordinary people who had suddenly appeared — women and children in loose-woven tunics, standing near a group of small houses made of reeds.

She had never noticed these little houses before. None of the people seemed to notice her.

The women took the children back inside the huts, silently. When Aili looked into one, she could see one woman rocking a child, her mouth moving as though singing a lullaby.

"You have to get out," Aili said urgently. "There's something happening here. You have to go–"

"Aili!" Tairei's voice was in her ear. "Aili, come back away from Zhu Guiren. What are you doing here?"

"They're too close. This can't be safe for them–" Aili backed out of the house, Tairei's hand on her arm.

Tairei looked up at her, a little frown between her brows; Liu Chenguang's eyes a thousand years ago. *Are you all right? You look unwell.*

Aili grabbed Tairei's hand and put it on the hut. "Can you feel it?" she demanded.

Tairei shook her head. "Aili, there's nothing there. There's no one here."

Aili looked around wildly. The women and children were coming back out of the houses now. She could see from their faces that they were screaming, some wounded and bleeding. Gunfire — she assumed it was gunfire, since she couldn't see any arrows — was tearing through the little reed houses. The women trying to run were being gunned down. The children, too.

Aili screamed as well and tried to stand between them and the gunfire, but it made no difference. She knelt down next to an injured woman and slashed at her own hand with a knife of golden flame, trying to heal her, but nothing happened. The woman died with her eyes open, her chest torn to pieces by the bullets. Two bearded men in ragged clothing walked by, their mouths agape in silent laughter.

*"Aili!"* She could hear Tairei shouting for her, but she was too busy — too busy trying to save these people, why couldn't she save them?

Zhu Guiren's voice, chanting, slammed through her head in a language she couldn't understand, his melodious voice terribly altered into something high and empty. The smoke curled around her feet, curled around the women and children, who lay down in it, and died. She looked around wildly for help.

In the center of the field, Zhu Guiren fell to his knees. Tainu dropped with him, still helping to hold him upright. The sound of his chanting reached a crescendo, shaking the air; he held the cup of ice high, pouring out the long, long stream of blood into the earth. As the last drop fell from the cup, the tendrils of smoke suddenly rushed back, and Zhu Guiren simultaneously slammed the cup of ice down onto the ground, smashing it.

Something rippled through the earth, through the air, through their bodies. The trees and grass whispered as though a heavy wind moved through them.

Zhu Guiren slumped over, eyes closed. Tainu held him, keeping him from falling over completely, but there was no resistance to gravity left in his body. At last, he opened his eyes and sighed. "Well, that was the easy one," he said. He grasped Tainu's arm and tried to struggle to his feet, failing the first few times.

"Do you need anything?" Tainu asked him, clearly concerned.

Zhu Guiren's head hung down as though he didn't have the strength to lift it up. "Nothing you can do," he said, but he still held on to Tainu's arm, and Tainu did not let go of his.

# CHAPTER 23
## SEPARATION

AILI'S EYES WERE fixed on a corner of the field near the stream; she held a whip of flame in one hand and En in the other. Tairei held the whip hand down hard.

"Aili," she said, over and over again, trying to sound calm. "It's Tairei. What's happening?"

At last, Aili's blue eyes frowned down at her. "Didn't you see them?" she asked. "The women and children? All dead…?" She wiped her mouth as though she were nauseated.

Zhu Guiren limped up slowly, Tainu supporting him. "Those were the mortal souls caught in the founding event of the array," he said after Aili explained, haltingly, what she had seen. "It's gone now. Do you feel any different?"

Aili didn't answer this. "Did the demon make them…do that?"

Zhu Guiren motioned to Tainu to help him sit down on the ground; his face was very pale. "Is it important to you to understand this for some reason?"

Aili's gaze moved to the white house and the red barn next to it. "Yes," she replied.

"No," Zhu Guiren said. "This was a weak array created by a weak demon. He just took advantage of what was already happening. He didn't encourage it to happen." He shrugged. "Lucky for us, this was not demonically initiated. It was…harder than I thought to break it." He looked down at the ground.

"Tainu," he said abruptly, "I need to rest."

They all looked at the house, then at Aili.

She said, "Fine, go on in. The door is open. I'll be out here. I need to think."

Tairei wanted to stay with her, but as she hesitated Aili met her eyes.

"You too," she said. "Just leave me here for a while."

Tairei followed Tainu and Zhu Guiren up to the house, turning around just once. Aili sat quietly by the water, her arms wrapped around her knees, watching the stream go by. She seemed well enough now, but very sad. Tairei didn't think she'd ever seen her look so sad, in this life or as Hong Deming. Surely, breaking the arrays...shouldn't it have made things better for her?

Tainu settled Zhu Guiren into one of the upstairs bedrooms to sleep, and then came back down into the kitchen. Tairei could hear him rattling around, probably trying to make some tea or finding whatever was to eat left in the pantries. They were all hungry now; she and Tainu had been cultivating heavily and hadn't eaten much in the spirit realm, and Aili and Zhu Guiren had been eating only what they'd been able to catch or forage in the forest around the refuge, much of which was not at all tasty. Probably that's part of the problem, she thought. Probably, Aili's hungry...

When dinner was ready, Tainu called her in. "Where's Aili?"

"She went into the barn," she said, sitting at the table.

He looked at her closely. "Have you been crying?"

She shrugged. Zhu Guiren came in and took a seat. He still looked pale.

Tainu had found potatoes and herbs, some unripe tomatoes growing wild, and eggs from some chickens scratching in the yard who had made nests on the back porch. "No time for bread or anything," he said. "And no rice here. Sorry, Tairei. Federatives don't usually use rice much."

"No problem," she said. "At least it's not meat. I've never seen so much meat in my life as in the restaurants in Easterly."

Not looking up, Zhu Guiren said, "Tainu, I need to talk to you. About the arrays." He didn't pick up a fork.

Tainu said, "Fine. Tairei, do you want to hear it?"

"I don't want her to," said Zhu Guiren. "It's private."

Tainu frowned, but Tairei nodded. "I'll just...take a plate out to Aili."

It was almost full night now, and there was no light. "Aili?" she called at the entrance to the barn. "Are you there?"

"Up here," came her voice from above.

"I brought food–"

Aili leapt down from the loft, using a tiny bit of qinggong to land lightly and easily next to her. "Good," she said, "I'm starving."

They sat on two hay bales near the opening to the barn so they could see the stars come out. Aili said, "It's good we did this. That those souls were freed. But it doesn't change what happened in the past." She ate some of the potatoes, then added, "Tainu's a good cook."

Cautiously, Tairei asked, "What happened in the past?"

Aili seemed to understand. "I'm wondering how much of it was my father and how much of it was the…array," she said. "If it makes a difference at all. I don't know." She ate more. "The stars are clearer now. It's as though there was a haze over this valley my whole life, as far back as I remember. Sounds were quieter. When…when there was noise, nobody seemed to hear it. Or maybe they just didn't care."

Tairei ate her potatoes, terrified of what she was going to hear.

Aili took a deep breath. "My two brothers died. Not accidents."

Tairei put her fork down.

"I couldn't protect them," Aili said. "My baby brother was crying, and my father was drunk and annoyed."

Tairei was silent, sick to her heart.

"My mother tried, but she couldn't either…There's a whip in the barn somewhere. That's what I came to look for."

Tairei could see Aili's face, turned up toward the stars.

"My second brother– He was already twelve. I don't know what he did to make my dad angry. But he was so scared that he– that he was up on the roof of the barn, and he fell. Or maybe he jumped. I wasn't here. I was at the hotel that day. I was fifteen. That was my job. I went to the hotel and helped behind the bar, cleaning and cooking and stuff like that, to make some money for us. We never had much money, and what we had my dad, would drink or gamble away. I could bring food home sometimes too, that way. That day, Mrs. Mitchell had some extra apple pie, and I brought it home for my brother. But he was dead."

After a while, Tairei said, despite knowing how completely pointless it was, "I'm so sorry, Aili."

"Did that happen because of the array? Or because my dad was just…like that?" she asked.

Tairei thought for a while, and said, "I don't think it matters. What matters is that it happened."

"That's what I think too." Aili was silent.

Tairei wanted to ask *what did your father do to you?* But she didn't dare, and in her heart, she wondered if she could bear to know it.

You survived, she thought, and you still have your kind heart, surely that means something…

But at that moment, she knew that it meant nothing at all. At least, not to Aili.

There is no good thing that has come to you from me, Tairei thought bitterly. Because of me, your first life was ruined. Because of me, you were born into this one.

Pulling up her courage, Tairei said, "Tainu told me that Nora died. I'm sorry."

"Yes." Aili's eyes remained closed. "She died."

"Are you all right?" Tairei asked eventually.

Aili laughed a little bit. "No. No, I'm not."

"Can I help you?"

"I don't think so." Aili ate some more of her potatoes. Then, suddenly said, "My head hurts."

Tairei checked her pulse. Aili's qi was unstable again; she calmed it, soothed the meridians back down, then took her hand. "Aili."

"Tairei," Aili sighed. "What do you want, Tairei?" she asked, as though she were very tired and trying very hard just to get through what needed to be done.

"I want you to be happy and well."

Aili shook her head a tiny bit. "I want that for you too."

It seemed to Tairei as though there was a glass wall between them that neither of them could break through. They sat there in silence, Aili letting Tairei hold her hand, neither moving, looking at the stars, and not at one another.

Eventually, Tairei said, "Aili, I wanted you to know…my name is Eftahede."

Aili looked at her, confused. "What?"

"Can you say it?"

"Eftahede," said Aili obediently, and then her eyes opened wider. "It feels…"

"You can feel it, can't you?" she asked. "If…if we are separated again and you want to find me, you can say my name and you'll know where I am. You'll be able to find a path to me."

"What if…you want to find me? I don't think I have a name like that." Aili frowned.

"You don't, yet," she said. "It's something that comes to you when you're ready, your name. Maybe someday you will, and maybe someday you will want to tell it to me. It's not something to be shared with anyone else, or spoken where other people can hear. You and Tainu are the only people in the world who know my name." She knew Aili couldn't really understand. But this was the only gift she had left to give her — the gift of her name.

"But…" Aili looked down. "What if you want to find me?"

"I can find you," she said. "It will just take longer. Like I told you, I have a general sense of your location from the binding. Hot and cold."

Aili nodded. "Eftahede," she said again, quietly.

"And…" Tairei said, "Aili, please don't– don't hurt yourself carelessly. I saw what you were doing with the soul-devourer. Just because you'll recover doesn't mean that your pain isn't real."

Aili gazed at her silently. Tairei had to look away.

"The same," said Aili, suddenly. "The same for you. Don't let yourself be hurt. Please."

Zhu Guiren stared at his plate of potatoes and eggs. Tainu leaned against the wall of the kitchen, waiting.

"I can't do it," Zhu Guiren said at last.

"Tell me more," said Tainu. "Were your calculations wrong somehow?"

"I underestimated how much power it takes to break an array," he said. "How much blood it takes. There's not enough blood in my body to do this."

"Even if I'm helping you?"

"I can't imagine how." He put his head in his hand. "You don't understand how…This is what I didn't tell you before. You know, I thought Hong Deming was bound by me, and Liu Chenguang said that he's not. But he is. He's both. Bound both by my array and Liu Chenguang's…whatever it was. There are a bunch of complications relating to the double binding there that I haven't worked out. Also, there's another array, although it actually may be connected to my array, I'm not sure."

Tainu sat down next to him, got a forkful of potatoes, and held it up to Zhu Guiren's mouth. "Eat," he said. "You need to eat. You're not making sense and you're exhausted."

Zhu Guiren opened his mouth and let Tainu put the forkful of potatoes into it, chewed, and swallowed. He looked at his plate some more. "Again," he said.

Tainu laughed and gave him another forkful, then another.

"You're a good cook," Zhu Guiren said, sounding surprised. "I can't cook at all."

"Late-night breakfasts in abandoned houses are my specialty," Tainu replied. "Are you better now?"

Zhu Guiren said, "Ok. Better."

"So, what's the real problem?" Tainu began eating his own dinner.

"There are two." He took a deep breath. "The first is that I'm not sure that I can break my own array. It is one of the most powerful ever made. It took me over two hundred years to set it up."

Tainu ate another forkful of potatoes. "So you started with the Fei Sukang uprising, then?"

"Around that time, yes. The fall of Zhashan, the end of the Feng dynasty… that was all me." He tossed that out casually enough. "I'm wondering if the second array on Aili is actually in Zhashan. I think Hong Deming was born there, which might mean that he is doubly bound by me. Although, Zhashan is full of arrays, not just mine…There are multiple nodes to my array because I set it up as an interlocking system over such a long period of time. The mortal souls caught in it number well over two million, spread out all over the central plain and throughout the Sorrowful River valley."

Tainu choked. "You–" he stopped, appalled.

"What?" Zhu Guiren asked defensively.

When Tainu just stared in silence, Zhu Guiren's face twisted a little bit. He pushed himself back from the table and walked outside.

Tainu finished eating his potatoes, sat there for a while, and then followed him.

Zhu Guiren was standing under the eucalyptus trees in the dark, looking out over the valley, his single hand holding his other elbow behind his back. When Tainu came up behind him, he said, "The earth is soaked with blood and hatred everywhere I've walked. Can you accept that so we can move on?"

"Continue," said Tainu.

Zhu Guiren didn't look at him. "My array is huge and powerful. I manipulated people in various ways to create the largest possible amount of resentment through cruelty and betrayal. In addition, I sealed it with the blood of a phoenix, as well as the rebirth fire and a final dose of mortal souls experiencing violent death, making the array both essentially impregnable and everlasting. The blood of a phoenix is…more powerful than my blood, of course. The normal way to seal an array is with the blood of a defenseless being." His eyes slid toward Tainu as though to see how he would take this.

Tainu didn't respond.

"Unlike the blood of any other being, the phoenix blood in connection with the rebirth fire will remain powerful and undimmed throughout time, constantly providing new life to the array. This was always going to be a challenge in trying to undo it. My plan was to begin around the edges, dismantling node by node, and at the end, the central seal would perhaps be at a manageable level of power for me to overcome with my own blood. Now here is the second problem: because it's my own array, as we begin to dismantle it, my own power will weaken. This means that my blood will have less and less effect as we come closer and closer to the central seal. Each time, I will need to use more and more blood."

Tainu remained silent.

Zhu Guiren said, "I've graphed it several times. By the time we reach the central node, my blood will not be able to overcome the sealing of the great array, no matter how much of it I use." He turned to look at Tainu directly. "I don't think it's possible."

Tainu asked, "Are you absolutely sure?"

"There are many variables. Not everything is clear yet. But, Tainu, I don't think it's possible." His gaze shifted away.

At last, Tainu said, "Do you still want to undo it?"

"I told you, I don't think I can. I don't think I can undo it."

"That wasn't what I asked," Tainu said. "Do you want to undo it?"

"Yes. I want to."

"Then I'll help you. That's all. We'll try together." He turned around. "Come finish your dinner, demon."

Zhu Guiren stood under the trees a while longer, breathing in their bitter scent.

After they had all eaten, they gathered together again, this time on the hill above the valley. No one wanted to stay in the house or near the creek anymore.

Tainu looked at all of them, gauging their energy for this. Aili looked pale, but otherwise all right; Tairei looked as though she had been crying; Zhu Guiren was looking at the ground and avoiding everyone's eyes.

Tainu sighed.

"All right," he said. "We need to decide what happens now, and how we do it. The demon and I are going to go try to break the remaining two arrays. They are in the Daxian Republic."

Tairei's head raised; Aili's dropped.

Zhu Guiren said, "Aili, when you were born as Hong Deming, was it in Zhashan?"

She nodded. "Yes. I was an orphan. Taiqian–" She shook her head. "Taiqian found me and brought me back to Crane Moon as a disciple. I was only around four years old. I don't remember anything."

Tainu said, "You do remember something. You don't want to remember it. That's how it is, with children of that age. I can try to bring the memories back. It will help us pinpoint–"

Aili shook her head. "No. I've had enough memories for one day. Let me think." After a few moments of silence, she said, "Taiqian told me that my parents were probably killed in the Wan Zhao rebellion."

"That doesn't exactly narrow it down much," said Zhu Guiren.

"That's all I can give you," she said fiercely. "No more memories today."

Tairei said, "You told me once that you– Taiqian found you in what used to be the marketplace of the east quarter. That there was a beggar who was earning money with you. You were able to dodge rocks and knives…that people threw at you."

Aili closed her eyes. "That's enough," she said sharply.

Tairei looked back at the ground.

"Anyway, that was how Taiqian knew I had potential," she said. She turned her back to them.

"Aili," said Tainu.

Aili shook her head.

Tainu said, "All right, I understand. No more memories." He put his hand over his eyes. He had spent thousands of years watching human beings suffer; it never got easier and so often there was nothing he could do, but at least he could offer. At least she should know that they cared for her, as she was now, not because she had once been Hong Deming. "Aili. Is there anything– anything we can do for you? That I can do for you?"

She said, "I need this to be over. I need no more of this. I need to be away from this. All this." She waved her hand to encompass the valley, the house, the three people standing near her, herself.

Zhu Guiren glanced at Tainu and said, "She doesn't need to come. I can find it without her being physically present. It will just take longer."

Neither of them mentioned that they had been counting on Aili for protection.

Tainu nodded. "All right, we'll head to Zhashan. Tairei, will you come?"

Tairei took a deep breath. "Yes," she said. "I'll come."

The demon said, "Next question. How do we get to Daxian? Ship?"

"No," said Tairei and Tainu simultaneously. Tairei continued, "Assuming that there's still a war, which I think there is, there won't be ships we can get on as civilians."

Tainu added, "I was able to enlist because I had a documented identity here, back in the rural provinces. None of you do. They're careful with papers."

"There's a dragon gate off the coast a few miles north," Zhu Guiren said. "And I can call the dragon…Never mind."

"What?" asked Tainu.

"It'll want a sacrifice to take us through its gate. You won't like how that works out…" He tapped his arm with his fingers. "We can go through the spirit realm. If we can get in, I can easily find a demonic gate that goes to Zhashan. That area is riddled with arrays."

"Ugh, spirit realm," said Tairei.

"Don't worry. Demonic gates are all over, and they're stable. Not rare and temporary like phoenix gates," he said. "It'll be a quick trip once we're in. The closest demonic gate here in the mortal realm is about twenty miles north. We can just start walking, I guess."

Aili said, "You don't have to walk. I can make a gate for you. I can call the fire whenever I want to now. I watched Tairei do it. I think I see how."

Tainu looked at her for a moment, wondering. "All right," he said. "Try it."

Aili looked down, placed her hands together, then drew them apart with a shout. Phoenix fire — more red than gold — spun out into a sheet of flame.

"Hold my hand," Tainu said to Zhu Guiren. "I still don't know if you can go through a phoenix gate without a phoenix." To Aili, he said, "Be careful." He wanted to say more, but then shook his head and grabbed Zhu Guiren's hand, leaping forward through the flame.

When Tainu and Zhu Guiren had gone, they stood together on the hilltop, the flame of the gate in front of them between Aili's hands.

Tairei said, "Aili."

The flames flickered in silence above the earth. Aili didn't speak.

Tairei thought perhaps her eyes were glittering. Perhaps she was crying, as Tairei wanted to, but in the shadows, it was hard to tell. "Aili," she said. She found that she couldn't say anything else. "Please find me. When you can, please come, please call my name."

Aili nodded. "Go," she said, her voice calm.

Tairei threw herself through the fire.

On the other side, she fell and rolled, hoping against hope that someone would follow her.

But as soon as she was fully on the ground, the flame behind her disappeared.

Tainu was waiting for her. "It'll be all right," he said. He hugged her, letting her cry. "It'll be all right, don't worry. You did the right thing."

They had entered the spirit realm near a river, perhaps because there had been a river near where Aili had sent them through. The sun was bright and high in the emerald sky. Zhu Guiren was standing a little way away, his eyes closed, holding two fingers in the air as though testing the wind. He turned slowly in one direction. "There," he said. "Not far at all. A gate to Zhashan. No one's watching right now. It's an old one. Let's go."

On the hilltop above Fallon, the flame disappeared. There was only starlight and the sound of insects.

Aili sat, dry-eyed, at the top of the hill for a while. It had rained not so long ago; the ground was damp.

When her mind was calm, she walked slowly down toward the stream and crossed it, letting it get her wet like it had when she was a small child, feeling the water on her feet. She had always loved that stream.

She stood in the yard in front of the house. She looked at it for a long time, then at the barn and the eucalyptus trees. She looked at the place where there had been a flower garden once and wondered how long ago her mother had gotten the telegram, whether the cattle had been sold then, or before. After her father had died, her mother wouldn't have been able to manage the cattle on her own. At any rate, they were all gone now, and the horses too.

She looked upstream and down. The other houses seemed to be empty. Fallon wasn't a prosperous place; the soil wasn't good, there was only so much forage for cattle, and everyone who lived there seemed to have bad luck of some kind or another. The town had mostly been abandoned by the time she ran away at sixteen. She supposed that she should check the houses and be sure, but she found that she didn't really care. Let them run, if they were there, if they had been there all this time and never lifted a finger.

She raised her hands, and there was a whip of flame in each one. She shouted, and called down fire from heaven.

# THE AUTHOR HAS SOMETHING SHE WANTS TO SAY

Thank you for reading the story of Liu Chenguang and Aili to this point. In *The Shoreless River*, their story continues – as does that of Zhu Guiren and Tainu. I hope you will continue on their journey with them to the end!

In writing this novel, I've been inspired by the work of contemporary Chinese web novelists in the danmei/BL genre. I love their work and the creative risks they take, the quick pacing and emphasis on story, the unapologetic focus on loving and complicated relationships, the playfulness around sexuality, and the frequent blending of pathos and humor. These writers publish under pseudonyms, and among my favorites are the works of MXTX (Mo Xiang Tong Xiu), Priest, Rou Bao Bu Chi Rou, and Fei Tian Ye Xiang. Many of these works are currently being published in licensed English translations and I highly recommend reading them!

I also draw heavily upon the Chinese contemporary genre of xianxia (cultivation or ascension). In xianxia, human beings, through meditation and hard work as well as luck and talent, can develop spiritual powers and even, in some cases, ascend to become deities. Spiritual beings (yao or yaomo, often translated as demons, and yaoguai, often translated as monsters) also cultivate in order to develop their powers. The yao are not demons in the western sense; like human beings, they can be good or evil, and the category of yao can include all kinds of spiritual beings, harmful and harmless, although yaoguai have more of a sinister or dangerous connotation. Xianxia builds upon wuxia, the genre of martial arts fantasy, and exaggerates the powers of wuxia martial artists into the spiritual realm, including the aspect of training in different cultivational paths that is handed down in different sects or clans. Chinese fantasy also includes xuanhuan, stories about mythological creatures and fantastic beings. While in some ways this may be considered a xuanhuan story, in other ways, it is not, as the phoenixes and demons here have many aspects that don't reflect Chinese traditions. The cultivation of resentment and the "demonic path" (mo dao) is a frequent trope in xianxia novels.

I'm grateful to an entire community of people who at various points in the writing process discussed the ideas in the books, or pointed me to learning resources, or read early drafts, or edited and commented, including Spencer Hatcher, Yilin Wang, Ali Lutz, Amy Snow, Zhui Ning Chang, and XM Moon, and of course, she without whom nothing is accomplished, my spouse, Tita Valeriano, and my child, who is very proud of my books even though they're a little above his age grade at the moment. As an indie author, community is central to being able to write and publish, and as a reader, you're part of that community too. Please consider leaving a rating or review to help other readers find a story they'll enjoy. And if you would like to keep up to date on future books and the writing process and occasionally get a free short story or novella, or stay in touch via social media, please sign up for my newsletter on my website, jcsnow.carrd.co, where I'll have all the most recent links, updates, and book progress.

# THE Shoreless River

J C SNOW

# PROLOGUE

IN THE CAVERN, there was a person being cut, over and over. The person lay on a stone couch, and the blood that flowed was caught in small drains carved into the stone, and from there fell into an open bowl, a thin waterfall.

The person was a young boy, about seven years old, with bright red hair and pale skin. If he opened his eyes, they were a clear green color, but he had kept them closed for a long time.

A creature sat near the stone couch, carving into the boy with his sharp claws. The creature looked something like a lizard, something like a cat; his edges were blurry and undefined, as though he wasn't quite sure what he wanted to be. His scales were silvery, and his wings and mane were like smoke. On his head were several small horns, pointing every which way like a thicket of ice.

Larger beings had come, cut harder, cut more often. For a long time, every time he cut the boy's skin it would heal. Now the wounds stayed open, and this creature, which was about the size of a large rabbit, could keep working on his own. As long as the boy was cut continually, the wounds wouldn't heal, so the process needed to not cease, day after day.

This was the creature's job.

It was a boring job.

One day, the creature got distracted, because his job was so boring, and how much blood did they really need, anyway? He went over to another part of the cavern and instead used his claws to make a design on the wall. The design looked like symbols and letters, although no one but the creature could read them.

"What's that?"

The creature whipped his head around. The boy had opened his eyes. The creature was struck by them; they were shaped in a fascinating way. He quickly calculated the degree of the angle between the bed and wall and leapt over. The creature liked to do math very much.

"Your eyes are the color of grass," he said.

"This time they are," the boy said, and closed them again as though he were very tired. "What are you drawing on the wall?"

"It's a system I worked out myself," he said proudly. "I can use it to calculate things precisely, angles and such, and predict where things will be at certain speeds within a certain period of time."

"Why do you want to know that?" the boy asked.

"Why not?" The creature brought his head back on his long neck like a snake getting ready to strike. "If I look at the stars at night, I see they are moving, and I thought it would be nice to know where they are and where they've been."

"Can't you just look?"

"No." The creature's head drooped. "I have to do this now. Just keep cutting you."

The boy actually laughed and turned his head to look closely at him. "Well, it's much worse for me. I can't see the stars either and I'm also getting cut all the time."

The creature looked at him curiously. He was very close to the green eyes now. Cautiously, he stretched out his neck and touched the boy's nose with his snout. The boy jerked back a little bit, but not much; he was restrained with silvery shackles around his wrists, neck, and ankles.

"Does it hurt?" the creature asked.

"Of course it hurts, idiot," said the boy. "Every time, it hurts."

"Oh," said the creature. "I didn't know. You never move or anything."

The boy sighed. "Well, better get on with it."

The creature lifted a claw and gently dragged it along his skin, but didn't cut into him. "Did that hurt?"

"No?"

The creature pressed harder. This time the claw sliced inside and drew blood. The boy frowned.

"That time it hurt, didn't it?"

The boy nodded.

The creature thought for a while. "A conundrum," he said at last. "I can't think of any way to do this without hurting you, but I have to do it. If I don't make sure you keep bleeding, the larger ones will kill me."

The boy didn't say anything.

The creature did his job and sliced him all over, making him bleed, but he noticed how the boy kept frowning, every time his claws cut. When he was done for the day, he went and curled up in another part of the cavern, thinking. Then, he drew on the wall some more, considering, and left.

After a while, a second boy entered the cavern and said, "Hello!"

The first boy opened his eyes, shocked.

The new boy was unconcerned that there was a person his own age tied up and bleeding on the stone couch. He sat on the edge and excitedly said, "Guess what!"

The first boy narrowed his green eyes. The second boy had black hair and eyes, and pale skin. "You are…"

"Look, it's me!"

The boy on the couch struggled and tried and failed to sit up, apparently forgetting that he had silvery bonds on all his limbs. "Why did you do that?"

"I can't hold it very long. This is my first time trying a mortal body." The other boy put his face down close so they could look at each other's eyes. "Is it good?"

Against his will, he smiled. "Very good."

The other boy's shape fluttered and dissolved, resolving itself back into the lizard-cat creature. "That takes a lot of energy," the creature said. "I have a plan to experiment with. I'll find a way to do this without hurting you. That's what the body is for. I'll test with it."

The red-haired boy looked at him pityingly. "Good luck with that."

"What's your name?"

"I don't have one," the boy said, "and I wouldn't tell you it if I did."

"Oh," the creature said. "I don't either. I'm not ranked high enough to be called anything yet."

The red-haired boy smiled. "I'll just call you demon, then."

"Then I'll call you phoenix." The creature sounded pleased, and began cutting the boy again. As he did so he said, "I asked why we have to have your blood, and they said that phoenix blood is the most powerful substance, useful for lots of things, spells and wards, and for cultivating power, and we need to cultivate so we can survive, although surviving really means we have to kill each other, it's all very confusing. Then they told me not to ask questions anymore."

Slice, slice. The boy frowned each time.

Talking more quickly, the creature said, "I've been cut a lot myself. I don't feel it anymore. That's why I didn't know it hurt you. If you let the big ones see that it hurts, they say you're a weak one and you should be culled, which means killing you. That happened to my friend, I had a friend once. There was a competition and he lost, so he's dead now."

Slice, slice.

The creature was getting a little frantic; he wanted to get it done quickly, but that meant he was getting sloppy with his technique and the cuts were deeper. The boy made a noise, and the creature instantly stopped.

"Are you all right?" the creature asked eventually.

"Of course I'm not all right, don't ask stupid questions," the boy said.

The creature noticed that there was water on his face. He reached out with his snout and gently licked the water off. It tasted salty. "What is that? The water?"

"It's crying. Shut up," the boy said.

The creature didn't come back for quite a while, perhaps several days although there wasn't a way to tell time. The green-eyed boy's cuts healed themselves, leaving pink scars.

When the creature returned, he was in his mortal body. "I have a solution," he said shyly.

The boy looked at him silently. There were dark bruises under his green eyes. He didn't ask if the green-eyed boy was all right because that was a stupid question.

"Here," he said, offering a cup of dark liquid.

The boy looked at him. "Have you not noticed that I'm tied up and can't use my hands?"

"Oh, I'll help you then?"

"What is it?"

"I made it. I tested it on this body," he said. "Look!" He took out a knife and drew it across his own arm without wincing. A great deal of blood immediately poured out.

The boy yelled, "Stop that! What are you doing?!"

"Don't you see?" he asked, crestfallen. "When you drink it, you can be cut and it doesn't hurt. And it also makes you bleed more, so I won't have to cut you as much."

The boy on the stone couch looked at him silently.

"Are you crying again?"

"Shut up."

He put the cup on the side of the couch, then transformed back into his normal self. "Will you drink it?"

The boy said, "No."

The creature curled up next to him. "You're warm," he said after a while. "I like being close to you."

The green-eyed boy turned his face to look at him. "I can tell it's you, demon," he said. "No matter what your body looks like, I think. You have the same expression in your eyes no matter what shape they are."

The creature put his head on the boy's arm and turned it to one side so he could see the green eyes better, considering.

The boy asked, "Do you know why they are making you do this? A little baby demon who doesn't understand what he's doing?"

"No? Why? I thought it was my job. I'm being punished for spending too much time looking at stars and making calculations. That's what they said, I need to be responsible."

"That's not why," the boy said, gently. "It's because they see that you are clever and will grow up to be strong if you can cultivate the demonic path. You can help make your clan more powerful, and thus make them more powerful, but they need to make you cruel as well. Otherwise, you're no good to them."

The creature stared into his eyes. "Am I not cruel?" he asked. "I'm a demon. I know...I know what we do..."

"Do you know what you have to do in order to become a true demon? To cultivate into your most powerful form?" the boy asked, still gently.

The creature looked at the ground, twisting his claw into one of the bloody channels in the couch. "They told me, but I don't really understand it."

"You can't do it if you're not cruel. You can't do it," the boy said, "so they need to make you hurt me, and get used to hurting me, and stomp out all the kindness you have. Anything that might rise up in you and resist — anything in you that is sad that you are cutting me and hurting me, they need that to be destroyed in your heart."

"I don't have a heart," he said immediately. "They said I don't."

The boy laughed. The sound was full of genuine pleasure.

The creature looked at him, unable to stop looking and listening.

"Everything has a heart," the green-eyed boy said, smiling at him. "You have one too."

"They don't know that I learned how to undo the wards," the creature said suddenly. "I watched them carefully when they captured you. I only need to see something once to remember it. I did the calculations already. I know how it can be undone."

"You figured that out before you came?"

The creature said, "I thought you might not drink it, so I planned ahead." He took his mortal form again. "But I don't want you to go. I wish we could stay together."

"Would you like to come with me?"

"I can't," he said. "I can't survive away from the clan yet. I haven't cultivated enough. I'd just be meat for other demons."

"Will they punish you?"

"Of course," he said, indifferent. He slashed his arm again, and blood gushed out. The boy gathered a handful and walked around the stone couch, murmuring in the demonic language, sprinkling the blood and wiping it on the shackles. The green-eyed boy watched and listened carefully.

The silver shackles disappeared and the boy sat up, rubbing his wrists and ankles. "Thank you," he said. "Be safe. I'll remember you." With visible effort, he transformed into a very small, red bird, the size of a hummingbird, and flew out of the cavern.

The black-eyed boy transformed back into his true body and went over to the cavern wall to continue his calculations.

# CHAPTER 1
## ZAI'AN

IN THE DEEP night of a quiet street, three people suddenly appeared from a blue-black slash in the air. They were a strange group: a young Daxian woman with gaping holes in the back of her shirt, a one-handed Daxian man dressed in travel-stained silk robes, his wide sleeves fluttering and long hair tangled, and a tall, dark-skinned man with a graceful bearing, dressed in an unremarkable shirt and pants that could have come from anywhere in any world.

Zhu Guiren looked around with distaste. "What a mess. This place reeks of resentment. And have they never rebuilt it?"

"It's called Zai'an now," said Liu Chenguang, putting her hair back behind her ears. Her voice sounded a little stuffy. "And yes, they've rebuilt it various times, but never again as it was under the Feng. Good job there."

"Enough," said Tainu in a calm, quiet voice. "Demon, can you find the array?"

Zhu Guiren closed his eyes and turned in a circle. "This place is…covered with arrays," he said. "Array on array…Some are very old. Those are the ones most likely to be associated with Hong Deming, but there are a lot. Any big, violent events here? What happened recently? There are some very strong new ones…"

"How recently?" asked Liu Chenguang.

He shrugged. "Past half-century or so?"

"Thousands of people in the Mitang quarter were killed here during the overthrow of the last dynasty," she said.

"That would do it. Hmmm…"

After a few moments of waiting, Tainu asked, "Hmmm what? What's happening? Can you find the array or not?"

"No," he said eventually. "Not…right now. Can we…sleep on it?" He looked a little abashed from what could be seen of his face in the moonlight. "I may need to do some reconnoitering. Talk to some people. The newer arrays have incorporated pieces of the ancient ones."

"By 'talk to people', do you mean talk to demons?" Tainu asked.

"Correct," he said. "For that, I need sleep first. In a bed. Do you realize that I haven't slept in a bed since…"

"Since last night?" Tainu asked dryly.

"That doesn't count. That was just a nap in Aili's uncomfortable abandoned house."

Liu Chenguang turned around and walked away down the darkened street.

"Wasn't she the one who decided to come and leave Aili?" Zhu Guiren asked.

"You are so…" Tainu shook his head. "Never mind. Come on, we'll find a place to sleep."

Quietly, Liu Chenguang called, "We should also get some decent clothes tomorrow. Especially him."

"Why?" Zhu Guiren looked down at himself. "What's wrong with this?"

"I think I'll just let you wander the streets like that tomorrow so you can find out." Liu Chenguang came back toward them. "I haven't been here since I left this area to look for Aili," she said in a steady voice. "About seven years ago now. The town has been through a lot, but it seems as though it's still Daxian territory–"

Zhu Guiren looked at her. "Of course it's Daxian territory."

"There's a war," she said. "Remember? A very complicated and protracted war with at least three sides, and the ordinary people are caught in the middle of it. There's been some kind of war or disaster constantly for the past hundred years, although not all of it affected Zai'an directly. Don't you read newspapers?"

"I've been in the Common Federation for centuries," he protested. "The newspapers don't have a lot about the Daxian Republic. Also, I've been doing other things. Also, since when do you know anything about politics? What did you do with Liu Chenguang?"

Tainu said, "Liu Chenguang, just take us to a place where we can sleep. Do you have money?"

"Not here. I don't even know what currency they're using now."

"Fine," Tainu replied. "Well, I agree with the demon. I'm tired. He and I can fly off and rest in a tree somewhere, but—"

"No," said Zhu Guiren. "No, I cannot. I want a bed and a bath."

"My goodness, people." Even in the dark, Tainu's eye roll was visible. "Demon, do you have money?"

Zhu Guiren closed his eyes, muttered something, and held out his hand. "There," he said. "Gold — the universal maker of friends and buyer of comfortable beds."

"Is that real?" Liu Chenguang asked skeptically.

"Of course it's real," he said indignantly. "Don't you remember how I hid gold in all those places?"

"Fine, gimme." She took the gold out of his hand and walked away. "Come on," she called, "there used to be a few places down this way. I'll get the best one for us. The one where they don't ask many questions."

The inn was dilapidated and the food poor, but at least there were beds and hot water. The owner was almost pathetically glad to have paying visitors, especially as the payment was in gold. Liu Chenguang got a suite with a large shared central area and several smaller bedrooms and alcoves since money wasn't an object and she thought they might be staying for a while. Once upstairs, she opened a window to let in fresh air, as well as a small red bird and a large black crow with an unusually long tail that had been waiting in a tree outside.

"Why did we have to do that?" asked Zhu Guiren crossly once he was transformed and standing on the wooden floor. "For the record, not having a hand translates into missing something important in my wing. Not sure what it is, exactly. I can't fly far, so let's not do that again."

Zhu Guiren massaged his handless arm until Tainu came over and started massaging it for him. "You did look a little bit like a sick chicken trying to get into the tree," Tainu remarked. "Next time I'll get up to hawk size, and if you downsize to a sparrow, I can carry you."

Zhu Guiren went from slightly flushed to bright red. "That's—that's embarrassing."

"Isn't it?" Tainu flashed him a smile. "But how can you be offended when I'm being so helpful?" He completed whatever he was doing to the muscles of Zhu Guiren's forearm. "That should make it better. Liu Chenguang can probably make some ointment for you tomorrow to help too."

"Liu Chenguang's going to be doing a lot of shopping tomorrow," she said from the table where she had watched all of this, unsmiling. "Zhu Guiren, give me your measurements. You too, Tainu, even though you're not quite as embarrassing as that one."

"What exactly is embarrassing about my robes?" Zhu Guiren demanded. "Once they're clean– Or I can get a new outfit–"

"Not like that one you can't, unless you're going to a theater and rummaging through their costumes. No one dresses like that anymore since the fall of the last dynasty, and most people well before. Not in the cities, anyway. It's Federation-style trousers and buttoned shirts and vests for you gentlemen unless you want traditional peasant wear. Cheaper that way, if you want to wear loose trousers and knotwork tunics instead." She sighed. "But I am not wearing those damn dresses. You can barely breathe or walk in them. I'll get some pants for me as well."

Tainu said, "I'll have the Federation style. Get me a hat, too."

"You're probably going to be mostly in your bird form during the day, so you don't need to worry about your accessories," she said. "You'll be highly visible. There are almost no foreigners in the Daxian Republic now with the war, and you'll immediately be taken as a Federative." If Aili came, she would have the same problem; she quashed that thought quickly. "But truthfully, given what people are going through here, I doubt most people will care much. It's just that if we want to hide in the crowd it becomes more difficult."

Tainu sat down. "I'll be glad to get new clothes, but who do we have to hide from?"

Zhu Guiren tried to comb his fingers through his hair and got stuck in tangles immediately. "I need a pincrown."

"No one wears pincrowns anymore. You need to get a haircut," Liu Chenguang said impatiently.

"No," he argued. "I like my hair long and I'm not cutting it for a bunch of mortal peasants."

Liu Chenguang snickered. "I'll get you a hairpin, Tainu can help you put it up."

Zhu Guiren glared at her and continued trying to unknot his hair.

"I'm excellent with hairpins," said Tainu solemnly. His own hair was still in the military cut, nearly-shaved to show the shape of his skull. "Anyway, who do you think might be looking for us?"

"As I mentioned, there's a war on," Liu Chenguang said, trying to keep her patience despite her complete exhaustion. Tainu was used to always being with humans. He was social that way, and interested in them — one of the many things which set him apart from most phoenixes. He would have to be more careful, this trip. "Zhu Guiren and I look like Daxians in our mortal bodies, but you definitely don't. There aren't any people here with skin as dark as yours. Most people won't care, but anyone from the Kunorese invasion force certainly will, and anyone reporting to them or spying for them will pass the word. Why would we want that kind of trouble?"

"All right," Tainu said, "I see what you're saying. We don't need additional complications. But this city is held by the Daxian army, isn't it? So it should be fine here."

"Who knows?" Liu Chenguang stood up. "There's paper and pen on the table. Leave your measurements for me, and anything else you want me to get. I'll be heading out early in the morning to the market. Bath and bed."

The inn had running water. Zai'an was a city after all; they weren't out in the villages, so she poured herself a bath and washed her hair, listening to the two talk softly in the main room, their voices — Tainu's deep voice and Zhu Guiren's lighter, quicker one — comforting probably precisely because she couldn't understand what they were saying. Sometimes, she heard Zhu Guiren's pointed laughter, or the warm tone of Tainu's voice that meant he was smiling while he talked. They seemed to enjoy one another's company, something she never would have imagined, but she remembered that when she traveled with Zhu Guiren, it really hadn't been so awful. He hadn't smiled or laughed like he did now, but as a traveling companion, he was quite pleasant aside from…well. She wondered sometimes why Zhu Guiren was doing this, but in the end, she was just grateful that they could do something to help Aili. Anything at all.

She had left Aili only a few hours ago, but across the world, on the other side of the great ocean. She had left her alone in the place that had killed her spirit, the place she called home. Aili had sent them away. Opened the phoenix gate and sent them from her.

After a thousand years of waiting, Liu Chenguang had found her person again. For nothing.

She wished that Aili had a true name so she could know it and say it to herself when she missed her, which was almost every moment that she was not fully focused on doing something else. But after everything that had happened, she was too exhausted for it to even hurt too much. It was more that the hope she had had for the last thousand years was gone now, and there wasn't any other hope to replace it.

Fully outfitted, Zhu Guiren went out after lunch the next day to "talk to some people" on his own; he didn't want anyone to know he was traveling around with two phoenixes. He returned several hours later and immediately settled down in a corner and began to scribble calculations on the walls with a pencil he'd found.

"Why do you always use walls?" asked Liu Chenguang. "We have paper." She was seated at the table, surrounded by piles of bark, roots, fungi, and herbs, making up packets and grinding things into powders.

"Paper is limited. My ideas are not," he said. It was certainly true that his diagrams were beginning to cover large portions of the wall. "What are you doing? That's a lot of powerful material you have there. What's the prescription?"

"Just making preparations. We're going to have to pay to get that cleaned."

"Who cares?" After he had scribbled a while more, he sat back on his heels and looked over what he had done. "Where's Tainu?"

"Oh, he went out to talk to some people too," she said vaguely. "He has old acquaintances."

"Why didn't he tell me?" he asked, frowning. "He doesn't know the right questions to ask."

"I have different questions." A red bird flew inside and transformed into Tainu. He smiled. "It's nice to see old friends. I've got the word out to let me know about any place where they've seen demons congregate, or anything they know about an array if they've heard demons talking."

"Who are you talking to?" Zhu Guiren asked, sitting up.

"Some fox spirits, some harmless bird and beast yao…"

"Fox spirits aren't harmless."

"To me they are," said Tainu, winking.

Liu Chenguang rolled her eyes.

Zhu Guiren shrugged. "Fine. All right, I think I've got some ideas here."

Tainu came over to stand behind his shoulder and look at what he had drawn on the wall.

"I'm pretty sure the array we're looking for is one connected to Hong Deming's birth. We know that there was one connected to Aili's birth, and one connected with Hong Deming's death, so that's the last option. Unless there was an array he was bound into as one of the perpetrators of violence…Was he ever involved in an unjust killing? That time the cultivators attacked Gunan, did anyone else set an array? I know I was too busy then…" He tapped his fingers on his handless arm. "Well, let's eliminate this option first. There are two ways for a living being to be bound into an array from birth: either you were conceived or born within an array's geographic center of influence, or your parents or ancestors were bound into the original mortal event."

From behind them, Liu Chenguang asked, "Can you remind me of what happens to a mortal who's born into an array? As opposed to the souls that you catch in it at the…event?"

"Maybe just bad luck, maybe not much, maybe a horrible life. It all depends on a lot of factors," Zhu Guiren said absently. "To be bound into an array — as opposed to just having an awful life for other reasons — means that it's more likely that bad things will happen, which leads to more bad things happening. The suffering and resentment of that person belong to the demon who set the array, as does the resentment produced by the original array event."

Liu Chenguang and Tainu were silent.

"You asked," Zhu Guiren said coolly. "Do you wish you hadn't?"

"Yes," replied Liu Chenguang.

Zhu Guiren turned to look at Tainu, who continued to study the diagram.

Eventually, Tainu said, "I don't understand all your figures here, but in general, it sounds as though the…cultivation material…produced by the array is exponential for the demon who made it? And continuously increases resentment over time throughout the population of those affected by it?"

"Correct."

Tainu said, "Let's destroy them all."

Zhu Guiren turned back to his diagrams. "As I've mentioned, I don't have the power for that. Ironically, I'd have to set more arrays to get enough cultivation to destroy just what's in Zai'an, much less the great array I made myself. We have to be strategic if we want to destroy the array here that is specifically affecting Aili. So, to get back to specifics, I've looked around and talked to some of my subordinates here–"

"You have subordinates here?" Liu Chenguang interrupted.

"I have subordinates in most of North Daxian," he said. "I haven't been physically in Daxian, in my mortal body, for several centuries. Now that I'm here, and therefore more vulnerable to attack, my subordinates are starting to move. Either toward me, to demonstrate their loyalty, which I wouldn't believe in anyway, or against me, to try to break free and take the array for themselves, for which I have to be prepared."

Liu Chenguang said, "I can now see why you enjoyed imperial court politics, actually."

"True. It felt very homey. Now back to the point of all this. Under normal circumstances, an array's power will dissipate over time as the mortal event begins to lose cogency, and particularly as living mortals are more weakly connected to the event. My subordinates have confirmed that the arrays that are in this area and are over a thousand years old are mostly just relics at this point–"

"But the mortal souls are still caught in them?" she asked.

"Yes. That's pretty much forever. Until the demon that created the array dies. I suppose I should tell you that that's one possible shortcut to destroying my array."

"Not funny," said Tainu.

Zhu Guiren risked a glance at him over his shoulder. "It's also not my preferred method. And if I'm killed by a demon stronger than I am, which I suppose it would have to be, logically speaking, that demon could set things up in advance so they take over the array. That will be the hope of at least some of the strong demons in the area, even in my own clan and certainly in others." He put his thumb against his teeth. "Where was I?"

Tainu reached over his shoulder, took his hand, and pulled it from his mouth. "Stop that. You're going to chew that thumb ragged."

Zhu Guiren took his hand back. "You can fix it. Anyway, there are very few arrays that are of the right age to be connected to Aili. There are two possibilities for the one that she is connected to: an ancient array that has been taken over by a strong demon killing a weaker one, and so it's still functioning because of that new connection, or there is one ancient array different than all the rest. It still has one living mortal bound into it. I propose we try that avenue first, because it's easiest to check for that and we can rule it out before trying to look for arrays that have been taken over. I'm hoping we don't have to do that, as I'll have to fight the owner."

"I thought you would have to fight the owner anyway," said Tainu. He was standing next to Zhu Guiren now, his expression concerned.

"True, but someone that's taken over other demons' arrays will be stronger than someone who owns a thousand-year-old thing that's barely functioning." He smiled. "And look at my secret advantage — I have a phoenix if I get hurt."

Liu Chenguang said, "You're taking a risk, for Aili."

Zhu Guiren shrugged. "I'm taking a risk. I don't know what it's for, to be honest."

"I'll...I'll forgive you. A little bit," she said. "For doing this for her."

Zhu Guiren stood very still.

She got up and walked out.

"What was that for?" Zhu Guiren asked Tainu, turning back to the diagrams.

"Why *are* you doing this?" Tainu asked quietly. "I didn't realize how risky this was for you until right now."

"I want to. I want to undo it. I'm…not sure why? Maybe there's more than one reason." He reached out with his finger and traced one of the diagrams.

Tainu watched him closely.

"Since I completed it…I haven't wanted to…" He struggled with something he couldn't quite manage to say, and shook his head at last.

"All right," Tainu said. "It's also that I didn't realize just how much your fellow demons are out for your head."

"Oh yes," he said, smiling. "Everyone wants to kill me when they get to know me."

"I don't."

"Well, you're a phoenix. You couldn't even if you wanted to, so I guess I'm safe with you." He turned and said, "Come with me. I'm going to start looking now. If I find it, I'll need you with me."

Tainu looked at the scribbles again, then followed him outside.

They began near the center of old Zai'an and walked out from there in a rough spiral as the roads allowed, which was not very well. Every so often Zhu Guiren would stop and mutter incomprehensibly to himself, or hold up two fingers as though to test the wind, or reach out and grab the air for invisible strings. Tainu amused himself by smiling in a friendly way at the citizens of Zai'an, who stopped what they were doing to watch a tall, dark foreigner and a very handsome, but very peculiar Daxian man walking down the street together.

"I wonder where Liu Chenguang got to?" he asked during one of Zhu Guiren's pauses.

"Eh," Zhu Guiren responded. "This really only needs two of us, why did you encourage her to come anyway? Back to Daxian, I mean. Aili would have been useful, but I already have a phoenix."

Tainu shrugged. If Zhu Guiren couldn't see that Liu Chenguang and Aili being together was just going to keep hurting both of them, it wasn't surprising; he couldn't have too much emotional sensitivity toward their relationship, given all that had happened. "It was better," he answered vaguely. "Any hints?"

"No," he said, annoyed. "We'll have to check the outskirts. Let's go away from the river first."

After more wandering and muttering, in a field between the edge of the city and the rise into the mountains, Zhu Guiren sat down in a lotus position and held his single hand in a seeking seal. "Again, so much would be easier with two hands. There are some seals that require them."

Tainu sat down next to him. "Can I help?"

"I don't know, set your hands into seals and see what you can find," he said grumpily.

"What am I looking for?"

"If it's a live array with a living mortal bound into it, you'll sense corrupted qi moving in a rough spiral from this spot."

After a few moments, Tainu said, "Ouch. That stings. Yes." He winced and shook his hands out. A little blood dripped from his left hand.

Zhu Guiren watched the drops fall without comment. He stood and said, "Next step." He closed his eyes and took out his sword, turning in a slow circle. "Damn."

"What?"

"Strong demon, strong array, medium strength binding," he said. "Aili's resentment is very strong right now. It's feeding into this like crazy. I can actually tell it's her."

"You can tell?"

"It's got a certain…flavor," he said, eyes still closed, "and since this array is from the time of the Wan Zhao rebellion, she's the only living mortal strongly tied to it. Previously, her resentment was probably feeding at the first level into the weak array of her birth, but now that that's destroyed, this is getting more of the resentment fed into it. It has probably already attracted the attention of the demon that owns this array, so we won't be able to do this quietly."

He opened his eyes and looked at Tainu, seeming to consider his options. "I am definitely going to have to fight," he said, "and also manage the spellcasting at the same time, with one hand. I can't also protect you. It's better if you're not visible when I start. Don't stand next to me."

"But then how will I heal you? Won't this take a lot of blood?"

He nodded, slowly. "I'll have to– I don't know. I'll call some subordinates, although I don't fully trust any of them not to turn on me, to be honest. I'll prioritize completing the spell. Once that's done, I can turn my attention to fighting the demon protecting the array. Do not under any circumstances come out while there is still another demon here." He didn't sound very hopeful, but he took a deep breath. "All right, let's get started. You transform, get over into those trees, and stay away until the other demons are gone."

Tainu stood still. "I don't want to leave you here if you're going to get hurt."

"Just go," he said impatiently. "If I have to fight more demons to rescue you, how does that help anything? Get into the trees. Set a ward." He turned his back and called his halberd, striking down onto the ground and shouting something in the demonic language.

Tainu reluctantly transformed and flew away, settling in a branch close to the edge of the copse.

From the earth, two yaoguai crawled up, one a snake and the other a beetle; from the sky, three crows flew down. All of them prostrated themselves before Zhu Guiren and listened to his instructions. Tainu saw them disperse around him in a circle, facing outward. Zhu Guiren looked very small in the middle of the circle of yaoguai and yaomo — smaller than any of them — and when he slashed his handless arm on the sword so the blood came pouring out, Tainu winced.

There was a lot of blood.

Tainu couldn't help noticing that, as the blood continued to flow and Zhu Guiren's chant began to get louder, first one and then another of the yaoguai turned to look at him, and then at one another. Uneasy, he watched from his perch as the blood continued to fill the cup, minute after minute. Zhu Guiren was beginning to look pale, even from this distance.

Suddenly, there was a rumbling noise from the trees below him and something like a boar rushed out onto the field, transforming into a huge man with a dagger-axe, hair tangled in knots down to his waist. He screamed at Zhu Guiren in the demonic language and chopped down, hard.

One of the crows flew at the demon's face, but the others remained still. The demon chopped down the crow and roared at the others. The beetle came at him, but was also crushed to the ground easily by the axe-demon. The two other crows flew away, while the snake turned to look hungrily at Zhu Guiren, still kneeling on the ground, his blood flowing into the cup of ice. The demon raced up to Zhu Guiren and swung the dagger axe again, this time slashing into the left shoulder. Zhu Guiren nearly collapsed, but then righted himself and continued to chant, bleeding now from the axe wound as well as the cut for the spell. The attacking demon reached down to grab his throat, choking him, but Zhu Guiren continued to hold his arm over the cup — half of the blood hitting the ice and half missing — chanting in a garbled, horrible voice as he tried to breathe.

Tainu couldn't stand watching this anymore. He flew straight upwards, as high as he could over the site, until Zhu Guiren was a tiny figure below him, then stooped to dive at his top speed, changing his bird shape into a falcon.

Qi spun from his wings as he dove, golden sparks that fled through the air. He beat his wings heavily in front of the yaomo with the dagger-axe, sending sparks into his eyes to distract him, then transformed next to Zhu Guiren, slamming the ground with his hand and setting a ward in the same moment. The dagger-axe caught him in his other wing as he transformed, but that actually saved him time now. He simply brushed the bleeding limb on Zhu Guiren's wounded shoulder and knelt next to him, breathing hard.

Zhu Guiren glared at him, the expression in his sharp black eyes furious, but didn't stop the chant. The yaomo began his own counterchant to undo Tainu's ward, while the snake yaoguai slithered around the edge of it, striking here and there to find a weak spot.

At last, the ice cup was full of bright blood. Zhu Guiren brought the cup to his heart, still kneeling; it seemed that he was too weak to stand, and his lips were completely without color. As the smoke began to pour out from the cup, Tainu grabbed his handless arm and healed the cut there, but giving Zhu Guiren's strength back wouldn't happen so quickly. He remained kneeling, swaying as Tainu held him upright and sometimes faltering in the chant as sweat streamed down his face. Small trickles of blood started seeping from his nostrils and ears. Tainu felt a sense of dread in the pit of his stomach. If there was a qi deviation or Zhu Guiren used too much qi and fell into a coma, there was no easy or quick way to fix it.

The smoke started pooling against the inner edge of the wards. Zhu Guiren narrowed his eyes at Tainu, still chanting.

With a sinking heart, Tainu nodded and removed the ward. He immediately transformed, flying upward and beating his wings in the face of the dagger-axe demon. From behind, the snake yaoguai grabbed one of his wings and began shaking him; Zhu Guiren's voice rose behind him, still in the chant, but with a note of panic. Tainu quickly transformed into a hummingbird and got out of the thing's mouth, then back into his human body.

He ran. He couldn't fly far until he healed from the ragged bites and the dagger-axe attack; his arm was spilling blood everywhere he went.

The dagger-axe demon roared and came for him, as did the snake. Zhu Guiren's voice took on an edge of fury as he began pouring the cup, the blood's long stream back into the earth. Tainu stumbled among the tendrils of smoke, far more complex than the ones from the array near Aili's birthplace. Hundreds of people must have died here.

The smoke burned his clothes, and then his legs where it touched his bare skin, as he dodged the strikes of the dagger-axe and the fangs of the snake; as he fell into the smoke, crying out at the burning of his body and face, he sensed someone leaping over him. The person threw something at the snake yaoguai, which hissed in rage and pain before withdrawing behind him into the woods. Then, the person grabbed him and rolled over the ground with him, wrapping him in something that seemed to protect him from the demonic smoke.

Almost as though they were flying, the person leapt away. Tainu couldn't see well out of his smoke-burned eyes yet — the healing would take longer since it was a demonic wound — but the demon with the dagger-axe had turned back to Zhu Guiren. Zhu Guiren's voice began to crescendo as the blood stream neared its end. The yaomo threw a talisman, but the person did something to make it spin away from him and tried to distract the yaomo, seemingly unable to make the attacker retreat, but constantly blocking him from Zhu Guiren. The person took the dagger-axe strikes meant for Zhu Guiren into their own body, mostly in the shoulders but occasionally a stab to the abdomen; their movements became heavier and slower, but they stubbornly remained standing between them.

The person blocked another talisman, then a strong spell that exploded with demonic qi, almost as though surrounded by a strong ward wherever they went. Tainu rubbed his eyes. Wards were not mobile that way; they were based in the earth where they were set, and in any case, whoever it was had been wounded by the dagger-axe, so it couldn't be a real ward.

Again, at the sound of the smashing ice cup, all the smoke tendrils rushed back into the last few drops of Zhu Guiren's blood, and Tainu felt the world explode around and inside him.

Tainu staggered to his feet, still unable to see well. Zhu Guiren was on the ground, collapsed and apparently unconscious, and the person defending him was lying on top, shielding him with their body as the yaomo screamed in rage, smashing into both of them with the dagger-axe. He himself wasn't healed yet, and couldn't fly again for a while, but with only one demon and the array broken, he could at least do something. He became a scarlet sparrow and hopped over to the yaomo, trailing his broken wing so it was obvious that he was vulnerable.

As he had hoped, the demon turned to follow him, growling. He dodged the creature's talismans and nets and dagger-axe as fast as he could with unpredictable little hops and flutters, baiting him back into the woods where he could duck into a little hole at the base of a tree. The demon transformed into a boar and began to dig with his tusks, finally pushing him against the roots of the tree. He couldn't dig, he couldn't get smaller, and he was beginning to be crushed and cut by the tusks. Blood poured out from his skin, feathers soaked with it.

Suddenly, the tusks disappeared. The demon roared and then screamed, a long gurgling shriek that ended in silence. Blood seeped down into the hole — demon's blood. Cautiously, Tainu peered outside. The boar demon was slumped there in its mortal body, viciously impaled through the mouth by a double halberd.

Zhu Guiren knelt next to the hole. His face and clothes were striped with blood, his hair clotted with it. His hand shook as he reached in to pick Tainu up. "I'm going to kill you," he said, his voice also shaking.

Next to him, also drenched in blood, stood Liu Chenguang.

Tainu decided that this was as good a time as any to pass out.

# CHAPTER 2
## CRANE MOON

Tainu woke up in his comfortable bed back at the inn and sighed with happiness. "Liu Chenguang?" he called. "Demon?"

Liu Chenguang came in. "You're better," she said. "You've been out for a couple of days. You got serious internal injuries from that boar-thing while you were being a sparrow in a hole. What were you thinking, Tainu?"

He sat up. "The same thing you were thinking, I imagine."

"Were you thinking that if Zhu Guiren dies, we have no way to break the arrays?"

He shook his head.

"I didn't think so. When we were there, he was— I've never seen him like that. He sat up, bleeding from various orifices, and said, 'Where is he?' over and over again. I wasn't in any good shape myself and could barely move, but when I told him that you'd allowed the yaomo to chase you…Well, anyway. He was frantic. He staggered over there and killed that thing and wasn't able to say any actual words again until he got you out of that hole."

She added, "And then he collapsed and you were unconscious, so we were all just sitting there in the forest until he woke up and I was healed enough to move on and heal him, and then he was frantic again because you weren't waking up, even though I explained to him that some kinds of injuries take longer for us to heal than others, and you would be fine."

Stunned, Tainu said, "He was that upset?"

"He was that upset," she replied solemnly. "And for all I know he's still that upset, but once we got back here and you transformed back into your mortal body — lucky you didn't while we were in the forest; we'd still be there — he left. I haven't seen him since the day before yesterday."

Tainu shook his head, wondering. He wouldn't have expected Zhu Guiren to be that upset, given his familiarity with phoenixes, but it must be a visceral thing. Unlike any mortal being, Tainu knew with absolute certainty through countless painful experiences and dreadful wounds, that he wouldn't die and that he would heal. In his mortal body, any injury aside from amputation or decapitation would heal; if the mortal body received a fatal wound that couldn't be healed, he would enter the rebirth fire. This endless, inescapable life was his reality, the reality of the phoenix. Perhaps nothing that had the ability to die could really understand what it meant.

He knew, also with absolute certainty, that his healing ability — unless constrained through his own weakness, qi deviation, or blood loss — would heal almost any wound in others. Yet, he had to admit that even though he knew that as long as he got there in time, the demon would always be healed, he felt very disturbed about seeing him wounded or hurt. Upset enough that he disobeyed his orders. But as long as he got there in time, always, all would be well.

*But what if he hadn't gotten there in time?* His mind veered away from that question. He would always get there in time. That was all. The demon would have to understand that this was an unshakable priority, whatever orders he might give before the event.

He was touched that the demon was worried about him. And happy. It made him happy. That was also the truth.

Liu Chenguang looked at him curiously. "Why do you trust him?" she asked unexpectedly.

He smiled again and shook his head. "If he doesn't come back by the time I've eaten dinner, I'm going to look for him. Oh, and Liu Chenguang," he added sternly, "I think you have some explaining to do as well."

They were sitting down at the table to eat when Zhu Guiren came back. Tainu noted that he stopped a brief moment in the doorway, looking at him, and then his face returned to its usual closed expression.

"You're awake," Zhu Guiren said, sitting down. "Good. We need to talk."

"Where have you been?" asked Liu Chenguang. "Have you eaten?"

"No." He took some rice and vegetables. "Didn't you get any meat?"

"Next time if you want meat, just say it. We didn't know you were coming back," replied Liu Chenguang.

He was silent for a minute. "I went to find and kill that snake yaoguai," he said. "That's done. But I don't know whether he told others before he died that there's a phoenix with me."

Tainu looked at him. "Is that why you were so worried about me being there?"

*"Yes,"* he said emphatically. "You have to understand how…how vulnerable you will be if they know where to find you — even where to look for you."

"You shouldn't worry so much," said Tainu, trying to reassure him. "We live all of our lives knowing that demons are looking for us, we're good at hiding–"

"Don't you understand that you are *not hiding?!*" he asked angrily, looking Tainu full in the face, his eyes narrowed. "You are with me. If they know that you are with me, they know where to look. I am going to be destroying arrays. I will be attracting the attention of every demon in North Daxian. I am leaving a path that's easy to follow, and I won't always be able to protect you. My own power– my own clan will start asking questions, and they–" His face paled.

Liu Chenguang looked down and coughed slightly. "Zhu Guiren," she said, "since when do you care about phoenixes being captured by demons?"

Zhu Guiren put down the chopsticks and walked out.

Tainu looked at her.

"What?" She looked back at him defiantly. "It's a legitimate question."

He sighed and followed Zhu Guiren outside.

The demon was pacing the yard of the inn — a rather ramshackle collection of dying bushes and a few sad sheds. When Tainu came out, he said, "You understand, don't you?" an amazing combination of plaintive and furious.

"I do," he said, leaning against the outer wall and crossing his arms. "But you can't expect her to understand that things could have been worse. I'm not even going to try to tell her that, and I suggest that you don't either."

Zhu Guiren looked at him, then nodded curtly. "All right, I'll just tell this to you. My clan has always been angry that I let her go. That I sent Liu Chenguang into rebirth and didn't recapture him. We hadn't had a phoenix for millennia before I caught him, and none since. It would have been a great source of power for us to keep her. Knowing that I'm with a phoenix now is going to– They are not going to leave me alone. They will not trust me to…keep you."

Tainu nodded. "You also have to understand that I make my own decisions about what I am willing to let you go through. I won't just let you be wounded and in danger of your life in front of me if there's anything I can do to stop it, or to help you."

Zhu Guiren stared at him.

"I can't do much. I think Liu Chenguang can do more. That's what I wanted to ask her about when you came in. But I will do what I can do to stop you from being hurt, and to ensure you can be healed." He added, "You have to understand that from our point of view, you are the most vulnerable person here. You are the only one who can die."

Zhu Guiren said, forcefully, "Yes, I can die. You can't. It's you — you and Liu Chenguang — who can spend eternity being tortured if they catch you."

"I know," said Tainu. "But we always know this. We'll be careful."

"You were not careful." He closed his eyes and took a deep breath. "You need to be more careful. We'll make a better plan for next time."

When they went back inside, Liu Chenguang made a point of being friendly to Zhu Guiren. It was completely unconvincing, but at least smoothed things over a bit. She had ordered some meat for him that the innkeeper brought up halfway through the meal: a sad bit of fried pork. Meat wasn't easy to come by now.

"So," said Tainu, after they had eaten, "Liu Chenguang, you came to the demon fight with some phoenix stuff. How did that go?"

She laughed. "Well, not as anticipated. It was these." She looked at them, nodding.

"It was…what?" asked Zhu Guiren.

"Is there something I'm looking at now?" asked Tainu.

"Don't you see them?" She stood up. "I can see them…"

Tainu came closer. "Are you saying the wings are there? That you've transformed?"

"Yes." She looked to one side, then the other. "They're right there."

Tainu put his hand out, cautiously. "Ah," he said.

Zhu Guiren also reached out.

"Don't," said Tainu, but too late.

Zhu Guiren hissed and pulled his hand back; it looked as though it had been burned. Tainu quickly bit his lip and stroked some blood on it, then turned back to Liu Chenguang.

"Pure qi," he said. "Made…semi-tangible." He reached out again and tugged hard.

"*Ouch!*"

Tainu looked down at his hand. If he narrowed his eyes in just the right way, it looked as though a small streak of light was lying in his palm. "What was that?"

"A primary," said Liu Chenguang, wincing and stroking the air. "Don't do that again, please."

"So..." he said. "I couldn't see well when you came in, but it seemed as though suddenly the smoke couldn't hurt me anymore. I would guess you wrapped me in the wings."

"Just instinct," she said. "I didn't make the decision to do that. They just... appeared. And when I was trying to defend Zhu Guiren, they blocked talismans and spells, but not the weapon itself." She winced again. "Whenever he struck my body with the dagger-axe, it went right in. But the wings blocked demonic qi."

"Hmm." Tainu walked around her, thinking. "I still can't see them, even though I know they're there...All right, so you came in not knowing this would do anything. What was your plan?"

Liu Chenguang said, "I'm taking the wings back in now." Nothing at all changed, but after a moment she said, "I learned qinggong at Crane Moon. You know that. So, I knew that I could at least leap around and be distracting, maybe block something with my body. But more than that, after I...came back...I kept thinking about Hong Deming and how I couldn't help him at all, and I wanted to...avoid that happening again. I thought a lot about how I could fight yaoguai when I can't fight with weapons or even my own body. Anything with killing intent will disintegrate if I try to use it, so what doesn't have killing intent? I can only be defensive and harmless, but maybe there were ways I could be more...I developed some...strategies." She reached into her pocket and took out a small packet. "This is one of them. I came up with some medicinal blends that are offensive to corrupted qi. They'll not do anything more than annoy a yaoguai, or for a weaker one, put it to sleep, but it's better than nothing. Back at the place where I lived for the last cycle, I have more things. If we're anticipating that we'll have to fight yaoguai, I'd like to go back there and get them."

Tainu and Zhu Guiren exchanged glances.

"I agree," said Zhu Guiren.

Tainu nodded. "Bring the wings back out again. I have another idea," he said. "Demon, touching the wings burned you, but when she was defending you, did that happen?"

"No. Not that I noticed. Although at the time, I was barely conscious."

"So, it may be that the intention to protect is important," Tainu said, thinking out loud. "Demon, do you have any demonic talismans on you? Ones meant to attack?"

Zhu Guiren rolled his eyes. "Please." He snapped his fingers and a rectangular strip of yellow paper with red characters appeared between them. "What for?"

Tainu gingerly reached out to take it in his own hand.

"Watch out," said Zhu Guiren sharply.

"I know," Tainu said, wincing. He took the talisman in his hand, and then covered it with the other, closing his eyes and drawing his hand sharply down against the length of the talisman. He said, "Now, demon, stand still," and quickly threw the talisman at him.

Zhu Guiren did not stand still.

This was a good thing, as the talisman exploded next to him. Suddenly, he was on the ground, gasping for breath and coughing blood. Tainu immediately knelt next to him and placed his own blood on Zhu Guiren's lips.

Zhu Guiren said, "What. The hell. Was that?!"

"Sorry," Tainu said sincerely. "You're the only demon we have to test things out on."

"Warn me next time!" He lay on the ground some more. "That was damaging," he said at last. "I'm still feeling it, even with the blood from you. For a weaker demon? Probably fatal."

Liu Chenguang said, "You put the feather from my wings on the talisman. And then you can use it as a weapon?"

"Because the killing action is not from you, I would guess," Tainu said. "The killing intent of the talisman is demonic. I reordered the spell to put pure qi at its center rather than demonic qi, but the attack itself, the attack function…" He shook his head. "You understand," he said to Zhu Guiren, who was now sitting up.

"Yes," he said slowly. "Well, I have a lot of those. I would feel better if each of you had some with that adjustment made. Keep them on you at all times," he said, sounding oddly formal.

"I'll go pull some feathers," Liu Chenguang said. "Better me than you, I'm going to go look in the mirror so I can pick good long ones." She headed toward her bedroom.

Tainu sat down next to him. "You're all right?"

Zhu Guiren just shook his head. "You are just…guessing about these things? Just trial and error?" he asked.

"Well, it's not like we have a manual." He picked up Zhu Guiren's hand, which was still showing blistered burns, and started putting more blood on it.

"You people are surprisingly chaotic," he said. "*We* have a manual."

"I would very much like to see this manual," replied Tainu.

They left Zai'an the next day, walking up the Cui Valley toward the gorge that led to Crane Moon. Liu Chenguang felt an ache sometimes as she saw the familiar places; the last time she had been here, she had been searching for Aili. They had to stop frequently, as there were both soldiers and refugees on the roads. Liu Chenguang and Tainu both healed surreptitiously wherever they could; done is done and pain is pain, and wherever pain could be assuaged for whomever was suffering, it must be.

Zhu Guiren watched and shook his head. "Doesn't it occur to you," he asked as they left behind one sleeping group, several children cured of dysentery, "that there's not a lot of point in healing people who are still starving and have no likelihood of getting decent food? Or healing soldiers that have just been attacking the other people you healed?"

"It doesn't matter whether there's a point," Liu Chenguang said. She remembered having the same conversation with Hong Deming, centuries before, but she had far less desire to try to explain things in any meaningful way to Zhu Guiren.

Tainu looked at her, and then said, "There's a point, demon. Think about it."

Zhu Guiren just rolled his eyes.

As they neared the village at the foot of Crane Moon's mountain, Liu Chenguang stopped and looked upward. The sunset would soon strike the place where she knew the waterfall came down, though it couldn't be seen from below; the ruins of Crane Moon were hidden from view from the bottom of the gorge. She didn't think they'd ever been found by anyone who was not a cultivator. Certainly not by the people in her village.

"Is there an array at Crane Moon?" she heard Tainu ask Zhu Guiren.

"Not that I set, or that was there when I was present," he said. "Maybe since."

"It was destroyed by violence," said Liu Chenguang, "so it's possible there's one now."

Zhu Guiren shrugged. "If so, it wouldn't affect Aili. Hong Deming was dead by that point. We have to–"

Liu Chenguang quickly walked away from him, but not quickly enough to avoid hearing Tainu say, "Demon. Can you try to be a little sensitive?"

"What do you mean?" he asked, frustrated. "Why is *she* so sensitive? She could be with Aili now. It's her choice not to be. We all know how Hong Deming died. Why does she have to get so upset? We're trying to do something to help now, but we have to be strategic…"

Behind her, she heard Tainu's expressive silence.

"*Fine.*" Zhu Guiren said. Stones rattled, probably because he was kicking them. "Fine, I don't understand anything, fine, it's all my fault, fine. Let's just keep going."

Liu Chenguang walked even faster, not wanting to be near him, especially as what he said was true. She could have stayed; she could have been with Aili now. It had been her choice to go, but it felt like…she didn't have a choice.

Because Aili didn't want her to stay.

Because Aili didn't want her.

She thrust that thought down hard and put a smile on her face as she always had when coming into the village beneath the cliffs: the pale brown wooden houses scattered on the deep green hillside, the terraced fields below.

"Doctor Liu! Doctor Liu!"

It hadn't been so long this time that the people she remembered were old or dead; only seven years or so, but still, what a difference. The children were teenagers now, the babies were children. There were some missing faces, but not many. It looked as though the war had not come here yet — neither the armies that contended for the land nor the bandits and looters that followed them. She breathed in relief.

"Doctor Liu?" Old Zhao pulled himself up short, frowning. "Is it?"

She smiled, and said, "I'm Doctor Liu's sister, Liu Chenguang. He sent me to see how you all were doing. I'm a doctor too."

"Ah!" several people said, but she knew they were looking at each other behind her back. Doctor Liu was the divine doctor. How could he have a sister?

But she just smiled and ignored it. They had never known that her first name was Chenguang; it had always only been Doctor Liu here.

Someone finally said, "Welcome! Please come, please come in, Liu Chenguang!" It was the current headman of the village — still Fang. Half the village were Fang. "Doctor Liu's house is still ready and clean if you want to go there?"

"Certainly, I will. Thank you for your hard work," she said.

One of the old women called out, "Will you introduce your husband, Liu Chenguang?"

She looked around and realized that they could only be speaking about Zhu Guiren. Tainu had transformed; he was sitting on Zhu Guiren's shoulder in his sparrow form, his head in Zhu Guiren's hair. She could almost hear him spitting with laughter.

"Ah, yes," she said. "This is my husband, Zhu Guiren."

He gave her a look of death.

She smiled. "Please, husband, go up the hill to my brother's house," she said sweetly, gesturing toward the little building set apart from the rest of the village.

He audibly hissed at her as he walked away.

"Ah, Liu Chenguang," said Grandmother Wang, hobbling up next to her as Zhu Guiren stalked away, to the disappointment of a gaggle of village girls. "Forgive me for saying so…your husband is very good-looking, but seems bad-tempered. I am sure Doctor Liu would not approve. He's such a kind man."

"You're correct to say so, grandmother," she said. "My brother does not approve at all. We'll be getting a divorce soon."

The faces of the girls brightened visibly.

"Good, good. That's best." Grandmother Wang nodded. Grandmother Wang was the oldest woman in the village, and had been when Liu Chenguang left seven years ago; clearly, she thought that her advice was welcome, necessary, and appropriate.

Liu Chenguang found it rather heartwarming.

Grandmother Wang added, "Since you've said you are a doctor also, would you be able to receive patients tomorrow? Since Doctor Liu left us, we haven't had anyone to take care of us. Some people have died. I'm sure it would make him sad."

"Certainly, certainly," she said.

"I'll send my granddaughter with a meal for you and your husband. Rest well," Headman Fang said. "We're glad to welcome Doctor Liu's sister."

Up at the house, Tainu was transformed back into his mortal body and apparently had been teasing Zhu Guiren mercilessly; he was bright red and stuttering.

This was absolutely wonderful.

Liu Chenguang smiled at the glorious sight of an embarrassed and flustered Zhu Guiren and said, "Dinner's coming soon. Tomorrow morning, I'll be seeing patients. We'll be here for a few days, most likely. We can rest and plan better than we have."

"Agreed," choked out Zhu Guiren. "Better plans are needed."

"There's hot springs at the base of the mountain, if you remember," she said. "Why don't you two relax, do whatever."

"Where are you going?" asked Tainu, looking at her as though he knew very well.

"Up to the ruins of Crane Moon," she said. "There's a place there I need to visit."

Since dinner would be coming late — the villagers had already eaten when they arrived, so close to sunset — Tainu and Zhu Guiren went up to the hot springs. The hottest spring was inside the mountain itself; it poured down into progressively cooler pools, the last few of which were outside under the stars. They chose a pool under some trees, with maple leaves swirling around in it. Tainu stripped down first and got in, gasping at the heat.

"Ah, that's better," he said, relaxing. His mortal body never really had bruises or aches for very long, but it still got tired and tense. That conversation between Zhu Guiren and Liu Chenguang had been difficult to hear; the demon really couldn't understand what the problem was, though he knew there was one, and Liu Chenguang was still in so much pain, which she wouldn't talk about or acknowledge. At least he had gotten Liu Chenguang to laugh before they came here, though he was sure that she was up at Crane Moon to cry on her own right now. Hopefully, it would do her good to let it out.

He sighed and looked up to see Zhu Guiren struggling with the buttons of his shirt. He wanted to offer to help, but was afraid the demon would be embarrassed so he looked away and busied himself ducking his head under the water a few times. When he came up, Zhu Guiren was completely naked and carefully touching the water of the pool with one toe.

Zhu Guiren naked was quite as beautiful as Zhu Guiren with clothes on, if not more so. Normally, Tainu greatly appreciated seeing beautiful naked people of his own mortal gender, whatever that happened to be at the time, but he felt differently about Zhu Guiren, so his mind didn't immediately go there. Instead, his eyes noticed that Zhu Guiren was covered with scars, large and small, strikes as though from whips, cuts from blades, old burns, pitted lumps from who knows what. It hurt to look at them. No wonder he had recognized Aili's whip scars just from touch.

Zhu Guiren noticed where he was looking and flushed from his face all the way down into his chest. "They're old," he said shortly, and got in the water.

Tainu struggled with whether to ask more; he didn't want to make Zhu Guiren feel ashamed.

But in the end, Zhu Guiren offered it on his own, after he had ducked his own head underwater a few times and was squeezing out his long hair. "Most of them are from my childhood. Or from when I was much younger, anyway. I don't even remember what most of them were from originally." He added, "None of the things that you've cured for me have scars. That's nice."

"Sometimes it scars," he said. "Even if I heal it. It depends on the person and on what caused it and other things that I don't necessarily understand. I can't always predict– The healing isn't just about the body." He didn't really know why he felt the need to explain that.

After they'd soaked for a while, Zhu Guiren said, "I've been curious. Why do you always call me demon instead of my name?"

"I can't call you your true name in front of people," he said. "And I know that you didn't really intend to tell it to me, so…"

Zhu Guiren nodded, looking at the water. "Why not call me Zhu Guiren?"

He deflected the question by asking, "What do other demons call you?"

Zhu Guiren ducked his head under the water again. "You couldn't say it, but the meaning is 'Third'."

"Third? Like…third brother?"

"No, just third. It changes. Third means that I'm the third strongest in my clan."

"Hmmm." This was interesting; he hadn't known all these things about demons. "You people really are very organized."

Zhu Guiren laughed. "Well, I don't miss it. I've been avoiding the clan since…" he waved his hand. "All this."

"So, if you're Third, there's a First and a Second?"

"Yes, and many hundreds below," he said. "The First and Second of my clan are very old. The older you are, the longer you're likely to live. Many demons die in the low ranks, in the ranking pits…I've been Third for about two thousand years now. At my rank, I can only be challenged by the demon directly below me, unless I'm directed to answer a challenge by First or Second. For those in the lower ranks, below Tenth, any of the top ten can direct anyone to fight anyone else."

"So, the demons within your clan fight each other, as well as fighting demons from other clans?" Tainu frowned. "That seems…awful."

"It is," he said shortly. "That's why I've been avoiding them for centuries. But now that I'm here, it's likely that I'll receive a challenge or directions from First or Second."

"What would happen if you lost a challenge? Would you become Fourth?"

"Ha, no. I'd be dead. I've never lost a challenge," he said casually. "Obviously."

Tainu frowned more. "I do not approve of your clan. I'd like you to be more of a free-range demon."

Zhu Guiren laughed. It was good to hear. Tainu smiled at him.

Zhu Guiren suddenly stopped laughing and looked at him, tilting his head to one side as though trying to understand something better.

"It's nice when you laugh," explained Tainu. "That's all."

Clearly self-conscious, Zhu Guiren nodded.

Feeling he should offer something personal in return, Tainu said, "You know, I didn't grow up with anyone. There are so few of us, and when I came to consciousness, I was alone. That first cycle was very strange because I didn't know what I was, or what to expect. There weren't many mortals then, and the spirit world was different too. It's gotten much more dangerous since my awakening. When I entered the rebirth fire for the first time, I was completely shocked. I didn't know that was going to happen…" He stopped.

Zhu Guiren was looking at him, and he didn't want to continue this story.

"Anyway, that's one of the reasons that when I was able, I tried to find the new phoenixes whenever they awoke. So they wouldn't be alone, so they would know what they were."

"You were always alone?" asked Zhu Guiren.

"Mostly," he said simply. "Mostly alone."

His effort at making the conversation lighter had failed miserably. The demon, of all people, looked sad for him.

He tried to change the subject. "What do you think of this place? That Liu Chenguang's been here being a doctor all this time?"

Zhu Guiren agreed to be diverted. "It makes me glad," he said. "That what I taught Liu Chenguang really meant something to him. That he was able to continue with it, too. It makes me feel as though…well."

Tainu smiled at him again. "You must have been a good teacher. I hope you get to teach someone again. What would you teach now?"

Zhu Guiren said, "I don't really know. These centuries since Liu Chenguang, have I learned anything new? Anything to pass on? It's been a strange time. Like a holding time. Like…waiting." He shook his head again. "But there are things I'd like to learn about the ancient making of the earth, about the stars…there's so much happening now in the sciences…"

Tainu noticed his eyes shining a little bit. This was good. "Maybe when this is over, you can do that," he encouraged.

Zhu Guiren looked back at him. "What would you like to learn?" he asked.

"I don't know," he said, surprised. "No one's ever asked me that before…I've just always learned whatever I needed to learn to be wherever I was, I guess."

"So you could…help people," Zhu Guiren said.

"Yes, that's why. I learned spells and such to try to defend myself and hide when necessary…how to extend my power for those who needed it as much as I could. But now, when I'm with farmers, I learn to farm. When I'm with sailors, I learn to sail…What would I want to learn, just for me, just because I'm curious?" He put his mind to it and tried to imagine. "Do you know, really, I can't…? I've never thought…"

"It's the best way to live, learning things," Zhu Guiren said, intently.

"Is it?" Tainu felt as though his whole being was smiling. Something about the demon made him feel this way; he had no idea why. "I'll have to try it."

# CHAPTER 3
## GRANDMOTHER WANG

Liu Chenguang came down from Crane Moon slowly, using her qinggong only when necessary. In her heart, she thought she might not return here. After so long, the pain was finally too great to even remember. But then, she lifted her body up for the next leap and she remembered so many things. Of course, most of them were from Hong Deming's lifetime. There was so much more to remember. So much more time they had had together, then. But Aili, too: that first meeting in the alley, when she had looked up at Aili's face with so much joy and excitement. Even through the confusion and bewilderment in Aili's eyes, she could see that Aili knew her, somewhere deep down, that she was drawn to her.

She remembered seeing her that very first time — sitting in the bar in Easterly, watching everyone else — and how their eyes had met, Aili's blue eyes widening as they took her in. The shock she had felt, realizing that her person was now in a female form, then dashing out into the alley to make the change of gender for her mortal body and getting caught by those annoying sailors. She had leapt out in front of Aili with her qinggong before her mind was consciously aware of it, taking the knife in her forearm. That had hurt, but she was so excited she could barely feel it. Reaching up to touch Aili's hair, dark gold, braided back in that complicated way. She could still sense Aili's heart; it was her person's heart — open and brave and kind — desiring and responding to her. She could feel it. How could she have mistaken it?

What had gone wrong?

She remembered her terror when she realized what kind of nursing Aili was training to do. She knew that her mind hadn't been clear, that she had made decisions badly. She'd been so upset, too, by discovering Aili's terrible family. At the time, she had barely known how terrible it was, but it had been enough that she was disturbed beyond sense — rejecting all of this as Aili's reality, wanting only to make reality change, make it be different. As though some blood and good intentions were enough to heal the abuse and suffering Aili bore in her soul and make it as though it hadn't happened.

But it had.

Deep night had fallen when she entered her old house to see Tainu and Zhu Guiren chatting happily at the table, both looking clean and relaxed.

"The demon wants to challenge me to a drinking bout," her sibling said to her solemnly.

"Zhu Guiren, I'm telling you now, and I'm sure Tainu has also told you, that there's no winning for you there." She sat down to eat her own dinner. "There's not enough alcohol in this village and probably the next one over to get a phoenix drunk."

"Demons are also quite capable," he said. "When we get to a town, Tainu, let's see."

Liu Chenguang looked at him, considering. At least going up to Crane Moon had helped her realize that not all her troubles were of Zhu Guiren's making. "You're a doctor too," she said. "Why don't you help me with the patients tomorrow? It will go faster that way. I guarantee everyone in the village will be in."

"Me?" To her surprise, his face lit up. "Yes, of course."

Tainu smiled.

After they had eaten, she took out the materials she'd come for: a stockpile of the anti-demonic powder, though probably it had lost strength over time, and her own talismans, which she could use to set a ward, though they were weak compared to Tainu's. She had never been as good at wards and spells.

"I'll look them over and strengthen them," Tainu said, examining them. "It'll give me something to do while you're physicking the town tomorrow."

Last were her deerhorn knives. She lifted them up — two double-crossed crescents with blunted ends.

Zhu Guiren frowned. "Show me," he said, and took out his sword.

"You have to come at me. I can only use them defensively."

When he did, though she could tell he was trying to hold back, she was able to capture the sword and disarm him effectively.

He looked at her, shocked. "Again," he said, and came at her with more force.

This time, she needed to use qi, but was still able to block and disarm.

Tainu looked on, wide-eyed. "What are those things?"

"They're designed for defense and disarming," she said. "Other people can use them offensively as well, but I can't. They're from a sect that developed about two hundred years ago. I studied with them for a while. It's a form that is well-adapted to a purely defensive, close-combat style. Of course, I can't follow up with a strike when I disarm an opponent, but I can at least run away. Or give someone else an opening."

Zhu Guiren seemed to be deep in thought. "You've been busy," he said at last. "You've used the time well."

She felt oddly proud to hear it from him.

"Can you teach Tainu?"

"Yes, of course," she said, "but it will take a while before he's proficient enough to be able to really use them in combat. I have, and I'm confident in my skill, but I also have the qinggong foundation, which he doesn't."

"I've never studied any martial art," he confessed.

"You were quick to turn that knife at my throat back in the spirit realm, remember?" asked Zhu Guiren, smiling at him. "Your reflexes are good, you're clever, you already know how to cultivate. You can learn."

Liu Chenguang noticed them looking at one another and wondered what exactly was going on between the two of them. She added, "About fifty years ago, some people decided that this sect's martial arts were good enough to deflect bullets during a major rebellion."

"Not?" asked Zhu Guiren, rolling his eyes.

"Not," she said. "They're only good against traditional weapons. Not guns. But let's practice daily. The three of us, so you'll know how you can work with us and how we can work with you. That's my first suggestion."

Zhu Guiren nodded.

"My second suggestion," she said, putting the knives back in their case, "is that we think carefully about the issue of guns. There is a major war going on, and we're walking through it. Our healing powers can't always protect against guns. Of course, your sword," she nodded at Zhu Guiren, "would easily kill mortals—"

"No," he said flatly. "It wouldn't. I don't kill mortals."

Both of them stared at him. Liu Chenguang bit down on several things she wanted to say.

"I don't. Not if there's any other way. Not if it's avoidable," he said defensively. "I only do what I do because I need the power I gain from it, and the power comes from what mortals do to each other. That's what produces the suffering and resentment we use for cultivation. There's no benefit to my power from killing with my own hand. Only from…" He flushed. "There are demons who kill mortals directly because they're just sadists or like the taste of blood, but I've never been one of them, and I don't want to start."

"You killed people when we were traveling," Liu Chenguang said. "I clearly remember it."

"That was different. We were being attacked, and I used ordinary mortal weapons, remember?" he said. "At that time, I was pretending I didn't have any spiritual power. It was an even fight."

Liu Chenguang looked at him.

"Fine, not *even*, but as even as I could make it."

She looked at him more, but this time he lifted his chin and refused to respond.

Tainu said, "Liu Chenguang, don't encourage him to do something he feels is wrong. Please."

"Well," she said at last, "you're still not a phoenix, so you may have to fight mortals if they attack you. You should think about how you want to go about it."

"As even as I can make it," he said stubbornly.

"Fine." This conversation was reminding her painfully of how upset Hong Deming used to get about how easy it was for him to kill ordinary people with En — not even a demonic weapon; how he wanted to fight yaoguai instead of cultivators. "But think about the guns, and how we can avoid them. You especially."

He nodded. "Let's focus on the arrays as much as we can, and any fighting should only be with the demons if we can manage it," he said. "That's our business. I agree that avoiding guns is also a good idea. We're not here to get involved in a mortal war."

The next morning, she and Zhu Guiren sat at first light in the open area of her little house, eating congee that Fang's granddaughter had brought up and watching the line of excited villagers form outside.

"We're the best entertainment this village has seen in years," remarked Zhu Guiren.

"Husband and wife team," Liu Chenguang snickered.

"Hush, Student Liu," he said in his old haughty tone. "Treat your teacher with proper respect."

As they began to see patients, each on opposite sides of the room, a red bird would fly in every so often, usually perching on Zhu Guiren's shoulder, though sometimes on hers. He never stayed for long, and seemed to just be checking on them, but the villagers were quite taken by his antics, of which he was well aware. Tainu had taken a form more like a swallow than a sparrow and swooped acrobatically above the people in line to keep them entertained. Liu Chenguang sometimes looked up to see Zhu Guiren watching his flight with a strange expression on his face that she couldn't read. Perhaps Zhu Guiren was not irredeemable after all.

She remembered that his theoretical understanding of medicine had been unsurpassed when she learned from him, and that was still true. As an actual doctor, though, he was awful, and his bedside manner was laughable. After she sent him a couple of warning glances while he loudly discussed his patient's yang deficiency — to the delight of the people waiting in line — she sent everyone out for a break while she tried to explain basic human interactions to him.

Tainu flew back in and joined them to eat the noon meal. He laughed out loud at the yang story while Zhu Guiren pouted at the table. "Just don't send him any of the unmarried women," he said. "They're all chattering about your gorgeous, soon-to-be-divorced husband out there."

"We're getting a divorce?" Zhu Guiren stabbed a mushroom. "I can't wait."

"Unmarried women should definitely come to me, my husband," she said. "Do not chance it. Your virtue must be protected."

Tainu snorted. "Anyway, let's finish this up today and leave by tomorrow morning at the latest. I flew up to Crane Moon just to take a look–" he said, carefully avoiding Liu Chenguang's eye, "–and from up there I could see that there is a group of men on the way. Hopefully, they mean no harm, but…better for us to not be here."

"Ordinary men?" asked Liu Chenguang, feeling a chill. "Revolutionaries or Republic? Or Kunorese?"

"Would it matter? Could I know from so far away?" he asked.

"If it's revolutionaries, they're probably just recruiting," she said. "Although the village might miss the young men and women, it won't kill them to go. At least, not right away. Army of the Republic, probably the same, but they're less likely to come to a little village like this. Kunoru…" She sighed. "Kunoru would raze this place to the ground. I have to give this some thought. Can you go out and check again when we're done eating? And see if you can get close enough to hear where they're going. Maybe they'll skip this village."

"No, do not fly close enough to listen. It's not safe," Zhu Guiren said sharply.

Tainu said, "It's all right, I'm fast."

"Not as fast as a bullet."

Tainu smiled. "I'll be fine," he said, and left.

Zhu Guiren looked at Liu Chenguang accusingly. She was not used to receiving that kind of look from him.

"You've changed," he said.

She ate some more tofu. "It's been a thousand years, Zhu Guiren," she said. "You were right when you said I wasn't paying attention, back then. If I had been, I would have realized that something was wrong much sooner. If you wanted a stable dynasty, why were you backing the most unstable and paranoid candidate for emperor?"

"It's always been amazing to me that no one noticed that at the time, but there was so much violence and paranoia built into the structure of the imperial court that people couldn't perceive how genuinely terrible Zhu Wen really was. And you're changing the subject."

"It was Tainu who taught me first," she said. "To heal people. But it was always accidental for me…not something I sought out. Most phoenixes don't. Tainu's different that way."

Zhu Guiren raised an eyebrow.

"It's important to him. But for me, it was only after…after living with Hong Deming," she said, "After that, I decided that trying to help people suffer less would take more than just healing skills. I would need to pay attention to all those things. To try to understand what was going on in the human world and intervene when I could."

"Was that for Hong Deming too?" he asked, curiously. "Like the deerhorn knives?"

"It was. And it wasn't, also. It was something we shared together — that we wanted to try to save what…to save the one that was in front of us, yes, but also…he had so much compassion. That's what drew me to him to begin with," she said. Another thing that she'd never shared with anyone before, and now it was with Zhu Guiren of all people. "He always felt people's pain and wanted to stop it. He always felt sadness for those who were suffering, even if he couldn't stop it, even if it had nothing to do with him. So, I decided to…keep going."

Zhu Guiren looked at her in silence.

Someone knocked on the door. "Liu Chenguang? Doctor Zhu?" called a man's voice. "Are you able to receive visitors now?"

Liu Chenguang stood up. "Come in," she called, and smiled in preparation. "Unmarried women should see me, please."

The last person in, close to dinnertime, was Grandmother Wang herself. She insisted on being treated only by Liu Chenguang, so Zhu Guiren was left to sit staring out the window and waiting for Tainu to return. Liu Chenguang found that Grandmother Wang was suffering from a cancer of the uterus — not something that could be fixed with traditional medicine at the stage it had already reached — so she slipped some sleeping medicine in her tea, and then quickly treated her with blood. By morning, she would be cured.

As Grandmother Wang slumbered face down on the consulting table, Liu Chenguang stretched and went over to the window.

"He's been gone a long time," Zhu Guiren said abruptly.

"He's fine. Tainu is very fast and very clever. He doesn't take undue risks without good reasons, and if he thinks it's not safe to get too close, then he won't." Privately, she admitted to herself that Tainu took undue risks all the time, especially when he thought it necessary to help people, but…a bullet wouldn't really hurt him for long, after all, and he was always very careful to avoid the notice of demons, which was the only real danger to a phoenix in the long run.

Zhu Guiren snorted and went back to staring outside. "They're bringing dinner."

Fang's granddaughter brought the meal in, accompanied by two teenagers who were all eyes for Zhu Guiren. He sat down at the table and was joyously served, but he didn't appear to notice.

"Thank you, you've worked hard," said Liu Chenguang.

One of the girls asked shyly, "Madam Liu, should Grandmother Wang stay here?"

"She's fine," she said. "She'll wake up in a little while, it's just the medicine she took, it's not unexpected."

As the three were leaving, a red bird swooped in through the open door, making them cover their hair and laugh.

Zhu Guiren looked coldly at him. "You were gone a long time," he said.

Tainu transformed and sat back down for dinner. "I waited until it was getting darker to get close. They're Daxian. Army of the Republic. They're not planning to come here. Just headed to Zai'an, and then east toward the coast."

Liu Chenguang sighed with relief.

He kept talking as he began picking out vegetables for his plate, unsmiling: "I listened to get more of a sense of what's going on. It is…extremely bad. The Kunoru are in all the eastern provinces. Hai'an is a disaster, there's scorched-earth war in the central provinces, massive flooding of the Sorrowful River…the Army of the Republic breached the levees."

"On purpose?" Liu Chenguang's eyes grew wide.

"On purpose, to block the invasion from going further inland, but you can imagine…At least four provinces are flooded. There's famine because people can't plant. They keep trying to rebuild the levees, but the Sorrowful River doesn't like being controlled. Since the Kunorese have been blocked from easy invasion by land, there've been planes bombing most of the major cities. Even Zai'an — that's why it seemed so miserable there. The soldiers were talking about it since that's where they're headed. There are refugees fleeing everywhere." He raised his head and met Liu Chenguang's eyes. "A lot of death. A lot of suffering."

Zhu Guiren tapped his fingers on the table in an irregular pattern.

Liu Chenguang and Tainu looked at him.

"We were going to travel in that direction," he said. "There are a lot of nodes in Hureng and Hai'an that I wanted to break before we attempt the central one. For the array I made."

"Where is the central one?" Tainu asked.

"Somewhere on the north side of the Sorrowful River, west of Hongye. I can't narrow it down for us more than that till we get closer. It's not geographically in the center of the array — it's central because it's the central seal."

"Well, we knew there was a war on. I'll gather as many medical supplies as I can to take with us," Liu Chenguang said. She felt the sadness of knowing what she was going to see, the hundreds of thousands of unnecessary deaths that accompanied great wars and famines.

Zhu Guiren was clearly thinking in another direction. He said, "With that level of resentment and suffering, there are going to be a lot of demons attracted. That explains why we haven't had many problems so far…"

"We haven't had problems?" asked Tainu, raising an eyebrow.

"Not really," he said bluntly. "Not as bad as I expected, to be honest. We destroyed an array and no one has come after us. Only one demon showed up to fight me. It was ridiculously easy. I've been wondering why, but this would explain it. They've all flocked east for the banquet."

Liu Chenguang winced, then thought more about that statement. "We've destroyed two out of three of the arrays," she said. "Would Aili be…better? Has it helped her?"

Zhu Guiren replied, "Her resentment was very high before we destroyed that array. At least, the destruction would have taken away something that was…exacerbating that. I can't feel her in my own array. It's too large to feel one person's resentment, but I expect that…well, it should have helped her in some way."

Liu Chenguang could tell he was trying to avoid saying something; he kept glancing over at Tainu, as though asking for help. Tainu, however, was looking down at the table, lost in thought.

Zhu Guiren finally got desperate and said, "Tainu, what do you think? How is Aili?"

Tainu started. "Aili? We won't know till we find her again, will we?" He looked at Liu Chenguang.

Liu Chenguang said, "I don't know if I'll find her again." She felt the sadness in her own voice, in her heart. "I wish I understood what went wrong. I don't understand. Not really."

Tainu looked at her and opened his mouth to say something, but suddenly, Grandmother Wang grunted and snapped upright; Tainu transformed and fluttered over to Zhu Guiren's shoulder.

Grandmother Wang seemed to have heard a little of the conversation just before she awoke. She yawned and asked, "What's that, Doctor Liu? You have someone you're looking for?"

Liu Chenguang sat down next to her. Grandmother Wang couldn't see well, she knew, but surely her voice sounded different now than when she was male? She said, "It's Doctor Liu's sister, grandmother." On an impulse, she added, "It's not me looking for someone. It's really about a friend of mine."

Zhu Guiren looked at her. "But it's—"

"Shh, you don't know this person," said Liu Chenguang, blushing. She could imagine the faces Tainu would be making at her if he wasn't currently sitting on Zhu Guiren's shoulder wearing red feathers. "Yes, this friend of mine has someone that she was in love with when they were young, and this person loved her too, and they promised to be together. But then, they were separated."

Zhu Guiren stared at her, mouth hanging open. It was worth it just for that.

"Ah, that happens so often!" said Grandmother Wang, shaking her head. "So, they married other people?"

"No, no—"

"Why not?"

"Because they didn't want to."

"What does that matter? Young people don't know what's good for them…" Grandmother Wang muttered under her breath. "So, they were alone, but they couldn't be together? Why was that? Doesn't make sense."

"You're right, grandmother, but that's how it was," she said.

"So did they miss each other?"

"One person missed the other, but the other person forgot about them."

"Eh, can you be clearer? That doesn't make sense."

"So, ah…Chenguang missed Deming, but Deming forgot about Chenguang."

"So they didn't really love each other, then?"

"Ah, there were circumstances."

Zhu Guiren left the room in evident disgust; the red bird immediately flew back in and perched on the rafters.

*Anyway,* said Liu Chenguang loudly, "after they'd been apart all of this time, Chenguang found Deming again."

"And he was married, I'm sure."

"No, he didn't get married."

"It's fine if he did. Chenguang can still be the concubine."

"No, that's not–"

"Or is that not allowed anymore? I'm so confused with how things are changing these days. Deming's a beautiful old-fashioned name. I'm sure he's happy with his wife. If Chenguang isn't planning to be his concubine, she should stay away. How long were they apart, anyway?"

"Twenty-five years."

"Ha, that's too long. Chenguang probably can't have babies anymore. What's the point? She should just enjoy her age, I suppose. That's my advice for your friend."

The red bird deliberately flew down to the ground in front of them and started rolling around on the matting.

"Stop that," hissed Liu Chenguang.

"What's that now?" asked Grandmother Wang. "Or Chenguang could become a nun?"

"But grandmother," she tried again, "after twenty-five years apart, could they still love each other?"

Grandmother Wang considered this seriously. "Did one of them really forget the other? I forget the names now."

"They didn't really forget."

"Well, perhaps they could still love each other, then," said Grandmother Wang portentously. "But not right away."

Liu Chenguang froze. "What do you mean, not right away?"

"Well, twenty-five years…That's a lifetime, isn't it? They would have to get to know each other again." She nodded. "Really though, if Deming didn't take his chance and get married, there wouldn't be any babies for anyone, with this situation."

"No, there wouldn't be babies," she said, a little dazed. "But why do they need to get to know each other? They knew each other so well. They grew up together."

"All the more, then," said Grandmother Wang firmly. "People who grow up together…they only know the beginnings of one another. And then they've been apart, so they've missed so much. Maybe they're not the same people anymore. And maybe they do still love each other anyway, but it's not for sure. They would have to try together just like any couple does, no matter how they came together to begin with. Like me and my old husband. I didn't know him at all when we were married, but we grew to know each other." She nodded. "I tell you, there are ten thousand ways for people to fall in love at first, but loving one another past that, you have to work at it. Doesn't matter which of the ten thousand ways got you to where you are. You have to choose the way from there together." She smiled suddenly, showing her few teeth.

Liu Chenguang walked out slowly, and Tainu flew up to her shoulder.

Zhu Guiren was leaning against a wall, looking bored and beautiful. Several of the village girls ogled him as they walked by on made-up errands. "That was certainly a good use of time," he said. "Did you attain enlightenment?"

Tainu flew to his shoulder and pecked him on the ear.

"Ow! What was that for?"

Liu Chenguang walked over to the edge of her clearing, where she could look up at Crane Moon. Had it been a lifetime for Aili, truly? Only twenty-five years?

It was nothing to her, but Aili was mortal — time was different, a lifetime was different…Liu Chenguang's time with Hong Deming had only been ten years, after all, and those ten years had become the heart of her life. Aili had truly lived longer away from her than with her, and she herself had lived far longer away from her beloved person than with them. Even Zhu Guiren had said it: *she had changed.* Aili had changed also. They were not the same people that they were when they parted.

*Nothing that exists is a finished thing.*

She looked up at Crane Moon one last time…the old place from the old life.

"Liu Chenguang?" asked Zhu Guiren. Tainu was perched on his shoulder, his golden eyes peering out at her between the black strands of Zhu Guiren's hair.

She said, "I'll gather the medical supplies — as much as we can carry, and everything else I came for — and then let's go. We can make some good time tonight."

"East?" asked Zhu Guiren.

"East," she said.

# CHAPTER 4
## LITTLE DAXIAN

THE SUN WAS far too bright, and the sidewalk was far too hard. Also, there seemed to be something sticky on it.

Aili turned her head so she wasn't looking at that too-bright sun and noticed that the sticky stuff was right next to her hand. She tried to shuffle vaguely away from it and found that there were several clay jars next to her. There were also several people standing around her, but because of the bright sun, they were just painful silhouettes.

"White liquor only?" someone asked.

Someone else replied, "She drank all the golden liquor first, old Liang said. All the golden! Everything he had in stock!"

"Ahhhh!" said several others.

"More liquor," she said, and closed her eyes.

"Doctor?" whispered someone.

"Priest?" asked someone else.

Someone knelt next to her, speaking in Anglish. "What on earth happened to you? I thought you were dead."

With effort, Aili opened her eyes again to see Edna Lee's face. She started laughing. "Edna," she said, "Edna, you know what? It's so hard for me to get drunk now."

Edna's face paled. "When did you learn Daxian?"

She laughed and laughed and laughed some more. "Good liquor," she said, and passed out.

When Aili woke up again, her head was clear. She sat up and found herself on a couch in a small living room stuffed with knickknacks and decorated with Daxian landscape scrolls. There was incense burning somewhere. It reminded her sharply of Liu Chenguang.

"You're awake," came Edna's voice. She walked slowly into the room, carefully sitting down on the chair nearest the couch. "Do you know who I am? And who you are?"

"Yes," she said. "Well, mostly. Why do you ask?"

"You've been raving in Daxian and Anglish and some other languages for a few hours now," Edna said calmly.

"Well...it's hard to explain why that is."

"Can you explain why I just found you passed out on a sidewalk in Little Daxian?"

"I was trying to get drunk," she explained. "It took a while."

Edna stared at her. "I saw you get drunk on one bowl of liquor at the restaurant," she said.

"Yes. That's different. I also discovered getting drunk from here on in is going to be an expensive proposition."

"You also don't...sound like yourself."

Aili shook her head. "Well, it turns out I'm the same person all the way down...Anyway, I know. I can't explain anything to you in a way that makes any sense. But thank you for picking me up off the sidewalk." She stood up. "Also, congratulations."

"No, you're not leaving now," said Edna sternly. "Sit. You owe me an accounting."

Aili sat meekly.

"Let's just start with why you got drunk," Edna said. "And you can make it snappy. My husband will be home soon, and you'll have to start all over if he's here. Do you have a place to go, by the way?"

Aili sighed. "No," she said at last. "I lived with Nora...and Nora's..."

Edna's face grew quiet. "Were you with her?"

"I was. And she asked me to come tell her mother about it, but...I never met her family...and I don't know...what to say."

"Is that why I found you on the sidewalk?"

"One reason."

"Her mother's already gotten the telegram," she said. "You didn't come back either, so I assumed…but you survived."

Aili looked down. "In a sense."

Now that the liquor had fully worn off, everything was coming back to her. The long walk from Fallon to Easterly. Days without food because she couldn't think of how she could go into a restaurant with human beings and ask to be fed even though she had money in her pocket that she'd taken from the house before it was burned. Two days out from Fallon, wandering to find a way to cross the Tamer River without using a bridge or coming near people, she had come across a snake yaoguai and fought it and killed it, then staggered on. Nothing felt real except pain, but Little Daxian felt familiar and homey to her — hearing Daxian, even in a dialect different from the one she'd spoken with Liu Chenguang.

"Ah," she said out loud. "Oh, it hurts." She bent over, feeling the hot spike in her heart again, and the ache in her head. When the pain had passed, she remembered Nora again. "I thought it would be a good thing I could do," she tried to explain. "It didn't seem like…like there was much point in me…existing, though. Besides that." It had been easier in the spirit realm, being flayed nightly by the soul-devourers. It had taken her mind off of all of the pain that couldn't be healed, ever. After she had destroyed Fallon, what else was there to do?

Edna stood up, her pregnant belly visible in her dress. "Do you need a doctor?"

The pain in her head was unbelievable. "Needles."

She heard Edna call someone on the telephone in the other room, speaking in a rapid southern Daxian dialect. "My husband will be here soon. He's trained in both styles. Although he can only practice among Daxian," she added with a little bitterness. "His office is just down the street."

"Your husband," Aili said, trying to act like a civilized human being instead of a lump of quivering demands. "Can you remind me his name?"

"David Lee. He's happy to have me home, obviously," she added, patting her belly. "The generals decided married women couldn't be pilots, so here we are…"

Edna's husband was her height exactly, a neatly dressed man in glasses, with a kind face and a gentle voice. Unlike Edna, he spoke Anglish with an accent.

Aili said, "We can speak Daxian."

"Either is fine," he replied, his expression not showing any surprise at all. He took her pulse and asked her symptoms, then had her lie flat as he began to insert the needles and burn incense.

The pain disappeared almost immediately. She lay there with her eyes closed, enjoying the sense of being free from it. Then, she wondered where it was coming from; after all, with her situation…as it was, should she be having these repetitive bouts of pain and weakness? She remembered Liu Chenguang checking her pulse at the barn in Fallon. Her face had been worried…her expression when she turned into the phoenix gate to cross into the spirit realm, she had been so determined, and in so much pain. Aili could see it in her eyes.

Ah, there it was again.

"What's that?" muttered Doctor Lee; he started moving needles around. "There's something…"

"Chenguang," she said. The pain in her head subsided.

"Who's Chenguang?" he asked in his quiet voice.

"A friend," she said. Then she added, "Chenguang's a doctor too. She used to do this for me." Because they were speaking Daxian, she knew, he wouldn't be able to tell whether Chenguang was male or female. Just as well, though probably Edna would tell him later.

"Did you often have this kind of complaint in the past?"

"No, it's recent…"

He nodded and finished resetting the needles. "Wait here."

When he came back in, Edna was with him. He said, "My wife and I are concerned about you. Since you're a friend of Nora's and you have nowhere to go, would you consider staying with us tonight?"

"I couldn't trouble you."

"It's no trouble," Edna said. "When you're better, we'll go see Nora's mother together, all right? So you can keep your promise to her."

Aili nodded under the needles. "Thank you," she said. "I hope I can repay you someday."

Doctor Lee said, "No worries. I'm going to leave the needles for a while. Sleep if you can."

Edna sat down next to her one afternoon a week later and said, "I need to talk to you before we go see Nora's mother." She looked a little uncomfortable. "I know that you and Nora both had…interests in women. I've known that about Nora since we were kids together. And you and that woman had…well, whatever that was. She's gone now, right?"

"She's gone now," she said. "Yes."

"It doesn't bother me. You know, when we were growing up, there weren't a lot of places for me, as a Daxian girl. There weren't a lot of other Daxian kids. My parents weren't born here…Nora was kind to me ever since we were little. She protected me from bullies…" She wiped her eyes.

Aili felt her eyes tearing up as well. "Nora was like that," she said. "To me too."

Edna took a deep breath. "It's still not real to me. So, I want to hear what you have to tell her mother, too…and it's fine for me to be there. Her mom really likes me. She'll like me even more now since I'm married and pregnant." She rolled her eyes. "But what I wanted to say is that the reason Nora's been living on her own since she was seventeen is that her parents kicked her out when they found out that Nora had a girlfriend. They were able to accept her back into the family when she was older only because she never mentioned it to them, and they never asked, and she always wore dresses when she visited. So, don't bring it up…don't mention it, all right? And…I'm going to come right out and say it. Aili, I'm going to need to get you into some more…Nora would say *femmey* clothing."

Aili snickered, hearing Nora's vocabulary from Edna, and Edna giggled too.

Aili said. "I don't think we need to go that far. I can just dress the way I did when we were on the base. We had regulations for dresses and stuff like that, remember?" Aili had arrived in Little Daxian wearing the old clothes she'd gotten from the house in Fallon, which at least weren't the bloodstained rags she'd worn out of the spirit realm but were definitely more farm*boy* than farm*girl*.

Edna nodded, relieved. "That's right, like that." After a while, she said, "That person– What was her real name again?"

"Liu Chenguang," she said steadily.

"And you really liked her, didn't you?"

"Yes," she said. "I really liked her a lot."

Edna rocked in her chair, her hand over her belly protectively. "So, what happened? Can I ask?"

Aili sighed. "You wouldn't believe it…"

"Not any unbelievable stuff, please." She held up one hand. "Just the love stuff. That's all I'm interested in."

Aili thought for a moment. "It…it can't really be explained without the unbelievable stuff…But it comes down to– I love her, and she used to love me, but I don't think she can love me now."

"Didn't you only know each other for a few weeks?" Edna asked, frowning.

"I told you, there's unbelievable stuff."

"Love is a strong word," she said sternly, "for someone you've known so briefly."

Aili shook her head and started laughing — laughing in a good way for the first time in ages. "Edna, you are so right. Can you take it as given that we haven't known each other briefly, but for a long time? But…the version of me that she knew and that she loved– That's not who I am anymore. So…"

Edna rocked her chair a little more. "Ok," she said firmly. "You know what? I'm going to go for it. Tell me the unbelievable stuff."

That evening, they went to visit Nora's mother. Aili wore a dress and told her that her daughter had been brave up until the very end; that she had been trying to help wounded soldiers on the battlefield, under fire; that she had been the best of friends and cared for all those around her; that her death had been quick and painless.

Nora's mother cried, but said she was glad to know, glad that she hadn't been alone. Aili found that she couldn't cry herself, though she wished she could.

When they left, Edna eyed Aili carefully. "All right, now come on. My parents live down this way."

Aili found the dress to be incredibly constricting, thanks to the foundation garments she had to wear beneath it. "Ugh," she said. "Clothing in ancient Daxian beats this by a long shot."

"From what you told me, you didn't wear women's clothes in ancient Daxian, so you have no basis for comparison."

"True."

They walked down along the seawall of the bay, then turned a corner back into Little Daxian. Edna stopped in front of an old house with a large collection of orchids on a rack on the porch, alongside a lot of drying laundry.

"I can't believe I'm doing this," she muttered. "Promise you won't tell David."

Aili sighed. She felt no anxiety about this at all. "If I was Liu Chenguang, I could diagnose and probably do this much more effectively," she said. "But all I know how to do is put blood on his tongue, ok?"

"Don't tell David," Edna muttered again, "or my mother."

"I think she's going to notice when I slash my hand in front of her and start dripping blood on him."

"I'll bring her out of the room. I'll– I'll tell her I need her to feel the baby–"

An old man was lying in bed, deeply asleep or unconscious. The room smelled like incense burning and bitter medicine. Aili closed her eyes at the scent. Edna, as promised, hustled her mother out of the room with some excuse, saying that Aili was a visitor from the worship house; she discreetly stuck a sacred book in Aili's hand to make this a little more believable. Her father had lung cancer, but it didn't matter. After all that training with the Navy, in the end, Aili knew only one cure.

Two days later, Edna sat down next to her again. Aili was lying still, covered with needles; David insisted that she needed regular treatment to ensure that the terrible headaches wouldn't come back.

"He's cured," she said. "He's up, puttering around with his plants again. Can breathe normally, eat, sleep…No pain, no coughing."

"Yes," said Aili, unsurprised.

"So, you told the truth."

She nodded.

"So," Edna said. She leaned forward and took Aili's hand. "Now, you have to tell me the rest of the truth. Why you were drunk in Little Daxian, and why you are in so much pain."

Aili didn't want to keep depending on the Lees, but she didn't have enough money to rent an actual apartment of her own. She found a room just outside Little Daxian and mostly sat in it, alone. Edna, she knew, was worried about her, but what could she say to make her feel better, when she herself felt…as she did?

She began wandering around Easterly at night, remembering how Liu Chenguang had been able to help people by doing this. Like Liu Chenguang, she found quite a few people lying in the alleys who needed help. More importantly, she started to see the people who were hurting them and thought that she should probably put a stop to that. One night, she found herself standing in front of an old house with wooden shingles rotting off, hearing the rowdy customers inside it, and a girl screaming in pain and fear. Of course, she had always known these places were here. These were the places where runaway girls who trusted friendly men were taken. Luckily for her, she never did trust friendly men, so she was still lying on a bench at the bus station when Nora had found her. She never told Nora that she had had to fight off two men before she showed up; Nora probably thought the bruises were from her dad.

Aili didn't bother bringing En out for this. Qinggong and bare hands were enough. One by one, she threw all the men out into the street. The women followed, some of them wailing that she was interfering with their business, others silently running for whatever safety they could find.

Well, she couldn't give them safety. But she could give them this.

The rage was sunlight and lightning inside her, washing away the pain of Liu Chenguang, all the shame and humiliation of her two lives, her cowardice, and her utter and complete failure at protecting the people she loved. She lifted her hand, shouted, and lashed down, the whip of phoenix fire striking her anger on the world.

The remaining women also screamed and ran away.

Aili stood there, breathing deeply, eyes closed, enjoying the feeling of the flames on her skin. When the fire department arrived, she used qinggong to leap away — back to her lonely, dark room — and fell asleep soundly for the first time in weeks.

She did it again the next night.

And the next.

And the next.

This time, to her surprise, a few of the prostitutes were young boys. Like the girls, most of them ran away, but not all of them.

A teenager walked out after his customer and looked at her, frowning. "What are you doing?"

"What does it look like I'm doing?" She pulled the phoenix whip out of the air and showed it to him. "I'm burning this place down."

"Why are you burning down my home?" he asked evenly. "You think people like me don't deserve a roof?"

"You should have a better home than this," she said. For some reason she felt herself tearing up. "A better life than this."

He laughed bitterly. "Well, go ahead and burn it down," he said, walking away. "But all that happens is I don't have a place to sleep."

The night after that, there were patrols organized by the brothelkeepers and the organizations that profited from them. Someone shot her. She burned him, as well as the house he was guarding. The night after that, there were large groups patrolling and almost no customers. She was pleased with this situation, but there was nothing to burn. No one to hate. She needed someone to hate, so she went looking across the bay in San Toma and found some places there to destroy.

The seventh night, she went back to the bar where she had met Liu Chenguang and drank. Beer wasn't nearly as effective as white liquor, but she did recognize one of the sailors who had attacked Liu Chenguang. She followed him out into the alley and broke both his arms. When he fled, begging for mercy and help, she laughed out loud and looked up to see a crow watching her. She threw her whip at the crow, and almost caught it.

On the eighth, she went down to the waterfront and waited silently at the water's edge until the quietest part of the night. A drunk man slept on a rock next to her, covered in tidal slime and deeply unconscious: perfect bait. When the yaoguai arose from the water, one yellow eye still dimmed, she leapt in and tore it to pieces with En and the demon-quelling seal. The drunk man was still sleeping as she staggered back to her apartment.

The following night, she went to San Toma again, taking the ferry from Easterly. As the boat crossed the bay, she watched the waves sheet over the water and wondered who else in the world she might usefully hate. She found that she couldn't really hate the Kunorese, even though they were the ones who had killed Nora; those had already been punished. Who else was there, besides her father and grandfather and great-grandfather — murderers, men who abused women and children?

She stood in front of a pleasure house she had found in San Toma — a large one, not far from San Tomas Little Daxian neighborhood, which was decorated for tourists with red lanterns and dragons. Even though it was completely false, the red lanterns made her feel homesick. She looked at them for a while. Someone somewhere in that street was playing a qin. The sadness and the rage were fighting with one another inside her; it seemed that there was nothing else left in the world but those two things to choose between.

She sighed and looked back at the house. At least with the rage, she was doing something. Something that would help people. Being sad was just…nothing.

As usual, she went in and used her hands and feet to knock down and drag out the customers, one by one. Someone hit her with a knife this time, which she blocked casually and then grabbed, stabbing the person in the shoulder before she remembered that she was trying not to kill people, then realized this person was a woman, not even a customer; this was someone she was trying to protect. Aili quickly slashed her hand and healed the wound. The woman spat in her face. She ignored this, and went back outside when she was sure the house was empty, ready to burn.

As she lifted up the hand with the whip, she felt someone grab her wrist.

Doctor Lee. "No," he said sternly. "Stop it."

She stared at him, uncomprehending.

"Edna sent me," he said. "Edna. My wife. Sent me. Stop it."

She raised her empty hand for a palm strike to his chest, ready to send him flying down the street.

"No," he said. He looked at her calmly.

She couldn't kill Edna's husband. She slowly lowered her hand, looking at him, though the whip was still burning.

He glanced at the whip, and she realized that he wasn't as calm as she had thought; he was trembling a little bit. This was an ordinary person, after all — not a cultivator.

She flicked the whip out of her hand, out of existence.

He brought her over to sit on the curb across the street from the unburned house. The prostitutes and their customers started to stealthily sneak back in.

In his quiet voice, Doctor Lee said, "Edna sent me. She's worried about you. So am I. Someone told me you got on the ferry tonight, so I came too."

"Aren't you also afraid of me?" she asked.

"Well, yes, since you're burning things down with your hands," he said calmly. "You didn't mention to Edna that you can do that."

"There were a lot of things I didn't mention," she said. She hadn't told Edna anything about being a cultivator, or En, or the yaoguai and the soul-devourers, or burning down Fallon.

Doctor Lee thought for a minute. "Edna would be here herself, but I didn't want her to risk it in her condition," he said. "In case things got out of hand. But if she were here, I know what she would say to you. She'd ask you to think about the people you love, and who love you, and ask yourself if they would want you to do this. You shouldn't only be doing things out of hatred and anger."

"That's all I have left," she said, almost in a whisper. "The people I love are dead, or don't love me."

"I doubt that," he said. "I'm here for you, Edna's here for you, and we hardly know you. That doesn't even begin to count as love. Just the beginning of friend-ship, and look at us. There are people who know you better, who love you more." He paused. "Even if they're dead, they still love you. You can still question if they would be happy with this — with you becoming like this."

"Can I not burn all the pain out of the world?" she asked, wondering aloud. "If I destroy all the evil, will all the pain go away?"

Doctor Lee said, "What do you think?"

Aili sighed. She reached out and pulled En into her hand, looking at its blade. David's eyes widened slightly. "My sword. I named it En. Isn't it funny to have a sword named for gratitude and benevolence, owing a debt to the one who saved me? Can a sword also be like that?"

Doctor Lee looked at her. "I…don't even know how to think about that question. My guess is that gratitude comes from life, not from death." He was silent for a little bit. "I also know that death and life are not easily separated, neither is good from evil. They're too deeply intertwined. How can you cut one without also cutting the other? Better to grow the good than cut the evil."

She shook her head. "I don't know. We didn't go to worship growing up." The only sacred book in the house had been in Sammish. It was somewhere on a base in the islands now, unless they had shipped it back with her belongings.

"It seems to me, as long as good is growing, that's the important thing. So, the question would be, can this sword be something that helps what is good to grow? Can you be something like that? Can your life be something like that?" He looked at her, very earnestly. "There's a lot in my life that I am angry about, I'd like you to know. Not as much as you have, you might think, but everyone has their own pain. It's not that I'm not angry, but there's good in my life. There are people I love. We're going to have a child — making a good life for them so they can live well, doing whatever good thing is in my power…isn't that better than seeking revenge and destroying what has hurt me, even if it's in my power to destroy it completely?" He nodded at her sword. "It's in your power to destroy. More than most, I would guess, so you need to think about it, very carefully."

She was silent, staring at her hand wrapped around En's hilt and remembering Liu Chenguang in the caverns, his hair brushing his wrist. Liu Chenguang would not want this, she knew. More for her to be ashamed of.

As though hearing her thoughts, David said, "There was something Edna specifically wanted me to tell you, and I'm sorry if this is getting into too much of your personal business, but Edna's very perceptive, and we share our thoughts a lot. I'm a doctor, too, so don't think that…well, there are lots of confidences I keep."

After a while, Aili said, "All right, what is it?"

"Edna wanted to tell you not to be ashamed of anything. That you've never done anything to be ashamed of, and whatever's been done to you, that's nothing to be ashamed of either. She wanted me to tell you that you can't blame yourself because of things that other people have done."

Aili was silent.

He continued, "She also wanted me to tell you, if I found you, which I have, and if it seemed important, which it does, that whatever happened to you as a child or in your past, that's not your whole life. Just because bad things happened to you before doesn't mean that good things can't also happen. Just because someone you trusted betrayed your trust doesn't mean that everyone will. Just because love wasn't enough to protect you when you were young doesn't mean that love is nothing."

Aili looked over at the red lanterns hanging outside the stores in Little Daxian and listened to the qin music. "I've done things I'm ashamed of," she said at last.

"It's better to do something different, I think," he said thoughtfully. "To do something to make amends. Just being ashamed…it doesn't make anything better."

When she didn't respond, he stood up, brushing his pants off where the dirt of the curb had stuck to them. "That's all I had to say. I know it probably is just words to you, but I wouldn't have said them, and I wouldn't have come all this way, and Edna and I wouldn't have spent so much time talking about you if you weren't a person worth all of this and more. I hope you know that."

"Thank you," she said. She looked at him seriously. "I'm…I'm grateful."

He nodded and stood nearby as she sat there a while more, watching the prostitutes and their customers go in and out of the house. Aili thought of Wu Fan and wondered what had happened to him. Maybe she would light an incense stick for him if there was a place in Little Daxian, even if it only was a place for tourists and not a real shrine. She decided to go ahead and do it, and stood.

For the first time, she realized that she had been wearing Liu Chenguang's jade pendant around her neck through everything: the spirit realm, the destruction of the array, the madness. She put her hand on it, feeling its shape and the warmth of the jade, the wings of the crane from so long ago. She should give it back. It had always been meant for her — for Liu Chenguang — but perhaps she had needed to be reminded, too.

"Will you come back to Easterly?" he asked.

"Not tonight."

She took a late-night bus from San Toma and reached the hotel outside of Fallon the next day. As she had thought, her mother was staying with Mrs. Mitchell, helping out around the bar and hotel for room and board. After she had gotten over her joy that Aili was still alive, they sat in a room together, Aili's mother's eyes constantly filling with tears.

"You look tired," she said to Aili. Her Anglish had improved a great deal, but being able to talk to her in Sammish made her even happier. She completely bought Aili's story that she had learned Sammish on the ship to the base.

"A lot has happened," she said. "Mama, I can't stay. There's somewhere I need to go."

She nodded. "That girl."

Aili started. "How did you know?"

Her mother smiled. "I didn't have enough Anglish to tell you what I knew. I always knew that you liked girls. I'm not a fool or blind. It was obvious that you liked her, and she liked you. She liked you very much, I could tell." She smiled again. "As she should, my beautiful Aili. You deserve to be loved very much."

Aili looked down. "Her name is Liu Chenguang," she said. "Or Tairei, that's her...nickname."

Her mother said, "Your father died, of course you knew."

"Of course."

"I'm glad," said her mother. "The best day in my life, the day they told me he was dead."

"Why didn't you leave sooner, Mama?"

"I was afraid," she said. "First it was for you, because if I wasn't there, I thought it would be...even worse. After you left, he said...he said he knew where you were. You were in Easterly. And that's where you were, wasn't it? Even now, I don't know if he really knew or was just guessing to threaten me, but he said he would kill you if I left, and then he would find me and kill me."

She looked at her hands. It was not necessary for either of them to say that they believed he would do exactly that.

"I couldn't think of anything to do to be free, to free you." She sighed. "So many times, I thought about killing him, but I didn't dare."

After they were quiet for a while, she added, "I wish I could have protected you better, my Aili. That's the great sadness of my life. It wasn't because I didn't want to. Only because I was too weak to do it."

Aili said, "You're like a phoenix, Mama."

Quizzically, her mother looked at her with blue-gray eyes that were the same as her own. "I don't understand. What is that?"

Aili hugged her, feeling the scars on her mother's back through the thin fabric. "You didn't have any weapons, but you tried to stand between us anyway."

Aili slept that night in the hotel and had a good breakfast with her mother and Mrs. Mitchell before starting west. She didn't want to walk through the burned remnants of Fallon, but she thought she would need to hike along the coast itself to see what she needed. As Zhu Guiren had said, she didn't have to go for many miles; by mid afternoon, as she walked north along the high cliffs above the boulders and the foaming waves, she saw a huge arched rock about half a mile out. She'd known it since she was a child, and she was fairly sure that this was the dragon gate. There was no point in her trying to take the phoenix gate into the spirit world, since she couldn't enter a demonic gate to go to Daxian and would just end up fighting yaoguai endlessly.

Just to be sure that she was doing what was necessary, she stood at the very edge of the cliff and whispered. "Eftahede."

In her mind's eye, she saw a brilliant line of white-gold light leading from her own heart outwards, straight across the ocean.

So it was necessary, then.

She settled into a lotus position, first to cultivate, then, as the sun drifted toward the west, to consider how Zhu Guiren would call a dragon. She held En in front of her for confidence and tried to send out some sort of intention into the ocean, asking for a response. It was enormously difficult, probably because she was doing it wrong, somehow, and it took nearly two hours. As the sun began to shine blindingly across the water, as it did near sunset, she saw something break the surface near the rock. Several somethings.

She moved toward the edge of the cliff again, shading her eyes with her hand. Yes, there it was. At first, it was like dolphins — regular curves clearing the surface again and again — but she knew that this wasn't dolphins.

From far below came a clear, thin voice that cut through the sound of the waves. "What is it?"

Aili cleared her throat. "Lord Dragon, I need to cross the ocean. I beg the favor that you take me through the dragon gate with you."

"My gate requires a sacrifice. A mortal life."

She had been pretty sure that would be it, since Zhu Guiren had decided that Tainu wouldn't agree. "I am amenable."

"Send the sacrifice to me and come to the shore."

She walked back from the edge of the cliff several steps, then several steps more, then again. The cliff here was at least three hundred feet tall, at least; "very high" in her childhood's recollection, and still more now that she was doing this. She felt that things would go better if she missed the rocks at the very edge and at least got into the water. When she turned around, she took several deep breaths and closed her eyes, digging her toes into the earth. She bounced up and down a few times, like a runner at the beginning of a race, then put her head down and

flew forward with all the qinggong she had.
　When that ran out, she fell like a stone.

# CHAPTER 5
## REFUGE

THE ROAD EAST was brutal.

Mostly, the crowds of refugees were headed west, inland, away from the Kunoru-held provinces. Many of them were sick or wounded, and since Tainu and Liu Chenguang kept stopping, blending with crowds — Tainu usually in his bird form, as his tall, dark-skinned figure was very noticeable — and finding ways to surreptitiously heal people, sometimes they would travel less than three miles in a day.

"It's so much easier when they're sleeping or unconscious," sighed Tainu after several days of this.

They were seated around a campfire a mile or so off the main road, in the ruins of a nameless village. It had been burned and broken, but the corpses at least were buried in a recent line of mounds.

Zhu Guiren looked around and said, "No one even bothered to set an array here after it was attacked. The pickings must be very good to just ignore something like this."

Liu Chenguang just put her head in her hands and sighed. "I'm so tired. There's so much…so many people."

After some dispirited silence, Zhu Guiren said, "Why do you two have to do this? Can you just…stop? We're not making any progress on our actual goal of destroying arrays because I have to constantly watch the two of you mingle with crowds of sick and suspicious mortals and keep an eye out for demons."

Tainu and Liu Chenguang looked at each other. Tainu finally said, "We could stop, but we don't want to."

Zhu Guiren moodily poked the fire with a stick. "If anyone has been wondering how I spent my day, I've been off fighting with random demons that are stalking the refugees."

Tainu said, "Well, that explains why you look like that." He reached over and took the stick out of Zhu Guiren's hand, then laid his own against Zhu Guiren's forehead. "Why didn't you tell me? Where's the wound?"

Zhu Guiren unbuttoned his shirt, feeling slightly embarrassed; unbuttoning and buttoning were difficult. How had Tainu even known he was wounded? There was nothing visible until his shirt was peeled away to show a large patch of burned skin oozing a viscous dark liquid.

"Talisman," he explained.

Tainu looked closer, bit his hand, and gently brushed the wound. He held up his hand and closed his eyes, whispering. A gentle golden glow surrounded his fingers as he laid his hand against Zhu Guiren's chest. It felt warm; Zhu Guiren realized that the wound on his body had been leeching a freezing cold inside him. He hadn't even noticed.

"You've never done that before," Zhu Guiren said, watching Tainu's face. He didn't wince when his wound was touched, but Tainu did.

"You've never had a wound like this before. At least, not since we've been with you," Tainu replied, eyes still closed. His hand trembled slightly. "This couldn't have come from an ordinary demon. It's eating away at you. The true wound is inside. This is just the mark of where it's poisoning your meridians…" He took a deep breath and removed his hand.

Zhu Guiren's skin was smooth and unwounded.

"I've never seen anything like that before. What was it?" Tainu met his eyes, but Zhu Guiren looked away.

"I told you," Zhu Guiren said brusquely. "Talisman strike. I've had wounds like that before. It's not that different."

He worked on buttoning his shirt with his single hand. He did not want to tell them who had given him this wound, but eventually, he decided he had to. They were partners now. He had never had partners before — people that he needed to trust and coordinate things with. It was something new to consider. But every morning, they practiced together for an hour, and of the three of them, he was the only one who could really propose strategy. Neither of the phoenixes understood what they were facing, and Tainu still had no martial arts to speak of. It made his skin crawl to imagine demons coming after Tainu if he wasn't there to protect him. He looked up and saw that Liu Chenguang had slumped over, asleep already, but Tainu's dark eyes were watching him. Belatedly, he realized that Tainu was concerned he couldn't button his shirt.

"I'm fine," he said. "I can do it."

Tainu replied, "Of course. But I'm wondering where that wound really came from. It's not from a normal demonic weapon."

He nodded. "It's a weapon sent by the First of my clan. His special talisman. It's not something he would send out lightly or give to just anyone. It carries a good amount of his power. He doesn't have many of those."

Tainu frowned. "You fought First? Does that mean you're now the head of your clan?"

Zhu Guiren snorted. "No, if I fought First…I don't think I'd survive that. Probably, I couldn't beat Second either. I fought Seventh."

Tainu gave him a quizzical look.

"She would never have tried against me without a direct order from First, and he had given her weapons that would be effective against me."

"She's dead?" asked Tainu.

"I'm alive," he said shortly, "therefore she's dead."

Tainu was quiet for a moment. "Tell me, though. You're Third, she was Seventh…There was no way she was likely to win against you, given that she's not your nearest ranked demon, from what you've told me. What was the point of sending her, even with a powerful talisman? What would have happened to you with that wound if I hadn't been here?"

"Those talismans are used for punishment. If Seventh didn't kill me, I would have eventually been paralyzed until First could send demons to pick me up and bring me back to him for discipline." He would also have been in atrocious, mind-breaking pain, but he didn't feel the need to mention this. "It didn't affect me immediately. It would have taken a while to work, so I…forgot about it."

In a very level tone of voice, Tainu said, "You should not wait for me to ask you before showing me a wound. Do not do that again."

Zhu Guiren looked up, surprised. He had never heard Tainu angry in quite this way before. Annoyed, yes, but actually, truly, angry? No. Well, wounds were wounds; sometimes he didn't notice them.

"I'll do my best," he said. "I didn't mean to hide it from you. I was just concerned about what this means for us. First is looking for me, and clearly is not sending me a polite invitation to come chat. His assumption is that I will not obey discipline unless I'm forced to, which means that he is currently treating me as an enemy and finds me suspicious. If Seventh was out looking for me, certainly I can assume other top-ranked demons are also out there looking, and we haven't even destroyed any arrays yet."

Tainu stirred the fire with the stick, saying nothing.

"I'm not sure what to do," Zhu Guiren said. "We're moving very slowly, and I am now a visible target. I am wondering if there's a safe place you can wait while I...deal with this."

"What do you mean, deal with this?" Tainu asked quietly.

"Demons only solve problems in one way," Zhu Guiren said, annoyed that he had to explain obvious things. "I need to go kill ten or twenty or so of my clan."

"How do you propose to do this?" he asked, still in that quiet voice.

"It's not an unfamiliar exercise for me, or for them, for that matter. All of us know what we're doing and have done it before or we wouldn't be alive and where we are. I'm not exactly sure what kind of details you want from me." He felt oddly defensive, as well as strangely...sad? Sad. Had he ever felt sad before? He imagined poking the feeling like Tainu was poking the fire.

"That fight was draining. I need to cultivate," he said, and stood up to go over to the new cemetery — a convenient little store of resentment for him.

He settled in a lotus position on one of the graves, the dust on it still loose; this village hadn't been destroyed long ago. The souls of the dead — except those held to earth by strong obsessions — would mostly have gone already since they weren't caught in an array, but the resentment of the dead was still here for demonic cultivation.

As he closed his eyes and focused, resentment poured into him, sharp-edged and bitter like the wind filling the sail of a broken ship, a drink like sweet soy milk hiding shards of glass. He remembered the first time he had cultivated, long before he was able to form a mortal body: how much it had hurt, how the teaching demon had to force him and the others to settle to it, to learn to drink the pain and find it good. Not all of the others could. He remembered the examples made of those who failed or gave up. It was all a lesson learned.

The glassy edges smoothed as the flood of resentment became thicker; now, instead of sharp slashes it was a river of heat — acid, burning and blistering — the layered resentment of war and destruction, far beyond a few mortal bodies lying in the soil and their wasted lives. This was the resentment of death multiplied ten thousand times, the breaking of all dreams, the loss of all hopes, the burning of the earth and the wasting of the waters, the betrayal of trust and the futility of love.

He took a deep breath, as close to truly drunk as he had been since he first set his own array — since Liu Chenguang's blood and destruction had sealed the array that held two million mortal souls. This was why demons were here, flocking to the eastern provinces. So much thick, rich resentment. So much power, so close at hand, ready for anyone who would take it.

He would have to cultivate more regularly if he was going to fight so many in such short succession. Others would be gathering power, setting arrays even now. If he really wanted to survive, to win, he should also be setting his own… He should be in among the mortals — spreading lies, fomenting more cruelty, more betrayal — increasing the flood of power that could be his own, as he once had done. Once his power was great enough, he wouldn't need to fear any other demon, allied or enemy. His life would be his own, then. Why was he wasting his time here?

Zhu Guiren opened his eyes to see Tainu sitting in his own lotus position, the light of the fire on his face. He looked very tired. Liu Chenguang had lain down from her slumped posture earlier, not visible behind the flames except for one out-flung hand and her shoulder-length black hair hiding her face. Tainu had covered her with a blanket.

Suddenly, Tainu seemed to feel Zhu Guiren's gaze and turned his dark eyes toward him. Zhu Guiren closed his own eyes again, embarrassed, though he didn't know why. He couldn't quite get the flow of cultivation again either. Something seemed to be interfering with his focus, though he tried for what felt like hours.

Could he really leave the phoenixes? They were good at hiding. They had said so themselves many times. He wasn't a monster. They had been friendly to him; he didn't need to capture them or betray them. They had their things to do and he had his. That was all. It wasn't his job to protect phoenixes or to destroy his array. He was a demon. His life was what it was.

"Demon?" Tainu's voice was very close to him.

When Zhu Guiren opened his eyes, he saw Tainu had come up to him silently, and was kneeling in front of him. The light was very poor, and the fire had died down low.

He felt something trickling down his face and froze in shock. Why was his face wet?

"Demon," said Tainu quietly, "you're tired. Come to sleep."

He felt Tainu's hand take his, pull him up, walk with him back toward the remains of the fire. There was a blanket ready for him; Tainu helped him lie down and put another one over him.

"I'm tired," Zhu Guiren said at last.

Tainu put a hand on his forehead again, then gently on the blanket lying over his chest where the wound had been. "You're very tired," he said. "Sleep now. Tomorrow's another day."

He seemed to be hesitating, thinking about saying something else. Zhu Guiren watched him, his mind in a fog. Truly, he was tired. It must be the effects of the talisman. He had never heard of anyone escaping the punishment talisman before; there was no knowing what Tainu had saved him from.

"Thank you," he mumbled, and closed his eyes, sinking further into the misty world of sleep. As it enveloped him completely, pulling him down into unconsciousness, he dreamed that Tainu kissed him on the forehead, very softly.

The next morning dawned gray and sad. The ruined village surrounded them as they wearily ate some stale oilcakes together.

"Demon, do you need to leave?" Tainu asked.

Zhu Guiren shook his head. Let them come find him, he thought. With all the resentment around, he should have an easy time cultivating enough power to deal with them. "I shouldn't stay too close to you, though. I'll be off to the sides as much as possible."

Liu Chenguang yawned. Zhu Guiren decided he'd let Tainu fill her in; he didn't want to talk about it anymore. He had never liked Seventh much — who did he like? Who was likable among demons? — but he had known her for millennia. They were close in age. At one point, three or four thousand years ago, before either of them had reached their advanced ranks, Second had ordered them to bear offspring together. This idea had so infuriated him that he had immediately left the clan home to wander for several centuries. He wondered how Seventh had felt about that. If perhaps she had wanted offspring; if she had borne any before she died.

Why was he thinking about these things? It was none of his business. Seventh knew what she was getting into when she came for him.

"Should we practice this morning?" Liu Chenguang asked.

"Every morning," Zhu Guiren said firmly.

He brought out the sword. First, he attacked Liu Chenguang, then Tainu practiced diving at him to block his eyes. Liu Chenguang practiced disarming him. Then, the two of them drilled in ways that they could work together to defend him during those crucial moments when he was weak and unable to fight while spellcasting: warding, diving, disarming, blocking, Liu Chenguang's wings. Zhu Guiren's role at this point was to watch and suggest ways they could coordinate more effectively, to show Tainu how to block without getting injured, and occasionally to play the demonic attacker. They didn't practice using the phoenix-infused talismans; they were too painful for Zhu Guiren to receive and too valuable to waste. Zhu Guiren privately considered them for emergency use only — if the phoenixes were attacked and he wasn't able to protect them.

Zhu Guiren finally called a halt. "Your energy is low. Do you need another day to rest?" he asked. "Do you need to cultivate? I've been taking it easy on you but no other demon will."

Tainu and Liu Chenguang looked at each other again, just like last night.

"We should cultivate," Tainu said reluctantly. "We really are…too weak now. Liu Chenguang, I don't think I could heal anything serious right now. How about you?"

She said, "You seem worse off than me."

Zhu Guiren remembered the talisman wound last night and wondered if this was why Tainu was so tired. He opened his mouth to ask, but Tainu spoke first.

"This place isn't a good place for us to rest," he said. "This whole landscape isn't good for our cultivation. It's full of death. We would need to get somewhere else — somewhere better…but I can't just leave all these people."

Liu Chenguang nodded, and wearily sat down next to him.

Zhu Guiren couldn't stand it anymore. "Are you two literally the only people in the world that can help others?" he asked sharply. "Why is it all your responsibility alone?"

Tainu smiled at him, which made him feel a little confused. He was so frustrated with these damn phoenixes.

"Even with everything we can do," Tainu said, "it's nothing compared to the flood, you're right. But there are things that only we can do, so we have to do them."

Liu Chenguang asked, "Isn't there anyone else, though?"

Tainu whispered softly under his breath for a while, and then shook his head. "Kunoru, Innam, Tomasines, the great plateau," he counted off. "We're the only ones in North Daxian."

"No, we're not."

Tainu's head came up sharply. "Yes. We are."

"There's that–"

"Don't be ridiculous. They haven't come down from their mountain in what, three thousand years?" His eyes narrowed. "Did you know I went to her and begged her to let you come to Mount Shi, back then? She refused. Even if you had made it there, she would have warded you out."

Zhu Guiren looked back and forth between them, intrigued. "Are you saying there's someone who can help that's at Mount Shi? That's not so far, if it's just me going. I can be faster than you. I could go get them, and you could stay here and rest and wait for me…cultivate for a while. Although, it's not very nice for you. It's really more my kind of place," he added, looking around at the burned buildings and the cemetery.

Tainu said, "Don't bother. She won't come, the shameless coward."

Zhu Guiren smiled, "I've never heard you swear about someone before. You must really dislike this person."

Liu Chenguang poked Tainu in the shoulder. "Don't let him fool you," she whispered very loudly to Zhu Guiren. "Beneath his kind attitude is boiling rage."

"It must be difficult to be a phoenix with an anger management problem."

"Oh, you're not wrong," said Liu Chenguang sincerely.

Tainu just glared at them. "This is just a distraction. Liu Chenguang, it's just us. Let's cultivate a few hours and head out."

"Oh no, I want to meet this person," Zhu Guiren said. And, he thought privately, this would be a good opportunity to get away from the phoenixes for a few days. Fight some demons perhaps…get them off their trail. The phoenixes could hide and rest, and he would draw attention from them. And perhaps, if he got someone else to take care of all the mortals, they would remember the reason they were here at all and get back to work.

"I'm telling you, she won't come," said Tainu through gritted teeth.

"I wasn't planning to *ask* her," Zhu Guiren replied, smiling. "This is a phoenix, correct?"

"It's warded. Heavily warded. She never goes out." Tainu frowned at Zhu Guiren, clearly seeing through his ruse to get away from them.

He shrugged. "Nothing ventured, nothing gained. Where?"

Liu Chenguang smiled. "I would love to see this if you can get her to come."

"Don't encourage him," Tainu said. "Demon, don't try it. You'll be injured at best, maybe seriously. Her wards are strong."

"As strong as yours?"

Tainu was silent.

"No," said Liu Chenguang.

Tainu glared at her again.

Liu Chenguang continued, "Tainu, what can it hurt? He can at least ask.

Look at all of this — all of these people. At some point, she has to have some compassion."

"No. Do not." He stalked away, his shoulders stiff and furious. Over his shoulder, he yelled, "Liu Chenguang, come on, let's go. Demon, don't do it. I'm telling you."

Zhu Guiren leaned down to Liu Chenguang. "Tell me where she hides, how to find her," he whispered, "and you two go back down the path a little bit. Where we camped night before last was better than this for you, probably. Those trees, remember? I'll meet you there in three days. Rest and cultivate."

Liu Chenguang looked after Tainu, irresolute, but finally she told him.

A week later, Zhu Guiren marched into their camp and tossed a woman bound with glowing, blue-black chains on her ankles and wrists in front of Tainu. Tainu looked at her in horror, then at Zhu Guiren in fury.

"Fix me!" Zhu Guiren crowed, holding out his arms wide. He was covered in blood, burns, and bruises, and his clothes hung off him in rags.

"Liu Chenguang," gritted Tainu, "you do it."

"Oh no," said Zhu Guiren. "I get to pick. You do it. I want you."

Liu Chenguang shrugged.

Tainu stiffly moved over to Zhu Guiren and began dabbing blood on wound after wound.

Zhu Guiren felt almost giddy with blood loss and success. He'd killed Eighth, Sixth, and Fourteenth, in addition to several other demons from other clans. No one else had gotten a talisman on him, and he'd broken the wards to capture this annoying phoenix after she insulted him and told him that all the mortals could die and the two busybody phoenixes could rot in their self-righteousness as far as she was concerned. While he appreciated her point of view, no one spoke to him that way. She wasn't particularly strong — not nearly as powerful as Tainu or as clever at self-defense as Liu Chenguang — so it hadn't been difficult once he had gotten a spellchain on her so she couldn't transform and fly away.

"You have a lot of internal damage from her wards, didn't you notice?" Tainu said. His voice finally lost a little bit of its edge of anger, which made Zhu Guiren feel secretly relieved.

"No," he said honestly, "I was busy with all the other damage. I might have cared if I didn't have a phoenix to come back to." He smiled guilelessly up at Tainu.

Liu Chenguang laughed. "Zhu Guiren, let her go. I didn't really mean you should chain her up and force her to come. What good is that? She can only help if she wants to."

He snapped his fingers and the spellchains disappeared.

Tainu finished by touching his mouth with his bloody fingers, which felt rather odd; Tainu had only done that twice before — in the spirit realm when he had lost his hand, and after he was attacked with the phoenix talisman — and he supposed those times, he'd been in too much pain to really feel it. Tainu's fingers pressed inside his lips, parting his teeth and brushing his tongue lightly with blood. He didn't remember that part. He raised an eyebrow, but Tainu was already walking away from him, looking grim, to sit by the strange phoenix.

She sat up and tossed back her long, unbound black hair, rubbing her ankles where the chain had been. "How dare you, sibling," she hissed at Tainu. "Both of you. How dare you partner with a demon to insult and abuse me in this way."

"I apologize," Tainu said tightly. "We didn't intend this. We only wanted him to ask you if you could come down and help the people. There's a lot of suffering, war, flood, famine–"

"Why should I care about this? Let nature take its course. Let the mortals do what they need to do. Why do you need to interfere? You've insulted me, inconvenienced me, and set me back in my cultivation. Look at the two of you — what's the effect of constantly interfering with mortal lives? You are only increasing suffering, and you are covered with the world's filth. You," she said coldly to Liu Chenguang, "are barely a phoenix anymore, and you," she glared at Tainu, "eldest, century after century you keep trying to fix what can't be fixed, cure what can't be cured, and you wander the world in pain. For what? Stupid. Let the dying die. You're only prolonging the inevitable."

Tainu clenched his fists and closed his eyes.

Zhu Guiren stared at the phoenix, then back at Tainu. He leaned over by Tainu's ear and whispered very loudly, "You want to hit her, don't you? Do you want me to hit her for you?"

Tainu snorted, and then laughed out loud. His fists relaxed. He looked away from the phoenix and smiled at Zhu Guiren.

Zhu Guiren grinned back. Tainu laughing was the best sound. Also, he would very happily hit this phoenix if she called Tainu stupid again. He shot her a nasty look to make sure she understood that.

Despite being glared at by a demon, the phoenix opened her mouth again, but Liu Chenguang spoke first. In a reasonable voice, she said, "We're sorry for the inconvenience, but after all, you're already here. Why not walk with us and heal for a while? You've been alone a long time. Surely it would be good to be out in the world for a bit. There are so many–"

"No," said the phoenix coldly. "I'm leaving now." She held out her arms in preparation to transform, then suddenly stopped. She looked consideringly at Tainu, then at Zhu Guiren. Abruptly she said, "Those wards were the strongest I could devise, but this demon barged in with no problem."

Zhu Guiren lazily examined his fingernails. "Your wards were pathetic. I'm sure you're the weakest phoenix I've ever met. Probably you couldn't heal people even if you wanted to."

The phoenix ignored this and turned to Tainu. "Did you give him a talisman or spell to break the wards?"

"No," he said. "He did it himself. While they damaged him internally, they didn't kill him, obviously."

"And now you've healed him, for no reason I can see other than to annoy me. Well, I have a bargain for you, eldest sibling. Make me a refuge. As strong as the ones in the spirit world. A refuge that's only for me. If you promise to do that, I'll walk back to the sacred mountain with you and heal along the way. I want it just like the refuges in the spirit world. Just as strong, a cultivational focus, but one that won't let any other being enter but me. Do that, and I'll help."

Tainu looked at her very seriously. Liu Chenguang looked at Tainu. Liu Chenguang's face was shocked, but for Zhu Guiren, it was as though he had always known; of course Tainu had made the refuges. Who else could it ever have been? But with a trickle of unease in his stomach, he saw that Tainu looked… not afraid, exactly, but as though he was carefully considering whether he could accomplish something. As though he was bracing himself.

Tainu turned to Liu Chenguang and Zhu Guiren first. "If I agree to this," he said, "I'll be incapacitated for a while. I don't know how long. Weeks, most likely, if not more. Completely incapacitated. I won't even be conscious."

"I don't want you to do it," Liu Chenguang said.

Zhu Guiren nodded. "No. To hell with her. Why should you do anything for that piece of garbage?" He felt suddenly that this was his fault — his fault for bringing her here, even though he meant it all to help. He glared at her, but she ignored him. Stubborn like all phoenixes.

Tainu was quiet, thinking, then he said to Liu Chenguang. "There's no one else. And she's been cultivating nonstop for more than three cycles. There are so many thousands. We can't help them all, but she'll be able to do…a lot."

"I will," the phoenix said. "I'll heal as many mortals as you like between here and Mount Shi. It's a waste of my time and my power, of course, but I'll have a refuge to cultivate in afterward, so it's a good bargain."

"Isn't it." Tainu's voice was flat. "Sibling, your selfishness will eat you from the inside out in your dark prison."

Zhu Guiren was stunned. He had never imagined Tainu condemning anyone in this way, his face cold with disgust.

The phoenix, however, was unimpressed. "Sibling, your wasted compassion is dissolving you in despair," she said just as coldly. "I desire solitude and peace. You walk in pain wherever you can find it to step in. No thank you."

"I'm tempted to build it without a door," Tainu said, "but since my wasted compassion isn't quite dissolved in despair yet, I'll make sure it's possible for you to leave whenever your heart wakes up and realizes it's alive."

"Don't," said Liu Chenguang.

"Will you stay with me afterward?" he asked, looking at Liu Chenguang, and not at Zhu Guiren.

"Of course," she said.

"*I* won't," Zhu Guiren said, feeling irrationally angry. "This is stupid. Don't do it."

Tainu smiled at him. "I'm doing it," he said, his voice composed and determined, "and I hope I'll see you when I wake up. Let's go." He started walking.

Zhu Guiren stood still, watching him walk away, followed by the other two phoenixes. Finally, he walked in the same direction.

Later that morning, Tainu found him walking alongside the column of refugees and fluttered to his shoulder. "It's because she's never been with people enough. She doesn't have a real name — either a true name or one that others call her."

Zhu Guiren didn't answer.

"Demon?" Tainu asked, his tone a little uncertain, but Zhu Guiren kept walking.

"I don't want to talk to a stupid bird," he said, although of course he knew that Tainu couldn't be in his mortal form among all the Daxians; he was far too visible. He could feel Tainu's little claws clutching at his shoulder and his feathers brushing against his skin and it annoyed him immensely.

"It will be worth it, demon. It's good you brought her. It's only been a few hours and she's already healed dozens of people. She's awful at self-protection, but she has enormous stored power for healing because she's almost never used it. And for the other thing, truthfully, I don't mind doing it. Now that I see how frightened she is and how weak her wards are…When we're done with this, she'll be completely drained as well. She'll need protection."

Zhu Guiren felt that unreasoning fury again. "Waste of time. Get off my shoulder. I have things to do." He barely restrained himself from pushing the little bird off by force. As Tainu fluttered upward, Zhu Guiren raced away toward the hills above the roadside, looking for yaoguai, wanting to feel something die.

At evening, he looked down and saw the red bird — still hovering, still swooping down to touch people. That night, he didn't come back to the camp.

Several nights later, Zhu Guiren stalked into the firelight to see that Liu Chenguang was already wrapped in a blanket and passed out. He didn't look for Tainu. The strange phoenix, who he had mockingly named Feng Huang, cultivated neatly to one side. He walked over and kicked her. "Heal me."

She opened her eyes and glared at him in disgust. "Ask Liu Chenguang."

"She's asleep."

"I was cultivating. It's more important than sleeping."

"Sword cut to thigh, calf, left shoulder. Stab wound in upper left chest. Talisman strike."

"Ask eldest sibling. He's the one that'll cure anything that crawls out of the mud."

Zhu Guiren said, "No. You."

"What if I refuse? It's not like you'd attack me."

He snorted. "How is it possible you don't think so?"

She finally snarled, stood up, and bit her fingers to get to work.

While she healed him, his eyes slipped against his will around the fire. "Where's Tainu?"

"How should I know? With the refugees most likely."

"Alone?"

"He's always alone. I'm done." She went back into her cultivational pose and ignored him.

Zhu Guiren wavered a bit, but then went to look. It was very late; mostly the refugees were asleep, scattered along the side of the road for miles. There were thousands of people. He couldn't be sure. Perhaps Tainu was there somewhere, but he couldn't find him among all the moaning masses. Such a waste of energy.

Infuriated, he ran back down the road looking for yaoguai preying on the stragglers. Now that he was healed, he felt very much like killing something again.

He tracked a yaoguai through the woods — a centipede — and killed it. He hadn't been wounded by that scum, so no need to go back to the phoenixes yet, but the slime had gotten on him and he didn't like the feeling of it, so when he found a stream, he knelt by it to wash his face.

"Getting the blood off?"

He whirled around to see Tainu, sitting on the ground with his back to a tree. He must have walked right past him. There was a child asleep with its head on his lap, a little girl holding onto Tainu's hand.

"What are you doing here?" Zhu Guiren asked, and turned back to the stream to splash the water on his skin. He hadn't realized he was covered in blood. Somehow, he had gotten used to it.

"This one was left for dead," Tainu said. "I found her on the road. I can't leave her alone." He added, "I must have fallen asleep myself."

Zhu Guiren flicked the water off his arm and bit it back as long as he could. Then he said, "What are you doing, Tainu?" He turned to face him. "Why are you wasting our time and energy for this? We've lost weeks, and we're just flailing around getting nowhere with arrays. That girl's going to die no matter what you do. It's only temporary. She's still starving to death. No one is going to give that child food when you leave her behind. Were you planning to take her with you and feed her?"

"No," he said. He stroked the girl's hair gently. "I can't take her with us. I know that. A child couldn't be safe with us. I can't fix anything. The world is what it is. It's only temporary. I know." Looking at his hand on the girl's head, he said, "You have to understand, demon. Everything is temporary for me. Nothing lasts, everything dies. Except this one thing."

"What, feeling sorry for people?" Suddenly enraged, Zhu Guiren said, "You must feel sorry for me too."

"No. I don't feel sorry for you. Why would I?" He shook his head and said, "Do you want to understand? No one really understands…It's tiring sometimes."

"I don't want to understand. I want you to stop doing this. Look at you. You're exhausted. We have so much else to do. There's a reason we're here and this isn't it. These people are all going to die. Or if they live for a little bit longer, that's beyond your control too—"

"I *know*," Tainu said, as though trying to emphasize something. "I know it's beyond my control. I'm not trying to control it. It's just that they are beautiful, demon. Can you see? Every one of them. Beautiful and temporary and suffering and I want them to— I want them to know that they matter, however short it is, however temporary. It is the most amazing and beautiful and true thing in the universe that they exist, that this little girl exists, and I don't—" He struggled for a moment, then continued. "I don't know her name, but it matters that she is here, and her suffering matters, and her love and yearning matter."

"So, these people," Zhu Guiren said furiously, his fist clenched so the nails cut his skin, not understanding why he was so angry at Tainu, at his gentleness and kindness. Why was he so angry? "These little, short-lived vermin whose names you don't even know…they matter more than the whole reason we're here? More than Aili? More than Liu Chenguang?"

"What are you talking about?" Tainu asked, confused. "Why is there a measurement? Of course, if I had Aili in front of me or someone I don't personally know, I would– But it's never like that, or almost never. I can do both."

"No, you can't! You can't do everything! You have to– Even if you decide you want to care so much, you still need to– It's so–" He took a deep breath and calmed himself. "Whatever, I don't know why I'm trying to talk to you. You have limits too. You're not inexhaustible."

Tainu raised his eyebrow. "Well, to be fair, I'm pretty close to inexhaustible, in certain circumstances." He gave an exaggerated leer.

"Are you– What– Are you bragging to me?" Zhu Guiren spluttered. Why was Tainu always going in the direction he least expected? "Really? What are you even–"

Tainu laughed until he choked. "It's so fun to tease you," he said, coughing.

"How can you still be laughing?" demanded Zhu Guiren. "You can barely stand up. You just fell asleep, unwarded, with a hunting yaoguai ten feet away. Did you even know? I just killed it! It was probably stalking you."

"I'm not that foolish," he said, clearly a bit stung. "I did have a ward set."

"Why–" Zhu Guiren stopped mid-sentence, appalled at the implications.

Tainu said it anyway. "My wards recognize you now."

"That's…permanent?"

"More or less," Tainu said. "I can revoke it, but I don't really see the need."

Zhu Guiren bit out, "The yaoguai didn't trip your wards because I was with it."

"All right, I see your point. But I'm still not going to revoke you."

"You. Are. An. Idiot."

"Thank you," Tainu said, serious again. "I know. You're right. I'll do what I can do. I know I can't do everything. But I won't revoke you. And I can't ignore a dying child in front of me."

Zhu Guiren stared at him, his heart roiling for some reason. How could Tainu bear to live this way, seeing every being he encountered as beautiful and worthy of his attention and sacrifice? Tainu's eyes were locked with his, pleading for understanding that he had no desire to give.

"Ignore it," he said, finally. "And don't do whatever it was you promised that trash phoenix."

Tainu laughed again and broke the lock of his gaze. After a moment he said, "She's also my sibling. There's a lot of people who owe their lives to her, and even if they never know it, even if she doesn't care, still she did it. It still matters." Tainu stood up, carefully lifting the child in his arms. "There's some people that take in lost and orphaned children. I'll bring her to them, leave her there before she wakes up. It's the best I can think of. Do you have any other ideas?"

Zhu Guiren said, "The one thing that doesn't matter to you is, apparently, my opinion. It doesn't matter, does it, what I say."

"It matters," Tainu said. "It matters a lot, because you wouldn't say it if you didn't care about me." He held the child against his shoulder and met Zhu Guiren's eyes, smiling at him as though he were something that could be trusted.

Zhu Guiren laughed out loud. Even to himself, the laugh sounded strange and brittle. What was wrong with him? "Do you have some misunderstanding of me," he asked harshly, and walked away from him, looking for something to kill.

Three weeks and uncountable hundreds of people healed later, they stood on Mount Shi, at the entrance to the hidden cavern where Zhu Guiren had found the phoenix.

Zhu Guiren wished more and more that he had never come. He hadn't spoken to Tainu since that day; had only followed behind and to the side, watching as they healed, and healed, and healed, and healed — never thanked, never noticed, always hiding. Even Feng Huang had found ordinary mortal clothes to replace her cultivator's robes, braided up her long hair, smeared dirt on her face, and blended in, dabbing blood here, there, everywhere among the thousands and thousands of refugees flooding the roads, huddled in the makeshift camps, hiding in the cities, starving, wounded, sick. Every day, he saw Tainu in his bird form, hovering above the crowd, choosing a person that was weak or faltering, looking for his opportunity to claw himself and drip blood on their wounds and then swooping down, or waiting until they slept when he might be able to approach in his human form and put blood between their lips.

He remembered Tainu's fingers between his lips. The taste of his blood. Zhu Guiren clenched his fist in disgust. Every time Tainu did that, he became weaker. Why did he have to do it? Why did they all have to do it? For what benefit?

What goal?

Every night, he found a graveyard or unburied corpses — there was no shortage — and cultivated, drinking in the pain of the people, alive and dead. Tainu's efforts made no dent in this flood of delicious resentment. He felt it pouring, pounding through his meridians, almost too much to hold, tearing him with its bitter edges, sensuously exciting in its turbulence. There was no point to what Tainu did. It didn't stop death or suffering. It didn't change anything. Night after night, he took in resentment till he was gasping trying to contain it all, and then he would leap out, seeking death; seeking other demons to kill, and finding them.

When he was wounded again, he went to Liu Chenguang. She asked him once why he was avoiding Tainu.

He just stared at her and said, "Fix it."

Tainu must have heard; he hadn't kept his voice down in response to Liu Chenguang's whisper. He was cultivating nearby, though really almost falling asleep — his head was tipping toward his chest. He looked up at Zhu Guiren, his eyes tired and bruised underneath, but didn't say anything.

Zhu Guiren hated seeing him like that. When Liu Chenguang was done healing, he left again.

He didn't know why he was here, looking into this damn cavern, standing next to the three most annoying creatures in the world. Maybe just to see it end. Tainu wrapped his arms around himself as though trying to reassure himself that he could do something. Liu Chenguang just looked at the ground. The strange phoenix stripped off the mortal clothes with complete disinhibition until she was naked. She had a perfect body, silken hair falling past her waist, but Zhu Guiren mostly looked at her and wanted to kick her. Hard.

"Do it," she said coldly.

Did none of these people consider going back on a promise? Zhu Guiren could kill them all just for being such idiots.

"Don't do it," he said to Tainu, the first thing he had said to him in half a month.

Tainu looked at him and smiled. "It's all right. It's not a bad thing to do."

Zhu Guiren turned his back on him.

Tainu kept talking. To Liu Chenguang, probably, since he himself was very obviously not listening, but of course he could hear it as though Tainu was speaking to him too. "I've only ever done this in the spirit realm before," he said, "and normally I would go into a refuge immediately on completing it to cultivate and heal. I have no idea how long it will take me to heal after this, since I'll be creating a refuge I can't stay in. Once the work is complete, I think it will bring me outside since the wards will only recognize that one and repel all others. But I will heal, you know I will, so don't be worried."

Liu Chenguang said, "I'm worried, Tainu."

He continued as though he hadn't heard. "I don't want you to watch. You stay outside. Both of you," he said, as though Zhu Guiren was actively listening, which he was not. "I'll be unconscious at the end, remember I told you. You'll have to bring me somewhere to stay. Somewhere safe, all right? Where we can stay for a few weeks, at least."

Liu Chenguang said, "Zhu Guiren, please. I won't be able to carry him."

Zhu Guiren nodded curtly, still not turning around.

"Demon," said Tainu, "thank you."

He finally turned and said, again, "Don't."

Tainu smiled at him, a smile that blazed like sunshine through the clouds. "You know, I can remember anything I've seen. I only need to see it once."

Zhu Guiren watched him turn and walk into the cavern, frozen in place. That smile like sunlight…there was something inside him, something that was locked, and the sunlight fell on it and warmed it.

He shook off Liu Chenguang's hand on his arm, pushed the naked phoenix out of the way, unseeing, and followed Tainu into the cavern.

Tainu stood inside it, on an even part of the floor, his arms outstretched like wings with his hands in seals, and he was murmuring words that Zhu Guiren knew — words in the demonic language.

"No," Zhu Guiren said sharply. "No, what are you doing?"

But Tainu was already deep in trance, working the spell. If he tried to physically touch him now, he might hurt him — hurt both of them — seriously. The qi was gathering into the shape he was calling it, but Zhu Guiren knew no phoenix could speak the demonic words without pain. And there was pain. He could see it in Tainu's posture, throughout his body, holding himself upright by sheer will. That was a posture Zhu Guiren was familiar with. He had experienced pain like this many times, but this person had never let anyone see him in pain, had always hidden it so well.

"Stop it," he whispered, but helplessly. It was too late now.

What Tainu had begun, he would have to complete.

The demonic words were ripping Tainu's mouth and throat. Zhu Guiren could see the blood dripping from his lips as he chanted, moving his hands into a new seal. The golden qi was spiraling around him, surrounding him as he was held by it in midair, slowly expanding into a perfect sphere with him at the center.

Zhu Guiren narrowed his eyes. It was hard to see through the golden net, but he thought— There was something happening to Tainu's body.

To his shock, he saw…rips…begin to open in Tainu's skin, small tears, then larger ones, as though many, many old scars had simultaneously ruptured, spilling out his blood, so many that it looked as though he had been flayed, more wounds than whole skin, everywhere, all over him. He couldn't imagine the pain.

"No," he said. "No."

Even knowing it was impossible, he reached forward, trying to grab him, trying to stop it, but the qi blocked him; the anti-demonic spell was already working, throwing him backward to the floor. Inside that net of gold, he could see Tainu still chanting, the words even louder now, though his eyes were closed tight. Suddenly, as he reached the crescendo, the blood dripping and trailing from him burst out in a mist, following the curve of the golden sphere so that its inner wall was a delicate membrane of blood.

The golden sphere suddenly solidified, became opaque, and faded into blue-gray stone.

Tainu appeared on the floor next to him, not breathing, covered in blood.

"Liu Chenguang!" Zhu Guiren screamed, kneeling next to him. "Liu Chenguang, come! Come now!"

The other phoenix came first — naked and beautiful as a creature from before the mortal world was made — running gracefully past them and diving into the place Tainu had made for her with his blood. Zhu Guiren heard himself growl like an animal, reaching out his hand to grab her and tear her apart, but too late. She was gone.

Liu Chenguang was there, kneeling next to him, calling him.

"Zhu Guiren," he heard her say at last. "Zhu Guiren."

He looked at her, stunned past bearing. The rips in Tainu's skin, his sunlit smile, those two things did not belong together, but they did, they went together, somewhere in his heart there was a place these two things had lived together a very long time, behind a door that was locked and the lock had been broken so the door couldn't be opened anymore except by force, and now the force had come, but it hurt, it hurt to open it.

He looked at Liu Chenguang without seeing her.

"Zhu Guiren," she said, her voice quavering, "I can't heal him with my blood. Phoenixes can't heal one another. We need to get him to somewhere safe and clean, and treat him as best we can with mortal remedies, and beyond that we need to let his body heal itself. Our bodies will always heal. This is why he reminded us. He knew that it would be like this. We just have to— to follow his instructions."

He didn't respond.

"Please, Zhu Guiren," she said, sounding desperate, "I need you to carry him. I'm not big or strong enough."

He finally understood this part. His mortal body was not as tall or heavy as Tainu's, but he was a demon with a demon's strength. He could do this, except that Tainu's blood was everywhere. It was so slippery. "Get the cloth."

Liu Chenguang handed him the white cultivator's robe that the other phoenix had discarded. He carefully and gently wiped off the blood as well as he could. The cuts were still bleeding, but this was all he could do for now. He put his handless arm under Tainu's knees and his other arm beneath his back, holding him cradled against his chest. Tainu's head lolled against his shoulder.

"I have him," he said.

# CHAPTER 6
## AFTER THE REFUGE

ZHU GUIREN SAT next to Tainu, watching him sleep.

So much of his past wasn't clear to him — it had been very long, and he had done many things, and many things had been done to him by others — but this he remembered. Sitting by this person and watching them sleep. Worrying about them.

He seemed to recall that it would be better to be closer. Tainu's skin was dark, his eyes closed. Underneath his eyes were darker bruises. He remembered the bruises under his eyes.

"Tainu?" he asked, quietly.

Tainu didn't respond, except for a little wrinkle in his eyelids.

"It's me," he tried. He didn't know why it seemed so important to tell Tainu that it was him speaking. Who else would it be? Obviously not Liu Chenguang. Who else was even here? Why did he think that Tainu would be comforted by knowing he was close? Why did he even care about whether Tainu was comforted or not?

Why was he doing this at all — undermining his own cultivation, undoing what he'd spent thousands of years preparing to accomplish?

The question came and went in his mind without any answer. He slowly reached out with his single hand and interlaced his fingers with Tainu's, their pale and dark skin making a pattern together.

He had never held hands with anyone like this before, trying to give them comfort. He remembered how Liu Chenguang had asked to hold Hong Deming's hand after he died and squeezed his eyes shut so he wouldn't see that anymore. Something about it made him hurt inside. Every time he saw it, every time he saw Liu Chenguang reach for Aili's hand while Aili slept in the spirit world, it ached. Even when it happened — when Hong Deming's dead body lay next to Liu Chenguang and he knew that Liu Chenguang would soon be destroyed and reborn. Even though he would never change his mind about any of it. He had come so far, done so much; he wouldn't stop so close to the end. Even then, even so, at that moment, he felt something he had no name for, something both sharp and sad. Liu Chenguang's eyes, his voice saying, "Please."

As he watched, Tainu's eyelids wrinkled a little bit. Was he in pain? Should he come closer? Would that help him?

Zhu Guiren laid down on his side on the edge of the bed and carefully reached out across Tainu to hold him. His head rested on Tainu's shoulder, so he could still see his face. He closed his eyes after a while, feeling Tainu's breathing calm, his heartbeat become peaceful. "It's me," he whispered, hardly moving his lips. "It's me. It's Arciniang. I'm with you."

"What are you doing?" came a hissed whisper from behind him. "Get away from him."

He raised his head to see Liu Chenguang, eyes wide with shock, holding a bowl with water and herbs and a clean cloth to wipe Tainu's wounds. "I want to be close to him," he explained, although it should have been perfectly obvious. He wasn't really his usual self right now, unable to destroy those who would block his will; he felt very soft inside.

"What? I don't care. Does he want to be close to you?" Liu Chenguang replied. "I don't want you close to him like that. Let him go. Get away."

Reluctantly, he untangled himself and sat up, careful not to wake him. "Now he'll be cold," he said accusingly, still in that strange, unknown space in his heart.

"That's what blankets are for." She covered him up, trying to push Zhu Guiren aside.

He wouldn't go.

"What is going on with you?" she asked, exasperated. "This isn't like you at all. What's happening? Are you having some kind of qi deviation?"

He reached out to take Tainu's hand again, interlacing their fingers.

Liu Chenguang firmly reached out and took Tainu's hand away from him.

He looked at her, confused. "Please?" he asked.

Her face was filled with a mix of disgust and resignation. "I can't deal with this right now," she said, and left the room.

That was perfectly fine. He held Tainu's hand again and watched him sleep.

Liu Chenguang had found an inn close to the road near the base of Mount Shi, probably once one of the finer accommodations in Shi'an; under war conditions, everything was shabby and poor, but the room was still a decent one, and it had a window looking toward the mountains. Zhu Guiren vaguely felt that this was good for the phoenixes; much better than the landscape full of resentment they had been walking through, a good place for Tainu to heal.

But week after week, it didn't seem that Tainu was healing beyond the superficial closing of the wounds. He didn't wake for more than brief intervals during which he didn't speak or seem to perceive where he was, his eyes clouded and quickly closing. Liu Chenguang was worried, and he himself felt a sense of deep distress whenever he couldn't be near Tainu. Liu Chenguang had finally accepted that she would have to let Zhu Guiren do some of the watching. There wasn't much to do, other than sit there, but he always felt a sense of relief when she would let him in, so he could hold his hand, and look at him. Zhu Guiren would try to go cultivate, or do something, *anything*, but all he wanted to do was sit near as Liu Chenguang would let him. He knew, as though watching himself from a distance, that his behavior was ridiculous, but his sense of dignity had fled completely, and settling into cultivating resentment had become impossible, some block in his spiritual body resisting it.

Some four weeks after Tainu had set up the refuge, Zhu Guiren noticed that his hand suddenly felt warm. Much warmer than usual. At almost that same moment, Tainu opened his eyes and looked over at him, his gaze clear and serene, and smiled.

He looked so happy.

Zhu Guiren felt something inside him opening up at that smile and those warm, dark eyes on him. "Tainu?" he asked cautiously.

"I feel a little unbalanced," he said. "Can you help me get out of bed? I want to look out the window."

Zhu Guiren helped him up, wishing for the millionth time that he still had two hands. "Come on. Do you need a chair?"

"No, I'm fine, I want to stand…" At the window he looked out at the sea of green running up into the mountains. "It's beautiful here. Are we in Daxian?

That looks like Mount Shi."

Zhu Guiren looked at him in shock. "Yes…Are you all right?"

"I feel good. When do I ever not?" Tainu looked at him and smiled again. "And you're here."

Zhu Guiren felt that strangeness again, somewhere inside him, when Tainu looked into his eyes and smiled that way. He didn't have words for this feeling; he hadn't felt it before. "I'm…I'm here."

"Are you worried about something? Don't be worried." Tainu reached out and pulled him closer. His balance really wasn't good. When he pulled on Zhu Guiren's arm, he stumbled backward to lean against the wall next to the window.

Surprised, Zhu Guiren fell forward, so their bodies were fully against one another. He felt Tainu's arms around him, enclosing him with warmth.

Tainu laughed. "Arciniang," he said, very softly, and Zhu Guiren felt Tainu's lips gently covering his.

Zhu Guiren realized that his entire mortal body was trembling, and every inch of it was filled with light.

"I'm so happy you're here," said Tainu, murmuring against his lips. "Arciniang."

Then he fell over to the side and landed on the floor.

"Liu Chenguang!" shouted Zhu Guiren, panicked. "Liu Chenguang!" He picked Tainu up to put him back into bed and realized, not distracted by his lips and his smile, that his skin felt like it was burning up. "What's happening?"

Liu Chenguang rushed in and took his pulse.

I could have done that, Zhu Guiren thought, too late, I'm the one that trained her after all. But it seemed that any sensible thought in his brain had gone long ago and far away.

"Qi deviation," she said brusquely. "Stand back."

"But he was fine! He said he was happy! He wanted to get out of bed–" Zhu Guiren flailed inwardly, desperate to get Tainu back to that now-desirable state of simply sleeping all day.

Liu Chenguang didn't even spare him a glance. "His qi is very strange. Maybe it's a backlash from using the demonic spell?" She started to transfer qi to him, moving from one meridian to another.

"I can– I can help," he said, reaching out his hand.

She pushed it away. "No," she said, "you can't give him demonic qi. It would make it far worse than it is."

Zhu Guiren's eyes widened, and he took a step back, then fled the room.

Outside, he covered his face with his shaking hand. But Tainu had been strange before he touched him, before…kissing him. That hadn't been what caused this…Had it?

He took several deep breaths, trying to calm himself down, and found he couldn't.

He attempted to put his thoughts in order, kneeling next to the wall and scribbling frantically with the pencil he kept in his pocket. Tainu had used a demonic spell and the demonic language to create the refuge, combined with his own blood; that could only have worked if he was somehow manipulating demonic qi, resentment that he had gathered from the surrounding environment. Had there been some kind of reverse connection, where his blood had not only entered the spell, but the spell had also entered his blood? There had been those hundreds of cuts all over his body…

He closed his eyes and reordered his thoughts from that sense of horror. Tainu's skin tearing and bleeding in front of him, again…why did he think *again*, as though that had happened before?

If the demonic qi had entered him at that point, the pure qi would be attempting to overcome it and purify it. Perhaps this was a crisis point and it would resolve on its own. The heat and loss of cognitive focus would be ways in which the spiritual body was attempting to purify itself — removing various internal barriers to an increase of qi beyond what the mortal body could normally tolerate and attempting to make the spirit well inhospitable to the demonic qi — just as a fever in a mortal illness was a way in which the body overcame…

How was kissing him part of this process?

With great effort, he stopped himself from thinking about Tainu's lips on his and returned to the main point.

But perhaps it was part of the process, after all? He scribbled more, a quick diagram; was the phoenix's mortal body attempting to expel the demonic qi through connecting physically with a demonic mortal body? The demonic body would act like a magnet for the demonic qi…

This possibility made him feel somewhat sad, but at least it was a solution.

Would it have to be kissing?

He felt, truthfully, that he was a little biased about this question. Would holding hands also do? He decided that, purely objectively speaking, kissing would probably be more effective. Because they'd been holding hands for weeks already. Tainu said that in the past he'd only ever done this in the spirit realm and had entered each refuge to cultivate immediately on completing it. The refuges were anti-demonic; they would have done the work for him. Tainu probably hadn't realized that in the mortal realm, with a mortal body, he couldn't do it on his own.

Lucky he was here, really.

"Oh no. Hell no. You get away from him!" Liu Chenguang shouted. "Are you insane?"

He tried to explain his theory.

Liu Chenguang stared at him. "He kissed you?"

He nodded, blushing.

"You're blushing."

He blushed more.

"Anything else?" she asked, shaking her head and visibly retreating into *I'm a professional physician, nothing shocks me* mode.

"He called my true name."

"He knows your true name?!" she asked, professionalism immediately lost.

"Yes, so, he knew who I was, and what he was doing," he said. "You can stay here, and if it doesn't seem like it's helping, just…jump in and do more of whatever you're doing. You can tell me to stop."

She looked at Tainu, who was now lying in a pool of sweat on the bed, shivering. "What I'm doing isn't helping," she said, finally. "I can't get it under control and he's getting worse. All right. I'm going to keep my fingers on his heart meridian while you…do this."

She sat on the edge of the bed with her fingers on Tainu's wrist, then looked at him. "If you don't mind I'm going to close my eyes. I don't want to have to remember this image later."

He nodded nervously, then sat next to Tainu and tried to prepare himself.

After a few minutes Liu Chenguang opened her eyes. "Why aren't you doing it?"

He cleared his throat. "I don't really know how."

Liu Chenguang appeared to mentally count to twenty backward. "All right. Just lean over and put your lips on his. If your theory is correct you won't have to do more than that. The demonic qi will be attracted to you without any effort, right?" She squeezed her eyes shut. "Ugh, just do it. I'm never getting this picture out of my mind."

He took a deep breath, leaned over, and brushed Tainu's lips with his.

It was definitely working; he could feel the corrupted qi leaping toward him. He pressed a little harder. He hadn't cultivated much for weeks now. It was actually quite helpful—

Tainu's arms came up around him, pulling him closer, kissing him harder.

Liu Chenguang said "Ow!" and fell off the bed.

Zhu Guiren couldn't feel the demonic qi anymore, only Tainu holding him, kissing him back, it felt, it felt— Zhu Guiren kissed him back too, lips moving against his, lightly and then with more pressure, feeling the different parts of Tainu's lips, the corners and the fullness in the middle, sometimes separating a bit, then coming closer together—

Tainu sighed. His hands dropped to the bed, leaving him, and he turned his head to the side, asleep.

Zhu Guiren sat up, shaking slightly.

Liu Chenguang grabbed Tainu's dangling hand and checked the pulse. She breathed a sigh of relief. "Well, as bizarre as it was, your theory was correct. The corrupted qi is completely gone. He should probably wake up tomorrow or the next day and be pretty much finished with this. So, we can expect some awkward conversations at that point, I guess." She looked at Zhu Guiren. "Are you crying?"

"No."

"You are," she said. She sat up and looked at him more fully. "What's wrong?"

"Nothing's wrong," he said. "I don't think he'll remember this, so we probably won't have to have any…conversations."

"Zhu Guiren," she said seriously, "he should know what had to be done to heal him. This can't be kept a secret from him."

"Of course. You can tell him. He should certainly know that he can't do this again unless there's a demon ready to help heal him. He should know that the demonic qi gets into him during the spell. He may not really understand that."

"Then why are you crying?"

"I told you," he said, standing to leave. "He won't remember."

Zhu Guiren was sitting on the grass under some neglected trees at the outskirts of Shi'an, looking toward the summits of the mountains, when Tainu found him a few days later. Tainu stood looking at Zhu Guiren from a distance for a while; his shoulders were a little hunched, and his expression was very dull. Was something…was he upset about what he had had to do to save him? About kissing him? It must have felt very uncomfortable for him. Tainu winced.

Finally, Tainu walked to him and said, "Where have you been? I've been looking for you." He sat down next to him without being invited and noticed how Zhu Guiren inched away from him. Well, that was to be expected, probably. Tainu let his body experience the 'sitting on the ground' feeling, his muscles aching; he really wasn't fully recovered.

Out loud, he said, "I never realized exactly how much it took out of me, to build a refuge. I always had the refuge to cultivate in before, and even though it hurt, I healed on my own eventually."

After a while, Zhu Guiren said, "The way you built the refuge…You've been captured before."

"Yes." So this was why the demon looked so unhappy. "At the beginning of my second cycle. My first rebirth. There weren't any refuges then…That's why I'm the oldest. I'm really just the oldest surviving phoenix. There were others before me, but once the demons realized what they could do with phoenix blood… Well, you know. We were always captured as soon as we were reborn — when we were at our weakest. And since that was happening in the spirit realm, where we can truly die, all the oldest ones were killed before you figured out that if you brought us into the mortal world we would just have to…keep surviving it, over and over."

Zhu Guiren was silent. With a single finger, he drew a pattern on the ground. "How did you get away?" he eventually asked.

"My people skills, of course," he said. "There was a demon assigned to watch me. I think he didn't like to be doing what he was doing, so he started talking to me."

"Probably he was just bored," Zhu Guiren said.

"Probably. But also, he had a good heart. He didn't want to be hurting me. And he was brave, and clever."

"How can a demon have a good heart? It's not our nature."

"It wasn't his nature to be cruel," he replied. "They would have to make him into that." When Zhu Guiren didn't respond, he continued, "So he let me go, and I watched him carefully — saw what he did. I designed the refuges from what I saw him do. I turned the spell he created inside out to mimic the original spell that captured me, and then I changed its ordering and mixed it with my blood instead of a demon's blood, so instead of being a prison for a phoenix, it would repel demons. In a sense, the world outside the refuge becomes the prison for demons; the wall of their prison is the wall of the refuge, and they can't pass. There were some other pieces I designed into it, of course, to make it suitable for cultivation…"

Zhu Guiren had raised his head and was staring at him, unblinking. "What happened to the demon who let you go?"

"I've always wondered," he said. And he always had. "I've always wanted to see him again, and make sure he was all right."

Zhu Guiren just kept looking at him.

It seemed like the appropriate time to say it, so he finally did, although his heart was afraid to know. He looked in Zhu Guiren's eyes, the expression always the same, as he knew it would be, essentially always himself no matter what shape he took. "What happened to you?" he asked gently.

Zhu Guiren looked away. His voice even, he said, "I am sure I was punished. It must have been a very severe punishment. Enough that I don't…remember the details. I don't really remember you. Just…bits and pieces."

"Oh," he said, not knowing what else to say to that. But after all, even if Zhu Guiren remembered, what could he possibly say? He closed his eyes, remembering Zhu Guiren's cold, triumphant expression when Liu Chenguang's mortal body was destroyed, when Hong Deming lay dead. He breathed deeply, trying to release that image, the worst of all his long life.

"I'm glad I let you go," Zhu Guiren said suddenly.

Tainu opened his eyes to find Zhu Guiren looking at him intently, clearly wanting to see how he would respond, as though he needed some kind of reassurance. He smiled, impulsively reaching over to tousle his hair. "Look at you now, grown up all big and evil."

"Stop that. It's so undignified," said Zhu Guiren, batting at his hand.

"I know." Tainu grinned.

Then, he looked at Zhu Guiren's hair again. It was a tangled mess with a hairpin stuck in it at a strange angle. He realized that there was no possible way the demon could have put his hair up properly with one hand. Thinking of him trying to do it and never asking anyone to help him made his heart hurt. "Let me," he said, reaching forward. "Why didn't you ask me to help you? All these days."

He took the hairpin out and laid it down carefully, then stroked the mess of the demon's hair into a smoother fall. He couldn't get the knots out without a comb; that would have to wait. "Do you want it all up, or some down?" he asked.

"All up," Zhu Guiren said, looking at him again with that unblinking stare.

He knelt to get closer and reached back behind his head to gather it all. With a few quick twists, he made it into a topknot and smoothly slid the hairpin in. "There, that should last the day. I told you I'm good with a hairpin. Is it good?"

"Very good," Zhu Guiren said.

"Let me help you do it in the mornings," he said. Then he closed his eyes and drew a quick, harsh breath, suddenly assaulted by sensations: holding Zhu Guiren, kissing him, feeling his body moving against him—

"Tainu?" came Zhu Guiren's voice, "are you all right?"

Zhu Guiren grabbed his wrist to feel for his pulse. At that very moment, Tainu's imagination was overwhelmed with the feeling of his lips blended with what it had felt like to stroke his hair, the weight and warmth of it, and the heat of the nape of his neck under his hand—

"Your pulse is fast, but your qi seems all right…Tainu?"

"I– I–" He breathed himself back to normal. "It– it must be an aftereffect. That's all."

He was shocked by those images, those feelings. He had never thought of the demon in that way. It wasn't that he was inexperienced with such matters, but never with those few who were truly important to him — only those who could come and go and leave no mark in his heart.

An aftereffect of the demonic qi. That was all. Surely it hadn't been like that, kissing him. Surely the demon wouldn't have…it wouldn't have been like that. It would never be like that. It was just something still healing in his mind. He could calm himself. It would fade.

Without opening his eyes, he said, "Liu Chenguang told me what you had to do to save me. Thank you. I never knew that the demonic qi was entering me when I built a refuge. If you hadn't figured it out I'm not sure what would have happened to me. I'm sure it was very awkward for you."

"Do you remember it?" Zhu Guiren asked.

"No," he said, attention still on trying to get himself under control. "It's all just a blur since I started the refuge spell." At last he felt himself enough to open his eyes. He smiled again at him, wanting to convey his gratitude. "Really, now you've saved me twice."

Zhu Guiren shook his head, his eyes focused on the distant mountains. "It's nothing."

That night, after Tainu and Liu Chenguang were asleep, Zhu Guiren prowled through their rooms at the inn, unable to settle. He opened the door to Tainu's room and went in to watch him sleep; it felt strange to not do it, to not be close to him every day and night. Instinctively, he reached out with his hand to interlace it with Tainu's fingers, but then drew back. He was healed now. He didn't remember anything. He didn't remember calling his true name. He didn't remember that he said how happy he was to have him there. He didn't remember holding him or…anything else. He was peaceful and easy in his sleep. He didn't need anyone to be there for him now.

Zhu Guiren thought, I want to be close to him. Why do I want it so much?

Whatever had happened between them when they met, it was gone. Cut and burned out of his mind. Only those bits and pieces remained. Only his smile, and his blood.

Leaving Tainu's room, he returned to his own, the walls covered with his scribbles and diagrams. Viciously, he struck out the diagram of the phoenix and the demon together.

The other diagrams — the arrays, his notes, trying to recall exactly which nodes were where, which were strongest, which he should break first…He looked at them coldly. He didn't have the patience for this now.

Shi'an wasn't as full of resentment as the refugee roads, but there was more than enough. He ran through the dark streets, hunting for a good place, until he found a cemetery. There was another demon already there, cultivating; he drew his sword silently and the other demon wisely fled. He longed for his true body, for claws and fangs. This mortal body remembered too much and yearned to have more.

Zhu Guiren settled down among the graves and closed his eyes, welcoming in the familiar pain.

# CHAPTER 7
## YISUE

THE SOUND OF the waves was lulling, crashing nearby, spraying on her face. Every bit of her skin felt sticky and crusted with salt. Aili sat up and reflexively put her hand on her forehead, just to make sure her head was still attached given the level of pain she was feeling all over her body.

"That was funny," said a voice off to one side.

"Was it?" she said. "What was it?"

"You jumped off the cliff to be a sacrifice for your own passage through my gate." The voice's owner wasn't visible; wherever they were was very dark. "It was hilarious. You're not dead though, so it doesn't count."

She remembered that now. "You're mistaken," she said. "I did die. At least, my mortal body would have been dead if I didn't have some special medicine."

"True," said the voice. "You certainly did look dead when I fished you out of the water. You were all floppy and bloody and your limbs were in different positions."

Aili decided to let that go.

"Did it hurt?" the voice asked, a bit salaciously.

"Yes," she said. "So it should count as a sacrifice. Definitely."

The voice was quiet. Then it asked, very suddenly, "Are you a starfish? I've never met a starfish that cultivated a mortal body before."

Aili considered this. "Yes," she said. "Yes. I'm a starfish."

There was a softly-growing light that illuminated their surroundings: a wet cavern dripping with seaweed and lined with mussels and barnacles, and, closer to her than she had expected, the dragon.

It didn't look quite like she had imagined. It was smaller, for one thing — only ten feet long or so — and it had webbed feet along with its claws. It was pure white, lithe and serpentine, without wings, with delicate tendrils dangling from its jaw and temples. Its claws seemed to be like hands, and one of them held something that looked like a very large pearl; it was this that was the source of the light, shining through the webbing.

"Greetings, master dragon," she said formally. She tried to consciously ascertain what language they were speaking and realized that it was Anglish.

The dragon brought its head closer to her; she could now see that its eyes were a blue-green color. "All right," it said, "I don't really think it counts as a full sacrifice, but it was funny, so I'll accept it. My gate is here. Where did you want to go?"

"Can you take me to Zhashan?"

"I don't know where that is."

"It's a city in Daxian."

"Is it next to the ocean?"

She shook her head.

The dragon explained, "I can take you anywhere else in the world that there is a dragon gate, but dragon gates are only on ocean coasts or deep under the sea."

Aili thought about this, trying to recall the geography she knew of Daxian. Unfortunately, in her lifetime as Hong Deming, she had never crossed into the coastal provinces at all. "Can you bring me to a gate that's close to the mouth of the Sorrowful River?" she asked, finally.

"I've always wanted to go to Daxian," the dragon said; it sounded more excited. "I have relatives there, but I've never been, so I don't really know exactly where to go. I can just aim for a gate on the north coast. That will get us close, right?"

"Ummm…I actually have no idea."

"Let's go!" the dragon said happily. It held the pearl high, and it glowed fiercely: white, blue, green, purple.

Before she knew what was happening, the dragon had bitten down on the collar of her shirt and leapt forward into the light.

In no more than a moment of swirling confusion, the dragon dropped her and spat. "Ugh," it said, "your clothes taste terrible. We're here!"

'Here' was a small, flat cleared area covered in barnacles and seaweed under an arched rock, surrounded by surging water and waves. The mainland was about a half mile away.

Aili stood shakily. She still didn't feel completely herself physically; the battering of her leap into the ocean had been serious. "I don't think I can swim there," she said, holding one hand over her eyes.

The dragon looked at her. "You're going to the *land?* Really? I want to come with you."

"Ah, why?"

"I told you, I've never been! Hold on to me." This time, it threw her on its back and leapt into the water. The dragon was an excellent swimmer — faster than a dolphin and just as graceful. Moments later, it pulled the two of them onto the rocky shore and shook itself, apparently delighted with the exercise.

Aili coughed, wondering where they were. Looking around, she didn't see any obvious place where people lived, but the northern coast of the Federation was like that too, after all, if you were looking from the ocean at the shore. People lived inland, mostly. They seemed to be near the tip of a rocky peninsula, surrounded by the ocean on three sides.

The dragon looked at her expectantly. "Where are we going now? Are we going to see human people? Are we going to see dragons?" It wiggled in excitement.

Aili was beginning to develop a suspicion about this dragon. "How old are you?"

"Oh, five hundred, maybe? I haven't left the ocean much before…just near the coast where you jumped off," it said casually. "I haven't seen a lot of people. Do you want to see my other form? My name is Yisue. My parents live in the deep ocean but I like the coast, so they let me stay there by myself." Its long white body shimmered and transformed into a light-skinned boy of around ten years old, with long white hair and blue-green eyes. "This is my other body! I haven't used it much. Let's go!" He turned to walk and immediately tripped over a rock and fell down.

"Ah, you should get some clothes," she suggested.

"Why? Ow! This hurts." He rubbed his bleeding knee. "Scales don't rip like this. Are we going to the Sorrowful River? My parents told me I have an uncle there."

Aili whispered Liu Chenguang's true name. The white-gold line went inland to the southwest. "All right," she said. "Yisue, listen. Thank you for bringing me, but you should stay here, or go back to the ocean right away. It's really not a good idea for you to come with me. I'm probably going inland and not coming back, and truthfully, I don't know how long it will be before I find the Sorrowful River. And there's a war happening. Mortals will be attacking each other. This isn't a safe place for you and I'm sure your parents wouldn't want you to stay here–"

"Look! There's a little starfish like you in this one. It's eating something…Do you have relatives here?" Yisue was ignoring her in favor of tide pools.

She turned and walked in the direction of the light — toward Liu Chenguang. She didn't have any sense of how close or distant Liu Chenguang might be, but the light had gone straight over the horizon; certainly several hours' worth of walking, if not a full day.

Behind her, Yisue yelled, "Hey, wait for me!"

The little dragon boy didn't stay close to her, wandering and exploring and occasionally jumping in the water, but gradually, they came closer to signs of human habitation: garbage, cemeteries, old buildings. It looked as though war had passed through here, more than once. Yisue drew closer to her and more silent, looking around. When they first saw actual people, they gathered and pointed, whispering in Daxian about Yisue, who certainly caught the eye.

"Can you become a bird or something?" she asked, a little worried about how much attention they were drawing.

"Can you?"

"No, I only have one body," she said.

"I'm a dragon. This is my real body, just like my dragon body. We have two true bodies — not just one and a mortal body — but obviously I can't become a *bird*," he explained. He picked something up off the ground. "What's this? Can you eat it?" He stuffed it in his mouth before she could respond, then immediately spit it out, choking and grabbing his tongue.

"No," she said dryly. "Are you hungry? You should probably go back to the ocean then."

"No. I don't want to. The ocean is boring."

The occasional houses and outlying villages coalesced into a city, which she soon learned was called Zhaishou; Aili didn't remember this city from her life as Hong Deming, but she'd never entered Hai'an in that time. There were a surprising number of foreign people — soldiers and merchants of the Twin Empire — scattered among the Daxian in the streets, and many, many Kunorese in imperial military uniforms. They looked curiously at her and Yisue, making her very nervous about how to keep the boy safe.

The sound of spoken Kunorese made her shiver; she still hadn't forgotten Nora.

"All right," she said at last. "Put these on."

Aili handed him a shirt and pants she had stolen, unnoticed, from a rooftop string of laundry using her qinggong. She felt awful about this, but she had no money that would be accepted here. She would have to find some somewhere; she had no idea how they could survive otherwise for a long journey unless Yisue proved more willing to eat rabbits than Liu Chenguang had ever been. Of course, she would then also need a bow. Could she create a spirit weapon that would shoot rabbits? Were there even rabbits in Hai'an? Many of the people looked starved and beaten, most likely anything edible had long ago been eaten.

Yisue was holding the pants and shirt as though he had no idea what to do with them.

"If you put these on, I'll feed you," she said, a little desperately.

"I don't know what these are," he said, dignified. "Also, they stink."

"They've just been washed. Don't be so picky…" She helped him put them on, remembering helping her little brother when they had been growing up. They'd only been three years apart, but he hadn't always wanted to wear clothes properly either. As she looped together the knotwork buttons around Yisue's neck, she stopped suddenly, surprised. That had been…For the first time since his death, that had been a happy memory of her little brother, Eddie. She had… happy memories. There had been more to their life together than coming home the day he died. Why had she never been able to realize this before? To remember him as he lived — the good things, and not only the bad ones?

"What?" Yisue said. "These are itchy."

Aili tried to think of what she could do to earn some money, or at least a meal, with what she had to offer: strength, cooking, swimming, healing…Healing, yes — people would be willing to pay for that…Of course, she would do it for free, but she needed to get them something to eat. Surely it would be a fair trade.

She found a woman running a noodle stall who was suffering from a toothache; she cured it easily with a bloody finger for a few bowls of noodles. Yisue put them away in shocking fashion. The stall owner watched in resignation.

"These…They are so…Amazing…" he mumbled through his full mouth. "Never going back. Noodles."

Well, that was a bit of a misfire, then. She tried one last time: "Yisue, I am really afraid this will be dangerous for you, and I can't get you back to the ocean anytime soon once we leave the coast. I don't know when we will be at the Sorrowful River. The cook says it's on the other side of the province, and I'm not going in that direction. And she said there's flooding, too. The dikes were broken inland, so the Sorrowful River is probably a mess anyway. I would really, truly, feel much better if you went back to the ocean now."

He slurped his last noodles and looked at her with his blue-green eyes. "No," he said. "More noodles."

Conversation with the stall owner led to a deal: the stall owner would spread the word that a healer was available, and people would come pay Aili; the owner would get a cut and let them eat and sleep in the stall until they had enough money to move on.

"You've got a good deal with me if he's going to eat like that every day," the noodle-seller said, but she didn't sound too angry. The tooth had been giving her a great deal of pain. "Excuse me for asking, but why does he look that way? Does he have an illness?"

"He was born like that," Aili said. "Don't mention it, he's sensitive."

"Ah, yes," the woman said. "I remember, my sister's husband's cousin had a child like that. Couldn't bear the sunlight. Well, I have an extra hat. I'll give it to you for him."

Aili was grateful for it, and when she had a little money, she decided to buy another for herself — one of the large conical woven hats that she could tuck her hair beneath to try to look a little less unusual. She braided Yisue's hair as well, warning him to try to keep out of the sight of the Kunorese soldiers while she worked.

Earning the money to leave took a good number of days.

Aili's plan was to stock up on Federation-style medicine as much as possible, since she knew how to use that in addition to blood healing, but in the end, she had to be satisfied with some anti-diarrheal medications, some bandages, and a curved needle and thread for sewing stitches; truthfully, she doubted she'd ever bother with this, since blood healing was so fast and easy, but it was part of the kit. All other medical supplies, like almost everything else, were tightly rationed. At least it gave her some kind of cover for what she was really doing, and in any case, she couldn't help but notice that most of the ordinary Daxian people she met simply assumed that as a Federative she knew all kinds of powerful medical secrets. She bought additional clothes for herself and Yisue and considered buying a riding animal, but decided it was likely to just get eaten. That left all the rest of her savings to buy food along the way.

Three weeks later, she asked Yisue if he would return to the ocean, and as she had anticipated, he refused. She whispered again; they took a ferry across the bay of Zhaishou, and then began walking due west.

Aili stood still, frowning.

Yisue said, "What are you looking at?" He tilted his head to one side, looking at the road in front of them, which looked very much like the road behind: pitted with ruts, with groups of people who tried not to talk to one another as they hurried along.

"So many," she said, dazed.

"So many people?" Yisue sat down on the ground, dissatisfied. "There are so many people always. Soldiers and people who are sick and scared. That's all we see."

"Ocean is due south. Just turn left and go home," she said, something she said several times a day at this point.

"No," he said, equally automatically. Really, he was just stubborn.

There were so many people on the roads, always, but there was something else too. People speaking without sound, being speared, impaled, cut apart, dying in front of her. Silently. Unnoticed by the plodding groups of ordinary people.

"Don't you see them?" she asked. She moved forward and tried to touch one — a young man wearing the armor of the Feng dynasty, shot by multiple arrows, lying gasping with his eyes staring upward. Her hand tingled, but she couldn't touch him.

With that one, tingling sense, something rushed through her body and she could hear: the screams, the yells, the clanging, and that nameless sound of flesh being parted by sharp metal. Her head snapped up, flooded with memories from her life as Hong Deming, from the Western Sea.

"What is it?" Yisue asked, sitting up. "What's wrong?"

The young man she had tried to touch looked at her and said, "Sister, tell my mother, tell my mother–"

And then, he died.

Aili calmed her shaking mind and body and settled into a lotus position, out of the way of the road. She waited. And waited. Yisue curled up and fell asleep, then woke up and asked for food; she absently pointed to the travel container, continuing to watch.

She watched several thousand people die violently over approximately eight hours. After that point, the remaining living — those who had killed but not been killed — wavered and disappeared. The bodies remained.

Another person appeared, a man she recognized. Zhu Guiren.

But he had two hands.

He knelt on the ground near the center of the corpse-laden field, refugees walking through his figure as they used the road west. In his hand, there was a glimmering container made of some substance she couldn't name. From it, he poured a liquid out on the earth, chanting, and then knelt and struck the earth with his hand.

Something raced out from where he touched the earth — a spider made of smoke, leaping from corpse to corpse, shooting out into the air to fasten onto things she couldn't see that went beyond the field's boundaries. The refugees stumbled through, unfeeling, unaffected, but the corpses all shivered and then disappeared. Zhu Guiren also stood, his hand held in a seal as the smoke spider returned to him. Then he, too, evaporated.

Aili took a deep breath and stood up. "Yisue–" she said, and then stopped.

The field was full again of screams, metal, blood.

Yisue yawned. "Are we going anywhere today?"

Aili sat down again, chin in hand, then switched back to a lotus position to cultivate. "No. Get out the sleeping things. We're staying here."

Eight hours later, she attacked Zhu Guiren. He didn't notice. Nothing changed.

The sun came up.

"Now?" asked Yisue. "I'm *bored*."

"Eat," she said, handing him the bag. "Go climb some trees or something. Go exploring, but don't go far. I'll be here."

Every so often, she jumped into the battle just to see if she could change anything, first with En, then with the phoenix whip. No one noticed; nothing changed.

Eight more hours later, she stood next to Zhu Guiren and tried to take the container away from him with her hands, then with En. He didn't notice. Nothing changed.

She tried to catch the stream of what she was now sure was Liu Chenguang's blood, glimmering in its thin waterfall. It went through her hands. Nothing changed.

She brought out the phoenix fire and let the blood pour through it. She felt the heat of Chenguang's blood against her skin and closed her eyes.

"Eftahede," she whispered, and the world exploded around her.

It seemed that she was always being knocked unconscious and being woken up, which was annoying; but after all, most of these times she probably should have been dead, so, overall a win. Aili laughed out loud.

Yisue was staring at her, as were a good number of the refugees walking past, giving them a wide berth. Whatever she had done, she had done it in the middle of the road. She sat up and wiped blood from her mouth.

"How long have I been out?"

"A day," he said, eyes wide. "I've been sitting here, keeping people from trampling you."

"Thank you."

While she hadn't been paying attention, Yisue had apparently decided that his hair would look especially attractive in a blend of braids and knots with some random pieces of metal, cloth, and shell stuck into it. "Isn't that piece of glass in your hair a little close to your throat?" she asked diplomatically.

He silently took it out and handed it to her, staring. "Your mouth is bleeding," he said.

She nodded.

"Also your ears. And your nose. And a little bit out of your eyes."

"Ah," She tried to stand up and found she couldn't. "What happened?"

"You were standing in the middle of the road and you took out your sword. You never told me you had a sword," he said accusingly.

"Sorry about that. Do you want to see it?" She tried to call En, but it wouldn't come. "Sorry...I must really not have anything left..." She felt very vulnerable knowing that. "I need to cultivate..."

"And then," he continued, "you were moving your hands around, and kind of muttering to yourself, and then there was a big flash of light, and almost like an earthquake, and a wind that blew everything around. Everyone was very scared. When the light went away, you were lying in the road. All the people who were nearby ran away, and since then, people have just been ignoring you, and no one would help me move you somewhere safe," he added, glaring at the people who continued to walk by without paying them any attention except looks from the corners of their eyes. "I was thinking about transforming and picking you up in my mouth when you finally woke up."

"Don't do that," she said, and stood up, dizzy. "We're not near the ocean. I don't know if it's safe for you."

Yisue reached out and took her hand. Surprised, she looked down at his face and realized that he was frightened and trying not to show it. "Don't worry," she said, "I'm fine. I think...I think I did something that's good. Can we wait here just till it gets dark, to be sure?"

They waited all night. Yisue curled up to sleep next to her, and Aili alternated between sleep and cultivation. The battle and Zhu Guiren did not reappear.

They worked their way across Hai'an slowly and with greater and greater horror. Yisue sank into silence, eyes wide at the mortal word in an endless death throe: flooding, corpses, orphaned children, famished families, shattered cities, soldiers marching, soldiers killing.

Aili was aware of the host of demons that followed the suffering as well — both yaoguai and the more powerful yaomo that, like Zhu Guiren, had cultivated human forms and hid among the human beings. She fought them when she found them. They were almost in a frenzy, an ecstasy of resentment; they rarely chose to hide or run, and some of them had started preying directly on the mortal beings, murdering and torturing the stragglers. No doubt, others had blended into the flood of humanity, encouraging more brutality, betrayal, and cruelty as Zhu Guiren had at the imperial court.

Because of all this, and because Aili needed to cultivate regularly to manage the drain on her powers, they moved very slowly through the misery of Hai'an in wartime. The people on the road had gone through too much to easily befriend strangers. They were suspicious of one another, and of possible collaborators and informers — afraid of being robbed of their meager belongings and keeping others at a safe distance — so despite the crowds, Aili most often felt they were alone. There was hardly any wood to be had for a fire, so their nights were cold as well. Yisue curled up shivering close to her, and she wrapped him in the blanket to keep them warm together.

"This can't be good for you, little dragon," she said eventually. "Go back home. I'll walk with you to the ocean."

He was quiet for a while. "But that's not where you're going," he said. "Where are you going?"

"Did I never tell you?" Aili shook her head. "I should have told you. It's just been so...well, we didn't get time, I guess. I'm looking for someone."

"You know their true name." he said astutely. "I hear you whispering sometimes."

"You don't actually hear it, do you?" she asked, flustered. "I don't think anybody is supposed to hear it."

"No, I hum so I won't hear. It would be very bad manners," he said, sounding very prim. "But you should probably be quieter. But, if you know their true name, you must be very important to each other. That person must be waiting for you to come."

"I hope so."

"I don't have a true name yet," Yisue said. "I'm too young."

"Me too," said Aili.

"What are you?" asked Yisue seriously. "You can heal like a phoenix, but you can also fight and do other things, so you're not a phoenix. What are you?"

"You guessed it already," she said, bopping his nose with her finger. "I'm a starfish."

After a while, Yisue said, "Well, I don't want to go back to the ocean. It's lonely there. My parents live very deep and if I'm with them, I don't see anybody. They don't like mortals. They hardly ever even come to the surface. But I like mortals. I like them and I'm sad that they're sad now."

Aili nodded. "Me too," she said again.

"Also, noodles are good," he added sleepily.

That night, airplanes flew low over the refugees camped along the road, sending people into a panic as they tried to cram into whatever little shelters they could find. Aili had heard of the terror of the air raids from many people. Though this whole province now was Kunorese-occupied, and therefore not bombed anymore, too many people had lost their homes and loved ones to planes to be able to think about that clearly; the panic started and flowed everywhere, and people were crushed and trampled.

Aili moved from place to place, doing her best to heal surreptitiously when people were desperate enough to let a stranger come close. These were the kinds of wounds that really required blood healing — bandages weren't going to do anything for crushed internal organs — but it was starting to become obvious, as she was so physically visible, that people were miraculously healed wherever she went. She wasn't the only foreigner among the refugees. There were missionaries, journalists, and others, but far from enough for her to blend in, especially with Yisue at her side.

Two nights after the panic, Aili was cultivating when she heard a quiet voice murmur, "Not quite a phoenix, but something interesting. An experiment, he said."

Another voice coolly said, "Well, take her alive, then. We can experiment some more. Kill the dragon."

Aili swore and rolled to one side, getting space between her and Yisue. "Run!" she yelled at the boy, and jumped up, calling out En as well as the phoenix whip.

A woman like her — though much more beautiful, light-skinned with golden hair — stood off to one side while a man with black hair and dark eyes in a Kunorese imperial uniform came racing at her. He was using a ranged weapon she was unfamiliar with, small disks he threw with vicious sharp edges, incredibly fast and unpredictable in the air. She knocked several of these out of the air with En, but one caught her in the thigh and immediately she felt something cold and sharp climb through her veins from the wound, damaging her spiritual power more than her body.

Now that she was moving more slowly, the woman came from the other side so she had to deal with two at once. She released En and took out a second phoenix whip. She needed something more powerful and unpredictable than the sword for this, and started whipping out, aiming primarily at the man to begin with, then quickly switching when the woman came close. Both the man and the woman were also fighting with double weapons: the woman with a sword and spear, the man alternating the throwing weapons with two swords.

Aili used her qinggong to leap up onto a ruined wall, trying to think.

She couldn't see Yisue. Hopefully he was hiding.

She needed a ranged weapon too. She attempted to form the phoenix fire into a bow, but it was too unstable, so she let it go and tried to summon a spiritual bow. It didn't work. I should have practiced this kind of thing, she thought, annoyed with herself. She gave up and called the whips back.

The woman jabbed at her with the spear. Aili wrapped a whip around it and pulled it out of her hand, but she immediately summoned it back to herself.

They had reached a stalemate, neither of them able to get close enough to her, and she was unable to do enough damage to would end this.

The woman said, "We want to take you alive, creature. Come with us, or we'll hunt down the dragon child instead. He's far less able to fight or hide than you — it won't take us long."

"Not a very attractive offer," Aili said, breathing hard and trying to think.

The man spoke to the woman in the demonic language, and she nodded.

"Where is Zhu Guiren?" she asked. "Tell us where he is, and we'll let you go. For now."

"I don't know where he is. Why would I know?" Aili jumped down with the whip, aiming for the woman's arm. She seemed to be suffering there from an old wound that limited her mobility, and when the phoenix fire wrapped around it she gave a muffled scream and jerked away.

The man laughed, as though he found this amusing.

The woman snapped, "Shut up. Just get her. She must know how to find him."

Aili was starting to feel the effect of the wound in her thigh; the physical wound had closed, but the spiritual damage continued to grow. She didn't have any other ranged weapons in her training but the bow and arrow, and she couldn't seem to make one, but maybe…She switched the phoenix fire to a looped rope. She had learned this as a child for fun — how to lasso the calves and horses — although they'd not been armed or quite this fast and the phoenix fire didn't have the true weight of a rope, but she could try…

It did confuse the man, at least; he backed up quickly when she threw the rope at his feet, and then at his arms or his head, while attacking with the phoenix whip in the other hand. Clearly, this was a fighting style he was unprepared for. He finally became frustrated and came close to her with his two swords, blocking the whip and letting the rope hit him in an effort to get inside her guard. The rope didn't catch him, but the phoenix fire burned him. He leapt back, yelling in shock.

She followed up quickly, striking with the whip again and again. His upper body was starting to catch fire, and with one final scream of rage he turned into a hawk and fled, dripping sparks across the sky.

The woman swore and backed away. Aili moved toward her, switching one hand back to sword, and then started to run. The woman backed up more quickly, then feinted to one side and came at her with the spear again. The spear took her under the ribs; she hacked down with En to break it, then lashed with the whip, catching the woman around the neck. She screamed and scrabbled at her burning skin, then she also fled.

Aili sat down, bleeding, and closed her eyes. She had been healing so much and not cultivating enough; it was taking a while for her own body to heal — longer than it should. That spiritual damage was also still there. She settled into cultivation and attempted to purify it, but she was so tired.

"Aili?" Yisue stood, uncertain, a little space away.

"Stay away for now," she said, "in case they come back tonight. Just stay where you are so they can't get both of us at once, ok? If they come for me again, you need to run."

He nodded and settled down, his white form dim in the darkness.

Aili sighed and closed her eyes. She whispered again. They had crossed most of Hai'an already and were nearing the mountains. It would be good to see the eastern sacred mountain at last.

# CHAPTER 8
## REUNION

TAINU WAS STILL weak, so for days on end, they remained at the inn in Shi'an. Zhu Guiren mostly disappeared, either in his room scribbling or out cultivating at night. When Tainu went looking for him, he was never to be found.

"Is the demon upset about something?" he asked Liu Chenguang one day.

Liu Chenguang looked at him. "Did you two talk about what happened?"

"That he had to kiss me? Of course we did."

"And that was…fine? He was ok?"

"Why would he not be ok?"

Liu Chenguang leaned her chin on her hand; she was working at the table over some maps. "Tainu, I don't want to interfere if he didn't want to talk to you about it, but he was…upset. At the time."

"Oh." Zhu Guiren had to kiss someone he didn't want to after all, so it was to be expected, but Tainu felt a little hurt. He had thought it was all settled. "Well, I'm sorry he was upset."

Liu Chenguang was still looking at him. "Are you worried about him? Why don't you just ask him?"

"I can't find him," he said, frustrated.

"Oh." She looked back down at the table.

Tainu sat down. "Let me guess," he said, "it's only me he's avoiding."

"I'm afraid so. What can you do, Tainu? Let it be — he'll get over whatever it is eventually. He's off cultivating resentment and killing other demons. I'm sure that is his medicine for all ills. Meanwhile, he has me trying to draw up accurate maps that compare the landscape during the Feng dynasty with the landscape now, and it's difficult, as you can imagine. The bed of the Sorrowful River has shifted at least three times, and of course now it's flooded all over. Current, accurate maps are classified material. If I keep trying to buy one I'm eventually going to get targeted by either Daxian guerrillas or Kunorese spies."

Tainu looked over the papers on the table. "Do you want me to go survey?"

"Are you strong enough?"

"For flying? Of course."

"All right then. Can you fly over to Hongye and check where the Sorrowful River is compared to this map?"

He looked, memorized the map and nodded. "Probably three hours," he said, and left.

It took far more than three hours. He had to go to ground repeatedly to avoid gunshots and planes, and really he didn't have enough energy for this; he was still weaker than usual. By the time he returned, exhausted to the bone and very much in need of a bath, it was well after dark.

As a reward, though, Zhu Guiren was sitting at the table with Liu Chenguang. He looked very pale, and a little shaken.

Tainu stopped in the doorway for a moment to look at him. "Is something wrong?" he asked, concerned, as he walked in.

Zhu Guiren growled, "Where have you been? You were supposed to be back hours ago. Don't do that again."

"I've been to Hongye. It took longer than I expected because I was being careful and safe," he said, soothingly. "Liu Chenguang, show me the map." He went to stand next to Zhu Guiren, who edged himself away.

Ignoring his own sense of hurt, he traced his finger down the line of the Sorrowful River to just west of Hongye, then skewed north. "Here," he said. "It's moved far closer to Hongye than in this map. Hongye is right on the bank now, at least of the actual bed. Water is low, though, since the levees were broken upstream."

Liu Chenguang nodded and made the corrections, then bundled the maps off to her room for further work. "You should eat," she said over her shoulder. "We already have."

"Well, that's important to know," Zhu Guiren grumbled. "Some of my contributing arrays might be underwater."

"Would that break them?" Tainu asked curiously, sitting down with a bowl of cold noodles. It wasn't lost on him that Liu Chenguang was trying to give them some space to talk; he was grateful, but also very hungry.

"I don't know," Zhu Guiren said shortly as Tainu slurped his noodles. "But something is breaking them. Something other than me, since I haven't done anything at all about arrays for months on end at this point."

"What do you mean?" Tainu frowned. "Do you think it's another demon?"

"I don't know. It could be someone trying to weaken me, I suppose," he said. "But as I said before, demons would want to keep the array and just take ownership — not destroy it. And I don't know any other way of destroying an array than the one I came up with."

Tainu ate more noodles, then asked, "Are you all right?"

"I'm fine. But I feel it, when an array is destroyed. The larger, the more…The arrays are part of my internal cultivational structure now. They've been there a long time, feeding me resentment. I feel something…rip…when it's destroyed." He paled and put his hand on his abdomen, just above his hip.

Tainu touched his arm, a little uncertain. "Do you want– Can I help you? Are you in pain?"

"I think I just have to adapt. That's all," he said, shaking off Tainu's hand on his arm. "You don't have to touch me."

"Ah," he said, taking his hand back as quickly as he could. "All right." That really did hurt, but he let it go, and ate some noodles, avoiding Zhu Guiren's eyes.

"I'm sorry," the demon said eventually. "I didn't mean that…that way. Just, you can't heal me."

"Will it get worse?" Tainu asked. "What will it do to you when we start destroying more? When they're all destroyed?"

He shrugged. "I don't know."

They sat in silence for a while, Tainu still smarting inwardly from Zhu Guiren's rebuke. When his noodles were finished, he stood to retreat to his room, dispirited.

"I'm sorry," Zhu Guiren said again, with more force. "I didn't mean it that way, I told you."

Tainu nodded — he really must be very tired; he felt close to tears — and turned to go, unspeaking.

Suddenly, Zhu Guiren stood up and grabbed him, hugging him fiercely.

"I'm sorry. I didn't mean you can't touch me."

Tainu froze in shock. Zhu Guiren's embrace was so strong it was almost painful, imprisoning him, yet not at all as though he was angry. Not angry at all. Just…desperate. For something. For what, exactly? At least Zhu Guiren didn't hate him after all, wasn't disgusted by touching him. Tainu was relieved, his heart felt light.

"Thank you," he said, and hugged him back more gently. "It's all right. I'm just tired, you are too. I'm just going to sleep. I'm not angry with you."

Zhu Guiren's face was hidden on his shoulder, invisible to him, but Tainu could feel him take a deep breath and sigh it out, his body relaxing.

"Is there anything I can do to help you, Tainu?" the demon asked, still holding on to him.

Another wave of shock. Tainu tried to count on his mental fingers how many times in his life people had asked him if he needed help, if he wanted it, if they *could* help him. It was so rare. He couldn't remember the last time; he was always the one other people came to. So this was a question that required a serious and honest answer, and he gave it thought — forgetting that he was still in Zhu Guiren's arms — long enough that Zhu Guiren raised his head to look at him, questioning.

At last he said, "Just don't go away from me again. Don't hide from me. I've missed you, these days."

Zhu Guiren put his head down again and held him a moment longer. "Yes, of course," he said. "I'll be around."

Tainu reached out and touched his hair. "You promised you'd let me help with your hair every morning," he said, half-stern.

"Did I promise that?" Zhu Guiren smiled at him as he let go and stepped away, seeming more himself. "Well, I will."

Liu Chenguang went out shopping again the next morning, fortified with some of Zhu Guiren's never-ending fortune. The markets in Shi'an were as impoverished as anywhere else, from famine and war and occupation, but at least she could buy what was available in them. She paid the innkeeper for their food, so what they needed tended to be things like clothing, and paper and ink, and information, and of the three of them, she was best suited to find information. Zhu Guiren was too imperious — although he insisted that he could be very convincing, she seriously doubted he could ever pass as a poor or even common person — and frankly, too good-looking. People would remember him. Similarly, Tainu was too noticeable in his mortal body; for brief flyovers or for quick dips into enemy territory, she'd ask him. Not as far as Hongye again until he was fully recovered, though. He had looked half-dead last night, so it had probably set him back in healing. She herself looked ordinary enough: Daxian, perhaps a little more tanned than a city woman, wearing ordinary peasant clothing, which she found much more comfortable than western-style dresses, attractive but not too much so, her hair roughly cut to her shoulders. She could be friendly, but not too friendly. She could sit and eat and listen to others, unnoticed.

Today, she looked in the bookstore, where she was well-known at this point. Not a lot of people were buying books under the circumstances, and the owner was eager to please her. He went into his back storage area, looking for any old maps he might not already have sold her or books on the history of Hongye. She needed a better map of the district around Hongye — Zhu Guiren thought that the seal of the great array would be somewhere to the west of that area and wanted maps to remember where that final battle where Hong Deming had died had been held — but she would buy almost anything even remotely relevant to her request, though she knew most of it probably wouldn't be very useful. Zhu Guiren's gold would have a good purpose if it was supporting a family here.

With the maps and books in a package under her arm, she went back out and wandered toward the apothecary to pick up some additional medicines for strengthening Tainu's vital energy. Of course, he would heal on his own eventually, but it didn't hurt to add support. After some thought, she devised a prescription for Zhu Guiren as well. While they were waiting for Tainu to return last night, she had had to listen to several hours of Zhu Guiren's anxious sniping, and had taken the opportunity to check his pulse. There was definitely something off about his qi circulation. It was very ragged and turbulent, as though he'd sustained some kind of injury. She tried to adapt the remedy she would normally use for natural qi to take consideration of what corrupted qi would require, avoiding purifying substances since that might hurt a demon's cultivation, but she'd have to see if it would work for him or not.

Next, she went to her favorite noodle shop, where she was well-known as someone who would sit, reading quietly and eating noodles, for a few hours at a time. It had been destroyed in the original bombardment of Shi'an, the owner had told her, but the reputation of his noodles was such that he was able to open again immediately, even just under a ragged cloth, as soon as he could get flour and oil to cook with.

She sat and listened, trying to gather news about the war, and the road ahead. The official newspapers, everyone agreed, were full of lies, but the gossip in the market was not necessarily any more accurate. Zhu Guiren had said there was a major sub-array in Hai'an that he wanted to tackle first, so it would be good to know how the roads were and whether the Kunorese were setting up roadblocks. The roads were broken, and the railways had long been cut, so transportation now was by walking. She'd have to plan to bring food with them; it didn't sound as though there was anything to be had on the roads east of Shi'an and Zhu Guiren was never to be bothered with that kind of planning, as she well remembered.

"I'm so *hungry*," whined a little boy's voice.

"All right, all right, I know you want noodles," said another voice, tolerant and amused.

"It's been so *long* since we had noodles."

"Look, see that character? Can you read it? That means this shop sells noodles."

Liu Chenguang sat with her noodles halfway to her mouth, her body shocked into complete stillness. Then, she very carefully put the noodles back in the bowl, placed her chopsticks at a polite angle, and stood. There was no way.

*There was no way.*

She turned around to look out the doorway to the street. There was a little boy with tangled white hair beneath a straw hat, blue-green eyes staring up at the sign, looking bored. Next to him stood a tall woman, her thick, dark blonde braid lying over one shoulder and ending just down past her collarbone. She was pointing at the sign above their heads and outlining the order of the strokes to the little boy, who was rolling his eyes and following her movements with his hand. When he drew the character in the air on his own, she nodded and laughed, and walked into the store with him. She met Liu Chenguang's eyes.

They both stood still as statues, staring at one another, but it didn't last long. The boy grabbed Aili's hand and dragged her over to the counter, talking about everything he would get on his noodles. Aili looked back over her shoulder, and Liu Chenguang continued to stare at her, but neither of them said anything.

Liu Chenguang sat heavily in her seat, still watching them. Her heart was pounding so hard she thought she might faint. *Aili, Aili. Aili was here.* Her mouth was dry, her eyes unable to look away. She could see — could tell, because she knew this person — that now Aili was feeling self-conscious; her easy posture and open smile were gone as she bought noodles for the little boy and then brought him over to sit with her.

"Aili," she said finally, hurriedly making room by shoving all of her books and medicines onto the floor. "You're here."

"Liu Chenguang," Aili said, her voice thin and tight. "Are you, how are you?"

The boy slurped noodles and ignored them for a while. When he was getting near the bottom of the bowl, he looked up and said, "I'm Yisue. Are you the person Aili was looking for?"

"Yes, she is," said Aili.

Liu Chenguang flushed all over.

Yisue looked at her doubtfully. "Aili knows your true name?" he asked, as though this seemed very uncertain.

"Yes," Liu Chenguang said. "I told it to her so she could find me."

"Oh," he said. He held up his bowl. "More noodles please."

Liu Chenguang gestured to the owner. "Just, just go up to him and tell him it's my treat, then tell him what you want."

His eyes lit up and he ran off, leaving her alone with Aili.

"I'm so glad to see you," Liu Chenguang said, the words so weak for what she was feeling.

Aili nodded, then said, "You are– you're well?"

"I'm fine. We've been busy. A lot has happened…" She felt as though she was staring too intently at Aili's face but she couldn't stop herself; her eyes were very blue today — they sometimes looked more gray, but now they were a deep, multi-layered blue — and Aili looked tired — very tired, but not tormented, not in that horrible, endless pain that she remembered from leaving her through the phoenix gate. Was that because they had broken arrays? Had that helped her? She hoped so much that it had.

"Tainu and Zhu Guiren are here too. We're staying in an inn. Will you come there with us?" she babbled, still staring.

Aili smiled. "Of course."

"How did you get here, anyway?" Liu Chenguang asked, realizing there was no obvious way. Then, she looked at the tangled white hair of the boy at the noodle counter; he had bits and pieces of metal and cloth woven into it. "Oh, no, Aili, is he– What did you do? Did you–"

"She did," said the boy, bringing his bowl over. "She made a sacrifice to come through my gate." Yisue settled down and began slurping. "This is really good. She was all bloody and floppy," he confided.

Liu Chenguang's initial horror evaporated because Aili covered her face in her hands, but was clearly laughing.

Sternly, Liu Chenguang said, "Aili, I do not want you to do things that make you bloody and floppy again under any circumstances, please."

"She's a starfish," Yisue added.

Aili seemed to be dissolving into helpless giggles behind her hands.

"That's really good to know," Liu Chenguang replied very seriously. "I'm glad we cleared that up."

Since this conversation clearly wasn't going anywhere fast, she started eating her noodles again.

Aili looked up from her hands, her eyes a brilliant blue and filled with laughter, and Liu Chenguang smiled.

"Eat," she said.

Tainu was asleep and Zhu Guiren was in his room, scribbling or whatever he did, when she brought Aili in. He came out quickly for the map she had gone to buy, and Aili and Zhu Guiren stared at each other. Aili's eyes went to his missing left hand. Neither of them said hello. Liu Chenguang had forgotten that, of course, they still hated each other. Or Zhu Guiren was indifferent, as he put it, but Aili had not spent the last months with Zhu Guiren, as she and Tainu had, and she realized that she now saw Zhu Guiren very differently.

*How was that?* she wondered. *No matter what he does now, he still did what he did then. He's the same person that ruined our lives and so many others. He's still a demon, still cultivates resentment.*

But somehow, it had changed.

She handed him the prescription. "I came up with something for you. Try it out. It's for your meridians — your circulation is very strange now." She added, "Aili's back."

"I see," he said stiffly.

Aili nodded at him, but Liu Chenguang thought she saw a glint of laughter in her eyes.

She was sure of it.

She added, "And this is Yisue."

Yisue looked at Zhu Guiren and yawned. "Demon," he said in acknowledgment. "Where am I sleeping? Are there beds? I want to sleep in a bed."

"I don't care," Zhu Guiren said, and turned around to go back to his room.

"Zhu Guiren," called Aili. "Come back. I have something to ask you." She had noticed the maps on the table and said, "Look here," as she traced back east into Hai'an. "Here. Did you set an array here?"

He came over and looked where she pointed. "It's hard to say," he replied. "The maps don't give enough detail for me to remember the locations of all the arrays. I'm trying to devise a way to sense them magically, which is what I need to get back to right now."

"A large battle," she pressed.

He shrugged. "There was an array in western Hai'an that I created using a significant battle, yes. I don't remember who fought in it, if that's your next question."

"With Liu Chenguang's blood?"

He hesitated, just slightly. "Yes."

"I broke it."

Zhu Guiren's eyes widened, and he sat down heavily.

Tainu came out of his room, yawning. "Sorry, I fell asleep again after lunch. What's going on?"

Zhu Guiren looked at him and said, "Aili's back, and she can break arrays. And you owe me a drinking bout."

Later that night, Tainu let Zhu Guiren lean on him back to his room, then carefully helped him lie down on the bed. "Do you need to throw up?"

"No, no," he said, eyes half closed. "I'm fine."

"All right, then." Tainu carefully laid the blanket over him. "Sleep it off. I'll decide what you owe me as the winner tomorrow."

"Ha, you're not the winner. I'm not done yet..." Zhu Guiren suddenly reached out and grabbed his hand. "Don't go."

Tainu tried, unsuccessfully, to disentangle his hand, even attempting to peel Zhu Guiren off him finger by finger. He seemed to be falling asleep but was holding Tainu's hand as though his life depended upon it. "Demon?"

When nothing happened, he gave up and sat on the edge of the bed, waiting until full unconsciousness hit in the hopes that Zhu Guiren would loosen his death grip then. Since there was nothing else to look at, he looked at the demon's face and thought he looked very beautiful, as always — maybe even a little bit more so because he was a little sweaty and flushed from the alcohol. There were little strands of hair sticking to his face, which he reached over and carefully peeled off.

"Kiss me," mumbled Zhu Guiren.

Tainu froze. "What?" he asked.

Zhu Guiren opened his eyes, seemingly with a great effort. "Can you say my name?"

Helplessly, Tainu said, "Arciniang."

Zhu Guiren smiled and closed his eyes again, still not letting go of his hand; Tainu tugged a little bit to see if he could escape, to no avail.

"Have you ever kissed me?" the demon asked. "Will you kiss me?"

Tainu laughed, uncomfortably. "I've never kissed you, and I won't kiss you now. You are extremely drunk. You won't remember this in the morning."

"I will. Kiss me. Just kiss me on the forehead, if that's all you want to do," he said as though throwing down a challenge, his eyes still closed.

Tainu leaned over and pecked him on the forehead. "There."

Zhu Guiren opened his eyes and said, "That wasn't good. You can do better than that."

Tainu pulled his hand harder. "Demon," he said, trying to appeal to any bit of sobriety that remained in the mortal body lying in front of him, "I'm not trying to impress you with my skills, believe me. I don't want to kiss you."

"You don't?" Zhu Guiren sounded sad. "Oh."

"Can you let go of my hand?"

"No," he said. "I won't let go. Stay with me." He closed his eyes again and seemed to fall deeply asleep this time.

Tainu stretched as far as Zhu Guiren's steel trap of a hand would let him and hooked a chair with his foot so he'd at least have somewhere to sit beside the edge of the bed, and sat there, looking at Zhu Guiren sleeping. His mind wandered after a while, wondering where all this was coming from. He wondered if demons fell in love with people. They had children, certainly, not like phoenixes. From the hints he'd gotten from Zhu Guiren, it didn't sound as though demonic society was very pleasant. Probably, their relationships were fairly awful as well, although he really had no idea what demons got up to in their intimate lives. Maybe even if Zhu Guiren didn't have a relationship with other demons, there was someone else — some other spirit or yao or even a mortal. Who knew? He started snickering imagining Zhu Guiren trying to court someone; he would probably insult them all day long. Certainly Zhu Guiren wasn't courting *him*, this was just alcohol, but maybe there was someone he loved, or someone he wanted, or someone he had loved once and lost.

He himself had had no shortage of experience with physical intimacy. Sexual pleasure was just that: pleasant and comforting, one of the few genuine pleasures of the mortal world, and not threatening or dangerous at all. He had never fallen in love with anyone, though he had watched human beings love one another, shaping their lives by their desires to be with one another, growing old together, sacrificing for one another. It was so different from the solitary and endless existence of the phoenix.

What would it be like to love someone fully, mind and heart and body and soul, to give oneself completely to someone, and then lose them? He would always, in time, lose everyone except other phoenixes. If he were to love anyone the way that Liu Chenguang loved Aili, and then watch them die as everyone died, he thought he would very likely lose his mind, yet he would still live forever with the pain of it. He had always thought that mortals were so courageous to do such things when their loss was so certain, so inescapable, so inevitable. He thought a thousand years ago, and still thought, that Liu Chenguang was brave beyond belief.

Zhu Guiren's eyes had smoothed out with true sleep, although his hand hadn't loosened at all. He looked at his sleeping face, their entwined fingers, and the thought came: *what if? What if…if I did want to kiss him…*

He took a deep, long breath and closed his eyes, trying to imagine, then shook his head. That would never be. Not with this beautiful, strange, brave person. There was no one like him in the world. It was good as it was, just to be together.

"Tainu?" Zhu Guiren opened his eyes, just a little. "Your hand feels very warm."

He pulled, helplessly, as Zhu Guiren tightened his grasp and fell back to sleep.

Aili came back from checking on Yisue in the other room. "He's sleeping," she said, and sat back down. "Where did Tainu and Zhu Guiren go?"

"Zhu Guiren passed out and Tainu basically carried him away," said Liu Chenguang. Before Aili could change her mind and go back to her bedroom, she pushed over another bowl of liquor. "So, who do you think would win between the two of us?"

Aili looked up, smiling, her blue eyes very slightly unfocused. "Well, I'm bigger. That should make a difference, right? The last time I was really drunk in Easterly — it was an entire store's worth of golden liquor plus six or seven jars of white liquor…"

"You got drunk in Easterly?" Liu Chenguang asked. "Which store?"

"Old Liang's."

Impressed, Liu Chenguang nodded. "That is not a small store. What happened afterward?"

"I passed out on the sidewalk, Edna Lee found me."

"Edna," Liu Chenguang echoed, remembering. She felt a little jealous. Aili had so clearly admired Edna for being a pilot. She drank her bowl, refilled it, and reached out to refill Aili's. When she looked up, Aili's eyes were on her, but she quickly looked down at the table.

Liu Chenguang had completely run out of things to say. She didn't want to reminisce about Crane Moon, or talk about the war, or stupid Zhu Guiren and whatever he was up to, or arrays. She racked her brain for some topic that wasn't painful in Aili's life, because she wanted to know about Aili's life, but everything she could think of went right to the worst places and what good was that? The silence drew out between them, becoming more and more awkward.

She looked up again, and Aili was looking at her again. And she looked away. Again.

Liu Chenguang suddenly recalled Aili sitting in that bar in Easterly when they first met. Alone. Watching other people, as though from the outside, and realized...

Aili was shy.

Had Hong Deming been shy? Would she have even known? She'd never cared about how Hong Deming was with anyone else. In their years together, he had almost never spent time with Hong Deming among other people; it had far more often than not been just the two of them. As she had told Grandmother Wang, there were circumstances, and she herself had no ability to make friends with others, but it also had never occurred to her to wonder, except with jealousy, about whether Hong Deming had other people in his life and whether they made him happy too. She hadn't known better then, but now she'd spent a thousand years living in a village full of people who were family and friends to one another. She could understand now how important it was, but back then, she had never paid attention to whether Hong Deming had friends, or made them easily. Probably not. She'd only ever heard Deming talk about his martial brothers, and one time about Mo Xiang, who he had to fight. Maybe he...hadn't been easy with people, really. And now, since they'd lost the ease they had together in that life, Aili wasn't easy with her either.

But Aili wanted to be with her. Aili was here — had come all this way on her own, to sit with her at this table and drink with her — even though it was obvious that she was terribly uncomfortable about it. Liu Chenguang tasted the liquor, smooth and sweet and biting on her tongue, and thought, *my person is so very brave.* She felt warm all over, not only from the liquor.

"What are you thinking about?" Aili's voice broke into her reverie. Her eyes were on Liu Chenguang again, and she smiled.

She picked up her bowl and drank it, then poured a new one for both of them. *I'm so happy that you are here,* she thought, but that was too soon to say. She was sure Grandmother Wang would advise against it. She said, "Friends. I was wondering about your friends, your friends in Easterly. Edna, and Nora."

Aili's face lit up. "They're both such good people. Nora was really…well, she was so much fun to be with. And so kind. She was the one who helped me find a job when I first got to Easterly and gave me a place to stay. We went everywhere together."

"Really?" Liu Chenguang poured another bowl, sweet and stinging, one for each of them, and reached for a full jar. It was so wonderful to be with Aili, to see Aili happy; it warmed her inside, more than the liquor, more than anything that could be. "Tell me more."

# CHAPTER 9
## FOX SPIRIT

"At some point, we have to do it," said Zhu Guiren. "We have to go find an array and start breaking it." He pointed to the map. "I've triangulated four arrays within a few days' journey of Shi'an that would be worth breaking. We don't have to expect that the owner of the array will attack, since that's me, but we need to be prepared for other demons attacking. We just have to get started."

Liu Chenguang asked, "Tainu, are you strong enough?"

"I'm fine," he said. "I'm more worried about the demon."

Zhu Guiren impatiently waved his hand. "I'm fine, or as fine as I'm going to be. We have to do it. I haven't broken one of my own arrays yet and we need to see how it works."

"I can do it," said Aili, sitting in the corner of the settee, legs stretched out in front of her.

"Not all of them," Zhu Guiren replied impatiently. "From what you told me, the crucial point where you can intervene is when I'm pouring Liu Chenguang's blood. I made hundreds of arrays without doing that before Hong Deming was even born. You won't have an intervention point for any of them, and some of those would definitely need to be destroyed for us to have any chance at the great array."

"At what point, exactly, did you start using my blood?" asked Liu Chenguang, raising an eyebrow. "Not just that last year?"

"No. Why would I wait? I took blood from you once a year at least, since the first year you came to Crane Moon. While you were in seclusion, Taiqian would bring you the drink and he was always the person cutting—"

Aili turned pale, stood, grabbed Liu Chenguang's elbow, and pulled her out of the room.

"Well played," said Tainu.

Zhu Guiren put his head on the table. "Why? Why is everyone so sensitive? Everyone knows this happened! Everyone knows! It's important to be precise. Why is it always such a shock to these people?"

Tainu wasn't feeling very sympathetic, so he wandered out after Aili and Liu Chenguang. He saw them walking, talking together; it seemed that Liu Chenguang was trying to calm Aili down. He suspected that Aili had been about to go for Zhu Guiren with whatever weapons she carried around these days. Thank the heavens for Liu Chenguang, although rightfully, she should have been just as upset. The little dragon boy, Yisue, was shooting marbles in the yard with some of the local children. Tainu had taken charge of his hair, combing and braiding it decently, but he'd let him keep a few of the beads.

"Hello, Tainu," said Yisue. "Aili's upset."

"I know," he said, squatting down next to them. "She has a good reason."

After watching the game for a while, he went back inside.

Zhu Guiren was back in his room, scribbling. The demon looked up at him. "I want to undo it. I'm trying."

"I know," Tainu replied. Done is done — that was the basic way the phoenix approached the world — and pain is pain. "I know you're trying." He found he really couldn't say much else, but he came over and put his hand on Zhu Guiren's shoulder. Zhu Guiren didn't look up, though he stopped scribbling and stared at the floor.

"Come on," Tainu said. "Show me the maps. Your plan is to find an array that didn't use Liu Chenguang's blood and test what happens when you break it yourself?"

Zhu Guiren nodded. "There are four possibilities that would be good...test sites. The arrays that Aili already destroyed were not strong for the most part, there was only one strong one, but it has affected me significantly. When I made my initial calculations, I didn't realize that the loss of the sub-arrays would also damage my cultivation, or my ability to cultivate at all, in this way. That's going to change some of the calculations. I need to know if it's different if I do it myself."

They had walked back over to the map table to examine it. Cautiously, Tainu asked, "Does it matter that much? If Aili can break an array that was made with Liu Chenguang's blood, then she can break the great array, can't she? Why don't we go right there?"

Zhu Guiren said, "Well, it's good I didn't bring this up given how emotional she is over the whole thing, but I'm not at all sure she can break that one. I didn't exactly pour Liu Chenguang's blood for the final seal. It was…a different situation."

Tainu closed his eyes.

"You see," Zhu Guiren hurried on, "I don't think that there's an intervention point for her in the same way. At the moment the great array was sealed, the moment Liu Chenguang entered rebirth, I was already miles away in my crow form. Also, I'm not sure…"

"You're not sure Aili can actually watch it happen without trying to kill you?"

"Correct. That's it."

"I agree," Tainu said. "I would not be surprised, and frankly couldn't blame her. Could you?"

"No," he admitted. "To be honest, when we get to the point where we are breaking the central seal, I don't think she should be there at all if we can avoid it. Or Liu Chenguang, either."

Tainu nodded. He felt very conflicted about this entire conversation, but whatever the reasons, he could fully agree that Liu Chenguang and Aili shouldn't be put through that.

"The other thing…it's not directly relevant," Zhu Guiren said. "It's not about the arrays, but just about safety. We have a child with us, and this is not going to be a safe situation. Aili told me that the little boy wanted to go to the Sorrowful River. Some of these sites are close, or on the other side. I think we should bring him and let him stay in the river, instead of with us."

Tainu looked at him, surprised.

"You're surprised I would think of things like that," said Zhu Guiren, straightening and looking at him.

"I am, honestly," Tainu replied. "You're usually so…" He cast about for a word that wouldn't be too insulting. "Utilitarian."

"Well, then think of it in terms of efficiency, if that makes more sense to you," Zhu Guiren said. He sounded a little bitter.

Liu Chenguang and Aili sat together under one of the trees near the inn, watching Yisue play. Aili's face was still pale with shock. "I can't believe it," she kept saying. "All that time, he was doing that to you and no one knew. No one cared." Her eyes were a little unfocused, as though she was seeing something else.

Aili was almost visibly burning with fury; Liu Chenguang didn't dare hold her hand or touch her, as though touching her would scald the skin. She knew that Aili had been within a dust mote's width of attacking Zhu Guiren. When the demon had said that Taiqian had been cutting her since she arrived at Crane Moon, she had seen Aili's hand move in the air to call En, then had just as quickly twisted back before grabbing her and leaving.

"Aili," Liu Chenguang said at last. "Aili, it's done now. It's long done, and there's no undoing it. I don't want to remember it." But of course, that was unfair. The truth was that she didn't remember it. It was Aili who had seen it; it was Hong Deming who had rescued her and brought her out. She sighed, and finally laid her hand carefully next to Aili, open, in case she wanted to take it.

She was surprised to suddenly be engulfed completely in Aili's arms, to have Aili hold her tightly — almost too tightly for comfort — gulping air as though she had just come up from a deep dive without oxygen.

"Aili?"

"You're all right," she said, muffled, her face in Liu Chenguang's neck. "You're all right now."

"Yes." She carefully reached up to touch Aili's hair. "Yes, I'm all right now, Aili. I'm…I'm fine." Which was actually true, she realized. "I'm fine, and you're here. I don't want to spend all my life remembering the horrible things Zhu Guiren did. Zhu Guiren is not worth that much of my attention."

Aili laughed, shakily, and let her go. "Yes, I see that now…But how can you not hate him? How can you be…with him all the time like this?"

"I don't know. If I think about it, I know it makes no sense. He's still a demon. He hasn't changed. I had my time of hating and raging at him, but then it was just…done. We had other things to do. And other than coming out with little tidbits like that every so often, he's really…not awful." She added, "Tainu likes him, for some reason I can't comprehend, so I have to put up with it. And you know, Zhu Guiren and I had a decent time together, back then. He was boring and stuffy and bossy, but he did teach me a lot."

"That doesn't make up for any of it," Aili said, her expression darkening again.

"No, it doesn't," she agreed. "In some ways, it makes it worse. But it is what it is. I don't hate him anymore, that's all. I have other things to do."

Aili nodded. "All right. Well, I'll put up with him for Tainu, I guess."

"And because he can break arrays," Liu Chenguang said. She stood and reached down to pull Aili to her feet. This didn't work at all; she nearly fell into Aili's lap, laughing. Aili laughed too, and pulled both of them upright as she stood.

Liu Chenguang looked up at her, feeling…something. Like a little shock of electricity — as though their bodies were touching one another even though they weren't; aware of Aili's body near hers, like a bell's thrumming after a strike.

Ever since her interrupted regeneration when she had met Hong Deming, she had always been small in her mortal body. Hong Deming had been taller than her, as had most adult men in her previous life, but Aili was taller than Hong Deming. Standing so close, Liu Chenguang was suddenly very aware of how far back she needed to tip her head to see Aili's face, and how much that felt like she was asking to be kissed, and maybe she was.

She stepped back quickly, unsure whether Aili had noticed anything.

Aili just smiled. "All right, let's go back to the demon." On the way back, she patted Yisue on the head and said, "Yisue, dinner in an hour, don't go far."

"Yes," he said, staring at the marbles in the dust. "But Bai Chao says that his parents don't have much food for him. They have to save it for the little brother and the grandmother. Can he share our dinner?"

From behind Aili, Liu Chenguang said, "You can bring some bowls down to share with him, but he can't come up." It would just be too awkward trying to explain Zhu Guiren and Tainu and the maps all over the room. Yisue had already been told to be discreet, but he knew how to be discreet the way a fish knows how to walk.

Later, they settled around the table for dinner; Yisue came up and got his two bowls, and said, "There's someone downstairs looking for Tainu."

"Who?" Tainu frowned and stood.

As Yisue slipped out the door, his hands full, someone else came in without knocking. He was almost as tall as Tainu, his face as beautiful as Zhu Guiren's, but somehow more magnetic —attracting the attention of everyone in the room. Once noticed, it was almost impossible to look away. He stood just inside the door, his dark eyes focused on Tainu from under his thick lashes, and smiled slowly. His lips were beautifully shaped, and when he smiled a small, sharp tooth was visible, pressing into the pink skin.

"Who are you?" asked Zhu Guiren sharply. "Who told you to come in here?"

The man ignored him, looking only at Tainu. "It's good to see you," he said.

Tainu suddenly seemed to become a different person. He leaned back against the wall in a way that emphasized the long lines of his body, languidly hinting at its capabilities, graceful as a leopard, matching the man's gaze with half-lidded eyes and a lazy smile of his own. "You too. Who told you I was here?"

The man shrugged. "I heard that you were looking for information on the arrays and demons here. I thought you might like my help." He took a step inside the room, like an entranced wild animal, as though he couldn't resist coming closer to Tainu.

"We don't need your help," said Zhu Guiren loudly, looking at Tainu and trying to catch his eye.

Liu Chenguang began to feel as though she'd like to either start laughing or leave the room — one or the other of those things would need to happen soon — while Aili looked back and forth, clearly confused.

"Shall we talk in private?" asked the man, leaning forward. The very tip of his pink tongue brushed across his upper lip.

Tainu smiled.

"Don't," said Zhu Guiren, standing up so abruptly that his chair fell over with a clatter, his eyes glittering. "You, get out."

The man ignored him, as though he didn't exist, and took Tainu's hand, leading him out the door. Tainu looked back at them and winked before disappearing.

Zhu Guiren was breathing hard and fast, his eyes narrowed to slits. "That was a fox spirit," he hissed.

"Obviously," said Liu Chenguang. She picked up her chopsticks and kept eating. "That's why he's better looking than you."

Aili snickered. Zhu Guiren looked as though he was considering how many ways he could kill them both with a chopstick.

Then, Aili said, "Oh! I remember now, I met a fox spirit once."

"Did you?" Liu Chenguang frowned. "Were you…?"

"It wasn't a friendly encounter," she said. Her humor disappeared. "I wasn't in the mood, believe me."

Liu Chenguang glanced at her, then at Zhu Guiren, then at Aili again, meeting her eyes. She covered her mouth to stop herself from laughing, and Aili managed to smile too. "But Zhu Guiren," she said innocently, "I do want you to know that except for that fox spirit, you're really the most handsome man I've ever seen."

"Absolutely," agreed Aili. "You shouldn't feel bad."

"He does wear the clothes nicely," mused Liu Chenguang.

"True," said Aili. "Zhu Guiren, you should ask him where he shops."

Zhu Guiren went and sat down in the corner to scribble furiously on the wall, ignoring them. Soon, he said, "He's been gone a long time."

"He's been gone five minutes," said Liu Chenguang.

"Too long," said Zhu Guiren. He stood up. "I'm going to go get him. Probably he needs to be rescued."

Liu Chenguang laughed out loud. "Zhu Guiren, I promise you, my sibling does not need to be rescued from a fox spirit. He's very capable–"

"Shut up!" Zhu Guiren turned bright red. He ran out of the room, clattering down the stairs.

Liu Chenguang and Aili looked at each other and laughed hysterically.

"Oh, that was so worth it," said Liu Chenguang, wiping tears from her eyes, "I'm going to invite fox spirits in regularly. I've never seen Zhu Guiren upset like that, ever, even in our other life–"

"But he must be familiar with fox spirits," said Aili. "He sent the one I met, I'm sure." She prodded a piece of tofu, then said, "To be fair, I think I lived… as long as I did, because that fox spirit didn't want to kill me. So, I suppose I should be a little grateful…" Then she shook her head. "You know what, no. No I'm not."

Liu Chenguang laughed. "Well, I'm glad you're not grateful to a fox spirit. That wouldn't be a good favor to owe as far as I'm concerned." She looked at Aili, considering. "Also, if that fox spirit laid a hand or any other part of its body on you, I have some things I'd like to say to it."

Aili flushed. "Liu Chenguang, have you ever…"

"What?" Liu Chenguang smiled at her.

Aili opened and closed her mouth a few times, as though not sure what to say, then went back to eating.

Eventually Tainu returned, still smiling. "Well, that was worth it."

Liu Chenguang smirked at him. "Was it indeed?"

He laughed. "I meant he actually did have information–"

Zhu Guiren burst back into the room after him, panting. "Tainu!"

Tainu looked at him, "Yes?"

"Are you all right?"

"Yes…?"

"That was a fox spirit!"

"Of course he was a fox spirit. I'm well aware, demon."

"But fox spirits always– They always want…something!"

"I know what they want. I'm ten thousand years old, demon. I've met fox spirits before." Tainu looked at Zhu Guiren, smiling. "Come on, you've got to be near my age. You must have some experiences too?"

Zhu Guiren turned red, and then completely pale, as though he was going to faint. "Did he– did he–"

"Did he what?" Tainu started to laugh uncontrollably. "Oh no…oh no, demon, do you really not– Oh my goodness, how old are you?"

"Shut up!" Zhu Guiren shouted. "Did he kiss you? Did he– did he do other things?"

"A gentleman never tells," Tainu said primly.

Zhu Guiren ran out of the room again.

Zhu Guiren was knocking down trees with some kind of demonic unarmed combat skill when Aili found him, his beautiful face twisted in fury. She looked at him, feeling sympathetic; it didn't matter to her if Liu Chenguang had been with fox spirits or who knows what else for seven thousand years before they met, but obviously it bothered Zhu Guiren to think about Tainu…

Why would Zhu Guiren care about Tainu…

In fact, she really did care that Liu Chenguang had been with fox spirits.

She took out En and prepared to deal death to some innocent nature.

"You!" said Zhu Guiren, turning toward her. "Why didn't you stop him?"

"Me?" She pointed at her chest. "Me? What right do I have to stop him? Anyway, he said that the fox spirit had information. That's why he went," she said, trying to soften the blow.

"He didn't listen to me." Another tree met its splintery end. "I asked him not to go. Didn't you hear me? Do you think maybe he didn't hear me?" he asked, suddenly hopeful.

"I'm pretty sure he heard you," she said. "But really, I'm sure it was just to get…the information."

Zhu Guiren spun in the air and took out two trees at once.

Aili watched him for a moment. "Want to spar?" she asked suddenly.

Zhu Guiren looked at her. "You really think you're qualified?" he asked, sounding more like himself. "Hmph."

She called the phoenix whip and flicked it at him. He yelped. "Please, show me your skills," she said, smiling.

His halberd appeared. "Don't hold back because I've only got one hand."

"Oh, not a problem," she replied, and they launched at one another.

Zhu Guiren didn't come back until the next day. Aili returned after a few hours, covered in dust and splinters, and said that they'd been sparring and Zhu Guiren needed to go cultivate to recover. She herself, she said, just wanted a bath, but also disappeared till the next day's breakfast. Tainu and Liu Chenguang exchanged glances, Tainu trying not to snicker out loud at Liu Chenguang's overly-innocent smile. It was so typical of Aili's personality to be jealous, though he couldn't understand why Zhu Guiren was so upset. Probably he just didn't like fox spirits. Plenty of people didn't.

When Zhu Guiren did return, Tainu shared what the fox spirit had told him: there were a great many powerful demons in the area, and that there had been several battles between demon clans recently. Many of the less powerful or harmless yao were fleeing west to avoid being caught in the demon wars, including him. He had asked Tainu to go with him.

Zhu Guiren clearly wanted to kill something, preferably the fox spirit, on hearing this.

In a clear bid to distract him, Aili said, "Oh, I just remembered — I fought a demon who was looking for you, Zhu Guiren. She thought I'd know where you were. There were two of them, a woman with blonde hair and a man who might have been Kunorese. At least, he was in a Kunorese uniform."

Zhu Guiren sat up immediately. "Did they transform? What weapons did they use? How did you get away?"

After she had described it all, and much to Liu Chenguang's evident discomfort at imagining Aili having to fight two demons at once, Zhu Guiren nodded and began scribbling on the table.

"Stop that," said Liu Chenguang. "At least use a wall or something. I don't want to have to replace all the furniture in here too."

He shook his head. "My clan, two other clans. Those are not allies to one another, although the woman's clan is allied to mine, or at least used to be. The woman was probably the one I fought on the way to the refuge, Liu Chenguang. I wounded her in the arm."

"Did you tell her I was an experiment?" Aili asked, looking at the ceiling.

"Well, technically you are," said Zhu Guiren. "In the literal definition of experiment–"

Tainu covered his eyes and said, "Demon, I beg you, please just stop."

Zhu Guiren stopped. Then, he said, "There's so much going on right now. I need…I need to work this out. We're leaving tomorrow. Here." He put his finger down into the mostly empty map space due west of Shi'an. "Aili and Tainu, prepare the boy. We're bringing him to the Sorrowful River first. Liu Chenguang, get your supplies together. Food for four days in case we're delayed. Tell the innkeeper we'll come back here afterward. We need to have a safe place to return to. We leave in the morning." He turned and went into his bedroom.

Everyone else stared at each other blankly. At last Liu Chenguang stood up. "That's a lot to get together by tomorrow morning. I need to get to work."

Aili said, "All right, I'll talk to Yisue," and went downstairs.

Tainu stared at the closed door to Zhu Guiren's room, and finally walked over to push it open.

Zhu Guiren was kneeling against the wall, scribbling in his system of symbols and diagrams that no one else could understand. His hair was messy, Tainu noticed. He hadn't slept in his room, and Tainu hadn't seen him before this impromptu meeting; before that, it was Zhu Guiren running out of the room with all of them laughing at him about the fox spirit.

No wonder he was upset.

He went and knelt beside him. "I'm sorry."

"For what?" Zhu Guiren wouldn't look at him.

"For teasing you."

The pencil stopped moving for a brief moment, then continued. "Why did that fox spirit want you to go with him?"

Tainu tried very hard to answer this question without making a joke out of it. "We knew each other a long time ago," he said. "He remembers it fondly, I guess."

This time the pencil stopped completely. Zhu Guiren's body froze for a moment.

This truly upsets him, Tainu realized, feeling a deep unease about this situation. Why does it upset him so much?

"It's not that he was special to me," he tried. "Just…it was a nice time we had together, back then. Probably, fox spirits don't often get to see their partners again."

This definitely was not going well. Zhu Guiren began scribbling again, even more furiously than before.

"I didn't go with him," Tainu pointed out, a little desperate. "I didn't want to." When there was no response, he said, "Demon, won't you look at me?"

Zhu Guiren finally looked at him. To his shock, he saw that the demon's eyes were red around the edges.

"Demon?" he asked, panicking a little bit. He reached out for him, but Zhu

Guiren drew back, shaking his head.

"No," he said. "Not…not now."

"What's wrong? Why are you so upset?" He sat and waited in silence, determined to get a response out of him and unwilling to leave without one. Something was very wrong; something needed to be dealt with. "I'm not leaving until this is better," Tainu said at last. "I'm sorry. If anything I've said or done has hurt you, please tell me. I'm worried about you. I really–"

"You always look sad," Zhu Guiren said suddenly. He was still writing feverishly on the wall.

"Do I?" Tainu asked, surprised. "I don't feel sad. Just like usual."

"What would make you happy?"

"I told you, I'm not sad."

"Do you miss your family?"

"Where are all these questions coming from?" he asked uncomfortably. "What do you mean? You know my family's long dead. Now I have my little sibling. That's all. She's right here, I don't miss her."

Zhu Guiren scribbled even more furiously. At last, he sat back to look at what he'd written. "Tainu," he said.

"What?"

"What do you think you will do when we're done with this? When I've broken the arrays? Will Liu Chenguang stay with you?"

Tainu's heart fell a little bit. "Probably not. We're usually solitary. Maybe she'll be with Aili if that works out."

"Is Aili your family too?"

"I'd like her to be, one day."

"Where will you go?"

"Wherever the suffering is."

Zhu Guiren looked away from the wall, at last meeting his eyes fully.

*Still a little red, but better*, Tainu thought in relief.

"Tainu," he said.

"Yes?" Tainu frowned in confusion.

"What if I went with you? Would that make you happy?"

"You mean, you would be my family too?" Tainu smiled, warmed inside. "Would you?"

Zhu Guiren looked at him, unspeaking.

"No?" Tainu felt his smile disappear, a sense of loss. He shouldn't have asked; it was too much to hope for.

Zhu Guiren took a deep breath. "I don't want to be your family."

Tainu nodded, automatically accepting this even though he was still trying to understand what was happening. "Well, that's all right then. It's fine–"

"I want you to be in love with me."

Tainu's heart plummeted into the earth. He stared, his mouth hanging open. Then he closed it.

Zhu Guiren stared back, still except for the fingers of his one hand, which trembled.

"I don't do that," Tainu said at last, weakly.

"You've never done that," Zhu Guiren corrected. "That doesn't mean you can't."

When Tainu didn't respond, he said, "I want to make you happy. I want you to be happy with me. I want–" He breathed deeply. "I want you. I want us to love one another. Not as my family."

Tainu stared at him, unable to move or think or feel anything except that *this can't be happening.* This couldn't be. His mind could make no sense of what he was hearing.

"Why do you always have to be alone?" Zhu Guiren asked, almost pleading. "Why do you always have to suffer, and take care of everyone in the world, and never have any happiness for yourself? I want to be with you, I want to go where you go, I want to–" He closed his eyes. "So many things."

Tainu stood up, awkwardly. "I'll go now."

He stumbled once, as he walked out of the room in a trance. When he looked back, Zhu Guiren still knelt, his eyes closed, but he had leaned forward so his forehead was against the wall, as though he couldn't support his own weight. He ached to see him like that; he wanted to go back, to put his arms around him and say *it's all right, I'm here,* but he couldn't. He couldn't do it. His heart was beating so fast he thought he might faint. What if Zhu Guiren— what if— if that happened, if he let himself— He hadn't known, he hadn't imagined. He had thought only of friendship, only of being together, and now, everything was torn open. Everything was possible: the things he had never wanted, things he hadn't dreamed that he could want—

Tainu half-fell downstairs to the door outside, flung it open, and transformed to fly away.

# CHAPTER 10
## ZHU GUIREN'S ARRAY

THE NEXT MORNING, Tainu left before dawn without waking anyone up. On the table was a note that he was going ahead with Yisue to the Sorrowful River, Liu Chenguang would be able to find him.

Aili slapped her forehead and said, "No, I should be there, Yisue will want me," then asked Liu Chenguang to tell her Tainu's direction and ran out the door at top speed. Yisue wasn't a fast walker; she could catch up.

Liu Chenguang stood with Zhu Guiren by the supplies she had gathered and asked, "What is going on?"

Zhu Guiren just shrugged. "Can you find him when you need him? Can he find you?"

"Yes, of course," she said. "I know his true name, he knows mine."

"Well, he can find me. If he wants to. Let's go." He started walking.

Liu Chenguang yelled, "Someone has to help me carry this, Zhu Guiren, and you're the only one here."

Zhu Guiren turned around silently, chose the two heaviest bags, and then started walking again. Liu Chenguang made annoyed noises under her breath and followed. This was far too much like following Zhu Guiren around in her previous life; no one told her what was going on, and she wasn't going to put up with it.

She ran to catch up so she could walk next to him. "Zhu Guiren. Tell me what is happening."

"Nothing is happening. If you want to know why Tainu ran off before the sun came up, you'll have to ask him," he said. He looked straight ahead, not meeting her eyes, as they walked out of Shi'an and into the countryside. "Aili, same. Neither of them consulted me about their plans. We have about a day's journey to the site. It's not necessary for either of them to be there. I only need a phoenix." A little bitterly, he said, "Since you can also help defend me if necessary, you're better than Tainu for this. It's just as well."

"You're worried about him?" she asked.

He shrugged. "He's more vulnerable," he said flatly.

He refused to say anything else about what had happened between him and Tainu. Liu Chenguang knew that just a few nights ago they had been very friendly with one another — that they had been drinking, and that Tainu hadn't come back to them after he'd brought Zhu Guiren to his room. And then Zhu Guiren had been so upset about that fox spirit. *Had they...?*

She looked at his closed expression with horror and decided she really, really didn't want to know the answer to this question. Instead, she said, "Go over with me exactly what we'll do. Aili can find me. We can wait for her if you want real protection, but if you want to begin with only me, let's lay it out."

He nodded, and they discussed strategies as they walked. Liu Chenguang inwardly considered — as Zhu Guiren explained the timing of the blood and when he would need healing as opposed to blocking, assuming other demons showed up, which he was sure they would — Zhu Guiren and her sibling together. What a horrible thought. Surely Tainu hadn't been *that* drunk.

Aili caught up with Tainu and Yisue on a back road out of Shi'an, headed northwest rather than due north. Tainu was in his bird form, riding on Yisue's shoulder, which was stupid. *It's not as though Yisue isn't already visible enough,* she fumed, *there should be an adult standing near him at all times so no one will try anything.*

"Yisue!" she called.

Yisue turned, his face very glad. "Aili! You came!"

Tainu fluttered around but didn't say anything. Aili tried to give him a dirty look, but this didn't work so well with a bird.

She gave Yisue a hug, then said, "You're going to need to walk faster than this if you want to make it to the Sorrowful River today."

"Tainu said that we'll stop when we're tired and then keep walking until we get there," he said. "He said it's hard to tell, comparing flying to walking, but he thinks it would be about a full day if we didn't stop at all. So if we stop and rest and then walk more, we'll get there in the nighttime, but that would be ok. It doesn't matter to me."

She held his hand as they walked. Tainu sat on her shoulder now, which annoyed her; she wasn't pleased with Tainu at all. How could he just leave with Yisue like that, not even consulting with her? Didn't he think that they might want to say goodbye to one another?

"Did Tainu explain why you need to go?" she asked.

"You said last night," he replied. "I understand. You're going to do dangerous things, and so it's better for me to be with my relatives."

"That's it," she said, relieved. It was good he was going willingly. She had been afraid that he would refuse, in the end. "Will you have problems finding them in the river?"

"I don't know," he said lightly. "I haven't been in rivers much. There's no river dragon close to my coast. But I think that once I'm in the river, my uncle will know and he'll come look for me."

"You'll be safe there," she said, comforted. "And when you're finished visiting, you can go back down to the ocean and go home."

"No," he said, just as lightly. "When I'm done visiting I'm going to come out of the river and find you."

Ah, here it was. Aili coughed. "Yisue, how will you find us?"

"You can tell me your true name?"

"I don't have one, remember?"

"Oh." His face fell. "I could come back to that city. Shi'an."

"We may not be there. I don't know where we will be."

He thought about this for a while. "Will you be near the Sorrowful River at all?"

"I don't know, Yisue," she said gently. "That's one of the reasons we want to take you there now — so you can be in a safe place."

"Well, you can find me, then. When you're done with the dangerous things. Come to the Sorrowful River and throw this in." He twisted his hand and a small pearl appeared in it — not the large one that he had used to create the dragon gate, but a small one, like those she had seen on earrings. "I'll know. I'll come to you. Promise," he said plaintively. "Promise you will."

Aili took it. "I promise," she said, and put the pearl in her pocket. "Yisue, you're a good friend."

He beamed at her and ran ahead.

"Tainu," Aili muttered, "what's going on, why did you run off with him?"

Tainu didn't reply, but flew off above Yisue as though keeping watch.

The landscape was terrible — flooded repeatedly, full of ruined houses and empty fields. There were no people left here. They had all fled long ago. Aili had never seen anything emptier than this place, except the ocean from the deck of the troop carrier. Only birds flew above them, waterfowl especially. At last, Tainu decided that he might as well take his mortal form again, since there was no one here to see.

"Well, the ducks are happy, at least," Tainu said after Aili had ignored him for several miles.

"Why did you leave without telling me?" Aili asked. Yisue was jumping up and down in a flooded field ahead of them.

Tainu didn't reply at once. Finally he said, "There was something difficult with the demon. I just needed to get away."

Aili frowned at him. "Zhu Guiren? But what?" The sadness underneath Zhu Guiren's anger about the fox spirit when she was with him the other day was so clear to her. "Zhu Guiren wouldn't do anything to hurt you," she said, oddly certain. "For whatever reason he seems very…attached to you."

"I know," he said. "That's what's difficult."

"Oh," she said awkwardly. "Well. You don't feel the same for him? You seemed to…like him quite a bit too?" She'd only been there for a few days, but this had been almost painfully obvious. She tried to think what advice Nora would give, what questions she would ask.

Tainu kicked a puddle, splashing them both with mud. "I like him. I like him a lot."

"All right," said Aili, secretly thinking there was no accounting for taste, "then what's the problem?"

Tainu just shook his head. "I don't– I don't…have relationships like that."

This was extremely confusing and starting to get quite embarrassing, but she pressed on bravely. "Do you mean…not with men? But that fox spirit?"

Tainu turned back into a bird and flew away again. Aili gave it up as a lost cause.

It turned out that they didn't have to go all the way to the main channel of the Sorrowful River. A few hours later, Tainu landed and said that Yisue would be able to swim from a flooded area just ahead and Aili, at least, probably couldn't go any further than that.

Yisue turned to her and said, "Goodbye, but only for now. You promise!"

"I promise," she said. "Be good for your relatives."

"I will! You be safe. Watch out for demons." He hugged her fiercely, then turned around and ran splashing into the water. When it was up to his chest, he shimmered and transformed — a white dragon who soon turned a muddy yellow color from the silty water. He turned back and nodded his head, then dove beneath. Aili watched the track of his wake until he entered the deeper channels and it disappeared.

Tainu watched, the smile falling off his face as soon as Yisue was underwater. "Let's go. We'll have to find them now. I'll look for Liu Chenguang." He whispered and then said, "They've made better time than us. I'll fly ahead and tell them to wait until you come, so the demon has more protection." He transformed before she could say anything; clearly, he was avoiding any possible further conversation.

Aili looked one more time to where Yisue had disappeared and silently wished him well. If they didn't come back, he would surely give up eventually and go back down to the ocean, or perhaps stay in North Daxian with relatives who had more time with mortals; either way, he would be safe. He was so fascinated by the mortal world. She smiled, then settled into a more combative frame of mind. Time to get to work.

"Eftahede," she whispered, and started running down the white-gold path.

Liu Chenguang was glad Zhu Guiren was carrying the heavy bags. The countryside was sodden and often flooded, but Zhu Guiren walked quickly and by late evening, they had found the place he thought the array had been set. He settled into a lotus position and concentrated, then stood up and walked around, feeling in the air with his single hand, until he stopped with his feet in several inches of water. "Problem. I need to be able to pour the blood into earth. Pouring into water will just dissipate my own spell."

Liu Chenguang said, "I'm sad to say that shovels weren't part of my supply planning."

Zhu Guiren glared at her, clearly in no mood for joking. He stalked over to a ruined farmhouse and started digging through the detritus piled against the walls. He threw her a spade and took a rake himself. Together, they piled up enough dirt in the spot he selected so that there was a little island, just a handsbreadth wide and a finger's width above the water. He wiped his face, striping himself with dirt. Liu Chenguang stood up and stretched.

"Are you ready?" he asked, looking at her as though he hated her and everything else in the world.

"Is there something wrong with you? This probably isn't the kind of thing you should be doing if you're distracted." Under her breath she whispered Tainu's true name to gauge the distance. "Tainu isn't far away. Let's wait. It would be safer if Aili's here too."

"No," he said, even more bitterly than before. He turned his back on her, slashed his handless arm before she could say anything more, and started chanting.

Stunned that he began something so dangerous with so little notice, Liu Chenguang brought out her wings, invisible though they were, and readied herself, balancing her deerhorn knives in her hands.

The attackers showed up almost immediately: four yaoguai and three demons. Liu Chenguang swore to herself. Zhu Guiren was on his knees, still chanting. The cup of blood was nowhere near full.

The demons attacked first, evidently considering this their privilege. One of them shouted something at Zhu Guiren in the demonic language and threw a talisman, which she blocked with her wings. It was enormously strong, unlike anything she had felt before; it felt as though her wing had been broken by it, and the shock from the qi almost knocked her unconscious. Luckily, it did not, as she then had to block a sword stroke and disarm one of the demons — a man with blue eyes and short, ash-blonde hair.

"Little one," he said, "that was quite clever, but not enough." His other hand held a mace, which smashed down toward Zhu Guiren.

She could only desperately try to block. The force of the blow nearly broke one of the deerhorn knives as she dodged and circled behind him. If only she were able to actually fight...But this was all, and she couldn't even use all of her defensive skills of circling and avoidance because she needed to stay between them and Zhu Guiren.

The smoke of the spell was now curling outwards from Zhu Guiren's hand, moving over the ground in a complex woven pattern. The demons brushed through it, unconcerned. Behind the three demons were the yaoguai, misshapen creatures, circling hungrily. Liu Chenguang risked a look at Zhu Guiren. His face was contorted as though in pain and his voice was shaking, but he didn't stop chanting. One of the other demons took advantage of the fact that she couldn't protect him from all sides and circled behind him, stabbing him in the back with a short sword. Zhu Guiren grunted, but somehow managed to work it into the chant.

Liu Chenguang put more effort into her qinggong, giving up on the deer-horn knives to simply use herself as a shield — wings against talismans and spells, body against weapons — flipping and circling around and above Zhu Guiren as rapidly as she could. But now, there was a fourth opponent: a snake yaoguai who had circled in under her guard. She hadn't even had time to heal the cut on Zhu Guiren's arm as they had planned, and so even though now the cup was full and he was pouring it on the little pile of earth, his blood still sluiced from his arm into the water. His face was deathly pale. The snake yaoguai bit him in the lower back, its mouth nearly encircling his entire waist; he screamed, then continued the chant. His voice tried to crescendo, but he seemed to have nothing left. The blonde demon got through her guard and smashed Zhu Guiren with the mace, slashing his face with its spikes and breaking his left shoulder into meaty pulp. He screamed again and broke the cup on the ground, or tried to; the little island was too sodden with water and blood for it to actually break, but the smoke rushed back into the last drop of blood anyway. The spell was complete.

A violent ripple passed through earth, air, water, and all their bodies, shaking everything. Zhu Guiren screamed one more time — a long, drawn-out cry, as though something was being torn from him — and fell face forward into the water.

The surrounding demons didn't disperse. One of them laughed. The snake yaoguai slithered forward again. Liu Chenguang's wounds had almost all healed, but the talisman she had blocked was still affecting her qi. She didn't think she would be able to heal Zhu Guiren, but she leapt over to him and continued to block, taking the wounds in her body. She wasn't immune to pain by any means, and it was agonizing, but she would heal, if only she could stay conscious soon Zhu Guiren could fight, or Aili would come—

Suddenly, Tainu was there in his falcon form, sending qi into the eyes of the demons and beating his wings. He landed next to them and tried to set a ward, but the earth was covered with water and the ward wouldn't take. He shouted something she couldn't understand and turned Zhu Guiren over in the water.

She left Zhu Guiren to him. Once he was healed, they would have a fighter; meanwhile, all she could do was block, and block, and block. The demons and yaoguai circled continuously, stabbing and slashing at her. She gave up trying not to scream.

Behind her, she heard Tainu talking endlessly to Zhu Guiren, nothing she could understand under the circumstances; Tainu had taken several wounds as well, acting as a secondary shield over the demon. So far, the demons were satisfied with simply attacking them, knowing that if they refused to fly their capture was inevitable, but this would last only until the two of them could no longer heal themselves, she knew.

"Where's Aili?" she yelled at Tainu, spinning, blocking, being raked and stabbed, feeling talismans burst against her wings like burning embers. "And why isn't he getting up? We need him!"

"I don't know!" he yelled back at her. "I don't know!"

From the other side of the field, there was a splashing sound and a shout. Aili raced toward them at last — phoenix whips in each hand — so quickly that her footsteps seemed to not pierce the surface of the water. She lashed out at the circle of yaoguai and destroyed them one by one, almost in passing, then leapt up with qinggong and twisted to land in front of Liu Chenguang.

"Get back!" she ordered, her voice raw. "Behind me!" The phoenix whip lashed out again and again.

Liu Chenguang collapsed into the cold, bloody water, sobbing for breath. She and Tainu covered Zhu Guiren's body as shields, and she spread her wings over all of them, still blocking talismans. "Aili," she murmured.

She could hear Aili's wordless cries of rage over the demons and yaoguai howling and screaming at her and at one another, could smell burning flesh where the phoenix whip found a target, but all she could see was the bloody water under her.

Tainu was cradling Zhu Guiren's head, keeping it out of the water so he wouldn't drown — unless he already had? She frowned. No, she could feel a heartbeat. What was wrong with him? Tainu had clearly given him blood, and plenty of it, since he was wounded himself. The two of them were practically bathing the demon in phoenix blood, why wasn't he getting up?

At last, Aili collapsed into the water next to them with a loud, "What the hell?"

Liu Chenguang sat up with great effort and looked at her; she'd never heard Aili swear quite like that before. Her face was flushed and speckled with blood and she had a few small wounds, but there were two dead demons and four dead yaoguai in front of her. The blonde demon had apparently fled.

"Aili, are you all right? Can I heal you?" she asked, forgetting that Aili could now heal herself.

Aili was yelling again. "What the- what the hell were you two doing, starting without me?"

Liu Chenguang timidly reached out to her shoulder.

Aili shook it off, her blue eyes flashing. "What if I came later?" she demanded. "I ran as fast as I could! The two of you were being slashed into mincemeat

— how long could you have held out? This was just luck, you understand?"

"Aili–"

"Damn it!" She got up and staggered away from them, splashing through the muddy water. From a distance she turned around. "Zhu Guiren!" she yelled. "Zhu Guiren, get the hell up. I have things to say to you!"

Tainu had ignored all of this. Finally he managed to stand, holding Zhu Guiren in his arms. He walked slowly through the water and mud and blood, carefully so as not to trip. "He's not waking," he said at last when they reached drier ground. His face was drawn with anxiety. "Liu Chenguang, help me check what's wrong. I don't understand…"

Liu Chenguang tore her eyes away from Aili and helped Tainu lay Zhu Guiren carefully down in a place without visible water, though every inch of earth here was really just mud. His wounds were mostly closed already, and he was breathing. Liu Chenguang listened to his lungs. "He has some water in them," she said, "but trying to get the water out here would be counterproductive, I think. As soon as we reach somewhere warm and dry…" She went into her physician mind and began to check his meridians. "Ah, Tainu, feel this."

Aili came back over. Liu Chenguang risked a look at her and realized that she had been crying.

"What's wrong with him?" Aili asked, still not quite in a normal tone of voice.

Liu Chenguang said, "We're trying to find out. Tainu, do you feel it?"

He nodded. "All his meridians are irritated, and some are torn," he said. "Severed."

Liu Chenguang sat back on her heels and looked at him. "It's just as well he's unconscious," she said at last. "The pain must be very intense. Let's move him while we can."

Aili said, "It's a long walk back to Shi'an."

"We didn't pass anywhere better. To go forward instead of back, we would need to cross the river, and there's nothing there either," said Liu Chenguang, standing. "This whole area is just a giant floodplain now. The villages are deserted or ruined. Tainu, can you carry him?"

Tainu silently bent down again, and carefully picked him up.

"We'll take turns," said Aili.

When they reached Shi'an, muddy, bloody, and bedraggled, it was luckily well after dark. Tainu flew ahead to warn them of Kunorese patrols since it was after curfew and the last thing they needed was to be dragged in for questioning. Their rooms were waiting for them.

"Tainu," Liu Chenguang said, looking at Zhu Guiren's muddy figure on Aili's shoulder, "I can't put him to bed like this. Can you bathe him or do you want me to?"

Aili and Tainu both looked at her.

Liu Chenguang sighed. "He's filthy," she said. "We're trying to heal him, not give him amoebic dysentery or who knows what else from lying in that water with open wounds and getting it in his mouth and lungs."

"But I gave him blood," said Tainu meekly. "He won't get any of that."

"You people are ridiculous," Aili snapped. "I'll do it. It's part of my training, Liu Chenguang."

Now Tainu and Liu Chenguang both stared at her.

"What? I'm already carrying him anyway." She turned her back on the two ridiculous phoenixes and brought him into the bathroom.

Zhu Guiren was still very much unconscious; Tainu's treatment should have taken care of all his wounds, internal and external, but Liu Chenguang had said he was probably in pain from the meridians, so she was still careful with him as she cut off what remained of his clothing, wiped him down, and put him in the bathtub. She frowned at his long hair. It was a good thing that they cut hair short in the military, she thought, because it added quite a bit of complexity to getting him fully clean while he was unconscious; she had to be sure that he wasn't aspirating water while she rinsed him.

As she cleaned his body, she saw the scars of his old wounds and stopped briefly. "Zhu Guiren," she said quietly, "I'm sorry, I didn't know." At least she'd been able to spare him the embarrassment of having Tainu do this for him. She had a sense that his feelings for Tainu actually ran quite deep, as bizarre as that seemed.

*Stupid demon, stupid phoenixes,* she thought as her mind went back to what she had seen, running across that flooded field: the two of them being attacked, defenseless, bloody, stabbed and slashed again and again, not moving, not trying to get away; Liu Chenguang lying face down, half in the bloodstained water—

She finished drying him, wrapped him in a robe she found, and carefully laid him in the bed, then went back to her own room to get clean herself.

Aili stalked coldly from Zhu Guiren's room into her own without speaking to them.

"She's so angry," Liu Chenguang whispered, but Tainu couldn't respond; he was too worried.

He went directly into Zhu Guiren's room as soon as Aili had left. He was lying in his bed, completely clean, his hair still damp. Tainu touched his hair, his hand shaking a little bit. *Demon,* he thought, *demon, I'm so sorry.* He wanted to gather him up and hold him again. What was he thinking? Why was he so confused?

"What's wrong with you?" Liu Chenguang asked, following him in.

He shook his head. "His meridians– Check again."

"You too," she said. "Feel here...and here..."

The tearing was, if anything, increasing in severity.

"There must be some kind of chain reaction through his whole cultivation structure," Tainu murmured. "From the destruction of the array. It's become a part of him through the centuries."

"Did he expect this?" she asked, frowning.

"He told me it was a possibility."

"Then why did he refuse to wait for you?"

Tainu winced. He sat next to Zhu Guiren and took his hand, his face bowed.

"Tainu. Focus," Liu Chenguang said sharply. "Whatever happened between you two can wait. His condition is deteriorating. I've done what I can do. Trying to give him qi through the meridians isn't helpful. It's just becoming more turbulent. I can keep coming up with prescriptions for him, but until he's able to drink it's not going to do much. What ideas do you have?"

Tainu laid his hand on Zhu Guiren's side, where the damage was worst, and tried to feel it echo in his own cultivational structure. He winced again. "I'd have more to offer if he didn't cultivate resentment," he said at last. "Anything you or I could give him, it will feel to him like resentment does to us. It will hurt him."

"Hurt him as in painful, or hurt him as to worsening the injury?"

"Definitely painful, at least if he were conscious. It may not worsen the injury, it may stop the damage, but I don't think I can heal it. It's as though the resentment has left the meridian system and is simply rampant in his body now. Like internal bleeding. I can..." He closed his eyes and felt more deeply, intuiting as he did when going into a trance or creating a spell. "I can reconnect the meridians to others so that the system is closed again, and I can take the loose resentment into myself to remove it. That will hurt me, but I'll get over it. It's not much compared to...other things. But his cultivational structure — the damage will be permanent. He can still cultivate, but it will be more difficult for him… more painful, from now on. I can't think of anything more I could do."

Liu Chenguang nodded. "Tainu, if there's nothing more you can do, there's nothing more anyone could do."

"Maybe another demon could help him more. Another cultivator of resentment," he said, wavering. "I don't want to do this to him if there are other options. It can't be undone."

"Do you know of any demon who's ever done anything but try to kill him?" she asked. "Don't make up imaginary solutions, Tainu. If this is all there is, it's all there is. Unless this can be stopped, I think he's going to sink further into unconsciousness, then coma, then death, within two days at most. He won't wake up for us to ask him about it."

Tainu jerked. "No!" Then he said reluctantly, "Yes. That's also…what I foresee. Without doing this."

"Go ahead," Liu Chenguang said. "Do it now. He's only getting worse as we wait."

Tainu sighed, closed his eyes, and held his hand lightly against Zhu Guiren's bare skin, whispering in the phoenix language, calling healing for him. *Arciniang.*

A soft, golden glow bathed Zhu Guiren's side and began to travel through his body, veins of light spinning out from where Tainu touched him, connecting and reconnecting but avoiding the place where his hand lay, which he had shielded to cut off from the network. Tainu grieved inwardly for him — losing this piece of himself — but the demon had known that it might happen. They should have talked more, Tainu thought, about what to do if it did. Why had they not talked? Why had Zhu Guiren not waited for him to be there when he broke the array? Had he hurt the demon so much?

He reversed the flow, drawing the loose resentment bleeding through Zhu Guiren into his own cultivational system, feeling its sharp edges, the bitterness and pain, and wondered if it felt this way for the demon, too, or if it was just because the demonic qi was incompatible with his own. Gasping, he let go, a bit of blood coming from his own lips.

"It's all right," he said, holding up his hand as Liu Chenguang frowned. "It's done. I just need to cultivate and purify now."

He settled himself down to cultivate.

"Here?" asked Liu Chenguang, still frowning.

"Here," he said. "I'll stay with him."

"He won't wake up tonight, or probably tomorrow either."

"I know. He shouldn't be alone." He found that he didn't want to meet her eyes.

Liu Chenguang sat down next to him, wrapping her arms around her knees, and finally said, "Tainu, he can't hear us now. What is happening between you? Why did you run away this morning? Why didn't he wait for you if he knew something like this might happen to him? I didn't know it. He never said anything to me. He just said he wouldn't wait for you, and started right away."

"Was he angry?" he asked. "Or sad?"

"How should I know? I think you know, though."

Tainu considered a cowardly plea that he needed to cultivate and get rid of the resentment he'd taken in, but of all the beings in the world, who could he possibly talk to about this aside from his little sibling? "I ran away from him last night, not just this morning. I was avoiding him."

Liu Chenguang raised her eyebrows. "Did something happen last night?"

Tainu twiddled his fingers for a while, and finally said, "He told me something."

"That's all? He's told you lots of things — most of them incredibly insulting or deeply pathological. What did he finally say that got you to run away from him?"

Tainu cleared his throat. "He– he said," he coughed more. "He said…"

Liu Chenguang turned her whole body toward him. "Spit it out, Tainu. What on earth could it have been?"

"He said…" He took a deep breath. "He wants me to be in love with him."

Liu Chenguang stared at him, wide-eyed. "What?"

"He– he said that," Tainu said weakly.

"What does that even mean? It's not like you can make a decision about it," she said. "It's either something that is, or it isn't. Aside from whether it's a good idea, which obviously it's not, you can't control if you have that feeling for him."

Tainu was silent.

"You…do?" she asked, astonished.

"I don't know," he mumbled. "I don't know how."

"Tainu," she said, smirking a little bit, "come on. You surely do know *how*."

"Not like that," he said. "Of course I've had a lot of…pleasant experiences. But I think this is…not the same?"

"It's not the same. If you are asking me, no, it's not the same at all." She leaned forward, seriously. "Tainu, I'm sure there's nothing I could say to you about falling in love with a demon that you haven't already thought of."

He snorted. "I'm sure you could say lots of things because I have never in my life thought of this happening." He shook his head. "It does feel like falling…I'm so afraid."

"What are you afraid of?" she asked gently. "Of losing him?"

"Yes. Liu Chenguang, I don't know how you could bear it. Losing him."

"Is that all?"

"Isn't it enough?" He looked down at the ground, his eyes unexpectedly filled with tears. "I can't– I can't."

Liu Chenguang reached out and took his hands. "Tainu, there's no knowing what will happen. He's a demon, after all, not a mortal."

"That means he lives until he's killed," he said. "We live forever. Someday he'll leave me. Someday– If I let myself love him so much, how can I–"

His little sibling looked him, steady and serious. "Tainu," she said, "if you love him so much, what are you doing wasting time like this? Do you think that somehow, if you don't…well, have him as your lover–" Her face turned bright red. "Do you think that somehow that protects you from being heartbroken if something happens to him? You already have these feelings for him. How would you feel if you lost him and had never taken this chance to love him as much as you could?"

He closed his eyes.

"How long has it been like this for you? I think it's been much longer than you've ever told me."

He nodded.

She asked, "If you let yourself think about it — if you try to put the fear away just for a few minutes and let yourself know what you want — what is it?"

They sat quietly together beside the bed for a while, watching as Zhu Guiren breathed; Tainu lifted up his head to look at his sleeping face and tried to be without fear. Finally, he asked, "Liu Chenguang, if you had it to do over…knowing how it would end…would you still do it?"

"I would," she said. "Even knowing what I know now, I would still have tried."

# CHAPTER 11
## TALKING

THE NEXT SEVERAL days, everyone seemed to tread carefully around one another: Aili avoided Liu Chenguang, Zhu Guiren mostly slept, Tainu obsessively watched him while he was sleeping and avoided him while he was awake, and Liu Chenguang decided they were all ridiculous and went out to eat noodles and heal refugees in the shanty camps.

A week or so later, when she came back exhausted from a day in the camps, sneaking blood to people who thought they were getting traditional Daxian medicine, she found Aili waiting by the door of the inn for her. Passerby were staring at the tall foreigner in Daxian peasant clothes.

"Do you want to walk with me?" Aili asked.

"I'm tired," she said, and started upstairs. They would have to leave this inn soon. Both Aili and Tainu were far too visible. The Kunorese puppet government of the city would start paying attention soon if they weren't already. She was feeling pretty thoroughly done with Shi'an anyway.

"I know," Aili said. "I'm sorry."

Liu Chenguang shook her head. "I can't right now. Do whatever."

"Tonight?" Aili asked cautiously. "After you've rested? I really want to talk with you."

Liu Chenguang turned around on the stairs, already up several of them so she was a little taller than Aili — certainly an unusual point of view — so she could look down and see Aili's upturned face, serious and determined. Well, they would have to have this out at some point.

"All right," she said. "Were you planning to take me to a moon viewing platform? I don't think there's much to see tonight."

Aili's mouth quirked up a little bit. "That's an excellent idea. I'll look into it."

She turned and walked away, so Liu Chenguang continued up the stairs into the land of Tainu's personal drama, which she was also feeling very done with.

Just sleep with him already, she thought to herself uncharitably, the world has enough problems. His cultivational system is practically destroyed and he's pining after you on top of it? I feel sorry for him at this point, and I don't even like him. You're clearly in love with that person, who knows why, but it's obvious to anyone watching you two together. You're ten thousand years old. Put it in perspective; mortals love and lose each other every day — thousands of them, sibling...

She threw cold water on her face and fell down into her bed. "I am not able to talk to anything with any emotional issues for the next three hours," she announced to her pillow. She felt no anticipation whatsoever about seeing Aili later and thrashing out whatever was going on there. "There's a war going on. Has no one else noticed?" she said, also out loud.

"I'm here and I have noticed," Tainu said from the other room.

"Oh," she said after a moment.

He knocked on the door and stuck his head around it. "I saw you in the camps today," he said.

"You were there too?"

"Yes," he said. "Just so you don't think I'm only avoiding someone, I am actually doing things."

"Whatever. But good, that's good. How's Zhu Guiren?"

"He's been trying to cultivate, and as anticipated, it's very painful," he reported. "He's gone to find someplace with lots of resentment to cultivate in, so, for all I know, he's in the camps as well. Other than that, he's totally recovered."

"Good," she said. "And you?"

He hesitated. "We haven't talked," he said. "But we will, I promise."

"All right."

"You and Aili?"

"Tonight."

"Ah," he said. "Well, good luck."

"Ergh," she groaned, her face back in the pillow. "I'm going to sleep now."

Tainu laughed and closed the door.

She woke up several hours later, feeling refreshed, and went downstairs to find Aili waiting for her outside.

"It's almost midnight," Liu Chenguang said, yawning. "Have you been here all this time?"

"No, I thought if you were napping, I might as well too. I've just been here for a little while, thinking about what we should do."

"And?"

"I didn't find a moon viewing platform," Aili said seriously, "and there's no moon tonight anyway. So, it's just…" She smiled. "How tired are you?"

"Why?" she asked, suspicious.

"I've never been to the summit," Aili said.

Liu Chenguang laughed out loud. "Are you joking? If I could transform, maybe, but I'm not walking to the summit of Mount Shi tonight."

"Even with qinggong? Even if I carried you?" Aili asked persuasively.

"Really?" Liu Chenguang shook her head, still laughing. "All right, you can give it a try."

Aili knelt in front of her. "On my back, arms around neck, legs around waist," she said.

Liu Chenguang couldn't see her face, but she could tell that she was still smiling.

"I'll probably need to use my arms sometimes, so hold tight."

"Do you even know the way?" she asked, laying her weight on Aili's back and wrapping legs and arms around her as directed.

"Nope," she said in Anglish, sounding quite satisfied. "Assuming that going up will get us there eventually."

"Not exact–"

Aili laughed and started racing up the road toward Mount Shi, making her laugh out loud as well. Aili's qinggong was powerful and graceful; she took great leaps from boulder to boulder, up cliffs, dancing between the established paths and the peaks above and to either side of them. Liu Chenguang could feel the strength and sureness of Aili's moving body beneath her — and even more than that, Aili's sheer delight in what she was doing, in feeling life run through her in this way — and how Aili wanted to share this with her.

Every so often, Aili would stop and put her down, breathing steadily, so they could look out at the growing panorama beneath them and the stars above their heads. In the dark, the terror of the war wasn't obvious; occasionally planes flew past, but there were no bombs tonight, and the flooded Sorrowful River was simply a glint in the starlight. Once, Aili reached out and held her hand, and she let that happen. She had flown over Mount Shi so many times, and for thousands of years she had lived in mountains. She was familiar with the peaks and cliffs of the world, but it was different to share it with someone.

Aili smiled at her, her face nearly invisible in the dark, limned only slightly by the starlight, like the river below. "Come on," she said, kneeling again. "Let's go."

Slowly, the edge of the eastern world grew lighter, sharpening the shapes of things. Liu Chenguang had lost track of time. Delighted, she asked, "Will we be there at sunrise?"

"That's the plan," Aili said, breathing deeply but easily and continuing to leap up the cliffs. "Actually, we've been faster than I thought we would. I took some detours so it would work out for dawn."

Liu Chenguang rapped her gently on the back of her head. "Trickery," she said. "You didn't tell my brother you were planning to keep me out all night. My reputation will be ruined."

Aili laughed. "Could you have done this yourself?" she asked.

"Yes, but not with as much style, I admit," she said, and before she knew it, she bent her head to kiss the back of Aili's neck where her braid left it bare. Aili's skin was warm beneath her lips, tasting slightly of salt.

Aili stumbled, but then continued without saying anything.

Liu Chenguang said, "Sorry,"

Aili stopped and put her down.

"Are we there?"

"Not yet. I just lost my breathing rhythm for a minute. I have to get it back."

"Oh," she said, looking up at her.

Aili looked down, seeming very tall against the stars and the beginning of the dawn. "Liu Chenguang–" She shook her head. "I wanted to say to you that I'm sorry I was so upset at you. About the array. I just want to protect you so much."

Liu Chenguang sat down, and pulled at Aili's hand so she would sit down too. "I know," she said. "We all want to protect each other. But you can't always protect me from everything. There are things I'm going to choose to do because I need to do them."

How many times had she had this conversation in her mind, over the past thousand years? This time, it went somewhere she had never anticipated, as she blurted out, "Do you think I loved you just because you were good with a sword?"

Aili looked at her for a moment and then said, very seriously, "As I recall, I was indeed *very good* with a sword, so I think you did take it into consideration."

It took Liu Chenguang a full minute to realize what she was saying, and then she turned bright red. "Aili!" she yelled, laughing uncontrollably.

Aili just watched her, smiling.

"All right," Liu Chenguang said at last, wiping her tears. "You were good with a sword, I confess it."

"My work here is done," said Aili portentously.

"Behold, the dawn!" Liu Chenguang collapsed into laughter again.

"Really? In that case, I've failed. We're not at the summit yet." Aili looked up. "But I feel like this is a good place."

"It is." After a moment, Liu Chenguang said, "I'm really not saying this to trick you into hugging me, but I'm honestly very cold."

Aili reached out and pulled her into an embrace, holding her from behind so they could watch the sunrise together. "Sorry," she said. "I'm warm from the exercise. I didn't think about how cold it would be. If I was really good at this, I would have brought something warm for you to drink."

Liu Chenguang tapped her hand. "How would you have carried it?"

"True." As the sun started peeking above the horizon, Aili said, "Thank you for coming up here with me."

Liu Chenguang pulled Aili's arms around her more tightly and pressed back against her chest for warmth, shivering a little. "Someday," she said, "I'll take you to the place where I used to live, these past years. There are a lot of good people there. Although they'll be very confused about you. I'll have to tell them you're a missionary or something. Can you pull that off?"

Aili snorted. "Highly unlikely. Tell them I'm a nurse."

"Done."

She felt Aili nuzzle the back of her head gently — her lips brushing against her hair and her breath warm on the tips of her ears — and she felt a little shivery for reasons that had nothing to do with the cold.

"Chenguang," Aili said, her voice a little bit strange.

Liu Chenguang's heartbeat suddenly raced and her body lit up, but she didn't say anything else.

Aili's arms tightened around her, and then let go. "The sun's up. Should we go check on those two? What exactly is going on between them?"

Liu Chenguang laughed, and although she was tempted, she didn't want to gossip about her sibling. "Who knows," she said.

Aili hugged her one more time. "Let's go. Going down will be quicker. Let's get back for breakfast."

After Liu Chenguang left with Aili, Tainu sat at the table, looking aimlessly at Liu Chenguang's map projects. None of them had talked about how to continue breaking the arrays since Zhu Guiren's collapse. Probably, Liu Chenguang and Aili didn't really care, but Tainu was very worried; this hadn't even been the great array, and without Tainu's healing, the demon almost certainly would have died.

What would happen to him if they kept doing this? Did they even need to? Aili seemed fine enough now. Maybe just breaking those two arrays was enough to make her well. Maybe Liu Chenguang's binding protected her from Zhu Guiren's array…

Two million mortal souls.

The time passed slowly. Zhu Guiren didn't return.

He decided to go look for Zhu Guiren accidentally; really, he was just going for a walk because he was bored, and who knew — maybe Aili and Liu Chenguang would come back and want some privacy.

The streets of Shi'an were devoid of mortal life except for the government patrols and Kunorese guards stationed here and there, but there were many yao. As his fox spirit friend had said, the harmless and less powerful yao were fleeing from wars of demons and mortals, and Shi'an had become a resting place for those going west, since they preferred to stay near mountains. He saw mouse and rabbit yao, foxes and dogs snapping at one another, cat yao leaping from roof to roof, and even two deer yao, male and female, delicate and frightened, under the eaves of a building destroyed in the bombardment. Among them stalked the demons in mortal bodies, and the smaller yao drew back where they passed. Tainu took his bird form and fluttered among the sparrows.

He knew that Zhu Guiren would have sought a place of strong resentment — a cemetery, or perhaps a bombed building; a place where many people had died violently or were buried — but there were so many such places in Shi'an that he wasn't sure where to begin. Finally, he closed his eyes and tried to intuit where his own revulsion was strongest and headed in that direction.

It was a cemetery next to the refugee camp, or rather, a morgue where unclaimed bodies were placed until they were buried, graves unmarked, in the field next to it. He had been near here that morning, trying to heal a little boy. It was very difficult when he couldn't get blood directly into people's mouths — blood that didn't come from his own physical touch generally wouldn't work for healing, so putting it into tea or food was ineffective — and he hadn't been able to do it in time. The little boy's body was here somewhere, probably.

Zhu Guiren was in his lotus position on a recent grave, but as soon as he heard the rustle of Tainu's clothing he was up, sword against his throat. "Oh," he said awkwardly when he saw who it was. He immediately stepped back, releasing his sword. "Sorry."

"It's all right," Tainu said. "I was just worried about you. That's all. How are you doing?"

The demon shrugged and turned away, returning to his cultivation spot. "It hurts," he said, laconic, and closed his eyes again.

Tainu went and sat on a grave near him. He had already explained what they had had to do to heal him — the permanent damage to his cultivation system — and the demon had listened to that, nodded, and said nothing.

Nothing between them had been addressed; nothing had been discussed.

Tainu wondered if, some day, he simply would go out and not come back at all. It seemed that he was withdrawing from them all so much. "I don't want you to leave," he said aloud, surprising himself.

"Who said I was leaving?" The demon opened his eyes and looked at him.

"Aren't you?"

He considered it. "I suppose, maybe. If there's nothing else I can do about the arrays, then what's the point? If I can't cultivate, eventually I'm just going to have to run for my life anyway."

Tainu said, "I don't want you to leave. Even if we can't break the array."

The demon just stared at him.

"Please."

Zhu Guiren said, "I'm trying to cultivate. Can you leave me alone?"

He swallowed. "No."

Zhu Guiren ignored him.

"If you can't cultivate," Tainu improvised, "you should stay so Aili can protect you. And I can heal you if you're hurt."

After a long silence, the demon replied, "Do you think that I could stay with you and draw other demons to attack you just because I'm afraid of being hurt? Do you think I would risk you just in case it would buy me a little more safety, a little more time to live? If that's what my end will be, that's what it will be."

Zhu Guiren lifted his eyes to meet his and Tainu realized that he was genuinely angry. He also realized that he had never really seen Zhu Guiren angry before. Not at him.

"Do you think that I'm that kind of coward?"

"No, not at all, that's not what I–"

"I'm trying to cultivate so I don't have to go," he said flatly, still staring at him. "If I can continue to gather power and fight and defend you, I will stay. Otherwise, I'm not going to put a target on your back. Aili's good, but she can't keep you safe against my whole clan *and* everyone else who is looking to kill me and get a phoenix out of it."

Tainu was silent, trying to think what to say, what to do. At last, after Zhu Guiren had already closed his eyes and settled back into cultivation, he said, "Is it very selfish to say I– I would want you to stay with me anyway? Even if..."

He couldn't bring himself to say, *even if you aren't as strong as you were, even if you can't defend me*; he was sure the demon wouldn't accept those words from him, and they wouldn't be helpful.

He couldn't say, *if you're going to be attacked and hurt and maybe even, even die, I want to be with you for that. I don't want you to be alone. I don't want to lose you again. I don't want...I want...*

He couldn't figure out how to say any of those things.

Zhu Guiren's closed eyes wrinkled a little bit at the corners.

"Or," Tainu said, getting braver, "I'll go with you. If you leave, I'll just follow you. I know your name. I can do it."

Zhu Guiren shook his head. "I'll tie you up and bring you back."

"Then I'll just go again," he replied. This strategy seemed to be working; he felt quite light in his heart now. "You won't be able to get away from me, no matter what you do."

Zhu Guiren looked at him at last. "You are an idiot."

Tainu smiled. "I am," he said comfortably. "I am an idiot you are never getting away from."

Zhu Guiren's eyes followed him as he came over to sit on the same grave, next to him.

"I don't like this place," Tainu said conversationally.

"Of course you don't. You're a phoenix, and it's full of resentment," the demon responded. "Which, as I mentioned, I'm trying to cultivate right now."

"You said it hurts. Can I help you?"

"How could you possibly help?"

Tainu gave this very serious thought. He looked at Zhu Guiren; he couldn't see much of him in the dark, but he could see his eyes in the light of the stars, and that gave him a sense of where to place his hands on either side of his face. Before he could let himself think about this any more deeply, he leaned over and kissed him, lightly, on the lips.

Zhu Guiren's entire body jumped as though he had been hit by a talisman.

Tainu felt such happiness, he laughed and kissed him again.

"What are you doing?" the demon asked. "I don't understand."

"I don't know," Tainu said, because he really, truly didn't. "I wanted to kiss you. Is that all right?" He still felt very light inside. It felt good to be touching his face like this, looking into his eyes, to be so close to him, to not let him go.

Zhu Guiren continued to look into his eyes with that little frown he got when he was very confused. At last he said, "This doesn't really help me with my cultivation."

"Does it help with anything else, though?" Tainu leaned over to kiss him one more time. Zhu Guiren's lips were very firm and narrow, Tainu brushed his own against them and tried to see if he could feel their shape better, trying to learn how he felt in the dark, feeling little dangerous shivers inside.

"Yes. It helps me know that you really are an idiot." Very cautiously and lightly, Zhu Guiren leaned over to kiss him back.

They looked at each other in silence. Tainu felt as though he couldn't stop smiling. The demon looked very serious.

At last Tainu said, "I am an idiot. Is that all right with you? Will you stay?"

The demon nodded slowly. "I still need to cultivate," he said. "Go back. This isn't a good place for you to be."

Tainu reached out and touched his hair. "Promise you'll come back soon," he said, "and I'll go."

"I promise."

When Tainu woke up the next morning, he heard the three others in the main room having breakfast. He stretched and went to join them.

Zhu Guiren looked up immediately to meet his eyes, but didn't smile. Tainu sat next to him and reached for a simple steamed bun — all there was, since the rationing was getting worse even for people with Zhu Guiren's endless amounts of gold.

Aili and Liu Chenguang both looked very happy, though, as well as windswept and tangle-haired.

"What have you two been up to?" he asked.

"Mount Shi," Liu Chenguang laughed. Her eyes sparkled in a way he hadn't seen in ages; it was a weight off his heart.

Tainu caught her eye and winked, wondering just how far up Mount Shi the two of them had gone.

Zhu Guiren looked at Liu Chenguang and Aili and frowned a little bit, but didn't say anything. He didn't look at Tainu, either, which bothered him a little.

"Demon?" he asked.

To the table as a whole, Zhu Guiren said, "I'm able to cultivate now, but it's slow compared to what I'm used to. I don't know if it will get better over time."

Aili said, "That's good? Not good?"

"Good, as far as it goes," Zhu Guiren said.

Tainu noticed he wasn't eating anything and placed a steamed bun in his hand, but he just put it down on the table, still without looking at him. This was honestly getting a bit disturbing.

"The one thing we found out for sure when we broke that array was that it doesn't make a difference whether I break the array myself or whether Aili does it. It's going to damage me either way."

They were all silent.

"Sorry for the bad news," he added. "If it is bad news."

Tainu wanted to touch him but was uncertain whether that was all right to do now; Zhu Guiren had never acted like this before, ignoring him as though he wasn't there, and so he had never imagined that such a thing would be this upsetting.

Finally, Aili said, "Zhu Guiren, it is bad news. Did you really think we wouldn't care whether you're hurt?"

Silently, he got up and left the table, still without speaking or looking at Tainu.

After a few minutes of the three of them looking at one another, confused, Tainu followed him into his room with another steamed bun. "Demon?" he asked, cautiously.

"Why did you kiss me?" he asked. For once, he wasn't scribbling on the wall, but lying on his side on the bed, his back to the door so Tainu couldn't see his face.

Had he misunderstood all along? Was that not…what he had meant, when he said he wanted to be in love, to be together? He felt his skin getting hot with embarrassment. Feeling greatly ashamed, Tainu said, "I thought you wanted it. I thought that's what you wanted."

"Is it what you wanted?" Zhu Guiren asked. "Or did you just do it because you thought– For me?"

Tainu thought, if I did it just to make you happy, isn't that also good? But the truth was… "I wanted to kiss you. I just…I don't…"

"What about that fox spirit? Did you want to kiss him?"

"What about the fox spirit?" Tainu asked, a little angry. "It was literally centuries ago, demon. Probably I wanted to kiss him, but not in the same way. It's not the same at all. Why do you keep going on about that fox spirit?" He decided it probably wasn't the time to mention that in ten thousand years there had been a lot more than one fox spirit.

"Why is it not the same?"

"Ugh, demon, why are you asking these questions?" Leaving the bun on the side table, he sat down on the bed leaning over him to see his face at that strange angle, nearly upside down. "Because I told you– because I've never done this. It's new for me. It's all different."

"Being in love? Will you be in love with me, then?" He turned over and now Tainu could see him properly. His eyes were rimmed with red. "Do you want me?"

"What's wrong?" he asked, alarmed. Tainu lay down next to him, laying a hand on the side of his face. "Are you all right?"

Zhu Guiren looked at him with those clear, dark, serious eyes, still full of pain.

Why so much pain? Tainu stroked his hair gently, and looked at his eyes, and then kissed him again.

At last, his demon sighed and allowed himself to be soothed, but he said, "You don't look at me the way you looked at that fox spirit. You're still touching me and kissing me like I'm a child who hurt his knee. Someone you're trying to heal. Is that the kind of love you have for me?"

Tainu's hand froze on his hair.

"That's what I thought," Zhu Guiren said, and rolled himself over, away from him, to sit up.

"That's not..." Tainu protested weakly, still lying there, looking up at in him shock, his hand still frozen where he had been touching his hair. "I don't– I didn't mean– demon, please..."

"That's not how I love you," the demon said. "That's not what I meant."

So quickly that Tainu wasn't at all sure how it happened, Zhu Guiren was on top of him. Tainu's two hands were captured in his one and pulled up over his head, and then Zhu Guiren was kissing him with a rhythmic, desperate force, his tongue entering into his mouth and his leg pressing between Tainu's so there was no doubt whatsoever about exactly what Zhu Guiren wanted. Tainu's body was responding eagerly and he heard the demon groan softly in his ear as they moved against one another, but his mind was somewhere else completely; when the demon finally looked up into his eyes, Tainu knew that all he saw there was absolute shock and panic.

Zhu Guiren let go of his hands immediately and sat up. "I'm sorry. That's not what you want, is it?"

Tainu just stared at him — still lying down, still aroused, and still shaking all over.

"But that's what I meant," the demon said. "That's how I want to love you. Like that. Not like a child."

When Tainu still couldn't respond, his mouth unable to make words out of anything, he continued, very formally, "I'm sorry I frightened you. If this isn't what you want, truly, Tainu, you need to…stop touching me. Because I want to touch you like this. I want to love you like this. I don't want you to only love me like something you need to take care of — like everyone else in the world."

Tainu closed his eyes, still lying in Zhu Guiren's bed as he heard him walk out, and felt in his body how much he did want him.

How had this all gone so wrong? Somehow, it had, and he couldn't figure out what to say to make it better because it was very true of him; he took care of everyone, and he wanted to take care of the demon too. Wasn't that love? Didn't that count? He didn't love that fox spirit — he didn't even know his name — and that fox spirit didn't love him either. That's why things were easy with fox spirits.

When he came out of the room at last, not knowing what he could possibly say to any of them, only Liu Chenguang was there. She said, "Aili and Zhu Guiren went to go break another array. Aili will do this one and Zhu Guiren will protect her, but I guess it takes longer when Aili does it, so they'll probably be gone for a few days."

"Who will heal him?" he asked, confused. "Why did he go without us? Why with only Aili?"

"Aili can do it, remember?"

There was something about this idea that felt dangerous to him, but he couldn't think of what it was; his brain had stopped functioning completely and his body was still tingling all over, so he just nodded, and sat down. "Did you hear?" he asked. It wasn't a large space, and the walls were thin.

"Not the conversation," she said diplomatically. Then, she added, "We heard the part that wasn't really a conversation. If you and Zhu Guiren intend to do more of that sort of thing, we should probably make sure we're not here. Just, you know, give me a hint."

"Thanks," he said, putting his head down on the table. "I think it's unlikely to happen again."

"Oh…I don't understand. It was pretty confusing to us. Zhu Guiren came out looking as though he had not had a good time at all, which frankly was kind of surprising, all things considered, and told Aili his plan, and since I already had the supplies set up from last time they just went."

"Confusing to me too." Without anything else to do, he said, "I'm going to the camps."

"All right," she said. "I'll come too."

# CHAPTER 12
## ZHU GUIREN IS MISTAKEN

ZHU GUIREN AND AILI walked together in silence across the empty, flooded countryside. Neither of them were very talkative even under normal circumstances, and Zhu Guiren was feeling very much not normal. He could still feel Tainu's body beneath him, feel his own intense need for more; he could still see Tainu's eyes, begging him to go away. Tainu didn't want his love, not the way he wanted to give it. Only as someone to take care of, just like he took care of everyone else.

Zhu Guiren suddenly spun around and threw some qi toward an inoffensive wall, which had clearly already endured much in its life. It obediently crumbled to the ground.

"Fuck," he said loudly. He hadn't said that word since living in the Federation. It felt good.

Aili looked at him, probingly. "Zhu Guiren?" she asked. "What's wrong?"

He shook his head.

To his surprise, Aili continued to press him. "Zhu Guiren, you and Tainu. What's happening?"

He ran ahead of her, fast, wishing he could still turn into a crow. Unfortunately, Aili was also fast. She jogged up to him easily, not even breathing hard, and said, "Come on, I'll tell you a secret."

"What is it?"

"The secret is that you don't really have any secrets," she said solemnly. "Those walls are thin."

"FUCK!" He threw more qi toward a ruined farmhouse almost half a mile away.

"Impressive," said Aili, her mouth twitching.

"Did you hear everything?"

"Only the part that didn't involve words."

Zhu Guiren started walking much faster. "Well, nothing happened, so I don't know what you think you heard."

Aili didn't say anything.

Zhu Guiren oriented himself and tried to get his anger under control. "None of this matters," he said. "The array is southwest."

After they had walked for a while, Aili very seriously said, "It does matter, Zhu Guiren. It's not a distraction from important things to love someone. It is the important thing."

Zhu Guiren replied, "You're a mortal, that's why you think so. Also because– because you have been able to love someone, and they love you back, so you can say that." He didn't speak again for about two miles. Then, he said, "Not everyone has what you have, so we have to have other important things. Like surviving."

"There's a tree up ahead," said Aili. "Let's take a break there. It's around dinnertime."

When they had settled down, Aili handed over a cold bun left over from breakfast. "This is dangerous for you," she said. "Are you sure you want to be out here without either of them to help you? It's not too late to go back and get them. I can smear blood all over you, but it's not going to do what Tainu did to get you out of the coma. I don't know how to do that. Neither does Liu Chenguang, actually, she said."

"It's fine," he said, stubbornly, and ate some bread. He knew he was taking a stupid and unnecessary risk, but he couldn't bear having Tainu take care of him again, as though that was their whole relationship. Although apparently, it was. "Just..." He waved the bun in the air. "Just carry me back. If you need to. It might not be that bad this time."

"Why not?"

He shrugged. There was no reason why not at all. The sub-arrays they were breaking were all strong ones. These were the ones that might weaken the central seal enough for him to break it. He truthfully wasn't sure he would survive breaking it, but he was determined to do it now. He wanted it to be gone. He hadn't told anyone this; not even Tainu, though he was sure Tainu was beginning to guess. Those pitying eyes looking at him... He threw the bun on the ground.

"Don't," Aili said sharply. "People are starving. Don't just waste it like that." She picked it up and tried to brush it off.

Sometimes, he wondered how much of the incredible suffering he saw around him — this three-sided war, the mortals killing one another unendingly, the children dying, the famine and starvation — was from his array lying like a curse over this whole area, resentment built on resentment, a chain reaction of suffering. The sheer scale of death and devastation was beyond imagination. Of course, mortals were just like this. That was true. And of course, there were other demons encouraging things to get worse. That was true too. But what was absolutely undeniable to him was that he was benefiting from it. The net of his array had grown exponentially since it was set a thousand years ago, encompassing and binding millions of descendants. The resentment of the people dying all around him didn't all just bleed into the air. Some of it came directly to him, directly into his cultivational body, feeding his own powers, and he didn't want it there anymore. He just hadn't thought it would be so painful to remove, or that he wouldn't be able to replace it with more normally-cultivated resentment.

He was tired of drinking suffering and death. He didn't want to live this way anymore.

He wanted to live another way, but that wasn't working out either.

Aili was nibbling her bun thoughtfully while looking up at the gray sky through the branches of the tree. He felt incredibly envious of her.

"You and Liu Chenguang," he said. "You two love each other. I could see it, back then."

She nodded. "I'm told it was very obvious," she said with a little smile, looking up at the sky as though remembering.

"I could see it even though I didn't know what it was," he said. "Only that he wanted to be with you. It was annoying."

"No doubt." Aili looked at him, then smiled. "You know, I was very jealous of you. At the time."

"Those rumors...I never had those kinds of feelings for Liu Chenguang, but the rumors were useful in their way. It kept importunate people away from me. It used to happen pretty often, back then, that someone would throw themselves at me."

Aili raised an eyebrow like she wanted to laugh, but didn't.

"I knew about these things," he insisted. "From observation of others. I needed to understand those feelings because that's one way mortals were motivated to do or not do things, and that was my business then. Manipulating them. But I never…had those feelings myself."

Aili handed him his bun back. "You still need to eat," she said. "When you say never, you really mean…never? Aren't you as old as Tainu? And Liu Chenguang?" She added, clearly not happy to say it, "I wasn't the first person Liu Chenguang was with, by any means."

Zhu Guiren looked at her, stunned. "But you…but he…"

"I know," she said. "Not thrilled with the idea."

"I'm younger than Tainu. I'm around nine thousand, maybe nine thousand and a half…I don't really keep close count."

"That is a lot of never," Aili said.

"Well, you know…among demons…why would we voluntarily be with each other like that? It's pretty much all rape, or because we're forced to by the clan leaders. We don't trust each other at all, for very good reasons. Who could let down their guard that way? And unlike some people, fox spirits never–" Fox spirits had never even approached him, thinking, correctly, that he was far too dangerous to risk. "Anyway."

"Anyway. But you were able to avoid being forced, at least. That's good," Aili said, her tone odd.

"Some demons do it with mortals, but it's just more…it's no different, not really. A demon's relationship with a mortal is always to get something for the demon. Pleasure or power — that's all. I never did. I never wanted to."

She nodded.

"But I know what it is. I know from watching. I know that I want it now. And he doesn't." He savagely bit into the bun. There, he'd said it.

Aili finished her food, but she didn't stand up. "Zhu Guiren, this is important for you to know before we go ahead and do what we're going to do today. Last time, Liu Chenguang said you went into it all half-assed–"

"What does that even mean?" he said, repulsed.

"It's a technical term that means you didn't think clearly about what you were doing," she said seriously, "and you started before you were really prepared."

"Oh." He felt that this was a sadly accurate description.

"And that didn't end well. You shouldn't be going into something as dangerous as this is for you with your heart bitter and angry," she said. "I don't know much about resentment, but that must resonate with what you're trying to destroy, right? Maybe it causes you more damage because of it."

He nodded slowly. This did make sense. When Aili had broken arrays in Hai'an, it hadn't damaged him as much as it had during the last time, when he had felt so bitter and hopeless after Tainu had rejected him. The first time. Now, again.

"So, you should know that you can't know about it from watching. Not from watching others, not from study, or looking at books, or whatever exactly you think you know," she said. "You have to find what you want, and what your partner wants." She seemed to be trying very hard not to look embarrassed, but it wasn't going very well; her skin had more pink in it than a Daxian's, and she looked very red now.

Zhu Guiren stared at her, wide-eyed.

"If you're going off what you saw happening in the imperial court during Great Feng, I'm telling you right now that you know exactly nothing about anything meaningful between you and Tainu."

Zhu Guiren frowned. "Really? Nothing?"

"Well, maybe in terms of pure mechanics," she allowed. "Maybe."

"Oh." Zhu Guiren was finding this conversation incredibly illuminating. "Because those people didn't love each other. Is that why?"

"A good number of them, probably not," she said. "Most of the people you saw didn't have a choice about being there at all, or who their partners were. Or their partners were just there for their pleasure. Or power. It's not that different, is it, from what you said about the demons?"

Zhu Guiren nodded. It was true. It was certainly very true, what she was saying. He looked at her with new respect. "For someone who's lived less than fifty years, you know a lot of things," he said.

Aili smiled at him. "Mortals have to learn fast. We don't have long."

He thought about this for a while. "But he doesn't look at me that way. He doesn't want me that way."

"Why do you think so?"

"That fox spirit," he said, with difficulty. "Did you see how he was? How he…stood for him, and looked at him? He doesn't look at me like that."

"Zhu Guiren, you are not a fox spirit to him. Tainu cares about you very much."

He shook his head. "Not the way I want him to," he said. "Not like you and Liu Chenguang."

Aili laughed out loud. "Do you think that we just…like fox spirits?" She smiled at him. "It wasn't like that at all. I've only ever been with Liu Chenguang, so I'm not speaking from vast experience of this subject. But I think that just because two people love one another, it doesn't mean that suddenly you just," she waved her arm around awkwardly, "roll into bed with each other and everything's fine and easy."

Zhu Guiren decided this would probably be the only chance he'd ever get to say this to someone who could give him advice. Who else could? He steeled himself to say it. "I tried with him, and he just wanted it to stop. He didn't like it at all."

Aili coughed. "All right, the truth is that as soon as we heard you two doing more than talking, we left the room. It was too embarrassing. But it didn't sound as though he wasn't liking it."

"He was afraid," he said, looking down. "He was afraid of me."

"Maybe it was too fast for him. Maybe he wasn't ready. But Zhu Guiren, think about it. He loves to be with you, he loves talking with you, he loves to touch you and be close to you. Do either of you even know how much of the time you spend just looking at each other and ignoring everyone else around you? He is so sensitive to you, wherever you are, whatever you are doing." She smiled. "It's really rather sickening."

"Oh. Is it unusual?" He hadn't thought of this before. Then, he said his greatest fear. "Don't you think that he sees me just as one more person to take care of? Just a…healing project?"

"No, I don't think he sees you that way at all" she said, very seriously. She shook her head. "Zhu Guiren, do you feel less resentment now?"

He took stock. "Yes," he said, rather surprised. "I feel different now."

"Good." She stood up and stretched. "Let's run for a while. I want to get this done. I don't like leaving them alone without one of us."

Aili felt rather satisfied with that conversation, which was mostly drawn from her memories of Nora's advice. She smiled to herself, remembering Nora's long and fairly explicit lectures in the apartment before they went to the bar or out on double dates which had never worked out for her personally but nonetheless were, in Nora's opinion, important experiences for a young woman learning the ways of the world. Poor Zhu Guiren. Nine thousand and something years old and no one to teach him anything important at all.

"To the right," called Zhu Guiren from where he ran behind her as they came to a fork in the road.

She ran in that direction. The flooding now was quite serious, and after a while she was wading to her knees even in the higher ground next to the roadway.

Suddenly, she saw a body lying in the water in front of her — the body of a child. She sloshed over to it to turn it face-up, but her hand passed through, tingling, and then she could hear the screams. She stood still.

"We're here," she said to Zhu Guiren without turning around. Beneath the cries and the metal and the weeping and wailing of women, she could hear him wading up next to her.

"What do you see?" he asked.

"It's a village. Bandits. The men are already dead. The women—" She covered her eyes.

"Ah," he said calmly.

The water on the ground of the present was not visible when she looked at the people dying, just a film laid over reality, though which was the film and which was reality, she couldn't quite tell anymore.

Aili put her hand over her mouth. "The children," she said.

He nodded. "These weren't really bandits," he said. "It was a splinter group from a foray by the Emperor's forces to punish an upstart general who was trying to govern this territory separately. They had been given orders to take no prisoners, although as things were going, those orders weren't even necessary. It had become common practice."

"Who gave them those orders?" she asked quietly.

He didn't respond.

"Why do I see them?" she asked. "You don't see them. No one else sees them. Why do I?"

"I've given it some thought," he said.

His calmness disgusted her, but of course he couldn't see; all he was looking at was muddy water in a field, she had to remind herself. But he knew it. He knew what had happened. How could he be like this? She continued to watch the slaughter and rape of the women and children.

"Truthfully, I can't completely explain what has happened to you — the combination of the array and Liu Chenguang's binding. But you are a mortal soul caught in the array. I think you can see these things because they are connected to you. You are also part of this reality, though not completely, since you're alive."

"I saw Nora and others after they died," she said. "They weren't in an array."

"You must have been connected to them in some way," he replied. "Certainly there has to be some limiting factor, otherwise you'd be wading through ghosts every moment."

She nodded. "The attackers have disappeared," she reported after another hour of watching the horror. "There's only corpses now. So soon—" She started forward.

"What?" he asked.

"Chenguang," she said, her heart in her mouth.

She walked forward, the muddy water around her knees, but not feeling it. Liu Chenguang was there, moving among the corpses, bending down to check each one.

The scholar's robe he wore had only a gourd at its sash; he hadn't yet been given the jade ornament. It was before they had found each other again, before Hong Deming had met him that night in the yard of the Delicate Orchid. His eyes were sad but calm as he knelt next to a woman and closed her eyes.

Aili called, "Chenguang, Chenguang," tears falling down her face. It was so good to see him again.

"Aili," Zhu Guiren said. "Aili. Liu Chenguang can't hear you. He's not dead. His soul isn't here. This is just an echo of him in the event."

She had reached him, reached out to touch him. He ignored her and stood up, turning to look in another direction.

"Teacher Zhu," he called, "there are no survivors." His hair was falling forward over one shoulder and he pushed it back, annoyed.

Aili reached out shaking to touch his hair; he didn't have a pincrown yet. "Chenguang," she said, "Chenguang, it's me." He didn't look very different; Liu Chenguang male or female was very much the same person — small and lightly made, the beautiful eyes shining even through his sadness at all the death around him. She tried to touch his hair again, but her hand moved through his body. He didn't see her or feel her or hear her. He was not truly even a ghost.

The corpses around them lay still. Liu Chenguang stepped over them, going back over to another person: Zhu Guiren in his traveling robes; Zhu Guiren with two hands and a cold, haughty expression.

"I didn't think there would be," he said. "Go back to our camp. I will follow you in a few minutes, after I examine the field to report to the Emperor's forces."

Liu Chenguang bowed, and as he walked past the last corpse before the edge of the field, he disappeared.

Zhu Guiren watched him go. Aili clenched her fists and found that a phoenix whip had appeared in one of them.

The ancient Zhu Guiren walked to a spot near the center of the field.

"What's happening?" asked the Zhu Guiren who had come with her.

She restrained herself from lashing out with the whip at him, but it was difficult, very difficult. "You're here," she said. She forced herself to walk away from him, to not kill him, fighting the image in her mind — striking him down, avenging Liu Chenguang and the obscenity he had made of Liu Chenguang's trust, his healing lifeblood.

He didn't respond. Aili walked out to the center of the field to meet the other Zhu Guiren, who had taken a small container out of his sleeve and began to pour a dark liquid out onto the ground, chanting.

Aili knelt and placed her hands beneath that stream of blood, feeling its heat like the tears on her cheeks, calling the phoenix fire. "Eftahede," she whispered.

She woke up feeling that she was being bumped around quite a bit. "Put me down," she said.

Zhu Guiren carefully set her down on the ground. "You've been out for about twelve hours," he said. "It's nighttime now. There was no good place to rest near where you did it, so I've just been carrying you back toward Shi'an. We should get there in the early evening tomorrow, but truthfully, I need to sleep a bit if you can keep watch."

She nodded. "No demons came?"

"No," he said. "This is a clear advantage of having you do this. You're just a mortal and your presence isn't alerting them. We should have you do it as much as we can manage in the future. Assuming it's not damaging you?"

"I don't think so. When we get back Liu Chenguang can check," she said wearily. "It's just a lot of power, I think."

He nodded.

"You?"

He didn't respond.

Zhu Guiren held his body as straight as he could as he walked into the inn's courtyard, not wanting to let anyone see how much pain he was in. This was something he was quite good at; Aili had had no idea all the way back.

But Tainu came directly up to him and said, "What's wrong? How is it?" then reached immediately for his arm to check his meridians.

"I'm fine," he said, pushing his hand away. "Is that all you ever have to say to me when you see me?"

Tainu looked down at him from his slightly greater height and said, "Yes. Under the circumstances, that goddamn well is what I have to say to you. Sit the hell down."

Zhu Guiren sat down.

Tainu silently checked his pulse, then moved his hand over his abdomen.

"Are you angry?" he asked.

"Can't you tell?" Tainu's eyes were narrowed, and the movements of his hands over Zhu Guiren's body were jerky and sharp. "Yes, I'm angry. You went by yourself. With Aili. You knew she would see Liu Chenguang. You experimented to see if she would attack you–"

He nodded.

"You didn't ask me, you didn't bring me…" He took a deep breath. "The damage is severe. Not as bad as last time. But still."

Zhu Guiren nodded again. Tainu was kneeling next to him to check his meridians, and Zhu Guiren was stunned to see that there were tears in his eyes. "Tainu?" he asked, uncertainly.

Tainu got up, turned around, and walked away.

Zhu Guiren followed him inside. Liu Chenguang and Aili were over in the other part of the yard, holding each other and talking. Shouldn't they also be doing that? He was in so much pain that he couldn't think very clearly, but he knew he didn't want Tainu to yell at him; he didn't want to be angry with Tainu either. "Tainu–"

"Shut up." Tainu went into his room and shut the door.

Zhu Guiren pushed the door open and followed him. "Tainu, I'm sorry–"

"For which thing?" Tainu asked, turning around to face him. "For throwing yourself on top of me and then just leaving me there? For telling me I don't love you? Telling me not to touch you anymore? Or for running away and getting yourself hurt, or for not talking to me about what you're doing, or that you're risking your life and not letting anyone know? Which of those things are you sorry for right now?" His voice had gotten louder and louder, and by the end of it he was shouting.

"All of it," he said, shaken. "I'm sorry for all of it."

Tainu shook his head and fell silent, sitting on the bed.

Zhu Guiren sat next to him, heavily.

"You're in pain," Tainu said at last. "Do you want me to try to do something for you?"

"Not yet," he said.

"Why, do you enjoy being in pain?" Tainu pushed his shoulders down to make him lie flat. "Let me do it. It needs to be done before the damage spreads."

"Wait." Zhu Guiren grabbed his hand and tried to put his thoughts in order. "I wanted to tell you I'm sorry," he said finally, unable to remember anything else he wanted to say. "I'm sorry." Then, he remembered. "I don't want to just always be healed by you. That's not why I love you. That's not what I want."

"You've made that pretty clear," said Tainu, and put his hand against his side, murmuring as he began the healing.

Zhu Guiren heard him say his true name, and that made him feel warm, though the qi hurt him.

He winced, and Tainu said, "Sorry, I have to…" He removed his hand and sighed. "Not as bad as last time."

"Do you love me?" Zhu Guiren asked.

"*Yes,*" Tainu said. "For the love of heaven, how many times do I have to say it? How many ways?"

Tainu leaned over to him and kissed him, fierce and rough, jolting him inwardly so he gasped, trying to follow Tainu's lips as he pulled away.

"There, is that good enough, do you believe me now?"

Zhu Guiren just looked at him. "I'm sorry," he said again. "I'm an idiot."

"You are," Tainu said. "You are my idiot, and I am yours."

He reached his hand up to tug Tainu down to lie next to him; his face was still stained with tears, though he wasn't crying anymore, and Zhu Guiren laid his single hand on his cheek. Tainu just looked at him.

Zhu Guiren said, "Your eyes are so beautiful. I could look at your eyes forever." When Tainu still didn't speak, he said, out of bone-deep weariness and an inability to say anything that wasn't completely true, "I want to make you happy."

Tainu covered his hand with his own, turned his face to kiss it, and said, "Shhh. Go to sleep."

When he woke again, it was still dark, and Tainu was gently shaking him. "Demon," he whispered softly in his ear, "we need to go. Don't make a light, don't make a noise. There's a Kunorese patrol talking to the innkeeper. They're here to arrest Liu Chenguang. The bookstore owner that sold her maps has been taken into custody already. Liu Chenguang and Aili have already gone. They have all the maps and Liu Chenguang's fighting materials and medicines. We're going to split up and find each other later. Into the mountains at first. We need to go now."

Zhu Guiren sat up. "You should have woken me sooner," he whispered. "You transform now. Go, I'll go on my own."

"No—"

"Fly above me if you're worried," he said shortly. This was not the first time he had awakened and immediately needed to run for his life, but it was more dangerous now; he knew he wasn't as strong as he'd been, and he had a phoenix to worry about. "Go."

Tainu transformed and flew out the window. Zhu Guiren shook himself so his limbs felt loose and ready and threw himself out as well with a flip for momentum, leaping up to the courtyard wall and over it with his qinggong, then running toward the mountain. Shouts in Kunorese and Daxian came from behind him.

Just as he had reached the edge of the road, ready to move for the cliffs, he heard a gunshot behind him and felt a hot pain in his shoulder. He coughed a little bit, but kept going; Tainu would heal him. It would be fine. It was nothing to a demonic wound—

There was a second gunshot, and he felt it smash through his side where his internal cultivational structure had been nearly destroyed. He fell to his knees, putting his hand on the wound. It was very surprising. This must be how it felt to mortals to take a wound, to have their flesh torn and destroyed, unsupported by the strength of the spiritual body. Truly, it was more painful than he had thought it would be.

Then Zhu Guiren slowly toppled over, bleeding onto the dirt and mud of the road to Mount Shi.

# CHAPTER 13
## ESCAPE

ZHU GUIREN WOKE up not dead. The gunshot wounds in his shoulder and side were healed. These were the good things.

The less good things were that he was in a cell, tied to a chair, freezing, aching, and tired.

The good thing, again, was that these bad things had been done to him by mortals, not demons, so he would be able to leave more or less at will, at which point he expected to more or less demolish this place entirely, because he was not pleased.

The bad thing was that since he wasn't dead, and his wounds were healed, Tainu must have come down to heal him when he was shot. There had been guns and people very close to him when he collapsed. He couldn't imagine how Tainu could have gotten to him without getting seriously injured or captured, or both.

There was someone else in the cell with him; he spoke in Kunorese, asking where the Federative woman had gone. Zhu Guiren pretended he couldn't understand it.

A Daxian man entered and smiled at him pleasantly. Things immediately became much worse. This man was a demon, though luckily not one from his own clan; he might try to destroy him, but he wouldn't be carrying First's punishment talisman.

The demon spoke in Daxian. "We have already interrogated the innkeeper.

The Kunorese want to know where the blonde Federative woman and her Daxian assistant have gone, what your plans were, all such things." He smiled again and continued, "And other parties would like to know where the second phoenix is. The first one, we have."

Zhu Guiren said, "Make up whatever you want to tell him. I have no idea and no interest in these games." He kept his expression fixed and showed no concern, but his heart plummeted and his skin crawled. *Tainu.*

The man bowed and said, "I should introduce myself. I am Third of my clan. You and I are clearly destined to meet. The First of your clan is looking for you, we have heard. Perhaps you would like to challenge our Fourth and join ours instead? We are not allied to your clan and our First and Second have extended an invitation to you."

"If I was interested," he replied calmly, "I would of course challenge you. Why would I want to be Fourth?"

The demon bowed again. "That could be considered, but since I would kill you, my clan would not benefit from your joining us in that case. Challenging our Fourth is better, in my opinion, but the decision would belong to my clan leaders if you wish to make this request?"

"Why are your clan leaders extending this invitation?"

"It's not for me to ask." He raised his eyebrows. "Surely your First and Second don't share their thoughts with you? If so, no wonder your clan is such a disaster. I've heard that you've killed twelve of your own high-ranking clansfolk since returning to Daxian. For myself, I would keep you far away from us, but the choice isn't mine." He smiled, and turned to the Kunorese officer to translate something that would excuse the length of their exchange.

Zhu Guiren fell into the rhythms of thought that had kept him alive for nine thousand years. His near panic about Tainu disappeared, as though he had cut it off. He would kill this demon at the first opportunity. He would then find and take the phoenix, because the phoenix was his and no one took what was his. The first thing, before killing the other demon, would be to find where Tainu was held. The demon didn't know the phoenix's true name; a thread of worry came back, as he remembered there were others who did, that Liu Chenguang might be looking for him as well. He let that go. He breathed deeply and considered. The Kunorese thought Tainu was a Federative spy, thus he must have appeared in his human form rather than his bird form. This demon clan was pretending to work with the Kunorese, so the phoenix was likely held in an ordinary cell, but in order to hold him and ensure he didn't transform they would have had to place a strong demonic shackle on him, or else be bleeding him continually. It occurred to him that the phoenix might be undergoing interrogation already, and that this would be painful. This made him angry.

"Make the request of your clan leaders," he said suddenly. "I require an answer within twenty minutes. Otherwise, I will simply kill you, but will not join your clan afterward and the phoenix goes with me."

The Daxian man broke off his interchange with the Kunorese officer, nodded briefly to him, and said, "I am confirming the offer you are making: if you kill me, you will join our clan and will bring the phoenix voluntarily?"

Zhu Guiren nodded.

"And if I kill you," the other demon said comfortably, "we will take the phoenix, and I'll have had an entertaining hour or so. It's boring here." To the guard, the demon said, "He says that he needs a map to think about where the Federative woman has gone. I will go get one," and he bowed and left the cell.

The Kunorese officer remained, staring at him. Zhu Guiren considered his options, then decided to muddy the waters. In Kunorese, he said, "That man was lying to you."

The officer jumped. "What? What did you say?"

Zhu Guiren made his voice small and frightened. Hopefully the man wouldn't be alerted by the change in tone. "I didn't want to speak to you before. I didn't want the Daxian here to know I speak Kunorese, because some of them are spies. They kill people like me. My mother was Kunorese. My father brought me to Zhaishou when I was a child during the first glorious conquest." His mind quickly flashed back through the recent history Liu Chenguang had explained to him. "I didn't tell him what I knew. I tested him by telling him something that was true to see if he would tell you, but he didn't. I never asked him for maps. I told him that the Federative woman was from Zhaishou. He's a spy. Please save me from him. I was tricked by the Federative woman, she came to Zhaishou and hired me as an interpreter, that's all I know!"

"Our intelligence tells us the Federative woman speaks fluent Daxian," the man said. "Why would she need an interpreter?"

"I don't know! I don't know!" He cowered in the chair as though afraid of being hit. "I know she could speak Daxian, but she wanted me anyway. I don't understand her plans. The other Daxian woman too — she was just a servant. She was sent out to the market to buy things, but she didn't understand why. But the Federative man, he's the one that really knew everything."

The man said, "Tell me more." He shouted behind him for someone else to come. "If your information is accurate, we'll consider helping you to return to Kunoru."

"Thank you! Thank you!" He attempted to bow in the ropes. "You can see my hand," he said, "the Federative man is the one who healed it. He's a doctor of some kind, but he's here for other reasons. They go out in the countryside to look for things. I don't understand what."

A second Kunorese officer arrived, and they conferred just outside the door; he couldn't quite understand what they were saying. Time was getting short. If the other demon returned first, it was back to the original plan, but if this one worked, he could get the phoenix before fighting instead of after. That would be better.

As though he was suddenly seized by inspiration, he shouted, "I know! They must be going out into the countryside to make contact with the guerrillas! They must know where to meet with them, how to send messages to them! That's why that man lied to you. I knew it!"

The two Kunorese remained in the corridor, looking at him contemptuously, but as he hoped, they were unconsciously encouraged by his shouting to speak just slightly more loudly —still whispering, but his ears could catch it now. He closed his eyes to concentrate better.

One of them muttered, "Traitorous scum. Why would you trust anything that comes out of his mouth?"

The other replied under his breath, "He's the least valuable, but also the weakest. It doesn't hurt to check the story. It's the Federatives we need, but catching rebels is also a mandate if we can get information on that as well. He does speak Kunorese fluently. That's something unusual."

"Where's the one that was caught with him, the Federative man? We should see if we can test any of this with him before acting on it."

"The lowest floor. The commander is observing the interrogation."

That was enough to go on, and time was running short. Zhu Guiren smiled and twisted his wrist to call his sword of ice and smoke.

He ran down the corridor lightly and without anxiety. The two Kunorese officers and several other people that crossed his path were dead. He had not needed to use the sword for this; he disdained using a demonic weapon on mortals, and in any case, it was not necessary. His hand and his feet were more than enough.

He heard a delighted laugh from behind him and the other demon leapt and flipped over his head to face him.

"Finally," the other man said, his black eyes glinting. "*So* boring here."

Zhu Guiren said, "Do you really think you're qualified?"

"My clan leaders have permitted you to challenge me," he said. "If you kill me, you'll need to go to my clan, or else my own clan leaders will hunt you down for breaking your contract with them."

"What contract?" He called his halberd. "I have no contract with you. You're ten minutes late."

The other demon leapt for him, and Zhu Guiren jumped aside.

"That's your own fault. You weren't in the room anymore when I came back," the other demon said conversationally.

"Don't blame me for your failures. There is no contract. I'll kill you because I feel like it."

Two mortals came running around the corner; they were caught in the crossing waves of weapon energy and qi and more or less exploded into blood and flesh. The other demon laughed. Zhu Guiren threw a talisman at him, but he dodged.

This was wasting time. The other demon was Third in his own clan. He might be close enough to Zhu Guiren's normal level to delay him only slightly under normal circumstances, but he was not currently at his own full strength. He would need to hide this; he couldn't afford a drawn out fight that would display his weaknesses. The other demon held a sword and a close combat weapon he was unfamiliar with — a circle of metal with razored blades on one side. He himself could only hold one weapon at a time; with that bladed circle, close combat would not be to his advantage, and he could no longer use a bow and arrow.

As always when fighting, his mind was extremely clear and focused. While switching between spear and halberd to keep the combat at a distance, he considered what ranged weapons he could still use with one hand. He didn't even consider lowering himself to use a gun; that was far beneath any self-respecting demon. He could only think of the spear thrower, a weapon so ancient that even he could barely remember when it had still been in regular use, but he had once been quite good with it.

He threw a talisman in the air and switched to spear thrower, casting a spear of demonic qi so quickly that the spear impaled the talisman on its way to the other demon. Spear throwers were fast; it caught him in the throat. The combination of the talisman and weapon strike disabled him enough that Zhu Guiren was able to leap over and decapitate him. He laughed watching the blood spill out. What an arrogant fool. Who would want to join a clan that had that travesty as Third? His clan leaders were well rid of him.

Two more appeared around the corner. Demons, not mortals. One of them opened their mouth to say something to him. Lest it be something along the lines of honoring that dubious contract, he took one out with the spear thrower as well, then disemboweled the other one with his halberd.

And then he took *another* gunshot, this one luckily to his back, which was still protected by his demonic cultivation system. It hurt nonetheless. He turned and ran toward the unlucky mortal at the other end of the corridor, who trembled but aimed again. He released his sword and took the man by the throat just as the man shot him at close range, also in the throat. Luckily, the bullet missed his jugular, his brain, and his spinal cord, any of which would have been quite serious, even for him. He coughed and spat blood in the man's face.

"Where?" he said in Kunorese. "Prisoner. Federative. Show me."

The man nodded, eyes wide with terror. "The stairs. That way, three floors down."

Zhu Guiren noticed that he had pissed himself. *Disgusting.* He threw the man against the wall, which most likely killed him, and then ran for the stairs. He was bleeding heavily now; he needed his phoenix. His phoenix — no one else's. If there was anyone hurting his phoenix, he would kill them. The phoenix was only his.

The stairs were behind a locked door, which he blasted to smithereens. He didn't hear anything. Would he hear anything? That sense of anxiety started to return whenever he thought of Tainu being hurt, so he immediately stopped thinking of him and systematically began to check doors. He needed a phoenix to heal him. That was all. There was a phoenix here that he would find.

Behind one of the doors, he smelled blood and heard someone speaking in Anglish. There were several people behind the door. Because the phoenix might be there, he didn't destroy the door, but simply killed the two mortal guards outside. They screamed, and someone helpfully opened the door for him.

Tainu was shackled to a chair. One of the shackles was a demonic ward, the difference from the others visible to him, though the mortals wouldn't be able to see it. They had surely searched him, but not stripped him; he was still wearing what he had worn when they went to sleep the night before, his loose pants and shirt torn and bloody. He was not unconscious, but very close to it, and hadn't been disabled yet, though there was a great deal of his blood on the floor. His wounds were still healing very quickly, but they had injured him severely enough at some point that he didn't seem to realize Zhu Guiren was there.

Zhu Guiren felt as though something had struck him in the heart — so strongly that he actually looked down to see if he was wounded — but no, there was nothing, except seeing Tainu like that. He put it out of his mind. It was a distraction. He needed to focus.

"Hello, my dear," said a woman's voice in Anglish. "How nice to see you, Third."

Zhu Guiren froze, then turned and bowed. "Second," he said.

"Kill the mortals," she said.

He immediately released his sword and leapt to strike them one by one with his hand, so quickly that they were dead before they fell to the floor.

"Very good," she said. "Little Third, I take it this is your phoenix?"

"It is."

Second looked at him, smiling. He knew this middle-aged Daxian woman with a kind face was not the true appearance of her mortal body; First and Second rarely walked in the world without an illusion enchantment. In fact, they almost never left clan home at all.

"You're surprised to see me here," she said. "We're all out enjoying the banquet, of course, and all the entertainment that goes with it. I heard they had captured you. I had intended to come retrieve you myself from those insolent yokels when I was done here, but I see that you've saved me the trouble. Did they ask you to defect?"

He bowed in acknowledgment.

"Well," she said, turning back to Tainu, "I was only staying here to ensure that our new phoenix is well cared for. The other clan had at least put a shackle on him, but look how they've treated him, the idiots." She made a *tsk*ing noise. "I killed the mortal interpreter and took her appearance an hour or so ago so I could intervene. What a waste of phoenix blood…Look at it, all over the floor."

She walked over to Tainu and slapped his face. Zhu Guiren felt his fist clench at his side.

As though knowing what he was feeling, as almost certainly she did, Second whirled and threw a punishment talisman at him. It brushed his shoulder as he dodged, which was all it needed to do to start its work. He shuddered as the cold began to work its way through his meridians.

"Why have you ignored our summons?" Second asked. She simply dodged his attacks as he went for her with his entire range of weapons; she was incredibly fast as well as strong. "I don't want to hurt you, dear. You just need to come home and reflect a bit on your choices. We have the phoenix now. All will be well."

He could feel himself slowing. Before he could lose the power to do it, he slashed each of the mortal shackles on the phoenix, then slicked the demonic shackle with his own blood and began chanting.

Second laughed. "Really, dear! What good will that do anyone?" She threw a demonic talisman. Not at him, but at the phoenix; the phoenix screamed in pain, and the sound drove Zhu Guiren nearly out of his mind.

He attacked in a frenzy, coming at Second's face again and again using his sword — his favorite weapon. She had stopped smiling, and had finally called her own preferred weapon, a saber.

The phoenix was free. His chant had worked. He hadn't been sure it would since his own power was so diminished. Luckily, it hadn't been Second who set the shackle herself; he wouldn't have been able to break it.

"Go!" he heard himself yell. Why had he done that? Didn't he need the phoenix to stay with him, to heal him?

But instead, he shouted, "Get away!" and drove Second back from the phoenix so she couldn't hurt him.

Second hissed and threw another talisman.

He jumped in front of it so it couldn't hit the phoenix, but it was strong. Very strong. He fell down to one knee, choking on his own blood. The talisman had opened all the recent wounds in his body — the gunshot wounds in his side and throat particularly — and blood poured out everywhere.

The phoenix hadn't left. The phoenix stood behind him, putting his own blood on the wounds and saying something he couldn't understand. He turned. The phoenix seemed upset.

"Go away," Zhu Guiren said, and fell over.

Second ran toward the phoenix, another shackle in her hand, chanting the spell as she leaped toward him.

The phoenix took something out of his ragged clothing, something folded very small, and slapped it hard on her forehead. A bright white-gold light exploded silently in the room.

Second screamed as the talisman burned into her skin and hair. The false appearance collapsed into ashes and her mortal body showed: a tall, black-haired woman with deep blue eyes. Her golden skin was blistering and running, bleeding and burning, and she screamed again. She threw one last qi javelin and fled.

Zhu Guiren felt the phoenix roll him onto his back and continue applying blood to his wounds. He was talking feverishly. Zhu Guiren realized that the phoenix was crying. "Don't die," the phoenix was saying. "Don't, please, stay with me, don't go."

"Won't go," he said. "Not dying."

The phoenix laughed a little. Tainu laughed. He remembered now. All the terror he felt for him, all the rage at how he had been hurt, came back at once.

Zhu Guiren closed his eyes and shoved it back down. He couldn't afford this; they still had to get out. Tainu bent over and kissed him with his blood-stained lips, and he kept his eyes closed to feel Tainu's tongue flicker inside, a quick caress. He let Tainu's lips stay on his just for a moment.

"My shoulder," he said, as soon as his mind had recovered enough to start working again. "Punishment talisman."

Tainu used Zhu Guiren's sword to cut off the shirt — it wasn't worth saving anyway, just bloody rags now — and Zhu Guiren saw his face turn very serious as he laid his hand on the talisman mark. "Bad," was all he said before he closed his eyes to concentrate.

"Ah," said Zhu Guiren as heat poured into his body from Tainu's hand, clearing the bitter cold of the punishment talisman from his meridians and warming all the places that were hurt and aching that he hadn't even known about. When he opened his eyes again, his mind felt clear and his body was able to move. "Help me up."

Tainu pulled him upright, then to his feet. Zhu Guiren looked at him silently. There were no marks on him. Not anymore.

Tainu said, "I know you're angry at me. Can you tell me about it later?"

"I'm not angry. Not at you, anyway." He looked at the carnage in the room. "Can you transform?"

Tainu shook his head. "Not yet. That punishment talisman is very hard to deal with. I don't have much left. I need time to recover." He didn't say anything about all his blood on the floor from whatever they had done to him before Zhu Guiren arrived.

"All right," Zhu Guiren said. "There are at least two clans of demons here, one of them mine, in addition to the mortals. The mortals aren't a problem except for the guns, and the guns aren't a problem as long as I have you. And you are staying with me unless I tell you to run. You have to do exactly what I tell you, when I tell you to do it."

Tainu nodded.

He tried to think. "How long till you can transform?" He could carry Tainu if necessary, but not endless distances. "Once we're out, will you be able to fly?"

"I don't know," Tainu said. "It's not good for me, right now." He was swaying where he stood, as though his balance was affected.

"Damn." He no longer had time for nuanced decisions. "All right, just follow me as fast as you can. Warn me if you're falling behind or need to be carried. I can't always be watching." He called his sword and ran for the door. Tainu followed.

Zhu Guiren didn't bother trying to get out at ground level; instead, he ran up the stairs to the top floor of the three story building, killing all along the way. He looked out the window and realized that they had been taken to the south of Shi'an — the side of the city farthest from the mountains — and shook his head. "We should run west into the countryside first. We'll be caught if we try to circle Shi'an for the mountains from here. If we can get away, we can cross the river and circle back toward Hongye from the other side. Although Hongye is also Kunorese territory…" He gave it up. One thing at a time.

Tainu nodded. "Demon, I'm sorry. I'm keeping you here."

"Shh," he said absently, thinking. Well, it was what it was, though not ideal. "Get on my back. I'll take you down with qinggong through the streets, then you'll need to get off and start running with me."

Tainu nodded, looking determined, and put his arms around Zhu Guiren's neck to be carried.

"Hold on," Zhu Guiren said, grimacing a little. Tainu outweighed him, and of course he had the strength to carry him, but it wasn't something he could do without effort. He considered his path, then jumped out the window toward a neighboring rooftop and began running along it.

The yao of nighttime Shi'an scattered before him as he raced and leapt down and down, holding Tainu, focusing on the next step, the next jump, where to cross to avoid patrols, how to get out without using a guarded gate. Finally, he reached the ground to the southwest of the city and began racing forward to use as much of his momentum as possible before he needed to stop. They would hit the flooded areas soon; he had no idea what they would do then, but they needed to find somewhere safe and hidden where no one would look for them. They would need to rest, and he would need to cultivate. He would need it desperately if he was going to get them through this.

He let Tainu off and ran with him for a while, both of them slowing more and more with exhaustion. They waded through the empty, flooded fields in the dark until they found themselves on a low, wooded rise. There was a little house, mostly ruined, completely empty. It didn't seem to be a farmhouse. Belatedly, Zhu Guiren realized it was an old shrine. At least it had a roof.

He went inside and fell down. "What god is it?" he asked, rolling over on his back. There was still a very faint scent of incense along with mildew.

Tainu said, "There's no knowing now. It's all long gone. Just an altar cloth." He bowed before the altar and then went out.

"Tainu?"

He came back carrying an armful of small branches with dried leaves. "I'll make something to be a bed," he said. "You rest. We can't risk a fire here."

Zhu Guiren said, "I'll help you. You need rest as much as I do."

Together they piled up the branches and leaves, then Tainu went outside and brought back some long grass from the edge of the flooded area to soften it.

He bowed again and took the altar cloth. "We're going to freeze otherwise," he explained. "We both barely have clothes at this point."

Zhu Guiren shook his head. "I can keep us warm," he said sleepily, then realized what that sounded like and immediately amended it. "With qi. That's what I meant."

Tainu laughed and laid down next to him. "Keep us warm, then, demon," he said, spreading the altar cloth over them.

Zhu Guiren pulled him closer into his arms, wanting to feel that he was really there, but didn't say anything. He didn't know what to say. Falling back into the demonic world had made him feel very strange. Which was real? The blood and hatred, or this person and the months they had spent together, talking and laughing? Had that been the dream?

He could feel Tainu's eyes on him. It was so very dark that everything was by touch, or by guess: the warmth and weight of Tainu's body, his breathing and heartbeat, only an occasional glint of his eyes, a line of his face. The darkness made everything important — every little thing that he could glean of him, Tainu's warm, quiet voice when finally he spoke.

"That was one of your clan leaders?"

Zhu Guiren nodded.

Tainu reached out, fingers gently stroking his face. "Can I tell you something?"

"Yes," he said.

"I looked for you."

"What do you mean?" He frowned, then felt Tainu trace the fold between his eyebrows.

"You always frown when you're thinking hard."

"What do you mean, you looked for me?"

"After you set me free from that terrible place I found you," Tainu said. "I wanted to tell you this a long time ago, but I didn't know how. I was so young, I told you. That was my first rebirth, I didn't even know what had happened to me before I was in a child's body again, shackled to the stone couch and tortured every day for however many years it was."

Zhu Guiren closed his eyes; it didn't matter in the dark, but he couldn't bear to know. "Don't tell me this," he said.

"You have to know this," Tainu insisted, "because I met you there, and you were so beautiful to me. You were brave and kind and strong. Your heart was so innocent and you were so full of life and joy and everything about you was beautiful. And I loved you. Even then, I loved you."

Zhu Guiren felt his eyes grow hot. "I don't remember it," he said. "They took that from me."

"You were the best memory for me in that worst time. Your heart was so beautiful to me. I never forgot. You were so brave. You took such a risk for me — to set me free." Tainu leaned closer and kissed his lips, gently. "I have never regretted anything in my life as much as not being able to bring you with me. You stayed behind. To accept punishment. Can you forgive me?"

"I don't remember it," Zhu Guiren said, honestly, "but if I chose to stay, that was my choice."

"I looked for you. As soon as I was able. I established the first few refuges, and then I started looking. I went back to the clan home where I had been held, where you had freed me, but you weren't there. I looked and looked."

"How long?" he asked. "How long did you look?" It felt important to know.

Tainu caressed his face again. "I never stopped looking. I always hoped I would find you. I went all over the world, in the spirit world too. And about a thousand years ago, I started finding traces in North Daxian. A demon hiding among mortals, someone who loved to learn things, and study the stars."

Zhu Guiren's heart pounded hard. "Don't say it. Don't say it," he whispered.

"I went to Crane Moon," he said softly, "and I found you at last, torturing my little sibling."

Zhu Guiren flinched. The branches beneath him crackled.

"I didn't want it to be you, but I knew that it was. I would never not recognize you. Even when I didn't want to. Even when I wished so much that I had never found you." After some silence, he continued, "I helped Hong Deming get Liu Chenguang away from you. Did you know it was me?"

Zhu Guiren shook his head slowly. "I didn't know you were there."

"Would it have mattered if you knew?"

"No." This was the truth. It would not have mattered. It would not have stopped him.

"You chased them and persecuted them, engineered Hong Deming's death. You destroyed the life they could have had together. Then you...you cut my sibling into pieces."

"You were there." Suddenly, as he never had before, he felt shame. That Tainu had seen him, seen him doing that...

"I was there."

Zhu Guiren was silent. His heart was silent and despairing. "Tainu," he said at last, but he couldn't say anything else.

"And all this time since…Liu Chenguang." Tainu took a deep breath. "I followed you afterward, to see what you would do."

"And what did you see me do?" Zhu Guiren asked, his heart empty because he knew.

"I saw you go where the suffering was and cultivate from it," Tainu said bluntly. "You followed the Mitang invasion to the west. You followed the Imperial conquest of the southern continents. You were in the Common Federation for the past three centuries."

"Yes," he whispered. "That's where I was. That's what I did." He had been a crow following the path of carrion and cruelty and death, eager to feed on anything that suffered.

Tainu had seen him, all those centuries.

Tainu was still here, still looking at his face in the darkness. He knew because his cold fingers suddenly felt warmth, Tainu's fingers, interlacing with his. "Arciniang, it's all right," he said softly. "You always want to know why I won't call you by the name everyone else calls you…I don't call you Zhu Guiren because I don't think you are really Zhu Guiren anymore. To me, that name is a thousand years old, and I don't think you are the person that I watched do those things a thousand years ago."

Zhu Guiren looked at him. "How can you know that?" he asked, at last.

Tainu said, "Arciniang, I know…I know that you haven't built an array since this one. You have not made anything worse in the world. You haven't caused anything that wasn't already happening. I saw you try, sometimes. To be kind. I know that you wish you hadn't done this."

"If I hadn't done this," he said, "I'd be dead."

"But you still wish you hadn't done it."

"Yes," Zhu Guiren said. "But wishing doesn't change what I've done."

Tainu said, softly, "I love you, Arciniang."

Zhu Guiren felt something he still had no name for — a warmth and a desire and a pain — inside him. He bent his head to Tainu's face, finding him in the dark. "Tainu. I want to kiss you. Can I kiss you?"

"Yes."

He leaned over and put his arms around him, feeling him come closer, the leaves and branches underneath crackling under their weight. "I need you so much," Zhu Guiren said helplessly, "I don't even understand what this is. Do you understand it?"

Tainu lay on his side with one leg thrown over him. His hand gently traced the lines of his jaw, his throat, his shoulders, as though he was curious to explore his body even though he had touched it so many times to heal so many wounds.

"Tainu, I want you to kiss me," Zhu Guiren said again. "I want you to touch me. Do you want to?"

Tainu closed his eyes and whispered, "Yes, I want to. I'm just so afraid."

He was tired but still strong enough for this — to pull Tainu closer and press him into the leaves and branches, feeling the shape of him in the dark, stroking him, kissing his mouth and his throat, feeling his heart begin to race and his breath to quicken. He heard himself say, "Don't ever be afraid, not of me. I will always love you. I will always keep you safe. I want you to be happy with me, always. Always."

He kissed Tainu's throat so hard that it almost became a bite; Tainu gasped and pulled him closer, entwining their bodies against one another to reach him better, touch him more intimately.

Zhu Guiren said fiercely, "You're mine. No one else can touch you."

Tainu laughed softly, which was the best sound in the world.

"Yes," Tainu said. He traced Zhu Guiren's lips with his fingers, softly pressing in to touch his teeth and tongue.

Zhu Guiren caught his fingers in his mouth and teased them with his tongue, delighting in how Tainu cried out softly and arched his body to press hard against him. He shivered, at the edge of a deep need in himself, uncontrollable as gravity when he would let it take him.

"I want you," Tainu said. "I want you to be the one who touches me." His beloved one began kissing his mouth again, deeply, longingly.

Breathing hard and fast, Tainu's breath warm against his skin, Zhu Guiren said, "Tell me— Show me how to touch you. I don't know what to do. I want you to like it–"

And so, Tainu did.

# CHAPTER 14
## MORNINGS AFTER

THE NEXT MORNING, Zhu Guiren got out of their makeshift bed and began trying to cultivate. At least he did this after several times of beginning to get out of bed and then changing his mind because there were very important things to do in bed, so it was really lunchtime by the time he got up.

"It's not as though we have food anyway," he protested when Tainu told him this.

Tainu kissed his ear and told him to get up, which was also counterproductive. Then Tainu said, "Fine," and got up first.

He went out to cultivate, so Zhu Guiren followed him.

But he couldn't cultivate.

This was only partly because he was distracted and teasing Tainu. The pain was incredible, and he felt no more than a trickle of resentment flowing in, like ground glass flowing through his eyes. After an hour or so of this, he realized that he must have been making a noise because Tainu came to sit opposite him, looking serious.

"Demon," he said, "let me check you." Tainu ran his hand gently over Zhu Guiren's abdomen — not quite touching him, but close enough so he could feel the warmth of his hand — then closed his eyes and asked, "Can you cultivate while I'm observing?"

"All right."

After a few moments, Tainu said, his eyes still closed, "That is not helping your cultivation."

"But it's helping me with other things."

"Get your lips back where they belong and concentrate."

Zhu Guiren sighed and concentrated.

"Ah," said Tainu. After a while, he said, "Demon, I'm going to try something. Keep cultivating, but put your hand out, palm flat."

Zhu Guiren felt Tainu's hand extend just above his, not actually touching, but close enough to feel the energy of his skin.

Tainu said, "Now keep cultivating. Let me know if you feel something new." Then, after several minutes, "Stop that."

"You realize that you're sitting only a few inches away from me practically naked and holding my hand," he protested.

"Tomorrow, we leave and buy clothes. Concentrate."

Zhu Guiren concentrated. Surprised, he said, "Yes." There was something — something gentle, buffering the pain of the resentment as it flowed into him. As the pain lessened, his meridians were able to accept more and gradually, the trickle increased to a more normal volume.

Tainu carefully removed his hand. "Is it still working?" he asked. His voice was strained.

"Yes." Zhu Guiren stopped cultivating, then began again. "It still works." He opened his eyes. "Tainu?" he asked, concerned. Tainu was swaying where he sat; just in time he leaned over to catch him and hold him upright.

"Did it work? Did you feel it?"

"Yes. What was it?"

"Natural qi, purifying resentment," Tainu said, leaning against him. "Did it hurt you?"

His eyes widened. "No, not at all."

"I thought, since we've been doing…what we've been doing, you might not be so sensitive to pure qi anymore," he said, "so I could try to cultivate with you to strengthen your meridians."

Zhu Guiren kissed him gently. "What exactly have we been doing?"

"Shut up, demon."

"But you're hurt?" Zhu Guiren pulled him closer, so he was sitting in his lap.

"The resentment still hurts me," he said. "I haven't gotten less sensitive to it."

"But it always hurts. That's just how it is."

Tainu stirred. "Always? Every time you cultivate, it feels like that? Like something sharp is tearing you up inside?"

He nodded. "It's probably worse for you because it's new," he said. "When I first learned, it was very intense. I'm used to it now. It's just the injury that's making it hard."

Tainu just looked at him.

"Well," he said defensively, "wasn't it hard when you learned to cultivate?"

"I'm probably not a good example. My whole existence is based in pure qi, but I'm sure if you ask Aili, she'll tell you that it didn't hurt her to learn cultivation as a child."

Zhu Guiren frowned.

Tainu made himself more comfortable in his lap, sitting facing him with his legs wrapped loosely around his hips. Zhu Guiren decided he approved of this, but before he could take advantage of it Tainu spoke in a serious voice: "Arciniang, what will happen when we keep destroying arrays? When we destroy the final array?"

He said, honestly, "I don't know."

Tainu kissed him softly. "Arciniang, if you survive it at all, and I'm not sure you will, your cultivational structure will probably be completely destroyed."

"I've thought of that," he said, reluctantly. He knew that if he admitted this Tainu wouldn't let him go forward. "But I don't…I don't want it anymore, Tainu. I don't want to have an existence that depends on…that."

Tainu nodded, touching their foreheads together. Zhu Guiren said, "Last night you said that I hadn't made anything worse in the world. But I haven't made it better either. You know that. If you have been near me in the past five hundred years I have drunk your suffering too, the suffering of mortals you cared about. I don't want it anymore."

Tainu kissed him and said, "Yes, I know."

Zhu Guiren said, "Tainu. I don't want to benefit from that. I can't…go looking for it. Not anymore."

"But I want you to survive," Tainu said. "I know you don't want it, but I want you to do what you need to do. Promise me."

"I'll do what I need to do," he promised. "Also to protect you. But I want the array to be broken."

Tainu said, shyly, "Let me try something again." He closed his eyes and leaned in to kiss him, keeping one hand on Zhu Guiren's side where the cultivational structure was ruined.

Zhu Guiren gasped. An enormous amount of fiery heat passed through his body. A different kind of burning than the futile, lifeless acid of resentment — like a sun inside him, settling somewhere beyond his ability to feel it, nowhere and everywhere, as intangible as light. He felt Tainu collapse a little bit against him, breathing deeply. Zhu Guiren held him close and asked, "What is it?"

"I did something preventative," Tainu said. "For your meridians, so you will have a better chance of surviving the shock when the array is destroyed. I don't know what will happen with it. But cultivate with me, sometimes. That will strengthen what I've done. Can you try to cultivate natural qi in addition to resentment? Just to see what it feels like?"

"How do I do it?" he asked, frowning.

"Instead of seeking out resentment, seek out joy," he said. "Life, energy, movement, love, desire…It's better if you're in a place full of life, but even here, you could cultivate. There's trees, there's life in the water, the birds are flying…"

"You're here," Zhu Guiren said. "Can I cultivate by seeking out you?"

Tainu smiled, his eyes still closed. "Technically, yes. I am an endless fountain of spiritual energy."

"Excellent," said Zhu Guiren, and kissed him.

Tainu said, "Arciniang, my true name–"

"No," he said, very quickly. "Don't say it."

Tainu opened his eyes, surprised and clearly a little hurt.

Zhu Guiren said, "If I know it, and I'm captured, they will also know it. I won't be able to hide it from them. They'll be able to use it to find you." He put his arms around again and could feel Tainu's disappointment. Encouragingly, he said, "Someday. Someday, you can tell me."

In his heart, he didn't think that day would come; he didn't think he would survive the breaking of the great array, no matter what Tainu did to try to prevent it, but he felt no anxiety about it. All was well. All was *very* well. He kissed Tainu again and lifted him up to carry him back inside.

They really couldn't stay in this place longer than one day; they had no food, largely symbolic clothing, and while mortals would probably lose their path in the floodwaters, pursuing demons would not. Zhu Guiren let Tainu sleep through the afternoon and cultivated. He really couldn't feel anything when he tried to cultivate natural qi, but was successful in cultivating resentment, and by sundown, he felt much more confident that he could get them through the next stage. He went back inside and gently shook Tainu awake.

"It's dark," he said softly, "let's go."

Tainu nodded and whispered "Liu Chenguang has left the mountains. I think they are worried, and coming to find us. If we head northeast, we'll intersect them sometime in the next few days. From there, we can cross the Sorrowful River. You're sure the final array is there?"

"It's…somewhere," he said, not encouragingly. "The bed of the river has shifted and the topography is all different. We'll have to search. If Aili is with, us that will help. She's tied to it."

The stars came out as they walked, but the sky was cloudy, so the light was very intermittent — glinting off the water everywhere, the same off deceptively deep channels with strong currents and the shared surface of the shallow puddles on the roads. Zhu Guiren began to feel a sense of unreality in the landscape, full of trickery and shadows.

Tainu seemed to feel it as well. "This is a very yin landscape now…"

"Does that mean your powers are weaker?" Zhu Guiren asked, interested. He had always wondered about how things worked, being a phoenix. "Phoenixes are yang energy, aren't they?

"Not exactly. I have yin aspects too," he said. "Every phoenix is different. My yang aspect is stronger, so I need to consciously balance with yin, or I'll burn myself out and be forced to do it."

"I've seen you do that," Zhu Guiren said.

Tainu smiled. "You help me," he said simply. "You help me be more balanced."

Zhu Guiren felt that as a warmth in his heart — that he could be helpful to Tainu.

"I was just thinking about that as we're walking through all of this…Liu Chenguang naturally is more yin than I am. Whether she's in a male or female mortal body, that's just her personality." Tainu smiled fondly. "It's been good to be with her again, these months. We haven't spent this much time together in centuries."

"Why are you thinking about this?" Zhu Guiren asked. He stepped slightly to one side and got wet up to his knees, which didn't matter much as they were both already wet and muddy. "How are we going to get clothes, by the way?"

"You'll have to take care of that part when we get to a town…" After a while, Tainu said, "I was just thinking of the difference between yin and resentment, that's all. Yin energy has associations with death, isn't resentment death also? I was thinking about how it hurts you to cultivate resentment. It doesn't seem right. If it was part of the natural world, like yang and yin, it shouldn't be painful to cultivate."

Zhu Guiren shook his head. "I haven't thought about the pain part, but I've thought about resentment a great deal at times in my life, because I needed to understand how to create it and capture it for my array. The resentment is spiritual, beyond the cycles of the natural world. Resentment is suffering, loss, bitterness…Only spiritual beings produce it. The natural world dies and is reborn without resentment."

He continued, "Spiritual beings — mortals and yao — we produce resentment at death because our spirits long for what we can now never have, for what's been taken from us, for what we left unfinished and unsaid, for the debts owed to us and the debts unpaid, for what we've suffered in life and in dying. At death, our spirits know that there is nothing more we can do. Any failure is final, any loss is irrevocable, any suffering will not be healed, and our spirits release that into the world as the souls go wherever souls go. Or else, if the resentment is obsessive or it's caught in an array, the soul remains as a resentful ghost."

Tainu took his hand.

After they had walked for a while more, Zhu Guiren spoke again. "I spent two hundred years creating the great array by doing all I could to ensure that the suffering of the people was as great as it could be. None of it was by my hand, but all by my design, so that each person who died would produce resentment at the highest possible level. Those I caught in the array — they still feel it. Their descendants belong to me too, drawn into as much resentment as the array can produce in the circumstances of their lives. Every day, they relive it for me, and it feeds into me to strengthen me. I don't even have to cultivate it. It's like my heart pumping blood."

Tainu sighed. "Arciniang–"

"That's why," Zhu Guiren said. He knew Tainu wanted to say something comforting, but there was nothing to say. "That's why I need to destroy it."

Tainu nodded, and they continued to walk in silence through the dark watery land, hand in hand.

They came to a little village after sunrise, still with people in it. Zhu Guiren went in to buy some clothes for them, as well as a blanket and some food; no one commented on the bloodstained clothing he was already wearing. The villagers here had been through much. There were only a few younger men remaining. Most had gone to join the army, willing or unwilling, but their parents and grandparents sold their extra clothing to Zhu Guiren at a steep markup.

Tainu tore off his remaining rags, used them to wash himself as best he could in the silty floodwaters where he had waited outside the village bounds, and gratefully put them on. "Much better," he said. "Demon, the only problem is I have none of those talismans left. I wanted to tell you. I only had the one sewn into those sleeping clothes."

Zhu Guiren nodded, though his heart sank a bit. "How far is Liu Chenguang?" he asked.

Tainu closed his eyes and whispered, then he said, "About two day's journey walking, if we're all walking at the same pace toward one another."

"How long if you were to fly to her?" he asked. "Just to rendezvous, and to get some of the talismans from her? I don't like you being completely defenseless except for me."

Tainu shook his head. "Still several hours each way. I don't want us to be separated for that long."

Zhu Guiren smiled at him.

"Not because of that! My goodness." Tainu laughed as he came over and put his arms around him, looking down at him with his beautiful eyes. "I have clothes on now," he added. "So there."

"Clothes are removable," said Zhu Guiren.

"Not till tonight." Tainu started walking. "Let's go."

Zhu Guiren hurried to catch up. "Let's find a nice place to stop for tonight."

"I don't think there are any nice places here."

"A nice, abandoned house."

Tainu looked at him sideways, smiling. "Walk faster, then."

As they came closer to the Sorrowful River, the landscape became more and more dangerous. There were no landmarks left — no visible roads, only occasional rises above the level of the floods — and the walls of ruined houses sticking up from the yellow waters. Both of them were soon soaked and muddy again, tricked repeatedly into stepping into deep channels carved into the soil beneath them. Before sunset, they stopped at a treeless rise by common, unspoken consent, exhausted. There had been no usable shelters on the way, nor anywhere in front of them.

Zhu Guiren looked consideringly at Tainu. "Go," he said. "Fly to Liu Chenguang. You shouldn't have to slog through this for me. Find a safe, dry place with them and wait for me."

Tainu shook his head stubbornly.

"Tainu, even the food we bought this morning is wet. I want you to go somewhere better than this. I'm strong enough to defend myself well. There's nothing you need to concern yourself about."

"No," he said. "Arciniang, you know you can't find me if I leave. We'll have to come to you anyway and slog it out regardless."

"Tainu," Zhu Guiren laughed, "are you just using this so you can tell me your true name?"

He nodded. "If you're confident that you'll be safe, you'll let me tell you. Otherwise, I won't go."

"Tainu, just because I'm safe for a few days somewhere in wherever this is doesn't mean I'm safe forever," he tried. "You just go. I'll meet you somewhere."

"Where?" Tainu sat down in the mud. "You don't have a map. I don't even know where we are. No, I'm not leaving you like this. You don't know anyone's true name, and I'm the only one who knows yours. If something happens to either of us—"

Zhu Guiren said, "Fine. Stay with me in the mud, then."

"I will." Tainu yawned. "It's not so comfortable that I feel the need to stay here all night, though. Just…let's rest."

Zhu Guiren came to sit behind him so he could lean back and sleep. There was nothing else to lean on, not even a rock or a tree stump. The evening slowly drew down to a muddy, uncertain darkness. Something fluttered down from the sky to land next to them.

A bird.

A crow.

"Tainu." Zhu Guiren stood, bringing Tainu upright with him. "Tainu, wake up."

Another crow came down, and another.

Tainu shook himself awake. "What?" he asked, confused.

"Transform now, and go," Zhu Guiren said, his sword appearing in his hand.

Four more crows landed on the rise, surrounding them.

Tainu shook his head.

"Go!" Zhu Guiren shouted. "Now!"

The crows all transformed at once. He didn't recognize all of them — some must have been from the other clan he had met in the jail — but Tenth was there, and Fourth, and Fifth. All would be carrying punishment talismans, he knew.

He begged one last time, "Tainu, fly. Fly now."

"Demon, do you think I can outfly all of these?" Tainu asked. He knelt down and slapped the earth to set a ward.

It wouldn't last long. The earth was too saturated to hold it; the water would move its foundations, seeping through.

Zhu Guiren said, "I love you. Fly now, please," and leapt out of the wards to take the offensive.

He took down two of the strange demons immediately, but the first punishment talisman had already brushed his thigh. Tenth followed up with a strike with his favored weapon — a bladed whip that cut him heavily in the arm — but he paid for it by being impaled and then disemboweled by Zhu Guiren's double halberd. Fourth would be more problematic; he could see her eagerness to kill him personally. To take his place. Her preferred weapon was a bow, hard to defend against with only a sword. She sent arrow after arrow at him, and he blocked and blocked, but the second punishment talisman took him square in the back, and he fell to his knees.

Tainu rushed out of the wards to him.

"No, no," he gasped, but it was too late. Tainu was next to him, had set a new ward around them and was trying to heal the damage from the talismans so he could keep fighting, but the ward was weak. Another of the strange demons forced his way through it and grabbed Tainu around the neck with a garrote of demonic qi. Tainu gurgled in pain as it burned and cut the skin of his throat, and the other demon dragged him bodily away.

Zhu Guiren screamed in rage. He forced himself upright, chasing after the other demon, but already his reflexes were slow. Running was as though he was fighting his way through deep, cold snow; every movement was five times more difficult than usual, his striking ability taken as his meridians froze.

With relief, he saw Tainu transform into a hummingbird and dash upwards, but then there were two crows pounding up into the air after him, less maneuverable, but larger and much more powerful. A third crow rose up to herd the small red bird from every side, until at last one of them managed to pierce the little bird with its claws and it went limp, bleeding. Zhu Guiren screamed again and cast a spear, but it fell far short. The crow flew away to the west.

Zhu Guiren turned back to Fourth. "You're dead," he managed to say, and took her through the upper chest with a javelin. She pulled it out contemptuously and stood with the remaining demons, watching him flail, more and more slowly, against the muddy ground where he lay as the two punishment talismans took bitterly quick effect. They were so very strong, and he couldn't resist. The pain increased as his mobility lessened. All he could do was lie still and scream, and eventually, he couldn't even scream, trapped in frozen silence as his body and mind were torn apart by the talisman.

Fourth said, "First said to leave you here with the punishment talisman if we didn't kill you. He'll send someone to pick you up later." She viciously kicked his head, and he passed out.

He came to sometime the next day, being dragged bodily along the ground into an old farmhouse surrounded by the floods. The people dragging him talked over his head, laughing; he couldn't understand their words. The humiliation was worse than the pain, and he knew this was part of the punishment. His heart was nothing but hot, panicked terror. *Tainu.*

A paunchy middle-aged man sat behind the desk in an army uniform. "Brother," he said, winking. Then, "Dismissed."

The men holding Zhu Guiren threw him on the floor and left.

When they had gone, the man stood up. "Did you know I sent ordinary men to pick you up?" he asked. "You've damaged your own cultivation to the point I didn't even need to send demons once the punishment talisman had done its work." He strolled over, casually removing the illusion enchantment that had hidden his true appearance: tall, handsome, dead white skin, black eyes with a hint of red in them, white hair cut rough like a mane to the top of his shoulder blades. He moved his hand sharply, and Zhu Guiren's paralysis lessened, though the pain remained.

"First," Zhu Guiren managed, pulling himself up to a kneeling posture and bowing his head. "Instruct this person, what has he done to earn discipline?"

"Little Third," First chortled, "such a charming child. Do you have to ask?" He tipped up Zhu Guiren's chin to look at him better.

Zhu Guiren stared back at him, unblinking, his heart hammering so loudly that he knew quite well that First could feel it. He felt nothing for himself, but Tainu, Tainu — how could he save him now? He felt anger too; if only he had left when he was told, if only he had flown away, then he'd be safe. Then, he would have nothing to fear, if only Tainu was not also captured. They would be doing things to him already…

He knew what they would do. He thought he might go mad thinking about it.

First smiled down at him, stroking the line of his jaw, pressing his fingers into the soft place under his chin.

Zhu Guiren swallowed, against his will.

"Let us review. You let a phoenix go. Back then, we had a long discussion, similar to this one. Don't you remember it?"

Zhu Guiren shook his head.

"Ah, you wouldn't," said First. "It broke your mind a bit, as I recall, but you were quite good after that, for a long time. Quite good. Only a little bit of disobedience here and there, and that doesn't bother me. Our strongest children are always like that, needing a little freedom. But then…" He tapped Zhu Guiren hard in the forehead acupoint; it echoed through all his frozen meridians and he screamed out loud with the pain of it. "You let another phoenix go. You took what you wanted, set your own array, and let the phoenix go into rebirth. And then, we had another conversation. You wouldn't remember that one either. When we were finished, I let you go again. So many chances! You were supposed to find another phoenix to make up for it. And you did."

First knelt down, smiling, to look in his eyes. "You didn't bring the phoenix to me, as you were supposed to. You refused my summons. But all that is done now." He reached out and kissed Zhu Guiren softly on the lips. "My dear little Third…This phoenix is rather special to you, is he not? It's so good to know my little Third has finally grown up."

He shook his head and closed his eyes, his heart hammering with terror.

"Oh, my dear," First said, not unkindly, "do you think that if you don't intend to tell me, you won't? We will have such a good talk." First caressed his face with his long, white fingers, and then kissed him again, long and hard.

Zhu Guiren tried to make his mind blank in preparation — tried to empty it of all thoughts of Tainu, of everything he knew and felt — though he knew in the end, everything in his mind and heart would be spread out bloody for this being's entertainment.

"Let's begin, little one."

Tainu felt himself tied down to the stone couch again. He struggled weakly, panicking, tried to use everything he had, but it wasn't enough. It was nothing. The demons binding him barely noticed. It was the same, the same place; they had brought him to the clan home.

Because he had chosen, for millennia, to live his life in the riskiest possible ways, there was very little abuse that could be heaped upon a mortal body that he had not already experienced at some point; he had long ago lost the illusion that there was some limit to cruelty, or any saving grace in it. He did not trust these people, so trust was not broken. He knew what to expect, so he was not surprised. Thus, what the demons had already done to him did not injure his mind or his heart — only his mortal body, and that healed. They had done things to him in ways he would not choose to remember, but that was nothing compared to seeing his demon there, his Arciniang, looking at him indifferently, as though he didn't know him. His hair had been cut brutally short, and his face was calm and unconcerned.

When he had been fully shackled at the neck, ankles, and wrists, his demon came over to him, looking down. Tainu met his eyes, knowing what would happen now if they had done so much to him that his demon could see him shackled to the stone couch without his expression even changing, without his eyes looking the least bit distressed. His single hand held a knife of ice and smoke. With his hair cut short, his face looked colder and more distant — a harsher beauty, each line of his face clear and unhidden.

"Bleed the phoenix," called the ancient demon, sitting in a comfortable chair some distance away to observe with visible delight.

Tainu knew that this must be First. He could sense the cold, murderous aura radiating from him.

Without hesitating, Zhu Guiren reached out and sliced deep into Tainu's left bicep. Blood poured out.

"Demon," he whispered desperately, "it's me. Please, don't you remember?"

Zhu Guiren's dark, clear eyes met his. "I remember," he said. "I remember everything."

He sliced again.

"No," Tainu said. "No." He felt his eyes filling with tears — from the pain of the deep cuts, from the pain of knowing his demon's hand was wielding the knife, from imagining what his demon must have suffered from them to now be like this.

First, sitting with his chin in his hand, smiled and said, "He does indeed remember everything, and his will is free. He's no puppet. He chooses to do this to you."

Zhu Guiren looked back at First. "I'm choosing it now. I may not always choose it. Don't push me."

First laughed. "Do you see? He's still himself."

Zhu Guiren cut him again.

Tainu looked into his face, trying to find a trace of him, the one that he knew. "Demon," he said, softly, "you still have your heart. Don't you feel it? Please. You don't want to do this. This isn't what you want. Why are you obeying him?"

First had heard him, despite his efforts to speak quietly, and replied, "His heart is still there. I've made some adaptations. But he remembers everything there once was between you. He's told me all about it. Did you know that? He remembers it even now, while he's cutting you." He laughed out loud. "Third!

Make him say your true name."

Zhu Guiren turned to him. "Why would I do that? My true name's not for you to hear."

"You see?" First laughed. "He's still himself."

The cuts were closing immediately. Tainu hadn't lost much blood yet. It would take much, much more damage before his wounds would cease to heal; he remembered that, as well. He stared up at his demon, the tears streaking his face despite himself, and said, uncertain, "Demon?"

Zhu Guiren knelt down next to him, and met his eyes, his expression earnest. "I remember what happened," he said quietly, his face close to Tainu's. "I remember that there were feelings between us, but I don't feel them anymore. I don't have any animosity toward you. I just see no reason for my life to be governed by what I once felt, and do not feel anymore. It's…inconvenient for me. And you are a phoenix, after all. We need the power your blood gives us. This is just how it has to be." He struggled for a moment.

Tainu watched him, his heart breaking.

"I'm not being cruel," he said at last. "This is how it is. This is just what's necessary, no more."

Tainu looked at him — his beautiful face, his eyes trying to communicate something to him that he understood well enough. "Even now," he said, "you are still who you are. You don't want to do this. Even now. Don't let him make you do it."

Zhu Guiren touched his cheek, frowning. "It is what it is," he said at last, and stood up again, and cut him, again.

"Leave us," First said, suddenly. "I have things to say to the phoenix."

Zhu Guiren bowed and left without a backward glance. The other demons followed.

First came over to Tainu and stared down at him for a while. Then, he said, "Second should be the one explaining this to you, but she's out doing other things." He sat down in a chair next to the head of the stone couch so Tainu could turn his head and look at him. "You are the eldest living phoenix," he said. "The one who created the refuges. Third has told me."

Tainu didn't respond.

First nodded. "But I am far, far older than you are. Older than you can comprehend. You, Third — both of you are only children to me, and Second, and the leaders of other clans. Children only just learning to walk. You should know that we eldest demons don't cultivate from mortals at all. We cultivate from the resentment of other demons. All we do is meant to cultivate the suffering and resentment of the demonic people so we can drink it, and it is far, far more powerful than mortal resentment."

Tainu began to understand, and looked away.

"We are not people who need our children to grow up and replace us, after all. Our children exist only to feed us. Third is now ready for harvesting. Thus," he waved his hand over Tainu's body, "I have cut the connections between his heart and his conscious awareness. This was rather pleasurable for me, although not for him. I'd like you to know that he's suffered a great deal since he's come back to me. As much as I could contrive without killing him outright or rendering him into useless meat, and it is probably something of a relief to him that he can't feel at the moment. You should also know that his heart is still very much there, and that insofar as I can comprehend such things, he still loves you. He is actually *feeling* in his heart everything he is doing to you. I imagine that inwardly, he is screaming without cease. It's only that he is not aware of what he is feeling, as though I had given him an anesthetic, kind and thoughtful as I am, for his current condition."

He steepled his fingers together. "At some point, I will heal those connections, and he will know his own heart again. He will feel it all, all at once. I anticipate that at that point, he is likely to kill himself. If he does not, I will kill him. There is no path here that does not end with his death, but the longer he doesn't feel, the longer he will live. You should understand this, as I believe it matters to you in some way."

Tainu's eyes were closed, but he could hear in First's voice that he was smiling as he mused, "I've never cultivated the resentment of a phoenix. Perhaps I'll try, this time around."

# CHAPTER 15
## THE GREAT ARRAY

IT CAME SO fast, when it came. Aili and Liu Chenguang were still awake, drowsy but talking and drinking in the main room, when Liu Chenguang held up a hand and said, "We need to go."

"What?" Aili asked. She was feeling a bit odd after breaking the array earlier and seeing Chenguang. She hadn't wanted to talk to her about it — it was too strange — but she suspected that Liu Chenguang had figured it out anyway.

Liu Chenguang got up and said, "My supplies for a journey are already packed, luckily. Just let me roll up the maps."

"What is it?" Aili stood and started rolling the maps with her.

"Give me that one." She stuffed them all in a bag that was ready near the door. "There's someone speaking Kunorese outside. I heard them go past. They may not be here for us right now, but if they are here at all, they'll come for us sometime tonight. My medicine and talismans are already packed…Tainu?" she whispered loudly.

Tainu came to the door of his room, wearing his sleeping clothes.

"Wake up the demon, we need to run," she said. "We'll split up, head into the mountains, and meet there. Me and Aili, you and him. Do you have the phoenix talismans?"

He patted the seam of his shirt. "Always," he said. "You?"

She nodded. "Go."

Aili knelt. "Hold tight," she said brusquely. "This will be faster than before."

She felt Liu Chenguang clambering onto her back and set herself into her breathing to prepare. *Thank goodness we got Yisue out*, she thought. She bent her head and listened carefully for talking, for footsteps, and decided that the stairs were clear for the moment.

"Now." Aili stood up and began racing for the mountains.

There were people in the yard; someone shot at her, someone yelled in Kunorese. Her heart was in her throat, not so much for herself and Liu Chenguang — she knew she could survive a gunshot and could probably even still keep running through it — but for Tainu and Zhu Guiren. They were still in the room, and the demon was far more vulnerable to injury.

Liu Chenguang had the same thought, Aili could tell, but she bent her head and said, "Keep going, we can help them by drawing some of them away."

Aili didn't spend breath responding. Her previous visit to Mount Shi with Liu Chenguang had been a pleasure jaunt, but this was a race and she was very, very fast. She didn't take the main road, but ran off to the side immediately and started leaping for the cliffs, looking to get away from the places that were easy for mortals to reach.

"How far?" she asked after three hours or so of qinggong, when they were deep into the craggy hills. She had gone slightly west along the edge of the highest peaks, avoiding the temples and the well-known roads.

Liu Chenguang said, "This should be good. I need a rest anyway, even if you don't." She got herself off Aili's back and stretched out. "I know you're faster and stronger than I am, but from here on in, I can manage with my own qinggong."

Aili felt her way around the rocks. "I thought so," she said, "there's a good place here to get under cover."

It wasn't quite a cave, but a deep depression within the rock face that created a small, dark room, invisible from above, below, or the side. Liu Chenguang brought the bags in and took out a blanket to lie on and another to cover them.

"So prepared," said Aili, smiling.

Liu Chenguang laid the blanket down. "Come over here," she said, and made Aili lie down first. "If I knew we would be doing this tonight, I would have made you rest more. I know I said your meridians aren't damaged, not like Zhu Guiren's situation, but whatever you did was exhausting for you and now you've been doing this." She settled down next to her and pulled the second blanket over both of them.

"I'm fine," Aili said. In fact, she didn't feel tired at all, and better than when she had been sitting in the room resting; qinggong was invigorating for her, though she knew it was much more challenging for Liu Chenguang. She was very aware of Liu Chenguang's body next to her beneath the blanket, and the rhythm of her breathing and heartbeat. Out loud she said, "What should we do now? Should we aim for Hongye?"

Liu Chenguang snuggled up against her for warmth, and Aili automatically put her arms around her to draw her in; she didn't think about it until it was already done, and her face was buried in Liu Chenguang's hair. She still had that scent about her — incense and bitter medicine, uniquely Liu Chenguang's scent — and she breathed it in deeply. Her hair was so soft and smooth. As natural as holding her or breathing her scent was to kiss her hair, so she did that too. She could feel Liu Chenguang's breathing quicken and her body, seemingly as instinctively, press back against her, molding to hers.

Aili stopped immediately. "Sorry," she said.

Liu Chenguang was silent, and then she said, "Don't be sorry." She turned over in Aili's arms and looked up at her, as though wondering about something.

Aili said, "Your eyes are so beautiful, Chenguang."

Liu Chenguang smiled. "I like to hear you call me Chenguang." The silence drew out between them for a while, but at last, she said, "Aili, we haven't really talked. Not about the important things."

Aili felt her heart drop and drew back a little bit, but Liu Chenguang shook her head.

"No, I didn't mean that. I want you close to me. Do you remember, back in Fallon?" She sounded a little nervous. "You asked me what I wanted?"

Aili remembered that, very well. "I was…in a very strange place, then," she said. "When I asked you that, I was…a little…not completely in my right mind."

"You never told me about it," she said. "About Edna Lee and Little Daxian, but not about what really happened to you when we left you."

"I know. It's very hard…" When she trailed off, she felt Liu Chenguang's hand close around hers encouragingly. Finally, she said, "Something snapped in me, or something that was hidden came out. All the things that were hidden, I think. All the things that had always been hidden, in both my lives."

Liu Chenguang looked at her with her beautiful eyes — dark and quiet, like the depthless, still water that received everything given to it — so Aili continued, "I destroyed Fallon with the phoenix fire, and a lot of other places, too. I was so angry, and I couldn't hurt the ones that I was angry at, so I hurt the ones that I could reach."

"Ah," said Liu Chenguang. She picked up Aili's hand, gently unfolding her fingers to kiss her palm.

"I killed some people," she said, because it seemed important that nothing she had done be secret. "Not many, not on purpose, but there were people who sometimes got in my way, and I wasn't clear enough in my mind to control what I was doing."

Liu Chenguang nodded.

"I'll be honest with you, Liu Chenguang. It felt…it felt very good to do it. But it also felt pointless, in the end. The rage never would go away. It was like a fire that would never stop. The more I fed it, the more there was. Each time I felt better, and then it would be gone, and I would need to do it again just for that small relief of the burning." She shook her head.

"Were you angry at me?" Liu Chenguang asked quietly.

"You were part of it," she said. "Because…"

"Because?"

"Because I loved you, and you…you loved Hong Deming. How could you love me instead?" She felt the tears come to her eyes unexpectedly, hot and aching.

Liu Chenguang closed her eyes. "Aili," she said. She reached up and pulled Aili down close to her.

"Aili," she said again, and kissed her eyebrows and her nose and lips, lightly, softly. "What I want– What I wanted then, and what I want now…We are who we are. We're not like other people who have only met once, who have only one life together, long or short. It's not only you who's not the same person you were a thousand years ago. We have two lives, and this is our second time to know one another and love one another. So that's what I want." She smiled at Aili, her eyes shining again. "I want you to be happy. If you decide that you don't love me in this life after all, then I want your happiness however you will find it, but my selfish hope is that you will love me again. That I can make you happy."

Aili nodded, unconvinced, but sighed a kiss back onto her lips.

Liu Chenguang said, "I bound you to me when you died, but that's not a magic talisman that makes you love me. I know that."

"Who says I don't? That's not–" Aili said, flustered. Liu Chenguang's body was so warm and welcoming in her arms; it felt so very different than her memories and yet the same. Of its own accord, her hand began to lightly stroke Liu Chenguang's waist, her smooth skin beneath the loose jacket, and then tease a little higher. Liu Chenguang gasped a little bit, and she stopped herself, embarrassed that that had happened. *What was she thinking?*

Liu Chenguang laughed and put her head down. "Aili," she said, teasing, "you don't need to stop."

Aili shook her head, and Liu Chenguang kissed her lightly, accepting.

"Why did you love me, that first life we had?" Liu Chenguang asked. "Why would you love such a strange person that caused you such problems? I know I wasn't your only option."

After some thought, Aili said at last, "I just always loved you. Since I first met you. Before I knew what it was." Because they were being very honest with one another, she added, "There could have been others. I could have chosen someone else. Maybe I would have loved them too, but it was you. It was you I loved, it was you that I wanted, and so that was my choice."

Liu Chenguang said, "Do you know why I loved you? Because you picked me up and held me, and I had never had kindness like that before. And then I came to you, and I saw who you were. Who you are. And so, I made all my choices because I loved you, and then I loved you because I had made those choices."

They held each other in silence for a while. The tension in Aili's body, the heat and yearning, slowly faded; she wasn't ready for that. Not yet. Aili felt Liu Chenguang's breathing even out, her body relaxing, felt her own body drifting off to sleep, her heart deeply peaceful. It was a feeling she hadn't had in a thousand years, since the inn at Gunan, before they had lost one another: kissing Liu Chenguang's lips, trusting there would be time for them, time for everything.

Aili woke first the next morning, just after dawn. The shadows of the peaks still hung heavy to the west, where they loomed out over the lower hills and the Sorrowful River valley. She went to the edge of the cliff and settled to cultivate, watching the bars of the morning sunlight slowly slip over the world in the cold clear air. When Liu Chenguang came out, stretching her arms wide, Aili surreptitiously watched to see the shape of her body, and then mentally slapped herself and tried to focus on cultivation again.

Liu Chenguang, uncaring, sat next to her and looked out over the world. "It's a beautiful morning," she said quietly. "I love the dawn time."

Aili nodded, "Yes," she said. "It reminds me of you," which just slipped out.

Liu Chenguang brushed against her shoulder, smiling. She whispered, then frowned. "Tainu isn't in the mountains. They're south of us. Not far from Shi'an."

"What do you think? Are they all right? Should we go find them?"

Liu Chenguang looked irresolute. "I don't know," she said at last. "Tainu can transform and should have been able to get to the mountains easily. If he didn't, it's because something happened to Zhu Guiren."

Aili stood. "We should go."

"Let me think," Liu Chenguang said. "It's broad daylight and you're a tall, blonde Federative for whom I'm sure they've put out alerts. If only one of us could transform…" She looked at Aili, obviously frustrated. "If they've found a safe place to hide, it would only make things more dangerous for us to go stomping close to them."

"Show me on the map," Aili suggested. "The direction you think he's in, and the distance if you have any sense of it."

Liu Chenguang chose one of her maps of the Shi'an countryside, whispered again, and then drew with her finger toward the southwest. "This is a flooded area," she said. "They won't be able to go much further in that direction unless they find a boat. They'll have to turn either north, toward us, or west to get into the next province."

Aili examined the map and Liu Chenguang's notes on it. "There's literally nothing in that area. If we go there and the Kunorese are searching for them, we'll certainly draw attention." She stood straight and looked out toward the south. "Does it matter, though? Not to brag about it, but even before I had the phoenix whip and near-immunity to gunshots, I could handle ordinary people fairly well."

Liu Chenguang snorted. "Do you really think you can just wade in there and take on the whole Kunorese army?"

Aili considered. "Barring artillery or air support."

"You are really quite full of yourself, Aili Fallon," said Liu Chenguang, her eyes narrowed in mock disapproval. "Well, while that is technically a solution, it's not a good one in my opinion. Let's call that our last option. A better one would be finding them without alerting the people that we have to assume are looking for them."

Aili looked at the map again. "Then we have to come from the other direction," she said. "We can course correct as we need to if they start moving, but if we go make a circle northwest and then back south, I don't think we can possibly make things worse for them. Tainu will also be looking for you, won't he?"

They used qinggong to get back down to the plains west of the mountains and began picking their way west and slightly north. The ground was sodden and flooded in places, and mostly very empty. They walked in silence, listening to the sound of waterfowl splashing and calling to one another. There was almost nothing else to hear.

Liu Chenguang whispered under her breath every few hours and confirmed that Tainu was still in the previous location. "I'm worried that he hasn't set out to look for me yet," she said. "He's not moving at all. He could certainly fly to us from where he is now."

"Zhu Guiren could be hurt?"

"But then he would surely have healed him…"

Aili said, "I think that Tainu wouldn't leave Zhu Guiren alone for that long to fly to us, and Zhu Guiren wouldn't want him to go on his own either. We'll have to get closer."

Liu Chenguang whispered again, late that night. "They've started moving," she said, relieved. "Or Tainu has, anyway. He's free to move as he wills, so it must be all right. He must just be moving slowly for Zhu Guiren's sake."

"He does a lot for Zhu Guiren's sake," Aili remarked.

Liu Chenguang rolled her eyes. "I know. Not at all who I anticipated as a brother-in-law."

"I will admit, he has somewhat grown on me," Aili said. "I think he's a very lonely person."

"I don't think he can really blame anyone but himself and his charming personality for that," Liu Chenguang said wryly, but then added, "it's true, though. Tainu's always been very lonely too. I never realized until I saw how happy he was to have someone he could talk to, even if it was Zhu Guiren. It's…it's nice that they have each other. If that's what's happening."

Despite knowing that Tainu was on the move, getting closer to him wasn't easy, since neither of them could fly. A flooded area lay between them and where Liu Chenguang thought Tainu was.

"There's just, just nothing," said Liu Chenguang, days later, as they retraced their steps trying to find a place where it became shallow enough to cross. Already, they had had to turn back three times at sudden channels, one of which nearly swept Liu Chenguang away before Aili swam over to catch her and bring her back.

Aili shook her head. "I'd suggest swimming, but these currents and the depth are so unpredictable." She thought she could probably make it herself, but Liu Chenguang didn't seem to be a strong swimmer. She wrung out her clothes and Liu Chenguang carefully patted all the talismans dry.

Finally, Aili said, "Let's look at this another way. Our real destination is across the Sorrowful River, isn't it? Why don't we just look for the main channel and a way to cross? There must be bridges somewhere. They can follow and meet us there, or we can try to walk along the north side and find another bridge closer to them. Didn't you say that the flooding was only south, not north? They didn't break the northern levees."

Liu Chenguang nodded slowly. "All right."

They worked their way along the side of the flood channel, going more directly north toward the great barrier of the river itself, the dike rising high above the land where it hadn't been breached against the Kunorese. Because the original breach of the dike had been further southwest, the river level was relatively low within the levees here, and they were able to find a usable bridge without much difficulty within four days, though they had to keep a watch out for Kunorese patrols. By the time they crossed, it was almost night, and Liu Chenguang found them a room at an inn near the edge of a mid-size town. Aili jumped up into the window after she was inside.

Liu Chenguang pulled clean clothes out of one of the bags. "I'm sorry. They're all kind of wet, but maybe less filthy?" she said helplessly, then sighed.

Aili took them from her silently and laid them out in front of the room's brazier. "Let's hope for the best for tomorrow. Go have a bath, I'll go next."

While Liu Chenguang took the bathing room, Aili stood at the window, musing. There was something strange about the night, or the place. Something about having crossed the Sorrowful River. She could no longer remember where she had crossed as Hong Deming, during those last days of his life; he had been more or less delirious with infection, she realized, looking back. The river itself had moved, and the floods had changed everything, but there was something here. Her mind drifted, as though the river had its currents, and she were on it, beyond her own volition.

When Liu Chenguang came out in her nightclothes, toweling her hair dry, she came over to where Aili stood staring out the window, arms behind her back. "What is it?" she asked softly.

"Don't you feel it?" Aili asked.

Liu Chenguang closed her eyes. "No," she said, "but I don't know what I would feel."

"When I find an array," Aili said, dreamily, "it repeats over and over in front of me. I wonder what I'll see in the great array?"

"Aili," said Liu Chenguang next to her. She put herself in front of her, blocking the view of the window. "Aili," she said more sharply.

Aili shook her head. "What?" she asked in a more normal tone of voice. "Chenguang? Are you done in the bath?"

Liu Chenguang looked up at her.

"Chenguang? Are you all right?"

Liu Chenguang asked slowly, "Who are you?"

"Hong Deming," Aili said, smiling.

Liu Chenguang felt all the hair on her skin rise. "Aili," she said. "Aili."

Aili's blue eyes focused. "Yes," she said a little impatiently, "I'm here."

"Aili," said Liu Chenguang, very seriously, "come away from the window." She put her hands on Aili's shoulders and deliberately turned her around so that she was facing into the room. "Come with me." She walked backward, pulling her away from the window. "Look at my face," she said. "Look at my eyes, don't look back there."

"Liu Chenguang?" Aili asked as Liu Chenguang made her sit on the bed. "What's happening?"

Liu Chenguang sat firmly on her lap, putting her knees on either side of Aili's hips so she couldn't get up again and she couldn't see anything but her.

"Liu Chenguang?"

"Aili, listen. You became very strange when you went to the window. Are you sensing the great array is somewhere near here?"

Aili closed her eyes. "Yes. It's near."

"Is it having an effect on you?"

"I don't know…Chenguang?"

"I'm here."

Aili's eyes were still closed, but she reached her hands up into Liu Chenguang's hair and pulled her down into a kiss.

Liu Chenguang sat still in shock, feeling Aili's hand on the nape of her neck, the pressure of her lips and tongue entwining hers in the way she remembered so well, but was so different now.

"Chenguang," she murmured, "you're all right. I found you. I've been so afraid…"

She struggled to pull herself away, but Aili was much stronger and pulled her in more tightly. "Aili," she said helplessly, "No, not like this– please–"

Aili shook her head and let go of her. "What? Liu Chenguang, what's happening?" She seemed to suddenly realize what she had been doing and tried to back away from Liu Chenguang on the bed.

Liu Chenguang said, "Tell me who you are."

"I'm Aili," she said, looking at her, hurt.

"Where are we?"

"Somewhere in the Daxian Republic, north of the Sorrowful River. We just crossed…" Aili's eyes lost focus.

"Who are you?"

"I'm Hong Deming. Chenguang, don't you know me?" The exact same hurt expression crossed her face. It would have been funny if it wasn't so horrifying.

"Where are we?" Liu Chenguang asked, keeping her voice calm. "Why are we here?"

"I came looking for you," Aili said. "You've been gone so long. I've been looking for such a long time...I've checked all the battlefields. I always have to check the bodies to see if you're there. I've been so afraid that I'll find you that way..."

An expression of such pain crossed her face that Liu Chenguang's heart clenched inside her. Panicking, Liu Chenguang tried to think what was best to do. She said, "Deming, you've already found me. It's all finished now. It's been finished for a long, long time."

Was it a ghost? was Aili possessed? But Hong Deming could have no ghost, he was alive, just as she was.

But they must be near the place that Hong Deming had died.

Liu Chenguang hid her face behind her hands; Aili's hands gently covered them and removed them.

"Liu Chenguang?" she asked, looking at her. "Liu Chenguang, there's something wrong, isn't there? Because we're near the array. That's why you're asking all these questions. Am I–" she swallowed. "Am I forgetting who I am?"

Liu Chenguang nodded, putting her hands on either side of Aili's face and leaning forward so their foreheads touched. She felt, suddenly, a huge and unexpected fury that this was happening to Aili. "Let's destroy it. Let's just go do it now. But you have to always look at me. Promise that you'll always look at me. Think of what you'll see on the battlefield — of what you're going to see — get it all into your mind now, and then remember that I'm real. That it's me you need to look at. Remember that I'll always tell you what is real and true."

Aili took a deep breath and nodded. "Chenguang, I don't know how long the battle went on before I got there, or how long after I died," she said at last. "We may have to wait for hours, or even a day before we get to...where it happened. Where Taiqian did what he did to you."

Liu Chenguang nodded.

"When I do these things...when I break arrays," Aili continued, "I've been... what happens is..."

Liu Chenguang took her hands. "Look at me," she said gently. "Look at me, Aili." She leaned down and kissed her. "I'm real. You're real. We're real together. What is in the past is only a memory of what happened. You don't have to be afraid of it. You don't have to be afraid of talking about it with me or describing it."

Her kiss had been only for comfort, to help Aili focus, but she unexpectedly felt a rush of arousal, sitting straddling Aili's hips like this, and closed her eyes. This was obviously not the time. Aili also seemed to feel it and come to the same conclusion, drawing back very slightly. Neither of them mentioned it.

She cleared her throat and kept her eyes on Liu Chenguang's. "What happens is at a certain point, when the event is done and the victors or survivors have left the area, Zhu Guiren appears and pours your blood. The way I'm able to stop it is by placing my hands into your blood, catching it in my hand with the phoenix fire, and calling your true name."

Liu Chenguang's eyes widened. "How did you figure out that would break an array?"

"Trial and error," Aili said, with a little of her familiar half-smile. She reached up to Liu Chenguang's nape and pulled her down to kiss her, again, even more thoroughly.

This time, Liu Chenguang felt almost dizzy with excitement as their mouths met — as Aili's hand caressed her jawline and throat, feeling the outline of her ear — and then they parted again, both breathing quickly.

Liu Chenguang said, "What...I..."

Aili shook her head, confused. "That was me," she said, and took a deep breath. "Not Hong Deming."

Liu Chenguang nodded, shaking a little bit. "What's happening? I don't want– I don't want us to...just because of the array," she choked out.

"I know. This isn't right," Aili said. She put her arms around her and held her for a moment. "Not that I don't also want to kiss you," she added, "but it's as though the world is fragmenting. Things aren't holding together the way they should..."

Liu Chenguang felt it now too — the sense that there were too many realities overlying each other in this place, conflicting and opposing powers, something trying to tear down, something else building up, a net across the world that was being realigned, pulling everything in a different direction — and suddenly she realized what it was. "There's another demon," she said. "Another demon is trying to take over the array. Zhu Guiren said that might happen. It's– it's undoing things, and then re-doing them in a different direction."

"I wish Zhu Guiren and Tainu were here," Aili hugged Liu Chenguang one more time, firmly, and said, "But I think it's going to have to be just us."

Liu Chenguang nodded.

"Can you transform?" Aili asked. "Your wings might help keep us focused — protect us from whatever's flying around, at least a little bit."

She nodded again.

"Get your talismans and your weapons…Something to tie our hands together, in case we get disoriented by whatever is happening out there…And something to blindfold me."

They felt their way out past the last buildings in the town toward some low hills. Houses had been built on them, but not many, and most of them were unlit, unoccupied. Crows flew and cawed in the dark above them as Aili, blindfolded, directed Liu Chenguang toward where she felt the center was. The illusions had become dizzying for her, the ghosts disappearing and reappearing, changing direction around her as though north was now south, everything rearranging like iron filings shifting their shapes in response. Aili tried to find the magnetic pole that drew everything to it, and said, "There's two centers — the old one and the new one. The old one is straight ahead. The new one is to our right."

Quietly, Liu Chenguang said, "Straight ahead is a low place between hills. To our right is a hillside."

Aili nodded. "The old center is what we need. Take me straight in. On that hillside, there's probably the demon that's trying to take the array. Try to stay away from it. Once I tell you to stop, sit down and don't move till I tell you."

Liu Chenguang led her in, grass brushing against her legs. There was no other sound until she felt a tingling in her body, and there it was — the screams and the sound of broken flesh.

"Sit down here," she said.

"We're near an abandoned house," Liu Chenguang said, pulling her down to sit. "There are some trees ahead of us–"

Aili shook her head. "None of that matters," she said, trying not to sound unkind, but her head was going to explode with the noise. She took off the blindfold and looked.

In the dim light of the stars, the battle was shadowy and unclear, for which she was profoundly grateful. She looked for the copse of trees where she remembered Chenguang had been trapped, but there were several and of course, it had been a thousand years. The real trees and the trees of the ancient battle were no longer the same. She had come in from the top of one of the hills last time, probably where the demon was waiting now. She didn't care about that demon, though undoubtedly it would care about her once it realized she was breaking the array, but Zhu Guiren had said that demons wouldn't be alerted to her as a danger. She was just a mortal, not worth their attention. Her priority was destroying this evil thing.

It was evil. She hadn't really thought about it in that way before. As awful as Zhu Guiren was, she rarely thought of him as evil, but the array itself was an evil thing. They would break it tonight, she thought fiercely. Not one more day.

She stood up and tried to gauge where the battle was and if it looked at all familiar to her. The generals on their hillsides helped her reorient, but truly everything was changed around, not only her own different angle of view. There was a copse of trees not far from them; was that Chenguang there?

"Hong Deming."

She turned around and saw an older man in blue cultivator's robes, handsome and proud, only the faintest hint of gray in his hair and beard. His sword was strapped across his back, and he stood next to a beautiful man in traveling robes. Zhu Guiren.

"Hong Deming," the cultivator said again, more fiercely.

She saluted formally. "Taiqian," she responded.

Liu Chenguang whispered, "Aili?"

"It's all right," she said softly. "I know who I am."

"How dare you call me Taiqian," he said, but it was said weakly. Taiqian looked at her with such weariness in his eyes.

"Taiqian," she said more gently, "get away from Zhu Guiren. Walk with me." She put her hand down to Liu Chenguang, and murmured, "They can't see you or hear you, Liu Chenguang, but I still can. Tie your hand to mine and come with me. Wake me up if I seem to be getting…away from myself."

She felt Liu Chenguang's hand tie the ribbon around both of theirs — loosely, so that she could free herself quickly if she needed to — and felt the tug as they began walking. Nothing else was solid around them: the shadows of the men dying and killing moved and shifted everywhere; the trees seemed to change their positions; the bloody stream was partly beneath her feet and partly above her head, as though she was swimming in the blood cauldron. To one side, Zhu Guiren stood, a fixed point, but everything else was slowly tugged toward a new pole.

Zhu Guiren, Hong Deming, Liu Chenguang if she found him — they alone were not real here. All the souls surrounding them were real, the souls of the dead who had fought the same battle and died the same deaths for a thousand years. Because Zhu Guiren's soul wasn't in the array, he didn't notice that Taiqian had walked away from him, nor could he see Aili. Taiqian was more solid than Liu Chenguang in Aili's sight, but she knew that Liu Chenguang was there; she could feel the weight of her, always tugging on the ribbon as they walked together. Every so often Aili said, "Liu Chenguang," and she would hear her voice respond, "I'm here."

Taiqian said, "Who are you talking to?"

"It's Liu Chenguang, Taiqian," she said. "Do you know what has happened?"

"I don't know. It seems that things happen, and then they happen again. But things can only happen once, can't they?" He looked at her, questioning. "I'm so tired."

She nodded.

"Liu Chenguang is dead," he said suddenly. "Zhu Guiren lied to me."

"I know. He lied to all of us."

"But I can never– I can never stop doing it," he said, confused as a child. "Even though I know it's always the same, even though the end is never different, I have to keep doing it. I kill Liu Chenguang. I cut him and make him bleed, I cut off his arms and legs, and then, I cut off his head and the fire comes. There's never any other ending."

"Do you want another ending?"

"Yes," he said. "I wish I could stop doing it. I wish I had never done it."

Aili felt Taiqian's hand grab her shoulder.

"I see you too. I see you dead, every time. And I step over your dead body as though you meant nothing to me. I wish that I could tell you that wasn't true. I wish that I could go back and never meet Zhu Guiren, never bring Liu Chenguang back with us, so things could have been what they should have been for you." His face twisted as though he was trying not to cry. "Are you a ghost?" he asked. "Are you Hong Deming's ghost come to haunt me? But everything is haunted, all the time, forever."

"Liu Chenguang," she said, needing to know what was real.

Liu Chenguang's voice came, "I'm here."

Aili couldn't see her anymore, but she could feel that Liu Chenguang had taken her hand. Knowing Liu Chenguang could hear her too, she said, "Taiqian, it's all done now. It's long gone for me. For Liu Chenguang, too. We forgive you. I'm not here to haunt you. I'm here to set you free."

He said, "Is Liu Chenguang here too?"

"She's here."

"Can I speak to him?"

"She can't hear you or speak to you," Aili said. Given how Taiqian felt about

Liu Chenguang, it was just as well, she thought.

But to her surprise, Taiqian said sadly, "If he could hear me, I would also tell him that I am sorry. I was tricked. But even if I hadn't believed Zhu Guiren's lies, I was not kind to him. He had a burden none of us understood, and I failed him as his Taiqian. For no reason except I was tired and didn't want another disciple, I didn't like him. I should never have taken him as a disciple, not because there was something wrong with him, but because my abilities were limited. I was too old to change for him."

"I'll tell her," Aili said. "But she was your last disciple. Taiqian, when Crane Moon vanished from the earth, it was only Liu Chenguang who remembered you."

"I never truly treated him as my disciple," Taiqian said. "I am sorry. Tell him."

This was what it meant to be a resentful ghost, Aili realized — forever tormented by failures and pain, always lost among the most terrible version of one's life and death, never able to make amends or receive redress, never to be free of it. She looked up at the thousands of men on the battlefield, trapped in this reality for a thousand years. At last, she said to Taiqian, "It's good to be sorry for mistakes, Taiqian, but it's more important to try to do something different. Something better."

"What could it be?" he asked sadly.

"Bring me with you when it's time," she said. "Just bring me with you."

"Time has no meaning here. It is always time."

The phoenix fire was now part of the horizonless, perspectiveless world, mixing with the blood and the ghosts. Zhu Guiren was firm and solid against it, his outline clearly marked, as Taiqian stepped over a body and stood next to him. Aili looked down and saw Hong Deming.

"Liu Chenguang," she said, panicked, but she could no longer feel or hear her. The only remnant of Liu Chenguang now was that she couldn't freely move her left arm.

Hong Deming was lying on his back, his eyes closed. There was blood on his mouth and all over his torn robes. Aili saw himself — a young man, handsome once, like the thousands of others who had died and would die on the battlefield, his long hair clotted with blood, his body full of wounds, all of his dreams and hopes and efforts come to nothing. There was a sword next to him. En.

Aili twisted her right hand and called En to it; the En that had lain on the ground disappeared. Carefully, she said, "Liu Chenguang, I can't see you or hear you or feel you. If you're here, I need you. Come closer to me."

She felt something touching her, as though arms were around her. She looked down and saw Liu Chenguang, an arrow in his lung, breathing shallowly through lips thick with blood. *"Chenguang,"* she said, panicked, then she felt Liu Chenguang's lips on hers and closed her eyes to focus on that. She reached up her left hand, shaking, and felt Liu Chenguang's hand against her shoulder. "Stay," she said. "Stay there till I tell you to move, I need you close to me."

The hand against her shoulder touched her face, gently.

Liu Chenguang said, "Let me hold his hand."

Zhu Guiren said, "That's a dead man, phoenix. Holding his hand isn't going to change anything."

Liu Chenguang looked at Zhu Guiren, and he looked back.

Liu Chenguang said, "Please."

Aili saw that Zhu Guiren's eyes flickered — as though something had hurt him or confused him — but it passed quickly. "Zhu Guiren," she tried, but he couldn't hear her.

Zhu Guiren laughed and put Hong Deming's dead hand in Liu Chenguang's.

"Chenguang," she said, shaking all over now, and she felt Chenguang's arms holding her tightly, Chenguang's body nestled against her. "Untie my hand," she whispered. When her arm was free, she touched Liu Chenguang's back with her left hand, feeling the warmth of her wings, and said, "Be careful."

Aili reached out with her left hand and called the phoenix whip.

Taiqian began to cut Liu Chenguang. His blood spilled softly on the ground. Aili made a whimpering sound, feeling the warmth of Chenguang's embrace. She had to think. It would be soon; what could she do to block it, to undo the final seal that held the array together?

"Taiqian, stop cutting. Stop now," she tried, but it was as though he didn't hear her at all.

She said, "Liu Chenguang, please. Can you hear me?" and felt Liu Chenguang reach up to kiss her, but Liu Chenguang remained on the ground, bleeding, almost unconscious now.

She said, "Chenguang, step back."

Liu Chenguang let go of her, and she knelt next to Liu Chenguang and kissed him.

He opened his eyes; Aili couldn't tell if he saw her.

"Liu Chenguang," she said, "I love you. I will be with you again. Don't be afraid."

She cried out, "Chenguang!" and felt Liu Chenguang's hand on her head, stroking her hair.

"He's unconscious," Taiqian said.

Zhu Guiren's voice came, "Dismemberment and decapitation. In that order."

Taiqian argued, and Zhu Guiren's persuasive voice smoothed over it, and Aili tried to think through all the madness of her heart. The agitation of the world surrounding them grew even greater. The few of them — Taiqian, Zhu Guiren, Liu Chenguang, and Hong Deming — were the only stable things; everything else was a wash of patternless color and senseless movement.

When Taiqian's sword came down for the first time, she tried to block it with En.

The second time, the phoenix whip.

She couldn't block the sword.

Liu Chenguang screamed only once. His body was now so mutilated that if she looked down, she knew she was very likely to lose her mind.

"Chenguang," she sobbed. Aili knew that Liu Chenguang was nearby, but she couldn't touch her anymore. "Chenguang, I can't feel you anymore. Stand away from me. I don't want to hurt you."

The third time, she screamed in rage and loss and frustration that she was here for nothing, for nothing.

On the fourth cut, she threw herself in front of the sword. It came down anyway. She felt nothing but a sharp tingle in her skin.

She turned herself on top of Liu Chenguang's body to face Taiqian's sword, her eyes streaming with tears. As the last strike came down, she held up her hands full of phoenix fire and called out, "Eftahede."

The sword went through her hands, through her body, through Liu Chenguang, and the world exploded.

# CHAPTER 16
## MEETING SECOND

LIU CHENGUANG WATCHED Aili live through their deaths again in the empty, silent field, only the night wind in the grass around them, and became more and more desperate to touch her, to bring her back. When Aili held up the phoenix fire and cried out her true name, she leapt over to catch her as she dropped to the earth, wrapping them both in her wings as they rolled in the grass. The air, the earth, all beings shook as though a great earthquake wrenched the foundations of reality. From the hillside, she heard a shriek of pain and rage and the cawing of many crows, flying off into the distance.

Aili was unconscious beneath her, breathing weakly; whatever she had done had taken enormous amounts of power. Liu Chenguang checked her pulse, and then tried to feel whether her meridians were damaged. She wished Tainu was there since he was so much better with cultivational injuries, but as far as she could tell, Aili was uninjured beyond draining all her qi. It would heal naturally, in time, but for now, she was unconscious on the cold, wet ground, and Liu Chenguang wasn't strong enough to bring her back to the warm inn.

She was shaken by the power released by the breaking of the array herself. This was far beyond what she had imagined. The very energy of the mountains and rivers had shifted, and the net of qi over the earth had been remade. Something had echoed in her as well — some things that had been caught and frozen in regret were free now to move and flow toward their true destinations.

Liu Chenguang looked at the woman lying beneath her and kissed her, very gently, holding her in her arms. She looked around for a place to take Aili, the best she could find, and she felt lucky that it was close, was a little shack that had probably once belonged to a farm. She apologized mentally to Aili and dragged her unceremoniously over. It was long abandoned, but the straw still inside was good enough. Liu Chenguang tried to get her comfortable on the straw, wrapped her body and wings around Aili, and slept.

Aili didn't wake that night or the next day, but Liu Chenguang's constant checks of her pulse showed nothing of concern beyond exhaustion. After she tried to make their little hovel more comfortable, she found some water which she dribbled into Aili's mouth and was relieved when her tongue licked at it, responding to reality appropriately. She also checked Tainu's location; that was more concerning. While they were in the array, he had suddenly gone far to the west, past Zai'an. Had he started flying for some reason? Had the time in the array been much longer than it seemed? Why was he going in that direction?

Sometime after midnight, Aili opened her eyes. "Liu Chenguang," she said immediately.

Liu Chenguang was already lying down next to her and holding her, but she said, "I'm here."

Aili looked at her, silently, her eyes a deep blue that Liu Chenguang could see even in the dark. "It's done," she said. "Isn't it?"

Liu Chenguang nodded, propping herself up on one elbow to look down at her face. "I feel it. I feel that something's broken. Something that needed to be broken — like a chain that I never knew was on me."

Aili nodded and said, "Yes." She reached up to bring Liu Chenguang's face close to her lips and kissed her, softly and then ever more deeply, pulling Liu Chenguang down to lie half on top of her and stroking the back of her neck beneath her hair. "Do you love me yet?" she asked with her little half-smile.

Liu Chenguang kissed her hand and nodded. She smiled at Aili again, teasing, "And I want to take you back to that inn, because there are things I want to do with you that I don't want to do in this straw."

Immediately, she realized she hadn't really been teasing after all. Her heart started racing when she looked at Aili's mouth and the shape of her hands, and felt the strength of her body, and realized that Aili's eyes were very serious about this. Before it could go any further, both of them froze. There was a sound of beating wings outside.

Aili looked up at the ceiling of the little shack. "Liu Chenguang," she whispered, "get your weapons and your talismans ready."

Outside, in the darkest part of the night, they heard crows cawing. Many of them — so many that they could hear the beating of their wings descending all around the little shed. There was no other sound.

Liu Chenguang looked out through a crack in the door. There were dozens of them, all silently sitting in the grass around the little shanty, all of them staring at the building where they were. She met Aili's eyes.

Aili nodded slowly and leaned to whisper in her ear: "Are you ready?"

Liu Chenguang showed her the deerhorn knives.

Aili smiled and kissed her cheek. "Be ready when I jump, I'll draw them away first," she whispered again. "Run for the river. If we're separated, I'll find you, just get to a safe place. Don't worry about me."

With only a moment's gathering of her energy, Aili lashed out at the ceiling with the phoenix fire whip, setting it on fire, and leapt upwards at the same time, gaining height through qinggong and then coming down on the other side of the ranked crows. As she landed, she flipped so that she was facing the demons and lashed out again, catching several in the flame.

While the crows were distracted, Liu Chenguang leapt out as well and made it to Aili's side.

"Run first," said Aili sharply.

Liu Chenguang ran, no need for pointless heroics. She knew that Aili was faster and stronger and would cover her retreat; she herself was Aili's vulnerable point. *But where to retreat to?* There was nothing in front of them but the high levee of the river, nothing around them but empty fields and shallow hills, nowhere to hide. The sense of unreality returned to her — the landscape where she and Hong Deming had died, the landscape with no cover, no safe place.

She ran and ran, hearing the caws and shrieks of the crows behind her, but other things, too. She risked looking behind her and saw that there were many demons in their mortal bodies chasing them, some fighting Aili, who was surrounded by a circle of them with their various weapons. Others were chasing her, and were getting closer. There were so many of them. For the first time she felt fear. She couldn't transform; if there was no safe place to run to, she wouldn't be able to get away.

Aili broke away from the demons surrounding her, using only the phoenix whips in both hands, each whip lashing out more than twenty feet on each side and setting all the grass on fire. When Aili caught up to her, Liu Chenguang saw that her face was set in rage and felt a sense of dread. Together they turned and ran, Liu Chenguang striving to match Aili's speed, faster than she had ever imagined she could run, but her heart was clamoring in her chest and even with qinggong, she couldn't defeat the flight of a bird.

"The river," Aili said sharply. "Can you swim, Chenguang? Be honest."

"No," she said. "Not well."

Aili swore and turned. "Behind me," she said. "Chenguang. Get behind me."

They were at the top of the levee, the river at their backs, with nowhere to go. The crows fluttered down around them in a multi-ranked half-circle and transformed, dozens of them; she had never seen so many demons in one place.

A woman stepped out in front of them. Dawn was just starting to lighten the sky, and by its light Liu Chenguang could see that she was very beautiful — smiling, tall, with golden skin, black hair braided with gold, and deep blue eyes. "Hello, my dears," she said. "Zhu Guiren sends his greetings." She turned to the demons surrounding them. "The phoenix is damaged and doesn't require a shackle. Neither of them can transform. Both of them are capable of healing themselves. No need to hold back, only avoid amputation and decapitation."

Liu Chenguang pushed out to stand in front of Aili.

"Liu Chenguang!" she said sharply, and tried to pull her back.

"Aili, jump in the river," she said, quick and low. "Go now. You can escape. You can come find me. Otherwise, there's no hope for anyone to come help us. They must have Zhu Guiren, and they probably already have Tainu."

Aili looked at her, already angry with her, she could tell, opening her mouth to argue.

Liu Chenguang reached up and closed her mouth by kissing her, smiling. "Go now," she said. "I trust you." It seemed as though time slowed down so that she could say what she needed — could look up to Aili's eyes and say, "You'll come. I'm not afraid."

She looked at her face so she would remember it when the pain would come. Then she pushed her, hard, from the top of the levee to fall twenty feet into the river's murky currents, and turned to face the demons, deerhorn knives in hand.

Aili had never been so angry while needing to focus on her breathing at the same time. The water of the Sorrowful River was so filled with silt that it was a deep yellow brown, completely opaque and gritting finely in her mouth and eyes. She knew that as long as she remained underwater, there was no possible way the demons would find her. But she didn't want to stay underwater. She wanted to get back up that levee and pick up Liu Chenguang and take her somewhere safe, and then yell at her for several hours.

However, this was not an option. The river was deep and wide here between the steep dikes, and without anything to stand on, she couldn't jump up even with qinggong. She would have to swim until she found some way out — a bridge, or a boat, or a dock, or anything sticking out into the water. The current was strong, and there was no easy way out. At least, not here.

She swore mentally, using all the best curses she'd heard during several months at sea and on a Navy base, and then began to swim purposefully toward the southern side of the riverbed. There, the levees had been breached — some deliberately as a defense against Kunoru, others accidentally as the entire levee wall had been weakened afterward. Nonetheless, it was more than an hour before she could find a place to pull herself out, and yell "FUCK!" at the sky. The phoenix whip came to her hand in pure rage, and she lashed at the river for no other purpose than to get her fury out at something she couldn't hurt. Then, she sat down and tried to think.

She whispered Liu Chenguang's true name and saw the path immediately move west. They had already taken her. She put her face in her hands and took several shuddering breaths, trying to get her terror for Liu Chenguang under control, trying to erase the images in her mind of Liu Chenguang on the stone couch, his blood falling softly into the basin, trying to think.

They had Zhu Guiren. Almost certainly, that was true — they had known how to find the seal of the great array, they had been able to begin to subvert it toward a new demonic owner. She was quite sure that that wouldn't be possible unless Zhu Guiren was incapacitated. He had said that his death would destroy the array, but the array had still been functioning. Therefore, he wasn't dead. He had said that powerful demons would try to take the array before his death. It was possible that since that the array was now destroyed, they would kill him anyway.

If they had Zhu Guiren, they almost certainly had Tainu as well. Tainu wouldn't have left Zhu Guiren; he would have stayed, as she should have stayed with Liu Chenguang. If Liu Chenguang wanted to try something like this, she could have said so; they could have jumped together, she could have helped her swim too. Of course, it would have been more dangerous and difficult with a weak swimmer but now...now. She clenched her fist and struck the ground next to her over and over, fire wisping out and suffocating in the mud. Damn her. No time, no time for this, no time to be angry or afraid for her. She had to move.

Would they all be brought to one place? She would have to hope so.

The golden white light to Liu Chenguang led her back upstream, along the course of the river. She shook herself out and began to run. Liu Chenguang couldn't transform. They couldn't fly with her. They had a head start, but they were on foot too.

Liu Chenguang couldn't kill anyone with her knives, but she managed to disarm two of the demons and use talismans on three before they took her down. She thought that this was probably a record for a phoenix. There was something so glad in her heart that she had been able to do something at last, and not only and always have to hide behind Aili and depend on others to defend her. Although she knew Aili would be furious, she also knew that Aili would come for her. This was the best plan. She could distract them and let Aili get away safely. Nothing could be done to her that wouldn't be healed.

"My dear," said the black-haired woman, walking up to her, "really, a pleasure to meet a phoenix who can demonstrate some self-respect when approached."

Two demons held her, one on either side. She had been injured — stabbed and slashed — but these had already healed. The black-haired woman reached out and took her deerhorn knives, calmly broke them between her hands, and threw them in the river. She then stood looking at Liu Chenguang. Just looking.

Liu Chenguang stared back at her, trying not to waver. But it was hard.

"Where is the other one?" she asked the demons holding Liu Chenguang.

"Answering Second, in the river," spoke up one of them. "Fourteen of the low ranked have gone to fly over the north and south shores to see where she comes up."

"Hmph," said the woman. "I want her. Until she is found, none of you return. If she is not found, none of you live."

Every demon there, crow or mortal-bodied, except the two holding Liu Chenguang, bowed their heads and immediately started running or flying downstream.

The woman walked around Liu Chenguang thoughtfully. "Show me the talisman," she said.

Liu Chenguang didn't respond.

The woman flicked her hand to hold a dagger and casually stabbed her in the eye.

Liu Chenguang screamed, and would have fallen to the ground, except she was being held upright by the two immobile demons. Hot blood dripped down her cheek, her eye blinded. In all her life, she had never had such an injury. Of course, she could and would heal from it, but the shock stunned her into tears and the tears hurt more because the tears flowed out through her broken skin, into her torn and mangled eye socket, stinging with salt.

The woman licked her dagger and released it, watching her.

"Third calls you the little phoenix, did you know?" she said, watching as Liu Chenguang sobbed and screamed. "He is quite fond of you in his way, or used to be. He told us that you can't transform anymore because you somehow have transferred some power to your lover — quite a bizarre story — so I can see that you are a creative little person, a problem solver. But my dear, don't delude yourself that you can change what is happening to you right now. There's no need to think I don't already know what I'm asking you. Third has already explained the talismans to me. I just want to see what it looks like…Just curiosity."

Liu Chenguang's eye had healed itself and she looked up, shaking, to see the woman's face very close to her — tipped first one way, then the other, as though trying to understand something. The woman brought her dagger out again, cut her own lips till they bled, and then drew the dagger's razor edge down Liu Chenguang's face. She traced a complex pattern for her own amusement, and then licked Liu Chenguang's blood while Liu Chenguang tried not to scream in disgust, feeling her tongue on her face.

"Hmmm," the demon said, her blood mixing with Liu Chenguang's in her mouth. "I've always wanted to try that, to see if phoenix blood heals if it's taken without your gift. Apparently not." She smiled and traced another design, this time below Liu Chenguang's throat, carving into the thin skin over her breast-bone. "This is quite fun, how I can cut you and you'll heal over and over…There are many things we can do with your blood when it's taken unwillingly. No need to be concerned. Nothing is wasted. We're quite grateful." She put her head down on Liu Chenguang's breast and licked more, lapping up the blood that spilled from the wounds.

Liu Chenguang struggled to get away, to get back from her, to no avail.

"Look," the woman said to the other demons, "what character did I draw?"

"Answering Second, En," replied one of the demons obediently.

Liu Chenguang closed her eyes, determined not to scream.

The woman's voice said, "Bring her. We return to clan home."

One of the demons said, "Please instruct this person as to our preferred mode of travel."

"Walking obviously," she said. "This one can't fly. Feel free to carry her to go faster as you need, bind her, do whatever is needful, but whatever blood she spills between here and there comes out of your skin later. Bring her to Shancheng by tonight. I wish to speak with her further."

Liu Chenguang felt the woman's fingers on her lips.

"Little phoenix, tonight, I want you to transform. I'm very curious about those wings of yours. Please be ready to do so the first time I ask. Consider that I know how to make it happen, if you do not." The woman kissed her, a friendly peck on the cheek. "Until tonight," she said, and Liu Chenguang felt the shift in energy that meant she had transformed and flown.

The larger of the two demons holding her, a man almost Tainu's height, threw her over his shoulder and began to run with her, long loping strides. But not as quick as Aili, she thought, not as fast. Shancheng…they were staying near the river, then. She tried to think what to do, but her mind was panicking. Zhu Guiren had kept her unconscious while they cut her for her blood and had talked about this as though it were a great favor, but now she realized that perhaps he was right; perhaps other demons would be far worse. She had never been captured before, but Tainu had once told her that one of the reasons phoenixes needed to be so careful, needed to always hide, was that there were beings in the world, demon and mortal, who would enjoy having control of a being they could constantly torture that would never die, that could never escape from them. She had never really believed it until now.

She knew one thing, though. That woman could do whatever she wanted with her daggers, but there was no way she would ever do what she asked. Clearly, it would make no difference to the final outcome. And Aili would come for her soon.

The demons ran until they dropped, then handed her off to others. It didn't escape her that the demons were as terrified of the woman, Second, as she was, if not more so. None of them spoke to her and she had no opportunity to escape, trussed up hand and foot and tossed from demon to demon. She had no talismans left, even if she had had hands free to use one. At one point, she silently transformed and beat her wings, striking the demons with pure qi, but they overcame her again and bound her more heavily, this time with a sort of lined net that hurt her skin wherever it brushed her, a constant pain as they ran.

Their path, as far as she could tell, lay mostly along the levees on the north side of the river. Across from Shancheng, the demons were met by others in a small boat waiting for them and they moved back to the south shore. The building they took her to was right next to the river since it was now in flood — an ancient stone warehouse of some kind. She had stopped being able to think at this point. Despite her bravado, the thought of seeing that woman again terrified her.

Second was waiting for her in a large room with a couch and a window overlooking the river. The sky was threatening rain, an increase in the flooding. "It's just us, little phoenix," she said, sipping something while she sat on the low couch. Liu Chenguang had been thrown on the floor in front of her, the demon guards waiting outside the room's closed door. Second's hair had been re-braided with silver. "When we return to clan home, perhaps you'll see your friend Third again. Or the other phoenix. But for now, just us."

The woman put her cup down and said, "Transform."

Liu Chenguang got herself together enough to kneel upright, but said nothing.

The woman smiled. "Delightful," she said. She walked around her in a slow circle. At one point she reached out and touched Liu Chenguang's hair. "You know," she said, conversationally, "my spouse, First, has a terrible habit of destroying all of our strongest children. I wish he would remember to let them reproduce first, but he says it's so enjoyable to dominate those who resist, as opposed to the obedient, that sometimes he loses his control. It's something I've always found annoying about him. But I do see the attraction."

She knelt down in front of Liu Chenguang, very suddenly, so her face filled Liu Chenguang's field of vision. After her languid circling, the swiftness of the movement was terrifying. She reached out and touched Liu Chenguang's lips. "I'm not my husband," she said, "luckily for you. But I also appreciate the importance of dominating those who don't obey. If you would like to have a slightly less terrible time when we reach clan home, it would be better for you to learn obedience now, so that you don't draw his attention to you. He has had his fun with Third already. He'll be looking for something else to play with." She smiled, and put her finger inside Liu Chenguang's lips, stroking her tongue.

To her horror and shame, Liu Chenguang found that she couldn't even bite down. Even that small piece of self-defense was impossible for her.

The woman noted her distress, smiled, and added another finger. "You see," she said gently. "I could rip your tongue out right now, and there's nothing you could do about it. Perhaps it would grow back? An interesting experiment." She leaned over and whispered intimately in her ear, "Transform, my dear."

Liu Chenguang closed her eyes. The woman dug her nails into her tongue until the blood came, and she heard herself making terrible noises, choking and retching, while the tears ran down her face.

"Still no?" The woman got up and walked back over to the couch. "The hard way it is, then."

When she came back, she was holding a silver instrument that looked like a small, flexible wand with sharp teeth. Before Liu Chenguang was aware, she had struck her on the back with it.

Liu Chenguang screamed. The thing was full of corrupted qi, ripping into her skin and muscles, burrowing down like razored insects, tearing her meridians and spilling into both her mortal and spiritual body. The woman struck her again, and again, and again.

She would not transform, she would not transform, she would not do it. She clenched her fists and closed her eyes. She could feel what was happening — that the qi was trying to force her mortal body to transform in self-defense; it would be the first and normal reaction for any phoenix — but she wouldn't do it. *She wouldn't, she wouldn't, she wouldn't.*

Every so often, the woman would stop and look at her, always in silence, listening to her sob for breath, as she felt herself beginning to heal and the pain beginning to subside. Then, Second would begin again, moving from her back to her shoulders, her face, her belly, her legs and hips, anywhere unpredictable.

Eventually, Liu Chenguang lay quivering on the floor, unable to move or speak or focus her eyes. Her throat was raw with screaming. She realized dully that she was not healing as quickly as before.

The woman kicked her onto her back and looked down at her, smiling, and then knelt by her. Taking her chin in her hands, she said, "Really, you are quite a pleasure, my dear. Much stronger than you look." She kissed her on her forehead. "First will enjoy meeting you." She kicked her again, in the ear, and then left.

Two demons came back in and bound her, but left her lying where she was. Apparently, this was her prison for the evening. Shaking from pain and the on-going torment of her meridians, she closed her eyes, and tried to sleep.

Aili followed the golden light without stopping, calling Liu Chenguang's true name every few minutes to be sure it hadn't diverged, but it followed the course of the river on the north side faithfully, and then, at Shancheng, crossed back over to the south bank, such as it was with the river deciding banks were completely unnecessary here. It was well after midnight when she had reached that point — slowed down by the flooding, almost two full days without sleep, food, or rest — and she knew she was drawing heavily on her cultivation to keep going, but there was no question of doing anything else. This was where Liu Chenguang was; the golden light ended here, in this city, in this street, in this building, a stone monstrosity with no lit windows.

She was sure that she could go in and get Liu Chenguang out, but unless she had a place to go with her, there was no point; it wasn't any different than it had been on the bank of the river days ago. A safe place, a safe place to run with a phoenix, with pursuit behind them. Or a place where someone would hide them.

Aili looked back at the Sorrowful River, its golden-brown water sliding by, showing nothing that was underneath, and threw in a pearl. Then, she closed her eyes to gather herself. The pearl would bring Yisue for them, or it wouldn't. Either way, when she came out with Liu Chenguang, they would jump into the river. She could think of no other plan. She would help Liu Chenguang swim… they would be so slow. She couldn't think of that. It was the only option they had; she would not leave Liu Chenguang here for one moment longer. She looked back at the building and whispered Liu Chenguang's true name. She was there. There were no windows at ground level, and only one door.

Aili realized she was very, very angry.

She took a deep breath, grasped a phoenix whip in one hand and En in the other, and ran for the entrance, slashing down with a sword pulse against the wood and stone of the gate. Demons boiled out — crows and mortal bodies, wings and weapons — and she started killing.

Liu Chenguang heard the shouts and clash of metal and saw the reflected light of the phoenix whip on her window, flaring red and gold, and closed her eyes in relief. Aili had come.

They had only bound her with rope, ordinary rope, not spells, but she struggled to loosen her hands and feet. Quite a bit of her own blood had spilled during Second's time with her — enough to make the ropes both slick and sticky — and she rubbed her wrists against them until they let her draw her hands out, then she worked on the knots around her ankles.

She could hear Aili now, hear her voice, yelling for her. She called back, "Aili!" Her voice sounded hoarse from all the screaming she'd done earlier, that still wasn't fully healed, but she heard the clash of weapons around Aili coming closer and closer. She stood shakily, and started walking toward the door, but it suddenly blew inward, raging with phoenix fire, and Aili was there, her whole body wreathed in flame.

And then, the fire went out and Aili fell forward onto her knees. Liu Chenguang screamed. A sword bearing a talisman was thrust into Aili's chest. Second stood there, smiling, holding the sword lightly in one hand. She had moved so fast that Liu Chenguang hadn't even seen her. She saw Aili's mouth moving, trying to say her name, but it was as though she were paralyzed.

Second smiled again. "Look, little phoenix," she said, turning to smile at Liu Chenguang, "your lover came. As expected. Perfect." She wrenched the sword out of Aili's chest, and as the talisman fluttered down,

Liu Chenguang saw a black, oily mark left on Aili's body.

"The experiment is successful," Second said, and kicked at Aili's shoulder so she fell down on her face. En and the phoenix whip had both disappeared. "Third helped me design that talisman just for you, whatever it is you are." She squatted down and looked at Aili with great interest, then reached over to stroke her face.

Aili's eyes followed the movement of her hand, but she couldn't turn her head.

"So, this one broke Third's array. Fascinating. He didn't think she would be able to do it."

"Get away from her," Liu Chenguang said, but she was held by two demons again. "Aili," she called, trying not to scream. She knew that if Aili could hear her, she would want to know she was all right, that they weren't hurting her. She would never ever tell Aili about what had happened before she came. "Let me go to her," she said. "She's hurt. Let me help her."

"No," Second said, "I want her to heal on her own. I want to see how this works." She went back to the couch. "Shackle the hybrid. Rope alone is fine. She can't transform."

Suddenly, there were screams from below them: the first floor of the building.

Second frowned and stood again. "What is it? You, you, and you, go see and report."

Several demons ran for the door, but the screams were coming closer, and along with the screams there was a strange noise: a deep, slow, regular pounding, with space between each strike. The noise was coming closer as well.

Since Aili had already mostly destroyed the doors, Liu Chenguang could see down the corridor leading to it, and turning the corner from the stairs came a man. He was both tall and powerfully fat, dressed in a fashionable Federation-style suit and vest, his hair long and graying, and a thin, gray, beard hanging to his large belly in three strands. He held a walking stick in one hand, and this made the pounding noise at each of his steps — a great, deep, booming sound from the little half-height cane — making the stone walls vibrate and shudder.

The man walked deliberately and without haste toward the door of their room. The demons who attacked him from all sides simply were thrown back violently into the walls, broken and dead, as though they were touching something that could in no way be affected by their feeble efforts, something that paid them no more mind than an elephant pays to an ant. He neither looked at them nor raised his hand, but merely kept walking. His right eye was covered with an eye patch and his face was set in an expression of deep disgust, as if for some unfathomable reason he had been forced to take a detour through a narrow alley filled with stinking waste.

Behind him came a little boy with tangled white hair, filthy and completely naked. "Aili!" he yelled happily, peeking around the man's arm. "Aili, my uncle came to see you!"

# CHAPTER 17
## BEILONG

LIU CHENGUANG DID her best to bow toward the man. He ignored her completely. "This is the one?" he asked, looking down at Aili.

Yisue ran to Aili and shook her, his happy face suddenly a caricature of shock. "Uncle, uncle, they hurt her–"

The man turned to sweep his gaze across the room. His expression of disgust intensified. "Any friend you have here, take them to the palace and wait for me while I clean up this trash." He added, without looking at him, "And put on some clothes, you shame our family."

"Yes uncle," said Yisue, and he transformed. The room was suddenly full of white dragon scales.

Second yelled, "Retreat! Grab them–"

But Yisue already had Aili caught in his mouth, and quicker than water had come to Liu Chenguang. Yisue's uncle looked at the demons holding her. His glance alone threw them, bones broken and vomiting blood, into the stone wall. Neither of them moved again.

Liu Chenguang clambered on Yisue's back. "Go, go, go," she said. "Yisue, go quickly!"

As Yisue swarmed back down the stairs, she saw the carnage all around them, the demon bodies, but she knew that worse would be coming. Above her head, she heard the voice of Yisue's uncle. "How dare you, demon, do this on my banks?" he roared. "What makes you think you can disrespect me in this way? Do you think I am unable to control my own territory?"

Second said, "There is no disrespect meant–"

A great booming noise came, as though Yisue's uncle had struck the floor with the cane grown to the size of a tree. The entire building shook, and stones started to come down around them, and although they were still on the second floor suddenly they were surrounded with swirling, unstoppable water the color and texture of milky tea, rising and rising at a rate beyond belief — dozens of feet per second.

"Here we go!" yelled Yisue. "Take her," and he turned his head so Liu Chenguang could pull Aili out of his mouth and hold on to her. "Hold your breath!"

They were surrounded by the deep brown water, impossible to see through or around. Liu Chenguang closed her eyes, kissed Aili with a seal over her nose to keep her from breathing in the water, and held her breath, and held her breath, and held her breath, and finally she had to breathe. When she opened her eyes they were in a room made of stones, lit by pearls set in the ceiling.

She half-fell from Yisue's back, trying to keep Aili — still paralyzed and seemingly unconscious — from falling heavily to the floor. Yisue immediately transformed and knelt next to her, hovering over Aili's body.

"What happened?" he asked miserably.

"There were demons. They attacked us." She didn't have enough attention to go into it further. The wound where Aili had been stabbed was not healing; black tendrils seeped out from it into her body, weeping a thick black fluid. When she tried to check her meridians, she found that the rot was moving through them, pushing all the qi that remained into her extremities to be trapped there, unable to circulate. The pain must be intense, but blessedly, she was unconscious. Liu Chenguang almost wept in horror at the thing. If only Tainu were here…she didn't know how to do this.

Yisue said, "Liu Chenguang, Liu Chenguang, you can fix her? You're a phoenix, you can fix anything!"

But she couldn't fix everything. There were some wounds a phoenix couldn't heal — not many, but some — and cultivational injuries were healed by skill, not only blood. Besides, "A phoenix can't heal another phoenix. It doesn't work," she said helplessly, trying to circulate qi in Aili's damaged cultivation.

"But she's not a phoenix, she's a starfish," Yisue said.

Liu Chenguang took a shaky breath. "Yes," she said. "Give me something sharp." Yisue ran over to a rack at the wall and came back with a dagger. She slashed her hand and lay it down over the wound, then bit her lip and leaned over to kiss Aili's wound, closing her eyes.

She could feel her blood circulating against the rot, bearing qi with it, forcing it back, but it was difficult, difficult — as though she herself had become part of her own blood, imbued into Aili's body, seeking out the uncorrupted qi, strengthening it into walls, pushing the walls back, back, back, meridian after meridian, toward the central wound.

Yisue yelled as she fell backward from Aili's body, too exhausted to continue. Something rose up from the sword wound, a misshapen ball, sending its tendrils out toward her, toward Yisue.

*BOOM!*

The man who had rescued them entered the room with his cane and scornfully poked the thing with it. It instantly dissipated, not purified with qi, but simply melting into nothingness. "It was sentient," he said. "Disgusting."

Liu Chenguang tried to stand, but couldn't yet.

"Don't bother. Yisue, what did I tell you?"

Yisue looked down at himself. "I'm sorry, uncle," he said. "We were trying to save Aili."

The man knelt down next to Aili, surprisingly agile despite his bulk, and lay his large hand on the sword wound. "It's healing now. She'll need to rest for a while before she comes back to consciousness, though. And you look as though you could use a bath and a rest as well."

Liu Chenguang bowed awkwardly from her sitting position.

He stood and said, "The jiaoren will tend to both of you. Rooms will be prepared. When you feel ready, tell the jiaoren to bring you to my audience hall." He sighed. "And you too, Yisue. Let the jiaoren bathe you and give you clean clothes. If you want to live among mortals you'll need to do this. I don't understand why it's such an issue for you."

"There's no mortals *here*," he said rebelliously under his breath.

The man looked at him.

"Sorry uncle," he said.

Yisue's uncle swept out of the room, this time thankfully not striking his cane on the ground with every step, and several people entered: beautiful young men and women dressed in the style of the Feng dynasty, flowing silks and ribbons and golden ornaments in their hair. Several of them had visible scale marks on their faces, but this only made them look more interesting. Their hair varied in color, white, red, orange, and black; some of them even had hair of more than one color. Liu Chenguang was intrigued. She had never met jiaoren in their mortal forms before. Two of the men brought a stretcher to carry Aili, and they walked together into a different part of the palace. All of it was made of stone and lit with the shimmering pearls hung in nets and strings from the ceiling. The men brought Aili into a room with a bed and a bath prepared and departed.

One of the female jiaoren bowed to Liu Chenguang and said in a very soft voice, hard to hear, "My lady, please come with me. You also have a room we have prepared for you."

"Who's going to bathe her?" she asked, frowning.

Two of the women bowed.

She wavered, feeling uncertain about this, but Aili certainly did need a bath, and she wasn't strong enough to lift and bathe an unconscious Aili by herself. She nodded and said, "Take good care of her, please," and followed the remaining two female jiaoren into another room across the corridor.

The bath attendants provided her with all she needed and offered to wash her hair for her, and then to rub it dry and comb it into a semblance of decency, which she accepted gratefully. Laid out for her when she was dry was a simple layered cultivator's robe. She was deeply glad that Yisue's uncle didn't expect her to wear women's Feng styles, so elaborate and so easy to trip over, though she would have done her best for politeness' sake.

Despite his invitation to rest for a while, Liu Chenguang knew very well that this person was not one to offend or keep waiting. As soon as she felt her appearance was acceptable, she asked the jiaoren to take her there, just peeking into Aili's room on the way to see her comfortably clean and sleeping.

The room was huge, with enormous golden pearls set along the sides so there was a delicate warm glow over all of the furniture, carved rosewood tables and chairs. The floor was shining polished black, inlaid with pale jade in complex patterns.

"This insignificant person expresses gratitude for the great lord's kindness and care for strangers," Liu Chenguang said, offering her most formal salute before Yisue's uncle.

The dragon of the Sorrowful River snorted disdainfully. He had changed his clothing for court dress of the Fu dynasty — brilliant yellow and deep gold embroidered with vermilion and jade — and looked all the more impressive despite the fact that he was lounging quite casually on a carved wooden couch with his feet up on the railing. "The other one has given care to this king's relative. A debt is owed," he said. "His parents certainly aren't doing the job. Come in, come in," he added, sitting up, "there's tea and more here. I doubt the demon fed you well since she was trying to whip you to death, or whatever she thought she would accomplish by torturing a phoenix."

Liu Chenguang came to sit opposite him at the tea table. Jiaoren brought over the teapot and some small delicacies, though she didn't have much appetite.

"That one," he said, "she has a dragon's heart."

"What?" Liu Chenguang asked, confused.

"Yisue told me about their journey here. She is a dragon."

"Great king, this person is confused by your statement."

"You may speak informally, and address me as Beilong," he said. "I'll let you know when I need you to be polite."

Liu Chenguang bowed her head, slightly nervous at the prospect.

Beilong slurped some tea with evident pleasure. "It's nice to have someone to talk to besides the jiaoren. They're all very quiet, hoping to become dragons someday, but they won't because they don't have dragon hearts. They're just fish when you get right down to it. Fish that have cultivated mortal forms. A dragon heart is different. A dragon heart knows the reality of sacrifice and risk."

"I don't understand," Liu Chenguang said. "That doesn't sound good at all."

"Of course you don't understand, you're a phoenix," he said. "Phoenixes are always about new beginnings, forgetting what was, transcending loss, done is done and pain is pain. You don't understand such things."

"That's not true," she said. "Not for me."

He looked at her, and behind his jovial attitude she saw a hint of his true nature, his single eye deep and unfathomable.

She bowed her head.

"I'm older than you, or any phoenix," he said, "and I have seen much. Sacrifice is also part of reality. It's not usually the nature of the phoenix to grasp this aspect of existence. But I see that you have done so." He bowed in return. "Does she know?"

"I haven't told her. There's no need for her to know. It's not certain. Who knows what will happen?"

The dragon's eye glinted at her. "True," he said. "Who knows? This may not be your last cycle after all. You may be reborn again. You just don't know. That's a sacrifice as well, to not know, and to take the risk anyway."

Liu Chenguang poured both of them more tea.

Beilong asked, "Would you prefer liquor?"

"Not at this time. I need my mind clear." She sipped her tea, and said, "No one knows, not even my sibling. I didn't know it myself when I did what I did, but I suspected it might happen. It would only make sense that taking another being into rebirth with me through my own power, giving her part of my own self, that this would weaken my own ability to continue in my existence."

"On the other hand, it may not," Beilong said. "Your existence may be strengthened. This is the nature of sacrifice. It is one of the levers that moves the world in ways that can't be predicted. Sacrifice brings the element of desire into all that is, and desire moves the world into new and unexpected paths."

"But what does it mean," Liu Chenguang pressed, "when you say that she has a dragon heart?"

"Courage, sacrifice, desire, strength, willfulness, unpredictability and violence — these mark the dragon heart," he explained.

"That's not all of who she is," she said. "Not at all."

"Of course not," he said. "It's not all of who I am either. I am also the source of life for uncounted millions who have lived in my valley for all of mortal history, back beyond any possibility of memory. But they always think they have to buy safety from me or control me for this to happen because to them, the dragon heart is only power and violence and unpredictability. And I do not like being controlled. Neither does she." Sipping his tea, he added, "You should not keep secrets from her."

Liu Chenguang said, "Someday I'll tell her. Now, she's too upset about anything that might hurt me."

"Hah, possessive and protective as well! She truly is a dragon." He tapped on the table. "As I said, a dragon is also a source of life — the life of the mortal realm, growing and dying, creating and destroying. It is because we are far more mortal than you phoenixes are, more connected to the mortal realm, that we are so. This is true for her as well. It is her mortal soul that permits her to give a different life to you. This is why I wanted to meet her. I have things I wish to say to her later, when she is able to listen. Meanwhile, tell me what was happening with that trash of a demon. I have never seen such blatant disregard for my power and dignity. Not ever. How dare she, on my banks, torture a phoenix!"

Liu Chenguang could very easily imagine him lashing his tail in fury.

"There have been great sacrifices of mortals lately," he said. "My banks were breached and my bed has shifted. Countless thousands gave up their lives to me. An unwilling sacrifice is still a sacrifice. In return, I must protect my people from being preyed upon by demons like that one."

"It's a complicated story," she said, and began.

On her way back from talking with Beilong, she knocked at the door and said, "It's me."

Aili's voice responded, "Don't come in."

She opened the door anyway.

Liu Chenguang stopped in the doorway to look at Aili. She was standing with her face to the wall, one fist clenched — the very picture of anger and rejection. Her hair had come out of its braid when they bathed her and hadn't been put up again; she had rarely seen it down. She realized that she very much wanted to touch it and smiled. All she could think was, I love this person so much. "Aili," she said.

Aili turned to look at her, silently. "Liu Chenguang," she finally said in a voice that shook with anger, "you should leave. I'm going to say things I'll regret later."

Liu Chenguang ignored this and walked inside. She felt very light, as though she had discovered a great secret. The world was encircled with a wall and there were no doors in it. As long as a person tried to get through the wall they would always fail, and yet, the wall was much smaller than the world's vastness; all one needed to do was look in another direction. In the end, she thought, it turns out that I am still a phoenix, after all.

She noticed there was a table set with delicacies, apparently untouched. "Have you eaten?" she asked.

"No," gritted Aili. "I don't want to eat. Liu Chenguang, I am–" she took a deep breath, "I am so angry at you."

"I know," Liu Chenguang said. She looked up at her. "But I'm hungry. Aren't you?"

Aili said, "No. I am not hungry."

Liu Chenguang picked up a dessert that she loved, made of soft tofu with sweet syrup. "Have you ever had this?" she asked, and tasted it. "It's delicious."

"I. Have. Not." Aili frowned at her from across the room. She was wearing a Feng inner robe tied only at the waist, the thin fabric showing the shape of her body — her broad shoulders and the curve of her breasts. Her dark gold, unbraided hair tumbled down just past her shoulders, thick and not very long. It made her face look more gentle, even though she was so angry, with her eyes narrowed and her fists clenched at her side, ready to fight.

Liu Chenguang stood silently by the table, rolling the sweet tofu on her tongue and reveling in looking at her.

"What is it?" Aili said at last. "Why aren't you talking to me?"

Liu Chenguang said, "I really think you should taste this."

"No. I don't want it."

Liu Chenguang walked over to her with a spoonful.

"I said I don't want it."

"Yes you do." She ate a little bit off the spoonful herself.

"No. I don't."

"Yes. You do." Liu Chenguang smiled at her and offered the spoon. When Aili wouldn't take it, she tasted some more, just a little, just touching it with her lips.

"I don't." Aili was looking down at her, her eyes still narrowed, but her voice was wavering.

"You do." Liu Chenguang held the spoon up to her mouth.

Aili took the spoon out of her hand, very carefully, and laid it down on the little table next to the wall, never looking away from her eyes.

Liu Chenguang looked up at her, her mouth partly open, not able to smile any more, feeling dizzy at being so close to her, at what would happen next, her own heartbeat pounding in her ears. "Aili," she said, and closed her eyes, feeling Aili meeting her lips, slowly licking at the sweetness there and in her mouth, tasting her and exploring her — her mouth and down the line of her throat. All her body went soft with yearning, so Aili had to put her arms around her and hold her upright. Still kissing her, Aili picked her up and quickly turned to press her body hard against the wall, her robe coming all loose in front so she could feel the heat of Aili's body through the thin fabric.

Aili whispered hoarsely, "Arms around neck, legs around waist," and so she did.

Since there were no windows, there was no day or night in Beilong's palace, but the jiaoren seemed to have some sense of times for waking and sleeping and knocked to bring breakfast to them sometime after they had slept, tangled and sweaty in Aili's bed. Neither of them had ever lived in a place that had this sort of service before and both of them felt very embarrassed to be lying there, naked and trying to hide under the blankets, but the jiaoren seemed to literally not see them, laying out the food on the table as well as washbasins, cloths, and clean clothing for both of them, then departing in silence.

Aili whispered, "They all seem to have bulgy eyes. I feel like they're looking at me even when they're not," and Liu Chenguang laughed.

After breakfast and getting dressed, Liu Chenguang brought Aili to Beilong's audience room again. He was already there, and this time, so was Yisue — clean and elaborately dressed in the style of a Mitang chieftain, his white hair braided with gold — practically dancing with excitement.

"Aili Aili Aili!" he yelled, and launched himself at her, grabbing her around the waist.

"Yisue!" she said, equally happy, and picked him up to spin him around. "Yisue, thank you for coming to us," she added more seriously, then bowed to Beilong. "Thank you for saving us."

Liu Chenguang was pleased to note that she seemed not at all intimidated.

Beilong said, "You have a dragon heart."

Aili said, "I promise you that I do not."

Beilong snorted with laughter, a vast sound that hinted at a creature much larger than could be contained in the room around them. "Hah, you are a good one." He stood up and stretched. "You have been good to my nephew, and so I wished to meet you. You have a dragon heart, but you are not a dragon. There are things you can do that a dragon cannot do, but you will do them in a dragon way."

Aili didn't respond. Liu Chenguang could tell she was confused.

"We will have time to talk more. I will learn you better. For now, I wish to ask you a *favor*," Beilong said. He put a great weight on the word. "My nephew needs to be cared for better than his current caregivers can, since they will not leave the deep sea, and he is drawn to the edges of the land. He is running wild and does not know how to be a dragon, nor does he know how to be with mortals. He wishes to be among them, and thus needs to learn the dragon's proper role among other beings. He cannot stay here with me forever, and he will not learn from me." He casually reached over and smacked Yisue on the back of his head.

Yisue grinned at him.

"You see?" he asked, making a terrible frown at Yisue. He flipped up his eye patch so Yisue could see his scarred and missing eye, and Yisue yelled with laughter. He turned and formally bowed to Aili.

Liu Chenguang watched in awe.

"I ask if you would take my nephew to foster and teach him," he said, remaining in a bow. "If you will care for him until he is ready to take his place among dragons and mortals."

"What about his parents?" Aili asked, frowning.

"Parenthood among dragons is not like mortals," Beilong replied impatiently. "Yisue's parents beneath the great sea have already let him depart. He will need a new home to grow to adulthood."

"Does he want to?" Aili asked uncertainly, looking at Yisue,

"Yes yes yes yes!" yelled Yisue. "I want to!"

She smiled at him and said to Beilong, who remained bowed, "I am willing, but I don't know how long my lifetime will be — how long it will take him to grow up."

"Hah," said Beilong, and stood upright. "It is done."

Liu Chenguang and Aili both stood still, looking at Yisue. Aili met Liu Chenguang's eyes, and Liu Chenguang nodded.

"Now," said Beilong, "we move. Your phoenix and I spoke last night about the other phoenix and the demon with whom you concern yourself. I have a second favor to ask you: go destroy these demons, their nest."

"That's something I would do for free," said Aili.

Liu Chenguang smiled.

Beilong said, "Indeed you would! But I am laying it on you as well. I will give you what help I can."

"Can you come with us?" Aili asked. Liu Chenguang had described to her Beilong's power — how the demons had fled before his face and were destroyed by his glance.

He shook his head. "A river cannot run uphill. No demon makes a nest where I can reach them. While I could come with you in my mortal body to the mountains, away from my bed and floodplain my power is limited. I would not be able to do much for you. But, I know that their nest is somewhere in the mountains above Ximersia, where I run narrow and deep. I will bring you to Ximersia, and I will give you what I can to help you. Return to the river at any time for safety. The jiaoren will be waiting to protect you if I am not there."

"Can I come?" Yisue asked.

"No," said Beilong and Aili at the same time.

Yisue pouted.

The palace seemed to exist in a strange netherworld beneath the Sorrowful River. When Beilong walked outside with them, Aili looked up and saw that the sky was a deep, swirling mass of brown and gold and white, like an ever-moving painting. Light did not come through it; it was far darker here than it was within the pearl-lit palace.

Beilong turned to Aili and said, "Take this." He gave her a flask full of swishing liquid. Consideringly, he continued, "Your power is that of the phoenix fire and a mortal soul. You are a mortal cultivator. There are other ways to find the qi of the world, in the powers of the mountains and the rivers. This is all qi. When your cultivated qi is exhausted, drink some of this. It will feel different for you, but will enable you to keep fighting. Fighting is what you will want to be doing!"

He slapped her on the back so that she almost fell over, and whispered, "Don't give any to the phoenix. It's not good for her. She's not of the mortal realm."

Aili nodded. "What about demons?"

"Hah, no idea. Demons fear the river, as they should. Water is life and movement and transformation. Demons cultivate the barrenness of resentment. I can't imagine it would feel good for them. But it is not a weapon." He stepped away. "Let's be off. Stand back."

Aili and Liu Chenguang stood against the outer wall of the palace. Yisue, glum, stood next to them.

Beilong transformed.

The yellow dragon filled all their vision, so enormous she couldn't take it in, the one glaring eye larger than a house, its body fading into the distance. It spoke in a voice that made their entire bodies vibrate, so large and deep that it was almost not a sound. "Get on," he said. "With me, you don't need to hold your breath. This will be quick. You," he said to Yisue, "go inside. When I return, I want you to recite two new verses from the Great Classic."

"Goodbye, Aili," Yisue said sadly. "Come back soon. Goodbye, Liu Chenguang." He turned reluctantly and walked back into the palace.

Aili and Liu Chenguang had to use qinggong to leap up to Beilong's back, and then they were off, moving upstream through the shifting, impenetrable waters.

# CHAPTER 18
## CLAN HOME

ZHU GUIREN STOOD over him, cutting him again. Tainu stared at the ceiling, trying not to look at his face. There was beginning to be pain now, pain that didn't go away. For a phoenix, injury was always temporary, and thus a phoenix didn't get used to pain; it was new every time. But now, there were things in his body that didn't heal, and thus he was getting used to them: the slashing cuts, the bedsores, the weariness of not being able to move his limbs from their fixed places. He knew that this meant whatever First had in mind for him would come soon. There was not much time left. Very soon, though not in the mortal realm, it would be possible to kill him.

He was not afraid to die. He had lived a very long time. He suspected that when the time came, he would even be grateful to have it over. This must be how his beloved family had felt — how so many mortals felt, tormented by a life that went too long and too far into pain and loss and memories — that a time would come to leave. That was all right. It was only for his demon that he was afraid to go. For his beloved one, who would suffer alone after he was gone, who would never forgive himself for what was happening right now.

Suddenly Zhu Guiren screamed and collapsed on the floor next to him, convulsing.

Tainu yelled, "Demon! What is it!"

But Zhu Guiren was beyond answering, bloody froth at his mouth.

First stood up, frowning. "Check him," he said shortly.

Another demon knelt next to Zhu Guiren and tried to check his acupoints, then shook his head. First walked rapidly over and passed his hand over Zhu Guiren's body. "Ah," he said. "His cultivational structure has been ripped again. There is a serious—" He jumped backward, and the other demon began backing up as well, as quickly as he could, as Zhu Guiren's body transformed.

There was a being lying there now, a glittering silver creature sprawled on the floor, something between a lizard and a cat, perhaps fifteen or twenty feet long, with a smoky mane tangled over its long neck, and bearing an impossible thicket of horns on its head, clear and shining as icicles just before melting, some several feet long. It was missing its left front claw, and its left wing hung at an awkward angle. The creature cried out and thrashed in pain.

Tainu begged, "I can help him! Let me help him, please!" He was terrified now. The demon had returned into his true body while in the mortal realm; he was extraordinarily vulnerable, anyone could kill him with hardly any effort, his true body unsheltered and unshielded by the mortal one. He tried desperately to pull himself out of the shackles, but of course, nothing happened.

First walked over to him and looked down, those red-veined black eyes boring into his own. After a moment he leaned down to him. "If you attempt to heal his heart, I will kill him immediately," he said softly. "Do not doubt how fast I am." He reached out and touched the shackles on his wrists and ankles, which disappeared. "The one on your neck remains. That is enough to keep you from transforming."

His ankles and wrists also had sores; he rubbed them quickly, then stumbled off the couch over to where the demon had subsided into quivering unconsciousness. "Demon," he said, standing near the great head, "I'm here, it's me." He slipped his hand, already covered with his own blood, into the crystal-fanged mouth and let his head lie, just for a moment, against the forehead of the creature. It was near his head's height as he knelt next to it. One of the ice horns grazed the top of his skull, sharp as a razor, and as cold. The glittering silver scales sent a shower of light all around him. He reached out to stroke the mane, softer than smoke; his fingers could barely feel its fineness. "You've grown so big," he said, his eyes filling with tears. Even with all that was happening, he was glad he was able to see his true body one time — how the lithe quickness of his childhood had become power and beauty.

The body shivered, shimmered, shrank back into Zhu Guiren lying unconscious on the ground. Tainu knelt next to him, awkwardly because his body wasn't flexible anymore, and held out his hand, forming his true name silently in his mouth, putting whatever qi he could still summon into it, feeling the damage to the demon's meridians. He could feel the block that First had placed around the demon's heart, but it was not something he could have broken even if he wanted to. In his current state, bled and weakened, it was far beyond his power. The demon's meridians had been torn — some of them completely severed, others violently jerked out of alignment. The damage was spreading through his cultivational body like wildfire, demonic qi flooding everywhere within him, ripping him apart.

Tainu drew deeper into himself, pouring it into his demon from the last reserves he had of his own power, closing the bleeding meridians, and pushing the demonic qi back where it could be contained, to keep him alive, to keep his mortal and spiritual bodies from disintegrating in pain and madness. At last, Tainu fell down over him, gasping, blood trickling from his mouth and nose. He had nothing left, and he didn't think Zhu Guiren would ever be able to cultivate again, but he would live.

Zhu Guiren opened his eyes and looked up at him, confused. "What happened?" he asked. "What is it?"

Two demons grabbed Tainu and made him lie down again. First re-established the shackles, then walked back to his chair. "Continue," he said.

Zhu Guiren frowned and shook his head. He stood up with difficulty, trembling as though his body pained him. Then, he took his knife out again, and continued.

At some point later, an unimaginable amount of time later, Tainu lay alone in absolute darkness, body and mind, heart and soul. This was the time he should sleep — when the lights were out and the demons had left, when no one was cutting him or hurting him — but he couldn't. There was too much pain. He had used all of his qi for his demon, and his mortal body was deteriorating far more quickly now with no chance to rejuvenate or heal himself. He wondered, if they didn't take him to the spirit realm, if he might just continue living forever like this, like a piece of meat being sliced every day. What had Zhu Guiren said so long ago? Meat that doesn't die? Dying would be better.

He heard someone approaching. Even though everything was dark, he knew. A thread of warmth came into his heart. "Demon," he said softly.

Zhu Guiren stood next to him, then sat down on the stone couch. "I remember being like this," he said. "I remember holding your hand while you slept."

"You did," he said gently, remembering. "Would you like to now?"

He felt Zhu Guiren's hand tentatively entangling with his, interlacing with his fingers.

"I don't feel anything," the demon said at last. "I thought I might."

Tainu felt his eyes tearing up again, but weeping wouldn't help anything. He said, "Demon, will you listen to what I have to say? I don't know if I'll have a chance to tell you anything in the future."

"All right," Zhu Guiren's voice came indifferently.

He took a deep breath. "Come closer," he said.

Zhu Guiren leaned down. He could feel the warmth of his face near his lips in the absolute darkness. "Arciniang," he whispered. "I want you to remember this. I love you and will always love you. You are beautiful to me. You have been the best thing in my life. I don't regret anything. Will you remember that?"

"All right," he said again. His face remained near. "Is there more?"

"Yes." He didn't want to miss this opportunity; who knew if they would have any more time, ever again? He knew that there was almost certainly another listener — First might have anticipated that Zhu Guiren would come to him privately — so he tried to keep his voice as quiet as possible, but he couldn't not speak. "First wants to kill you. Be careful of him, please. Don't trust him."

"Of course he does, and I am, and I don't," he said calmly.

Tainu said, "That's good, that's good. I want you to be safe." He breathed and tried to think how to say it, wishing he could move a hand to touch him. "Demon, I know you don't feel anything for me now–"

"That's true."

"But there may come a time when you feel things again, and I know that you'll feel badly about what's happening right now. I want you to know that I know in your heart you don't want this. I want you to be able to forgive yourself. You have to promise me that you won't harm yourself, and you won't let anyone else harm you. Promise me."

"Why would I need to promise you that?" He made a little sound of annoyance. "Don't worry if it's on your mind. My life is always my own highest priority."

"Good," Tainu said. "Your life is also my highest priority."

Zhu Guiren paused. "Even now?" he asked uncertainly. "What about your life? Don't you want to escape?"

"Of course," he said. "But if I can't escape, if I can't have what I want, then just preserving your life is my wish."

"What do you want?"

It was dark, and he couldn't see Zhu Guiren's face, but he remembered that tone of voice well enough, imagining him frowning, trying to understand something that confused him. He smiled a little.

"I want you to have your heart back, and for us to live together, and love each other, and be happy," Tainu said. "That's all. That is my only wish. If I can't have that, between your life and mine, I would choose yours."

Zhu Guiren shook his head; Tainu could feel the movement of the air. "You're a phoenix," he said. "You're not going to die."

Tainu had given this a lot of thought since First had talked to him. First's plans couldn't be fully predicted, but he had said he intended to cultivate the resentment of a phoenix. There was only one way in which that could happen. "I think that First intends to kill me in the spirit realm, and for you to do it." He could feel Zhu Guiren's body grow still, the vibration of his breath ceasing in the darkness. "If that happens," he said, "for your own sake, please, refuse to be the one. Refuse. Let someone else do it." He couldn't risk letting him go without saying this, without being very clear. He was very much afraid that if his demon killed him with his own hand, he truly would commit suicide later no matter what he said now.

"I won't do it," he said. "I promise."

Tainu thought that there was an overtone of anger in his voice.

"That would be…too much. That would just be him trying to control me, demonstrate his power, be entertained by my obedience. I won't do it."

"All right." Tainu sank back, relaxed. His mind felt at peace now; he wanted to rest. If his demon was angry, he would get stubborn. He could trust that, at least. No one could make him do it if he refused. "That's good."

"Is that all?" Zhu Guiren asked after a long silence, still close enough to him that he could feel the warmth of his body. Their hands were still interlaced. It was a comfort to him. "I remember that you were good to me. I would free you if I could because I remember that. But I don't have the power to do it. First set your shackles himself. He's far stronger than I am, and I can't break those wards even if I tried. I wanted you to know that I would do it if I could. Because I remember," he said, with that directness so characteristic of him.

It made Tainu smile. "It's all right," he said. "I'm glad to know that you would if you could."

Again, Zhu Guiren asked, "Is that all?"

"That's all," he whispered sleepily. "Just remember that I love you, my demon, my Arciniang, always remember it."

"All right." Zhu Guiren bent closer, uncertainly, and then, to his surprise, lips touched his forehead. "I don't feel it, but I know that I loved you too. I'll remember what you said. So…so sleep well."

"Will you stay with me until I fall asleep?" he asked. He knew in his heart that he would not have this again.

"All right," Zhu Guiren, said, one last time.

He felt him there, holding his hand in the dark, until he slipped into sleep. When he woke again, the demon was gone.

Beilong brought them to the reaches of the Sorrowful River above Ximersia at evening, depositing them on the southern bank and disappearing silently back into the water, which looked far too narrow to hold him. Aili thought that probably the actual size of his body was too large for the mind to encompass and that this was just an imprint, a suggestion to the mind of "dragon."

Liu Chenguang whispered and looked up. Here, far to the north of the wide floodplain, the Sorrowful River ran deep and fast and turbulent in a steep gorge, with only a narrow bank a few feet wide, where they stood among tumbled rocks between the water and the stone walls.

"That way," Liu Chenguang said, pointing slightly east of south into the steepest mountains.

Aili looked at her seriously. "I'm not sure you should come," she said bluntly.

Just as bluntly, Liu Chenguang said, "It's a little late to say that now, Aili Fallon." She smiled as if to take the edge off. "Let's go. My qinggong actually isn't as terrible as you think it is. I just like it when you carry me."

They spent days climbing the cliffs and wandering among the peaks, trying to find a way to where Tainu was. Undoubtedly, it was in a fairly inaccessible area since the demons could fly in and out; the opening to it might be very small, large enough only for a person to crawl through. Even when Liu Chenguang said, frustrated, that Tainu was right *here,* here seemed to be beneath their feet.

One night, they huddled together under some low trees to keep warm, without a fire. Aili knew Liu Chenguang was almost frantic with worry.

"If only Tainu were here," Liu Chenguang said. "He's the one who can manage wards and spells, I don't know how." She slammed her hand down on a rock next to her and said "Ouch. If I was the one captured, I know he could find me."

Both of them had been racking their brains to see if there was anything Zhu Guiren had ever mentioned about his demonic home other than that he never wanted to go there again, but they couldn't think of any clues at all.

"Did you ever come here with Zhu Guiren?" Aili asked, reaching for anything. "Before?"

"We went to the southern sacred mountain, once," she said. "He left me there for a week at one of the temples. It was the only time in all our travels that he left me alone for more than a few hours. But that's the closest we came."

"It surely couldn't have taken him three days from the southern peak? It must be closer than that…"

"But he could fly then, if no one was watching him."

They looked, dejected, at the ground.

"I could just try to blast down through the rock somehow and see?" Aili was running out of ideas.

Liu Chenguang gave her the look that idea deserved.

"All right," Aili tried to work it out the way Zhu Guiren might have. "What marks might demons leave? What clues? What do demons…like?"

"Resentment," said Liu Chenguang automatically.

"There can't be that much resentment here. There's no mortals nearby at all, no towns or villages or cemeteries…Can you sense a place with strong resentment?"

Liu Chenguang closed her eyes and breathed deeply, then held up one finger and pointed it slightly west of south. "That way," she said. "It's quite strong. Further down the slope, not at the peak."

They picked their way down the mountain slowly, without qinggong, to follow every subtle hint that Liu Chenguang's senses could give about their direction. "We're close," she said several hours later, deep into the night. "We should plan as though we'll find the entrance. What should we do? Just…walk in?"

Both of them looked at each other.

"I honestly have no other idea," said Aili eventually. "We've had this much trouble finding one entrance, I doubt there are more. Will they sense us? Will there be guards?"

Liu Chenguang shook her head. "I don't know. Let's assume so?" She shivered. "What if they have more of those special talismans that are just for you?"

Aili said, "Well, we can only go see and try. We'll just…attack frontally. Try to use your wings to block talismans for me?"

Even in her anxiety about Tainu, Liu Chenguang seemed pleased that Aili had actually asked her to do this. It showed in her face; Aili kissed her lightly. "I'll be advance guard," she said, "and if we need to retreat, I'll cover. Remember what Beilong said. The river is safety. All we need to do is get to the water." There was a substantial ridge of mountains between them and the Sorrowful River, but it was better than nothing as a goal. "Even if we're separated," she said anxiously. "No matter what. You go straight to the river, promise?"

Liu Chenguang nodded. "You have the water Beilong gave you?"

Aili patted the flask at her side as she stood. "Let's go," she said softly.

The entrance was not magically invisible, but nature had done a good job. It was a narrow crack in a rock face, overlapped in front by a jutting boulder, impossible to see unless you were coming at just the right angle or already knew it was there. It would also be easy to defend from attackers, but there were no guards at all. Aili found this incredibly suspicious; surely there was at least a ward that was alerting the demons of intruders as they crossed into the rocks, but there was nothing to do except go forward, creeping sideways in the dark along the unlit cave wall.

Gradually, light showed in front of them after the tunnel had widened and gone through several sharp bends. Like Beilong's palace, it was lit with jewels hung from the ceiling — not pearls, but rubies and sapphires, producing an uneasy, shifting purple light. Aili liked this even less than the darkness. She reached out to find Liu Chenguang's hand and pull her nearer. The shadows produced by the swinging, irregularly placed jewels seemed to constantly be on the edge of solidifying into a hand or weapon coming toward them, and the air of resentment was stifling. Aili started shivering with nervous energy, ready for anything; she stopped herself just before pulling out the phoenix whip time and again for something that was only an illusion of the light.

Liu Chenguang stopped and pulled her closer. "It's affecting you," she breathed in her ear. "I can tell."

Aili nodded, nauseous. Liu Chenguang reached into the air beneath her own right hand and plucked hard, then wrapped Aili's hand around something she could feel only as a warm caress on her palm. "Feathers. Hold them, put them in your clothes, against your skin," she whispered. Aili slipped them inside her shirt, where they felt comforting and real.

As they turned the corner, someone stepped out in front of them, a true person. Zhu Guiren.

They both stopped and stared at him. Neither of them knew what to say.

Zhu Guiren's face was dreadful in the purple light. His hair had been cut short, so that all the planes of his face were sharp and shadowed, and his eyes were bruised and dull. He looked at them and said, very quietly, "My ward told me you came. I set it out past the entrance, well back, because I thought you might come for him. I disabled the inner ward so I would be the first one to find you."

When they didn't respond, he said, "Are you here to take him? Can you break the shackles?"

Liu Chenguang moved in front of Aili to block her with her wings. She said, "Zhu Guiren, if you know where he is, take us to him."

He immediately turned and started walking. They followed him down the twisting tunnel, which began to branch off, and he unhesitatingly took turn after turn after turn, in silence. The lights shifted from purple to a sickly orange, and he started to walk faster. "It will be dawn soon," he said. "You need to take him now."

Aili thought, *what's happening? If he's free to move why hasn't he freed Tainu himself?* But what other choice did they have except to follow him? Her hand was half-twisted, ready to call a weapon; Liu Chenguang clearly didn't trust Zhu Guiren at all, and stayed firmly between them, not letting Aili get near.

They came into a dark cavern, so unutterably black that the darkness seemed solid, something they needed to push against to enter. "He's here," said Zhu Guiren. "Can you break the shackles?"

Liu Chenguang rushed over, able to sense where Tainu was as she whispered his name, and Aili followed her scent in the air. Zhu Guiren came behind her, which made Aili's skin crawl, but he only stood behind them as though he would watch, although there was nothing to see.

"Aili," said Liu Chenguang, "En."

She brought En out and held it up. The golden light fell on Tainu's exhausted, ravaged face. Liu Chenguang made a whimpering noise and brought her fist to her mouth. "He's not healing," she said unnecessarily. The oldest scars were pale on his dark skin, but in the warm light of En his skin was mostly red. "Zhu Guiren, take the shackles off him, now, please, please now."

Zhu Guiren shook his head. "I thought you would," he said in a disinterested voice. "If I could, I would have already. They're still making me cut him every day, even though he's unconscious almost all the time now."

Aili turned to him slowly. "What did you say?"

"I can't undo the shackles. I thought you could."

"The other thing," she said, her voice shaking in a whisper.

"They're cutting him every day, even though he's unconscious."

"Who? Who cuts him?"

"I do. First insists that it be me." He looked at her calmly while saying it.

She slashed at him with En. He dodged, but not as easily or quickly as he had in the past; he was injured somehow.

"Aili," hissed Liu Chenguang sharply, "get Tainu out. That's what we're here for. That's what we need to do now."

In a nightmare of time passing, Aili tried.

She tried with En; she tried with a dagger made of spiritual qi, then with hooks of qi to tear the shackles out of the stone; she tried with the phoenix whip, even knowing it might take Tainu's hand off. She tried with her blood. She tried with Beilong's water, which hissed, rageful, when it struck the stone couch. She tried with her bare hands; the shackles burned them, as though they were coated with acid.

Zhu Guiren watched it all, his face unmoving.

Aili looked at Liu Chenguang. "I can't," she said at last. "I can't get them off."

Liu Chenguang's face grew horrified, then empty. "Aili," she said. "Kill him."

Zhu Guiren finally showed interest. "What?" he asked, frowning.

Aili understood, but she shook her head. "No, Chenguang. No."

"There's no other way. No other way, Aili. If we can't rescue him, send him into rebirth, then he'll be free." She looked at Zhu Guiren, her expression tortured. "We can't leave him here to go through this forever."

Zhu Guiren shook his head. "You can't kill him. That's…he wouldn't want you to do that. He told me. He told me, don't kill him."

Aili held En up to see him better as he spoke. For the first time, he seemed discomposed, his eyes dazed and uncertain.

"He specifically told me—" he said again. "He made me promise, don't kill him."

Aili looked at Liu Chenguang. "Chenguang, he said not to kill him…"

Liu Chenguang shook her head. "We can apologize to him later if it's not his intention," she said, "but believe me, Aili, he wouldn't want this, no matter what Zhu Guiren thinks he said."

Aili lifted En, then let it fall. "I can't, Chenguang."

"It won't take dismemberment now," Liu Chenguang said in a voice of forced calm. "If he were anything but a phoenix, he'd be dead already, long ago." She held her hand near his heart, and tears fell off her chin, glinting in En's light. "He has nothing left, Aili. No power left at all. He needs to be reborn. Just…just do it. Decapitation is the…safest and quickest way."

Aili looked at her. "Chenguang," she pleaded. "No."

Liu Chenguang stepped back. "I'm sorry, Aili," she said, "but if Zhu Guiren is forbidden, and I can see why Tainu might have forbidden it, you're the only one." Her voice was shaking, but her tone was inarguable. "The only one who can. He'll– he'll be back, don't worry. It just feels bad to you because you don't understand how it is for us. Rebirth is just…normal."

Aili looked at her, remembering Liu Chenguang's mutilated body on the ground, and then cleared her mind. "All right," she said. She positioned herself for a clean blow at his neck, and raised En, praying that he wouldn't wake up as the sword came down.

But as the sword whispered through the air, Zhu Guiren's halberd blocked it, En staggering in sparks, the harsh music of spiritual weapons clashing through the darkness. "No," he said, his face contorted with the effort. "No. He said no, don't kill him. He said someone else could do it. He said…not me."

Aili said, "Did he say not me?" She twisted En and tried to come at Tainu from another angle, but her heart wasn't in it, so she didn't even come close before Zhu Guiren blocked her again. "Maybe I count as someone else that can do it?"

"No, but I'm sure…I'm sure…" Zhu Guiren struck the halberd at her, quick and vicious. "He said…"

Aili realized, as they spun and struck at one another, that there was more light now and she could see him. His face was troubled, confused, his eyes unfocused; something was very wrong with him. The jewels in the cavern were starting to glow a rather cheerful, calming blue color — like a morning sky. She swore as the light grew stronger.

Zhu Guiren had managed to back her away from Tainu and corner her with a swift series of attacks from his halberd, but it was only because she was distracted. She could tell that he was far below his normal performance; his injury, whatever it was, must be serious. She flipped over his head and ran back toward Tainu. Something like a spear of qi dashed past her shoulder and almost hit Liu Chenguang, which enraged her.

"That's enough, children," came a cheerful voice. "Third, come here."

Zhu Guiren immediately stopped fighting and walked toward the owner of the voice: a tall, pale man with black eyes and a mane of white hair. He looked delighted to see them all. "Third," he said, and briefly trailed his hand over Zhu Guiren's chest in passing.

Zhu Guiren shivered back from his touch, but showed no other concern. His face grew calm again and his eyes cleared.

The white-haired man nodded toward Aili and Liu Chenguang. "You'll have to tell me why you're here and my wife is not," he said. "She hasn't returned from hunting you."

Aili leapt back toward Tainu, her sword raised. The man laughed and threw a talisman, but Liu Chenguang blocked it and it fell harmlessly to the ground.

More demons entered, but none of them attacked yet. The man waved his hand negligently and a protective net of purple light enclosed Tainu, who remained unconscious. "None of that, now," he said. "I have plans for that one. Now that I have another phoenix, no need to put it off."

Suddenly, a cloud of something dark, shot with red like old blood, surrounded Liu Chenguang. She screamed and fell to her knees, then down to the stone floor, unconscious.

"Take her," he said to Zhu Guiren. "We'll clean up the couch before putting her there. Just bring her along for now."

Aili ran toward Zhu Guiren, phoenix whip raised, but at the last moment whirled and sent it at the white-haired man.

He raised a hand and caught it, laughing. "Quite nice, quite nice!" he said. He moved quickly — so quickly she didn't see him move at all — to stand directly in front of her face, still holding the phoenix whip. His hand was burning slightly, a stench coming from the skin, but he seemed uncaring. "Here you are, my dear," he said smiling, and slapped a talisman on her throat.

The sick pain rushed through her and she collapsed immediately, but she could still see, still hear. Zhu Guiren walked over to Liu Chenguang and picked her up. The white-haired demon removed the protective net and reached out to touch Tainu's shackles, one by one. They all disappeared. The demon leaned over to slap Tainu's face, over and over, until his eyes opened blearily; Aili saw the moment when he realized that Liu Chenguang was in Zhu Guiren's arms, and she saw how he closed them again in utter despair.

"Demon," he said, his voice hoarse and croaking. He didn't say anything else. Zhu Guiren's eyes were fixed on him, expressionless.

The white-haired man tugged roughly at Tainu until he sat up, then stood, leaning against him. The man put his arm around Tainu, almost lovingly. "Are you ready?" he asked. He stroked Tainu's shoulders, gently, and kissed him. Blood came away on his hands and mouth.

Tainu didn't respond; he didn't open his eyes again.

"Third, give the little phoenix to them," the man said, gesturing at the other demons. "Ninth, choose four others, you're coming. Tie her up. Rope is fine, she doesn't need a shackle. The hybrid doesn't even need to be tied. The talisman is enough."

Once the demons had tied up Liu Chenguang, who was still unconscious, and one of them had picked up Aili, who was still unable to move, the white-haired man said, "Now this one. Tie him to carry."

Two demons came over to Tainu and lay him down on the ground to tie him.

"No," he said, when they were done. "You're not the ones that will carry him. Third," he called again. "Bring him."

Zhu Guiren walked over to Tainu and picked him up, cradling him gently against his chest, but his face was still blank. "Not like that, Third," called the white-haired man, seemingly in high spirits. "Over your shoulder, like a sack."

"No," Zhu Guiren said. "This way."

The white-haired man stood still and looked at him, then came over to him and looked in his eyes. "Hmmm." He reached out with one finger and touched Zhu Guiren's chest. "Still good," he said, as though he had determined that some sort of machine was still in running order.

Aili stared at Zhu Guiren, unable to conceive of how he could be there, holding Tainu's bloody unconscious body, not fighting, not running, not…doing anything. Did he have a plan? What was happening? She was close to total panic. They had Liu Chenguang now, but they hadn't shackled her yet; it wasn't too late to get her away, except she herself couldn't move, paralyzed by the talisman, waves of pain crashing through her and blurring her vision.

"Asking First," said the demon called Ninth, a woman with black hair cut short and vividly purple eyes, "please instruct these as to where we are going? Should we prepare for a journey?"

"No need." With a sharp movement of his hand, First opened a red-black slash in the air. "Come," he said, and he stepped forward.

The demon carrying Aili, much like a sack over his shoulder, followed after Zhu Guiren and the demon carrying Liu Chenguang had gone first. When he put his foot down after stepping through the break in the air and threw Aili on the ground, she saw the golden-edged razor grass, and the deep green sky, and the crystal blue rocks of the spirit realm.

# CHAPTER 19
## TAINU

AILI HAD BEEN thrown on the ground near Liu Chenguang, who was still unconscious. Behind them, Ninth and the lesser demons made a half circle with First in the center, facing them.

"Third," he said, "bring the phoenix here. Put him in front of me."

Zhu Guiren hadn't thrown Tainu on the ground. He carried him gently to First, and carefully laid him down.

"Not like that," First said. "Make him kneel up."

Zhu Guiren pulled Tainu into an upright posture but he couldn't seem to stay there, though his eyes were open. Tainu looked only at Zhu Guiren, as though there was nothing else in the world to look at. Aili wasn't even sure that his eyes could focus to see as far as where she and Liu Chenguang were lying in the grass. Finally, Zhu Guiren managed to get him to kneel, and stood back with the other demons, his single hand and his clothing covered in Tainu's blood.

Aili, struggling fiercely, managed to finally move her hands.

Immediately, one of the demons noticed. "Asking First," he said, "this one can move now."

"How interesting!" First knelt down next to her and touched the talisman.

She screamed out loud at the shock of agony.

"And she can make noise now, too." He frowned at her and slapped her face. "Well, I want to examine her more closely later. We can't risk losing her. Tie her."

He stood up again and went over to Tainu, who was having difficulty kneeling upright on his own, swaying back and forth. He pushed gently on his shoulder and Tainu fell to the ground. First laughed.

Aili said, "Stop it." The words came out quietly; she seemed to be unable to put force behind them yet.

First looked back at her. "Very interesting," he said. "Make sure she can't get away."

She felt the demons tying her feet and hands tightly as she laid on her stomach, trying to wrestle away from them.

"Third," he asked, "why can she resist the talisman?"

Zhu Guiren said, "I have no idea. But we haven't had a chance to test it previously. It's all trial and error."

Aili realized that underneath her belly, pressed against her skin as she lay on the ground, the feathers Liu Chenguang had given her were almost burning hot, sending a sense of warmth all through her body. It was beginning to wear away the choking tightness of the talisman on her throat, and the paralysis was weakening as well. She stilled, trying not to give away that she was more and more capable of movement. She was tied, but that was temporary — rope was only rope. She risked a glance over at Liu Chenguang, who was still unconscious. This was worrying; what had they done to her?

First poked Tainu with his foot. "Phoenix," he said, "any last words?"

"Not to you," said Tainu. He struggled back up to his knees. His eyes were clearer now, and looked toward Zhu Guiren.

First watched him, then smiled and spoke at last: "Third, kill the phoenix."

Zhu Guiren straightened up. "No," he said. He stepped back, out of the circle of other demons.

"No?" First seemed amused. "I will give you one more chance."

"I will not," said Zhu Guiren. He looked calmly at Tainu, then at First. "Someone else can do it. It doesn't have to be me."

Aili yelled in shock. "Zhu Guiren! You can't– You have to protect him–"

One of the other demons slapped her face to silence her, but she still struggled and fought to get away, trying to bring phoenix fire against them, but the talisman still kept her from calling En, or any weapon.

First looked at her, smiling. "Later for you, my dear. As Third said, you are indeed an interesting experiment." He walked over to stand next to Zhu Guiren. "Please observe. This is also an experiment."

Tainu looked very fragile, his arms tied painfully behind his back, his ankles tied together, forced into a kneeling posture, the posture of someone awaiting execution. His expression was calm. He looked only at Zhu Guiren. "Demon," he called, "look at me."

Zhu Guiren turned to meet his eyes.

Tainu's bloodstained face was very gentle as he smiled at him. "Now look away," he said. "Don't watch. Remember what you promised me."

Zhu Guiren did not look away. He kept looking at Tainu's face.

First said, "Ninth, there are several vacancies in the ranks above you. Kill the phoenix, and I will consider you for promotion into one of them."

Ninth stepped forward from the surrounding half-circle of demons. "Please instruct this person as to the preferred mode of death," she said respectfully.

First seemed to consider. "Killing a phoenix is no easy matter, even here," he said at last. "Blood loss before the fatal strike is crucial." He smiled. "Let's start with slashing both wrists and the throat. Then, immediate disembowelment. After that, decapitation on my word."

Aili screamed again and struggled harder; two additional demons came over to hold her down. "Zhu Guiren!" she shouted. "Zhu Guiren, wake up!"

"I'm not asleep," he said, sounding slightly insulted.

*"Zhu Guiren!"*

Tainu said, his voice suddenly stronger, "Aili, don't blame him. It's not his fault. Don't you watch either." He kept looking at Zhu Guiren. "Demon, please, stop watching."

Zhu Guiren did not obey.

Tainu closed his eyes.

The female demon leapt forward, two small knives in her hands. She freed Tainu's hands and slashed his wrists to the bone in one quick movement, then slashed his throat. Bright red blood poured from all three wounds. Before he could fall over, she changed one knife to a short sword, and stabbed and tore at his stomach several times. Tainu screamed at last, long and hoarse. Darker blood and other things poured and slipped out. He fell forward on top of them, his limbs twitching against the golden grass.

Aili couldn't stop screaming. She could feel the demons holding her down, pushing against her legs and back to hold her on the ground as she thrashed in a desperate frenzy, but Zhu Guiren stood there, calmly, looking serious but in no way upset.

*"Zhu Guiren!* Let me go, I might still be able to save him—"

Zhu Guiren looked at her, frowning, then looked back to Tainu's body.

First turned to Zhu Guiren. "Third," he said gently, smiling. "Come here."

Zhu Guiren came a step closer.

First put his hand on Zhu Guiren's chest and murmured something.

Zhu Guiren suddenly threw his head back and screamed. Screamed without breath, as though he was tearing out his own throat with his pain as he ran toward Tainu. Aili stared in shock and horror.

First stepped in Zhu Guiren's path and casually threw him aside, seemingly without effort, certainly without weapons. "Do you see?" he said to Aili, strolling over to her. "Let's see what he does now." He turned to Ninth, standing next to Tainu's dying body. "Decapitation," he ordered.

Before the demon's sword could come down on Tainu's neck, Zhu Guiren had cut off the other demon's arm, then slashed her nearly in half with his halberd. He knelt next to Tainu, keening wordlessly, trying to pick him up and hold him with his hands and body covered in Tainu's blood.

"Zhu Guiren!" Aili shouted. "Let me go. I can help!"

"Too late," said First, satisfied. "He didn't need decapitation after all. The bleeding before we got here must have weakened him significantly. We'll have to add this method to the records for future reference. Although, I don't expect we'll need to kill phoenixes in the future. With his death, the refuges will dissolve. We'll be able to capture them on rebirth again, as we used to do. Interesting…I'm not sure the phoenix death produced any resentment at all." His tongue flicked out, as though tasting for something in the air. He added, kicking Aili in the face, "Now watch and see what Third does. He's been totally destroyed, I think. His death will produce outstanding resentment." His eyes glowed with anticipation, like coals showing the patterns of the flame.

Aili looked, horrified, at Zhu Guiren trying to cradle Tainu's broken body against him. "You did this to him?"

"Of course," he said.

Zhu Guiren's cries had words now; he rocked back and forth, calling Tainu's name over and over, crying for him to come back, saying he was sorry, sorry, sorry. Then, without any pause, he stabbed himself in the throat with a dagger of ice and smoke.

Aili screamed again. First laughed.

Because he was laughing, he didn't notice that Aili froze in place, but the demons sitting on top of her did, and relaxed. Tainu was suddenly kneeling down next to her. He reached over to her, and she felt that tingling sensation — a ghost trying to be heard. His voice was not distant or strange; it sounded just as it did when he was alive, but very agitated.

"Tell him!" he was shouting at her. "Tell him!"

First looked over at the demons holding Aili. He snapped his fingers, opening a slash in the air. "All of you, go," he said. "Go assist Second. Tell her we have the phoenix and the hybrid, and the refuges are destroyed as we planned. She should come home now."

The demons stood, bowed, and transformed to fly through the gate back to the mortal realm.

Zhu Guiren was too distraught to have hit a fatal point with his first stab. He pulled the dagger out of his own throat, gurgling with blood, and readied himself more carefully, closing his eyes and laying the dagger's edge along his jugular vein.

Aili understood at last what Tainu wanted. She screamed, "Zhu Guiren! Tainu is here! He says remember your promise!"

Zhu Guiren opened his bloodshot eyes and shook his head.

"He says–" she yelled. "He says that his name is Tielende! He wants to hear you say his name. He says he loves you. He says you promised!"

Zhu Guiren held the dagger at his own throat, his hand shaking, his mouth moving without making sounds. It was possible that he couldn't make sounds; blood was pouring from the wound in his throat.

"He's here," she said. "He's right next to you. He's trying to touch you." Tears streamed down her face. She could see Tainu — the deep distress in his features, trying desperately to embrace Zhu Guiren, to hold his hand back.

"I can't feel him," Zhu Guiren rasped, voice thick and bubbling. He laid Tainu's body down, very gently, and stood up. "I can't hear him. I can't feel him."

First frowned. "What is–"

Before he finished, Zhu Guiren had a sword embedded in First's chest. He drew it out, then slashed him across the stomach, then his throat, then his wrists. First winced. His body shifted, becoming far less human-seeming and more monstrous, cold and furious.

"Zhu Guiren!" Aili screamed, struggling.

First came at Zhu Guiren with a sword in one hand and spear in the other, but Zhu Guiren dodged out of the way and raced to her, slashing down to break Aili's bonds. She rolled over; he had also slashed her skin, but it would heal quickly. She screamed in rage and attacked along with him, a phoenix whip in each hand.

Zhu Guiren's energy was fading quickly. He was bleeding heavily; Aili grabbed him, swiped her own bleeding wrist across his throat, and spun back toward First, who came at her, his teeth bared in a grimace. She whipped him again, hard, but once more he caught the phoenix whip in his hand. This time, she let him pull her close and stabbed him with En, sending a sword pulse of qi into his body. He growled and slashed at her with his dagger hand, and she left En buried in his chest, flipped back, and held her hands in the demon-quelling form, sending more qi into his body through En. First raced at her, but veered off toward where Liu Chenguang still lay on the ground. Panicked, Aili leapt to meet him, but she wasn't fast enough.

Zhu Guiren got there first, standing over Liu Chenguang's body; he had something in his single hand that she didn't recognize, but he used it to throw spear after spear of qi at First. Several caught First in the torso and abdomen, but he ripped them out and crushed them in his hands. He leapt bodily at Zhu Guiren, bearing him down to the ground next to Liu Chenguang and lifting his clawed hand to tear out his throat. Zhu Guiren was still, looking upward at the sky as though this didn't matter much to him anymore.

Aili could hear Tainu shouting at her, could hear that he was terrified for Zhu Guiren. He ran over as well, his ghostly hands trying to pull First off of him. To her shock, she realized that First could feel Tainu, even if he couldn't see or hear him. First whipped around and growled at the air, yelling something in the demonic language, and then turned to spit in Zhu Guiren's face. Zhu Guiren screamed in rage and began fighting again, just as Aili reached them. She threw herself on First's back, reaching around his throat to slash it thoroughly with her dagger of qi, and then wrapping the phoenix whip around his neck like a garrote to drag him off Zhu Guiren. Gasping, Zhu Guiren raised his single hand and let it fall back to the ground again, weakly.

The stench of First's burning flesh was heavy in her nostrils, but he was both strong and unbelievably resistant to pain. He suddenly threw himself backward so that he landed on his back with her underneath him, and then twisted around, hissing and slashing at her over and over again with the two daggers in his hands — her arms, her throat, her face. *It will heal, it will heal,* she thought to herself, her mind rapidly going through her options before she reached behind him to stab through his spinal cord, En grating on his bones.

He screamed and scrabbled back behind him with his hands; they grew very long, claws extending out, and he grabbed En and threw it at her, shouting a curse in the demonic tongue. Just before it impaled her through the forehead, En disappeared, dissolving into a shower of qi.

Aili called En back, but it didn't come. She backed up quickly, trying to draw First away from Liu Chenguang and Zhu Guiren on the ground.

Liu Chenguang had sat up at last, her hand on her head.

"Zhu Guiren! Heal Zhu Guiren!" Aili shouted. Her own wounds were healing slowly, poisoned with corruption, she realized.

But Liu Chenguang instead ran toward her, trying to use her wings to block a talisman that First had thrown. Even with qinggong she was too late. Once again, the talisman caught Aili, brushing her shoulder, and she felt the instant power of it on her, freezing her meridians, stilling her muscles. First watched Liu Chenguang catch her, rolling over and over to protect her with her wings, which in the spirit world were visible — red and gold, each feather limned with light.

First turned from them and walked steadily toward Zhu Guiren, holding his hand out for a sword.

Liu Chenguang stared down at her, terrified. "What– Aili– Tainu?"

Aili couldn't respond; Liu Chenguang's wings were protecting her, slowly nullifying the talisman, but too slow, too slow.

Suddenly, she was choking on thick, silty water; Liu Chenguang had grabbed Beilong's flask and dumped it out on her. Aili gasped, trying to drink, assuming that was what the water was for, since that was what Beilong had said, but a lot of it was going into her nose and her eyes and her ears as well. Sand as fine as air mixed in the water, gritty and tasteless against her teeth and tongue. There was nothing sweet or refreshing about this water — mountains and rivers, eyes and ears and nose and mouth and breath and body — and she choked and choked and got it down at last.

Liu Chenguang rolled off her and ran for Zhu Guiren, and Aili stood up, shaking her head in confusion. The dragon was imprinted on her mind: the dragon that was too large for the mind to hold. When she moved she felt that immensity moving along with her, a huge shadow with her small, frail body, following her and obeying as though she were holding the sticks of a shadow puppet. Or perhaps, she was the shadow, and something was holding her. There was the small and colorful world, and there was the great and unseeable shadow behind all the delicate and solid lines that tried to divide one thing from another.

There was another shadow, shapeless, huge, bending down over Zhu Guiren, and next to it was a small, bright star. Zhu Guiren was a puppet — a small broken puppet — and the shadow was reaching into him and tearing out his heart.

Aili yelled, and in her own mind, it was a roaring noise of waterfalls and boulders crashing in the flood. She threw herself on the shadow, tearing it with her claws of qi and her teeth of fire and the weight of her being. The shadow tried to flee, but she was much faster, much larger. *Trash,* she thought scornfully, and ripped it to shreds, tiny screaming pieces of shadow fleeing in all directions, but her being was a flood that captured all the pieces, the sliding silt that sealed them beneath. Each little bit of it was captured under her own shadow and torn and torn and torn until it could never become one being again, until it would dissolve into the greater existence. The bits of shadow she had ripped apart faded softly into the earth, harmless now.

Aili stood still, quivering with violence and rage and power, her eyes closed until she felt that fade from her as well, and she was only herself again. She opened her eyes to feel Liu Chenguang's arms wrapped around her. Zhu Guiren was lying on the ground, Tainu's ghost trying to hold his hand. Everything felt very still. Aili collapsed to her knees and Liu Chenguang stayed with her, calling her name, keeping her from falling into unconsciousness.

Zhu Guiren knelt back down next to Tainu's body. He could feel that Liu Chenguang was placing blood on his wounds, trying to heal him now that Aili was settled and conscious again, but he merely stayed still, uncaring. It was better if he was bleeding and in pain, but he had no energy to stop her. Kneeling was not enough. He laid down, pulled Tainu's body close to him, and closed his eyes, unspeaking.

Liu Chenguang knelt on the other side. "Tainu," she said. "Tainu." She shook the body a little bit.

Zhu Guiren pushed her hand away.

Aili said, "He's still here."

Zhu Guiren didn't move. That Tainu's ghost was here was a comfort, but soon, even his ghost would be gone. There was nothing to hold him to existence. Tainu had died without resentment, satisfied that his demon was still alive. He buried his head in Tainu's neck and let the hot tears pour down.

Aili's voice came. "Tainu says he loves you so much. He doesn't want you to be sad. He's not afraid of death. Only of leaving you behind. Only that you'll mourn him too much."

Zhu Guiren made a high-pitched whining noise because there were no words to answer that. But Tainu was still here, Tainu could still hear him. How could he say his last words to him and have them be bitter? The words of his heart: *don't leave me, I will never stop mourning you, I will die even if I'm alive.*

"I love you," he said instead. "I love you. I'm so sorry– I'm so sorry I failed you. I wanted to keep you safe, I wanted to make you happy–" He found that he was sobbing, gasping for air. The world was black, because he would not open his eyes again; he would not open his eyes and see that Tainu was now not in it.

"He's touching you," said Aili. It sounded as though she were crying too. "He wants to know, can you feel it?"

He tried, he really did, but there was nothing. He shook his head.

Aili said, "He asks, can you say his name? He never heard you say his name."

Zhu Guiren whispered, "Tielende," and felt the connection — the golden light inside him that meant it was a true name buried forever in his heart.

Liu Chenguang's voice came, also choked with tears, "Look. The refuges. The refuges are dissolving."

Zhu Guiren didn't want to look, but the refuges were a part of Tainu, the last part that he would be able to see. So he looked, and everywhere throughout the landscape, bright golden beams were springing up to the heavens, from the hills and mountains and plains, far into the distance. There were so many — dozens that they could see from where they sat. So many refuges that he had built, with his blood and his pain and his love.

"The refuges are him," he said as they watched the sky be striped with light.

"Zhu Guiren," Aili said suddenly, her voice tight, "Tainu says, if you really want it, he will try to stay for you. Otherwise, he says he is ready to go."

Zhu Guiren's throat was healed now, but he choked. He managed to get out, "Yes. Tainu, yes."

"Aili, what are you talking about?" Liu Chenguang asked.

Aili said, "I don't know." She wiped her eyes. "I'm just saying exactly what he's saying. Zhu Guiren, he says you need to use his blood to set an array. Right now. It has to be before the refuges fully dissolve."

Already, some of the beams of light were thinning.

"Liu Chenguang, you have to come here." She moved Liu Chenguang's hands as though she were sitting with her palms pressed against someone else's. "He's here. Tainu says you are cultivating with him. He wants you to send him qi. His hands are against yours now. He says you can't feel him yet, but if it works, you should soon feel that the qi is circulating with another body. He asks, do you understand?"

Liu Chenguang nodded, her eyes determined.

Zhu Guiren knelt by Tainu's body, reaching out to touch it and then drawing back. There was already blood everywhere, the terrible wounds of his death and the wounds he himself had given him, all those days, carved into his skin one by one with his own hand. He couldn't even cry anymore. His hatred of himself was so great that he wanted to stab himself, over and over and over, until he had as many wounds as Tainu. It would hurt less than this. But Tainu wanted him, wanted him to do this — this one last terrible thing. "I can't," he said. "I can't do this to him."

He felt Aili next to him, speaking quietly. "Tainu says he doesn't want to say your true name, so instead he says this. He wants me to say exactly this. Only exactly this." She closed her eyes. "I want to stay with you. This is only my body, that would be reborn anyway in a few centuries. This is trying to bring about an early rebirth. That's all it is. When my body dissolves, the array will bind me here, to you, until there is a new spiritual body for me. Don't be afraid. Just do it, my demon. I need you to do it right now."

Zhu Guiren listened. The tears started rolling down his face again, but he reached into Tainu's ravaged body through the great wound in his belly, trying not to feel it. He brought his hand out full of thickening blood, and began to sprinkle it on the earth, chanting. He saw the smoke spider creature leap out and bind something invisible near Liu Chenguang. *Was it Tainu's soul? Had he captured Tainu as he had captured so many others for so many centuries for his own needs, caring nothing for their suffering?* The spider didn't go anywhere else before it leapt back to his hand and disappeared.

"I feel something," said Liu Chenguang suddenly.

Zhu Guiren's head whipped up.

"Zhu Guiren," said Aili, "he's telling me to burn his body with phoenix fire. It has to be right now. Get back." She raised her hand.

Zhu Guiren stumbled backward, and she slashed down with the phoenix whip. The body didn't burn, but like the refuges, it dissolved into a pillar of golden sparks, rushing upwards into the sky.

Suddenly the pillar bent; all of the pillars, all of the golden, dissolving refuges, bent and coalesced into the invisible person whose palms were held against Liu Chenguang's.

Liu Chenguang shouted in surprise, spreading her wings. The influx of qi was so enormous that she blazed with light, too bright to see. Aili covered her eyes, but Zhu Guiren strained his eyes toward the light, eager, hopeful. The light grew brighter and brighter, more focused, as if all the light in the world pressed down into a blazingly brilliant star sitting opposite Liu Chenguang. Her bright wings were a black silhouette against that sunfire, and it compressed and compressed, brighter and brighter, until it was a pinprick too brilliant to even imagine, simultaneously all colors beyond the world's holding and no color at all, burning existence around it.

And then, it disappeared.

Liu Chenguang collapsed, her wings crumpled beneath her.

Zhu Guiren felt a hot, burning sensation in the palm of his single hand. It grew and grew, hotter and stronger as though a fire was burning through his skin — a searing star of flame.

Just as suddenly, the heat went out.

Shaking, he unfolded his fingers. In the palm of his hand was a very small red bird — smaller than a hummingbird, not nearly as big as a sparrow. He raised it up to the level of his face, and it opened its golden eyes and stretched out to rub its bright-feathered head delicately against his nose. Then it settled down in his hand, and went to sleep.

# CHAPTER 20
## AFTER

TAINU WOKE UP in a warm place, feeling very tired. He looked up and saw the face of his beloved one, his demon, and it all came back to him.

His demon had fallen asleep too, lying still in the golden grass outside the refuge, but was still holding him in his hand, loosely cupped so that he could move and flap his wings if he wanted to. Cautiously, he stretched out his wings and hopped out of his demon's hand. He didn't yet have all his flight feathers, so he continued to hop up to his face and nestled close to him, close enough to feel the warmth of his breath. Gently, softly, he called, "Arciniang."

He opened his eyes. He looked so tired, so hurt, and withdrew from him, afraid.

"Arciniang," he said, "please don't let it hurt you so much. I'm here..."

His demon nodded and held his hand out to him again, but didn't speak as he sat up.

From his new, higher vantage point, he saw Aili sitting a little bit away with her back to them, her sword ready in her hand. Liu Chenguang sat next to her. The two of them were talking quietly.

"Liu Chenguang," he called.

Liu Chenguang turned to him and walked over, kneeling so that she was next to Zhu Guiren. She asked, very gently, "May I take him? I need to bring him into the refuge now."

The demon jerked slightly and nodded, holding out his hand.

"I'll be back," Tainu said, "wait for me, don't worry."

But he didn't respond.

Once they were in the refuge, Liu Chenguang let him out and he sighed, stretching his wings. "This is better," he said. "I'll grow quickly so I can come back out sooner."

Liu Chenguang said, "Tainu, Zhu Guiren is…not in good shape."

"Why? I'm back…"

"Like you told me with Aili," she said, "this is not normal for him. He can't understand that it's really you and that rebirth is what we are accustomed to. And this isn't a normal rebirth. You were dead, Tainu. You were truly dead. He saw your dead body, he touched you when you were dead, his hand was filled with your blood. That's what he remembers now. That's all he can think of. You were a ghost that Aili spoke to." Her eyes filled with tears. "You were dissolving. Do you remember it?"

"I remember." He remembered it — the sense of dissolution, of the spaces within him growing and the pieces of his soul shrinking and scattering. "I came back for him."

Liu Chenguang nodded. "He hasn't spoken since," she said. "I didn't want to bring you into the refuge until you two were able to talk because he's in so much pain. I don't think he can bear to be here with you. His cultivation system is completely haywire with a mix of corrupted and natural qi. And…" She stopped.

"I know," he said. From First's sick pleasure in tormenting the demon, he could well imagine what had been done to him when he was powerless to resist it, what had been involved in breaking the connections between his mind and his heart. *I can't be with him in that way anyway, not until I'm grown,* he thought. *We'll have time.* But a little anxiety wrinkled into his heart.

He tried the transformation, and it worked; he already had enough spiritual power back for that. "How old do I look?" he asked, his voice piping high.

Liu Chenguang smiled. "Around four," she said. "You're so cute."

"If I go out to talk to him, do you think…you and Aili could give us privacy?"

"Let's make a plan first," she said. "How long do you think it will take you to cultivate to adulthood?"

His heart sank. This was hard to calculate; the time in the spirit realm didn't match with the mortal world well. "A year at least," he said. "Maybe more. Between one and three years." Once, a year would have been a blink of an eye to him; now, it seemed forever. He wanted to be back in the world, back with his demon.

"He can't stay here that long," she said. "He's more or less defenseless right now."

He nodded, dejected. His emotions were rather childish at the moment too.

"We'll set up a phoenix gate here. Aili can do it," she said. "We'll be able to come back and forth."

"Where will you all be?" he asked.

"Aili and I will go back to the Common Federation," she said. "She wants to be with her mother. If he'll come with us, Zhu Guiren as well. I don't think he should be alone, and I don't think he should be in the Daxian Republic. Try to convince him."

He nodded and squared his childish shoulders. "All right, then," he said.

When they left the refuge together, Tainu saw his demon sitting right next to the outside wall. Liu Chenguang took Aili's hand and they walked further away.

Zhu Guiren's eyes followed them and then turned, reluctantly, to him.

"Demon?"

Zhu Guiren started crying silently, looking at him.

"Arciniang," he said, coming over and sitting next to him, "it's still me. I'm just small."

"I know," he said hoarsely. He wiped his eyes with his single hand. "I'm so sorry."

Tainu decided to use a different strategy. He simply couldn't have this conversation in the body of a four-year-old child. It was too strange. He transformed back. Already, he was slightly bigger — a sparrow rather than a hummingbird. *I should probably stay in my true body here as much as possible, the cultivation will be faster.*

"Arciniang, can you take your true form too?"

The demon's eyes were startled, but he nodded and immediately transformed. The creature of ice and smoke was there before him, the air around him glittering with silver sparks. Tainu hopped up onto his right claw, then onto his snout so he could look into his eyes. He laughed. "Demon, you really always do have the same expression." He felt so tiny next to him. "I love you so much."

His demon closed his eyes, which in his true body were not black, but a very deep blue that was almost indistinguishable from black until seen very close, like ice over a deep lake. "How can you still love me?" he asked. "I've failed you in every possible way."

Tainu shook his feathered head, not knowing what to say. At last, he said, "You didn't fail me at all. You didn't. None of that was what you wanted to do to me. You brought me back at the end. And now, can't things be good again?" He knew he still sounded like a four-year-old; he couldn't help it — that's how his emotions were at the moment. "I have you back, and you have your heart. We have each other."

His demon looked at him and gently laid his head down on the ground. "I'm getting cross-eyed looking at you," he said. "You're so little."

Tainu smiled, though it didn't show in his bird form. "I'll get bigger as quickly as I can," he promised.

"I'll stay here until you do."

Tainu thought about it, hopping off the demon's snout and a little way away so he didn't have to get cross-eyed. Then, he laughed and fluttered his wings; the primaries had come in. He flew up to the end of one of the icicle horns and landed there.

"That's also an awkward way to look at you," his demon said, but his voice sounded a little lighter.

Tainu fluttered back down. He said, seriously, "Demon, I want to complete my cultivation as quickly as I can. And that means I should probably be in the refuge as much as possible, and not paying attention to anybody. If you were here, I would want to always be with you." This was true, and he thought it was better to say it this way than to emphasize that Zhu Guiren shouldn't be alone in the spirit world right now for his own safety, for his own healing. He needed Aili's protection and he needed to be with other people who would talk to him and distract him from his pain, not waiting for a bird that was hiding in a hole, trying to cultivate.

The demon nodded his head. All his movements were very regal, with the weight of the icicle horns.

"You're very beautiful," Tainu blurted out.

The demon put his head down on the ground again and didn't say anything.

Feeling a bit as though this wasn't going at all how he had hoped, Tainu said, "Will you come visit me? Aili and Liu Chenguang can bring you. Will you stay with them? Then when I come back, we can be together."

The demon was silent, and then he said, "I don't know if– if I can…If you will want me."

"Why would I not?" His heart felt a little desperate. "I will always love you. I will always want you."

"I'm not like I was," he said. "I don't have any power. To protect you, or do anything else. I don't– I don't have…I'm not like I was before."

Tainu wished so strongly that he was able to take on an adult form right now, to take him in his arms, but as a four-year-old or a baby bird there was no such reassurance he could give. All he could say was, "I love you and I will always love you," as seriously as a sparrow could say it. "I love you in your mortal body and I love you in this one. I love you with power and without. I love you because I love your heart and I love you with whatever body I have."

Arciniang looked at him. "I love you too," he said, at last. "I love you, Tielende."

They brought Zhu Guiren back when Tainu had grown to the size of a falcon. When Zhu Guiren arrived, he flew up high in delight, and spiraled down around him, spilling golden qi all over silver scales. He could see that his demon was smiling inside even though it was hard to tell with his true body; smiles didn't really fit on that face. He raised his icicle horns and let Tainu dive in and out around them before they settled down together, Tainu nestling between his forelegs.

"How is it in the mortal world?" he asked.

The demon said, "Aili and Liu Chenguang are living in Sand Island with the little dragon. He's going to school there. Aili's mother is there too."

"And you?" he asked.

He hesitated. "I'm there a lot. Not all the time. I have a project I'm working on."

"That's good," he said, smiling. "That's very good. What is it?"

"A surprise. I'll show you when you come back."

"Are you cultivating?"

"Aili's teaching me how to cultivate natural qi, the way she learned at Crane Moon," he said.

Tainu smiled inwardly.

"You did that, didn't you?" the demon said, nudging him with his snout until he laughed and had to spread his wings to keep his balance. "That time in the flood, when you said it was preventative…you planted a new cultivation system in me."

"It worked!" he said, jubilant. "I didn't know if it would. That's why I didn't tell you. I put it in the place in your side where your old cultivation system was already destroyed. It wouldn't begin to grow into your meridians unless your old cultivation system became completely nonfunctional."

The demon's head swung back and forth, the icicles cutting a swathe through the silver glitter from his scales. "Tainu, how did you do it?"

"I don't know," he said. "Someone told me once that phoenixes are all intuition and no skill."

"That must have been a very rude person," the demon responded.

"The rudest person I've ever met," he said. "But I think the only person in the world it would have been possible for me to do that for, because…"

The demon tilted his head to one side, considering.

It brought back very ancient memories for Tainu.

"Because?"

"Because we were as close as it's possible for people to be," Tainu said simply. "Because I love him so very much."

The demon looked down again.

Tainu transformed into his mortal body. He was now somewhere around nine or ten years old, he thought. It was hard to tell without a mirror or any other human people around to compare with, but that seemed to be the size of clothing he wore; he had long ago asked Liu Chenguang to bring him a wide variety, to have it as he grew. He stood in front of his demon and said, "Look at me, Arciniang," very seriously.

He looked, and away.

Tainu said, "Demon, my mortal body is still here. Someday, I'll be grown again. I don't want you to reject me then. I don't want you to be afraid of me or think of me as a ghost."

Zhu Guiren said, at last, "It hurts me to see you in your mortal body."

"Because I died in it?"

"Because I hurt you in it," he replied. "I did it, with my own hand. No one forced me, I wasn't controlled, I wasn't a puppet. I could have refused. It just…" His lip curled, showing his crystal teeth. "It wasn't convenient for me to resist. I weighed the costs and consequences and chose to hurt you. Even knowing who you were, even remembering…everything…"

Tainu's heart ached for him, but he said, "Arciniang, I made this mortal body to be the one that you knew." He walked over to stand next to him and put his forehead against the ridge over his eye. "Do you hate it?"

He felt himself getting teary inside. It was true the mortal body had been his choice; it was true that a phoenix had great control over the mortal body, more than a demon or other spiritual creature. He could have remade a different body for himself, but this body — this was the body his demon had loved. He wanted so much to stay in this body. It wasn't only a piece of clothing that he could change or not change. He understood, now, why Liu Chenguang had reshaped her mortal body to be identical to the one she met Hong Deming in after his death.

Softly, his demon said, "I don't hate it. I could never." He pushed against Tainu, and he almost fell down.

The spirit realm time was not like mortal time. When the demon came again, he was close to sixteen, lanky and gangling, and his true body was much larger than any mortal bird. He didn't show Arciniang his mortal body that time. It felt too embarrassing; adolescence brought all those feelings and bodily responses that he wasn't sure he could control, plus pimples and general awkwardness. Who wants to show their life's love what they looked like at sixteen? In his true body, however, he was aware that he was quite gorgeous, and so he flew all around his demon, draping him with his long plumage of blood and sunlight, golden qi glittering to match the demon's silver scales.

"Will you show me your mortal body?" Tainu asked as he rested between Arciniang's forelegs after showing off. "Just…I want to see you."

Arciniang nodded and transformed, and there he was: Zhu Guiren's clear dark eyes looking at him, arms wrapped around his wings and covered with his feathers as they lay on the ground together. His hair had begun to grow long again, well past his ears toward his shoulders. Tainu found himself itching to touch it with his hands. Just as well that he was in his true body at the moment. His true body didn't have gender, and it also didn't have hands; embarrassing things could thus be avoided. He allowed himself to run his beak through his hair, just once. He then spread his wings and bowed, feeling like a very red-tinged peacock, but he wanted to do *something* to show him his appreciation. His demon laughed.

"I miss you," Zhu Guiren said, abruptly. "I miss you so much."

"I miss you too," he said. Truly, it had been a bit of a shock to see Zhu Guiren again in his mortal body. He felt such a yearning toward him, not only because he was sixteen years old, but because, because, because…His heart beat with it. "Soon," he said. "I'm cultivating as fast as I can."

"I know," his demon said, and transformed back to his true body. It was a relief to both of them. Tainu flew over to nestle under his chin, and they were able to sleep together like that in the sunlight while Aili and Liu Chenguang kept watch with their backs to them.

When his demon came again, he was almost done. His body was in his early twenties.

He thought a great deal about how to manage this. He was old enough now, and certainly he wanted certain things, but he didn't want to move too fast, and he didn't want his demon to be pressured, and he didn't want to be rejected or have everything be awful. He thought it would be best to appear in his true body, his tail feathers nearly ten feet long and sparkling with gold and sunlight every time he moved; it would be good for his demon to see him like that first, and then he would realize that now it was awkward for him to cuddle. The demon's true body was a good size too, but they wouldn't fit together very well, so then his demon might just go ahead and ask him to transform, and then it wouldn't feel as though he was pressuring him at all.

He was extraordinarily nervous.

It was all thrown off because Zhu Guiren appeared in his mortal body to begin with, so there he was feeling very awkward, standing with his head several feet above Zhu Guiren's, and desperately wanting him.

But instead of asking him to transform, Zhu Guiren just reached out and touched his feathers as though in wonder. "You're so beautiful," he said. Where his hand touched his feathers, it nearly disappeared into their softness, and golden qi spiraled out all around him, encompassing him in Tainu's aura.

"You never said that before," Tainu blurted out. "Wasn't I the same before?"

"You were beautiful then too, but now you're yourself again." He looked up at him. "Aren't you?" he asked softly.

He nodded his head. Now, he felt very embarrassed. Out of an intense desire to change this conversation, he asked, "Demon, would you like to fly with me?"

"That would be embarrassing," he replied seriously.

He reached down and very carefully ran his beak through Zhu Guiren's hair; he had to be careful about it because his beak was now larger than Zhu Guiren's head. "You can ride on my back," he said. "Not embarrassing at all. How can you be offended when I'm being so friendly and helpful?"

Zhu Guiren laughed, which was the best sound in the world, and Tainu knelt down to let him clamber on to his back. "What if the feathers fall out?" he asked conversationally. "You don't have a saddle or anything."

"I'll dive and catch you, of course," he said, and spread his wings and leapt up into the air. He could hear Zhu Guiren laughing with joy, and he remembered that his demon hadn't been able to fly since he lost his hand. He must have missed it.

He very carefully swooped down to a place he thought would be safe — a place with another refuge at their backs, but far away from Aili and Liu Chenguang. He wanted privacy for this.

Zhu Guiren slipped off his back and they looked at one another.

He took a deep breath and transformed.

Zhu Guiren's eyes filled with tears as he looked at him. "Tainu," he said softly.

He nodded, feeling his heart in his throat. "Demon," he said. "It's me. I missed you so much."

Zhu Guiren walked steadily toward him, never taking his eyes away, though he also didn't stop crying, and then his arms were around him, hugging him fiercely. "So long," he said, burying his face into his shoulder. "Tainu, it's been so long. I've missed you. I've missed you."

Zhu Guiren turned his head so his lips were against his throat and kissed him; Tainu felt his whole body shiver with it, and Zhu Guiren stiffened against him.

"Oh." Tainu had forgotten how it felt. He had forgotten what it was like to have his demon love him. He thought he remembered, but he really hadn't.

He sank down to the ground, pulling Zhu Guiren down with him, feeling his weight, the softness of his hair spilling around him. His demon kissed him harder, reaching down between his knees to push them apart so he could lie between them.

"Arciniang," he gasped, but he couldn't get out any other words. Zhu Guiren's hand was touching him everywhere that he was most sensitive — all the places that he had dreamed of since his mortal body cultivated into adolescence.

"Oh," he said, sharp and surprised, and reached up to tangle his hands in Zhu Guiren's hair and kiss him, everything about them entangled in one another, and he wasn't afraid. He wasn't afraid of this. He wanted this so badly, for so long.

His demon's voice trembled against his skin, calling his name, and Tainu was too breathless with joy to answer.

# CHAPTER 21
## THE MORTAL REALM

A FEW WEEKS after they had left Tainu in the spirit realm, Liu Chenguang showed Zhu Guiren around Little Daxian, including the apothecary where she had worked. She looked at it consideringly. "You know," she said, "if you still have access to your gold, I'd rather just open my own. And I can study Federative medical traditions too. There's a college nearby."

"You can study here?" he asked. "What kind of things?"

"Oh, all kinds," she said breezily.

Since Zhu Guiren knew the Liu Chenguang of old, he knew this meant that she had no idea. "Aili, what can you study here?"

"It's not in Easterly," Aili said, walking slightly behind them, holding Yisue's hand. "There's a college in San Toma. I don't know what they study. I didn't even graduate from high school."

"Why do I have to go to school then?" Yisue asked immediately. "It sounds so boring."

"Because you're five hundred years old and functionally illiterate in two languages. That's why," Aili said. "I'm going to go back to school too. We can go look at the college together some time, Zhu Guiren."

He nodded, slumping back into indifference.

Aili and Liu Chenguang looked at each other.

Yisue yelled "DUMPLINGS!" and ran down the street.

Liu Chenguang said, "I'll catch him," and ran after him.

Aili and Zhu Guiren walked together; he felt about as comfortable with Aili as he felt with anyone except Tainu, who was different, and who he couldn't think about now without hating himself, and who he couldn't stop thinking about. She was able to be quiet when he wanted to be, which was most of the time now. He hadn't ever cut her into pieces to collect her blood, either, which made things feel less awkward for him.

After they had walked aimlessly for a block or so, following Yisue's white hair down the street, he made an effort and asked, "Why are we living in Sand Island instead of here if you both like Little Daxian so much?"

Aili replied, "When Liu Chenguang and I met with his parents, they were very clear that Yisue needed to have frequent access to the ocean, even if he doesn't swim every day. If we were in Easterly, he'd just have the estuary and the port, and they're kind of dirty and filled with heavy machinery and lots of people. A child or a dragon in the water would be noticed for sure. Sand Island's got a beach, at least, although the water's really shallow."

She added, "I've been thinking that we might need to go up to Fallon again." She said this easily now, although Zhu Guiren remembered that when she had first mentioned Fallon at the dinner table a few weeks before, she had seemed to choke. "My mother's going to sell that land. I don't want it, but when we have the money from that, we should find some other place that has good ocean access for him so we can go stay there sometimes, near his coast and his dragon gate."

"Why don't you just keep the land in Fallon?" he asked, without much interest.

Aili looked at him, her expression complicated in a way he didn't understand. "I burned Fallon to the ground. Bad things happened to me in Fallon," she said. "Like what happened to you at the clan home."

He flinched. "Oh." he said. Then, rallying, "How do you know what happened to me at the clan home?"

"I don't know the details," she said, "and you don't need to tell me at all, unless you want to. But I know they hurt you. That's what happened to me, growing up."

"Oh," he said again. He was silent for a while more, then, "When you go there, I'll go with you." He added, "We don't have to wait for you to sell that land to find another place. I've got plenty of gold."

After Aili and Liu Chenguang were in bed, and the dragon child was asleep, and Aili's mother had finished puttering around in the kitchen, Zhu Guiren slipped out of his own room and went to the beach to look at the water. He couldn't sleep much, these days. He couldn't cultivate either. All he could do was wander and try to get away from the pain and the memories: the pain of what he had done, and the pain of what had been done to him. He knew that these two things were intertwined, but couldn't separate them. They were one thing. Even his memories of Tainu were poisoned by this pain; he couldn't think of them being together without the sharp claws tearing inside.

Occasionally, he tried to cultivate resentment, but trying to reach out to find the suffering and loss that permeated the mortal world just made him feel sick. And he couldn't do it anyway. Liu Chenguang had confirmed it; his cultivation had disappeared. Of course, he still had the meridians of his mortal body, the ones that every human being had, the liver and heart and all those things, but the well of qi — the center where he had gathered and stored corrupted spiritual power — was gone. He sometimes wondered if he was even a demon anymore. If he didn't cultivate resentment, then what was he? If he couldn't produce a spiritual weapon or use spells, at best, he was a long-lived mortal with good martial arts skills.

He looked across the still waters of the bay toward San Toma. The lights were out everywhere, since the country was still at war and there was anxiety that Kunoru might attack with planes or ships, so at least the stars were bright. He tried to remember what it had been like as a child, before he had learned to cultivate, and couldn't, really. They were started on cultivation very young at clan home, and his earliest memories had been broken by First as his punishment for freeing the phoenix. There wasn't much there, but he did remember that he used to love to look at the stars. That was how he had developed his system of symbols and calculations, trying to predict and understand the movements of the stars and planets. He looked at the stars now and imagined that he was back at the beginning and everything was still to come, rather than all over, all done, all ruined.

In the end, they all drove up to Fallon together. Liu Chenguang didn't want Aili to have to be there alone, and after all, the whole reason for going was to give Yisue a chance to swim in his own part of the ocean again. Aili refused to let Zhu Guiren drive, which he found irritating, but not worth arguing about. Yet.

Fallon was green again, after the burning. Aili walked quietly toward where the white house had been, Zhu Guiren remembered. Liu Chenguang went with her, holding her hand.

Yisue stood with Zhu Guiren. "Uncle Demon," he said.

"What?"

"Why is Aili sad?"

"This was a bad place for her," he said. "She doesn't have good memories." He added, "Should you call her Aili? Is that respectful?"

"That's how I first met her, so she said that's ok if that's what I want," he said comfortably.

"I have never in my life told you to call me Uncle Demon. You can call me Zhu Guiren like everyone else." *Except Tainu,* he thought with a sudden pang.

"I like Uncle Demon," said Yisue, "so that's what I'll call you."

He wondered what Aili saw when she looked at the burned places. The phoenix fire was not like normal fire; there was nothing left. The eucalyptus trees that he had stood under when he told Tainu about the array — those were gone.

Tainu had said, *We'll try together. Come back and finish your dinner, demon.*

Zhu Guiren said, "I need to walk, stay here," and ran away from Yisue and Aili and Liu Chenguang to the hilltop, then over to the other side of the hilltop where they wouldn't see him, and curled up in the grass.

The worst thing, the worst thing, the worst thing about everything was that even his dreams of Tainu were tangled up in all of what First had done to him, and what he had done to Tainu. Even the good things were ruined. How could Tainu come back to him? How could he let him be near? All his best memories, all that there had been between them, even those good feelings and good memories were corrupted now; there was no pure thing left in him that wasn't tainted, disgusting, horrible, not one memory or feeling or desire.

He must have lain there for a long time. Eventually, Aili came and sat next to him silently. She didn't say anything. He pulled himself up eventually and wiped his eyes.

She continued to be quiet, so he was able to say, "I don't know how it can ever be better. I don't know how he can love me." He thought maybe he needed to say more, but then he thought Aili understood.

After a while, she said, "It's different for everyone, I think. Everyone has to find their own way through it. But someone told me once — it was very important for me to hear at the time — that just because bad things happened to you doesn't mean good things can't also happen. That things were done to you is nothing you need to be ashamed of. And if you've done things you're ashamed of, it's better to do different things to make amends than to live in shame about it." She paused and seemed to struggle about whether to continue. Then, she finally said, "People hurting you is just that, Zhu Guiren. It's got…nothing to do with Tainu, with loving him. It's the opposite of that. Don't even put it in the same category. Let things that hurt you be things that hurt you. Let loving Tainu be loving Tainu. Let him love you too."

He shook his head. "I don't deserve it," he said. "I don't deserve him loving me."

Aili said, "No one blames you. We all know, Zhu Guiren, that you would never have hurt Tainu of your own accord. Even with First torturing you, you still tried to get Tainu away from him. You let us in. Can you give yourself some credit for how much you also love Tainu and how strong you were to resist First? And you also had to survive. Would Tainu be happier now if you had fought back so much that they killed you? Can you imagine how that would have been a better outcome? Without you, how would we have brought him back? Without you, Zhu Guiren, he wouldn't even have tried to come back."

He didn't say anything. None of this made him feel any better about any of it. Without him, would they have captured Tainu at all? Tainu would have been safe and hidden, as he had been for thousands of years, except for him.

"Zhu Guiren," Aili said sternly. "Stop finding ways to make everything your fault. You're not the source of all the evil in the world. You're really not."

Zhu Guiren looked up at her, surprised at her tone. She sounded very…the word that came to mind was *commanding*.

*Where had that come from?* Zhu Guiren frowned.

"What do you think Tainu will want, when he comes back?" Aili asked. "What will he want most of all?"

Zhu Guiren tried to think. "He said once that he wanted me to be a free-range demon."

Aili smiled. "What does that even mean?"

"Not…not like the other demons, not in a clan where I had to live like that."

"So, you should find a way to be a free-range demon," she said. "Because I think what Tainu would want most of all would be to come back and find you living a happy life. Because he loves you so much, and that's not ever stopping."

Zhu Guiren nodded and stood up. "So now you've been here," he said, rapidly changing the subject. "What do you have to do to sell it?"

From Fallon, they drove west to the great bluffs above the ocean. Zhu Guiren desperately wanted to drive the curvy road along the cliffs, but Aili still wouldn't let him. She was showing off for Liu Chenguang; Zhu Guiren very reasonably pointed this out and Aili ignored him while Liu Chenguang smiled at her. Yisue was hanging his head out of the window and letting his tongue flap like a dog. Zhu Guiren decided that he was very done with these people, and he should figure out how to be a free-range demon somewhere else.

"Here!" shouted Yisue suddenly. "Here, here!"

There was a little "For sale" sign off to one side of the road, on the ocean side. Down the cliff from the sign was the rocky beach with the crashing waves, and out to sea was an arched rock.

"Well," said Aili, driving up to the sign and parking the car, "this does seem pretty perfect. I wonder how far back the property line goes."

There was a good amount of grass-covered bluff between the road and the cliff, but Zhu Guiren was mesmerized by the glitter of the light on the ocean. He found himself settling into a cultivational posture and just watching it. Far below, he saw Yisue run naked into the violent surf and then come up again in his dragon form, blending perfectly with the foam and spray. Yisue leapt and cavorted in the waves and Zhu Guiren watched him, his eyes half closed, seeing the intertwined patterns of wave and dragon, the light and the water, the rocks and the tide, the complex unpredictability of the predictable movement.

Liu Chenguang watched Zhu Guiren, clearly curious; Aili put her finger to her lips and drew her away.

Zhu Guiren didn't know how long he sat there, but gradually, his body felt different — lighter, more relaxed, as though something dark and painful was leeching out of it.

He startled and realized that the light had changed; the sun was going down. From the brilliant white glitter the light on the water was now more golden-red, and the shadows were long. He looked away from the ocean, blinking his eyes to clear them, and saw that Aili was going through a simple sword form behind him, her eyes closed, holding En and moving gracefully through the pattern, over and over again. He thought he would like to try that; he hadn't seen a sword form quite like that before. He couldn't produce a sword, but he could just hold his hand out and pretend. He set himself behind and slightly to one side of her and began to mimic her movements. Soon, he had it well enough to also do it with his eyes closed. It felt very peaceful. Then, he heard more movement, opened his eyes again, and realized that Aili was going through the form again but many times faster, so that her sword became a flickering light in her hand.

He could do that, so he did it. Even though he didn't have a sword, still it felt oddly like he was flickering too with the swiftness of the movements, like the light on the water.

Aili laughed and put the sword down, not looking at him. "Yisue's back," she said to no one in particular. "Yisue, where are your clothes?"

He was stark naked. "Forgot them on the beach," he said.

"Well, go get them. We have a long ride back in the car and I don't want you naked."

"Too late, tide got them," he said, sounding very satisfied.

Aili said, "Well, then, the blanket it is."

"What blanket?" he complained, following her back toward the car. "What blanket are you talking about, do you mean the picnic blanket? But it's all *itchy* and it had *bugs* on it..."

Zhu Guiren heard their voices slowly drifting away. He turned back to look at the ocean and saw Liu Chenguang coming up from the beach as well, using qinggong to leap up the cliff instead of the narrow, curved path. She had found some abalone shells, which glowed in the sunset light.

She smiled at him. "Come here," she said, "let me check you."

He frowned. Liu Chenguang checked his pulse, and then carefully laid her hand over his abdomen, not quite touching it, the way that Tainu had done sometimes.

She smiled. "Very good," she said.

"What?" he asked, following her as he walked back to the car with her.

"Nothing," she said. "Nothing much."

Edna Lee brought her daughter over, a fat little baby sitting up and waving her hands at everyone and making babbling noises. Aili, her mother, and Yisue were absolutely enchanted. Liu Chenguang was standing with her back to a wall looking very freaked out; Zhu Guiren felt like Liu Chenguang looked.

He cleared his throat. "Ah, Liu Chenguang, don't we need to go check on the clinic?"

"Yes. Yes we do," she said, and fled with him outside.

They walked down the street to the storefront Zhu Guiren had rented to become Liu Chenguang's clinic. She had decided she didn't need to stock a full pharmacy since there was already a good one in Little Daxian, but there was a space for consultations, two table-beds for acupuncture, and today, there would be a delivery of furniture — the many-drawered cabinets that would hold her equipment and some of the more basic, frequently-prescribed materials for prescriptions.

Liu Chenguang said, "It's good to get you out of there, Zhu Guiren. Edna keeps asking if you're married."

"I heard," he said, annoyed.

"Aili's tried to explain, but she's never met Tainu so she doesn't really understand," she said. "Aili just says you're spoken for. But I guess Edna has some friends who are really in the market for someone as good-looking and sweet-tempered as you are."

"Shut up," he replied absently. They sat in the clinic drinking tea, waiting for the delivery truck. After a while Zhu Guiren decided he might as well ask. "So," he said in a voice as casual as he could make it, "Aili tells me you've been with fox spirits?"

Liu Chenguang spat her tea on the floor. "Why on earth would you– Why is that your business?" she asked, pouring herself more tea.

"Well," he said, "last time I was up at the ocean…by myself, you know… I was cultivating, and I think I met one? But I'm not sure."

Liu Chenguang's eyes grew wide. "What happened?" she asked.

"Well," he said awkwardly, "this very good-looking man…he just kind of… showed up. And then he…well, he tried to kiss me. And when I said no, he kept trying to kiss me anyway."

"Sounds like a fox spirit," she agreed. "And?"

"And nothing. I finally convinced him to leave." This had actually required a certain amount of physical intimidation, but he got there in the end. "But the thing is…"

"Mm?" Liu Chenguang sipped her tea again.

He was sure she was laughing at him, but this was important. He needed to ask someone — someone who might know.

"The thing is, I was interested," he said at last. "And I never…Never except Tainu. Had that feeling. So I am…is that part of what fox spirits do? Make that happen to you?"

"No," she said. She seemed to understand why exactly he was so upset, even though he was trying not to show it. "It's not just a fox spirit thing. It's normal, Zhu Guiren, to be attracted. It doesn't mean you don't love Tainu. It's a choice to love someone this way. It wouldn't be a meaningful choice if there was literally no one else in the world that you could possibly be with, as though Tainu were the last man on earth." She reached over and patted his shoulder gently. "There's nothing wrong with you at all, and nothing to be ashamed of, and it doesn't mean that you've betrayed Tainu somehow just by having feelings of attraction. It's just a way that you can remind yourself that you love him, because you are committing yourself to him and telling the fox spirit or whoever no thanks."

He nodded, thinking it over, and sat quietly, drinking his tea. "I miss him so much," he said at last. "So much. Last time I was in the spirit realm he wouldn't show me his mortal body at all."

Liu Chenguang smiled kindly. "He must miss you a lot too," she said. "He'll be ready soon."

Some months later, Zhu Guiren was alone in the house. Liu Chenguang was at the clinic, Yisue was at school, and Aili had gone out for a walk with her mother. He went into the little back yard to check the "Victory Garden," which he thought was the stupidest name ever for a bunch of vegetables, but Aili's mother had a good time with it.

He was kneeling down trying to look between the vines for ripe tomatoes when he heard Tainu's voice. "Demon?"

Zhu Guiren froze, then carefully got up, brushing off his knees, and turned around.

Tainu was standing there, looking shyly at him. He must have come through the phoenix gate that Aili had set permanently in the back corner of the yard. He looked just as he had when they first met in this body: in his late twenties or early thirties, tall and well-made, if a little on the slim side, skin a warm deep brown, high cheekbones and generous mouth, beautiful eyes looking only at him.

Zhu Guiren leapt over to him so quickly that Tainu almost fell over before he was caught in Zhu Guiren's arms. "Tainu," he said. "Tainu, you're really back? You're done now? You're back here?"

Tainu smiled down at him. When they had made love in the spirit realm, he had still not quite been to his full height and weight, but now he was just very slightly taller than Zhu Guiren. "I'm back," he said, and kissed him.

Zhu Guiren held his face and kissed him back, first on the lips, but then carefully on his eyelids and his ears and his nose, everywhere, all the precious places he had missed touching and seeing for so long. He found his eyes growing wet, and he could taste that Tainu was crying too.

At last, he said, "No one's home now. Come on, let me show you the house." He took his hand and brought him inside the little wooden house, showing him the kitchen, and the dining room, and the library-study-living room, and then his own bedroom, which was small and held only a bed and a shelf for his books.

He saw Tainu frowning at the size of the bed and laughed. "Don't worry," he said, "we're not staying here."

"We're not?"

Zhu Guiren dragged him down the hallway, laughing madly the whole time, but he felt so happy inside that he couldn't keep it in. "Definitely not," he said. He left a note for them on the dining room table and then brought Tainu outside, where he hot-wired the car. He had been doing this for a while, and Aili never said anything about it, but she also didn't give him his own set of keys, so this was how it was going to be. "Get in," he said, patting the passenger seat.

Tainu laughed too and sat down. "Where are we going?"

"It's a surprise."

When he pulled up at the ocean several hours later, it was just the right time. The sun was glittering on the water. Tainu came out and took a deep breath, energized by the qi, just as Zhu Guiren had hoped he would be. "What a wonderful place," he said. "I've never been here before…this part of the world."

"I didn't think you had," he said happily, "Aili said you just came to the Western Federation on the ship where she met you, for the war, so I thought you probably hadn't been up here before." He held his own hand against his handless arm to keep it from shaking as Tainu turned in the other direction, looking back at the bluff running up toward the high hills. There was a little house there — really just a one-room cabin.

Tainu looked at him. "Is that where we're going?" he asked.

He nodded, feeling anxious and trying not to let it show.

"Well, let's go up," Tainu said, taking out the groceries. "The milk will spoil if we leave it in the car."

Zhu Guiren carried the groceries since the hill was steep and he thought Tainu might be tired, but he came up easily and quickly enough, looking around at everything.

"The view's even better from here," Tainu said approvingly.

From the grass in front of the cabin, they could see out across the panorama of the bluffs and the little rocky castles and great cliffs of isolated rock scattered through the deep blue, glittering coastline.

"Is that the dragon gate, that arched rock there?"

Zhu Guiren nodded again. He still couldn't manage to say anything, his throat was dry.

Tainu turned and opened the door to go inside.

The cabin was not large, but it had a good kitchen and a large bed and a table and a wood-burning stove.

Tainu ran his hand over the door frame. "This was built pretty recently," he said. "Nice work."

Zhu Guiren smiled, still nervous. He'd forgotten that Tainu knew how to do so many things; he probably knew how to build houses too. "Do you like it?" he asked at last.

"I do. It's very nice," he said. "I especially like the bed." He went over and sat on it, smiling at him. "Why are you still standing in that doorway, demon?"

Zhu Guiren didn't say anything. Finally he said, "Aili's mother made the quilt."

"Very pretty." He held his hand out. "But I want you now," he said, simple and demanding.

Zhu Guiren just looked at him.

Tainu stood, went to the center of the room, and turned around slowly. When his eyes came back to Zhu Guiren again, they were shining. "You made it," he said. "You made it?"

He nodded. "There's a sawmill up the river. It's redwood, and the house was easy, really. It was figuring out how to get running water that was the challenge. That took me forever to engineer," he said, knowing he was babbling, and then Tainu was holding him and laughing and crying a little bit at the same time.

"It's so beautiful," Tainu said, holding him. "Arciniang, you made this. It's so beautiful." He bowed his head down onto his shoulder. "I've never had a home before. No one has ever made a place for me before, ever. A place to share with me."

Zhu Guiren put his arms around him and said, "This is for us to be in when we need time together, or to cultivate together, or whatever. Whatever we want to do. I was thinking that you wouldn't want to live up here always. It's so lonely, you want to be near your family, but there's no place there that I could build a house for you, and I wanted to build something for you. Just for you." He held him tighter. "When we go back, we'll look for a house there together. I didn't want to buy one without you seeing it too and helping to choose. But this will be our special place."

"Yes," Tainu said, and smiled at him again. "You've thought so much about it."

Zhu Guiren took a deep breath, feeling how their bodies fit together as they held one another; he was more than ready now. "I've thought so much about lots of things," he said, and kissed him, and pulled him over to the bed.

# THE AUTHOR HAS SOMETHING SHE WOULD LIKE TO SAY

Thank you for sharing the adventures of Liu Chenguang, Aili Fallon, Zhu Guiren, and Tainu. I hope you're as happy as I am that they've found one another and begun their lives together. They've come to a point where they can rest, but for beings that are immortal or nearly so, there will always be more to come.

Once again, I want to highlight the wonderful stories to be explored in the Chinese genres of danmei, xianxia, and xuanhuan which inspired me in these books. Works of Mo Xiang Tong Xiu (MXTX), Priest, Rou Bou Bu Chi Rou, and others are now being published in official English translations, and I hope that you'll enjoy them as much as I have.

With much gratitude, always, to my wife Teresita, to our child and our shared extended family, and to all the readers and writing community that share all these imaginary worlds.

If you enjoyed the book, please leave a review or star rating. This helps other people find the book and know if they'll enjoy it or not, and it's greatly appreciated! And if you'd like to stay in touch, read book reviews or musings on the writing and publication process, and get first news about future books, free short stories or novellas, and more, please sign up for my newsletter on my website, jcsnow.carrd.co.

# THE AUTHOR HAS SOMETHING SHE WOULD LIKE TO SAY

Thank you for sharing the adventures of Liu Chenguang, Aili Fallon, Zhu Guiren, and Tainu. I hope you're as happy as I am that they've found one another and begun their lives together. They've come to a point where they can rest, but for beings that are immortal or nearly so, there will always be more to come.

This story began with my excitement in exploring the Chinese contemporary fantasy genres of danmei, xianxia, and xuanhuan. Danmei novels are stories of two people falling in love who coincidentally are both men (there are relatively few baihe novels, where the protagonists are women who fall in love). While they can be set in outer space, college, or modern day life, they're often blended with fantasy in the genres of xianxia and xuanhuan. Xianxia is a fantasy subgenre blending the martial arts exploits of wuxia with Daoist and Buddhist mythology. In xianxia, individuals – human and nonhuman – can cultivate spiritual power through meditation, practice, and learning in order to use talismans, spells, spiritual swords, and miraculous medicines, attaining power and longevity far beyond an ordinary human. In addition, mythological beasts and spirits can also cultivate, and can sometimes take human form, typical of a xuanhuan novel. In some ways The Crane Moon Cycle might be called a xuanhuan novel, but in some important ways it isn't, as the phoenixes, demons, fox spirits, and dragons differ from Daoist or Buddhist inspirations. Nonetheless learning about the world of Chinese mythology and the fantasy worlds of Chinese writers, which I am continuing to do, has been incredibly enriching.

I continue to be inspired by the immense creativity and energy of these works, the pacing and clear focus on individual relationships, the complex narrative forms and interlocking arcs, the playfulness and critique of gender roles and expectations, and how they often work in a narrative tension not of conquering evil, but of protecting the ones you love from it. Works of some of the great danmei authors, including in the xianxia/xuanhuan genres, such as Mo Xiang Tong Xiu (MXTX), Priest, Rou Bou Bu Chi Rou, Meng Xishi, and others are now being published in official English translations and I hope they become more widely known and appreciated among English speaking audiences.

If you enjoyed the book, please consider leaving a review or star rating. This helps other people find the book and know if they'll enjoy it or not, and it's greatly appreciated! And if you'd like to stay in touch, read book reviews or musings on the writing and publication process, and get first news about future books, please sign up for my newsletter on my website, jcsnow.carrd.co, or find me on social media. One of the things I love most about being a writer is the community of readers.

When I started writing these stories, I was alone in the writing world, and now I'm so grateful for the community that I have found in writing and publishing. The world of indie publishing, and most definitely the fantasy and queer speculative fiction corner of it, is supportive, creative, rambunctious, and such a gift! I am very grateful in particular to the people who talked with me or gave me feedback at various points of the idea development and writing process, including Zhui Ning Chang, Amy Snow, Spencer Hatcher, Yilin Wang, and the editor for this omnibus version, XM Moon. With much gratitude, always, to my wife Teresita, who is my manager and confidence booster; to our child who is so proud of my books though he is too young to read them; and to all the readers and writing community that share all these imaginary worlds: thank you. Aili Fallon, Zhu Guiren, Liu Chenguang, Tainu, and Yisue wouldn't exist without you.

# ABOUT THE AUTHOR

J. C. Snow (she/her) is a queer fantasy author, scholar, and occasional musician, who wrote her first story in third grade in a blue journal stamped with a silver unicorn. It's still floating around somewhere in the box of memorabilia she's brought from upstate New York through Boston, New Haven, Los Angeles, and Chicago to her current home in the Bay Area. She holds a PhD in Religious Studies from Columbia University and has written extensively on religion and race in American history, including a book on religion and early Asian immigration to the United States. Her fantasy worlds are inspired by diverse historical and cultural settings, and her stories always center queer characters. She lives with her amazing partner and child and together they love to travel and have adventures. When not writing she is mostly wishing she could be writing, or wandering around unsupervised at night listening to Spotify character playlists.

# TWO HUNDRED YEARS AFTER THE END OF THE SHORELESS RIVER...
# THE DEMON CHILD

WHEN THE HANDS came for her, she hissed and slashed out with her long black claws. She wasn't very big, but the claws were quite impressive. The hands were human, pale skin covered with scratches that quickly faded. She gave the hands new scratches.

"That's a demon, Aili. Let it go."

"That explains the four wings, I guess." The hands lifted her up to look into a pair of human eyes, blue and surprised. "Hello, little demon, do you have a name?"

The man's voice was cool and precise. "She's just old enough that she may be able to cultivate a human form. Right on the edge. At that age, we don't have names."

She turned her head with difficulty: a mortal-formed demon, black-haired with pale skin and dark eyes. Though he was clearly a demon, his aura was like nothing she had sensed before. No corrupted qi around him at all, no aura of resentment. But he was very powerful, she could feel it, and all-powerful demons were dangerous. She squeaked and writhed in dismay, trying to free herself and flee, and then bit the hands that were holding her firm and tore at them with her teeth.

"Ouch," the woman's voice said, but the hands still held her, gentle and immovable.

She looked up into the woman's eyes — thoughtful and with an unfamiliar expression, so different from the trainers.

"Zhu Guiren, why does it look like this? It looks like a little furry thing with four wings, is that normal? And the horns?"

The other demon — Zhu Guiren — snorted. "You've seen me in my true body. You know what it looks like. In general, we always have horns and wings. Beyond that, it varies. We're not like humans that all look the same."

The blue eyes narrowed. "She's injured."

"She's in her true body. We're more vulnerable in that form. That's why we cultivate mortal forms here."

"What could have hurt her like this, though?" The woman held her higher, to examine her belly, where the larger wound was. She couldn't help it and squealed in pain.

"Aili, this is a waste of time. Put her down and let's go home."

"Does she understand what I'm saying, or do you need to speak with her in the demonic language?"

"I don't need to speak with her at all. Just put her on the ground and leave her, she'll be fine."

"I can understand you perfectly," she said to the woman — Aili — in the human language. "Put me down."

Very gently, Aili laid her back down on the ground, placing her on her side to examine her wound more closely. The woman had a dark gold braid that fell forward over her shoulder — tantalizing to play with if she wasn't in so much pain.

"Are you all right?" Aili's voice was gentle, but she was trembling all over from fear, and how much it had hurt to be lifted up like that out of her hiding place in the grass. "If you transform I can heal you."

"You can heal her now if you want to. It doesn't matter whether she's in a human form or not," Zhu Guiren said, sounding impatient. "She already bit you, might as well use it. Just drip some blood on her and call it a day, Aili. I want to get back home."

Something warm and soothing fell onto the wound in her belly, deep into her vitals.

"What hurt you?" Aili asked. Her hands, bloodied where she had scratched and bit her, began to stroke along the claw wounds near her wing muscles.

"A– a badger monster," she said, a little ashamed to say so in front of the powerful demon. A demon should always be able to best a natural spirit, corrupted or not. Natural spirits of the mortal world weren't nearly as powerful as demons were — everyone knew that. She hadn't ever thought she wouldn't be able to defend herself after running away. But it must just be that most demons out in the world were much older and more powerful than she was, and that's why little demons remained in clan home being obedient, as she had always been told.

Her wounds were healed. A rush of energy, a sense of well-being, prickled through to the outside of her skin. She took a deep breath of surprise and transformed. She had only done it a few times before, the quick thrill and thrum of spiritual energy reshaping her into a form of this world.

Aili made a noise of shock and then grabbed her, wrapping something around her limbs—

"No!" she shouted, struggling, trying to get out of the trap, forgetting that she could transform back and be too small for the constraints. The panic was so great she couldn't think clearly; would they hurt her, would they take her back to the trainers?

"Shh, shh, in your human form you should wear clothes," Aili said. "Just wear this for now. It's just my jacket. Sorry, it's a little dirty."

She stood still, trying to stabilize herself and find her dignity again. Of course, clothes. The other demon, Zhu Guiren, wore them too. The piece of cloth, the jacket, was stiff and itchy against her skin, but Aili quickly grabbed her arms and stuffed them into its sleeves, which fell over her wrists, and then just as quickly fastened it down the front so she was fully enclosed in a scratchy tube that covered her from neck to knees. She looked down at the fasteners — a long line of knotted buttons and loops. Now that she was in a human form in front of them both, she felt even more vulnerable, though of course, it was the true body that was the more delicate. It did feel better to be covered, even with such an inadequate shield as a piece of cloth. Her human body was unfamiliar and awkward, but it made it easier to look at the woman on a level of equality. A human form was much larger than her true body.

"Where did you come from?" Aili asked, still kneeling in front of her. That was helpful; the blue eyes were near the level of her head now. "Should you be out on your own? You only look around nine."

"I ran away," she blurted out.

Zhu Guiren's sharp dark eyes looked right through her. "You're not even old enough for the ranking pits yet. How could you fight your way out past the guards?"

She eyed him cautiously, hoping he would stay at a distance, and edged slightly closer to the woman.

Zhu Guiren shrugged. "Aili, let's go home, Tainu'll be worrying. And Liu Chenguang too."

"But is it safe to leave her? She's only a child."

"She's a demon, she'll be fine." Zhu Guiren tapped his fingers against his arm, and she realized that in his human form, he had only one hand. She hadn't noticed before.

Aili nodded. "Good luck, little demon."

The woman stood straight, very tall. Even in her human form now, she had to tip her head back to watch her. There was blood all over the loosely fitted shirt the woman wore, but she seemed unwounded. Had they fought other demons, before finding her? Other monsters?

Suddenly Aili spread her arms apart, quick and sharp, her fingers straight. The power within her surged up and out, a golden-red fire held and expanding between her hands.

Despite herself, she stumbled back in surprise, but Zhu Guiren stepped forward instead. He jumped through the fire and disappeared.

Not a fire. A gate. A way to escape.

"Wait!" She ran back towards Aili, holding her hands out, entreating. "Please, take me with you, I don't want to stay here, please."

Aili held her arms steady, the fire between them, and paused. The blue eyes examined her thoughtfully.

"It doesn't matter where you go," she babbled, "just– just away– just, please. Just take me. I don't want to go back to clan home, they'll come looking for me, I'm not strong enough on my own."

Aili said, her voice uncertain, "I don't know how to take care of you. You can't cultivate demonic power if you come with me, don't you need it?"

"I don't need it," she lied. "That other demon, he doesn't need it, does he?"

"Not anymore," Aili said. "But he's different."

"He can teach me, how to be a demon without corruption, can't he teach me?"

"I'm his teacher."

A human was a demon's teacher? How could that be? The trainers had always been very clear: humans were weak, easily controlled and manipulated, good for nothing but entertainment and the delights of corruption.

But no matter what the trainers said, she would trust her own senses. Demons were very good at sensing power and where it lay. And this woman— even though she was only a weak child who couldn't yet fight in the pits, even so, she could feel it in her, the power she held, unlike anything she had sensed before. It drew her like the sun, painful and necessary.

"Teach me," she said. "Can't you teach me?"

"We can…I suppose we can try." Aili's eyes weighed her, then she said, "Zhu Guiren is waiting for us, and he's probably not happy we're so late. Be polite to him, all right?" She smiled. "Where I'll bring you, there are natural spirits and other beings too. But you'll be the only demon, except for Zhu Guiren. It might be lonely."

"I'll be fine," she said, her eyes on that glowing red-gold gate in the air, ready to jump. Of course she wouldn't be lonely — how ridiculous. Demons were never lonely, what would be the point?

"You'll need a name," Aili said.

"This one hasn't yet earned a rank number," she said, automatically.

"Not a number," Aili said. "A name."

"Just give me one, whatever."

Aili paused, then said, "Sanmer. It was my mother's name. Will that be all right with you?"

"It's fine, let's go!" The powerful ones could come any moment, the ones that would take her back — unless she could get through that fiery gate with Aili, she would need to start running.

"Well, then, just jump through, Sanmer," Aili said.

And Sanmer jumped.

Sanmer landed awkwardly on a cold stone floor. A tall man with very dark brown skin and hair in long braids was—

She stumbled back in shock.

Aili closed the gate behind them, the fire dissolving between her hands. "What's wrong, Sanmer?"

"What, what are they doing?" she asked, horrified. The man was eating the other demon? Did they eat demons here?

Aili tossed a glance to where the tall man had Zhu Guiren captured in his arms, their mouths together, Zhu Guiren making noises as though he were in pain. "Tainu, there's a child present, tone it down."

"What?" The man turned around, laughing. "What do you mean, a child?"

Zhu Guiren stared at her, pressing his lips together in a thin line.

Sanmer backed away from him — better safe than sorry.

"Aili," he said, his voice very calm, "what the hell are you doing?"

"She doesn't want to go back to clan home, can you blame her? Her name is Sanmer."

"Sanmer," the tall man said, his long braids falling around his shoulders as he knelt down.

Zhu Guiren made an irritated noise.

"Welcome."

She couldn't understand why his eyes were so soft. She had never seen eyes with that kind of expression before; she didn't know what to make of it.

"My name is Tainu. That demon is my partner. Don't be afraid. No one will hurt you here."

She just stared.

Tainu turned to look inquiringly back at Zhu Guiren. He huffed and left.

"Hmmm," Tainu said, and went to follow him.

Aili said, in a very casual voice, "I don't think Zhu Guiren likes being reminded of growing up in clan home. It must be pretty awful,"

"It was fine," Sanmer said, which was a complete and obvious lie.

Aili didn't press her, only nodded.

Then she said, "Yes, it's awful."

"Do you want to talk about it?"

"No," she said firmly. "Not ever."

"All right," Aili said. "Officially, then." She smiled. The room they were in had no windows, and was very dim now that the phoenix fire gate had faded, but Sanmer could still see her smile. The trainers never smiled unless they had something particularly unpleasant planned. "Welcome to Crane Moon, Sanmer. I know you'll have a lot of questions. You've met Zhu Guiren already. He and I are the masters here."

Master was a word Sanmer understood. She immediately prostrated with her face on the ground.

"No," said Aili, sounding horrified, "that's not what it means. It means that we teach disciples. That's all it means." Aili's hands pulled her up, carefully, to sit upright.

"Teach what?"

"I told you, I teach— we teach how to cultivate spiritual power," she said.

"Instead of corruption?"

"Yes," Aili said. "The natural spiritual power of the worlds." She broke off, her gaze suddenly moving past Sanmer and her whole expression brightening.

"Liu Chenguang," she said, "look who's come to stay with us. This is Sanmer."

Another woman's footsteps paused, briefly, but long enough for Sanmer to be able to feel her shock. Then they came forward, firm and light. This woman was smaller, pale and black-haired like Zhu Guiren was, but clearly not a demon. There was some power Sanmer couldn't place in her. Both of the two women were strange beings. But clearly powerful, and that's what mattered.

"Power keeps you safe," Sanmer whispered to herself, "power keeps you safe." That's what they had been taught — why they needed to learn to cultivate — to become powerful and strong and cruel, so they could fight and kill and not die. So they could be free.

Someday.

But she had cheated them, and she was free already.

An irrepressible smile reshaped her face, the muscles so unused to such a movement.

"What did you say?" Aili pulled her to her feet.

Liu Chenguang looked down at her, not nearly as tall as Aili, her eyes thoughtful. "Sanmer? Did you– did you know that was Aili's mother's name?"

Sanmer wondered why they thought a mother was significant; she had never met her own, and most likely never would. "Aili gave me this name," she said. Already, she felt attached to it. Back at clan home, she would never have had a name like this — only a rank number, and only once she had earned it. How special, to have a name that was also a gift. She hugged it to herself, secretly delighted but trying to keep her face expressionless, so no one would know and try to take it away.

She realized that Aili and Liu Chenguang's eyes were meeting over her head, communicating silently, perhaps, as the clan leaders did. Liu Chenguang looked away from Aili and back at her, long dark eyes creased in a smile.

"Sanmer," she said, "it's very late now here. Everyone is asleep, but we're happy you're with us. Aili and I have a house that has an extra bed. Why don't you come sleep there, just for tonight?"

Liu Chenguang took her other hand, a little more cautiously. Sanmer wondered briefly if they would put shackles on her, but there was no sign of it — no shackles but the women's hands, one on each wrist, both gentle and warm. It was a very strange feeling.

They walked together, still all hand in hand, out the door of the stone building. There were no walls around it, no wards to prevent flight. If she wanted to leave, she could, at any time.

If she wanted to leave…she could. She mulled that over, chewing on it, as the two women walked with her up a steep and twisting hill path. There were no trees — only long grass and some bushes, rustling in a strong, cool wind. The moon was bright enough to light their way. As they climbed higher, Sanmer looked behind them and froze in awe. The long, low stone building was near the edge of a great cliff, and beyond was a shining expanse of darkness and glory, ever moving, shifting and shimmering, with a deep and inconstant roar.

"What is it?" she asked, frightened, longing.

"It's the sea," Liu Chenguang said. "I felt that way too, the first time I saw it. I hadn't lived near an ocean in any of my lives before."

Sanmer didn't understand this. She just looked; it seemed as though she could look forever, always the same, ever-changing. "It's powerful," she whispered, "and it's free."

"Yisue's home?" Aili asked softly. She was looking away from the ocean, up the hill that rose behind the building, mounting towards higher peaks far away beneath the stars. A little building stood there, a golden light inside shining out through holes in its walls.

"He came home yesterday," Liu Chenguang said. "We were just playing cards with Tainu and waiting for you to come back. When Tainu felt you open the gate, he flew down to you, and then I walked; Yisue said he would wait at home and make some tea for you. I'm sure Tainu's got Zhu Guiren home by now. We won't see them again tonight."

"Sorry we were gone so long," Aili said, as though responding to a hidden rebuke. "The array wasn't where Zhu Guiren thought it would be. We had to search for a few weeks."

At the door of the house stood a boy several years older than Sanmer, in their mortal forms at any rate. He was thin and very pale, his long white hair scattered with braids and beads. When he moved his attention to her, she stopped short, pulling back on Aili's wrist. The power she could sense within him was like the sea — overwhelming, depthless.

"A demon?" he asked sharply.

"A guest," Aili corrected. "Sanmer, this is Yisue, our son. Yisue, this is Sanmer. She wanted to come live with us."

The boy's eyes met Sanmer's, and she bowed her head quickly. He didn't seem very friendly.

"Were you going to give her my room?"

"Of course not," Aili said. "We have a guest bedroom, Yisue. Your room is always yours."

"Really?" The boy relaxed. "Well, I won't stay here anyway though. I'm too old to live with my parents."

"Of course," Liu Chenguang responded, very solemnly, "but we're always glad to see you, Yisue."

"Did you break the array?" The boy stood to one side at last, letting Sanmer sidle in behind Aili. Liu Chenguang came inside and closed the door behind all of them.

It was a small room with one very large window — the one she had seen the golden light through. Now the golden light was inside with them, a lamp on a table scattered with bits of paper marked in patterns and swirls. The building was wooden; very easy to burn she thought, and then she felt ashamed for thinking that, and then she wondered why she felt ashamed. It wasn't as though she would burn it herself. It was only practical to think about defense. It was why all demon clan homes were stone, underground, more defensible and strong. Wood was vulnerable to so many things.

And when she stopped thinking about how the house could burn, she really saw it, and then, then so many colors; her eyes couldn't take them in all at once. On the floor, blue and dark gold, and on the walls there were things hanging pale and dark with scribbles, and there was a thing in one corner that held racks and racks of other things, and the table of polished wood, and the cups on it, the scent of something sweet like flowers, the flowers in the meadow where she had fled and been attacked — where Aili had found her — incense and food, she could smell that there was food nearby, through that other doorway where the white-haired boy stood, but what else was here, where were the dangers, she couldn't understand where the dangers were—

She closed her eyes and clenched her fists, frozen.

"Sanmer?" Aili asked from a distance.

"It's too much for her," Liu Chenguang said. Through the ringing in her ears, where she was straining them to hear any hint of attack, she could barely hear her.

Another hand took hers, this one bony and light. She didn't open her eyes.

"You two get rest, it's really late," Yisue said. "I made tea for you. I'll get her to bed in the guest room."

She felt herself led into a quieter place — safety where the walls were closer — and at last took a deep breath and opened her eyes.

"You're a dragon," she said to the boy.

"I know," he said. "You're a demon, what of it?"

She watched him, a little afraid, as he took cloths out of a box and spread them on a platform beneath a small window.

"This is the bed," he said, patting it.

She stared at it uncomprehending.

"You sleep on it," he said, sounding impatient. "Don't demons have beds?"

"Not like that." The youngest demons slept on the stone floor, tangled with one another for warmth. Platforms were for other things. For training. But maybe more powerful demons had…beds.

She cautiously sat on it.

Yisue said, "Lie down."

She kicked off the heavy cloth, panicked, when he tucked it down on her.

"Come on," he said, and firmly spread it back over on her again. "It gets cold when the wind gets up. It's to keep you warm."

She lay beneath it, too frightened to move a muscle until she was sure it wouldn't do anything to her.

Yisue sat next to her, cross-legged on the floor, and stared at her for a while. The platform of the bed was only a few inches off the floor; if she turned her head she would be staring at him, and she didn't want to, so she just looked out of the corner of her eye. A dragon was far too powerful to antagonize — more powerful than any demon, even if this one was skinny and young.

"Do you want to stay here?" he asked.

She considered how to answer. A question with a question. That was safest. "What is this place?"

"It's where my mother and Uncle Demon train beings in cultivation," he said. "I used to study too. But I'm not good at it, so I'm done now. With cultivation, anyway."

"How did they punish you?" she whispered. "For not being good at it?"

"What do you mean, punish?" he said, repulsed. "I did my best. and I just can't, that's all. What punishment would there be? Uncle Demon says perhaps dragons can't really learn this way."

"Oh," she said. "Are there– are there other dragons here?"

"No," he said. "Only bird and beast spirits. A lot of shore creatures, otters and seals. Deer, foxes, squirrels. You know."

She didn't know, but nodded as though she did. "And they can all learn?" If they could, she could too. She was good at learning.

"They can all learn." The boy sighed, as though thinking of something else. "How old are you?"

"I don't know," she said honestly. "How old are you?"

"Six hundred or so," he said. "I've never met a young demon like you before. Only Uncle Demon. And other grown demons, when they attack us."

"We don't normally leave clan home till we're very strong," she said. "They bring us there from the spirit realm to teach us to cultivate mortal bodies. We can't leave until we're strong enough, and have rankings."

"Rankings?" He shook his head. "But how are the rankings done?"

Quick hot panic, terror, blood, death, entrapment. The blanket was heavy on her limbs, she was surrounded by others more powerful, a wooden house, a dragon, the dark eyes of the powerful demon, all wrong things could happen. She made the mistake of turning her head to see him, and then she was so afraid that he would be angry that she squeezed her eyes tight, pretending to go to sleep.

Yisue said, "Never mind. You don't have to tell me. No one will make you do things you don't want to do."

She could leave at any time, they hadn't shackled her. But a young demon wouldn't be strong enough to survive alone; that much was clear. She had run away in the hope that she could escape, but she needed a shelter, at least for a while. Until she could become powerful. Until she could fight. Until she could be safe.

Unexpectedly, Yisue said, "You'll be safe."

She opened her eyes again. He sounded so confident. Like he wanted her to be confident too.

"I know it's all strange. But you can trust Aili and Liu Chenguang. Everyone here."

She pulled the piece of cloth up under her chin. Warm.

"I'll sleep now," she murmured, and then, surprisingly, she did.

www.ingramcontent.com/pod-product-compliance
Lightning Source LLC
Chambersburg PA
CBHW022008300726
48970CB00003B/798